Four Hours

Elite Escorts MM 4

Lynn Burke

Four Hours

Cupid did me no favors when he pierced me with Preston's arrow straight through the heart. He's everything I've ever wanted.

He's also my stepbrother.

I've loved him since high school when I became his protector, a safe place of refuge from his mother's stern, backward ideals. Our attachment gave him comfort, but my heart craved more, putting us both in danger.

Distance seemed the answer to escape my forbidden desires, but eleven years later, I'm still obsessed.

When an accident leaves us stranded with no means of escape, I learn I'm not the only one with fantasies. The draw between us is potent. Too many emotions erupt, laying us both bare, and me desperate to make his dreams come true.

But our four hours of heaven jolt to an end, leaving us on unsteady ground.

Can I convince Preston that we are two perfectly fitted parts of a whole? Or will he allow the tyrannical matriarch of his old money family to dictate who he ought to love?

Chapter 1

Drake

Thirteen Years Ago

I'd been to downtown Boston countless times, so I thought I knew what a city smelled, looked, and sounded like.

But Manhattan?

Crowded and chaotic didn't begin to describe what I gawked at out Dad's SUV windows. The stench of the streets seeped through the vehicle's seams, filling my nose with greasy food and acrid exhaust while I peered up at towering skyscrapers that stole the beauty of the sunset. Obnoxious car horns and gut-rumbling bass from other vehicles drowned Aerosmith's "Dream On" from Dad's speakers when we stopped at a red light.

And talk about fucking pretentious. Not just the people with their noses in the air, either.

The building Dad's new wife lived in—hell, *we were moving into*—lay directly ahead of us and looked like it was made solely out of glass.

Fucking forty-two floors of *glass*!

A doorman assured Dad our boxes of shit would be delivered upstairs and that a valet would see to his old SUV.

Not trusting strangers with the important stuff, I grabbed my duffel that held my laptop and Xbox.

Dad and I walked into the vast lobby, and I tipped my head back to take in the three-story space laid bare to the bustling world beyond. Everything was either see-through to the pandemonium outside or white furniture with chrome accents. Pops of red and orange littered the walls in funky artwork that didn't make a lick of sense to me.

Everyone was in such a damn hurry too, not even taking time to make eye contact or say hello as their heels clacked or shoes squeaked while passing us commoners by. The men and women were dressed in expensive clothing and carrying purses or briefcases that probably cost more than Dad made in a month.

He clasped my shoulder once we stood in front of an elevator, waiting for the doors to slide open. "Okay, son?" he asked, assuring me he still cared even though he'd turned my world upside down.

Not wanting to dampen his upbeat mood, I nodded, fearing that me and my dad's closeness was about to be completely obliterated by the fancy bitch with money who'd whisked him off to Vegas but had refused to take his last name.

Like a Hemmings was beneath her or something.

I followed him into the elevator, relieved to leave the ruckus behind. Glancing over at my father, I wondered if he felt the same sense of being misplaced as I did. A blue-collar worker, he dressed in jeans that had seen better days, a black button-down, and old slip-on shoes he called classy.

He pressed the button for the thirty-fifth floor. A smile I'd become familiar with the previous few days stretched his lips. His blue eyes, the same cornflower shade as mine, were filled with a happiness I hadn't seen on his face since before his and Mom's divorce years earlier.

I clutched my bag's handle a little tighter as though trying to hold onto some sanity in my new reality. I'd enjoyed living in Boston's suburbs with Dad, but he'd dug us up like a clod of dirt and flipped us wrong-side-up. "Who did you say this woman is?" I muttered.

"She's the reason my heart is beating again," Dad said without hesitation or a hint of questioning in his tone. "The love of my life," he continued as though to himself.

My chest ached a bit at Dad's statement. His and Mom's divorce had been the first earthquake in my childhood when I'd been in sixth grade. At least splitting time fifty-fifty between them hadn't been bad since Dad chose to get along with the woman who'd crushed him.

He hadn't seen the divorce coming, he'd told me when I was older. There'd been no cheating, no lies, just Mom feeling as though they'd grown apart for whatever reason.

Sounded like bullshit to me, but what did I know about love? In my dreams, it meant a white picket fence, kids, and romantic dinners by candlelight until death do us part. Their divorce fixed in my head that happily ever afters were a fantasy and nothing more.

Mom had met Bob and his two young daughters, Lyla and Kayla, when I was in ninth grade, and when she'd agreed to move into their Rhode Island house, I'd stayed in Boston with Dad. I wasn't about to leave my hometown, my high school, and my best friend, Sean.

But Dad went to New York on a business trip a couple of weeks ago, met Jacqueline Casswell, took off for Vegas in her private jet, and returned a married man. *Then* he informed me he would be relocating to Manhattan...yeah.

Talk about balls. I was more than a little annoyed to say the least.

Since sixteen was too young of an age for me to stay in Dad's rental on my own, I was given the choice of going with him or moving in with Mom and my two whiny soon-to-be stepsisters, who were wicked annoying.

With my sophomore year starting in a month and having no real choice, I decided I would experience New York until I could return to Mass for college where I would spend the rest of my life.

Parents or no parents nearby, Boston would *always* be home to me.

Dad glanced over at me. We stood eye to eye at six foot, both of us brawny with wide shoulders even though I'd just gotten my driver's license. His grin slowly faded, and I realized I scowled.

"Coming to New York isn't going to change anything between us, little buddy," he stated quietly.

I scoffed. "I'm not little."

Dad grabbed me in a big hug, squeezing the hell out of me. "Love you, Drake. More than anyone or anything, no matter what. Don't you ever forget that."

The elevator slowed, the ding announcing we'd arrived.

Tears stung my eyes at Dad's declaration, and I gave him a few bro pats before we both stepped away.

Regardless of Dad's assurance, fucking Cupid's arrows could suck a dino dick and choke on it for all I cared. Didn't the angelic shithead with wings realize I'd had it good back home?

I mean, I wanted to be happy for Dad finding love after Mom broke his heart, but come on. New *fucking* York?

Grumbling internally about the second disaster of my

life, I followed Dad into a hallway spanning to the left and right. A single door lay at either end.

He strode toward the left, his footsteps quick and light while I lagged behind.

The door yanked open before he got there.

A petite redhead threw herself into Dad's arms with a squeal. While stumbling together into the penthouse, they kissed as if they'd been separated for a year rather than the three days it had taken Dad and I to pack up our shit and leave Boston behind.

My steps slowed as I approached the open door.

Redheads had always been my kryptonite from the minute I figured out what a dick could be used for. Guess Dad and I had that in common too.

But the same as my best friend Sean, my cock didn't get hard for females. While my buddy from back home was out and proud, I'd yet to share my sexual orientation with my dad.

Later, I told myself as I'd been doing for the past two years since he already had enough on his plate.

Foreheads together, Dad and the supposed love of his life whispered a few words I didn't catch as I stepped over the threshold, shut the door behind me, and glanced around.

My jaw dropped again.

Fucking floor-to-ceiling windows lay straight ahead past a living room decked out in off-white furniture. A massive grand piano sat on the left, a silent Manhattan spreading beyond in a dizzying display of buildings reaching for the sky. The walls, windows, and insulation of the skyrise blocked all the noise of the city we'd left outside, while light jazz-like music filtered through the condo in surround sound.

Smooching noises drew my focus back to the couple clinging to each other beside me. Their size difference was laughable, but rather than snickering, I cleared my throat because *one*, I had to piss, and *two*, their PDA kinda made me nauseous...and a little jealous if I was being honest.

I was a sucker for affection, even though I didn't have a boyfriend I could cling to like a koala.

"You must be Drake." Jacqueline finally ripped her attention off Dad, coming into my personal space without hesitation to wrap her arms around my waist.

Expensive perfume and the scent of crisp one hundred dollar bills clung to her, or at least what I figured freshly printed money smelled like. I'd never held any in my rough palms that were scarred from all the sports I played.

Awkward as fuck, I glanced at Dad.

Talk about heart eyes. He stared at the small woman hugging me, and in that second, I recognized the fact Dad planned to spend every day he had on earth beside her, same as Mom with Bob.

They'd both found what they thought would be forever, but my parents had been in love once upon a time too, and look how that had ended up. While I didn't hold onto hope either of them had found something that might last, I'd already set the one boundary in cement for myself. I wasn't up for adoption to either Bob or this Jacqueline woman, who Dad swore walked on water.

I could admit her money would make shit a hell of a lot easier for as long as the two of them lasted though. Wouldn't complain about that, but I already had two parents. I didn't need a third or fourth.

Dad's wife stepped away from me, clasping her hands together beneath her chin, her eyes like glittering green jewels as she peered up at me. "You're a picture image of your father, Drake. So tall and *manly*."

"Thanks," I muttered, wondering over her emphasized last word.

Dad got plenty of attention when it came to the ladies. He only had a touch of gray in the dark hair at his temples, and he'd yet to have a wrinkle show up and announce he approached forty. Good genes meant I would hopefully look the same when I was older. But, I could do without the women.

"Uh, bathroom?" I tacked on, my bladder grumbling as much as my mind.

"Of course." She gestured for us to follow her into the... house?

I had no fucking clue what to call it. Whatever title her place officially had, it would be home for the next three years at the very least.

After telling me I could leave my bag on the steps leading to the second floor, Jacqueline showed me to the half-bath in a back hallway. I took care of business and washed my hands before slipping out and heading toward the open concept main area where I'd left her and Dad.

There were windows *everywhere*.

Fucking hell, I'd never seen anything like it. Not a fan of heights, I wasn't too keen on the view from practically every angle. I hoped whatever room I ended up calling my own was either an interior space or had blinds to block out the city far, far below that made me woozy.

I turned the corner into the living room and slammed into somebody. A grunt pulled from whoever it was, and I grabbed his slender arms to keep them steady. "Shit—sorry."

Another tiny person with a mop of red, wavy hair stood inches away from me.

But unlike Jacqueline's smooth, blemish-free skin that had probably cost a fortune to maintain, pimples littered the kid's face. He peered up at me with emerald eyes framed by pale lashes before flitting his focus to my chest. Cowering in on himself, he hitched his narrow shoulders, sending a sudden pang through me.

I dropped my hold on his arms, fisting my hands as though he'd burned my skin.

The young teenager was cute as a button and would be a heartbreaker when he was older, that was for damned sure.

"H-Hi," he croaked, his voice breaking like a pubescent kid as his face flushed the color of a cherry. He stepped back and continued to stare at my chest, which was eye level for his short height. Everything about him screamed bashful and insecure. "S-Sorry about that. I t-tend not to look where I'm g-going."

His stuttering hit me in the gut and made me want to soothe him somehow.

"Preston?" I asked, figuring out who the kid was.

Dad had told me Jacqueline had a boy a year or so younger than me, and I'd been kind of excited to have a stepbrother to play sports with.

From his appearance, I didn't think Preston would be joining me on any field. His long, slender fingers looked like they belonged on the ivory keys of that piano out in the living room rather than grasping a football or baseball.

"You must be Drake." He held out his hand, acting all posh and shit with straightened shoulders, his words more articulated than before, even though his extended arm shook.

I swore if the floor opened and swallowed Preston whole, he would sigh in relief. At least he hadn't sneered at my ripped jeans and old Aerosmith T-shirt when he wore a starched button-down and perfectly creased slacks.

"Hey." I clasped his hand, wishing I could wrap my arms around him in a big hug instead and tell him we would be best buds and that everything would be okay like Dad had promised me.

Preston gasped at my touch and quickly stepped back, wiping his palm on his thigh.

My eyebrows dented inward.

"S-Sorry," he rushed to say. "I-I'm not normally this n-nervous."

So he wasn't scrubbing the lower class of me off his palm. Good to know, because I didn't want to spend the next three years with a rich snob for a stepbrother.

"No worries, kid." I clasped his shoulder with a light touch.

He still shied away from me again, nodding.

I guessed I needed to keep my hands to myself.

"You—have an accent l-like your d-dad," he said, his voice barely above a whisper.

"Boston," I stated, the first hint of a smile on my face. Fuck, did I love that city.

"It's...c-cool."

I grinned even though he hadn't taken his focus off my chest. "Thanks."

"Mom wanted me t-to tell you that d-dinner is served," he stuttered and spun.

I followed on his heels, noticing he wore fucking loafers or some shit while my right big toe threatened to push through the thinning material of my old Vans.

Preston had serious self-esteem issues if his stooped posture and lowered head were any indication. I wondered how he would handle high school in a couple of weeks.

Unless he had a solid group of friends, I expected it would be a rough transition for him from middle school.

Hopefully, New York teenagers wouldn't give me shit for the accent Preston liked. As long as no one started talking shit about my Pats or the Sox, we'd be okay.

Dad seated Jacqueline at the foot of their small dining room table before heading to the other end. Preston and I sat across from each other on the longer sides, the cushioned chair beneath my ass white and in serious danger of getting stains with how little manners I had when it came to eating.

A woman dressed in all black appeared out of nowhere with filled plates in hand before anyone had a chance to speak.

Outside the 99 Restaurant back home, I'd never had someone serve me. Who the hell had waitstaff in their houses for fuck's sake?

Eyebrow raised, I eyed Dad on my left.

He smiled at his new wife, oblivious to everything but her.

I mean, the woman was easy on the eyes, no doubt about it. It was obvious where Preston got his cuteness from, but come on. Did Dad not notice the *richness* around him? How his wife ignored the men in black who silently moved through the condo with boxes of our shit? They sure as fuck weren't invisible, but Jacqueline felt they were beneath her for all the attention she paid them.

If she knew I used to stock shelves at Market Basket alongside Sean on the weekends, she'd probably turn a blind eye to me too.

Our new lifestyle was about fifty rungs up from the ladder Dad had attempted to climb back home.

Neither of us fit it.

At. All.

How long before Jacqueline grew bored with Dad's modesty and proved to me yet again that forever didn't exist? Sure, he was a good-looking guy, but he didn't come from old money like the Casswell family. He also lacked the refinement I figured she would expect when around *her* type of people. She would see that soon enough and send us packing—not that I would complain.

A plate suddenly appeared in front of me, and I checked out the funky white sauce artfully dripped over a seared chicken breast. Asparagus spears stacked alongside small, elongated potatoes, the likes I'd never seen before, their pale flesh sprinkled with some green shit.

Parsley, maybe?

My cell dinged with a text, but while I fished it from my back pocket, Jacqueline cleared her throat.

"No phones at the table," she stated firmly with a fake-ass smile.

"Sorry," I murmured, ignoring the text from Sean and powering the thing off.

"Next time, leave it in your room, Drake," she ordered, her tone suggesting she wouldn't listen to any argument on the topic.

I glanced at Dad. His unwavering smile directed at her annoyed me.

Jacqueline's home meant her rules, I realized when Dad didn't speak up. Either the woman had a magical pussy, or she'd lobbed his balls off.

Whatever.

As long as he was happy, I could put up with Jacqueline until I could escape New York. But when she eventually ripped his heart out like Mom had done, I wouldn't keep quiet.

Mom's choice to find another man and move to Rhode

Island had been forgivable but only because we shared blood.

Jacqueline?

She meant nothing to me. Not even a purse for me to take advantage of. With her snobbish attitude, she could keep her fancy meals, penthouse, and jewels for all I cared.

Three years.

I repeated the two words in my head, turning my focus to my plate.

The meal looked like a work of art, but the steam rising toward my nose smelled fucking divine regardless of it silently screaming I shouldn't mess up its beauty. I dug into my food like the starving teenager I was while the newlyweds chatted, Dad's wife filling me in on the private school I would be attending with Preston.

Of course, Jacqueline had family connections that allowed her to sign me up for classes much later than normal at the elite school. I couldn't begin to imagine how much of a sore thumb I would be regardless of the school's uniforms. My stomach churned.

Jacqueline bragged that a big donation had the headmaster bending the rules before my less-than-stellar transcripts could even be an issue.

Dad had told me she came from money, but seriously.

The diamonds around her neck? In her lobes? On four of her ten fingers for a weeknight dinner at *home?*

And her driver would take us in a limo—a damned *limo* —to high school.

What the actual fuck?

I was in another dimension. At least I was the steady sort and didn't get too flustered with change. Outwardly, anyway. Inside? I attempted to cling to a deflating floatie of normalcy in the ocean I'd been tossed into.

Preston sat across from me pushing his food around his plate with a fork rather than eating. I wondered if he felt the same. Our gazes caught, and his face flushed before he jerked his eyes back down as though afraid I would punch him for looking at me.

The poor kid. He seemed terrified of me. Or, maybe he was all uptight about the school Jacqueline continued to go on about.

Had Preston been bullied in eighth grade?

The thought roused heat in my chest. Made me want to curl up my fist and smash something. I'd always had my best friend Sean's back, so I recognized the rising protective instinct for what it was.

"The first day will be here before you know it," Jacqueline said with excitement in her voice, and I realized she spoke to me. "Less than two weeks!"

A flash of nerves lit inside me as I nodded, unable to smile. I expected Preston and I would *both* be half-sick while being carted to a new school. I might be calm by nature, but I wasn't above first day jitters. Swallowing shit down and putting on a brave front would be my top priority if for no other reason than to help keep Preston from tossing his cookies.

"Will...Dad be here to see me off like he used to?" Preston asked, his voice as quiet as a mouse.

The air cracked like an impending lightning strike, same as that time Dad and I had gotten caught in a storm while fishing up in New Hampshire.

Tension hovered over the table stifling *everything* as though awaiting the thunder.

My new stepbrother stared at his plate, fork poised over a spear of asparagus, his cheeks pale compared to moments earlier, shoulders hitched up around his ears. That need to wrap the kid in my arms sparked to life inside me again. It was too bad he didn't like me all up in his space because he could definitely use a good hug or ten.

I glanced at Jacqueline—the source of the disturbance in the atmosphere.

She glowered at Preston, her lips pressed into a tight line and cheeks mottled red. My forehead dented into a frown. Dad eyed her funny too, like he had no clue what the fuck was going on.

Married or not, you couldn't know everything about a person's past a few days after meeting them.

"*Nancy* is no longer allowed in this building," Jacqueline snipped, the name spat out like a curse, "or the high school for that matter, so no, he will *not*."

The fuck?

Dad and I caught each other's gazes. He shrugged.

"That...*man* is an abomination," Jacqueline continued, waving her hand as though her ex-husband was nothing but a pesky black fly. Her hard, annoyed tone hinted at the same. "You will not speak of him—*her*—or whatever it is *Nancy* believes himself to be these days."

Tears welled in Preston's eyes at Jacqueline's harsh statement, and empathy and anger bolted through my chest.

One of Sean's and my classmates had come out as trans the year before. I guessed Preston's dad had done the same, and Jacqueline couldn't handle Nancy's truth.

If that were the case, Dad's new wife, while rich and beautiful, reeked of transphobia, which made me assume she was probably homophobic as well. That whole *manly* word's strangeness took on meaning.

My heart fell even though anger for Preston caused it to beat harder than the norm.

Guess I'll be staying in the closet a little bit longer.

I wiped my mouth with the linen napkin and set it atop my plate. "Dinner was great, but I'm beat," I lied, needing to get the hell out of there. "Hey, Preston, want to show me my room? Dad told me we're across the hall from each other."

Preston pushed back from the table immediately, scurrying away without a word like his ass was on fire.

Jacqueline's face reddened further, and she opened her mouth, most likely to bark about us not asking to be excused or finishing our dinner. She seemed the sort to do both.

"Darling," Dad cooed, distracting her before she spoke more hatred, "it's been three days of agony not being by your side. I've missed you terribly."

Wanting to gag, I followed after Preston, who headed toward open stairs along the far wall as Dad continued with his lovey dovey bullshit about sharing a bottle of wine on the balcony. At least he'd allowed Preston and I to escape without a fight.

I grabbed my bag off the first stair, and my chest lightened a little in knowing he *did* still have my back.

I caught up to Preston at the top of the stairs.

"B-Bathroom is straight ahead. This room is yours," he whispered, his voice cracking, but I expected it was from the tears wanting to roll down his cheeks rather than late puberty.

Once more, I had to fist my free hand, but the second Preston entered my room on the right, I dropped my duffel, grabbed his arm, and pulled him against my chest.

His entire body stiffened, and I shushed him before he could argue, squeezing him tight. Whether he liked physical touch or not, the kid desperately needed some damned comfort.

"You can cry if you want to," I murmured, my tone light and unthreatening. "I won't judge. Promise."

Preston released a heavy exhale, sagged against my chest, and broke into silent tears. I expected with a mom like Jacqueline, he'd learned how to keep his hurt on the quiet side. He clutched at my T-shirt, his leaking eyes soaking the thin, ratty cotton within seconds.

I kicked my bedroom door shut behind us, glancing around the vast area with its queen-sized bed—and the windows beyond.

Fuck.

Those blinds would be closed twenty-four seven from here on out.

I gave my attention to the thin kid clinging to me.

"If you wanna see Nancy at any time, you just tell me, okay?" I said. "I've got my license and will drive you in my dad's SUV wherever the hell you want to go. Your mom doesn't even have to know about it."

He cried harder, and my throat thickened at the sobs spewing from my new stepbrother. How long had he been holding that agony in? Even though my parent's divorce had hit me hard, I couldn't imagine the bullshit Preston had faced with his dad transitioning into a woman when his mom was downright vile about the whole thing.

At least, I was pretty sure I had figured the situation out.

"Your dad." I paused once he quieted a bit, not real sure how or what to call them. "Nancy...she's trans?"

Preston hesitated, once more tensing, but jerked his head in a nod.

"Sweet. I can't wait to meet her," I stated firmly while holding his shivering body just a bit tighter. While a fraction of my size and easily half my weight, Preston fit in my arms perfectly.

I didn't give a shit Preston's bitter mom was Dad's new wife or the reason his heart beat again.

I would be in my stepbrother's corner no matter what. He was now mine to look after. Mine to protect—even from his mother if it came to it.

Chapter 2

Preston

In typical Jacqueline fashion, Mom had ruined what I'd hoped was finally the beginning of something good in my life for a change.

But I'd made the mistake of opening my mouth to ask about Dad, since I'd been all but freaking out about the first day of high school in the not-far-enough-away future.

I knew better.

Mom's harsh words about Nancy had hurt worse than dull blades ripping through skin. I'd bled countless times from her spewed hatred but had learned to hold in my grief until I was behind closed doors where no one would see my emotions but me.

Drake had offered me escape, and I'd been desperate to get away regardless of how Mom would berate me later like she always did. I planned to show Drake to his room, then hide in mine where I could cry silent tears into my pillow until she showed up to remind me of who I was. How certain expectations came along with the Casswell name.

But the almost-man crushed me to his chest the second we were alone, keeping me from wallowing.

I gave into my need to be held. His strong arms wrapped around my back, his exhales hot on the top of my head as I sobbed like a baby over my inability to please my mom and gain her affections.

Drake didn't judge, just like he'd promised. Didn't snap at me to get ahold of myself and act like a man like Mom would have done. He gave me freedom to grieve the life I'd lost when Dad had transitioned.

While Drake's father Devlin seemed great and all, he would never replace the person who'd sat with me every night before I went to bed. There would be no sharing about my day, playing duets on the piano downstairs, or discussions of books we both enjoyed reading with Drake's dad.

Because he wasn't mine, nor would he ever replace my biological father.

Sure, I had a cell phone and was allowed to talk to Nancy, but it wasn't the same as having him—*her*—be a part of my daily routine like she used to be, the only person I'd had to count on for acceptance and love.

Drake promised to take me to see Nancy whenever I wanted.

And his hugs were better than warm glazed donuts.

I could stay right there with my face smooshed against his hard chest, his heart beating calmly beneath my ear forever, but I didn't want my new stepbrother thinking I was a total loser.

Sniffing, I pulled away, swiping my arm over my eyes. "S-Sorry."

"Don't be." He half-punched, half-squeezed my shoulder in some sort of bro action—affection, maybe? I didn't have any close friends, so I wouldn't know.

I liked it though. Loved how the feel of his hard body and warmth lingered along the front of me.

"Shit." Drake stood, hands on his hips, and glanced around.

His bedroom was similar in size to mine but lacked in personal effects that would reveal his personality. The half-dozen boxes and a few trash bags to his left had been brought up by staff as we'd sat down to eat dinner.

"I'll, um, leave you to g-get settled in," I said, my voice cracking like usual. Growing up sucked, even more so since my hormones had started to kick in long after the other guys in middle school.

"Stay."

I glanced up at Drake, his vivid blue eyes searching my face. Heat rushed to my cheeks, and I swallowed, turning my focus to the hardwood floor in front of us. "Sure. I c-can help if you want?"

"Sweet. Just give me one minute." He fished his cell from his back pocket, reminding me of Mom chiding him as though Drake was her real son.

I'd been embarrassed that she'd shown her true colors so quickly, but Drake did live in Jacqueline's penthouse now. He would learn she was Napoleon in female clothing, and nothing we did would make her appreciate us.

A huffed laugh rumbled from his chest, and his fingers flew over the screen after he powered it on. "My best friend is an asshole."

Even though Drake smiled while texting his friend, I could see sadness on his face.

"You miss him."

"Fuck yeah." Drake's grin faded, and he shoved his phone away. He didn't look at me but started for the pile of his belongings.

"New York isn't so b-bad." I offered what I hoped would be comfort. Not that my stuttered words would ever feel as good to him as his hug had to me.

"I can handle it for three years." He tossed one of the two black trash bags toward the bureau against the far wall.

"You'll go back after you graduate?" I picked up a smaller box, proud that I hadn't stumbled over my words.

"Yeah. Boston is my home, you know?"

I didn't but nodded all the same while sitting the box atop Drake's bed. Evidence of his sporting accomplishments lay wrapped in old, frayed towels.

I glanced over at Drake. He stuffed clothing into drawers, not even bothering to fold the items first. Hopefully, Mom didn't go through his stuff like she did mine to make sure I kept my belongings tidy.

"Where do you want these?" I asked, holding up an old trophy with a baseball player atop it.

Drake looked around the room, blanching a bit as his eyes drifted over the windows. "Uh..." He hopped up and fumbled with the blinds until they closed us in from the outside world.

I bit back a smile at finding Drake wasn't completely perfect like I'd thought. He obviously didn't like heights, same as me. But I'd only ever known living high above the rest of the world. He would get used to it eventually.

"You can put those on that shelf." He pointed at the bookshelf I'd had to empty of my book collection overflow. Unfortunately, Mom had made me go through my fantasy books and pack up older ones for donation, since I had to now share the upstairs with someone else.

At first, the idea of another teen imposing on my space had twisted my stomach. I hadn't slept much since Mom had told me about Devlin and Drake, but neither of them had made me uncomfortable.

Drake especially wouldn't be anything *near* a bother since his hugs were freely given and just...*perfect*. Even if he farted around me, peed all over the toilet seat, or smelled like sweat after working out, which I expected he did a lot of considering the muscle on his huge frame, I wouldn't mind sharing the penthouse with him. Maybe it would finally begin to feel like a real home.

Smiling when I'd expected to be miserable, I carefully made a shrine to Drake's athletic abilities on the top shelf.

"Are you going to play football this year?" I asked, setting up the final trophy and angling it just so before breaking down the box.

"Nah. Too much going on, and I'm sure the season has already started."

I wouldn't know. "Does your best friend play too?"

"Sean—and no. He's got two left feet and is too small for the gridiron." Drake sounded like he smiled again.

Sure enough, when I turned from finishing with the cardboard, he grinned.

"You guys are pretty close even though you're opposites?"

"We've been best buddies since elementary school."

"Must be nice to have a friend like that," I murmured, more to myself than Drake.

"You don't have any close friends?"

I shook my head, hating the tightening in my stomach.

"Well, I'm here now. I'll have your back."

Warmth spread through my chest, and my face heated. "Thank you," I whispered.

He used his foot to push a box toward me. "That's shit that can go on the desk. In it, or whatever. I'm not picky."

Nodding, I set to work unpacking a mess of items that appeared to have been tossed in without care. School supplies, framed pictures...old chargers, and even an empty Sam Adams beer bottle.

"You drink?"

Drake glanced my way, saw what I held, and chuckled. "That's the first bottle I ever cracked open. But yeah. Sean and I love the shit."

Shit was right. I couldn't stand the smell of hops. "Dad —*Nancy*—loves Sam Adams too. I think it's gross."

Drake laughed again, and I couldn't help my smile over hearing the lighthearted sound. "She and I will get along without issue."

My throat tightened even though my lips still curved upward. Drake had no problem using my father's pronouns, something I still on occasion struggled to remember even though it had been a couple of years since she'd been forced from our home. "Nancy is great."

"She took part in making you, so I'm sure she is."

Eyes welling and heart fluttering at the first genuine compliment I could ever remember hearing outside of Nancy, I swallowed hard. I focused on keeping the tears from falling while arranging pencils, pens, and old markers in the desk drawer. After the divorce, Mom had legally changed my name to Casswell, erasing all evidence of Nancy from my life. She also had the money and lawyers to strip my dad of all rights even though no court of law should have granted it. My age allowed me to suggest who I wanted to live with, but Nancy had a new future to figure out. She'd hugged me goodbye, promising she would be waiting for when I was old enough to visit without needing Jacqueline's permission.

But now?

I could go whenever I felt like it. Drake's offer to sneak me to dad's place had filled me with a willfulness I'd never experienced before. For the first time, I was ready to go against Mom's rules and thought I might finally have found the balls to do so.

Maybe someday, after a few more baby steps of independence, I would even reclaim the surname Mom had stolen from me.

Guts clenching at the thought, I focused on the steadiness of Drake, his strength, and his promise to have my back. My nervousness had eased a lot thanks to his awesome hug. It helped that Drake didn't have an intimidating bone in his body even though he towered over me by at least a foot. Hopefully, I had some of Nancy's height still hiding in my DNA even if the rest of me was almost a spitting image of my mom.

"So are you nervous about high school?"

I snorted at Drake's question, not upset over the conversation change in the least. "Considering we aren't in the same grade and I have more bullies than buddies, you could say that."

"Bullies?"

Shrugging, I broke down the box I'd emptied while hoping a non-cavalier tone bled through my words. "I'm the only *carrottop* in my class, I'm the last to hit puberty, and my voice still cracks with every other word. Add the pettiness of other rich kids who are jealous of your status, and what do you expect?"

"For people to be decent human beings," he stated, his voice pissed off. "But yeah—it hardly ever happens. Teenagers especially are assholes. But don't worry. I'll be there for you. Anyone gives you shit, you let me know."

"I wouldn't want you to get into trouble." And I could

only imagine how Jacqueline would go into a rage if he caused any drama for the Casswell family even though his surname was different than ours.

"Taking care of what's mine will never be trouble."

I stared at Drake's wide shoulders as he shoved an armload of jeans into his bottom drawer. He thought of me as *his?* A strange twinge radiated through my chest, a feeling I'd never experienced before. Appreciation, probably since most days I swore even my own mother would rather I hadn't been born.

I'd always wanted a brother, someone I could confide in, someone who had firsthand experience of living with a particular mother who found everything about me lacking regardless of how hard I tried to please her. Gain her love.

Now I do.

My throat tightened, and the sight of Drake's back went hazy. I shuddered with an exhale.

He turned, but I couldn't make out his face. "Hey." He hopped up, arms opened as he moved toward me.

It was easy as breathing to step into his embrace. I closed my leaking eyes and clung to his old Aerosmith T-shirt again. He smelled like soap with a hint of dryer sheets. Clean. Untouched by Mom's negativity and money.

Drake Hemmings was the most real guy I'd ever met.

I wanted to keep him forever.

Chapter 3

Drake

It had been ten days since I'd arrived in New York, and Preston hadn't escaped the penthouse once. I'd asked him to show me downtown Manhattan, but he claimed to dislike crowds and noise. Seeing how easily he grew anxious around just his mom and my dad, I'd eventually left him alone. I ended up checking out the city by myself since even Dad couldn't be bothered to leave his new wife's side and had accepted a lowly position in her family's business.

One afternoon was all it had taken for me to know bustling New York City wouldn't ever grow on me with its noise and people who couldn't be bothered to make eye contact. Central Park might be okay for the occasional morning run instead of the treadmill, but that was about it. I'd returned to sit inside the glass building that would be my whole world until I graduated.

There was a gym on one of the lower floors, exclusively for those who lived in the building, but Preston had no interest in joining me there either even though I'd begged him often enough. I thought I'd intimidated him when we'd first met, but I quickly learned he avoided people as a whole. Even the seamstress who'd come for our uniform fittings had made him uncomfortable. That and the how Jacqueline kept snapping at him to hold still or turn a certain way.

Fuck did I hate how she made her son cower in on himself. She, without doubt, was the sole source of his low self-esteem. It was too bad he couldn't just tell her to fuck off and go live with Nancy.

But he'd explained how Nancy had her own life to figure out and couldn't afford to provide for her son.

At least we had school to disrupt the boredom and allow us an escape from Napoleon reborn.

"I've got this."

I barely made out Preston's whisper to himself as he stepped onto the elevator in front of me.

We both carried backpacks, his fuller than mine with supplies for his freshman year.

That promised limo waited downstairs to take us to Dupont Prep for our first day of school, but there was no hiding both of our underlying nervousness.

Dad and Jacqueline had seen us off at the front door, Dad's hard hug hurting my ribs. Upon seeing how Dad bid me goodbye, Jacqueline put her arms around Preston in an awkward as fuck half-hug that seemed to make both of them uncomfortable. Even her smile in wishing us good luck looked fake as hell.

I didn't know what the fuck her problem was, but I didn't like it—or her—at all.

But my father was happy for now, and I had a clock counting down the minutes until I could return to where I belonged. Sure, I would miss Dad when I went off to college, but I felt sure we had the type of friendship bond atop our dad/son thing that wouldn't ever be broken. If he and Jacqueline even lasted that long.

I doubted he and his new wife would miss us that morning though. They couldn't keep their hands off each other, so rather than going into the office like they usually did on workdays, I expected they would spend the day in bed since they had the place to themselves for the first time since we'd moved in.

Sickening and envy-provoking all the same.

Preston turned to face the panel once inside the elevator, and I stepped in to stand beside him. His freckles stood out from his paler than usual skin. He pressed the button for the ground floor.

"You okay?" I asked, nudging him with my elbow, wondering how badly he missed Nancy and if his stomach churned like mine.

Preston jerked his head in a stiff nod. Nostrils flared, he looked like he had trouble breathing rather than fighting off tears over Nancy's absence. According to Preston, she used to take him to school every morning but hadn't the previous two years. He'd kept how he felt about that fact to himself, but his face was an open book. It'd hurt like hell.

The elevator doors slid shut, and I swore I heard him whimper.

"Hey." I nudged him again.

We started down, and he shuddered, his eyes closing.

I grabbed hold of his hand clutching at his backpack strap. "*Preston.*"

Another shiver wracked through him. "Hey," I repeated, fighting his grip so I could twine my fingers through his. Tingles slid up to my shoulder as our palms squashed together, but I didn't know what to make of them. "Did you finish that book last night? I saw your light beneath your door at one this morning when I went to the bathroom."

"W-What?" He blinked his eyes open as I squeezed his fingers, tugging his arm down so the back of his hand pressed against my hip.

"That novel with the elf dude on the front."

"Y-You s-saw what I was reading?" He sounded breathless and swallowed hard.

"Yeah. You left it on the coffee table a few days ago. Looks pretty cool. What's it about?"

Preston rubbed his free palm down his slacks, his other hand gripping tightly to mine. "Uh...he's a d-dark elf."

"Does he have magical powers and shit? Like that Legolas guy?"

Blinking, Preston lifted his head to give me a rare, steady study with those emerald eyes of his. "You—You know who L-Legolas is?"

"The blond elf from Lord of the Rings. Yeah." I shrugged like it wasn't the big deal he seemed to think it was.

He blinked again like a cute baby owl. "You...wow." A shaky laugh lifted his lips, and I grinned.

"I'm not a total jock."

"L-Legolas doesn't have magic," Preston said, seeming to settle, his shoulders relaxing. "He just has natural abilities b-born to an elf. Exceptional eyesight. Endurance to t-travel for hours and d-days without tiring. Those sorts of things we mere mortal men could never do."

I tried not to grin too hard. He was such a nerd and adorable at that.

The elevator slowed as we neared the fourth floor, and Preston yanked his hand from mine, once more clutching at his backpack strap.

I curled my fingers together, missing the feel of his sweaty palm against mine. As one, we moved away from the door to make room for others heading down. Smiling, I nodded a greeting at the man in a business suit with a cell pressed to his ear who stepped inside.

The asshole ignored both of us, turning his back toward us without a word like all the other assholes I'd seen so far in the city.

We descended again, and at the hint of a shudder from Preston, I shifted closer to him so our bare forearms touched.

He glanced up at me.

You okay? I mouthed as our elevator companion spoke into his cell about a midmorning meeting.

A half-smile curled Preston's lips before he nodded. "I j-just hate enclosed spaces," he whispered.

Behind our companion, I pressed my hand against Preston's lower back.

He leaned in closer to me and sighed.

Lifting my focus off his too-cute face, I studied the seam of the elevator doors atop the rich jerk's head in front of us.

The first day of my sophomore year was going to kick ass. I would fit in. Make friends. And keep a close eyes on my stepbrother as best I could. Fuck knew the kid had anxiety issues enough for the entire school's population.

FF
MM

Nothing about this middle-class Bostonian with a heavy accent fit in with the elites at Dupont Prep.

D.P.

Whenever I thought about the prestigious school's

initials, I snorted. Sean had gotten a kick out of it too. While he was vers, he'd never taken two dicks at once. I'd yet to have one up my ass and wasn't sure how I really felt about being penetrated, but I was open to maybe try it someday. I'd topped twice to Sean's...twelve? Twenty times having sex? The guy was a total horndog.

I'd lost my virginity the summer before, but he'd been thirteen when he'd first been blown by another guy.

I missed the fucker, his constant upbeat attitude and laughter.

New York could do with a dozen Sean Foxes. D.P. especially. Every student walked around like they had two dicks shoved up their ass. Noses in the air, they sniffed at me as though I was beneath the soles of their designer shoes.

Three years.

Those words were still my mantra, my focus beyond passing high school so I could return to Boston for college. Sean and I would both get our MBAs then go work for some company or start our own and make a million so we could donate to politicians who believed guys like us deserved equal rights.

That last bit was a stretch, but why not shoot for the stars?

At least Preston had made a new friend. He told me about a Manhattan-born boy who'd recently switched schools, and like Preston, he was small and timid.

Benjamin Byron Baldwin-Barclay.

Who the fuck named their kid that? Pretentious assholes, and New York was fucking full of them.

"Drake!"

I recognized the high-pitched voice calling to me. Quad-B I'd nicknamed Ben. Turning, I scanned over the teenagers in the hallway as we all headed for our next class.

A dark mop of hair bobbed up and down, skinny arms waving frantically.

Frowning, I started toward him, not bothering to excuse myself as I jostled other students out of my way. I'd found no one else had a lick of decency in how they treated non-friends, so why should I?

"Drake!" Ben's face was white as a sheet. "Preston needs you!" He spun and sprinted back from where he'd come, and I hoofed it hot on his heels, my pulse picking up pace.

"The fuck is going on, Quad-B?"

"The Shipley bully and his minions," he gasped, out of breath.

Shit.

Teeth clenched, I readied to break a nose or three. Hell, maybe a couple of arms. Smash in some teeth, at the very least.

Jackson Shipley was one of the richest brats in New York and the fucker who had picked on Preston throughout middle school. He'd ignored my stepbrother so far this year, but it sounded like things had gone back to the way they used to be.

It was time to stop that shit from continuing once and for all.

Dad—Jacqueline especially—had warned me to be on my best behavior and would skin me alive if I caused unnecessary drama that would soil the Casswell name. Made me want to misbehave just so she'd send me away, but with my only option being Mom and those two annoying daughters of her husband's...yeah, no.

I would have to play nice.

Somewhat.

We rounded a corner, and sure enough, Preston was on

his hands and knees, attempting to gather up a mess of papers strewn over the floor. Two guys stood with Shipley, who loomed over Preston, both laughing at whatever the fucker had said. A smaller group of kids lingered around, the girls snickering behind their hands and manicured fingernails.

Shipley play-slapped Preston's pale cheek. "Look at the pimple-faced faggot on his knees like he's desperate to blow me."

Preston jerked away from him.

"Hey!" I hollered, drawing everyone's attention, but it was Preston's wet eyes I sought.

Fucking red hazed my vision over the embarrassment and pain reaching out toward me.

Knowing I couldn't really wreck Shipley's face and get away with it, I simply barreled forward. I used my line-backer body rather than my hands to send him crashing into his asshole buddies like they were a couple of guys on the football field.

"Don't fucking touch what doesn't belong to you!" I growled as the three guys slammed into the lockers behind them.

One cursed while Shipley straightened, brushing himself off like my touch had soiled his starched button-down. "Carrottop is *yours?*" He snickered.

"Damn right he is," I shot at him before grasping Preston's shoulders and giving him my full attention. "You okay?" I whispered, uncaring my back was to the three bullies. I hoped they *tried* to take me so I could claim self-defense as reason for sending all three to the floor.

Pink coated Preston's cheeks as he nodded.

"Come on." I helped gather up his things as the small crowd around us dispersed, the three assholes included, unfortunately. They muttered beneath their breath about faggots and my stupid accent, but I couldn't help who I was.

Fuck them and their elitist, homophobic bullshit.

All that mattered was Preston.

Arm slung over his shoulder, I glared at the few kids still hanging around. "Don't you have classes to go to?" I barked, giving them my harshest glare.

They scampered away, and I squeezed Preston tight against me.

He melted into me, and Quad-B flanked his other side.

"That was so cool!" Quad-B whisper-hollered, his voice giddy. "You're like a brick wall! A…an *oak* tree! Damn, I wished I had your height and muscle."

I preened a bit, thankful as fuck I had both of those in spades.

The better to look after Preston.

We stopped at the door to his next class he had with Quad-B, and I dropped my arm to face my little step-brother. "You going to be alright?"

He gazed up at me like I hung the damn moon to chase away the night's darkness.

I fake-punched his shoulder before giving it a quick squeeze like I always did, hoping to ease the strange ache in my chest.

His smile wobbled, but at least his tears had dried. "Thank you, Drake."

"Anything for you, kid."

"Not a kid," he muttered what he always did, even though I'd explained that calling people that regardless of their sex or age was a Boston thing.

"This is last period," I said, walking away backwards since I was going to be late for class and couldn't hang out any longer. "Meet me here when it's over—I don't want you leaving the building without me."

He nodded, his shy smile still in place.

Fuck, Preston was going to break hearts when he got older.

Jaw clenching, I spun on my heels and hurried to class. That ache in my chest lingered long after the bell rang, and I made excuses for being late to geometry.

The way Preston had stared at me was a lot like how I felt for him, even though I couldn't exactly put it into words. But Preston *was* just a kid even though he claimed he wasn't. He looked up to me like I was some sort of super-hero or such shit.

Fucking heart eyes and all, but we *were* stepbrothers.

I needed to remember that.

Chapter 4

Preston

The summer after my sophomore year, I finally shot up a few inches, quickly outgrowing my pants and proving to myself that Nancy really had taken part in giving me life. Unfortunately, I didn't fill out at all and was still as "skinny as a string bean," Mom stated. Her lips pursed as though annoyed with my DNA showcasing that "thing," which was how she referred to my dad.

I couldn't help the way I looked and was damned proud to finally have some outward appearance of Nancy.

Sure, anxiety oftentimes made eating damn near impossible, which added to my skinniness, but I also had zero desire to hit the weights or run on a treadmill for hours on end like Drake did downstairs in the gym. Physical activity didn't interest me.

Whenever Drake disappeared and I didn't have him to distract me with his Xbox or listening to Aerosmith together, I would sit and read to my heart's content. Mom and Devlin left us alone a couple of nights a week or for special weekend getaways, and I would sit at the piano and reminisce about the many hours I'd entertained Nancy when she lived with us.

Mom hated the sound of the piano—it reminded her of what she'd lost when Dad transitioned. At least she hadn't tossed it into the trash along with everything else Nancy hadn't packed up in her rush to leave. I'd have been in a hurry too seeing as how Mom had rained hell down atop her head with screams and curses.

Sometimes, I would come up from the world I escaped into through music to find Drake sprawled out on the couch, eyes closed, his lips curled up a little. The first time, I'd been embarrassed as hell, but he'd told me how good I was, how he'd never heard anyone play like I did.

Red-faced and stuttering my words, I'd thanked him.

The next night he joined me, I gave the ivory keys all my lovin', anything for Drake to relax and smile again. He preferred the more haunting type classical pieces, so I'd made it my goal to learn as many as possible regardless of what Mom thought of my practicing.

"What are you going to do after you graduate?" he asked, as the last notes from his favorite Bach piece faded into silence.

It was the weekend before our last year of school together. In ten months, Drake would hightail it back to Boston, never to return, and I would lose the only person who showed me a bit of attention. I'd hoped Mom's marriage to Devlin would make her appreciate me like Drake's dad did him, but no such luck. I still felt like a stain on Jacqueline's resume.

Slowly releasing an exhale, I slouched on the piano bench and glanced out over the city lights against the night sky Drake had gotten somewhat used to. At least he no longer demanded we close the blinds the second he entered a different room.

My heart lay heavy in my chest, a sadness I wasn't yet ready to face. "Not sure," I said, my voice barely audible.

"Aren't you going to work at Casswell Global? It's all Jacqueline talks about."

I shrugged, daring a quick glance at Drake, since I had to get my fill while I still could.

Eyes closed, he lay on the couch as usual, bare-chested, arms angled upward and hands clasped behind his head. Muscles rippled from his forearms down to where the dark hair on his lower abs disappeared into his sweats.

Clearing my throat, I tore my focus off him before he opened his eyes and caught me staring. The guy had the body of a god. Something I'd recently realized was sexy as hell. Life stirred in my groin, and I shifted, mindlessly playing a few scales in an attempt to distract my libido.

"I'm not really interested in the family company," I finally voiced for the first time to one of the two people I could trust with that information.

Nancy had understood. I expected Drake would as well.

"Your mom will shit a brick if you don't take over as CEO someday."

She would, even though I'd never been good enough for anything in her eyes. Some part deep inside made me want to believe her annoyance with my existence was merely a front, a way to teach me how to be a "real man," since she'd often spoken her hope for me.

Doubtful though.

Huffing, I dropped my hands to my lap, peeking once more at the guy who'd introduced me to wet dreams.

He studied me where I sat in sweats and a baggy T-shirt.

"What?" I asked, self-consciousness welling inside me as it always did whenever he looked my way.

A slow grin lit his bright blue eyes.

"*What?*" I repeated, my face growing hot.

"Make sure I'm around the day you tell her you're going to head off and do your own thing. *Please.* Fuck, do I need to see her face when you drop that bomb."

I snorted. "If I ever find the balls, I will. But you know me. I'll be stuck behind my grandfather's desk. Two PAs will be up my ass all day every day like they are hers, and I'll shiver and shake like a leaf whenever I have to attend a board meeting. I'll have an electronic leash by way of a cell phone, so my mom has twenty-four access to me to ensure I don't mess something up if she can ever be talked into retiring—which I *highly* doubt."

My shoulders sagged at the truth vomiting from my lips. I would never escape her, nor would she ever love me how I yearned for.

"I hate that for you." Drake all but growled the words, scowling, his eyes hard. "It's your life, Preston. Be who you want. *Do* what you want. Don't let some antiquated expectations from the illustrious Casswell line dictate your future."

I snorted at his use of the big words he always tossed out when talking about any of New York's richest families. Even though his way of speaking amused me, he'd made statements with such passion, such brutal honesty sometimes that I wanted to cry.

"What's your idea of the perfect job?" he asked, not ready to give up the conversation. He made my heart soar.

At least someone cared about me. Listened.

"Something with computers," I admitted, my chest fluttering. I'd bought myself a new Mac desktop halfway through my freshman year, and I'd been addicted to all things coding ever since I'd learned how the world wide web worked.

And Drake had thought I was a nerd before.

"You're a damn wiz with them. I can only check my email and social media. Even those fucking Google Docs we use for school mess with my head."

My poor stepbrother was not technologically inclined.

But he knew how to make me feel special. He could bring a smile to my face with a quick hug. He had my back as he'd promised, snuffing out the bullying against me before our first year at D.P. had ended.

As far as I was concerned, Drake was worth a million bucks.

"Our parents aren't coming home until tomorrow night," Drake said, sitting up and leaning forward, elbows on his knees. "Want to give Nancy a call? See if she's up for some company since she won't be around Monday morning before we head to hell?"

My heart squeezed tight inside my suddenly aching chest. "Yeah," I rasped. "I'd love that."

Forget that million. Drake was priceless.

We slogged through traffic in Devlin's old SUV with Drake behind the wheel, but we got into Queens without too much difficulty for a Saturday night.

Jacqueline's parents had demanded a prenup before she'd married my father, so when Nancy got kicked out of our home and Mom filed for divorce, she'd been left with close to nothing.

I wasn't sure what my mom had done with Devlin and how they'd gotten married so quickly, but knowing how tight she and her lawyers were, I expected Devlin had to sign something before she'd agreed to say "I do" again.

My second mom was left to work retail during the day, since she'd lost her position at Casswell Global in the human resources department. It had been five years, and she still hadn't been able to find a job worthy of her degree or kindness.

The world sucked, plain and simple. You'd think with how liberal New York could be that a trans woman in her forties would be accepted and hired for her resume regardless that she didn't always pass for a female.

Why couldn't people just be free to *be*?

Nancy greeted me with a hug, and I got teary-eyed at the scent of her new flowery perfume surrounding me. While she no longer smelled like my dad used to, she felt pretty much the same. Perhaps a bit softer, but I would love her no matter what she wore or how long she grew her hair.

"Drake." Nancy squeezed Drake tight too. "Thank you for bringing Preston to visit me." Her voice broke, and Drake held onto her while she sniffled a bit.

Throat tight, I looked on, loving how Drake accepted Nancy for who she was and how he gifted me the opportunity to spend time with her since I didn't have my license. The thought of driving sent my anxiety spiraling.

"Beer?" Nancy asked, and we both agreed, settling in her tiny living room with its love seat and recliner.

While we were far from twenty-one, Nancy didn't give a shit about the two of us having a drink while we hung out with her for a few hours. I still wasn't a huge fan of beer, but the occasional one shared with family was kind of cool.

The hops were growing on me.

"So." Nancy smiled, what looked like real happiness

shining from her face for the first time in longer than I could remember. "Your junior year starts on Monday."

"Ugh." I rolled my eyes. "Don't remind me."

Drake elbowed me and sipped his beer. We were squashed together from knee to shoulder on the tiny couch, but we didn't care. Affection and physical touch came easily between us. I craved his nearness even if all my thoughts weren't always appropriate toward him.

He never talked about girls like Ben did, and he'd never once been on a date that I knew of. Like me, he spent weekends at home, hanging out. We'd watched countless movies while lounging in my bed in front of the flat-screen TV I had hanging on my wall.

A few times, he'd even fallen asleep, and I let him stay, curling onto my side to stare at him like a pervert while he slept.

But I only allowed myself that special treat when our parents were gone for the evening.

Devlin and Jacqueline rarely visited the penthouse's upstairs, but if Mom found us lying down together like that, no matter how innocent, she would lose her shit and scream like a banshee.

But yeah. Those nights with Drake in my bed? Best. Ever.

I always woke with a warm body wrapped around mine, hot breath on my hair. How often I'd slipped from his hold to scamper to the bathroom before he woke I couldn't say, but I made enough racket to ensure he was awake and gone from my room before I returned.

"Will you come to my graduation?" Drake asked Nancy.

Her smile doubled in size. "I would love to, but that can't happen. The last thing I want is for my ex to throw a tantrum and embarrass you and your father, never mind my son."

"Jacqueline wouldn't dare," I said, spinning my sweating bottle of beer between my fingers. "She would be pissed as hell for sure but would hold everything inside until we got home. You know how she is about not making a spectacle of herself out in public."

"True," Nancy agreed, "but I wouldn't wish her wrath on your family behind closed doors either. I'll be there in spirit, Drake. I promise."

"So what's new?" I asked Nancy, pressing my knee a little more firmly against Drake's. Any excuse to be closer to him even if he only saw it as the comfort I wished to give him.

"Well." Pink flushed her face.

"Oh, this is gonna be good," Drake said with a chuckle.

"I met a lovely man." Nancy sounded breathless.

Joy welled up inside me at the happiness on her face. Same as always whenever I got emotional, my throat swelled. "That's great," I whispered, smiling. "Tell us all about him."

She did—and from what she said and the light in her eyes, I expected that Nancy wouldn't be struggling to pay rent on her own for much longer.

Nancy might be broke, living quite a few hundred steps down from where she'd lounged in luxury as Jacqueline's husband for over a decade, but she was content. Right where she was meant to be.

I hoped that when the day came for me to stand on my own two feet that I would find the same courage to seek out true happiness as she had.

Chapter 5

Drake

Those three years dragged by slow as fuck, and yet they suddenly ended.

Both of our parents were out on a dinner date, Dad still surprisingly as madly in love with Jacqueline as the first time I'd seen them hug and kiss. I didn't get it, but whatever. Preston and I declined the invite to join them as we always did.

Staying home alone with Preston had been my favorite pastime while living in New York. I sat and listened to him play a sentimental song by Beethoven on the piano.

His long, slender fingers glided over the keys with grace, his head bowed and floppy red hair hiding his eyes. But I knew what they looked like. Had memorized every varying shade of green and the golden rings around his pupils. How tears caused his irises to glimmer like freshly shined emeralds and pain dulled them. Happiness made them sparkle. The memory of sunlight glinting off their brilliance etched in my mind and visited me in my dreams.

They were the most beautiful windows I'd ever seen, open-looking glasses into the soul of the guy I desperately needed space from even though I longed for the exact opposite.

He never shied away from my affection, the little touches I couldn't help from lavishing on him since his mom couldn't be bothered to give him what he craved from her. I didn't get that either, but I'd never been without a parent's love and wasn't sure how I would react in his shoes.

He'd grown taller, an even more perfect fit against my chest whenever I hugged him close. But in our three years as stepsiblings, I'd eventually had to keep my lower body from him as things had slowly changed for me.

The instinct to protect him had grown into a barely tamed beast. Something more dangerous to him than it was to me. It was for the best I would leave the following evening. My bags were packed except for the track pants and T-shirt I would wear beneath my graduation gown the next day.

Most of the snobs in my senior class would be in slacks and a tie, but fuck that. I would be me as always. Comfortable and without two fucks to give. Jacqueline had insisted on dressing me in some designer suit that cost a few grand, but once I left the penthouse the following afternoon for the graduation ceremony, I would never return.

So fuck the suit.

And fuck Jacqueline and her hold on my dad. At least he and I were still pretty close considering who we lived with. Had Jacqueline taken him completely away from me like I'd originally feared that first day we'd stepped into her glass tower, I'd have gone feral on her ass. Soon, she would grow bored with her blue-collar husband, ditch him, and he would once more be all mine back in Boston.

Preston pushed up from the piano stool and stretched,

his T-shirt riding up enough to give me a peek at auburn hair trailing beneath his sweats's waistband.

Saliva flooded my mouth, and I tore my focus off him for the lit cityscape beyond him. That dizzying, stomach-churning view, while no longer puke-worthy, was enough of a distraction to keep me from getting hard.

"Ready for bed?"

Fuck.

I scrubbed a hand over my face, wanting to drink a few more beers from Dad's collection without him noticing. "Yeah," I rasped, wishing I could snuggle the hell out of Preston rather than lying alone on my own mattress.

He shuffled toward the stairs, and I stared at his bubble butt, my fingers itching to reach out and squeeze his flesh. Trail my fingertips down through his crack. Spread his cheeks wide so I could see how pretty his hole was. Because it had to be. Everything about my stepbrother was mouth-watering and perfect.

We paused in the hallway, strange tension thick between us.

"Mom and Devlin won't be home for another hour at least," he murmured, studying the hardwood floor beneath his bare feet. "Want to watch a show or something?"

A curse dragged through my brain, but I rasped a "Yes" anyway.

I followed on his heels into his bedroom.

Preston locked the door behind us as he always did. Not that we had or ever would ever fuck around—I wasn't sure if he rolled my way—but Jacqueline was a grenade that could explode at any second.

A shiver slid down my spine as I yanked my T-shirt off overhead, but I didn't look over to see if Preston watched. I knew he did. Could sense what felt like appreciation in his stare. But the last thing I wanted to do was cause him embarrassment or open a can of worms that needed to stay tightly sealed.

Bad enough I'd woken while sleeping in his bed to find his hard dick pressed against my thigh from where he sprawled all the fuck over my body. Morning wood, I reasoned it away. My cock twitched at the thought no matter what I told myself, but I put Jacqueline's face in the forefront of my mind to calm the fuck down.

Worked like a goddamned charm.

Preston crawled onto his bed after I did, situating himself a few inches from my left side.

Couldn't have that. Not when it was the last night we would have together.

"Get your ass over here," I muttered, wrapping my arm around his shoulder and yanking him closer.

He released a shuddered exhale and sank into me as always, his cheek on my chest.

"Gonna miss my snuggle buddy," I muttered into the silence as the scent of his bodywash—vanilla and spice— filled my nose.

Preston had forgotten to turn on the TV. "Same," he whispered, his hand a fist atop my stomach.

A few seconds later, a tear dripped onto my skin, and I closed my eyes as my own throat swelled shut. I wrapped him up in my arms, holding him tight until he slept.

Sometime later, I heard the front door shut and alarm reactivate.

Jacqueline and Dad were home.

My pulse picked up, and I inhaled shallowly, taking stock of where I was and *how* I was.

On my side, spooning the hell out of Preston.

Dick hard and nestled against his ass.

Fuck.

I bit back a groan, clenched my eyes shut again, and listened as my dad and his wife eventually entered their suite below us. Breathing a bit easier at the silence downstairs, I nuzzled my face in Preston's silky hair, wishing I could stay there all night.

But that would be playing with fire.

My balls throbbed, and I shifted, hoping to ease the ache just a little. Preston's backside was just so damn welcoming. I moved my hips again and shuddered an exhale at thoughts of releasing my dick from my sweats to rub against the cotton keeping his skin from mine.

Jesus, I had it bad.

Preston sighed in his sleep—or perhaps he stirred toward wakefulness?

I didn't move. Didn't breathe.

How often had he woken up and slipped from my embrace over the years when we'd been gifted the freedom to spend the night together? I'd always made sure to have my hard dick away from his ass, but in that moment, our last few hours together...I didn't want to.

Couldn't.

He definitely roused. I could feel his heart rate kick up beneath my palm on his chest.

Tension, thick and delicious, slid through my veins.

Preston swallowed and rolled onto his back, his head continuing to turn until sleepy green eyes met mine.

The world disappeared as I swam straight into his soul and frolicked like a kid in the baby pool for the first time. Wetness glazed over his beautiful orbs, and even though I wanted to smash my lips to his, lick into his mouth and taste his sweetness, I couldn't.

I wrapped my arms around him and pulled him against

my front. We touched from toes to chest, hard dick be damned, my lips against his forehead.

Jesus fucking Christ.

He was mine. Always would be, even after I put distance between us and decades passed with us living separate lives as we had no choice but to do.

"D-Drake," he whispered, his voice as broken as my heart.

"I have you, Preston," I rasped, fighting off tears.

He cried until he once more passed the fuck out.

Climbing from his bed knifed at my chest, leaving me shredded and bleeding.

It was the last night I would get to hold my stepbrother.

The following afternoon, I graduated. All my shit sat packed in the back of the Land Rover Jacqueline had gifted me that morning, ready for my escape to Boston. Dad hugged me, teary-eyed and proud, reminding his *little buddy* to shoot for the stars. Jacqueline offered me her best wishes, but I barely returned her embrace, unease making my skin crawl over the fact she gave me more affection than her own son.

And Preston...

The last to bid me goodbye—in front of our parents.

Swallowing hard, I ruffled his hair, wishing I could sink my fingers in deep and pull him toward me, right into my arms where he belonged. "Take care, kid."

He couldn't even find his voice to chide me. A single dip of his head, and he stepped back from my reach.

A blade of anguish stuck in my chest long after I left New York in my rearview mirror, but I had no choice but to leave him behind.

No matter how badly I wanted more with Preston Casswell, he could never be mine.

Chapter 6

Preston

Five Years Ago...

I stood in front of Jacqueline and Devlin's door to their new loft in Tribeca, my palms damp with sweat, my button-down and slacks chafing. The ache in my chest beneath my breastbone intensified from the anxiety attempting to squeeze the life from my lungs.

The man I dreamed about every night stood beyond the painted oak I stared at.

It wasn't until after Drake had left New York for Boston after high school graduation that I'd realized the true extent of my feelings for him. My longing had gone far beyond a teenage crush.

I loved him.

With every facet of my being. Every atom that made up my body yearned for him. Every beat of my heart thumped with agonizing want.

But he'd returned to his home, something I could never be for him no matter how badly I wished otherwise. I already fought hard for Jacqueline's affections and couldn't begin to imagine the fallout if she learned about my sexuality. Memories of Nancy's pain over that whole affair promised an emotional upheaval I wouldn't be able to handle.

Staying in the closet wasn't what I would wish on any person, but as a Casswell, I didn't feel I had a choice.

When Drake had left New York, we'd kept in touch for a few months. But eventually, he'd fallen off the map. I'd reached out to him a few times my senior year, but he rarely answered with more than one-worded replies. Eventually, I got the hint.

He'd moved on even though I hadn't.

Insecurities pushed me to believe I'd meant nothing to him, that the connection between us had been nothing but the fairy tale of a pimply-faced nerd. A dream made up for me to find solace and strength in order to make it through the toughest years of my existence.

College had proved easier.

I had needed to be near Drake even though I couldn't have him in the way I wished, so even though I'd been accepted to a few Ivy League colleges across the country, I'd chosen Harvard. I'd finally been physically free at least from Jacqueline, as I'd started referring to my biological mother at her insistence my final year of high school.

Nancy became Mom in my eyes, the nurturing woman who'd taken the place of the person in my life who had never loved me unconditionally, nor would she *ever* if she became aware of my truth. Nancy had no problem with me being gay. Knew of my longing for Drake. Hugged me every time I'd cried over losing him.

But still—I craved for Jacqueline to accept me. Love me. See me as more than just a weak man in the Casswell line.

It wasn't until I'd graduated college that something had finally gone my way.

Jacqueline had seemed to take a turn in her thought

processes, recognizing the fact I would never be enough to sit upon the Casswell Global throne. While, yeah, her admittance to that hurt like hell, I'd been thrilled to hear she planned to have someone else take over as CEO when she was ready to step down.

Drake hadn't been at my graduation or heard the news that had given me immense relief—because he'd been working, too busy to be there for me. It had been six years since he'd driven away from New York and out of my life.

Yet another thing to lament and wish had gone differently.

Jacqueline had requested both of our presences at her and Devlin's new luxury loft in Tribeca, same as she did at least once a year. Last I'd heard, Drake finally agreed to attend, so I had too. She and Devlin had one spare bedroom, but I had zero intent of staying overnight like Jacqueline insisted on.

Nancy had a room waiting for me where she lived with her boyfriend, Michael.

Knowing I would be uncomfortable being in Jacqueline's presence while waiting for Drake to arrive, I'd decided to be late. A half hour, an unacceptable amount of time that would lead to Jacqueline being pissy as hell.

She would have something to focus on rather than the fact I would be shaking in my shoes and probably acting like a lovesick fool over my stepbrother. I planned to keep my cell in my back pocket while sitting at the table too, just in case I needed further distractions from how I would salivate over Drake.

"I've got this," I whispered to myself the same words I always did whenever facing an event that turned my stomach inside out. A swipe of my palms down my pants and I rapped smartly on the wood separating me from the one I could never have.

The door yanked open.

Jacqueline glared at me. "Preston." She pursed her lips, her tone as annoyed as I'd expected. "You're late."

"Sorry, Jacqueline," I murmured, dropping my gaze to the hardwood floor.

She spun on her heels without a proper greeting. Not that I'd expected otherwise. In the few times I'd seen her since I'd left New York for Boston, she'd definitely taken to and appreciated my coolness at having become an adult in the world she'd grown up in.

God forbid we show affection or display our emotions freely in front of others.

I could sense Drake's presence before I laid eyes on him, but Jacqueline's husband approached. He hadn't aged a bit, still an older version of the dark-haired, blue-eyed man of my dreams and just as kind.

Devlin greeted me with a firm handshake and a grin. At least Jacqueline's snobbish attitude hadn't changed his easygoing nature. He was decent enough to notice I wasn't exactly comfortable around Jacqueline, but he never stuck up for me, which would stir her wrath. I couldn't blame the man, but I liked him all the same. "Good to see you, son."

I nodded, cringing at the label he'd given me even though no adoption had taken place. "Devlin," I managed.

At least my voice no longer cracked or words proved difficult for me to stutter through.

"Dinner is served," Jacqueline snipped, and movement in my periphery caused my already accelerated heartbeat to spin out of control.

My eyes flitted toward the living room regardless of my

determination to keep my focus on the dining room straight ahead.

Head down, Drake fiddled with his T-shirt. His hair had grown out a bit since high school, and a neatly trimmed beard lined his strong jaw. The arms that used to hold me tenderly appeared to have doubled in size, his wide shoulders even more broad and muscular. The man was a beast—and a sexy one at that.

Blood pooled in my groin, drying my mouth.

Same as always, Drake wore jeans that looked worn and soft as butter. He was no longer of an age that Jacqueline could demand he dress properly for dinner.

Shaking internally, I bit back a satisfied smirk to find him unchanged at least in that way and quickly glanced away before he noticed my stare.

Devlin seated Jacqueline, but before I could pull out my chair, warmth cradled my entire backside.

My breath caught, and I froze as Drake placed a hand on my lower back and did it for me the same as Devlin had for Jacqueline.

"Good to see you, kid." Drake's low voice caressed over my skin like a sweet kiss, leaving goose bumps in its wake.

"You too," I whispered rather than arguing his nickname. Unable to help myself, I fell into my chair and watched him round behind Devlin to sit across from me.

Our gazes caught, the flower arrangement low enough it didn't impede our line of sight.

Drake shuttered his blue eyes with a maturity he'd lacked as a teenager. Or maybe he no longer had the feelings for me he definitely had when we were younger. I'd felt the evidence of his desire that last night he'd been in my bed.

Perhaps I had been right all along and had only been

dreaming his comforting arms when I'd been heartbroken over his imminent departure the following day.

Drake's face remained unreadable, closed off and obvious in his disinterest for *more* when it came to me.

Swallowing hard at the thickness wanting to shut down my throat, I glanced at Jacqueline.

Her lips still pressed in a thin line as she glanced between us.

Fuck me, I had to keep my eyes off Drake before she learned the truth about my sexual orientation and who my heart longed for.

She shook out her linen napkin and lay it over her lap, glaring the entire time. "The board has settled on the new CEO, since you're unable to take your rightful place, Preston."

Disappointment coated her words, and I barely managed to keep from sinking deeper in my chair from the wish to disappear beneath the floorboards. "I'm glad to hear it." I managed to strangle some words out.

"Your second cousin Frederick *hardly* qualifies to occupy the seat meant for a Casswell. He's just as fragile and timid as you are." She sniffed with a haughty glance around the table as though looking for support.

Both Hemmings men knew better than to offer a comment.

Doing the same, I simply listened to Jacqueline drone on about family and responsibilities as a woman dressed in black served our meal. I didn't taste the scallops or risotto. Barely sipped at the sharp white wine in my glass.

Awareness of a silent Drake kept my nerves on edge and my heart in my throat, making eating difficult.

Why had he accepted the invitation to dinner when

Jacqueline had told me he'd brushed off countless ones in the previous six years?

Jacqueline soon answered that question by offering Drake a job in the family business, since her *other son* didn't have what it took to properly represent the family.

I couldn't find it in myself to care she did so with the intent to hurt me. I focused on the fact she'd in a round-about way called him her son, something she'd never done in the years since Devlin and Drake had come into our lives.

Risking a glance over at Drake, I found him pale, muscle ticking in his jaw. Blue fire raged in his eyes.

Breath once more held, I waited for him to finally lay into her, to give her a piece of his mind as he'd often told me he'd wanted to do.

He opened his mouth but hesitated when my cell played a Bach notification loud as fuck.

Heat rushed through me, flushing my face, and I pulled my phone from my pocket to glance at the screen.

"Preston!" Jacqueline admonished, but I tapped on the text regardless of her displeasure. "You know better!"

Nancy had texted me at the perfect time—and with the perfect news.

A shaky laugh erupted from my lungs, causing Jacqueline to hiss.

"Preston—"

"Nancy just got engaged to Michael!" I cut Jacqueline's admonishment off and lifted my head to meet Drake's gaze.

His eyes softened.

"What did you say?" Jacqueline hissed, her fork clattering onto her plate.

Here we go...

I turned toward the woman who'd birthed me. Face

mottled red, she glared at me with wild eyes, a sneer curling her lips.

"N-Nancy," I repeated since Drake's presence gave me courage to face her sure fury, "just got engaged to the man she's been seeing for eight years."

Drake chuckled at Jacqueline having been rendered speechless, the tension around the table making it near impossible to breathe.

"Darling," Devlin crooned in his usual voice when attempting to calm the raging beast about to explode. "We talked about this possibility."

Bless the man for trying, but Jacqueline ignored him.

"That sick *bastard!*" She erupted with what I'd expected.

I returned my focus to Drake, shutting out the tirade that poured from Jacqueline's lips. The blue eyes I wished to lose myself in slowly hardened again, and same as that first night we'd sat down to dinner as a family, I recognized the second he'd had enough.

Drake stood and tossed his napkin onto the table, making his wine goblet wobble when the linen hit it. "Dad. Jacqueline."

She cut off abruptly, mid-rant with her usual trans-phobic bullshit at Drake's gall to interrupt her let alone stand without excusing himself.

"Thanks for dinner, but I have to go. Preston?" He once more gave me his full attention.

I hopped up without a word, my own napkin fluttering to the floor as I hurried across the loft, our footfalls loud in the stunned silence we'd left behind.

"Jacqueline, my love," I heard Devlin murmur behind me, but whatever he intended to say in order to calm

Jacqueline's ire silenced as I clicked their front door shut behind us.

We didn't speak while trekking down the stairs. Didn't even look at each other once we stepped into the night.

My car sat directly out front, waiting to whisk me to the safety of my real mom's.

Drake stopped when he realized I didn't follow, turning to face me.

"My ride," I whispered, nodding toward the Audi. The shakes suddenly hit me as the adrenaline crashing through my system slowed. I swallowed hard, every inch of me aching for Drake's arms, his warmth, the steady thrum of his heart beneath my ear.

His hands fisted at his sides as he glanced up at the three-story building towering over us. He returned his focus to me, his face once more unreadable.

"D-Drake?" I choked on his name, stepping closer as my eyes welled with tears.

Without a word, he spun on his heel and stalked off, his shoulders hunched.

I took an invisible boot to my chest, losing my ability to breathe.

For the first time since we'd met, Drake didn't reach for me when I needed him. He'd given me his back rather than the comfort he was so damn good at offering. I'd been rejected with coldness when I needed affection and assurance that everything would be okay.

Perhaps in his world, things *were* downright peachy.

But those few, short minutes at Jacqueline's dining room table promised I would be thankful in the weeks ahead that I lived in Boston rather than Manhattan. She would reach out though, heaping her disappointment in me atop my head.

And I would take it because I was a coward, a desperate little boy, when it came to her.

Drake disappeared around a corner, leaving me feeling more empty than I'd ever been. I'd gone from flying high above the world at finally seeing his gorgeous face and strong shoulders to wallowing in my loneliness.

No one waited for me back home in Boston. Hell, Drake wasn't even aware I lived minutes away from him. We had no interaction—his doing, not mine since I'd given up after he'd made his desires clear years earlier.

And tonight only reiterated what he wanted.

Or rather, what he *didn't*.

Me.

Anger boiled up inside me, and I clung to the emotion like a raft in the turbulent ocean. Heart still breaking, I lifted my chin and turned toward my car on shaking legs.

Fuck Drake Hemmings.

I didn't need him in my life. I could choose to change my unattainable dreams about him, those fantasies of settling down with him and having a dozen babies together. Children who would be loved regardless of their sex or orientation.

There were no kids in my future, and there would be no grandbabies for Mom, since I didn't want any if they wouldn't have Drake as their Papa.

Climbing into my car, I kept my thoughts on my mom and Michael and the joy I would feel once I reached Queens. I would be happy for them and give all my energy to celebrating their engagement.

And try not to cry once I buried my face in the pillows on their guest bed.

Chapter 7

Drake

Present Day...

I stroked into a hot, tight ass, imagining the passion-filled green eyes peering up at me were Preston's rather than my Friday night client's.

But what else was new?

While I enjoyed the hell out of easy ass and getting paid for fucking it, I always imagined it was Preston Casswell sprawled beneath me, clinging to me, or bent over and begging for my cock.

Fucking Cupid. The batshit crazy asshole had hit the wrong fucker with Preston's arrow. I'd lost my faith in love when my parents had divorced, so I had no fucking clue what made him even aim my way.

But he'd struck me through the heart. Hard.

All I dreamed about was Preston's mouth and his bubble butt I'd lusted after for-fucking-ever.

But that could never be since we were stepbrothers. Even worse, our hooking up would inevitably end my dad's marriage, something I couldn't allow since he remained madly in love with his bitch of a wife.

Still, my heart wanted the man who owned me regardless of the necessary chasm of time and distance between us.

"Goddamnit," I muttered. I grabbed hold of Andy's cock to get him off before I blew my load into the condom to thoughts of sinking balls deep into my stepbrother I hadn't laid eyes on in years.

Andy whimpered, head tipping back, those gorgeous green orbs of his fluttering closed. Sweat dampened his brow and dark hair as he panted, "Yes, yes, yes..."

"Come for me," I coaxed, rubbing my thumb over his wet slit while burying deep inside him.

"D-Drake!" Andy sputtered my name, and ribbons of white shot up and over his smooth chest, soaking my hand.

I hissed, slamming in hard, seeing Preston in my mind. His red hair mussed from fucking, his eyes hazed over from climaxing around my dick, his plump lips parted while stuttering my name.

Only in my fucking fantasies.

I clenched my jaw and came, head tipped back and teeth gritted.

It had been eleven years since I'd taken off from New York like my feet were on fire and almost five since I'd last seen Preston.

He'd been broken and bleeding inside thanks to that fucking bitch of a woman who'd been responsible for giving life to his tender heart. Half of me wished Dad would leave her so I could have more time with him, but somehow he was happy. I couldn't take that from him.

Preston and I had stood on the cobbled sidewalk beside his Audi, my hands fisted so I wouldn't reach for him.

And those goddamned emeralds with the hint of gold around his pupils that peered at me like I hung the stars in the sky?

I groaned before shuddering out a breath as one last spurt emptied from my balls into the rubber encasing my dick.

"You with me?" Andy's familiar voice jolted me back to reality.

I heaved a heavy exhale, nodding. "Yeah. You were amazing as always," I claimed.

He smiled up at me, rumpled and sleepy as I imagined Preston would be after—

Nope.

Thinking about him was only allowed while fucking clients. After that? The forbidden desires inside me got squashed flat as a pancake so I wouldn't spiral like a damned fool wanting things I shouldn't and couldn't have.

With Andy, the pleasure came a little easier than with others though. He was by far my favorite client of Elite Escort's gay branch, since all but the dark hair atop his head reminded me of the man I was still crazy about.

I lowered some of my weight on Andy's slender body, enjoying how his legs clutched at me and hands ran down my spine and back up again.

"Have you changed your mind about dating outside work?"

I chuckled at his question before planting a gentle peck on his pouty lips. "No, but if I did, you'd be the first man I'd call."

While I adored the kid—not really a kid at twenty-five—I didn't do relationships.

Hard. Stop.

My heart had been claimed by a pimply redhead when I'd been sixteen, and there was no one who could ever replace him.

It had taken me over a year in New York to figure I'd

fallen head over heels for Preston, and I'd settled that truth in my head. But I'd also accepted the fact that we could never be.

I dreamed about the picket fences and children we could have had together though. Every goddamned night.

Why that winged bastard with the bow was cruel to me yet gifted Jacqueline the kind of love read about in fairy tales, I didn't know. Sure didn't make sense, nor was it fair.

Preston deserved to be outwardly adored and thoroughly loved on for all he'd endured in his life, but last I'd heard through the grapevine of Dad, he wasn't dating either.

At least I'd been there for three years of high school with him, protecting him whenever someone gave him shit for his cracking voice, blemished skin, and small stature, never mind Nancy, whose transition hadn't been private due to the richness of her ex-wife's family.

Fuck, how I'd soaked up whenever Preston had run to me and slammed into my chest, his long, elegant fingers clutching at me. I'd fucking *loved* being his safe place. Those same hands I could still see running over the piano's keys whenever Jacqueline and Dad were out of town.

I used to sit for hours listening to him play, lost in a fog of fiction and fantasy where we would make out against the baby grand before I carried him upstairs to my bedroom. Stripped down, he would peer up at me from my bed, reaching for me. Begging—

"Hey." Palms ran over my damp hair before cupping my cheeks.

I blinked open my eyes to find Andy peering up at me with concern. "Where'd you go just now?"

"Nowhere important," I lied as reality crashed into me like a mudslide, churning unpleasant emotions inside my chest. With one last kiss, I held the base of the condom and slid out of his warm clasp.

Back to business and reality. "You okay?" I checked in when Andy winced over the sudden emptiness.

"Yeah. Just gonna be sore for a few days."

I huffed a laugh, knowing he loved that shit. It was why he booked with me every couple of weeks. He wasn't a talker, and I wasn't nosey, but I'd learned a few things about my favorite client.

Andy Jefferson was rich, timid, and shy as fuck.

He was also Preston's mirror image, except for black in place of red hair. And, like me, he wasn't shopping for a man of his own. He'd hinted that his dates were only ever interested in the fame and fortune that would come from being hooked to one of Boston's most eligible bachelors.

With me, Andy knew he would get good dick without the drama.

I cleaned him up and was out the hotel door an hour later, having allowed myself a few extra minutes of cuddling since Andy enjoyed the fuck out of being the little spoon as much as I did the bigger.

I'd lost track of how often I'd wished it was Preston pressed all up against me, sighing in my arms as my soft dick snuggled against his ass crack, sated and warm.

Rubbing a hand over my chest, I hit the start button on my key fob. My Mercedes's engine purred to life, but the sweet sound was cut through by my cell phone blaring Aerosmith's *Dream On*. Dad and I had gotten to see them three times down at the Garden and once in New York after we'd moved there. That had been Preston's first rock concert way back when, and he'd become a fan too.

That was the one thing the three of us had bonded over,

since Jacqueline hadn't allowed for much else with how much she clung to Dad like she couldn't live without him.

Preston and I had been left to our own devices more often than not, but I'd never complained. Every minute with him had been perfect, even if I hadn't been able to touch him in the ways I'd wanted.

"Dad, what's up?" I answered while pulling out of the parking garage, my brow furrowed over his late call.

"Hey, little buddy."

I shook my head while grinning. I now stood taller than Dad, but he still refused to give me a different nickname.

"Jacqueline asked me to reach out to you about next weekend," he continued.

Valentine's Day was meant for lovers, so I had no fucking clue why he'd be calling *me*.

"What about it?" I asked, merging onto State Street.

"She requested your presence for dinner Friday night. It's been a while since you've been down for a visit, so we won't accept any excuses this time."

"I have to work, Dad," I told the truth even though he wasn't exactly aware of how I made my money. I'd finally admitted about my being gay, which he'd suggested I not share with his wife, considering her continued trans and homophobic stance. But in true Dad fashion, he'd accepted me for who I was, no questions asked. Part of me felt bad for making him keep a secret from Jacqueline, but it was for the best, he'd said.

That didn't mean he needed to hear about me being one of Elite Escorts gay branch's highest paid sex workers though. As far as he knew, I put my MBA to good use in my best friend, Sean Fox's family business—which was kind of true, just not the type of communications Dad figured I'd meant.

"You're going to have to get someone to cover you this time, Drake. It's important," Dad insisted.

"Important?" I asked, wariness creeping over my skin like a tendril of frigid air.

"Jacqueline hasn't shared details with me just yet, but she promised the news will be life-changing."

I needed more before I would ever agree to stand in her, let alone Preston's, presence again. Fuck knew it'd been hard—*I'd* been hard—last time I'd torn out my own heart when I'd walked away rather than offering him comfort.

I'd broken my promise to him and could only imagine how badly he hated me because of it.

"Life-changing...in what way?" I asked.

"Hugely," Dad said.

"Dad."

"Drake," he countered, his voice snipped short like mine.

I huffed at his unwavering tone. He wouldn't bend or give me anything more even if he had it. Probably Jacqueline's doing. She'd taught him a thing or ten about being manipulative to get what she wanted. "Fine. Your place in Tribeca?"

"Well, no," Dad said, a little hesitant. "We're staying at The Bloomberg on Fifth Avenue Friday night. We'll meet you for dinner at the lower level's restaurant at seven."

Jacqueline had sold off the penthouse after Preston had graduated and escaped her for Harvard, but I'd only visited the luxurious place they'd bought in Tribeca twice, the second on a day that Dad's wife had been out of town for a meeting.

I'd had Dad all to myself, and it'd been like old times. Smartly, I'd left before she'd arrived home.

"Can I ask why you're staying at a hotel rather than your home?" I asked.

"We decided to sell—but we'll discuss the reasons when you're here. Jacqueline already booked a suite for you and your brother."

Stepbrother.

I cleared my throat, my gut tightening and groin tingling. "We're sharing a room?"

"No. She got you both suites of your own. Check-in is at four, so you can settle in and dress for dinner."

Thank fuck we wouldn't be tossed into close proximity because the last time I'd been near Preston, I'd almost caved to my need to touch him in ways that would have caused a complete disaster for all parties involved.

Agreeing rather than continuing an argument I wouldn't win, I wished Dad a good night, or what was left of it. It was closing in on eleven.

I would need to reach out to Sean, who managed the gay branch at Elite, but it was late, and he and his professor boyfriend were probably fucking. Or in bed at the very least. I could wait until the following morning to drop the news of having to leave over Valentine's Day weekend.

Sean had stated once that he couldn't wait for the day when some ginger grabbed hold of my heart and stuck a fork in it like Matteo had done to him. Little did he know, that had happened years ago, long before he'd met his Teach.

And in one week, I would be faced with the man my thoughts couldn't quit. No one would ever compare to Preston, even though I'd often joked with Sean about finding a redheaded lover and having his babies.

I'd only ever wanted Preston. No one else.

That was why escorting had been an easy decision when Sean had asked me to join Elite. Dating and a relationship weren't in my future, so the easiest way for me to find release outside my hand was through a booking agency.

Unbelievable pay was the whipped cream topping, and pretending Preston was the man I pleased every time was the cherry on top.

A shiver slid down my spine at the thought of seeing him in the flesh again. The hairs rose on my nape in some sort of premonition.

I had a feeling Dad hadn't been lying about things changing.

But never how I wished for whenever I managed to catch sight of a star in the city's night sky.

Chapter 8

Preston

"**Y**our presence is required next weekend."

Typical Jacqueline. She didn't bother asking me if I had plans.

Huffing quietly to myself, I pushed back from my desk where I'd been doing some backdoor sneaking into a computer system for a client. Hacking came naturally and padded out my bank account that already overflowed. But it was work easily done from home, something that didn't require being among people.

Cell pressed to my ear, I strode out of my office, needing movement to release some of the nervous adrenaline that always coursed through me whenever she called. That was usually a couple of times a week to check up on me, unfortunately.

Jacqueline cared about me in some fucked up way, or so I told myself. But if she knew the truth...

Guilt slammed me in the gut, and I hated—despised—that I had to hide myself from the one person who ought to love me unconditionally. But she'd proven she wouldn't do that with Nancy, so what hope did I really have?

Best to keep my distance as much as possible and cross my fingers she never found out who I was in the deepest parts of my soul—and the man I longed for.

"I can't make it," I tried, already knowing the denial was simply a waste of my breath.

"You can, and you will," Jacqueline stated firmly as I'd expected.

While I'd grown quite a bit taller than her five and an inch or two height, she still ruled like Napoleon, never accepting no as an answer to any of her demands. "We're having a family dinner at The Bloomberg at seven, and I've already booked a room for both you and your brother."

Shit.

My eyelids slammed shut, and I sank onto the edge of my couch, pinching the bridge of my nose. Considering my ardent and taboo crush on Drake wouldn't relent, I refused to see him as anything other than the perfect man who fit me and my issues like a puzzle piece.

Even if he was an asshole who'd let me down, and I would have preferred to hate him if I could.

"Why?" I heard myself ask, questioning not just Jacqueline but life for fucking me over as it always did.

"I have made some decisions about your grandfather's business, and they affect you as well."

"Does this have anything to do with Franklin's failure as CEO?" I asked, my voice already resigned.

"That man is an absolute waste of sperm," Jacqueline snipped like the bitch she was.

Still, I blinked, thrown off-balance by her blunt words.

"But no matter," she continued, and I could imagine her waving a bejeweled hand. "Dinner. Next week. Don't be late."

I sighed heavily, rather than attempting to argue a fight I would never win.

She required one weekend. Two, possibly three days, when I hadn't seen her or Devlin for months.

I'll survive.

But my heart might not considering how I'd grieved the last time I'd seen Drake in the flesh.

"I'll be there," I agreed, my voice weighty even though a thrill of unwanted excitement flooded my bloodstream.

"You needn't sound so put out, Preston," Jacqueline chided in her usual snippy tone when displeased with me. "After all I've given you, you're still an ungrateful, whiny brat."

I was nothing of the sort, but what Jacqueline considered truth in her mind wouldn't be overturned. "I'm sorry," I stated on autopilot, since an apology would shut her up from going on and on about how much of a disappointment I was—same as Nancy had been to her.

Shoving aside thoughts of my *real* mom, the kind-hearted person who would always hold residence in my heart, I focused on my condo's view of downtown Boston. The capital's dome glinted in the winter's weak sunset, a golden color that suggested warmth regardless of the frigid temperatures outside that mirrored Jacqueline's heart.

The sight of snow would have made the cold more bearable, but it had been a drab, lifeless winter.

"Seven," she reminded me, and I agreed, trying for a more upbeat tone.

I hung up, cursed her as well as myself, and tossed my cell aside. My head tipped back, and I closed my eyes. The new couch I'd bought a few weeks earlier cradled my backside, the soft cushions hugging me. The plush piece of furniture wasn't nearly as relaxing as Drake's arms though.

He'd denied me the comfort I'd needed that he'd always willingly given without hesitation or question.

What had changed?

What had I done to make him look at me with distaste before turning away without a backward glance?

Drake had never left me wanting for affection and assurance during the years we'd lived together. He'd been there for me whether it was with ready fists he'd never had to use to fight my bullies or with muscular arms to tug me close when he insisted I soak his shirts with my tears.

I'd done so countless times in those three years we'd shared the second floor of the penthouse in Manhattan, and I missed that closeness with the only man to ever catch my eye.

He'd become aware of my hatred of elevators after that first day of school when we'd headed to the lobby where our driver waited for us. Once we'd been in the limo, far from the elevator, I'd explained how anxiety over small spaces left me gasping for breath. Add in the first day at a new school, and I'd been on the verge of panic.

From then until he'd moved home to Boston for college, if we were alone in an elevator—anywhere—Drake had sought out my clammy hand and clutched it tight, giving me something other than claustrophobic thoughts to focus on.

He'd noticed the other small things too. My slumped shoulders, tears in my eyes, my gaze on the floor...every shift in my demeanor that indicated I hurt inside. He'd been my hero, my protector, and he'd owned my heart when I'd been a young fourteen-year-old who'd hit puberty late enough I caught shit for that too in school.

But then he'd gone without a backward glance.

Knowing he would never be mine in the way I wished, I'd forced myself to give in to the closeted guy from college who had wanted to "rail my bubble butt" our junior year. He'd sauntered away from my apartment Jacqueline paid for, sated and smiling, while I'd been sore and unsure of how I felt about penetrative sex.

I'd never fantasized about topping. In all my daydreams featuring my stepbrother, I had been on the receiving end, but losing my virginity hadn't even been enjoyable enough to make me hard.

I opened my eyes to glance around my condo. Bookshelves lined the walls not dominated by glass, at least ninety percent of the shelves full of signed paperback or hardcover special editions from my favorite gay romance authors. A few fantasy titles were tucked in here and there, but my tastes had changed once I'd learned how sex could actually be enjoyable.

My second time beneath a man had been a hell of a lot better even if there hadn't been a happily ever after at its end—not that I'd been wanting or expecting one with him.

Mason hadn't looked anything like my stepbrother, but the silver fox showcased on Elite Escort's website promised a lifetime of experience in pleasing a young man. He'd given me something real to think on when fantasizing about my stepbrother.

He'd taken things slow and had been gentle with me, making for a beautiful evening worth every penny I'd dished out for the pleasure of his company. We'd spent two other nights together in the following months, and not once had he shown annoyance at my word vomit during our pillow-talk hours where I treated him as a therapist I ought to see but wouldn't. I never opened up to anyone. Ever. But the NDAs both Mason and I had signed assured me whatever I shared with him would never be repeated.

Mason had taken a vacation, and having gotten too used

to monthly meetings, I'd agreed to book with a different Elite when their secretary told me that my silver fox was no longer available.

Kellen, the third and last man I'd bottomed for, had given me the greatest gift, prompting me to role-play and going along with my desire to pretend he was Drake, one of his co-workers I'd admitted to finding hot as hell.

Thank fuck Kellen hadn't inquired as to why I didn't hire Drake instead of him.

He'd spooned me from behind and jerked me off while whispering all sorts of naughty things in my ears. I'd pretended that warm clasp around my aching length had been Drake's. The hoarse tone of his voice the low timbre of my stepbrother's wrecked with want for my body.

That night had been over a year and a half earlier, and I'd been celibate ever since. I'd grown too nervous that rumors would spread of what I did and my sexuality would somehow be found out by Jacqueline.

I often wondered if Kellen had told Drake about me, but the agreement every party had to sign was there to protect us—same as my surname change to Gibbons, which belonged to Nancy.

Kellen hadn't been aware Drake was my stepbrother...or had he? Had they laughed at my expense over drinks at some swanky bar downtown? Did nausea stir in Drake's stomach over the truth his stepbrother lusted for him?

The not knowing unnerved me.

I hopped up and paced my living room, rubbing damp palms down my sweats.

It had been five years since I'd last spoken to Drake, long before I'd snooped to find where he worked. Bitter jealousy rolled over me like a tidal wave whenever I thought too hard on what Drake did for a living.

Originally, it'd been an act of rebellion and a broken heart that made me decide to book with an Elite. I'd found the balls to embrace my gayness and spent good money to hide my need for release with someone other than my own hand. I'd specifically chosen one of Drake's fellow co-workers as a "fuck you" he didn't really deserve.

I'd stumbled upon Elite's website thanks to my constant online stalking of my stepbrother. It hadn't taken much to figure out how he afforded his condo in Boston. My honed hacking skills located the company he'd told Jacqueline he worked for, but they didn't have a Drake Hemmings on payroll. Nor did any other communications businesses in the Boston area.

Drake and his friends posted pictures on social media, which led to my discovery. His best friend he'd told me about, especially. Sean Fox revealed his brother, Micah Fox, which eventually pointed to their family business after a little digging.

Elite Escorts.

I hadn't known Drake's sexual identity until the day I'd found his profile on their website. While he'd never dated anyone in high school, he'd never shared his thoughts about girls or boys with me either—and vice versa.

Our conversations as teens hadn't focused on anything other than good music, movies, and what we planned to do once we escaped Jacqueline and her penthouse that had always felt more like a jail than home to both of us.

For the longest time, I'd assumed Drake was ace regardless of his morning wood, but I hadn't been about to ask, which would then make me have to admit to being gay.

And if my mom ever found *that* out? Poor Devlin would find himself in one hell of a pickle, having to choose between his son and wife, and the man was too decent to be put in that situation.

I shuddered at the thought of the hatred she would spew at him, choosing to focus on the better life I'd made for myself outside of New York and away from her toxicity.

Elite had opened a gay branch prior to my finding out about them, and I'd become a monthly supporter because surprise, surprise, I actually enjoyed sex. But that night with Kellen had taken me to an edge of messing with fire.

I'd been scared to book again, sure that somehow, Jacqueline or Drake would find out about me and my little crush.

Little.

I snorted and grabbed a bottle of beer from my fridge, choosing to reminisce over the best years of my life.

Those high school days had seemed to drag in endless agony, but looking back, they'd passed too quickly. I'd tucked dozens of memories away, finding comfort in them in my moments of need when I had no arms to hold me, no words of edification to ease my emotional pain, and no affection to fill up the void in my soul.

Drake had stood in back then, watering the desert-like areas in my heart. He'd been my rock, my only safe place outside of locking myself in my bedroom. A beautiful, giving man I would rather hate than love in the all-consuming way I did.

Pouting, I sucked down my beer, wishing I could erase the last time I'd seen Drake from my memory. Despising too that I couldn't eradicate my need for him from my body.

Seven days until I would see the forbidden fruit whose flesh I would never be able to taste.

My stomach twisted, my guts roiling even though my groin roused to life. I rubbed over my lower abdomen, my pinkie sliding beneath the band of my sweats to stroke over the tip of my cock suddenly straining to escape.

It had been days since I'd sought release, feelings of guilt assaulting me the same as they always did whenever I lay face down on my bed, cum beneath my belly, a dildo shoved deep inside my ass.

A whimper escaped me, and I squeezed the head of my dick to calm down.

But there would be no stopping my body. I had the choice to pull out the toys I kept hidden in the back of my bedside table's drawer or wake up with a mess in my boxers tomorrow morning.

I chose the first means of release, allowing myself to live out the fantasy of my stepbrother.

Daydream Drake with the filthy mouth and bruising fingertips could fuck me in the privacy of my own home where no one would ever be the wiser.

The real him included.

Chapter 9

Drake

My tie choked me.

My goddamned dress shoes pinched my toes.

The beard I kept trimmed close to my jawline bothered me for the first time ever.

And the slacks I'd chosen to wear for our family dinner downstairs in the hotel's restaurant had somehow shrunk. That, or I'd been working my thighs too much the previous couple of weeks at the gym.

But all three items of clothing were a requirement at The Bloomberg. Jacqueline had texted me a few days earlier, so I put them on before leaving my room.

Probably because I'd last shown up for dinner in Tribeca in jeans and a ratty T-shirt just to piss her off. She'd gone off as usual, but I'd just ignored her until she shut the fuck up. That first night at her dining room table I'd been given a pass too since I hadn't known any better, same with the cell phone rule. But throughout the rest of my time while a part of her household?

There had been no question who ruled the roost of that

penthouse in Manhattan then their loft in Tribeca. Not once had I seen a glimmer of hope she might change her mind toward the queer community either. I'd hidden in a damned closet for those three years, finally breathing freely when I'd stepped foot on Boston College's campus.

Sean and I had our fun as freshmen, partying hard and enjoying dick whenever we found guys to hook up with. Well, I'd thought we had a blast, anyway. Sean had been insatiable, living for sex, but had quit school before the second semester had even ended.

We'd stayed best friends over the years, hanging every weekend and enjoying a few too many beers. The day I quit my job in the sales department in a communications business and went to work for Elite, I'd realized I'd chosen correctly.

Elite had lined my pockets, allowing me to splurge on a kickass condo and luxury vehicle.

Jacqueline wouldn't ever believe I'd made something of myself if she knew the truth of how I earned my money though. She still clutched those invisible goddamn pearls when last I'd spoken with her five years ago and she'd flipped over Nancy's engagement.

Preston had never once admitted to his emotions, but I'd always been good at reading him. It had been outside beneath a streetlight that his heart had reached for me, needy and hurting, his eyes wet, chin trembling.

But during dinner, I'd been fantasizing about sucking Preston's dick rather than paying attention to Jacqueline bitch about the future of Casswell Global. My cock's rock-like state hadn't relented at Jacqueline's rant about her ex, so rather than giving Preston what he needed, I'd turned away.

Hiding the sight of my jeans that would reveal what he did to me.

Breaking my own goddamn heart just as much as I'd probably done to him.

But I didn't have a choice in that moment. Preston would despise me same as Jacqueline did Nancy if he knew how badly I wanted him. He would question how I'd held him when we were younger in a way that couldn't be passed off as morning wood. All those simple acts of affection I'd offered that had bordered on being greedy. Soothing my hands over his soft hair, his back, the warm skin of his arms.

I had wanted more each and every time he'd cuddled up against me, sighing relief at being able to hold him again.

And if Jacqueline ever found out how I lusted over my stepbrother?

I hated the ground that woman walked on. Loathed the fact she'd torn me from Boston even if she still made my father happy as shit. I had to attribute his ridiculous focus on his wife to that fuckface Cupid's goddamned arrows and resulting blind love.

A sentiment I unfortunately understood too well. While I hoped Dad's happiness continued for his sake, I wished my feelings for Preston would just shit the bed already.

Lips pressed into a tight line, I stepped into the elevator that would take me down sixteen floors to the hotel lobby where Jacqueline and Dad would be waiting for me. She'd called a family meeting, which meant the four of us. My pulse thrummed with the thought of Preston being by her side, his thick hair a mess of flaming waves, his emerald eyes meeting mine for the briefest of moments before flitting to the floor as they always did whenever our gazes clashed.

His fingers would be clasped in front of him in a white-knuckled grip, but he would release them to accept my outstretched hand in greeting. He would then rub damp palms down his dress pants.

I pulled at my too-tight collar.

The nervous little nerd—the beat of my heart—the goddamned bane of my existence wrecked me before I even laid eyes on him this time.

"Fucking hell," I muttered to myself, punching the down button.

There had been complete silence between us the previous five years, but I hadn't known how to fix the situation. The distance between us made shit easier. Out of sight out of mind—well, not really. Preston was in my thoughts twenty-four-seven.

Those years of silence stood like a necessary wall between us. And every passing day without hearing his voice or reading a text gifted from his elegant fingers had been harder rather than easier.

A muscle ticked in my jaw when the elevator slowed as it neared the thirteenth floor. I tucked myself against the back wall, readying for more people to join me in the space that suddenly felt too cramped and lacking in oxygen.

While I'd become a pro at small talk and social niceties, I wasn't in the mood. Nor was I ready to face the one woman I could say without question I hated. She didn't know how to love her precious son in the way he longed for and deserved.

Jacqueline would try my patience.

Preston would make me feel things I lusted for, emotions and actions that could all too easily be revealed if I wasn't careful—

The elevator doors slid open.

My breath fled from my lungs at the sight before me, the

quiet huff of agony torn from my chest lost in the continued dings ringing in my ears.

Pale and head tipped sharply down as always, Preston shuffled forward into the elevator his teenage self had often called a trap of death.

Silence settled, oppressive and spine-tingling regardless of the fact he stared at the floor.

A rush of saliva filled my mouth as the sweet scent of vanilla and spice wafting off Preston's freckled skin flooded my nose. He still used the same damn bodywash as when we'd been teens.

God. Damn.

I shuddered, having to yet again swallow down a groan as my groin stirred.

I'd jerked off countless times with his gel in our shared shower once I'd figured out my sexuality and recognized how badly I'd wanted to touch Preston with more than step-brotherly love.

My balls ached as my dick thickened, making my slacks even more tight and uncomfortable.

Without lifting his head, Preston spun to face the doors that remained open, unaware of the electrical currents zapping over my skin toward my tingling balls.

My heartbeat pounded in my ears, and I fought to keep from panting loud enough he would realize he wasn't alone.

The doors slid shut, leaving us in close proximity, and I curled my hands into fists so I wouldn't seek his out to offer the comfort I *knew* he needed.

At least he stood with his back toward me, unaware—

His head lifted when I'd expected him to curl in on himself and start counting aloud so he wouldn't lose his shit over the confined space that had always made him need my assuring touch.

A shudder ripped through Preston at the initial movement of descent, and he stiffened.

I gritted my teeth, my nostrils flaring. I fought to fill my suddenly desperate lungs as the elevator sped us toward the ground floor.

Don't turn around. Please. Wait—no. Do it. Grab hold of me and hang on for dear life. Press your face into my chest. Tremble against me, tell me how much you need me—

"D-Drake?" he whispered without turning, like he didn't want to lay eyes on the man who'd broken that promise to always have his back.

"Hey, Preston," I rasped, my voice ragged and desperate. "You okay?"

"N-No."

Shit. Instinctively, I reached for him.

The elevator jolted to an abrupt stop, inertia buckling both of our knees.

I grabbed hold of Preston's arm on my way down, spinning him around to land atop me as we crashed to the floor.

His weight slammed into my chest, punching the air from my lungs.

"Oh fuck, oh fuck, oh fuck..." He whispered the words with a heightened tone, scrambling to get his limbs beneath him. Panic widened his unfocused eyes.

I clasped his smooth cheeks in my hands before he could push off me. "Hey!" I gasped out with the first exhale I could manage once I caught my breath.

He blinked, those gorgeous green orbs closed flickering briefly with reality. His frantic movements to stand slowed, but he struggled to fill his lungs as he rested on my chest.

"You're okay, Preston. Breathe, baby." The pet name escaped me without thought, but I doubted he'd heard.

Sweet exhales smelling of wintergreen panted over my face, his plump lips mere inches from mine.

My dick started to stiffen again, and I quickly sat up to get my stepbrother off the telling evidence of what he did to me. He curled into a fetal position on the floor, and I threaded my fingers through his like I'd done hundreds of times, squeezing and rubbing my thumbs over the backs of his hands.

"Preston," I stated firmly glancing over his twitching, slender form.

He stared up at my lips from where I knelt beside him, eyes still glazed over—beautiful as ever.

My goddamn pants felt like a tourniquet regardless of the fucked up situation we were in.

"Preston!" I half-hollered, taking note of the still unmoving elevator trapping us together in the suspended unknown.

He didn't answer.

"We're all right—you're *fine*," I stated on autopilot, glancing around us, too fucking aware of the silence outside his gasps for breath and my thundering pulse.

There was no alarm screaming. No voice hollering or fists pounding on the closed doors to make sure we were okay.

What the fuck had happened?

Chapter 10

Preston

My lungs burned, but the muscles needing to fill them wouldn't work.

Couldn't think.

The vision of Drake wavered above me, vibrant blue eyes hazy rather than intense with worry as he murmured something I couldn't hear.

Can't breathe...

Darkness crept in along the edges of my vision, swallowing—devouring—the one my body burned for day and night as he glanced around the tight space we were stuck in.

My pulse throbbed in my fuzzy head.

Warm palms cradled my face. Even hotter exhales caressed my parted lips, making me linger in reality for a few seconds longer.

"Preston!" Drake's voice lay behind a thick veil, muffled and upset. "I've got you, but you need to breathe, baby."

Baby.

Did I smile?

I blinked.

"Come on, Preston—take a goddamned breath before you pass out!"

My eyelids grew heavy. I started to drift away into darkness.

"Jesus fucking Christ," Drake muttered.

Soft warmth pressed against my mouth, deliriously sweet in the midst of prickling facial hair he always used to shave.

A rush of air shoved past my lips, straight into my lungs.

I coughed, jolting in Drake's hold as he ripped his mouth from mine.

My chest exhaled on its own, another ragged sucking in of oxygen.

"Fuck." Drake still held my face, and I gained my focus as an unconscious inhale filled my starved lungs. "You okay?"

Drake kissed me...

No.

He'd forced oxygen into me to snap me out of my panic.

Thick black lashes blinked over his blue eyes, and a delicious, agonizing ache crept through my chest that had nothing to do with my heart scrambling to get oxygen through the rest of my body.

I lay curled up on the elevator's floor—

Reality hit my brain, shooting adrenaline through my bloodstream. Air became scarce once more as my eyes widened.

"No. Fucking stay with me, Preston," Drake demanded, sounding calmer than he should. "Breathe with me."

I fought to focus on his counting, trying to inhale and exhale when he did, but I didn't succeed fully until he sat against the back of the unmoving elevator's wall and pulled me onto his lap. Those fingers of his I'd clung to countless times threaded through mine, and I closed my eyes, shoving my face against his chest.

The familiar warmth of him surrounded me, slowly filling my lungs with his scent.

His other hand held my hip, thumb stroking in a comforting gesture that flooded me with equal amounts of arousal and gratitude. Slowly, peace settled inside me as it always did when I was with him, quieting my panic until my lungs relaxed and functioned without prompting.

The elevator hadn't moved, nor had the doors slid open, but in that stolen moment in the arms of the man I loved, I didn't care. Time could stand still, and it would never be enough.

"Are you all right?" Drake asked, his low tone rumbling pleasure down my spine along with the heat of his breath against the top of my head.

"Mmm," I agreed, knowing I had to escape his tender hold before I did something stupid like attempt to give *him* mouth to mouth. With tongue.

"Your mom is going to shit a brick over our being late."

Talk about a jolt back to reality.

We both chuckled, and I forced myself to straighten a bit so I could see Drake's face.

This close, I could make out the hint of freckles over Drake's nose. The darker ring of navy around his pupils.

He stared at me with an intensity that lit my body on fire. My cheeks heated, same as whenever our eyes met.

Space—need space.

But I couldn't move, trapped by desire and his large hand still firmly clasped on my hip. His grip on my fingers tightened.

Drake's focus flitted over my face as though drinking me down like a cool glass of water on a hot summer's day. His gaze stalled on my mouth, lingering for a pregnant moment that left me breathless for a whole other reason.

Did he want to kiss me?

A shudder ripped through me, and I swallowed hard, my palms growing damp.

With a slow, shaky exhale, Drake untangled our fingers and physically moved me to sit on the floor beside him. "I left my cell in my room. Do you have yours on you?"

"N-No," I answered, butterflies having a party in my stomach.

He grimaced. "Should have figured. It would have been blowing up with Jacqueline's calls by now if you did."

I huffed a snort of shaky laughter, forcing myself to relax against the back wall. While cool, the metal was solid. Safe. I breathed a little easier, pulling my knees up a bit so Drake wouldn't see how he affected me. "What d-do you think happened?"

Drake lifted his head, peering into every corner of the jail cell pressing in against us. "No fucking clue, but the entire panel is lit up, and I smashed the call button while trying to calm your anxiety attack. Nobody answered. But don't worry," he continued before panic could come knocking again, "this is The Bloomberg. I'm sure they'll have us out of here with a refund for your mom and a bottle of their finest wine in our hands in a matter of minutes."

"Jacqueline," I corrected him. "I don't refer to her as my mom anymore."

"Glad to hear it." He sniffed. "The woman doesn't deserve that title."

The sight of his profile—strong brow and nose, square jawline covered in the neatly trimmed beard he'd had the last time I'd seen him—grounded me regardless of where we hung suspended by cables. While I'd somewhat gotten over my fear of confined spaces, being trapped as we were poked at my weak tether on sanity.

If I could keep my attention on Drake, I wouldn't lose my shit again.

He glanced my way, his intense stare erupting even more butterflies in my belly, making bodily functions necessary for existence difficult.

I shifted my focus to the blue carpeted floor between my knees, unable to even think beneath his perusal.

"What room are you in?"

"1322," I whispered, thankful for something, *anything*, else to focus on. "You?"

"1654."

I nodded, expecting he would continue to ask me questions to occupy my mind as he'd often did on our daily descent to the limo for those long rides to school.

"Any idea why Jacqueline asked me to come to New York?"

Shaking my head, I considered his question. Did he still not know I lived in Boston, a mere couple of blocks from the condo he'd bought?

"Us," I said, hating the reminder he held no interest in my life like I did with him.

"Huh?"

"Jacqueline called *us* down here." At least my nerves settled enough I no longer stuttered.

"Wait—you don't have a place here in Manhattan?"

I shook my head again.

"I thought you'd move back after getting your degree at Harvard."

"Are you kidding me? And live close to Jacqueline *Napoleon* Casswell?" I huffed another laugh, this one sarcastic. "Don't you know me at all?"

Our gazes once more clashed, Drake giving me that damned inquisitive look that rushed blood to my groin.

I held my breath, wanting to squirm. How I managed to hold his gaze for all of two seconds before looking away, I didn't have a clue.

"The Preston I remember wasn't brave enough to stand up for himself," Drake finally answered as I fought the need to pick at a fingernail. "I'm guessing that's changed?"

"Not exactly," I muttered. "I managed to leave, but she still manipulates from afar." I tipped my head back against the elevator's wall, closing my eyes to keep from having to make eye contact with him. In my mind, I could imagine we sat at a picnic table somewhere or a bench in Central Park where dappled sunlight reached us through overhead branches and leaves.

Warmth licked at my skin, but it felt more like Drake's gaze rather than the sun's golden rays.

A shiver slid through me, goose bumps erupting over my arms.

"So where do you live?" he asked rather than poking at my emotions he probably expected I wouldn't share. He'd be right.

But answering that question might open a can of worms.

"B-Boston," I whispered.

"The fuck, Preston?" He sounded startled—annoyed even—and I rushed to explain.

"You didn't ask last time we saw each other, and w-with how you l-left..." My voice trailed off. I didn't want him aware of how badly he'd hurt me, how his leaving me behind in every way the past five years had almost destroyed me.

"I'm an asshole," he muttered, shifting in my periphery.

"Mmm," I hummed my agreement. Rubbing my palms down my shins from where I sat with my knees to my chest, I opened my mouth to fill the silence, but he beat me to it.

"What have you been up to?"

I guessed we weren't going to discuss the why or fallout of our losing touch with each other.

It was for the best that he didn't know how desperate I'd been for him and still was.

"Working," I croaked out, fighting against the draw to scoot closer to him. Climb on his lap. Lick up his neck. Rip open his shirt and run my hands over his thick chest and eight-pack of abs Elite's shirtless profile picture had shown off.

Jealousy sneaked through my gut yet again.

"What do you do?"

I fought off a frown. "Private contracting." I went with the easiest explanation of all the odd jobs I took on to keep busy.

Hell knew I didn't need steady income to survive. The inheritance Grandfather had left for me fifteen years earlier even after giving half of it away would easily see me through to my death.

"What sort of contracting?"

"Computer programming. Cybersecurity. Hacking."

"Hacking?" Drake's voice rose a couple octaves.

My forehead smoothed out, but I kept my eyes closed since it was easier to dismiss our situation and talk to him without reality all up in my face.

"Get the fuck out." Drake laughed.

"Wish I *could* get out of this death trap, but nope."

"Like government shit or civilian?" he asked rather than joking about our predicament as I'd attempted to do.

"If I answered that question, I would have to kill you."

A bullshit reply, but I enjoyed hearing Drake's lighthearted chuckle in response.

"Strait-laced Preston Casswell. You naughty boy, you."

Fuck. If he only knew.

He also obviously wasn't aware I'd secretly changed my last name in attempts to somehow distance myself emotionally from Jacqueline. She herself still hadn't found out and hopefully never would.

"I'm just kidding," I admitted with an uneasy chuckle, making myself lift my head. I still couldn't look Drake's way though. It was tough enough having the warmth of him along my left side and his long legs, muscular enough to fill out his black dress pants, in my periphery.

Every button on the elevator's panel was lit up like he'd said and blinking. At least it was silent. There was no phone on the wall, no evidence of cameras either.

The emergency button wasn't glowing, but he'd already attempted to reach someone.

I pushed to my knees and pressed it just in case. Nothing happened. No buzz, no intercom, not even a red light like the rest of the ones above it.

Sighing, I sank back, ending up closer to Drake without meaning to.

Our shoulders brushed, but I didn't pull away, needing to soak in his calming nature. It had been the jolt, the slam against his body, the surety of sudden danger and possible death that had freaked me the fuck out what seemed an hour earlier. There was no way it'd been that long though.

"Shouldn't they be prying open the doors or something?" I asked, wondering what the hell was going on and why no one was trying to rescue us. "I mean, even if we're between floors, they can do that, can't they? Pretty sure I've seen shit like that on TV."

"No fucking clue." Drake stood and pounded on the door, giving me a nice view of his ass and how well he filled out his slacks. "Hey! Anyone out there?"

No one answered, but I wasn't surprised, considering there hadn't been an attempt to contact us.

I tore my focus off him, my mind launching into reasons for the complete lack of communication from the outside world.

"What if there's a fire?" I whispered, my throat wanting to tighten.

"Alarms would be screaming."

"What if time stood still, frozen by like...aliens or something?"

Drake chuckled and sat back beside me, his shoulder tight against mine. "Don't let your imagination mess with your head. We'll get out eventually. Just gotta be patient."

Not easy to do with Drake Hemmings all up in my space.

I released a slow, steady exhale, ridding my lungs of the familiar scent of him. "How long have we been stuck in here?"

Drake shifted, lifting his right wrist to check his watch. The clean smell of soap wafted of him in a thicker cloud as more of our arms brushed together at his action. "A half hour."

"We're *officially* late for dinner."

"Jacqueline is going to be pissed," he said.

"It didn't feel like we'd descended very far—what do you think? Tenth floor? Seventh?"

He shrugged, and I rubbed my palms down my thighs at the thought of being stuck so far off the ground. What if the cables suddenly snapped? What if we plummeted downward? Were we still high enough we would be smashed to death rather than landing in a heap of limbs?

My mind started to whirl, taking my pulse on a rollercoaster ride that bottomed my stomach out.

"Where do you live in Boston?" Drake asked as though he'd heard the beginnings of a spiral in my brain.

I appreciated him wanting to distract me even if I didn't believe panic would truly be an issue again. "I have a condo downtown."

"What? Me too!"

I already knew he did but didn't admit that aloud.

"You could have called me," he said, bumping his shoulder against mine.

"I don't have your new number," I offered a lousy excuse.

"My dad does."

"And Jacqueline has mine!" I shot back, unable to help myself or keep the hurt from my tone over how he'd moved on so easily. He'd changed his a handful of years earlier, and I'd gotten one with a Boston area code after becoming an official Massachusetts resident my second year of college.

We both shut down for a minute after that quick back-and-forth. With every second that passed, my need to shift, climb onto him, or escape to the opposite wall, intensified.

The internal draw toward Drake pulled and pushed with equal force, making my heart speed up once more. My pants became bit tighter again too.

"I owe you an apology," Drake finally broke the silence.

I waited rather than attempting to ease the sudden awkwardness between us.

"From five years ago, when we got together with our parents at their loft in Tribeca. It reminded me of the first time we'd had dinner as a family and Jacqueline spouted off shit about Nancy." Drake stated what I remembered all too well.

I hummed in agreement, wrapping my arms around my bent knees and lacing my fingers at my shins.

"You were hurting, and rather than hugging you like I'd done that night in my bedroom, I walked away," Drake said, his voice full of remorse. "Left you standing there on the sidewalk while I turned my back, something I promised I would never do to you."

"What was different that night?" I asked, my voice low and uneven, the pang of pain still lingering in my chest.

Drake sat silent long enough I dared to glance over at him. His eyes were closed, lips were pressed tight, and forehead was dented by a deep frown.

I had no clue where his mind was. What had caused him to act like that when he'd been nothing but nurturing and protective since the day we'd met?

"Did I do something wrong?" I asked what I'd always assumed.

He huffed an exhale loudly through his nose. "No, Preston."

"Then what?" I asked, stretching my legs out and angling slightly to face him.

"It was me." Those blue eyes of his turned my way, freezing me in place. "*I* did something wrong."

Chapter 11

Drake

Preston held his breath, waiting for me to fill him in on what I'd done.

But could I go there? Did I have the balls to admit to him how much he had crawled beneath my skin that night? To the yearning I'd almost given into as we'd stood out beneath that streetlight, the warm spring air and scent of hyacinths surrounding us?

I'd been on the verge of taking what I wanted, fuck Jacqueline and fuck whatever reaction I would get from goody-two-shoes Preston, but a simple glance at the house looming on my right had shut me down.

What if she saw us?

I couldn't begin to imagine Jacqueline's reaction to me kissing her son—my stepbrother. The fact I was gay would be enough to have me banned from her house and life, but if I soiled her heir?

What kind of position would the truth have put Dad in? While I felt confident in our relationship, I wasn't so sure the bond would stand against the onslaught of Jacqueline's trans and homophobic storms that built whenever the LGBTQ community was mentioned in her presence.

"It doesn't matter anymore." I finally decided on a nonanswer, which would be healthiest for all of us. "I was... struggling then. Trying to figure some personal shit out, and I'm sorry for not being there for you."

"Please don't turn away from me like that again." The hurt in Preston's voice hit me hard, right in the chest. Add in the fact he hadn't stuttered, his tone confident in knowing what he wanted, and I squirmed.

"Fuck." I scrubbed a hand over my face, that shitty feeling doubling inside me. "I'm so sorry, Preston. I'll have your back next time. Promise."

No matter how hard my dick might get, no matter the temptation he proved to be, I would give him whatever he needed.

"I could really use a hug right now."

Fuuuuuuuck.

Swallowing hard, I lifted my arm, inviting him to snuggle in.

He did so with a sweet sigh, his exhale warming my neck rather than my chest like normal.

Jesus, the tightening in my groin tempted a groan to rise up my throat.

Preston shifted onto his hip to better face me, getting good and comfortable with an arm around my waist. I clasped his lower back with one hand and his forearm with the other, keeping him close, talking my lust down the entire *fucking* time he invaded my personal space.

He fit perfectly against me, same as he'd always done. He'd grown a few inches and put on some manly weight since our first hug all those years ago, but we connected like puzzle pieces created to be one, same as always.

"Okay?" I asked, my tone slightly harsher from anger over my arousal than I'd hoped for.

"Perfect," he stated with a quiet sigh.

Temptation set in rather than a possible few hours of platonic alone time I would prefer to have drag on and on. I needed to make the minutes pass faster. "So, what do you do to keep busy these days?"

"A little gaming but mostly I read."

"Are you still into those Salvatore novels about that dark elf? What was his name? Drazzle? Drizzle?"

"Drizzt," he said with a snicker. "I forgot all about him, actually."

"Not into fantasy anymore?" He'd always had a book in hand back in the day. His "escape", he'd called those worlds of wizards and warlocks.

"Uh, not really, no."

"What kind of books are you into?"

I fought to keep from rubbing my thumb over the soft skin of his forearm resting on my stomach.

Preston hesitated.

"Someone has a secret," I said with a low laugh, poking him in the side.

Preston squeaked and shied away but didn't take his face from my neck. Still ticklish but too needy to leave me. Thank fuck.

"No tickling!" he gasped.

"Answer the question."

"Fine," he huffed. "Romance."

I opened my mouth to rib him some more, but the thought of Preston reading about pussy and getting hard over tits turned my stomach. While I'd always thought Preston was ace or maybe demi, I didn't want to know the truth about his sexuality. Better to assume he had no interest in men or dicks. Being aware he walked the same path as me would make it even more difficult to keep from crossing into unsafe territory. Thanks to his mom and society's thoughts on stepbrothers getting together, that line between us had been drawn in Sharpie.

Doing so wouldn't just put Dad's marriage and continued happiness at risk but probably Preston's inheritance as well, considering how Jacqueline had treated Nancy when she'd come out as trans.

"Reading romance is nothing to be ashamed of." I decided to go with. "Spend any time at the gym? You've put on some muscle since I saw you last."

Preston snorted as I squeezed his bicep while asking. "A little."

At least that hadn't tickled and given him the opportunity to pull away from me. Now that I had him in my arms again, I didn't ever want him to leave.

Fucking fuckface Cupid. Asshole prick.

I smoothed my hand over Preston's arm to rest on his hip, squeezing lightly in an attempt to calm myself down.

I loved physical touch. Craved it from Preston when I cursed Sean for getting all up in my face while teasing me about cramping my personal space.

My eyes drifted shut, and I allowed myself to thoroughly enjoy the feel of Preston's warmth against my side. "Where do you work out?"

"My building has a gym in the lower level. It's free to the condo owners, so sometimes I sneak down when it's empty. If it's not, I just use body weight workouts in the privacy of my home."

I kept asking questions, loving his soft voice filling my ears as thoroughly as he'd done my heart. We shared food tips, mostly me telling him how to up his protein intake in healthier ways than powders and bars full of chemicals.

We talked about macros. Bulking and cutting, both of which I'd done a few times, but he had no interest in either.

"Why bulk? You're already a beast," Preston said from where he'd perched his cheek on my shoulder. He poked at my pec. "You're hard as granite."

My mind went straight to the gutter, the thought bringing life to my dick again. "I love the challenge. We should hit the gym here tomorrow morning if you want. Burn off whatever calories Jacqueline insists on serving us if we make it out of here before the restaurant closes," I suggested.

Knowing her, she had the meal ordered already and wouldn't give us a choice in what we ate.

Fucking control freak.

"I didn't pack any gym clothes," Preston said.

"Then I guess we'll just have to lift naked," I tossed back.

He snorted a laugh, and I grinned, loving the hell out of him being fully relaxed for a change. I hadn't seen him like that since...fuck. Before I'd moved out for college.

"Are you happy, Preston?" I asked on a whim, expecting our light conversation might turn grim, but I needed to hear how he'd fared in all our years apart.

"Happy enough," he answered, sitting up a bit so he no longer rested against me.

I kept my arm around him so he had freedom to lean in again if he needed to.

"I have a gorgeous condo overlooking Boston's state house, a job I enjoy, and I'm rich as hell." He shrugged. "What more could I possibly ask for?"

Definitely ace...maybe? Fuck it. I needed to know.

"No woman in your life?" I asked, a little hesitantly.

Pink rushed to his cheeks. "Uh, no."

"Man?" I held my breath.

A sarcastic snort left his nose. "Could you imagine what Jacqueline would say if I told her I was dating a guy?"

"Nothing good," I answered honestly, disappointed he hadn't exactly answered my question. "Have you come here to see her very often?"

"*Hell no.* I avoid New York like I did any and all social gatherings in high school, except for Nancy and Michael's."

"You went to some of the dances with me," I pointed out, tugging him against me again because I couldn't *not* take advantage of the situation we were in.

"Yeah but only because you promised to stick by my side." He snuggled in, and I sighed, my eyes closing in bliss. "You're the only one I felt comfortable with and the strength I needed at my back to exist outside of the penthouse."

My heart swelled at the truth I'd helped him to enjoy more normal teenage years he wouldn't have had without me. "You grew past all that, though. You went to college by yourself," I pointed out, hoping he would own that confidence too. "Graduated with honors, my dad said."

"Because it was that or hide away in my bedroom where Jacqueline would have eventually forced society—*hers*—on me." Preston snorted. "No thank you. I may come from old money, but I want nothing to do with others who have the same."

I'd seen enough of the Casswell family society to know what he spoke of and thoroughly understood.

"Dad told me Jacqueline turned your world upside down when she said that you wouldn't be taking over as CEO of Casswell Global."

"At first, I was sure she was trying to manipulate me. Then I wondered if she might actually care about my desires." Preston shrugged, but I could tell it hadn't been a small thing. "Wishful thinking, perhaps, but I'm pretty sure you know me when it comes to Jacqueline."

He hadn't spoken of his feelings about their relationship, but he hadn't needed to with me.

"Has anything changed between you since I've been gone?"

Preston hesitated before answering as though gathering his thoughts. Or wracking his brain for a hint of a positive. "She calls me a few times a week, and while it's mostly to nitpick whatever information she can get out of me about my life, I think it's proof that she cares."

How he chose to see that in a positive light, I had no fucking clue.

"Well, I for one am fucking proud of you, kid."

"Not a kid," he muttered, and I laughed, loving how easily we fell back into our friendship.

"You left her domain. Made Boston your permanent residence after graduating. That took some balls if you ask me."

"Guess I grew a pair after you left." He sounded proud of himself, and I couldn't help giving him a little squeeze.

"So tell me about college," I said. "Did you come out of your shell? Party hard? Get some action?"

"Some, no, and—a little."

It took me a second to put the answers to the questions I'd tossed out in order to know him as I used to. "What's a *little* action?" I asked with a teasing lilt to my voice.

"I lost my virginity," he stated blandly, "and I wasn't impressed."

Jealousy erupted in my stomach like singeing fire.

Oh, the questions wanting to spill from my lips and the need to punch something. Rage in possessive obsession over what I could never have owned my heart. I flushed with heat, my guts tightening into knots.

"How about you?" he asked before temptation to speak my feelings landed me in shark-infested waters that would reveal way too fucking much. "You've never had a shell you needed to escape from, but what about the rest?"

I realized he referred to my inquiry about his college days and inhaled a slow, deep breath to calm myself.

"I partied pretty hard," I admitted, focusing on memories of me and Sean doing keg stands. I'd hit the slow-motion chug faster than him every goddamned time, even though I'd had an easy sixty pounds on his ass that year.

"Women?"

I actually chuckled, trying to think of what to say. "No."

"Men?" Preston didn't hesitate to follow up.

Shit.

I rubbed my free hand along my jaw. Guess we were going there—but same as with Dad, I could trust Preston. "Would you be grossed out if I said yeah?"

He whipped his head off my shoulder, emerald eyes wide. "Why would you think that?" he asked rather than scowling or curling his lip.

"Because of your mom's stance on the LGBTQ community."

"Jacqueline's," he corrected me. "And her thoughts are not mine. Surely you know that."

I managed a stilted nod.

"What else?" he asked, his tone pushy for a change.

"What do you mean?"

"You said grossed out—not just wrong as Jacqueline would think. Why?"

I shrugged, my heart beating a little faster. "Because of how affectionate, handsy, I've always been with you." I squeezed his shoulder to remind him how close we sat.

He didn't pull away, which made my pulse thrum harder. "You're the only person in my life since Nancy moved out who has shown me any type of physical touch, Drake." Preston rested his soft palm against my cheek, his eyes luminous, fucking beautiful in the fake light shining down on us. "I love it. Gone too long without it."

Yearning swept through my body, tightening my chest to the point my eyes stung. Tension rose between us, the obvious sexual sort that couldn't be denied. The same desire I had for him shone in those glorious emeralds I wanted to own as much as I did the rest of his body.

My heart bounced against my ribs. Tingles raced over my skin, leaving bumps in their wake.

"Preston," I murmured his name, not exactly sure what I asked, what I ought to say in that moment. Question how he felt about me? Bring up the fact that us crossing a line would only rouse trouble? Ask if he'd been with anyone since college—I guessed guy—and the bad experience that made me want to smash shit?

Preston tore his gaze away first. He clasped his hands on his lap and stared at them, his face a gorgeous shade of pink.

"Talk to me, Preston," I begged, needing more. So much fucking more.

"And say what, exactly?" he whispered. "That I'm gay? Queer as a seven dollar bill? That I figured you were into guys ever since I found out where you worked?" Preston's lips snapped shut, cutting off his tumbling words, and he held his breath, his body going tense.

The fuck...

I stared at his red face. He obviously knew about Elite and seemed almost...guilty. "Does what I do bother you?"

He hesitated before shaking his head. "You have to know I would never judge you."

He shifted on his backside, intensifying my thought he'd done something he considered to be wrong.

I slid my arm from behind his back and pulled one of his tells, wiping my hands down my thighs. We'd stepped over that Sharpie stain, all right. Just not in a way that would preferably end with mutual orgasms.

I inhaled a steadying breath. "Got something you need to confess, stepbrother of mine?"

Chapter 12

Preston

"No?" I squeaked, lying through my teeth.

"Bullshit. You're twitchy, blushing, and biting your lower lip the same as you were that day your mom—sorry, *Jacqueline*—caught us sneaking sips of wine from the bottle she'd left out on the kitchen counter."

I released my teeth's hold on my lip, lifted my chin, and flitted my gaze toward him for a brief second. He stared me down with an inquisitive stare rather than anger, thank fuck.

And even though I hated revealing private things about myself, I wanted that connection we used to share, the openness between us we'd had as teens when I *hadn't* needed to disclose my feelings. He'd always seen.

"F-Fine," I admitted and blew out a long exhale. "I'm a computer geek. It didn't take more than one minute for me to track down your social media."

"I don't post anything online about my job." He still didn't appear upset over what I'd done.

"No, but Sean had pictures of his brother Micah, which

led to their family business." My voice barely escaped, the guilt inside me easily recognizable to anyone with ears.

"You little nerd, you," Drake said with a surprising chuckle.

My shoulders relaxed the slightest bit, and I braved another glance his way.

Those vibrant blue eyes lit with what looked a lot like pride. My lips twitched in response.

"What else did you learn about me?" he asked, leaning into my personal space with that smirk lingering on his mouth, close enough my heart began to pound.

Where you live—a mere three blocks from me.

What kind of car you splurged on—a Mercedes.

Your favorite bar—O'Malley's.

The comfort food you go to on dreary days—Stouffer's frozen lasagna.

"Nothing," I lied, not about to out myself for being a serious stalker who was obsessed with his stepbrother.

Drake studied me intently but without a hint of judgment in his gaze. I didn't want to look away, which would only make me appear even guiltier than I already felt.

"What?" I finally asked, too antsy to sit still and be patient for one more second.

I could see Drake's mind working, but he didn't share with me what he thought about.

"What?" I pressed, my voice a little louder, annoyed that I had opened up, and he hesitated.

"Did you ever..." He shook his head and looked away first, rubbing a weary hand over his trimmed beard.

I eyed the slightly more than stubble darkening his strong jawline. Would it be soft on my face? Rough between my thighs?

Oh God.

A strangled sound ripped from my lungs, drawing Drake's full attention to my face. Time paused, the air around us coiling with sexual energy. His vivid blue eyes bore into the deepest reaches of me, searching.

Knowing.

"Fuck," I whispered, slamming my eyes shut and pushing against my aching length while trying to think about anything other than his mouth, his body, his *dick*.

"Preston."

I shook my head, the low, suggestive tone of Drake's too damn close to my face. No way could I look at him—

He grasped my chin, and I gasped, my eyelids flying open. Evidence of his giving in, the hold he kept on his desires shone as clearly as the hard ridge in my slacks if he chose to glance down at my lap.

I whimpered, shuddering beneath his perusal, so damn needy for him I expected to pass out.

"Well, baby?" he murmured, his tone full of insinuation. Drake flirted with me, and every spasming muscle in my body died to melt into him.

Gulping, I focused on his lips rather than his eyes, which would be my undoing.

"Did you?"

"D-Did I what?" I asked, completely brain-dead beyond everything but that Cupid's bow and how much I wanted to lick it.

"Think about booking with an Elite?"

I had. *Fuck*, had I ever. Heat rushed to my face at the truth it'd been him I wished I'd met with rather than Mason and Kellen.

"Naughty boy." He tsked with a teasing tone while threading his free hand's fingers into my hair and tipping my head back slightly.

Guess I hadn't shielded my thoughts too well.

"Who?"

Oh. My. God.

The way he held me screamed of dominance, him taking what I now knew he wanted as much as I did. "Who, Preston?" he murmured, his breath so damn close to my lips that my dick oozed pre-cum.

A quick shake of my head and I swallowed hard as I salivated for a taste of Drake.

He leaned forward, bypassing my mouth in a teasing swoop for my ear.

I shuddered as his hot exhale ghosted over my lobe.

"Which Elite would you pay to fuck you if you'd done it, Preston?"

"Oh God." I gulped, flinching as my cock jerked between my thighs. I was so hard, the ache in my balls an intense throb on the verge of release.

"Me?" Drake suggested. "Someone else?" He growled at the second option, his displeasure over anyone but him touching me evident in his tone. "If the latter, would you at least have been thinking about me while they fucked your gorgeous ass?" Drake flicked his tongue over the shell of my ear, and every muscle in my torso clenched. "So sensitive," he murmured, trailing his lips along my jaw to where he still grasped my chin. "You're a needy little bottom, aren't you? I'll bet you would beg and plead to be filled up. Caressed and kissed—you're insatiable, aren't you, baby?"

"D-Drake." I licked over my lower lip, finally looking at him.

A breathtaking sea of blue filled with lust and everything I'd always dreamed of seeing peered back at me.

"P-Please."

"Please what?" he murmured, inches from my mouth.

"Cross a line I promised myself I would never do? Lay claim to lips I've been fantasizing about since I was a teenager? Finally taste the sweetness of your mouth like I've been wanting to do for half of forever?"

Yes to all of that. Please.

A whine built in my chest, and I couldn't contain it.

"Tell me what you want, stepbrother of mine," Drake demanded.

I slammed my eyes shut at his words but had no strength to deny myself what I'd dreamed about since high school. There were no cameras in the elevator. We were shut away from the rest of the world, so why not take advantage of what we could secretly share in that moment?

"You," I admitted, my voice betraying my desperate need. "Always you, Drake."

His hold on the back of my head tightened, and he urged me forward.

I went willingly, crashing my mouth against his.

My heart stuttered at the feel of his firm lips, the slickness of his tongue as he licked between mine and the soft scratch of his short beard. There was nothing gentle about the intimacy we finally shared. No softness or affection, simply a hunger, a craving left to simmer for too long without being sated.

His exhales filled my lungs, and I couldn't get close enough. I half-sobbed over finally having what I'd only ever expected to see fulfilled in my dreams. Even though we were starved for each other's kisses, half-mad for fulfillment, tenderness lay beneath his rough ownership of my lips.

Our tongues dueled, mine meeting his stroke for stroke, and I licked into his mouth to taste the warmth of cinnamon as he did the same to me.

I grasped at his shirt, my fingertips frantic to map out

the torso I'd been lusting to get my hands on. Drake was pure muscle and hardness, his thighs equally rock-like as I scrambled to straddle his lap.

And his dick... Jesus, he had a steel rod trapped between our bodies.

Groaning into my mouth, he grabbed my ass and squeezed to the point I gasped. He shoved his tongue in for another taste, stealing my breath.

Life erupted inside my chest like sunlight breaking through clouds. Happiness thrived in my heart like a bubbling spring.

Both from Drake's kisses, and I would never get enough.

"Fuck, Preston." He sucked my lower lip then my upper while grasping my face to hold me still. "Want to lick you—every fucking inch of your skin."

"Yes," I gasped against his mouth. "A thousand times yes."

My world flipped, and I found myself on my back. He paused to study me, spread out for his taking.

"Jesus," he whispered and swallowed. "Never thought..."

"Same," I choked out. "Please, D-Drake."

A groan rumbled his chest, and he made quick work of my belt and fly, his shaking hands letting me know I wasn't the one completely overwhelmed with emotion. He yanked on my slacks, taking them and my boxer briefs to my knees with one vicious tug.

"Goddamn." He stared down at my aching cock, his chest heaving while I shivered beneath his hungry stare.

My entire length bucked, pre-cum welling at my slit to drip onto my stomach.

One corner of his lips rose in a sexy-as-hell smirk. "You're leaking for me."

I whimpered, my pulse thrumming and my hands clenching and relaxing as I fought off the need to grab onto something, sure of the tsunami ahead of us.

Drake chuckled while grasping the backs of my thighs and shoving them toward my chest, my pants trapping my ankles together. "Hold on, naughty boy. Things are about to get messy."

He shoved his face between my ass cheeks.

"Oh shit!" I bowed as he licked over my hole. Once. Twice. Slurping me up like an ice cream cone and moaning his approval.

"Fuck, you taste good, Preston." His words escaped on a groan more potent than I'd ever imagined while fantasizing about him.

Heat swamped through my entire body, igniting my skin on fire as he dove in.

He nuzzled my firmed sac while tonguing my taint. His blatant, deep inhale made me flush from self-consciousness even though I'd showered right before leaving my hotel room.

Another low rumble escaped him, and he closed his hot lips around one of my balls.

"Oh fuck, oh fuck, oh fuck," I blabbered, lost in the exquisite feel of the heat, the slickness of his mouth suckling me.

Drake hummed his pleasure, and I thrashed, reaching around my thighs to grasp his hair.

"Drake—oh my God—seriously?" I choked on a laugh while wanting to cry and come at the same time. My emotions ran rampant from relief to delirious joy to agonizing need for more.

He licked up my aching length, pushing my thighs as wide apart as my restrictive slacks allowed. Strong fingers bruised the tender skin on the backs of my legs, but I didn't care. Drake could leave marks on me every damned day of the week like I dreamed about, and I wouldn't complain.

My ass lifted fully off the floor as he shoved me higher.

"Gonna suck your dick, Preston."

"Yes—fuck yeah," I gasped as he glanced up to my hot face.

Lust blazed in his bright eyes, causing another droplet of pre-cum to drip onto my skin as I fought to fill my lungs. Eyes were the windows to a man's soul, and I was sure he felt the same toward me as I did for him. In that moment, I didn't care what would come later—the truth we couldn't be together, that our affair had a time limit.

"Want to rile you up until you're begging to give me every drop you've got, baby."

Drake's desire ramped my own, forcing me to stay in the present.

If I had believed in angels, they would have broken into the Hallelujah Chorus as Drake took me to the root with one downward glide over my swollen cock.

"J-J-Jesus!" I stuttered, my body attempting to buck beneath his strong arms holding me still.

Wet heat clasped tightly around the tip of my dick lodged in his throat as he swallowed.

"Oh shit. I'm gonna come. Drake! Fuck, I'm gonna come."

He backed away so damned quickly my cock slapped against my belly the second he popped off.

"Ugh!" I jerked. "Shit...oh shit, Drake. That was close."

"Mmm." He licked his saliva from the back of my length and took me into his mouth again.

Teeth gritted against the orgasm of a lifetime, I tried— *fuck*, how I wanted to hold off coming too soon.

Did he have a condom in his pocket? Lube in his wallet?

"Want you to fuck me," I panted out the words, so damned desperate to feel him inside me. Filling me. *Owning* me.

He released my dick again and nuzzled against my tight sac, nipping at my taint with the perfect amount of sting. "Now's not the time, baby."

"*Please*," I begged, my hole so empty and needy. I did not give two shits where we were, the late hour, or anything else other than what I experienced in that second—intimacy, the connection I'd craved from the moment I realized I loved him.

Drake licked over where I wanted him most, his tongue probing at my hole but not breaching.

"Put it in," I demanded, and he chuckled, lifting his head enough our gazes clashed.

His laughter intensified. From amusement or happiness, I couldn't tell, but fuck did I adore the comfort between us, the lack of a wall hiding our deepest desires from each other.

Eyes on mine, he fluttered the tip of his tongue over my hole.

"Fuck you," I spat out without any heat behind my words even though a deep frown dented my forehead. "You...you *tease!*"

Growling, he leaned down and lapped at the new bead of moisture at my slit, holding it on the tip of his tongue extended from his mouth. He lifted my legs higher and shoved my pre-cum right up my ass as far as his stiff tongue could reach.

I cursed, my eyes rolling back into my head.

Drake was inside my body. Not exactly how I'd

dreamed about, but I would take what I could get. That beard between my thighs?

Exquisite. Absolutely delicious. Better than any fantasy I'd concocted after first seeing his permanent scruff all those years ago.

"Drake," I whimpered, trying to grind my ass against his face while holding onto his hair with a death grip. "Need you. More. *Please.*" I sounded like a whiny brat, but goddamnit, I'd waited for so long to be at his mercy. Never expected to have a single one of my dreams fulfilled.

And being gifted the perfect opportunity to be in our own little world of stolen time, he had kissed me. Sucked my cock. His tongue slicked in and out of my hole, taking me to the breaking point. I wasn't above begging since we might never have a moment like this again.

"D-Drake," my voice caught.

"Later," he promised, gently kissing my pucker. "I'll wreck you later. But for now..." He swallowed my length in one go, working me over like a cum-starved animal who was as desperate for my load as I was his dick up my ass.

"Oh...I'm close, Drake—close."

He didn't back off but doubled his efforts, fucking his own throat on my cock.

I hissed, my taint pulsing. "C-Coming— Ugh!" I shot off with a grunt that ripped from my chest with the force of a jet engine. I soared higher than any bird, losing all sense of gravity or reality as every muscle in my body tensed and flew in the clouds.

Shudders ripped through me, stealing my breath with every pulse of my balls.

Drake's throat tightened around my cockhead as he swallowed each spurt of my more than normal ejaculate that erupted up my shaft.

"Sorry. Oh hell, that's a lot—sorry. So good. Holy hell," I blabbered on as twitches continued to wrack my body.

Drake suckled on my tip as though wanting one last dribble from my spent cock. "Fuck, what a load. You're so damn sweet, baby." He licked me like a lollipop. "Better than I'd dreamed about."

He'd...what?

I went limp, sprawling as much as my dress pants allowed while trying to grasp what he'd claimed. My lungs fought for oxygen, my entire body overheated and tingling as Drake's words clarified in my buzzed brain.

Had he always wanted me? Longed for a physical connection? Or was it more, the overwhelming need to be one with each other in every way?

Basking in the afterglow of the best orgasm of my life, my eyelids fell closed. I set aside the deep discussion thoughts and just enjoyed the moment.

"What *was* that?" I murmured, my heart still racing.

"Me fulfilling what I'm guessing was our shared fantasy."

The *first* of many, I wanted to say, but I knew better than to hope. At least he'd answered one of my questions.

We could take advantage of our close proximity, the hours allotted to us by fate, but at the end of our time trapped in the elevator, we would both have to walk away.

A sudden sting struck my eyes, but I swallowed against the grief already wanting to tear my heart in two.

Chapter 13

Drake

Had Preston's slacks not acted like handcuffs around his ankles, he'd have sprawled across the elevator floor like an octopus. Flushed and glowing, he'd never looked more beautiful.

Sated, emerald eyes watched me as I gently lowered his legs and pulled back up his boxer briefs and pants. Who the fuck knew how quickly or exactly when we would be rescued. The elevator could begin moving at any second, and even quicker, the doors could be sliding open to a dozen concerned people getting an eyeful of what neither of us wanted known outside the four walls enclosing us in privacy.

My dick ached like a motherfucker, but I ignored the need to shove into his waxed, pink hole that had been too pretty for words. He was everything I'd expected him to be and then some. I zipped him up and buckled his belt.

As much as I would love to roar my ownership, my obsession, over my stepbrother to the world, even though I'd had nothing but a teasing taste of how potent we could be together, I couldn't.

Everything between us had changed, but our circumstances had not.

Leaning over him on hands and knees, I peered at the face I'd memorized years earlier and continued to dream about every night regardless of the distance I'd had to put between us.

Attempting *not* to love him had proven futile.

And I was okay with that now that I had him in my grasp.

For a short while, anyway.

Luminous eyes peered up at me full of trust and emotions I couldn't begin to name even though it looked like he felt the same as I did. He smiled up at me as though hearing my thoughts and tugged on the back of my neck, one leg wrapping around my waist to pull me down atop him.

"I'm heavy," I warned, settling some of my weight onto him, unable to keep from grinning.

"Don't care. Need to feel you and taste my cum on your tongue."

"Jesus, baby," I whispered but gave him what he wanted.

I'd called him sweet, but more salt lingered in my mouth after swallowing the cum he'd shot into my throat. He loved the flavor of himself if his sighing and one last shudder rippling through his body was any indication.

"Promise me this won't be the only time I get to have you, Preston," I begged, beyond desperate for another taste, another stolen moment with the one my entire being belonged to.

"We c-can't—"

"We *can*," I cut him off, my tone firm. "When this shit is

over tonight, I'll sneak to your room," I murmured, my dick throbbing with every beat of my heart.

"No! I-I mean not that I don't want you, but I'll come to you. It's better for Jacqueline to find me missing from mine if she checks in on me since you being in my bed isn't as easily excused."

Preston *had* grown some balls.

"I don't care where just as long as we're together." I slid off his body, stretched out onto my side, and tugged his back to my chest. My eyes closed, and regardless of my hard as nails dick and the unforgiving floor beneath us, I rested in bliss over finally having Preston in my favorite snuggle position again. "I never asked all those years ago, but do you mind being the little spoon?"

He muttered a curse while grasping hold of my arm around his middle.

"What?" I tucked his hips tighter against my aching groin.

"This," he whispered as he shivered in my arms. "Back then. When we...when you fell asleep in my bed. I always ended up in your arms like this."

"With my dick desperate to burst through the material separating us and claim your ass?"

"Fuck." His whimper heated me to the point I wanted to rip my clothes off and do exactly that.

"You would wake up," I reminded him, unable to help my grin. "Think I was sleeping. Sometimes grind against me the slightest bit before hopping out of the bed like I burned your skin. Sometimes, I figured it was just wishful thinking."

"I-I didn't believe you were interested in me. Morning wood, you know?"

"Mmm." Unable to help myself, I ran my hand over his

groin, tempted to rouse him back to life just so I could taste him again. "It was all you, baby. Every time. Even the mornings I was in my own bed, I was hard for you."

"Same," he whispered, his strangled word making my dick jerk in the confines of my pants.

"What else?" I pushed since the dam between us had been obliterated, and I needed everything. Physical *and* the mental intimacy our emotions could swim in.

He huffed a snort. "You want all my fantasies?"

"To hear them *and* fulfill them," I murmured, rubbing my nose in his soft hair. Sweet as vanilla. I considered sucking on his nape but didn't, since I wasn't about to leave a single telling mark on his body that could fuck us in the worst way possible.

The thought dampened my mood slightly, but I pushed it aside since I only had a short time to indulge before the real world appeared once more beyond the elevator's doors.

He shivered in my arms. "That would take months. Years, even."

Forever sounded even better, but again...I couldn't allow my thoughts to go there. But knowing he'd dreamed up that amount of fantasies?

Fuck.

"My naughty little nerd," I said with a chuckle before pressing my lips where I'd have preferred my teeth nip and bruise his tender flesh.

Preston elbowed me lightly.

"Do you hate me saying you're a nerd?"

"No, because it's the truth, but you can't call me *yours*. You know that can't ever be."

I wanted to argue past the sting in my chest his words pierced me with, but he didn't lie. Best to focus on the here and now. "So...what would you have me do to you, hmm?" I slid two fingertips between the buttons of his shirt to rub over the soft skin of his stomach.

"Jerk me off while fucking my ass."

I groaned, squeezing him while giving in to the need to grind my dick against his bubble butt. "If I was sure we'd be trapped for another two hours, I would gladly fulfill that request, baby."

Preston sighed. "Later tonight? If we ever get out of here?"

"Fuck yeah. Gonna fill you up and swallow my name from your lips when I make you come."

"D-Drake," he whispered, reaching over my arm to press on his cock.

"Am I making you hard again already?" I murmured while nuzzling his soft hair I couldn't stay away from.

"Yes, damn you. I-I'm insatiable when it comes to you."

Talk about a goddamned ego boost. My dick was making a mess of pre-cum in my black briefs. We needed to change the topic before I took shit even further than I already had.

I glanced at my watch.

"What time is it?"

"9:55."

"We've been in here for three hours."

"And you haven't panicked again."

"It's easy to remain calm when you're around," Preston admitted quietly. "It always was."

"I wish..." I trailed off since I hated thinking about the what-ifs. Having experienced a little of what Preston and I could be together, I would definitely go back and change shit if I had the chance.

"What?" Preston threaded his fingers through mine atop his stomach.

"I wish we'd had this when we were younger. Those three years together would have been crazy different."

"If Jacqueline found us in a compromising situation, she'd have kicked you out. Probably me too."

"We could have lived with my mom and my two annoying stepsisters since we weren't old enough to be on our own."

"Your mom is tolerant of queer people?"

"Yeah." I sighed over the fact my dick finally began to relax. "My dad too."

"Devlin knows you're gay?" He sounded surprised.

"I came out to him while I was in college."

"There's no way he told Jacqueline, or you wouldn't have been invited to their home or here for dinner tonight."

"She doesn't know," I confirmed. "I hated putting my dad in the position of having to keep a secret from her, but he's chosen not to rock his boat in any way."

"You're lucky to have such a father. Mom too, for that matter."

"There's nothing wrong with Nancy," I argued about his other parent he'd taken to calling his mother. "She adores the ground you walk on."

"Oh, I'm not saying there is," Preston hurried to add. "It's just...different." He snapped his lips closed, but I'd seen the hurt Jacqueline's words had caused. I doubted there was much I didn't already understand when it came to Preston's inner workings

Well, all except for the fact he was gay and wanted me. How had I been blind to those feelings? Probably fear over him being too much like Jacqueline, regardless of his love for his biological father.

"Did you go to Nancy and Michael's wedding?" I asked.

"Yes." I could hear the smile in Preston's voice. "It's was

beautiful. Michael's family loves Nancy. Welcomed her with open arms and celebrates who she is."

"I'm glad she found her place."

"She asked about you."

I grinned. "She did?"

Preston nodded. "I told her you were living in Boston, and she said the next time I saw you to thank you again for making sure I got to spend time with her when Jacqueline denied me the right to visit."

Nancy was a beautiful soul. Instinctively caring and nurturing, the same as me. She'd also been super affectionate with Preston, which had left him needy when we'd returned to the penthouse together in silence after sneaking off to visit with her.

"Thank you for always holding my hand on our way home," Preston said, his voice quiet.

"I was just thinking about that."

"Every drive back to hell, every elevator ride."

I squeezed his fingers, rubbing my thumb gently over his warm skin. "They fit together rather nicely, don't they?"

"Yes." Preston lifted our clasped palms, eyeing how I stroked over him. "I've had dozens of fantasies about your fingers."

I snorted a laugh. "Is there any part of me you haven't?"

He thought for a moment. "Nope. I would even suck on your toes if you asked me to."

Why did that image make my semi want to swell back to full, aching agony?

"Foot fetish, huh?" I asked.

"Not really," he said with a shrug against my chest, "but they're a part of you, and I lo— Well, every inch of you is perfect so..."

"You haven't seen all of me," I reminded him, my heart tightening in my chest over what he'd almost said.

He shifted, and I lifted an eyebrow.

"Something you need to tell me?"

"I, um...may have gotten a good look at you after you hopped out of the shower a few times?"

"Is that a statement or question?" I pressed since Preston rarely gave anything away. And that secret? Fucking gold.

"Okay, so five occurrences allowed me to see you butt naked. Yes, I'm a sicko who snuck peeks through doors left cracked open whenever given the chance." He huffed the words, and I lifted onto my elbow to check out his face.

He'd flushed a gorgeous shade of pink.

I rolled Preston onto his back, throwing my leg over his waist and spearing my hands into his hair. "I love that you obsessed over me as much as I did you."

The color in his cheeks grew darker, mottling. "You *didn't*."

"Oh, I definitely did. You want to talk about being a sicko? I would stand outside the bathroom door just to listen to you shower. Couldn't begin to count how often I jerked off right there in the hallway while imagining you washing your body."

"Oh my God, Drake." He gulped, his pupils swelling.

"I even got lucky enough to hear you jacking yourself—twice in the shower and at least a dozen times while hunkered outside your bedroom door when our parents slept."

"Jesus." Preston threw his arm over his face, but I pulled his wrist, pinning it beside his head so he couldn't hide from me.

"Hey."

He blinked open those gorgeous green eyes and managed to hold my gaze. At least I now understood why he couldn't stand to look at me for longer than a few seconds and why he'd been quick to wipe the feel of me off his sweaty palms.

"I made you nervous back then. Did you ever hate that about me?"

"Never," he hastened to assure me, shaking his head. "You're just so damned potent. Hot. The muscles. Your Cupid's bow." His gaze dropped to my mouth, and I rubbed my tongue over my upper lip.

"What about it?"

"Iwannalickit," he murmured, the words rushing into one.

"Then do it," I said with a smirk, lowering my face so he wouldn't have to make much of a move to take what he wanted.

A delicious whimper I'd gotten off to a thousand times leaked from his mouth. Blood rushed to my dick at the sound.

Rather than lifting his head to kiss me like I'd expected, he flicked his tongue out to literally lick my upper lip.

"Taste good?" I asked, still smirking.

"More."

As if I could deny Preston.

I settled in and kissed him. Explored his mouth while running my fingers through his thick, wavy hair. Gentleness replaced the hunger from earlier, but that didn't stop either of us from seeking out more friction.

He panted against my mouth, clutching at my back as we rutted against each other.

Lust to sink into his tight heat, stroke inside his ass until we both exploded raged through me, but I kept hold of my need.

Like I'd said, we could be rescued at any second, and while I would have loved to flaunt what I did with Jacqueline's son, Preston coming out to his biological mom had to be his doing. His choice and at his time.

And while he'd changed slightly from the young man I remembered, I wasn't sure he would ever find the balls to tell his truth.

Nor did I have any desire to wreck my dad's marriage. Because not a single doubt rested in my head that Jacqueline would make my dad's existence a living hell if he refused to cut me out of his life like she would demand.

Preston and I were both stuck. Emotionally glued to each other and yet unable to freely live our truth. Want who our hearts longed for. Love...

I sighed, closing my eyes while my lips lingered on his.

Preston was the one man I could see myself settling down with. The only partner I would allow myself to be vulnerable to future hurt at our sure end.

But we could never be to begin with.

The reminder sobered me, and I slowed our kisses until I pulled away, soothing his hair off his forehead. His hungry gaze tempted me to dive back in, to take everything he would give once lost to passion, but the possible consequences once more made me pause.

Later.

Chapter 14

Preston

I jolted awake—no, the *elevator* jolted, ripping me from sleep.

Drake scrambled off the floor where we'd been snuggling.

My heartbeat sped, adrenaline crashing through me as I peered up at him.

We descended at a normal clip, not free-falling.

Our time together had ended.

Sadness flooded his eyes, and he held out a hand to me.

I accepted his help up off the floor but didn't cling to his fingers like I'd have done as a teenager. A flood of people would be awaiting us on the ground floor.

Stepping away from him, I held his pained gaze, hating the feet separating us like a mile-wide chasm.

"Four hours of heaven," he murmured through the thick silence between us.

"Four hours of perfection," I whispered back, my throat tightening over how much deeper I'd fallen in love with him during our too-short hours of being stuck in close proximity.

The movement around us slowed.

Stopped.

Still, we stared at one another, our breaths loud in the stillness before the storm.

"Later," he stated quietly, a hint of inquiry in his voice.

The door slid open before I could respond.

Voices raised, and a ruckus of questions and wandering hands assessed us. Jacqueline's teary-eyed mess of makeup on her face hit me more than I'd expected. I'd never seen her so unkempt and ruffled.

Sudden surety that she truly cared about me in some way flooded me with wary hopefulness that things were about to change. That I might have a future with her that wasn't fraught with grimaces and flinches on my end.

Even though she could be a bitch—*was* a bitch at her core—she acted as though she'd been concerned for my welfare. I hugged her for the first time in years, rubbing her back as she cried in my arms, clutching me as though afraid of losing her only child. My eyes stung, and I swallowed repeatedly to keep from blubbering like the little boy inside me who was still desperate for his mother's love.

Devlin grasped Drake tight to his chest too, tears in both their eyes.

Emotions rose and dipped like a roller coaster, and I tired quickly, wishing the reunion, the EMTs insisting on checking out both Drake and I, would just go away. Authorities loitered around the lobby, and the explanation of a technical glitch answered my question as to why I'd been allowed those precious hours alone with the man I loved more than life.

Exhaustion lined every face I took in, but Drake's eyes burned with desire whenever our gazes caught over the next forty or so minutes of chaos.

"The restaurant closed," Jacqueline stated, still hanging

onto my arm with a death grip, "but we have meals kept aside for you both."

At eleven at night atop the drama and emotional upheaval I'd endured the entire day, I wasn't sure I could eat. I wanted a bed.

And Drake's arms.

After assuring everyone, hotel staff and authorities included, that Drake and I were fine, we settled at the bar. I picked at my food while Drake chowed down like a starving animal.

Jacqueline started in on assuring us The Bloomberg would face the consequences for the mishap. "I called my lawyers," she stated, petting my forearm.

I didn't pull away from her attempts at an assuring caress even though it felt...strange. A part of me had longed for the display for years, and now that she offered it, I would be a fool to withdraw from her touch.

"We're fine, Jacqueline," Drake interjected before she got worked up again. "Accidents happen, so unless there's evidence it was more than that, don't waste your energy."

"But it *shouldn't* have happened!"

"Jacqueline," I said, patting her hand clutching the stem of a wine glass she'd gulped from for the previous three or so minutes, "it's okay—*we're* okay. No harm, no foul."

Devlin slid his arm around her back from where he sat on her other side. "Our boys weren't injured, darling. I'll bet they even enjoyed getting caught up after all these years apart."

My face heated, and I feigned serious interest in the pasta dish that no longer steamed in front of me. I shifted on my barstool, remembering exactly how much I'd enjoyed Drake's mouth on my dick and balls. My groin tingled to life, and I fought against the need to look at the man on my right.

"This evening has *not* gone to plan," Jacqueline stated with a huff of annoyance at not having gotten her way. "I had everything perfect, and now it's ruined."

"We already discussed this," Devlin soothed, his tone low and firm as always with her. He murmured a few more things near her ear not meant for ours, and jealousy snaked through me as it did when I witnessed their love. I envied their freedom to openly show affection to each other.

"Boys, we're going to meet for brunch tomorrow at ten," Devlin finally addressed us. "I think it's best if we hold off on discussing the reasons for Jacqueline having you come to New York until the morning."

I nodded, more than happy to end the evening with them sooner than later. Jacqueline's unusual frantic nature over my safety, while kind of nice to see for a change, had begun to grate on my nerves. I wasn't used to her attention, nor did I know how to respond to it.

"Fine by me," Drake said, wiping his mouth with a linen napkin. He slid off his stool as though his dad's words had been etched in stone. "Think you can handle an elevator ride to the thirteenth floor, or do you want to take the stairs?" he asked me, ignoring both our parents.

Our gazes caught and held, making my blood heat.

The stairs, although easier to handle, would waste time and tire me out even more. While I'd had a short nap, I expected I was going to be up quite late. At least, I hoped I would be.

My face went even hotter as I tried to tamp down rising fear over being trapped again. "Elevator is f-fine," I croaked, my heart rate fluttering from both lust and trepidation.

"I could try to get you a room closer to ground level,"

Jacqueline started, but I shook my head, shifting my focus off Drake's gaze before we outed our want for each other.

"I've gotten over my phobia of confined spaces. I'll be fine." I hoped so, anyway.

"Are you sure, sweetheart?" she pressed, her gaze still troubled and emanating worry for me while glancing between me and Drake.

My heart ached at the term of endearment I couldn't ever remember hearing off her lips. Anxiety flooded me that she would read the sexual tension between him and I. "Yeah," I rasped, unsettled—unsure of how the evening had changed my life.

Jacqueline squeezed my hand, acquiescing for a change, thank fuck.

We left my half-empty plate atop the bar, the four of us making for the elevator not covered in caution tape. Drake led the way with sure, steady steps as always.

Adrenaline pumped through my bloodstream, half for the ride ahead and half for the *other* ride I would enjoy atop the man striding in front of me. Or he could be on top, I had no preference. I just wanted Drake inside me, making the rest of the world dissolve around us.

I was the second to enter the elevator, a mirror image of the one Drake and I had been trapped in. My heart outright raced, making me a little breathless. He moved to the far wall, and I followed on shaky legs, turning as Jacqueline and Devlin stepped in as well. Their room lay up on the twenty-something floor.

"If you need anything..." Jacqueline's voice trailed off, sounding exhausted as hell, and I nodded. Her assuring smile wobbled before she snuggled against Devlin's side as though seeking out his warmth and strength like I refrained from doing with the other Hemmings man beside me.

"Okay?" Drake murmured to me as the doors slid shut. He stepped close enough our shoulders touched.

"Yeah," I whispered, reminding myself to fill my lungs. That tight space issue might have healed, but new PTSD arrived in the form of fear of getting stuck between floors again. With Drake? I wouldn't mind. But it would be hell on earth to be confined for longer than five minutes with Jacqueline Casswell and her newly formed whacked-out responses to me.

Drake brushed his knuckles over mine, and while I wanted to entwine my fingers with his, I made do with the fact we had bare skin contact behind our parent's backs.

The elevator glided upward without issues, and I glanced over at his eyes darkened by desire as we slowed nearer my floor.

We couldn't speak of what we wanted. I couldn't double-check we shared the same plans.

But he nodded as though seeing the questions in my eyes.

I released a slow exhale and stepped past Devlin to exit the elevator.

"See you in the morning, sweetheart," Jacqueline called, and I dipped my head, forcing myself to turn away.

Shoulders hunched, I listened as the door slid shut once more, taking my love three stories higher where he would wait for me.

I didn't trust Jacqueline not to check on me in person. Knowing her, she probably had a key to my room and would march right in rather than call. I didn't want to ride the elevator alone so soon after being stuck in one, but I could handle three flights of stairs. All for the safety of Drake's room, where she wouldn't dare enter without knocking.

Shaking, I hurried to my suite. I cleaned myself out the

best I could with the removable showerhead before scrubbing the rest of my body. At least I kept myself waxed for personal preferences regardless of my celibacy, which Drake had already seen. Did he like it?

He'd groaned enough over my scent and taste, so I had to assume he held no complaints over my hairless groin.

I should have eaten more, I realized as tremors continued to plague me, probably from low blood sugar. Dressed in sweats and a T-shirt, I hightailed it for the stairwell regardless of my weakness, quickly losing my breath even though I walked on a treadmill three times a week.

My pulse thrummed in my ears as I exited the stairwell onto Drake's floor. A quick glance at the wall directly ahead showed me with golden arrows which way I needed to go. Left.

1650... 1652...

I stopped in front of his room and wiped my hands down my sweats. "I've got this," I whispered to myself.

What I'd wanted since I was a young teen lay within my grasp, and every inch of me trembled from fatigue, adrenaline crash, and heady desire for what I was about to do.

Nothing was going to stop what fate had finally gifted me.

Chapter 15

Drake

I'd kept my focus on Preston throughout the long moments after our rescue. He'd been pale, flushing when our gazes met but back to seemingly weak and exhausted seconds after he would glance away as he always did after making eye contact with me.

His timidity broke my heart, as did the bond between us screaming for the right of visibility.

I wanted to wrap him in my arms, assure him that no one knew what we'd been up to, that things would eventually calm down, and he would once more be in privacy where we could act on our desire for one another.

First, I would love him. Give him what we both craved. And I would cuddle him, lavish my pent-up affection on him until he passed out and snored in my embrace.

He ate only enough to sustain him until morning, and all it had taken was Jacqueline's starting to rant about suing The Bloomberg for me to draw the line. I'd had it—with the entire affair and how she'd clung to him like she suddenly remembered she had a child when she'd ignored him the whole time I'd lived with them.

Sure, sometimes it took almost losing what you loved to remind you that you had feelings for that person, but her actions still pissed me off. Probably because she had the freedom to touch him while I didn't. Fucking jealousy could choke on a dick and not in the fun way.

Dad backed me up about getting rest, eyeing me a little strangely while doing so. Had he noticed the hint of beard burn around Preston's mouth? Jacqueline hadn't, or she wouldn't have been so damned lovey-dovey with him.

Knowing Dad wouldn't say shit until we had a moment's privacy, I'd pushed to end the evening.

Preston had the balls to ride in an elevator again. I'd been sure he'd jump on the change of room Jacqueline offered to get for him so he could just take the stairs. But remembering the plans we'd made, three flights rather than sixteen would be worth the agony of being enclosed in another elevator. Without a second of privacy to insist on going to his room, I had to keep my fingers crossed he showed up.

I stood as close to his side as I dared, hoping my energy and warmth would give him the strength he needed not to panic.

He'd handled the elevator ride like a pro, but watching him turning his back on me—fucking *walking* away—stung like a bitch. Was that how I'd made him feel five years earlier? Even expecting he would be in my arms within the hour, I couldn't stand the pain of him leaving me for a minute now that I'd gotten a taste of him.

Being separated from Preston was worse than any laceration or injury I'd sustained on the gridiron. There was no way we could only have tonight. Depending on Jacqueline's plans, maybe I could talk him into a second night of sneaking around with each other.

Hell—Jacqueline never visited Boston. How would she know if we continued to hook up after returning home?

Hope sprang to life in my chest with a luscious ache, and I clung to the feeling, desperate for his agreement.

But first, tonight.

"Goodnight, son," Dad said as I slipped past them onto the sixteenth floor. "I hope you get some rest."

Jacqueline didn't murmur a word to me or inquire about the obvious suggestion in Dad's voice.

He fucking *knew*.

Had to with how I'd been unable to keep my gaze off my stepbrother. At least Jacqueline had been too wrapped up in her son to see how I stared at him with all the want in the world radiating from my eyes.

Same as with my sexual orientation, I trusted Dad with my secrets.

"Night, Dad." Excitement raced through me, but I didn't hurry to my room.

Those moments of listening at the bathroom door when we'd been teens assured me Preston couldn't take a quick shower. And also knowing his penchant for being clean made me confident he would be thorough in the bathroom before coming to my room.

I would give Preston an hour, and if he wasn't at my door by then, I would go to him, Jacqueline be damned. Now that I'd had a taste, I wasn't about to cower like he might do in his mind.

Since I didn't have his number, I couldn't text. I thought about calling Dad and asking for Preston's cell with the excuse to make sure he was okay, but I wasn't about to stir up any concern on Jacqueline's part. Best to leave things as we had.

With the stench of wine I'd smelled on Dad's wife and

the haggard lines that had broken through the mask of makeup she always slathered on, I expected she would lay down and not get up until morning.

And Dad wouldn't leave her side. His wishes for a good night's rest doubly assured me of that fact.

Freedom from possibly being found out lay ahead of me, and I planned on taking advantage of that shit all damned night long.

At least, as long as Preston allowed or stayed awake.

I'm a selfish prick.

Lips in a thin line, I stripped, telling myself I would not keep my sweet nerd up until morning no matter how much I wanted to. Big spooning the hell out of him while he slept would suffice.

After I had him naked and writhing beneath me at least once.

I climbed into the shower, propping the bathroom door open with the trash can so I would hear his knock. If he got there before I finished, he could join me.

My semi swelled fully at the idea of a soapy, needy Preston rubbing all over my front, but I ignored my hard length to finish up. The hot steam and steadily pelting water eased sore muscles from those four hours of sitting and lying on the elevator's hard floor.

I had twice the padding on my body as Preston, so I expected he might not be physically feeling the greatest either. Perhaps a nice massage after I left him boneless and sated on my bed was in order.

"Fuck yeah." I tipped my head back into the spray, rinsing shampoo from my hair. The thought of finally having the chance to touch every inch of him, kiss and suck on his freckled skin, made my dick throb.

Thank fuck I had years of practice denying myself a

quick release, or I'd be in danger of blowing my load prematurely. I'd learned how to please clients, so I didn't doubt my ability to fulfill Preston's fantasies.

What we had time for, anyway.

I lingered a few extra minutes in the shower, considering the weekend ahead. It was after midnight, so Saturday had officially arrived.

Valentine's Day.

The holiday for lovers and a little cliche, but it was the perfect moment of the year to make Preston mine.

I rubbed a hand over my balls, tugging gently to get them to relax.

Jacqueline had booked our rooms through Monday, so hopefully, events and plans ran in our favor, and it wouldn't be a one-night thing while we were in New York.

A knock sounded, sending a bolt of adrenaline and lust through my blood.

"Hang on!" I hollered, hopping out of the shower and grabbing a towel just in case the visitor wasn't my kryptonite.

A quick look in the peephole revealed a flushed Preston glancing up and down the hallway.

I ripped the door open and yanked him inside. It slammed shut behind him, and I tossed my towel aside.

"I—this is so wro—," His voice cut out as his gaze dropped to my dick straining toward my belly button.

"There's not one goddamn thing *wrong* about us, baby," I assured him, pulling him into my arms.

Our mouths came together with a crash, and I sucked whatever argument he might think off his full lips. The little noises he emitted just from my tongue in his mouth made me more desperate than I'd ever been for him.

I stepped back only to rip his shirt overhead.

He shoved at his sweats and kicked aside whatever sneakers he'd worn.

We backed farther into the suite, stumbling, nervous laughter escaping him between my kisses over his entire face.

"So sweet," I murmured before sucking his upper lip. "Damn, baby." I hefted him into my arms and tossed him onto the bed.

He bounced, squeaking, his lips already swollen and face a gorgeous shade of red. His hard cock leaked for me, and I gripped the base of mine tight while taking in the sight of my stepbrother sprawled out like a feast ready to be devoured.

Mussed red hair, lust-filled emerald eyes, his freckled pale skin heated with a pink flush...

Preston was the most beautiful man I'd ever seen in my life.

"You ready for me?" I asked, my voice raspy with desire denied for too many years.

Preston reached out, making a grabby motion with his shaking hand. "More than—want you so bad, Drake. I can't wait any longer."

I climbed over him, slow enough he cursed at me, and chuckling, I licked over his mouth again.

He grabbed hold of my back and thighs with all four limbs, yanking me down with a strength that surprised me.

"Hungry, huh?" I murmured.

"Starving," he corrected me.

"How do you want me?" I asked, rutting my hard length against his. Enough pre-cum oozed from both of us to ease our frotting, but I needed more than getting off on each other's stomachs.

"In me—I don't care how. Just need to feel what it's like

to be one with you, Drake," he whispered. "Please don't tease me by making me wait."

"Not a fan of edging?" I flexed my ass to stroke over his cock again with my length, loving the feel of his satiny skin along mine.

A deeper shade of red flooded his face, and he finally looked away from my stare. "Um...maybe? If you're behind me? You could...talk dirty to me while toying with my body until I begged you to let me come?"

I grinned. Someone hadn't lied about those fantasies.

"Fuck yeah, we're doing that but later. Right now, I just need inside your ass."

I'd brought along a bottle of lube since I knew I'd be jerking off a lot over the weekend due to being near Preston. I'd also fished a condom from my wallet before hopping in the shower, but we would have to acquire more for all the plans I had for the rest of the weekend if we got lucky.

"I'm already prepped a bit, so you don't have to stretch me," Preston admitted as I snapped open the cap, his sparkling eyes and pink cheeks so damn fine.

"What if I want to take my time becoming acquainted with the silkiness inside your hole?" I asked while oozing lube onto my hand. "Maybe use my fingers to stroke you to climax before filling you up?"

"Oh God." He gulped and shifted his hips.

I smirked, setting aside the bottle. "Hold the backs of your knees, baby. Wanna feel how hot you are inside."

Red crept down his hairless chest, and I leaned between his spread thighs to nibble on his hardened nipple.

"Ung." He bowed as I flicked my tongue over him.

"Mmm," I moaned my approval at finding him so sensitive. Pausing from playing with his tight nub, I watched his face while rubbing his asshole with my slick fingertips.

Lips parted, he stared back at me, pupils blown wide enough hardly any green remained.

I sank one finger inside him with no resistance, hissing at the heat of him sucking me in deeper.

Preston whimpered, a delicious sound that made the base of my spine tingle. I twisted my wrist so I could rub over his prostate. He gasped as I stroked over the roughened patch.

"Oh." He gulped. "Oh, God."

Smirking, I repeated the motion.

"D-Drake..."

"Fuck, I love when you stutter my name, baby." I gave him two fingers, my dick bucking as he closed his eyes and tipped his head back, tendons rising in his neck when I reached deep into his slick warmth. "Shit—you're so ready for me, aren't you? This needy ass is begging for my dick."

"Yes. Oh yeah. P-Please."

I kissed his belly button then the tip of his wet dick, taking a second to lap at the pre-cum waiting for my tongue. A few slow, steady strokes of my fingers into his hole, a little nibble on his taint, and I'd had enough teasing.

My hands shook as I sheathed and lubed my dick. An ache settled low in my groin, the promise of filling the rubber up. I'd rather empty my seed deep into Preston and watch it ooze out before shoving it inside where it belonged, but that would come after we had a chance to talk.

I'd been patient enough.

Preston grabbed the base of my dick and guided me to his pretty pink hole. "Wanted you forever," he murmured and bore down.

I sank past his ring with a slight push. "Jesus." I clenched my teeth and hissed. "I'm inside you, Preston. Fucking hell, you're tight."

A shudder ripped through him, and he wrapped his heels around the backs of my thighs, tugging me closer.

My dick burrowed in another inch, and I planked over him on my hands, watching his expressive face.

Hazed eyes. Flushed face full of freckles. A slight furrow of his brow appeared as I worked in farther, his channel like a warm, welcoming glove made just for me.

"Okay, baby?" I asked, my body quaking with the need to fully slam home.

"Yes," he gasped and licked over his lower lip as I pulled out and sank in again, gaining even more ground. "Fuck, you feel so *good.*" He choked on the word, eyes welling with tears.

"Christ." I swallowed hard, feeling the same goddamned sentiment. Giving him my weight, I licked into his mouth, needing more of a connection, since we both hovered on the verge of big emotions.

I longed to burrow into his soul where our spirits would intertwine, never to be set apart again.

Love you—fucking love you.

The words echoed in my head, but I held them back. We weren't at a place I could declare the true extent of my feelings for him, but I could show him.

I pulled out to the tip and sank in until my groin rested against his.

Mine.

Fucking finally.

Chapter 16

___

Preston

No two men could be closer than Drake and I in that moment. Nothing mattered but how deeply he impaled me, how thoroughly he'd worked his way into my body and heart.

We paused when he filled me completely, our mouths tender in tasting, sharing more unspoken vulnerabilities than I'd ever experienced. My throat ached with the need to cry, and Drake swallowed every whimper I couldn't contain.

Tearing his mouth from mine, he lifted enough to see my face. His arms weaseled beneath my shoulders, hands gliding upward to cradle my head. We lay face to face, heart to heart, sharing breaths as if we were one.

As we are meant to be.

I didn't doubt that truth but pushed aside reality wanting to enter in the moment and ruin the perfection I'd finally found beneath Drake. "You're my dream come true," I whispered without thought of consequence, my voice laced with the tears once more welling in my eyes.

"Preston." Drake made my name sound like a prayer

while rubbing his thumbs over my cheeks and temples. Lower lip sucking between his teeth, he slowly backed out of my ass in an agonizing glide until only his tip rested inside me.

Our eyes held each other captive as my body welcomed him until he filled me completely.

My breath left in a rush, my pulse thrumming with the overwhelming desire for more.

"Fucking *hell*," Drake groaned, slowly repeating the action that teased over my prostate and made my cock leak. "You're so hot inside, baby. Don't ever want to leave."

I clutched at him, my fingers trying to find purchase in hard muscle and skin slicking over from his shower or sweat, I didn't know.

Another long, drawn out stroke, and I couldn't handle any more. I squeezed my ass around his girth and leaned up to take his mouth.

He grunted—and fucked into me hard enough I slid over the mattress.

Oh fuck, oh fuck, oh fuck. I gulped, frantic in my need to taste his tongue, suck on his lips, and soak in the heat of his heavy body atop mine clear into my innermost parts.

"Jesus," Drake whispered harshly against my mouth, releasing his hold on my head with one hand to snake down along my side and grasp my ass. "Fuck."

I lifted to meet his thrusts, every thought but him abandoned in my lust to be closer. Whining, I shoved his face into my neck, and he gave me what I wanted, all his weight as he grabbed hold of my other ass cheek.

His grip would leave bruises as he pounded into me with full, steady strokes, his balls slapping against my body.

Hard muscles bunched against me, his pecs like rocks on my chest, his abs a glorious rippled board for my straining length to rub against. I wouldn't need a fist or tongue. My balls were going to erupt with nothing more than the friction between our bodies getting me off.

"Close," I whispered, eyes shut and cheek pressing against his still-damp hair.

He moaned and panted against my neck, his hot breath sending shivers over my arms. "Preston—baby."

I clung to him, rocking with every undulation of his hips, whispering curses and praise over how well his dick rubbed inside me like no one ever had. We were a perfect fit in every way.

"Never gonna get enough of you." He groaned, fingertips digging into my ass cheeks. "Fucking never."

"Oh—yes."

He punched the words from my lungs with harsh stabs into my body.

"Drake—God."

A guttural groan rumbled from his chest, tightening my balls.

"Gonna come for me, baby?" he asked, panting as he slammed into me over and over.

"Ye-es." The word ripped from me in two syllables thanks to his delicious ramming of my ass.

"Just like this?" His lips latched onto my throat with an open-mouthed kiss.

I gasped—and erupted. Curses spewed from me as cum shot from my slit, smearing between our rubbing abs.

"Fuck." Drake shoved up onto his hands while gifting me long, steady strokes, lips parted as he watched my cock continue to pulse untouched between us. "Jesus, you're so goddamn hot, baby. Look at you shooting off for me."

"Come on me," I gasped as another tremor ripped through me, tightening my core.

He hissed and backed out before he ripped off the condom, using one hand to stroke himself, the other firmly planted beside my head. Grunts rushed past his parted lips, and while I wanted to watch his cum spurt atop mine, coating me, I needed to see his eyes more.

"Look at me, Drake," I whispered, grasping his face, my empty hole clenching and aching to have him again.

He gave me his focus, the vivid blue eaten up by swollen pupils. I drowned. Lost myself as wet heat splattered over my belly and chest.

"Preston," he choked, gaze never wavering from my eyes as his glazed over, lost in his climax.

So. Gorgeous.

I pulled him down atop me before he finished, kissing his mouth. Licking his lips. Inhaling his panted exhales deep into my lungs so a part of him would pump throughout my entire body.

One final shudder, and he gave me some of his weight, winding his arms around me to hold me tight.

Our combined cum smeared between our torsos in a hot, sticky mess, but we clutched at each other, hesitant to break the physical bond between us. Every inch of my skin tingled, Drake's exhales causing shivers to raise the hairs on my nape and arms.

A smile settled on my face as our heartbeats slowed, and breaths came easier as I luxuriated in the euphoria of an empty mind sated by absolute bliss.

"Goddamn," he finally groaned, nuzzling my neck.

Fighting off the tickles and the need to shy away from his beard, I soothed my hands up and down his damp back. My fingertips dipped in and around his muscles. A shuddered sigh rippled through me, sending a rush of satiated relaxation through my extremities.

Comfortable silence rested between us, and I could have stayed there forever in his arms. Perfect peacefulness like I'd never experienced swept over me, weighty yet delicious.

My balls still tingled from the release he'd given me, my ass burning from the desperation with which he'd fucked me. But I wouldn't change a single thing about how we'd come together for the first time. Those four hours of perfection in the elevator had been nothing compared to our handful of minutes becoming one body.

Drake was the first to move. He kissed my neck, my collarbone, my chin, before lifting onto his elbows to gaze down at me. I'd never seen his eyes so open, a beautiful shade of blue like a clear afternoon sky.

I loved him. Wholeheartedly.

He tapped my lower lip, a soft smile curving his.

I nipped at his fingertip, and he growled in warning. Raising an eyebrow, I repeated the motion.

"You're going to test my endurance, aren't you?" he asked, his voice husky from those hours of talking then fucking.

"I've got a lot of pent-up need inside me," I stated, smiling up at him, so damned happy I could float away like dandelion fluff on the slightest breeze.

"Good." He gave me a quick, hard kiss. "'Cause I'm feeling the same, baby. But right now—" he kissed me again "—I want to clean you up and hold you while we sleep."

"I'd rather suck your cock until you're hard again so you can shove my face into the pillow and fuck me until I pass out." I guessed my nervousness had been beaten down by his cock and kisses.

"Jesus, Preston." Drake huffed a laugh and winced while climbing off me. "We ought to get some rest, or we'll end up missing that brunch Jacqueline is insisting on."

He had to bring her up.

"Ugh." I pouted but rolled to the edge of the bed, determined to ignore the world outside his suite. I didn't want our short time together tainted by thoughts of anything other than sated bliss. "You might need to carry me into the bathroom."

"Gladly." Drake stood and pulled me up into his arms as though I didn't weigh a buck-seventy.

"Jesus, Drake." I laughed. "I was kidding."

"Mmm." He pecked me on the cheek. "Always wanted to do this."

I wound my arms around his thick neck like I'd dreamed of doing, wishing instead that he strode over our forever home's threshold rather than into a hotel bathroom.

Can't go there.

Even though I yearned for it with every fiber of my being.

My legs were a little wobbly when he set me down, more drunk-like than buzzed. High enough the reality in the back of my mind didn't take away my joy.

He caught me grinning. "Someone's feeling fine."

"Better than," I breathed, staring as he bent to turn the shower on. Fuck, what an incredible backside he had. And those *thighs* rippled with muscle.

I shivered, wishing that just once I felt the urge to sink between firm ass cheeks and bury my dick inside a lubed hole. Drake's would be spectacular, no doubt about it.

Glancing down at my dick, I waited for the flaccid flesh to twitch.

Nothing.

I wasn't surprised. Drake had always topped me in my

fantasies. I would be perfectly content to bottom for him every day—twice a day—until I breathed my last.

He stepped into the shower and held out his hand to me. The longing in his eyes revealed our thoughts and emotions toward one another aligned.

My heart had already been ruined for anyone but him.

But we could never be free together in the way I'd always wanted: accepted and loved by our families.

Chapter 17

Drake

I washed Preston from head to cute toes, kissing every inch I mapped out with suds and trickling water. His sweet ass tempted me to have another little taste, but I knew if I started anything, we'd end up fucking again.

I'd been serious about needing rest.

Exhaustion had lined Preston's eyes when he'd shown up at my hotel room's door, but no fucking way would I have been able to sleep without being inside him first.

Our lovemaking in the beginning and the harsh fucking on its heels proved a better reality than any daydream I'd cooked up in the years since I'd met him. Even though I stood close to six inches taller than him, his longer torso allowed us to fit together perfectly. His mouth was in easy reach while I'd driven us both out of our minds with slow, teasing strokes.

And his ass...

Fuck, I'd never had anything so lush, so hot, clasping at my dick.

I wanted him bare. Needed to feel him skin on skin with nothing between us.

Pressing against his back, I rubbed my hands over his slightly swelled pecs, down to his soft cock and balls. "Are you negative, baby?" I murmured against his ear.

"Yeah. You?"

"Yeah. Elite provides a full panel every week, and I never go without condoms. Ever."

"Neither have I."

"Next time..." I wrapped my arms around his waist and held him tight.

Preston nodded against my shoulder before turning his face toward me. "I trust you."

"Same." I sucked the shower water off his lips, top and bottom, before pressing my mouth to his in a chaste, lingering kiss. "We need to sleep first."

He huffed and pouted, making me chuckle.

"Come on. I'll get us towels and tuck you into bed."

I did as promised, smiling as two yawns cracked Preston's jaw before I got him between the soft sheets.

He curled up on his side, and I flicked off the light and climbed in behind him where I belonged. Still grinning, I pulled him in closer against my chest, his hips and ass cradled by my groin and thighs.

A relieved sigh sagged him in my arms, and I closed my eyes, my nose against his wet hair.

"Feel free to push that perfect dick of yours back into my ass during the night if you need to," he whispered. "You don't even have to wake me up first. Just lube up and slide right in."

I groaned, squeezing him tighter. "Kinky fucker."

"Mmm," he agreed, sounding sleepy.

"Good night, baby."

"Night," he murmured.

His breathing evened out in a matter of seconds, and I

nuzzled in closer, soaking in his warmth, the rightness of finally having him in my arms again. Being stuck together in the elevator had been close to perfection.

But this?

Relaxation drugged my muscles, and I sank into oblivion.

I woke in the same position sometime later, already hard against the soft skin of Preston's ass.

"Fuck," I whispered, sure I'd dreamed the previous however many hours. But my stepbrother still lay in my arms, warm and tempting.

My groin ached for him again, and no matter how many times I sank into his heat in the future, it would never be enough.

I rolled, blindly reaching for the bottle of lube on the bedside table. Suddenly shaking hands made me fumble, but I grabbed it before it fell to the carpeted floor. I flipped the cap and squirted a shit ton over my length. The coolness made me hiss, but a few strokes warmed me right back up.

Preston hadn't moved a muscle.

Once more on my side, I scooted closer, sliding my slick fingers through his crack. God, he was hot. Soft. His pucker still lax. I groaned at the thought of what I was about to do, heat flushing through me.

He'd said I could slide right in, so I shifted forward, holding the base of my dick to rub over his ass.

A shuddered sigh rippled through him, and I eased in just a little, his ring sucking on my frenum.

"Jesus," I hissed, closing my eyes against the clasp of his body around me. I flexed my ass, burying deeper, gliding into his silken warmth. Nothing lay between us. Nothing man-made kept us apart.

I'd never fucked without a condom and had to swallow

against a sudden rush of emotion while winding my arms tightly around his torso.

He squeezed his ass around my rigid length, letting me know he'd roused from sleep.

"Fuck," I grunted, my hips instinctively trying to bury me even deeper. "I want to wake you up like this every night," I murmured against his ear, nipping at his lobe. "Your ass is so hot, baby. Tight and slick around my dick. Fucking heaven."

Preston sighed, arching slightly as though thinking I could penetrate him deeper than I already was. Great minds and all that shit.

"Feel me?" I pressed his palm against his lower abs, his thickening dick rubbing over the back of my hand.

"Mmm," he moaned, and I pulled out with a teasing but steady stroke. He whimpered when I didn't shove in right away. "D-Drake."

"I've got you," I promised and released a groan of appreciation while sinking my slick cock into his body.

He shuddered. "Oh, fuck yeah."

"Mmm hmm," I agreed, slowly repeating the motion.

"More."

"Nuh uh," I disagreed, wanting to savor loving on him skin to skin. "Gonna take my time. Drive you insane until you're begging for me to stuff your ass full of my cum."

He shivered and cursed.

"Like when I talk dirty to you, baby?" I asked, bottoming out once more deep inside him.

"So much—you have no idea."

I gyrated my hips, my balls rubbing all over him. "Fuck. You fit me like you were made for me."

We both went silent for a few strokes, our panted breaths loud in the stillness accompanied only by the quiet hum of the heater beneath the window. The wet sounds of a slow fuck, the slick glides of my dick through his tight ring, ratcheted my desire to soaring heights.

My throat thickened as overwhelming need and love for Preston swelled inside my chest.

I bit back the words wanting to spill from my lips. Undying love. The promise to stand beside him, hold his hand when Jacqueline disowned him for being gay and for agreeing to be mine.

I wanted him in my bed every night until I breathed my last. To cradle him while he held our babies. Wished I could grow old with him and experience every single thing life had to offer.

Together.

Resting my palm over his heart, I clutched him close, unable to lose myself in his soul like I wished for until death parted us.

I settled for fucking into his body. Kissing his neck. Offering him words of praise about how perfect he was in every way. How much I lusted for my cum so far up his ass he would taste me in the back of his throat.

My balls firmed long before I expected, but I kept my movements languid. Slow and luscious.

"D-Drake."

Fuck, when he stuttered with need like that...goddamn, did he heat my blood.

"Right here with you, baby."

Whimpering, he turned his head, and I took the gift he offered, licking and sucking on his lips. Tasting his tongue and delving into his mouth in time with my cock up his ass.

I slid my hand down his tightened core, finding his dick leaking.

"Mmm," I groaned over his lips, smearing his pre-cum down his length. "You're so damn hard and wet for me."

He gasped as I snapped my hips in deep while stroking him.

"Ah, fuck." He arched his back while reaching for my hair. "Again."

Our mouths hovered less than an inch apart, our panted breaths bathing the other's lips as I gave Preston what he wanted. Small noises escaped him with every sharp stab at the end of those slow delves deep inside his hole.

"So good for me, Preston. Fucking hell, I'll never get enough of you."

He shoved his tongue into my mouth, his entire body tensing in my hold. His cock jerked in my palm, his ass clenching around me.

"Fuck, yeah—give it to me, baby." I rammed into him, drawing out his climax and biting on his lower lip.

"Ung!" He grunted, his core convulsing with every spurt out of his dick.

"Fuck."

"Want. Your. Cum," he gasped through my thrusts. "Inside. Me."

Growling, I rolled him onto his stomach and set to fucking him clear through the mattress like he'd said. My balls slapped against his ass, his cries for more—harder— fueled my lust.

"Gonna fill you with it," I gasped my promise.

"Yes!" he cried, his voice muffled by the pillow he clutched at.

I sank onto my haunches and gripped his hips, not losing my rhythm. "Shoot so far up your ass you'll be leaking for days."

"Oh fuck, Drake."

I pounded into his tight heat, sweat dripping down my face and back while he writhed on the bed. "Want it?"

"Fuck, yes!"

"It's yours, baby—take it."

My heart. My goddamn soul.

Teeth gritted, I came, my dick pulsing deep, throbbing inside his body.

"I-I...oh shit." Preston writhed, humping the bed as I flooded his ass with my cum. "Fuck!" He convulsed, his ass milking me with sucking pulls.

"Jesus," I hissed through my teeth, managing a few short strokes to draw out his second climax.

We stilled at the same time, both of us gasping for air.

No one had ever satisfied me like Preston. Hookups back in college or afterward and not even needy, insatiable clients had wrung me dry. Depleted. Completely and utterly fulfilled.

Rather than pulling out, I stretched over the man I loved, twisting his head so I could eat at his mouth.

Fucking love you. Always and forever.

Chapter 18

Preston

I woke to a hot mouth sucking down my flaccid cock. The softness didn't last but a few breaths and I was thrusting into Drake's throat. I'd only had one other man's lips on my dick, and regardless of his experience and years on my stepbrother, his skills paled in comparison.

Drake had been born to suck dick. Songs could be written about his talent. Sonnets praising his tongue. Prayers slid from my lips as he took me deep into his throat, swallowing around my girth.

Fighting to keep from erupting too quickly, I thrashed against his tight grip on my thighs holding me to the bed. "Need you in me," I begged, desperate for more of his cum up my ass.

Drake slid up my length, twirling his tongue over my swollen head. "Not this time, baby. Want to swallow your seed so a part of you is in me all day."

"Oh God." I gulped and grabbed hold of his head.

"Mmm." He slid back down my length, and two thrusts later, I fulfilled his desire. "Jesus, Preston." Drake suckled and licked, stabbing his tongue into my slit in search of more. "You taste so good."

He kissed my tip then both hip bones. Sleepy blue eyes met mine across my still-shivering body. His slow grin made butterflies erupt in my stomach.

Love you.

The words lay unspoken between us, but I didn't doubt both of our feelings. Putting them into the air created a reality I couldn't live with though. Hell, I already struggled to keep depression at bay over not being allowed what I wanted most in life.

But I'd seen Nancy's pain. Had experienced Jacqueline's wrath even though her anger and hurt hadn't been directed at me.

Never—fucking *ever*—did I want to be in Nancy's shoes or experience what she had. Sure, she'd found love again, but the agony...she'd endured unbelievable emotional pain.

I wasn't strong enough. Couldn't imagine having to hunker down in my condo in Boston with Jacqueline beating down my door, her shrieks renting the air and announcing to the world what a disappointment and abomination I was. Hell, her calling me a spoiled brat throughout my childhood had hurt enough for two lifetimes.

And even though she'd seemed somewhat changed after the whole elevator affair, I knew better than to expect she would simply set aside her homophobia because her son was gay.

"Hey."

I blinked, realizing I'd disappeared on Drake for a few minutes.

He crawled up my body, planking on his elbows, his rigid length pressing against my spent dick. "You okay?"

"Mmm," I hummed an agreement, even though I wasn't really.

"What's going on in that pretty head of yours?"

Pretty—why did I love him calling me that? Jacqueline would have a fit over the adjective. I'd never been manly enough for her even though I wasn't exactly effeminate. But yeah. I was a lot more like Nancy with her tenderness than Jacqueline's hard aloofness.

"Scared," I admitted to one of the many emotions grappling for front and center in my brain, knowing Drake would never judge me. Sadness over our non-future reigned supreme, but that wasn't something I wished to dampen our stolen moments together.

He wrapped his arms around me, placing a gentle, chaste kiss on my lips. "I've got you."

I clutched at his back, wrapping my heels around his ass.

Drake groaned, fucking his dick over mine. "Damn, baby."

"Come on me," I murmured against his ear. "Rub it into my skin so you can't be washed away."

"Fuck." He set to work, grinding and quickly sliding through his pre-cum along my body. "Why do you feel so good?" Huffing, he lifted to his elbows once more and clasped his warm hands on my face. "Wanna kiss the fuck out of you, but the beard burn from during the night is fading. Can't make it worse for when we go downstairs."

"Love how you look out for me," I whispered, my eyes burning.

Gazes latched, we settled for silence as he rutted against me.

Never had I held eye contact with another person like I

did in our time together. There could be no hiding from Drake any longer. He'd laid claim to my soul, the emotional barriers between us long gone.

My dick attempted to swell back to life, enjoying every glide of his cock along mine. I'd never experienced frotting before, and although I'd read about it aplenty in my gay romance novels, Drake getting himself off on my cock was so much better than I'd imagined.

His lips parted in a quiet gasp, and wet heat spurted between us.

"Fuck yes," I groaned, tingles racing through me over him finding release.

Panting, he emptied himself on my skin, marking me with his hot seed.

"Baby," he murmured, winding his arms around me to squeeze me tight. "Never want to let you go." His adamant words whispered into me, wrapping the deepest part of my soul in his warm embrace.

JF
MM

I could feel Drake's eyes on me as I scurried to dress for brunch.

We'd showered in his room, already short on time due to lazing in his bed until the last possible second. A quick scamper down the stairs together to my room had ensured we wouldn't be seen, and if Jacqueline happened to come by while I changed, I could explain his presence as simply him checking in with me.

"You can't look at me like that!" I muttered while yanking on clean boxer briefs.

"How's that?"

Heat flamed my cheeks. "Like you want to eat me alive."

Drake made an appreciative noise deep in his throat. "That's because I do."

Cursing, I pulled on some slacks, glancing his way. Those blue eyes of his were latched on my backside, heated and full of lust. "Jesus, Drake." I chuckled a nervous laugh as he licked his lower lip and bit it. "You're insatiable."

"No more than you," he shot back, teasing as he lifted his focus to my face.

I couldn't help the eruption of a smile from the happiness bubbling inside me.

"You're beautiful," he stated quietly, his gaze full of adoration.

But I didn't have a spare minute to swoon or fall at his feet to worship him.

"We gotta go."

He stood, retrieving my loafers from along the wall for me while I fumbled with my shirt's buttons. A quick tuck, and I scurried to put on my belt.

Drake knelt before me, and I stared down at him with a tightening throat as he helped me with my shoes. He peered up at me when done, and I didn't know how it was possible, but I fell in love with him a little more in that moment.

"Drake," I choked out his name, and he stood to cradle my face in his hands.

His gaze bored into me, easily reading every secret, and knowing and understanding filled his vivid eyes. A heavy sigh, and he pressed his lips to mine, careful of his beard.

Our foreheads rested together for the span of a few heartbeats, and I wished the world could stand still so we could share all the words since I had no clue what awaited us. Who knew what else Jacqueline might have planned for the day, or if Drake would take off after breakfast if she lost her shit over one thing or another.

"Come on," he murmured, his cinnamon-laced breath filling my lungs. "Jacqueline will be pissed if we're late."

Once on the elevator, we stared at each other, my heart beating only slightly faster due to the knowledge of our close proximity in a small space.

What I wouldn't have given for another four hours trapped with the man I loved.

People joined us on the eighth floor, and I had to let go of his hand. Our shoulders still brushed though, and I soaked in every second of his touch, since it would end once we reached the ground floor, perhaps never to happen again.

We hadn't discussed the future—tonight, tomorrow, or next week. Regardless of how I wanted to savor every minute allotted to us, it couldn't continue. We would never be accepted as a couple, and I wouldn't survive the emotional upheaval from being found out.

"Ready?" Drake asked as we stepped off the elevator and headed toward the restaurant.

"No."

He gave my lower back a quick stroke, flooding me with warmth and a little bit of peace.

It would have to be enough.

Jacqueline and Devlin already waited for us, which was no great surprise. If you weren't five minutes early, you were late in Jacqueline's book.

She appeared like her normal self. Put together, a full face of makeup, hair without a single strand out of place, dressed to perfection, and jewels showcasing her wealth.

But that new motherly shit the night before had stuck.

"Preston." Jacqueline stood from her chair, rounded the table, and threw her arms around me. "How did you sleep?" She stepped back, keeping hold of my upper arms to study my face.

Thank fuck Drake thought to avoid beard burn.

I shifted and glanced at my lover before flitting my gaze to the floor as heat rushed to my cheeks. "Um...okay, I guess."

"You still look tired, but after our brunch, you can go back to your room and rest. You're booked through Monday, so please take advantage of being pampered by the staff. Come." She grasped my hand and tugged me toward the table. "You need something to eat. I already ordered your breakfast, but coffee awaits."

I warmth flooded my chest over her attentiveness, and heart hopeful, I slid onto my chair, fumbling with my linen napkin.

Drake sat in my periphery after having shared a few quiet words with his dad while Jacqueline had fawned over me.

My hand shook as I raised my steaming cup of coffee to my lips. It had been sitting long enough I didn't scald my tongue on the bitter brew.

"So." Jacqueline smiled at Devlin, who glanced between me and his son with an unreadable expression. "I'm sure you're both wondering why we requested your presence."

Neither Drake nor I spoke.

Jacqueline turned her focus on me. "I've sold Casswell Global."

I blinked, her words taking a few seconds to process. Surely, I'd heard her wrong. "You...what?"

"I've sold the family business."

"W-Why?" Not that it mattered or I cared, but I wasn't sure what else to say at the bomb she'd dropped. Her father's business had been her world, the reason for her existence long before kicking Nancy out of our home, and she was far from retirement age.

"Because you want nothing to do with the empire your grandfather built, and it's time I've focused on my own happiness."

As if she hadn't been doing so since Nancy had left us. Jacqueline never spared expense in what brought her joy, so what the hell was she talking about?

"What are you going to do?" I asked, still baffled and staring at her sparkling eyes. Was she drunk? High? Had I entered some other dimension? I looked quickly at her husband, who glanced between me and Drake.

"Travel," Jacqueline replied with a giddiness that suggested she hadn't already visited every continent already —which she had. Countless times. "Devlin and I are embarking on a three-month world tour this afternoon, thus the rushed weekend."

I sat back in my chair, still staring.

She glanced over at Devlin, and he tore his focus from us, took her hand in his, his eyes growing soft, same as always when gazing at his wife. I wished I could be happier for her, but what she'd done to Nancy didn't allow the sentiment.

"You're probably wondering what this means for you," she said, once more turning her attention on me, pink staining her cheeks.

Not really. I'd already gone off on my own and had my inheritance from my grandfather to cushion the rest of my life.

"Two million." She flitted her gaze from me to Drake. "Each."

"What?" I asked.

"I'm giving both of my boys two million from the sale." She beamed as though she'd just given us the greatest prize on earth.

I would've rather had had her attention and love as a child than a drop in the bucket of her wealth.

"You didn't have to do that," Drake stated quietly. He radiated tension and not over the gift but Jacqueline's words.

My boys.

I shuddered. The truth she saw Drake as her son sickened me to imagine what she would think about our being together. Swallowing against the bile wanting to rise, I tore my stare off my stepbrother. Remorse would never swamp me over what we'd done, but I couldn't help the unease wanting to creep through my mind and cover the joy I'd stashed away from the hours I'd been gifted with Drake.

"Thank you, Jacqueline." I managed to get the words out and a small smile, even though I didn't feel anything remotely happy about the situation.

Her face radiated pride, and I suddenly couldn't wait to be rid of her presence.

"When is your flight?" I asked, glancing up as a waitress approached with our meals.

"Three, so we are a little short on time," Jacqueline replied even though it was her own personal jet waiting for her.

I managed to choke down half of my omelet stuffed with vegetables when I would have rather slathered thick slices of French toast with maple syrup. After years of watching me eat while a child, the woman ought to know my preferences when it came to breakfast foods.

Drake devoured his meal without complaint, clearing his plate while all I could think about, what made my stomach nervous, was what would happen if Jacqueline found out what her "boys" had been up to since the evening before.

Chapter 19

Drake

My feet itched to move. To the elevator. Back to my room where I could strip my lover of every article of clothing covering his freckled skin so I could soothe—and taste—him again. Dick stirring, I fought to keep from shifting in my seat as everyone else finished their breakfast.

Jacqueline and Dad's bags had already been packed, and a limo waited to whisk them away to the airport.

While I'd rather have headed straight back upstairs once we stood from the breakfast table, I found patience enough to walk them through the lobby and outdoors beneath a cold yet sunlit New York sky.

"Take care of yourself," Jacqueline said to Preston as she hugged him. I'd only ever seen her hold her son once before—last night.

Part of me wanted to soften toward her, for the love she finally showed the poor kid, but I just couldn't. I clasped Dad tight, slapping his back. "Safe travels."

"You too, son." He squeezed my shoulder, giving me a direct stare. "And take care of Preston."

Preston. Not my brother. Not even my stepbrother.

Swallowing hard at his knowing yet assuring gaze, I nodded. Same as when I'd told him I was gay, there were no questions, no suggestions I attempt to live life another way. Dad had simply accepted who I wanted.

Maybe someday, he would be able to influence Jacqueline enough that Preston and I could try for forever.

Wishful thinking, but what choice did I have?

Dad turned to my lover to say goodbye while Jacqueline shifted to face me.

"Well." She tried for a smile, but the light in her eyes dimmed the slightest bit.

I nodded, not expecting affection. "Safe travels, Jacqueline."

Her gaze flitted to Preston, who glanced at me at the same time. I quickly looked back at Jacqueline to find a brief frown flitting over her brow, her eyes so like her son's filling with sadness.

"Come, darling," Dad said, grasping her elbow as though to hurry her along before she saw too much to handle.

Envying my dad's freedom to flaunt his affection for his wife to the world, I watched as he helped Jacqueline into the limo.

Once Dad was seated beside her, she glanced at me, her unsure stare making my feet itchy.

Chin lifting, I instinctively stepped closer to Preston.

Her green eyes welled with tears as she peered up at her son. "Love you," she told Preston and fluttered a jeweled, shaky hand at him.

The breath left my lungs like I'd been punched. I'd never heard her say those words to him.

Ever.

Preston swallowed audibly and nodded.

I fisted my hand to keep from reaching for him as hurt and need rolled off his shoulders like a ten-foot swell ready to crash him to the ground.

Dad closed the door, and the limo slowly pulled away from the curb.

Preston shuddered with an exhale, his breath fogging in front of his trembling lips.

A quick glance around and I leaned down close to his ear, needing to distract both of us from the excessive emotions that had surrounded the last ten or so minutes. "Since they're gone, how about we go back to my room and fuck until we both pass out from exhaustion?"

He shivered, his gulp making me grin. "Yes."

I spun on my heel rather than yanking him up into my arms to carry him bridal-style back into the hotel that offered us privacy and a place to lay our heads once we fulfilled another fantasy.

We had the elevator to ourselves for a few floors, and I didn't hesitate to get all up in Preston's face, owning his mouth since beard burn would no longer be an issue. He whimpered, clutching at my clothes as desperate as I was for him.

"Are you sore?" I murmured against his mouth, reaching around to palm his ass.

"A little, but not enough to stop you from having me again."

"You sure, baby?"

"One hundred percent," he declared, so I didn't bother arguing while resting my forehead against his.

"Thank fuck, cause I'm taking you the second we get in my room."

He gasped as I ground my dick on his. "Against the wall," he suggested, lust lacing his tone.

"Mmm." I licked over his lower lip. "I like the sound of that. Don't ever stop being honest about what you want with me. Fucking love it."

If only I could do the same with all the needs in my own head. Physically, we had three months until their return, a good portion of time to fulfill as many dreams as possible.

But after that?

I wasn't sure Preston would be up for sneaking around with Jacqueline stateside even with the distance between Boston and New York. No way had he grown that big of balls.

With how Jacqueline seemed to soften a bit over the fear of losing her son, I expected their relationship might be on a path toward healing. And while I hoped for that for Preston, my selfishness wished she'd written him off, so he could finally rid his life of her and be free to love and live how he wanted.

Or perhaps, she'd realized how much he meant to her, and his eventual coming out wouldn't tear them apart. One could hope she might even be willing to accept him and I together, but I knew better than to do so.

But in the meantime, I would take what I could and tuck away every minute in my memory.

We weren't in my room for two seconds before I shoved down my pants to mid-thigh, and Preston's loafers went flying, one leg freed from his slacks, the other stuck around his ankle.

I yanked him up into my arms where he settled, feet clasped around my ass. I held him against the entryway's wall as promised, kissing his mouth with desperate strokes of my tongue and nips of my teeth.

"Lube," I muttered as I thought of the need for it, rutting my hard, leaking cock against his.

"I'll be fine with spit," he argued, writhing in my hold. "Didn't clean out this morning—still can feel your load from last night leaking out of me."

I groaned, reaching around to rub a fingertip over his sticky hole. "Why the hell is that so goddamn hot? Fuck, baby." I brought my hand back to my mouth and sucked the flavor of him and my spunk off my fingertip before getting two nice and wet.

Our gazes locked as I once more reached between his cheeks, pushing my saliva up his ass.

Preston whimpered, his eyelids going heavy.

"You like my fingers in you?"

"God, yes."

"Want my dick?"

"So much. Give it to me."

Chuckling, I spat on my hand, reached between us, and got my dick nice and wet for him. "If it's too much or not enough—"

"Put your cock in me, Drake. Pound me until my spine aches from getting slammed against the wall."

"Since you asked so *nicely*..." I shifted, lifted him a bit higher, and rubbed my leaking slit over his crack.

"Drake, don't tease me," he whined, tipping his head back, peering at me with lust-hazed eyes.

"You're beautiful," I murmured what I'd done countless times in the previous twelve or so hours, lowering him and pressing against his hole. *You're mine*, I wanted to add but couldn't.

I popped through his ring, and he sank onto my shaft. Both of us groaned. A couple of gentle thrusts and I filled him completely.

Words wanted to pour from my lips, but I kissed him instead, needing to feel closer. Bury so deeply inside his soul it would be painful for him to eradicate me from his life.

I settled for short strokes, holding his cheeks open while tunneling into his silken heat sucking at my shaft. "So good for me," I whispered against his lips, my balls tingling over the little noises he made as I loved on his body. "Can't get enough of you."

Preston whimpered and crushed his lips to mine, his dick leaking and rubbing against my stomach. "Same. Want you always," he gasped into my mouth. "*Forever.*"

My heart raced even as my chest tightened at his declaration. He'd told me the night before that I was his dream come true.

Was Preston actually going to cross the line that would estrange him from Jacqueline? Was he willing to give up an eventual inheritance as her only son to be with me? Because fuck knew two mil a piece was pocket change for Jacqueline Casswell.

True hope made my skin burn at the prospect he was willing to imagine a future with me. In that moment, I couldn't even be bothered by the fact I would probably lose Dad in the process of Preston's coming out.

But fuck, I wanted to believe love was enough to sustain us both.

The way Preston looked at me promised it was, and my heart ached for us to just goddamn try.

Fingers crossed he wouldn't reject me or make me face abandonment in the future, I went with the swell of emotions tightening my chest.

"Fucking love you," I choked out the words, going all in, the world be damned.

"D-Drake." He sobbed, clutching at my back, his gorgeous orbs glinting gold and green fire from welling tears.

He didn't say it back, but he didn't need to. His eyes proclaimed his thoughts toward me loud and clear. We wanted the same thing.

And we would fucking have it. No one would ever love Preston like I did, and no one would lay down their life for him like I would.

I latched my mouth onto his neck, thrusting into him with abandon, desperate for his ass to milk the cum out of my balls. The need to fill him, mark him on the inside and out rushed through me.

"Oh God," he moaned as I sucked on his sweet skin, my fingertips without doubt bruising his cheeks.

I tore my mouth from his neck, panting. "Come for me, baby," I begged, rutting like a goddamn animal. "Soak my shirt with your cum."

Preston cried out, doing as I'd asked, and I stabbed upward, my dick erupting deep inside his body. Every spurt ripped a grunt from my lungs as I emptied myself, giving him everything I had.

"Preston," I whispered his name with a ragged exhale, rubbing my nose all the fuck over the dark purple mark I'd left on his neck.

Fuck. Yes.

He shuddered in my hold before going lax.

On shaky legs, I carried him into my bathroom, stripped him down, and took care of him.

We didn't speak. There was no need for words, since I'd said all I'd needed to and had seen the reflection of my feelings on his face.

I snuggled the hell out of him, petting his soft skin with trailing fingertips until he fell asleep in my arms.

Contentment flooded through me, and I buried my face in his silky hair, breathing in the vanilla, citrus, and natural scent of my love's freckled skin that bore evidence of my claiming.

No longer did I have to dread our going separate ways.

Preston was mine now.

And there was no going back. Ever.

Chapter 20

Preston

We woke Sunday morning wrapped up in each other's arms. My ass ached with a luscious burn, but I wasn't nearly done with Drake or his dick. He was a man of many talents, unsurprising to learn firsthand after having read all the rave reviews on EEMM's website. The idea of Drake being an escort didn't exactly sit well with me, but hadn't I hired two of his fellow co-workers? I wouldn't judge, but one thing I knew for sure...if the stars aligned and fate allowed us to be together, I would ask him for exclusivity.

But what were the chances of having my hopes fulfilled?

I hadn't meant to spill so many of my desires into the space between us. The *forever* I'd admitted to couldn't be promised, no matter how much I wanted him. Too many emotions had been overwhelming me for hours on end thanks to Jacqueline's actions and declarations. I'd been an absolute mess in my head, and Drake had held me through it all, not pushing for me to talk shit through.

He'd given me a safe place to rest while I tried to figure out my way forward—with Jacqueline and him.

Jacqueline definitely had a rude awakening from Drake and me being stuck in that elevator. She'd finally remembered she had a son who had needed her once upon a time. Regardless of the damage that had been done in years past, the longing for reconciliation between us had doubled. Wounds and bitterness had lain like a gulf between us for years, and the beginnings of a bridge spanned the distance.

Had her thoughts been jolted enough that she actually loved me like she hadn't claimed aloud since I was maybe in third grade? Would she be open and willing to eventually accept who I was?

Maybe even consider changing her stance toward Nancy as well?

Or was her softening a simple reaction, and she would go back to her usual cold, conservative ways after a few months' time?

I clung to a fragile thread of hope she'd turned a new leaf, looking forward to her and Devlin's return. If it took years of work to make things right between us, I was willing to put in the hours.

Anything to have peace between us—and maybe someday with Nancy as well.

Acceptance, at the very least.

"How'd you sleep, baby?" Drake's low voice against my neck sent shivers down my spine.

My waking inclination was to stretch, entice blood into my limbs, but I curled in closer to his warmth, soaking in the heat and strength of his body wrapped around mine.

That saying, heaven on earth?

I'd found it.

But with possible healing between me and Jacqueline, I

would have to play it safe. Those thoughts could wait though since I couldn't deny myself indulging for just a bit longer.

I rolled, snuggling my face against his rock-hard chest. His heart beat steady against my ear, and I clung to him, a sixth sense in the back of my mind telling me to hang onto him for every second I could.

I wanted to think that love could be enough for me to be content, that I didn't need healing and reconciliation with Jacqueline, but would it? Could I submit to my emotions and be happy with Drake while being estranged from the mother I'd craved a relationship with for my entire life?

The war over childhood needs and adult desires cluttered my mind.

My ass ached, but I yearned for silence in my head.

I reached for Drake's semi, and he grunted, hips flexing on instinct as I stroked him.

"Fuck, baby. Love having your hands on me."

His words and body's reaction to my touch roused my morning wood, and our breaths grew heavy. The thump of his heart beneath my ear was a welcomed cadence, steady and sure.

"Tell me another fantasy," he demanded, his large hand rubbing down my back to grasp my ass cheek he'd bruised the night before. I loved he'd done that—and marked my neck in his desperate need of me. "Let me make all your dreams come true."

My pulse raced, stomach flipping.

Love you too.

Swallowing hard, I decided to be as sexually blunt as I'd been since being stuck in the elevator. Why waste the moments allotted us, especially when Drake would never judge me for what I fantasized about with him?

Speaking what I wished for physically came ten times easier than the other vulnerable parts of me my tongue and insecurities wouldn't allow me to share.

"I want you to suck me off and use your mouthful of my cum as lube to fuck me," I stated without stuttering.

"Oh fuck." Drake huffed a chuckle against my hair, thrusting into my hand. "Jesus, Preston."

He moved in a rush, flipping me onto my back, his sleepy blue eyes peering at me from where he settled on his belly between my thighs. Butterflies erupted in my stomach at the grin lighting up his face as he pushed my legs wider. "You're so fucking hot."

I snorted. "Hardly."

His gaze focused with firm intent to convince me otherwise. "You said I was your dream come true, but you're my everything, Preston. Always have been."

I'd imagined about hearing those words. Had craved them. And now, they hung suspended in the air between us. The promise of him wanting that same forever I'd spoken of.

But.

My throat tightened over the war inside me. "Make me come," I rasped, desperate for release from my thoughts.

Drake swallowed me down, humming around my length and delivering my mind from its agony. I swam in pleasure, thankful for his experience, uncaring of the real world and the unknown that waited for us outside the suite's walls.

Time stalled, and I lost myself in Drake's touch. His coaxing lips and throat.

He feathered fingertips over my dry hole while swallowing me down, bringing me to the brink of release.

"Give me that mouthful of cum, baby," he crooned,

stroking his hand up my chest to rest over my heart. "Want it coating my dick when I sink into your sweet ass."

"F-Fuck." I choked on a gulp, my hips thrusting my spit-slickened cock into the air.

"Mmm," Drake hummed while sinking over me, the heat of his mouth and swirling tongue too much to deny.

I came with a cry, my hands grasping at his hair, spine arching, and body writhing in my release. Tingles raced through my blood, sending a rushing sound through my ears. I gasped for breath, going limp, limbs askew.

Drake spat, and I blinked him into focus.

He held my cum cradled in his palm, dripping between his fingers.

Stomach flipping with desire, I stared, still breathless, as he coated his stiff length with my spunk. He spat into his palm again and grasped the back of my right knee. "Hold yourself open for me, baby."

I palmed my rubbery legs, lifting them to expose my hole.

He groaned, his lust-filled gaze focused on my ass. "You're still red and puffy."

"Don't care," I whispered, clenching my pucker to entice him.

The teasing movement worked.

Drake swore and eased two cum-and-saliva-soaked fingers into me.

I hissed at the sting but forced myself to relax, watching emotion flit over his face.

The man was dead gone on me, same as I was on him.

"Drake," I whispered, unable to voice my need past the tightness in my chest and sting in my eyes. What was it about him that drew all my emotions to the forefront?

"I've got you," he murmured, rubbing the head of his

cock against my softened hole. He spat, saliva dangling from his lips to fall on my hole. "So fucking hot." He repeated the motion, groaning as I clenched my pucker again. "Exhale and let me in, baby."

As if I could deny him.

I did as told, and he sank into me with a groan, head tipping back, veins popping along his muscular neck. Unable to reach him from where he knelt between my thighs, I lifted my knees higher, inviting him to lean over me.

"Fuck." Jaw clenched, he opened his eyes to watch himself stroke into me with long, slow thrusts.

The initial burn eased, and sudden need made me restless. My dick lay flaccid on my stomach, but inside, I yearned for that closeness that brought life to my chest.

"Kiss me," I whispered, and he sprawled over me, giving me everything I needed.

Chapter 21

Drake

Preston refused to move. I threatened to carry him into the bathroom, but he begged me to let him rest a little while longer. Sprawled on the bed, still flushed and sweaty from our lovemaking, he looked like the sweetest treat I could ever dream up.

I at least cleaned our combined spunk from his ass, and he grunted a thanks before closing his eyes.

Unable to do anything but obey his every whim, I went into the bathroom to take care of what I'd been thinking about since the moment I'd given in to my desire to keep Preston. I would be his in every way.

Only his.

Sean answered after a couple rings. "Hey, boo. How's New York?" As usual, his tone held hints of a smile.

"This place sucks, but the company couldn't be better." I grinned at myself in the mirror, my face red from the thorough fucking of my stepbrother.

"Someone sounds happy. You know fucking on the side isn't allowed for EEMM employees."

I snorted. "You still haven't realized your brother lied about that to keep you in check?"

Silence met my ears, and I chuckled.

"That fucker," Sean grumbled, and I laughed louder. "Not fucking funny!"

"It kinda is," I argued.

"Fuck off."

"Already did that countless times," I stated, rubbing over my sweat-dampened chest.

"The fuck, Drake?"

"Long story short, I quit."

More silence, but I expected an explosion lay on the horizon.

"As in, no more escorting for me," I tacked on, in case Sean didn't catch my meaning.

"Goddamnit!"

I bit the inside of my lip to stop myself from laughing again.

"What the fuck is up with this love shit taking all of my best employees?" Sean's voice raised, and he tacked on a few more curses for good measure.

"You found the man of your dreams, the one who fits you like a worn, leather glove," I reminded him while turning away from the mirror to start the shower. "Would you deny the same for your friends?"

He huffed. "No, of course not, but this really sucks ass and not in the good way! Where the hell am I going to find another Drake Hemmings to put on the menu? Fuck! Who is it? And how the fuck do you fall so fast and easily when you've been anti-relationships your entire life? Whoever he is must have one hell of an ass because the boo I know would never give up his freedom at the risk of abandonment."

My smile faded. Preston was the biggest gamble, but for once, the possibilities outweighed any negative fallout.

"Talk to me, Drake," Sean demanded. "I can hear your brain whirring over the line."

"Jacqueline sold her empire and gifted me two mil."

"Chump change." Sean snorted the words, well aware of my dad's wife and her old money. But I'd never shared much about the boy-become-man I'd loved since high school.

"My stepbrother then gave me his ass," I stated bluntly, leaving Sean speechless.

His silence lasted a handful of seconds that seemed an eternity.

"Um...want to repeat that?" he requested, his words slowly articulated.

"Are you judging me?" I shot back, feeling more unsettled than I'd expected.

Sean should be the last person to think I did something wrong. He was one of the most accepting people I'd ever met.

"Of course not," he scoffed. "Just...goddamn. Since when did you have a thing for him?"

"Always."

"The fuck, Drake! You've barely mentioned the guy in the few times you spoke about those years living in New York."

I hadn't and for good reason. Until that weekend, I'd squashed my longing, my desires for the forbidden deep inside. Not out of shame but for the preciousness of those fragile emotions that I'd always felt could never see the light of day.

"There was never any point in telling you about him," I didn't bother explaining all my reasons since they no longer mattered, "but we got stuck in the elevator, and shit finally rose to the surface."

"Stuck? Jesus! What the hell happened?"

I gave Sean a quick rundown of Friday night's events. From the nerves over seeing my stepbrother again to the moment the elevator's doors slid open four hours later to release chaos on our asses.

Since then, it had been nothing short of euphoria experiencing everything I'd ever dreamed about.

"He told me he wants me forever, and I finally admitted after all this time that I love him."

"Jesus fucking Christ," Sean muttered. "Hold on..."

I could hear him murmuring indistinguishable words while he fumbled with his cell.

"Sorry. I'm back."

"How's Matteo?" I asked about his lover since he'd obviously been talking to him. They never went far on Sundays and were probably still in bed.

"Unbelievably delicious." Typical sassy brat sounded like he'd gotten some too.

I snorted at the light happiness in Sean's voice. He'd always been sunshine regardless of his childhood wounds, but Matteo had helped to heal all sorts of shit in my best friend's head and heart. They were peas and carrots together as much as Preston and I.

"He offered me the most incredible gift for Valentine's Day, and I was about to head south to show him my appreciation when you called."

"TMI, asshole," I said with a laugh.

"I only answered because it's you, and this damned trip you took last second had me curious as fuck. So the big news was she sold the company and wanted to seem like a gracious bitch by presenting a tiny portion of the proceeds to you?"

"She didn't even have to do that though. I'm not her son. Not really."

"Most people will see it otherwise," Sean said, his tone turning serious.

"I don't give a fuck," I stated, my chin lifted. "He's what I want, and everyone else can go pound sand."

"I'll always have your back."

"I know you will. Besides my dad, you're the most faithful person I have in my life, Sean Fox."

He fake sniffed. "You're gonna make me cry."

"Fuck off," I muttered, realizing the bathroom had filled with steam. "I need to shower."

"Where's your lover?"

"Probably passed out where I left him on our bed."

"Fuck." Sean huffed a small laugh. "I've never heard you sound this happy."

"For the first time in my life, I truly am."

"Then I'm thrilled for you, Drake. Honestly. I'll hate taking you off the website and scrambling to book all our clients for later this week, but if you've found what I have..."

"Yeah," I agreed with his unspoken question. Contentment flooded through me, peace in having made the right choice.

"Well, I can't wait to lay eyes on the man who snagged my most-wanted Elite."

I'd kept everything about Preston close to my heart. Sean didn't even know what he looked like or that Preston was the reason for my love of redheads. My type of kryptonite, I'd claimed to my best friend countless times. I'd even admitted to wanting kids and the white picket fence.

But Sean had no clue I'd imagined my stepbrother whenever I'd discussed those daydreams.

"Soon," I promised, ready for that hot shower to ease my tired, sore muscles. "When we get back to Boston, I'll bring him over to finally meet my best friend he's heard so much about."

"Am I going to lose my beer buddy?" A hint of worry actually coated Sean's question.

"Did I lose *you* to Matteo?"

"No, but you and I don't go out as much as we used to."

"And I'm fine with that because you're happy, Sean. You've figured out that you're fucking fantastic as-is. Add in the man who loves you fulfills all your needs, and I wouldn't wish for anything else. You've found your forever man, and I finally have mine."

"You're gonna make me cry."

"Shut the fuck up and go suck your professor's dick," I teased.

"Mmm. Sounds kinda fun. Hey, Teach!" Sean hollered in my ear. "Get your fine ass back over here. I want a little taste!"

Chuckling, I shook my head. "You're dead gone on that man."

"Can you blame me? He's hot as fuck. All stoic and shit. I love ruffling his feathers and turning him on to the point he becomes an animal." Sean made some sort of growly noise.

My fucking best friend. God, did I love him.

Chapter 22

Preston

I *quit.*

Drake's words echoed in my ears long after he hopped in the shower. I'd only heard the first part of his conversation with who I assumed was his best friend and employer, Sean Fox, manager of EEMM. Once Drake had turned on the water, I couldn't decipher his words.

I laid curled into a ball, my heart in my throat, a slog of thoughts attempting to choke the life from me even though he'd taken a step toward what I told myself I wanted with him—exclusivity.

A crossroads loomed ahead of me, one with paths that led in opposite directions.

It had taken me years to find the courage to reclaim Nancy's last name without Jacqueline knowing. It was only a matter of time until she found out I'd once more become a Gibbons rather than a Casswell.

She'd kept Casswell when she and Nancy had married, and I'd heard about the arguments they'd had over my birth when deciding whose last name would be on my birth certificate. When Nancy transitioned, Jacqueline had gone on a rampage, legally changing my surname to hers.

She'd stolen yet another part of Nancy from me when I'd been too young to do anything about it.

That feeling of being cheated had festered over the years until I'd found the balls to take it back. My first act of defiance, and I still dealt with daily anxiety over what would happen when she learned of it.

Jacqueline would shit a brick when it became known.

Or would her newfound softness toward me be forgiving of what she would have a month earlier seen as an affront?

The stress over that truth coming to light had lain like a heavy shadow in the back of my mind since I'd filed the papers to reclaim my legal name, but this thing with Drake? If allowed to continue for any length of time, it could very well be the final straw that would make Jacqueline lose her shit on me.

She'd yet to find Nancy's truth as acceptable.

Why would she see me as anything but filthy like she'd claimed countless times the LGBTQ community was?

Even more, why did I care? How could I allow fear of the woman to control me at twenty-eight years of age? I'd been on my own since college. Caring for myself, paying my own damn bills. Sure, I didn't have any close friends and never went out, but I was living.

Somewhat.

Since allowing myself a taste of the forbidden, I hadn't realized how much I'd been missing out on though. There was so much more to life than merely surviving. I didn't want to be done with Drake, but I couldn't find the strength inside my cowardly soul to stand for what I craved.

My conscience had been too conditioned to bow down

to the one who had ruled me from childhood. I ought to hate the woman who'd birthed me, but with her heart's change toward me since the elevator incident...

Exhaling heavily, I cursed the little boy inside me who still reached for his mommy with innocent love. Younger me longed to be coddled. Held in strong arms that promised to accept me, improper thoughts and all.

Had Jacqueline truly softened to the point of change?

Could she be swayed to accept the man that I was?

Did enough evidence exist that she could be schooled in sexual identity and fluidity and see it as truth?

Yearning for all three battled with my desire for Drake. Emotional versus physical. Which would prove stronger?

The shower shut off, and I had no answer to my dilemma.

My heart raced, and I tried to slow my breathing. The last thing I needed was a panic attack that would make Drake question what was going on with me. The man was damned nosey, prying into the corners of my mind for information I wasn't ready to reveal to the world. Too many new vulnerabilities hid inside me, shit that if found out would destroy my fragile existence.

He loved me, wanted to keep me forever as much as I did him, so I knew which way he would try to sway which path I chose.

Nancy would do the same as him, telling me that Jacqueline had given up the right to my love when I was a child.

But that fucking bond I still felt to her, that *need* to be loved by my biological mother, was stronger than any longing I experienced for things to be different.

If there was a magic pill, some concoction that would steal the connection with her from my soul, I wouldn't press charges at them taking it. I would gladly be rid of her, so I could have the man I yearned for beside me every day for the rest of my life.

The bathroom door opened, and I slowly exhaled, recognizing that I needed space to figure shit out. Otherwise, I might become so tangled up that I experienced the fallout of someone else's choices rather than ones I needed to make on my own.

Rolling to the edge of the bed, I kept my back to Drake while grabbing my briefs off the floor. "I'm going to go down to my room to shower and get clean clothes," I whispered, surprised I hadn't stumbled over a single word.

The bed dipped behind me, and warm, still-damp arms snagged my waist and pulled me back onto the bed. My traitorous body went willingly.

Drake sighed while tucking me against his chest. He nuzzled my neck then hair as I realized he was fond of doing. I kind of loved it too.

"Don't leave me," he whispered, squeezing me just a little tighter.

The exact types of words I feared. They sounded too much like manipulation.

Swallowing hard, I sank into his heat, the tension in my muscles leaking away regardless of how much my flight instincts screamed for me to leave before my truth and reality met in a head-on collision.

This had to be the end of us, but Drake would never understand. He'd always been strong, sure of himself and his actions, and having the chance, he would argue his case.

I didn't have the mental capacity to fight with him.

I could barely make sense of the conflict in my heart let alone discuss or choose which way would lead to a sense of happiness I could live with. I didn't believe having both of my heart's desires was a possibility.

Distance between Drake and I wouldn't be easy to ask for, let alone take. His body would coerce mine into giving him what he wanted, regardless of the ties that might wrench to the breaking point with Jacqueline.

The promise of her wrath, or at least, my expectation of it, turned my stomach.

Drake's palm pressed over my heart, and thoughts quieting, I held my breath, waiting for him to question me.

"I make your heart race," he murmured.

"You do," I admitted, rather than admitting the truth of why my pulse thrummed in a not-so-good way.

"As much as I would love to coax my dick back to life and love on you again, we need to rest, baby."

I hummed an agreement, my ass definitely on board with his suggestion to lay low.

"How about a cat nap then we can order room service?" Drake's hot breath wafted over my neck.

A shiver rippled down my spine but from the truth of what I was going to do rather than want for his attention.

He sighed as though in heaven, and I lay still, knowing from years of living with him that he would drift into sleep quickly as though he hadn't a care in the world.

Oh, to have the ability to turn off the mind like he did, not to worry about two opposing paths calling with the same intensity.

Within minutes, he breathed heavily, his steady exhales ghosting over my skin.

My throat tightened, and I gave myself a few extra seconds of soaking in his presence and comfort. All the fantasies, every daydream I'd had about my stepbrother, hadn't been fulfilled, but the time fate had gifted us drew to an end.

That crossroads waited feet in front of me, and I needed space to clear my head so I could make the most informed decision and not choose with my emotions.

Skin ripped from my frame, and muscle tore from my bones as I slowly pulled from Drake's embrace. Agony flared inside my guts, a searing burn that settled in my eyes.

I dressed in silence, not allowing myself to turn and take in his resting form that would be hazy from my tears. Enough memories etched in my mind from watching him sleep when we were younger. I didn't need more, especially after having tasted the sweetness of his kiss, the release his body had brought mine.

Wishing things could be different, I made my choice for distance until I figured out what to do.

Same as Drake had done to me that night at our parent's home in Tribeca, I walked away, well aware if he'd been awake, he would never have let me leave his side.

I had to stand on my own and find *my* strength for the decision I needed to make.

Chapter 23

Drake

A grin split my face before I even opened my eyes. No warm body snuggled against mine, so I reached out blindly, needing him close.

The sheets beside me were cold.

I cracked an eyelid open but didn't see him. "Preston?"

He didn't answer, and my straining ears didn't hear the shower either.

Rolling onto my back, I propped onto my elbows. "Preston?" I called a little louder.

Still no answer.

Hairs on my nape tingled, rising to life, and I shoved the blankets from my legs. A sense of foreboding leadened my feet, but I remained steady in my trek to the bathroom.

The door lay open as I'd left it earlier, the lights off.

I spun in a circle, taking in the truth Preston wasn't in my suite.

He'd wanted to go to his room, shower, and dress. Perhaps he hadn't been able to sleep and had gone down once I'd slept.

Assuring myself that's exactly what he'd done, I scurried to throw on some clothes. We'd been so caught up in each other that we hadn't exchanged cell numbers, or I would have simply texted to find out for sure where he'd went.

My heart beating too fast, I hopped on the elevator and cursed the slowness with which the doors closed. Only three floors rolled past, but they took an eternity to creep downward in blinking red numbers.

I should have gone for the stairs. They would have been faster than the fucking metal cage closing in on me due to my first brush with panic.

People waited on Preston's floor to enter, and I shuffled sideways through them, not even bothering to excuse myself or apologize for my hasty rush to get past them.

I turned a corner, intent on the room number he'd told me, pulling up at the sight of a cleaning cart beside his open door.

No.

No fucking way.

Heart stalling out, I double-checked the suite number. 1322.

A woman in her fifties exited the bathroom, noticing me standing there frozen in the doorway and fucking dying inside. "Can I help you?"

"The man who stayed here," I rasped, having to swallow against the sudden dryness in my throat. I opened my mouth but couldn't find words.

"I received notification they checked out an hour ago, sir."

An hour ago.

He'd taken off the second I'd fallen asleep.

My chest caved in on itself, and I fought to fill my lungs. Spinning on my heel, I made for the stairwell. The steps disappeared beneath my slapping feet, the echo of my stomps in time with my stuttering heart. Three flights later, I heaved for breath—but not from the exercise.

Preston had abandoned me.

Fucking left me exactly like I'd begged him not to do.

I crammed my shit into my bags without care, my movements hasty to get me the fuck out of there. Minutes later, I tossed my room's key onto the front desk without waiting to make sure shit was all taken care of.

My thoughts ran a riot in my head, battling it out in open warfare.

What had I done?

Had something kicked in his instinct to flee?

Jacqueline.

I gritted my teeth, knowing without a shadow of a *fucking* doubt that woman had somehow gotten into his head. Her conservative bullshit, her manipulations over his emotions he'd never spoke of as a kid but I'd seen more often than not.

He'd always been desperate for her love, and mine wasn't enough to fill that void in his heart.

Jesus fucking Christ, I'd been a fool.

My blood boiled even as my heart shriveled up from the coldness creeping through my chest.

I was going to lose my goddamned mind.

"Hey, Siri, call Sean," I bit out, needing someone to talk me down before I blew a gasket in my brain and ended up causing a twenty-car pile-up on the highway.

"Hey, boo—"

"He fucking left me!" I didn't even give him time to say hi.

"What?"

"Preston. Fucking snuck out while I was sleeping."

Sean hesitated rather than spewing curses to show he had my back as always.

"Say something!" I hollered, my insides shredded, my voice breaking from rage and pain.

"Preston," Sean repeated slowly.

"Yes! Preston—my stepbrother!" No fucking way Sean had forgotten already.

"That's not a common name."

The fuck?

"Neither is Casswell," I snapped, swerving to the right to pass a slow fucker cruising in the left lane. I glared at the fucker while flying past him.

"What, uh, does he look like?"

"Huh?" I steered to where I needed to be for my speed.

"Preston—what does he look like?" Sean repeated the words slower, almost warily.

"He's my kryptonite. My redheaded dream." I gave Sean the truth I'd always kept from him, my voice ragged.

"And you said he knows about Elite?" Sean asked carefully.

"Yeah. He's a computer nerd. Pretty sure he fantasized about hiring me too." My fucking chest ached at the memory of holding him in my arms and how he'd found the balls to just walk away without a word.

I'd done the same to him.

Fuck. I swallowed hard, hating that I'd caused him similar feelings to those coursing through me.

What had I done to make him leave me though? Why abandon me hours after I tore down my walls and gave him access to all the vulnerable pieces of my soul?

"Does this stepbrother of yours have an alias?"

"Huh?" I sounded like a goddamned dunce.

"Go by another name?" Sean explained even though I'd

understood what he'd meant but was baffled as to why he'd ask.

"No. Jacqueline would kill him if she found out he went by anything other than Preston Casswell."

"Does the name Gibbons ring a bell?"

"That's Nancy's surname—Preston's other mom. Why?"

"Oh, fuck me sideways with a ginormous dildo," Sean muttered.

"What?"

"*Preston Gibbons.* That's the kid who helped me and Micah with that pickle last fall."

"The attempt to exhort EEMM?"

"Yep."

"What aren't you telling me, Sean?" I asked, needing clarity for the brain fucking he was causing

"He's also a past client?"

"Is that a question?" I shot out.

Sean's exhale huffed throughout my car. "No—but NDAs and all that shit."

Memories flitted through my mind. The guilty look on Preston's face in the elevator when I'd asked who he would hire for the night from EEMM's lineup if he'd had the balls. The flush that had attempted to overtake his freckles had been etched in my mind.

"Fucking hell." I glared at the open highway ahead, stepping on the gas. The idea of another man touching him had flared jealousy inside me, but it being one of my friends? A fucking co-worker? Jesus fucking Christ, incinerate my guts right the fuck now. "Who did he book with, Sean?" I bit out the words.

"I can't share that information."

"You've got to give me something, you asshole. Please!"

"Two of our guys a couple of times, but no one in over a year."

Possessiveness flared to life, quickly heating me from the inside out. *Two* when I'd thought one was too many. Who would he go for? What gay escort had gotten a taste of his cum, enjoyed his tight ass milking their dicks?

Heat licked up my spine, and I knew what the Hulk felt like when he erupted through human skin.

Fuck, I couldn't even think about another man's hands on Preston.

"You're growling." Sean chuckled.

"Shut the fuck up," I snapped, my hands in a white-knuckled grip on the steering wheel. It would be a goddamned miracle if I didn't break the fucking thing in two.

"Someone is jealous—and you've no right to be considering all the ass *you've* had in the last couple of years."

"Fuck you, Sean."

"No thanks. Teach already took care of me earlier today. My hole needs a break."

I unclenched my fists to scrub a hand over my face, growling once more.

"How about an address?" Sean suggested. "If anyone asks, finding out where someone lives is easily done online. You can lie about how you located him and keep me from getting into trouble."

"Fuck yes. Give it to me."

Preston admitted to living close by to my condo, and he hadn't been lying.

"Are you shitting me?" I asked when Sean pulled Preston's file for the information.

"Nope."

"Fucking three blocks from me!" I spat the words. "How the fuck have I not run into him all this time?"

"Preston Gibbons is a self-proclaimed recluse according to his file," Sean said. "A tech geek who doesn't go out much."

"Yep, that's him, alright," I grumbled, some of my anger taking a backseat now that Preston couldn't hide from me.

"Good luck, my friend. Keep me informed."

"If you see anything on the news about Preston's disappearance or kidnapping, you don't know shit."

"Gotcha," Sean agreed with a chuckle. "Go get your man, and fuck anyone who gives you the side eye."

We would get a shit ton more than strange looks once Jacqueline's society found out her son shacked up with his stepbrother.

I needed to stop thinking of him as such. We weren't related. Neither of our parents had adopted the other kid, and we were grown ass men. Why would anyone give a shit if we were involved?

That question rang through my head long after I got off the phone with Sean.

Preston would care—because of Jacqueline. He didn't hide his desperation for his mother's love, her acceptance. And with her seeming to have a change of heart toward him, I couldn't begin to imagine my lover's conflicting desires.

He'd rejected me for her. Discarded me for something he saw as better, a relationship that could be more fulfilling.

But Preston Gibbons—Casswell—whatever name he went by these days, belonged to *me*. End of. He'd always been mine, and no rich, self-righteous bitch would steal from me the one person who felt completely right for my future.

He and I had some words to exchange whether he wanted to or not.

Running away.

I snorted. The fuck did he think would happen? That I wouldn't chase after him?

But did he even want me to? Was this his way of seeing how far I would go, how serious I was about him? A test to prove me worthy of owning his whole heart?

None of those suspicions rang true, but that didn't keep my gut from twisting into a painful knot.

Preston's heart was carved from pure gold. He wouldn't hurt a fly, and if he inadvertently did, he'd be crushed from having made that decision.

My thoughts warred as the Mass Pike's miles disappeared in my rearview. Woods faded into hints of settlement. Traffic slowed the closer I got to Boston. For the first time, the signs of life, the rush of the noise I couldn't even hear inside my car's interior, wreaked havoc on my overloaded brain.

Mind already crowded and rowdy, I didn't need a city pressing in on every side, exasperating my anxiety. I finally had firsthand experience what Preston dealt with when he got all up in his feels.

Teeth gritted against my need to escape—or hide—I exited the highway, making my way downtown. Traffic lights pissed me the hell off, but at least the other drivers used to Boston's fucked-up road system were aggressive and went with the flow.

Still, I cursed a dozen or so times, telling people to get the fuck outta my lane.

I had a man to confront and hopefully force into seeing things from my point of view.

My heart's ability to beat hinged on it.

Chapter 24

Preston

I'd been sitting at my piano for over an hour, attempting to lose myself in music. Every melody spilling from my fingertips reminded me of Drake. The way he'd sat in silence, listening to me practice when we'd been teens. How he'd close his eyes and smile as though what I'd played on ivory keys overwhelmed his soul with happiness.

Exhaustion weighed me down, but I'd been unable to sleep from the thoughts still clamoring in my brain. The almost five hours it had taken me to get home from Manhattan thanks to traffic hadn't settled anything in my head or heart. My split-path decision didn't lay any more straightforward before me than before I'd walked away from Drake hoping for clarity.

My shoulders slumped, my eyes exhausted from all the tears I'd shed while driving in the opposite direction of him.

Did he hate me for leaving him without explanation?

I couldn't begin to imagine his pain. Unlike me, Drake no longer withheld his thoughts and feelings like when we'd been young kids. He didn't stash part of who he was on a back shelf for safety's sake. He'd been open with me while I'd hidden the truth from him.

How could he *not* hate me?

Pain didn't begin to describe the dull throb in my chest. It didn't feel like the life-giving force of a heartbeat.

Until I figured the situation with Jacqueline out, it would be better to keep a low profile. I would utilize my usual self-restraint until I had a precise vision of what my future looked like with her.

Three months, she'd said they would be gone, but I knew she would get in touch with me countless times during their lengthy vacation. That was one thing I could trust her for, at least.

And didn't that loyalty reveal how much she cared about me?

Rather than stewing on my usual annoyance her regular check-ins inspired, I chose to focus on the positive aspect. Why call if she *didn't* care?

My fingers grew heavy, but I finished up Bach's Concerto in D Minor, one of Drake's favorites I'd fumbled through as a kid. He'd preferred the heavier classical music. Bach's Moonlit Sonata first movement had come easily, as had the second, but I'd learned the third years after Drake had left me alone in New York. I was no virtuoso but had continued practicing long after I'd quit lessons during college.

Playing spoke to my soul, or at least, reminded me of Drake. Perhaps that was why I still sat on the bench and filled my condo with haunting melodies. To keep him close, the feeling he sat and listened like he used to.

My hands fell to my lap, and silence descended.

With the music's fading went Drake's ghost, leaving me alone once more in my agony.

Lifting my watery gaze to the window overlooking the capital's golden dome glinting in the sinking sun, I allowed myself to just feel. Emotions given full rein, I sank into the experience of sadness.

The heaviness in my mind and tightness in my throat.

Lingering happiness bubbled beneath the surface, inspired by the contentment I'd felt being in close proximity to Drake.

Unease tingled along my spine with the knowledge of what lay on the horizon if I chose him without knowing Jacqueline's thoughts toward who I was at my core.

My eyelids fell shut, and I hunched, tears spilling down my cheeks.

I just wanted my mother to truly love me.

I wanted to be accepted.

I wanted to be free to love who my heart belonged to.

Write her off and walk away had been Nancy's recommendation. She'd done so but as a spouse, not a son. Jacqueline hadn't carried her inside her body for close to a year, hadn't borne her into the world, giving her life as she'd done with me.

Jacqueline, however, was the queen of decision-making. She domineered with her words and ordering those who'd upset her from her presence. Her fight instinct was strong as any I'd seen.

Me?

I was the prince of flight, a craven piece of shit who couldn't stand conflict. Too many arguments had raged in our home when I'd been a child, too much poison spewed from lips that had never offered an antidote for healing after Nancy had been kicked out. Even the *thought* of a dispute made my skin feel like I broke out into hives.

Perhaps I ought to see a therapist, but what was the

point of sludging through my childhood wounds again when I would never have the strength to stand up to Jacqueline?

I dragged my ass off the piano bench and started for my bedroom. I'd already showered, so it was time to close my eyes and escape into sleep were nothing but darkness mattered.

Hopefully.

A knock sounded before I crossed my condo, and I groaned.

I was not in the mood for company, solicitation, or any other bullshit person who had the gall to intrude on my misery.

Grumbling, I traipsed to the front door, cursing whoever I would see through the peephole.

Drake.

"Oh fuck," I whispered and stumbled back a step, heat rushing through me and pebbling my skin regardless of the knife stabbed into my chest. My pulse kicked into high gear, causing me to shake before a handful of seconds passed.

He knocked again, more insistent.

My feet moved forward, drawn as always to the man beyond the door. Resting my forehead against the cold oak slab between us, I cursed a few more times even as my hand reached for the handle. I should pretend I wasn't home—

Wait.

How had Drake found me? I hadn't shared my address or the fact that only three blocks separated our condos.

In the past couple of hours had he become some computer guru he'd claimed not to be? I hadn't told him of my name change either. Hadn't breathed a word of my personal life other than I had a place overlooking the state's capital, but dozens of Bostonians could say the same as I did.

So how the hell—

Another knock sounded, and I whimpered, well aware he wouldn't leave until he spoke with me.

Swallowing hard, I straightened and pulled the door inward.

"What the fuck, Preston?" He glowered at me, all light and love gone from his blue eyes. Their vivid hue had been overrun with anger and hurt. He stormed forward, and I shrank out his way before he barreled through me. Not that Drake would ever hurt me, but one touch, and I would cave to what my body craved.

He glanced around while stalking straight into my living room. Turning on his heel, he faced me, hands fisted at his sides as though he wanted to reach for me as badly as I yearned for him regardless of what I'd done. "Why?" He whispered, some of the anger bleeding from his gaze.

Trying to regulate my breathing, I tore my focus off him to quietly shut my front door and lock us in.

He wouldn't be leaving anytime soon even though I wished otherwise. Kind of.

I wiped my palms down my sweats even as my feet gladly took me closer to him. A couch sat between us, safer for both of us, I guessed. Unable to meet his gaze, I shrugged. "I j-just needed some space."

"Bullshit. You were clinging to me as though afraid *I* would be the one to walk out. What the fuck is going on with you? Why can't you just tell me the truth about how you're feeling?"

"Because I don't know!" I surprised myself by half-shouting. "There's too much in my head!" Tapping my temple, I watched the sight of him go watery as tears welled in my eyes. "Thoughts, feelings. They're confusing as hell, and while being with you makes everything go quiet, you also stir up things I can't want!"

"Why not?" Drake stalked around the couch, but I backed up, holding out a hand.

"Please," I whispered, swallowing as wetness dripped down my cheeks. "I-I can't!"

"Is it fear? Hmm?" Drake stopped in front of me, my palm against his chest. "Can't handle the stress of lying or sneaking around? You always were a nervous Nelly."

His words stung regardless of them being true.

My feet itched to spin and take me away from the vibrating tension, the energy of him tugging on my deepest desires. I longed for the warmth of his hard chest against my cheek. Longed for those strong arms of his to shield me from battling down a path that would lead to heartache one way or the other.

"Do you love me?" Drake asked, his voice low and strained.

I slammed my eyes shut, my fingers tangling in his T-shirt to keep him close even as my head told me to flee. My throat worked, but I couldn't...didn't know what to say.

"Jesus, Preston. Why won't you let me love you? Do you not trust me to have your back? To stick beside you no matter what *anyone* says about us finding happiness together?"

All my life, I'd squashed myself into the mold Jacqueline's expectations had formed around me. I'd been silent rather than standing up for myself. I hadn't told anyone about my hurts or secrets out of fear of her.

I hadn't realized before how much withholding myself, my inability to be vulnerable, was hurting Drake and causing a rift that might cause irrevocable damage for any possible future I dared to dream about.

That truth made me feel like a piece of shit, stirring nausea in my stomach.

I'd already told him, reiterated with my actions, that I was queer as a seven dollar bill. That bit of who I was hadn't been spoken aloud. Ever. But he deserved more.

"I'm af-fraid of this. Us. Jacqueline," I whispered one truthful emotion, a test so to speak.

"Thank you for sharing that part of you with me." Drake laced his fingers through mine atop his heart. "I can't imagine the anxiety you deal with, especially when it comes to Jaqueline and her nature. All I can do is promise to always listen without judgment and be here for you if you'll let me."

I believed him. He'd proven his loyalty time and again, having only walked away from me that once because of how much he wanted me.

I understood the choice he'd made that night. Thoroughly appreciated it now that I was aware of why. But I had no such reasoning. My timidity had sent me scurrying from the one man I could count on to stick by my side through thick and thin.

"I-I'm sorry for leaving without t-talking to you first. I... I'm just horrible with anything that rouses agitation or might become an argument."

"I know, baby," Drake murmured before releasing a heavy exhale. "I forgive you." His stomach growled loudly, making us both snicker even as my muscles loosened from his words.

"I have a lasagna in my freezer if you're interested?" I asked the obvious, thinking it was a good time to escape the heavy talk for a while.

"Stouffer's?"

Not trusting the sudden longing to spill *all* my damned secrets, I nodded rather than opening my mouth.

"God, yes," he groaned, his low tone making the skin on my arms pebble.

Face hot, I took my hand from his and started for the kitchen. "Sam Adams?" I offered, and of course he accepted.

I was well aware of all his favorites and had grown to love them, same as he did.

Chapter 25

Drake

It was only six-thirty, but darkness already claimed the sky outside Preston's windows by the time I wiped out half the pan compared to his single piece of lasagna. What were the chances we both shared a love of the same premade dinner I had packed in my own freezer?

His place was far nicer than mine with more square footage—which was a good thing, considering he owned a baby version of the grand piano like the one he'd had in New York. What I wouldn't give to just sit and listen to him plink on the keys, creating music out of ivory, strings, and hammers I thought he'd called them?

But we had to talk.

Or rather, he had to open up some more and tell me what all was going through his mind so we could move forward. Fear might be the underlying emotion, but I needed to understand where it rooted from so we could work through this shit together.

Knowing how easily he shut down, I would have to lower his defenses before weaseling into any serious conversation. That meant getting him to where he relaxed the most—cuddling, or at least as close as I could coerce him into.

We finished eating and cleaning up together before going into the living room.

"Sit here." I patted the couch cushion beside me when he hesitated over where to perch his cute ass. "I won't bite unless you ask me to."

Even with the distance separating us, I could make out the swell of his pupils.

Kink noted.

Grinning, I beckoned with my fingertips. "Come on, Preston. There's no one around. We have complete privacy, not that we need it. I don't know about you, but I'm beat and couldn't get it up even if you wanted my dick."

A total lie, but anything to get his body next to mine where my touch and close presence might lower his walls enough he would relax and eventually talk to me.

He huffed an exhale and listened, sitting primly on the couch's edge as I'd expected.

"Nuh huh." I tugged him into my side, my arm around his waist, and he melted into me same as he always did. "Much better," I murmured against his hair as he burrowed his face in my chest and sighed.

The scent of vanilla filled my nose, and I breathed him in, my own insides calming for the first time since I'd taken that catnap back in New York earlier in the morning.

We sat in silence for a little while. It would be up to me to break the quiet moment between us so we could get shit straightened out.

"I was fifteen when I lost my virginity," I said, sharing personal shit so he might eventually be swayed into doing the same. "It was the summer before I moved to New York. I actually bottomed."

"What?" Preston choked on the word, and I chuckled.

"Yeah, I'm not a size queen like Sean or anything, but I don't mind taking it on occasion. It's definitely not my preference though."

"I could not see you bottoming for anyone—ever."

I rubbed his arm absently, tipping my head back against the couch and closing my eyes. "I give off toppy vibes, huh?"

"Absolutely. But you...uh...did that for Elite?" I wanted to applaud his ability to vocalize his curiosity even though I was bummed he didn't sound jealous.

"Yeah, on occasion if no one else was available. What about you?" I asked, testing the waters.

"I was a junior in college," Preston muttered, surprisingly without hesitation. "A closet case senior wanted to 'rail my bubble butt' as he put it."

"You mentioned Friday night that you hadn't enjoyed your first time."

"Not really. I was left feeling as though I didn't want to bottom again, but the idea of topping doesn't do anything for me either. Never has."

"You seemed to enjoy yourself with me," I teased, poking his side. He grunted, and I realized I might have tickled him. "Sorry."

"No—it's okay," he said, going all lax again. "But yeah. I liked bottoming for you. A lot."

I knew the answer to my next question but tossed it out of feigned ignorance, not above stooping low to get him talking. "Was I your second, or have you had a dozen boyfriends in our time apart?"

Preston stilled. "I've uh, only been with two other guys since college."

I glanced at the hickey on his neck and squashed the possessive asshole in me that wanted to rise to the surface.

Sean was right—I had no fucking legs to stand on when it came hating the idea of anyone touching what belonged to me. Preston could count on one hand the men he'd had sex with while I'd lost track years earlier.

"Were they any good?" I had to ask, fingers crossed he would spill a few more of his secrets. I wanted the names of the Elites that had enjoyed his ass, damnit.

"The second was gentle with me. Kind. Extra patient." I could hear the smile in Preston's voice, which only made my jealousy burn brighter.

"He must have had more skills than that punk in college," I suggested, continuing to fish for information.

Preston huffed a laugh. "Yeah, you could say that. There was quite an age gap between us, which promised experience, thus my reason for sleeping with him."

So older. Silver fox, most likely. EEMM had a couple still on the menu, and along with Mason, another had recently left. It could have been any of them, but one had a very telling attribute he'd been teased about on occasion whenever my friends and other employees had gotten together.

"Did he have a massive cock?" I asked, my tone light, hoping Preston was clueless as to his secrets I was already well aware of thanks to Sean and his big mouth.

"Massive *is* an accurate word," Preston admitted.

Definitely Mason.

Okay. That I could live with. He was a decent guy and madly in love with his husband, Jasper, so there was no need to feed the green giant in my guts wanting to roar a very public claiming of Preston.

"And the second?" I pushed.

"We...well, we role-played." Preston's voice escaped as

no more than a squeak, but goddamnit, the kid made me proud with how vocal he was about sex.

That bit still wasn't enough though.

"Role-played, huh?" I poked him again, in supposed fun.

"Stop!" He jerked in my hold, but I clutched him tighter, wishing I could hate myself for manipulating him into giving me what I wanted.

"Tell me all the dirty details," I murmured against his hair, my voice low enough my chest would rumble against his ear and send shivers over his skin.

Sure enough, Preston shuddered, goose bumps rising along his arms. "He pretended to be you."

I grinned at his whispered words even though jealousy raged. "Kinky little nerd. And what fantasy did you play out?"

"The uh...one where you fucked me while spooning."

"Fuck that's hot." And surprisingly, it was. My dick plumped and everything regardless of the fact it had been someone else who'd gotten him off. It had been to thoughts of *me*, so maybe that was why? Who the fuck knew—and I didn't have time to evaluate my body's reaction. "Did he jerk you while talking dirty in your ear?"

I could imagine the red flushing Preston's face, since I couldn't see it and didn't want him budging from where he rested against me.

"Um, yes?"

The knowledge someone else had him like that still burned a sense of rage in my gut, but I grinned in pride over the fact Preston had the balls to ask for what he yearned for from one of my co-workers.

Ex co-workers.

"How long did you end up dating those guys?" I asked, all casual and shit, not a hint of jealousy in my tone.

It took Preston a few seconds before he answered. "They were one-night stands, but I met up with Ma—the first guy three times."

That slip. There was no doubt in my mind who'd had him.

Preston squirmed before I could cook up another question to get him to spill the beans of what he'd done. Considering the NDAs he'd signed, I couldn't outright ask, which would put him in the position of sharing information he legally shouldn't.

"What's wrong?" I asked when he shifted around a bit more without actually pulling away. "Getting hard?"

"N-No. Too t-tired."

"You're stuttering and have ants in your pants. What's got you feeling guilty?"

"Damnit, Drake." Preston huffed. "How do you always know?"

"You're an open book, baby." Most of the time, anyway. I kissed the top of his head. "Tell me what's causing your emotional response. Unload it off your chest so we can crawl into bed and get some much needed rest."

"They..." He swallowed audibly. "Were Elites?"

"Was that a question or statement?" I asked without a hint of judgment in my voice.

"Um. S-Statement."

"Hmm." I pretended to ponder what he'd shared with me, my fingertips once more active in caressing his bare arm to show him I wasn't upset. The caveman part of me was livid, but Preston didn't need to be aware of that just yet. "Let's see...experienced means older. Probably one of the silver foxes."

"He doesn't work there anymore," Preston said, his tone fond yet sad.

My hand stilled in its caressing. "You miss his massive dick?"

He huffed a laugh. "No. Yours is ten times better. A perfect fit."

My ego swelled, and I grinned. "Mason has a man of his own now, and would you believe he's a strict bottom?"

Preston jolted into a sitting position, his emerald eyes wide. "You... how did you... What?"

I chuckled, laying my arm across the back of the couch so I could rest my fingertips on his far shoulder. "There was only one silver fox on the EEMM's menu that would treat you the way you described, and yep. Long story, but he found his other half. Maybe someday he can share his truth with you."

"He was like the perfect Daddy though!"

I snorted an outright laugh. "Jasper is more the caretaker in their dynamic, and trust me when I say if any two men were made for each other, they're it."

Preston's lips slowly curled upward. "He never seemed happy, so I guess that stemmed from him not feeling fulfilled with his job."

"Probably. So, who was the kinky fucker who pretended to be me?" I asked, running my hand up his neck so I could play with his hair. "And does he know we're stepbrothers?"

"I didn't tell him who you were to me, so I don't believe so, no." Eyes closing, Preston pressed into my touch, his smile still in place.

The kid was putty in my hands. So easily swayed.

"Who gave you that gift, baby," I murmured, wanting the truth yet unsure how I would handle it depending on who he said.

"I—I signed an NDA, Drake."

"It's okay, baby. I won't tell a soul you spilled his name. Trust me."

"Fine. It was Kellen," he whispered, a gorgeous flush rising to his cheeks.

Kellen was hot as fuck. It was no wonder Preston had booked with him. "Smart choice," I stated what couldn't be argued. "Was he any good?" I asked and held my breath.

"He got the job done."

So not mind-blowing.

Jealousy took a backseat, and I stared at the man I loved, waiting for him to open his eyes again. A few minutes passed before he sighed and finally gave me those beautiful orbs I could get lost in.

"What?" he whispered.

"Were you sorry to see him go too?"

A frown flitted over Preston's brow. "Kellen quit?"

"Fell in love and moved to Maine. You haven't been on Elite's website for a while, huh?"

Preston's gaze dropped to his hands he clasped on his lap. "No."

"So I was the fourth man you gifted yourself to?"

"Yes."

"Meaning you've been celibate for over a year and a half? Because that's how long ago Kellen retired."

He shrugged, glancing out his dark windows. "I felt guilty on spending that kind of money and imagining it was you pleasing me rather than your friends and co-workers. It was kind of stalkerish? Sick?"

"Thank you for sharing those feelings with me—and I'm not upset," I admitted what I wanted to be true even though it wasn't one-hundred percent. "Can't believe you took that python in Mason's pants though. You're one brave soul."

"Like I said, he was gentle and made sure I was ready."

I held up my hand, stopping the words Preston had suddenly become liberal with. "I don't need details, baby. Bad enough knowing others enjoyed having you."

A memory flitted through my brain from when a group of Elite's employees had been at Jarod's wedding two years earlier. The retired worker from the straight branch married the woman he'd given up escorting for, and I remembered Kellen asking me something about a redhead...a client he'd been with.

Fucking hell.

Kellen *had* somehow figured out who Preston was to me. How had he been aware and Sean hadn't? Had Kellen fallen for Preston before JJ? Done some online stalking of his own and figured shit out? If he had, he'd kept his mouth shut, or otherwise, Sean would have been all over my ass about the entire affair.

My lips pressed tight as that damned possessiveness work back up with a vengeance. "No more Elites," I stated firmly enough Preston blinked at me. "You're *mine*."

"You're an Elite," he sassed, narrowing his gaze as though willing to go to war over who belonged to whom.

Fuck, did I love that new look on his face, like he was ready to throw down for the first time ever.

Over me.

A grin flashed my lips upward. "I quit."

"You seriously did? I-I heard you over the phone earlier this morning, but I wasn't sure..." He trailed off when he realized he'd admitted to eavesdropping. Not that I cared.

He'd given me enough for now, and I would prove myself by loving him regardless of his actions.

"I don't share when I'm invested, baby, and we belong to each other." My tone didn't allow for argument. "I've known that since the first night we sat down as a family at that ostentatious dinner table. Didn't recognize it then, but looking back, yeah. You were mine from the minute I first saw you, Preston Gibbons."

That gooey, melty expression erased the lines off Preston's face, and he stared at me with hearts in his eyes.

Talk about an ego boost and heartache at the same time.

"Come here, baby," I tugged on his shoulder, my voice gruff.

His cell rang—some fucking horrific ringtone that bled horror and death from my ears.

I snorted a laugh even though my stomach twisted. "Tell me that's Jacqueline."

"That's Jacqueline," he admitted, his voice shaky as he swiped his cell off the end table. His freckles shone out stark against his suddenly pale skin.

He answered before I could tell him not to.

"H-Hello," he squeaked and swallowed hard.

I couldn't hear what Jacqueline said but watched Preston's face. At the first sign of a grimace, I gestured for the phone.

No way! He mouthed at me, shaking his head, eyes wide.

"Give me the phone, Preston," I stated firmly but quietly enough Jacqueline wouldn't make out my words.

"Preston?" Jacqueline's voice came through loud and clear as I swiped the phone from Preston. "Did you hear me?"

I lifted his cell to my ear, holding him at bay with a palm to his heaving chest. "Jacqueline!" I greeted, trying for warmth in my voice. "Sorry about that—there was a spider in the elevator with us. Threw Preston for a loop, and he's a little shaken up."

"Oh! Drake, I'm happy you've chosen to stay in New York with your brother."

It was my turn to mirror a puke emoji. I fucking hated when she called me that. "It's been fun hanging with him again."

"He's always looked up to you." The saccharine in her voice triggered my gag reflex and not in a good way. "Idolized one of the best *male* role models in his life."

An agreeing noise sounded in my throat even though I'd heard an emphasis on that one word.

"Maybe now that you're reconnected—"

A snort almost ripped from me.

"—you can draw him out of his shell. Maybe take him out and help him make *friends*."

Annoyance slammed into me with the force of a nor'easter, cold and chilling me to the bone at the insinuation they be of the feminine sort. "I'm assuming you and my dad arrived safely?" I changed the subject, fighting to keep my voice level.

"Yes! And it's so beautiful here. And warm! I'm almost wishing we'd brought the two of you along so we could be one happy family together again."

Fucking. A.

"Sorry to cut you short, Jacqueline, but we really need to get going. It's late, and we're both exhausted."

"Oh! I'd forgotten about the time change. Give my love to my son, and I appreciate you looking out for him."

I hung up without saying goodbye, all sorts of pissiness roused back to life by the unspoken words between the ones she'd stated. Perhaps I projected, but I knew Jacqueline Casswell.

Preston, pale with panic-stricken eyes, stared at me. "Y-You...n-need to leave," he whispered harshly before swallowing like a frog choked his throat. "N-Now." He hopped up, rubbing his palms down his sweats. "Please, D-Drake. If you have any f-feelings for me at all—you'll go."

His sudden distress, the anxiety weighing on his face and shoulders rocketed compassion through me regardless of my anger at its source. His flight instincts always kicked in whenever Jacqueline riled him up.

The bitch still held complete sway over his mind, regardless of the distance he'd put between them by moving to Boston. Her claws had sunk deep into his psyche, her manipulations binding him to her in tighter ways than I could ever hope to experience with him.

I suddenly and *thoroughly* understood why he'd snuck out on me, the torn desires he needed to make sense of before he could choose between the two of us.

I also needed to relinquish any unrealistic expectations I had on Preston. While he hadn't yet given me all the reasons our being together dragged emotions to the surface atop his childhood wounds, I could empathize. His insecurities spoke to me on a deep level he might not yet recognize or even be ready to discuss.

I would remain loyal. Be there for him whenever he found his own inner strength and stood up to Jacqueline so he could be the man he hid from sight.

Knowing what I had to do didn't make shit any easier, but I chose to put him first.

Sean had been seeing a therapist for a few months. Perhaps it was time for me to do the same for my own shit that needed to be dealt with thanks to my parent's divorce, the uprooting from Boston, and my extreme dislike for Dad's wife. And maybe someday, hopefully in the near future, Preston would be open to the idea as well.

In the meantime, I would work on myself so I could be prepared for when that day came.

I would wait for Preston, no matter how long it took for him to accept the truth of who he was so we could be together.

Chapter 26

Preston

Drake left without any argument. No frown marred his gorgeous face, no vile words over my cowardly ass spewed from his lips. He'd always claimed to be able to read me, so I expected he'd figured out my issue, the divided path I hesitated in front of.

And rather than manipulating me like Jacqueline would have done into swaying me toward the decision he wanted, he gave me the space necessary to figure shit out.

He put my needs above his own desires.

I cried myself to sleep that night, sick with yearning for the solidity of him in my bed, the assurance of his presence alone that allowed me a glimpse of peace in my tumultuous existence.

Jacqueline had called at the worst time, or perhaps the perfect one depending on how a person looked at it. I'd been ready to cave to Drake's draw, the tender, loving care and protection he offered my exhausted heart and mind.

Her ringtone matched the emotions she always erupted in my guts. Maybe I ought to change to something a little more upbeat. A tune that reminded me of hope, because that was what I wished for, right?

For everything, not just with Drake, to be disturbance free. I needed reconciliation, all defenses down, and true acceptance atop what seemed like Jacqueline's renewed love for her son before I could even consider a future with him. I wouldn't be completely happy in a relationship with him otherwise—wouldn't be free to enjoy him to the fullest if Jacqueline's presence in the back of my head continued to nag and infuse fear in my thoughts.

I wanted both paths to circle back around and meet up in one road bracketed by gardens full of life and beauty, quietness and contentment.

But I stood rooted in unhealthy soil, unsure which way to turn to make that dream come true.

Jacqueline called every three days in the following weeks like clockwork, giving me updates on her and Devlin's jaunt from one country to another. Her dedication in using pet names and telling me she missed me inspired more hope of reconciliation. She sent me pictures of exotic places she thought I might like. Beaches and sand. Yachts and city landscapes in an array of colored sunsets.

And Drake?

He proved his thoughtfulness with similar gestures just as often.

Seeing as how I'd ignored the NDAs by admitting to which Elites I had been with, I couldn't be mad at Sean for giving his best friend personal information if that was how he'd gotten my phone number.

A part of me was glad to have that tether to Drake, a means of reaching out to him if shit hit the fan and I couldn't breathe on my own, because knowing Jacqueline, she could flip a switch at the drop of a hat.

Drake texted me every morning and night but with mere friendly messages. No booty calls. No hint of teasing or flirting. He'd promised to have my back, and he did without a hint of manipulation.

Twice, I'd called him in a huff, pissed at Jacqueline who'd regressed a bit toward her old self, asking if I ever left my condo for a night on the town with Drake to meet women. *Polished* ones, she'd hoped for aloud, not easy girls at like a dance club or seedy bar.

Drake offered to take me out after my second meltdown, but I declined. He also suggested going for dinner on a non-date.

But I said no to that too, still not ready to face him and have all my fragile walls holding his draw at bay dissolved into dust just by the sight of him in the flesh.

He told me he and his buddies were getting together on Saturday for the Bruins' game, but I also set aside that invitation due to my lack of balls. Especially when he warned me that Kellen and Mason sometimes showed up with their men.

Nope.

Definitely not.

Drake might be okay with my having fucked old acquaintances of his, but the idea of being in front of Kellen after I'd admitted to how much I wanted Drake—and him finding out his friend and co-worker I lusted over was my stepbrother?

Yeah, not happening.

I focused on computer stuff, doing some investigating for clients and website building for two others. Enough tasks sat on my to-do list to keep me busy for a month straight, but the problem?

I didn't allow time for me to work through my issues that would one day need to be dealt with.

Nancy reminded me of that fact. It was a Friday morning, almost three weeks since I'd seen Drake. She'd begun calling me on her way to work once a week, and I looked forward to connecting with her in ways I never had with Jacqueline.

"How are you, my sweet boy?" she asked, her kind voice, the affection bleeding over the line enough to make my eyes burn.

"Hanging in there." I'd told her all about New York. Drake. Him letting me go so to as not be a distraction while I figured my life out.

"Have you spoken with him lately?"

"A few days ago." I leaned onto my kitchen table, ignoring my piece of French bread toast.

"And he's still being patient and understanding?" she questioned, a hint of a threat in her voice if I said no.

I chuckled, glancing at the empty chair beside me I wished he sat in. "Always."

"That boy fits you like a puzzle piece, Preston."

"I know, Mom," I rasped, my lips flatlining over the ache in my heart.

"I wish I could give you the answers, show you the best route to take toward happiness, but that's something we have to decide on our own."

I picked at the cold crust before brushing my fingertips clear of crumbs. "Do you regret your choice to transition?"

"Not once," she stated without hesitation.

"Even when Jacqueline was screaming at you? Calling you all those vile names?"

"I won't lie and say it didn't hurt, or that cutting her from my life was an easy experience to endure, but I would endure it ten times over since doing so has allowed me to live my truth and I've once more found love. The kind that can't be broken. The forever, happily ever after you read about in your romance novels."

I swallowed hard, wishing I could have what she and Michael did.

"Have you considered going to therapy?" Nancy asked.

"No. You know I struggle with sharing my feelings about much of anything outside you—and now Drake."

"I never would have lowered my defenses or been vulnerable with Michael if I hadn't. Perhaps you should take a step that way first. Maybe dealing with the unresolved trauma from your childhood will make the other paths before you a little clearer."

But I didn't *want* to unearth my secrets. Couldn't imagine having to dig through the sludge of my emotions, dissect where they stemmed from, or study them in detail to better understand my inner thought processes and patterns.

Jacqueline lay at the root of it all, and some days I wished her away only to experience guilt for feeling that way about my biological mother. She'd never been the nurturing caretaker. That had always been Nancy.

And Jacqueline had made her leave.

I hung up with Mom a few seconds later since she'd arrived at work, but I didn't get up from the table.

The more I focused on the negative, the bitterness festering inside me intensified. Jacqueline didn't deserve my love or loyalty, but whenever she'd called recently, she'd sounded invested in my life and swayed me back toward wanting to have a relationship with her again.

An unexpected turn of conversation later that afternoon made me realize I wasn't the only one attempting to do some deep soul-searching.

"I'm sorry for not being around when you needed me most." Jacqueline's quiet admission stunned me into silence.

It had been a full week since my last pity party over the phone because of the woman who'd just blown my mind by apologizing to me for the first time ever.

I sat alone on my bed, hugging my pillow, speechless and bug-eyed at my cell on speaker on the mattress beside me.

"I was too focused on Casswell Global," she continued when I didn't respond. "Not that I can use that as an excuse for leaving my son behind on more occasions than I can count."

Holy fucking shit.

My throat tightened.

"Preston? Are you there?"

"Yes," I managed to whisper.

Jacqueline sighed heavily. "I...Preston, there's so much piled up in my head and heart I'm working through now that I'm focusing on myself, things I've never shared with anyone."

Didn't that sound familiar?

"You don't have to," I murmured but could admit to myself the curiosity attempted to kill this cat.

"No—Devlin has been explaining to me for years that I need to, and I'm ready for you to hopefully understand."

"Okay. I promise I'll listen. I won't judge," I gave Jacqueline what Drake had offered me, meaning every word —desperate for them, even. Anything to bring peace between us.

"My own mother wasn't there for me emotionally." Jacqueline's voice broke, prompting empathy enough my eyes stung. It took her a few seconds before continuing. "She loved her wine and pills more than her only daughter."

I closed my eyes, feeling as though I'd been punched in the gut. Jacqueline hadn't ever told me anything unsavory about her childhood before. Everything had always been rainbows and unicorns as far as I'd heard from her lying lips.

"It was no wonder my father spent more time in the office than at home," she went on while I sat like I'd been struck by lightning, my brain too fried to respond. "While I'm not an addict like my mom was, I recently realized I'm no better than she'd been. I was just as wrapped up in my own little world like both of my parents when you were at a vulnerable age. I was selfish in my pain I refused to admit or share, and I deeply regret whatever trauma I may have caused you."

I sat unmoving, unsure of what to say—what even to think as her words had blown my mind.

"Still with me, Preston?" A hint of fear came through her tone, and I longed to assure her but couldn't get out more than a whispered affirmative.

"I'm thankful Devlin and Drake came into our lives," she said with more hesitation than when revealing the sins of her mother. "That boy was there for you when I wasn't. He's been a faithful friend, hasn't he?"

"Yes," I managed to force the word out. How badly would she judge me if she knew the truth?

Jacqueline heaved a heavy exhale. "Have you been spending time with Drake since you both returned home?"

Again with the hesitation that made me question where she directed our conversation.

But I wasn't touching the topic of my stepbrother with her no matter how much she seemed open to a discussion. Swallowing hard, I imagined girding my loins before speaking to risk the fragility of this place we'd arrived at in our relationship.

"What about Nancy?" I held my breath, wondering whether her stance on the LGBTQ community had shifted with her new attitude.

Jacqueline didn't react by spouting off like I expected. She actually remained quiet for a few seconds, allowing me a sip of oxygen for my starved lungs. "I don't really know what to say. She chose to be something she's *not* in hoping it would give her peace, and I just can't wrap my head around that."

While she'd at least gotten Nancy's pronouns right, that whole *chose* revealed her thoughts *hadn't* changed a whole lot.

"I just..." Jacqueline released another loud exhale. "I'm not sure I'll ever be able to forgive her for the heartache she caused me all those years ago."

"But you have Devlin now," I said, gaining a little more gumption, even though I doubted I would ever be able to come out to her. "And you're happier than I remember you ever being with..." I wasn't sure what to say. My other mom? Nancy? Your ex? The last thing I wanted to do was trigger Jacqueline with the wrong word choice and ruin the progress we'd made with one phone call after an entire lifetime of zero connection.

Jacqueline didn't respond or offer to fill in the blank I'd left. I could almost feel her reflection through the cell line connecting us.

"Hey, Jacqueline?" I went with another test of sharing like I'd done with Drake—something that definitely took balls.

"Yes, sweetheart?"

"I didn't think I would ever be able to forgive you for the emotional pain I experienced as a child either—but I do."

A soft sob sounded through the speaker, and I swallowed a few times to keep from crying with her.

"I—I understand why you were selfish in your reaction to Nancy's truth," I went on, my voice wobbly, "and while I won't ever be able to forget about it, I promise I'm willing to move past it for the sake of our relationship."

I didn't know if she would acknowledge the point I'd tried to make or if her recent self-reflections would open her eyes to seeing the truth of my words. When she didn't respond, I grew antsy, my backside shifting on the bed.

"You said you're leaving Spain tomorrow," I reminded her, figuring we'd had enough of the deep, soul-tiring talk and had enough to think about until her next call. "Where are you headed?"

She sighed before answering, as though thankful I changed the topic. "Greece."

"*Not fair*," I stated with the same pouty voice I'd always done as a child when she'd eat two glazed donuts and only ever allowed me one.

Light laughter tinkled through my phone's speaker, encouraging a smile to my lips. Talk about a damned roller coaster. When had we last experienced a good memory, let alone one that inspired a positive reaction in both of us at the same time?

"You sound happy," I said. "A hundred percent more than when you slaved away in that office."

"Selling was the best decision I ever made apart from giving birth to you and falling in love with Devlin. He's an incredible man." Her voice broke again, and I wondered if she lamented Nancy's transition or was flooded with thankfulness for the second guy she'd given her heart to. "The absolute best," she whispered.

"I'm glad you found him." I almost tacked on *Mom* but

hesitated. We'd agreed on my calling her Jacqueline years ago, and it would take a lot of actions and words of healing between us before I would ever call her that again.

But I'd been truthful. I wouldn't change the fact Jacqueline had gone off on a whim and married Devlin Hemmings. If she hadn't, I never would have met Drake, and I couldn't imagine my life without him.

The distance between Drake and I caused every muscle in my body to ache. I cried at night. Whined to no one but myself during the day. Dragged to get anything done due to heartache. But this conversation was like a hint of sunlight through the clouds, making the future a slight shade brighter.

We hung up a few minutes later, and I lay back on my bed, emotionally spent, staring at the ceiling as the unknowns shifted around inside me.

Something was taking place in Jacqueline's heart, a new rhythm of thought that would eventually lead to harmony if she continued on her journey. Finally free from the burden to expand the Casswell empire I now believed her father had put on her, she allowed for some serious introspection.

She sought out a deeper meaning to her existence while enjoying vacationing with her husband, who still somehow adored the ground she walked on.

Perhaps when the day came for me to lay all the truth before her, she would understand why I wanted the same with the man I loved. Maybe I wouldn't need to choose one path over the other after all.

Maybe fate drew them closer together and *would* soon have them join where healing and love could be given and accepted all around.

Chapter 27

Drake

Saturday afternoon, I lounged on Sean's couch, my back to the wall of windows overlooking the wharf. The water was almost empty of boats due to it only being early March, and winter clung to Boston like a jealous bitch.

Zack sat beside me rather than Preston like I'd have preferred, Jimmy on my other side. Another couch held three other current employees, none of which I was super close with. Couldn't even wrack my brain to remember their names.

A bottle of Sam Adams sweated in my hand as I attempted to watch the Bruins take on the Lightning.

The absence of Preston lay heavily on my mind, keeping my spirits low as they'd been for going on three weeks.

Sean knew everything. I'd finally spilled what I'd kept from him about my time living in New York. He'd listened patiently rather than behaving like a brat, teasing or prompting me to hurry so he could get back to his Teach.

Like I'd expected, there had been no judgment, simply

a desire to rip Jacqueline a new one and welcome Preston into the fold whenever he was ready to take that step. That was why I had extended the invitation, in hopes that Preston would see that there were people who wouldn't look at us strangely or believe us being in a relationship was wrong.

My best friend knelt beside Matteo, who sat in a recliner, his cheek resting on his lover's knee. Never had I ever expected Sean to portray any type of submissive tendencies in front of his past and present employees, but that just went to show how much love could change a man to the point he didn't give two fucks what other people thought about how he lived his life.

He took pride in needing Matteo, and not a single guy in the room voiced a teasing word like usual whenever we got together. But it was all done in fun.

Perhaps if Kellen had been there with JJ, or Sean's brother Micah had joined, they would have given Sean shit for a daddy-dom type finally taking him in hand. But Kellen and his man were snowed in up at the camp in Maine, happy as pigs in shit according to Sean, and Micah's wife was pregnant, still suffering from morning sickness and miserable. Wild horses wouldn't have been able to drag him away from her side.

I was fine with Kellen missing the get-together that month. I wasn't sure how I would handle seeing the man who'd pretended to be me while railing Preston's ass—that lush, sweet-tasting hole that belonged to *me* and none other.

Fuck, did I miss him.

Jaw clenching, I shifted from equal amounts of annoyance and arousal, my focus flitting off my kneeling best friend for the TV in front of me.

Zack elbowed me gently. "You okay?" he asked, keeping

his voice quiet enough I would answer truthfully if needed amidst the noise of the game on screen and everyone else talking around us.

I shrugged, not really wanting to chat about where my body sat compared to where my heart longed to be.

"Sean still hasn't replaced you, and while I'm loving the money rolling into my account from the extra bookings," Zack continued when I didn't answer right away, "I'm kinda hoping he gets another tall, dark, and handsome on the menu. Know what I mean?"

I huffed a laugh. "Knees starting to hurt, old man?"

"Fuck you." He snorted and swigged his beer. "I only have a couple of years on you." Zack straightened and angled to face me fully. "That's why you quit, isn't it? Dick couldn't handle the workouts? Fucking finally became a chore? Blue pills weren't cutting it for you anymore?"

"Shut the fuck up," I muttered without a lick of heat in my voice.

All the guys bullshitted and teased more often than not. And while Zack wasn't usually one to poke fun at people, I was glad to see him opening up. He'd always been on the silent side, away from the group and in his own head.

Zack fucking chuckled, a rare sound. "Spill, man."

"I've actually fallen in love with a guy, and even though I haven't gotten him into my bed for good, I just can't imagine touching anyone else." I shrugged, smiling when Zack's jaw dropped.

"The fuck?" He stared at me like I'd laid down proof the earth was flat. "You're the most dedicated single-for-life guy I've ever met. Seriously. No one is more dead set against relationships than you."

"Love works in mysterious ways," I said, no longer wishing to curse that fuckface Cupid.

I'd spoken to Preston the night before, and he'd told me Jacqueline had apologized for some of the trauma she'd caused him. Talk about having my mind blown. I'd never expected to hear those words, and they'd only doubled my hope that the two of them would find healing enough that Preston would be able to someday tell her his truth too.

But the waiting fucking sucked.

I missed his warmth, the scent of his skin and hair, the sound of his voice. His smile and laughter. The way he melted against my chest and sighed over snuggling into his favorite place on earth. At least, that was what it seemed like, anyway.

Even more, I longed for the rightness of having that other piece of my life's puzzle in its place.

"So what's holding him back?" Zack asked, and I toyed over sharing personal shit.

He'd been nothing but loyal to Elite and the Fox brothers. He also didn't gossip like some of the others in the room —specifically Jimmy on my right, who probably listened in on every word we spoke.

I glanced over at EEMM's youngest employee to find him slouched down, head tipped back against the couch, mouth hanging open in sleep. "The fuck is wrong with him?" I asked Zack.

"His client kept him up, or rather *ass*-up, all night long, taking full advantage of having him until eight this morning. According to Jimmy, who isn't a size queen like Sean, the guy packed soda can girth. Poor kid had to pop a couple ibuprofen after soaking in a hot tub for a few hours after getting home."

I snickered, thankful as fuck I'd never been booked with a hung dude who wanted to wreck my ass. Sean had always known my preferences and wouldn't ever do me wrong like that.

Zack pulled his cell from his back pocket, frowning when he looked at the screen. A second later, his face turned a mottled red. "How the fuck did he..." His mutter trailed off, his fingers swiping over the screen as though replying to a text, lips pressed into a tight line.

"Everything okay?" I asked since I'd never seen Zack pissed before.

"Yeah." He shut down his phone and shoved it in his pocket. "Just some asshole from the past. It's nothing."

Didn't sound like or appear to be nothing. Zack shifted, glancing around the room, clearly uncomfortable.

"So, that question you asked," I said, getting back on topic, since he obviously had no wish to talk about whoever that asshole was. I checked to make sure no one else paid attention to us since I wanted to prove my suspicions no one would judge us. "He's my stepbrother."

Zack didn't bat an eyelash at my admission. "Didn't know you had a stepbrother."

"My dad married his mom when the two of us were in high school. We only lived together as siblings—not even legal ones—for three years before I moved back to Boston. We just reconnected a few weeks ago, and...yeah. Turns out we've both been pining for each other this whole time."

"Then what's the problem?"

I opened my mouth to respond, but some *loudmouth* answered for me.

"The problem is Preston's mom is a homophobic bitch, and Drake's too nice to put his foot down and demand the kid choose between the two of them!" Sean's outburst silenced everyone in the room.

"You're a dick." I glared at him.

"What?" Sean glanced around as I stared him down.

A pin could have dropped and gonged loud enough to wake the neighborhood.

Jimmy snorted, shifting upright to prove me correct. "Huh?"

"Fucking hell, Sean. You and your big goddamned mouth," I muttered.

Matteo grasped his nape, and Sean cringed, a look of contrition actually moving over his face.

"Why don't you take him back to your room and redden his ass for me, Matteo," I teased without a hint of jollity in my voice. "Teach that loose-lipped little boy of yours how to quit spouting off."

Matteo huffed a laugh. "Those kinds of punishments don't work on his needy ass."

Sean actually flushed, and I bit back a laugh. "Deny him a climax for a few days or put a cock cage on him. That'll make him see the errors of his ways real damn quick."

"Sorry," my best friend mumbled before Matteo could agree to two of the things Sean hated most. "I'm just pissed as hell for you. Want you happy and all that shit."

"I appreciate you having my back, but boundaries, dude. Fucking boundaries."

"Shit." Sean once more glanced around the room at the handful of other EEMM employees whose names I still couldn't recall. "Forget I said anything?"

"What'd I miss?" Jimmy asked, rubbing at his face as others chuckled or scoffed.

"Nothing," Zack stated. "Go back to sleep."

Jimmy shifted on the couch, grimacing.

"I heard your client from last night got his money's worth," I said, knowing exactly how to shift the topic of conversation when surrounded by a bunch of sex workers.

"Lordy, that man." Jimmy shook his head, his longer blond curls bouncing. Effeminate and kind of pretty in his own way, Elite's favorite bottom seemed to have finally found his limit when it came to how much dick his tiny, pert ass could handle.

He cracked up the room while going into detail about the dick he'd had shoved up his hole so many times overnight he'd lost count. Fucking soda can, no lie. Bigger even than Mason, he'd claimed, even though he'd never seen what EEMM's ex silver fox hid in his pants.

"How are he and Jasper doing?" I asked, glancing around at the other Elites to see if anyone had an update. "Haven't seen those two lovebirds in a couple of months."

"Really well, last I'd heard," Sean piped up, his being the only one of us who really kept in touch with the retired escorts when they didn't show up for our monthly get-togethers. "They're out in Montana again with Mason's sister. Coming home Wednesday, maybe?"

"Jasper still hasn't grown sick of his whiny ass?" I asked, even though Jasper loved taking care of his older man like the daddy he truly was. The man was an angel and like I'd told Preston, Mason's perfect match.

The chatter picked back up from there, various conversations taking place again.

Jimmy started snoring a few minutes later.

"So what are you going to do?" Zack pulled my attention back to our earlier conversation.

I glanced at Sean, who seemed to feel my gaze, because he lifted his head off Matteo's knee to hold my stare.

Do it, I could have sworn his eyes told me. *Put your fucking foot down and go for what you want. Don't take no for an answer. And you can thank me later for giving you the best advice ever.*

I snorted, and he grinned, knowing I heard him loud and clear. Fuck, did I want to follow his suggestion, but I put Preston first.

Always fucking would.

But maybe a short visit in a few days, a little poke to encourage a step in my direction wouldn't be a waste.

Chapter 28

Drake

I set the weighted barbell back on the rack and stepped away, my thighs fucking burning over the amount of back squats I'd done. Nothing better than jelly legs after a good workout on a Sunday morning. There was no day of rest in my books, especially since I hadn't yet found something else to keep me busy now that I'd retired from escorting.

Maybe someday, I would find a way to put my MBA to good use, but for now, I was relaxing and taking care of myself.

Sweat dripped down my chest, soaking my shirt. I lifted the hem and wiped my brow, content in my workout I would pay for later.

AirPods in my ears, I'd been jamming to my favorite playlist. Aerosmith's "Love in an Elevator" came on before I could take a few wobbly steps across the gym, and my grin broke out in full fucking force.

A call rang through the tune before Tyler even finished the first verse, and I groaned, wishing I could stay in my memories rather than answering.

Dad.

My attitude changed when I saw his name on the screen, my smile fixed back in my place. I hadn't talked to him since they'd left. Unlike Preston with Jacqueline, Dad and I only spoke about once a month.

"Hey!" I answered. "How's your trip around the world going?"

"Best vacation of my life," Dad said, happiness evident in every word.

"Glad to hear it. Where are you?"

"Greece, and it's absolutely gorgeous."

We got caught up for a few minutes, just the regular bullshit. I expected his wife was in the shower or at some spa, otherwise the conversation would have been short as fuck since she monopolized his time more often than not.

"So, I wanted to talk to you about something while Jacqueline is in her meeting." Dad's voice turned serious.

Sitting on an empty bench near the gym's far wall, I readied myself for what I expected was coming. "I thought she retired?" I hinted at, wishing I could put off the inevitable.

"This is something personal, she said. I'm not too disappointed, since her being busy gives me a few minutes alone with my little buddy."

Steeling myself, I asked, "So, what's up?"

"What are your feelings for Preston?"

Yep. There it was.

If I'd had on pants instead of short shorts, I would have been rubbing my sweating palms down them like Preston always did. "Pretty sure you already know the answer to that one, Dad."

He released a slow exhale that didn't sound disappointed or even upset. "You take care of him with more than stepbrotherly love and always have. It was obvious to me when you were both in high school—how you looked at each other when you thought no one watched."

I made a noise of agreement but didn't speak. He'd been aware of my feelings before even I was. Dad had always paid attention to me, but I hadn't realized how much he watched over me.

Had my fucking best interests at heart.

Jesus, could a man be any luckier to have such a father?

"Then that last dinner at the Tribeca loft," he continued, "you hadn't seen each other in years, but it was obvious as hell nothing had changed between the two of you."

Dad and I hadn't ever bullshitted each other, and I wasn't about to start now. The cards would fall where they were meant to, but nothing would change what I wanted for my and Preston's future.

"He followed me out, but I turned my back on him for the first time that night," I said. "Didn't speak to him for five years—until we got stuck in that elevator. They were the best four hours of my entire fucking life."

Well, *four* of the best. Having Preston in my bed trumped all else, but Dad didn't need to hear about everything.

Dad chuckled. "If anyone paid attention, they would have noticed the beard burn around his mouth. It was a little obvious what you boys had been up to."

Aerosmith's line about *living it up* ran through my head. I'd gone down all right. Wanted to again.

"Yeah, I was afraid of that," I said, pushing aside thoughts of sex. "At least Jacqueline didn't seem to notice."

"Or, perhaps she did and chose to ignore it in the face of the fear she experienced that night."

Could have been she was blinded by the onslaught of

emotions I'd seen smeared over her face with makeup. Who the fuck knew. At least she hadn't said anything if she had suspicions.

"Has she mentioned it to you?"

"No, but she's been extremely contemplative since the incident. Was there a reason you haven't told me before now?" Dad asked. "You've never kept a secret from me like this. Normally, we're very open and honest with each other."

"I didn't want to cause problems." Same as my reason for not telling him about all those trips Preston and I had taken to Queens to visit Nancy.

"There's nothing on this earth you could do to make me love you any less."

"I know, and I trust you with everything," I assured him. "But I wouldn't put you in a situation where you might have to lie to your wife. And, I would never make you feel you had to choose between me and her either. I had to do that between you and mom when I was a kid, and I wouldn't wish a heart being pulled in opposite direction on anyone."

"Shit." I could imagine Dad rubbed a hand over his jawline. "I'm so sorry, Drake."

"Don't be. Neither of you were happy—I get that—but both of you are now, and that's what matters."

"How does Preston feel about you?" Dad asked.

I studied the callouses on my hands. "It's not my place to say."

"Fair enough. I guess all I can suggest is to be patient," Dad said, kindly without a hint of resignation, thank fuck. "Jacqueline being retired is something...new. It's refreshing her in beautiful ways, and she's even more lovely to me."

I never thought she was *lovely* to begin with, but whatever. As long as Dad was content.

"Think she'll ever accept the fact Preston might be gay? Even better, what if he and I were madly in love like the two of you are?" I tossed out hypotheticals, expecting Dad was well aware both were true.

"I wouldn't suggest opening that can of worms just yet," Dad stated quietly, "but she's making large strides toward healing."

The fuck did she have to heal from?

Choosing to accept Nancy's truth ought to be enough for Jacqueline to move on. The woman had married an even better man in my dad, someone above her in every way that mattered except for money. But riches didn't mean shit when it came to being a good human being.

"She's writing in her journal a lot," Dad continued when I didn't say shit. "Reflecting over her life's choices, and I've seen amazing growth beyond what I ever expected. In the few short weeks since we were in New York, she's made changes for the best."

"I don't care how many new leaves she might turn over. She gets wind of Preston possibly being anything but straight, and she'll flip on his ass. Can't stomach the thought. Don't need him hurt even more because of her shitty attitude."

"Trust me, the last thing I want to do is cause issues between the two of them when they're finally finding some common ground. I'm well aware of how stirring up a hornet's nest for that boy would affect you."

I exhaled heavily and leaned forward, elbows on my knees. "You still love her like you did when you first got together?"

Dad chuckled, his happiness leaking through the line and making me envious as hell. "More, if you can believe it."

It'd been what? Over thirteen years? Not quite forever,

but the fact they'd stayed together regardless of her issues and their being opposites assured me love *could* last regardless of what I'd seen growing up.

"I expect your mom's and my divorce tainted your view of relationships," Dad said as though hearing my thoughts, "but trust me in this—love is worth the risk, son. Jacqueline has her issues, but there's no other place I wish to be than beside her. Holding her hand. Breathing the same air. Sharing the same space."

My throat tightened. I wanted that with Preston so fucking bad.

"You there, Drake?"

"I'm here," I rasped.

"I need to get going, and I promise I won't say anything, but if I had to bet her entire fortune, I would say she already knows."

"What?" I straightened, frowning across the gym.

"She was hawk-eyed over you both the morning we left New York. I could hear her mind working as she studied your every move while we ate brunch. She might have been distracted the night before, but sleep had returned her mind to its usual observant sharpness."

"But she hasn't said anything to you? At all?" I doubled-checked.

"No. She likes to figure shit out in her brain before making a plan of action. Our whirlwind romance and fast marriage was definitely out of the ordinary for her, but usually she's very calculated in her thought process.

"Lately," Dad continued, "she's been self-reflecting. Figuring out the rest of her life and what it looks like—who she is—outside the office. She's changing and definitely for the best. Yesterday, we were on the beach and passed two gay couples walking hand-in-hand, and Jacqueline didn't say a word. She didn't even scowl at them or mutter under her breath like she'd have done months ago. I think if you're patient enough, she'll eventually come around."

Patience. Something I fucking struggled with when it came to Preston.

"Did she tell you about the conversation she had with Preston on Friday?" I asked.

"I was in another room with the doors open between us and heard every word since she had him on speaker."

I shook my head, surprised by all Preston had told me. "I never expected her to get her head out of her ass and apologize for being a shitty mom."

"Like I said, she's doing a lot of reflection practices. Journaling. Recognizing her faults and admitting to them. That's the first step toward change, Drake. *That's* why I'm telling you to hang in there."

What else could I do?

The selfish part of me didn't want to wait to claim Preston publicly, but doing so might still cause waves when he and Jacqueline were rebuilding a relationship torn apart by hurt and bitterness.

Love came with the greatest of emotions yet the worst pain a man could ever experience.

Worth the risk, Dad had said.

I chose to believe him.

"Love you, Dad," I rasped.

"Love you too, little buddy."

Chapter 29

Preston

Drake stood outside my door on Wednesday night, his focus on the peephole I stared through.

My stomach fluttered, and I told myself not to answer, but my hand didn't listen. It'd been much too long since I'd seen Drake, and I couldn't help myself.

"Hey," he greeted me, his smile a little hesitant as I swung the door inward. "Can I come in?"

At least he didn't barrel inside like he'd done last time he'd shown up at my condo.

I stepped back, all of my senses going on high alert as he moved past me. God, he smelled good. Like soap, dryer sheets, and the love of my life. A shiver licked down my spine, and I swallowed hard, locking us in together.

Not exactly close proximity compared to what we'd experienced in that elevator but enough my skin tingled from his nearness.

I stayed close by the door, keeping distance between us. Unsure as to why he'd shown up unannounced and unin-vited, I gave him a quick once-over. He'd styled his hair, wore a blue T-shirt the same color as his bright eyes and dark jeans that hugged his thick thighs to perfection.

My mouth watered, and I tore my focus off his lower half for his face.

He grinned at me.

Shit. My cheeks heated over being caught salivating. "B-Beer?" I offered, my voice husky with nerves and want.

"Need you ask?"

Huffing a shaky laugh, I forced myself to turn away from desire for the kitchen, well aware of Drake following me. Every hair on my body reached for him, I swear.

"To what do I owe the pleasure?" I managed a measured cadence while popping the caps off two bottles of Sam Adams.

"Missed you." Drake's confession wasn't filled with heat or insinuation.

Missed you more, I wanted to say but didn't. I handed over his drink, shivering when his fingers brushed against mine. My groin had roused at the sight of him outside my door. His touch and the fact I hadn't jerked off in a couple of days only threatened to tent my sleep pants I'd put on after showering.

"Want to sit?" I suggested, needing to do so and hide what he did to me before he got any ideas.

Drake headed to the living room, allowing me a moment of privacy to adjust myself before following on his heels. He settled in the middle of the couch, but I claimed my recliner before he could tell me to sit beside him where I would end up tucked against his hard warmth, the space between us completely wiped out exactly like I yearned for it to be.

I sustained eye contact for all of five seconds before studying my cold bottle of beer, the potency of his draw too overwhelming.

"Have you spoken to Jacqueline since Friday?"

"No." I shook my head. "I expected her to call today, but she hasn't yet. I guess she and Devlin are having too much fun in Greece."

Drake crossed an ankle over his opposite knee, one arm along the back of the couch. Why was he so damn hot when he sprawled out with such confidence? I wanted to swoon along with the heart eyes I couldn't help but cast his way.

"I had an interesting little talk with my dad on Sunday morning."

I lifted my focus off how tightly his shirt pulled over his bulging bicep and shoulder. "Yeah?"

"Mmm." Drake drank from his bottle, his Adam's apple bobbing and making me want to lick his neck. "You're drooling," he said with a chuckle.

I glowered and tossed a throw pillow at him. He batted it out of the air to the floor, still laughing at me. "Shut up," I muttered.

"I love how much you want me, baby."

Heat flushed through me. "Tell me about the phone conversation," I demanded even though I would rather have him cross the living room to ravish me.

Jacqueline had explained to me how retirement had changed her. I'd heard that truth in her voice and the words of apology she'd offered me. But an outside perspective Drake told me his dad had given him only strengthened my hope that she and I were on the right course.

I swallowed hard, my eyes welling over the fact that she was probably already aware of my sexuality and how much Drake meant to me. A week earlier, fear would have swamped me at her finding out I was in love with my step-brother, but a strange sense of peace swam through my blood.

"Y-You really believe she knows?" I whispered at the tear-hazed vision of Drake across from me.

"She's more observant than my dad, who didn't doubt our connection since we moved to New York, so what do you think?"

I blew out a breath, turning my beer I hadn't yet sipped from in my hands. He had a point. "And you really believe she'll accept our being together?"

Drake smiled. "If she was smart, she would."

Jacqueline was one of the most intelligent women I'd ever met. "Why do you say that?"

"Because if she loves you like she's finally realizing, she'll want what's best for you—a man who will love you until your last breath. Someone who will stand by your side no matter what."

I swallowed hard. No one would ever take care of me like Drake did. No one understood or had ever been patient with me like him.

"You're everything I've ever wanted," Drake stated, leaning forward and staring at me intently. I couldn't have torn my eyes off his if I'd tried. "You fulfill my instincts to protect and nurture. I get off on affection—not just sex—and if you weren't super needy touch-wise, that part of me would feel robbed. You're my safe place, Preston, and I don't want to be anywhere other than beside you."

My throat swelled shut at his adamant declaration.

Boston had always been his home, and he would give it up.

For me.

Hands suddenly shaking, I set my beer on the end table and wiped my palms on my thighs.

What the hell was wrong with me that I wasn't sprinting down that path that led to our spending the rest of our lives together? The picket fence. The kids we would love unconditionally no matter what.

"You're perfect for me," I whispered the truth in my heart.

"And I love you with every part of my being," Drake said. "Every atom, cell, and strand of my DNA is yours, Preston. You fucking own me, heart and soul."

The swoon-worthy statement poured from his beautiful lips better than any romance novel hero.

"B-But how? I'm nothing but an emotional, geeky nerd who has trouble articulating what's in his head—unless lust inspires me to spill all my sexual desires."

Rather than snickering or his eyes growing heated, Drake scoffed. "Bullshit. You're the most decent and trustworthy man I've ever met—my dad included. You respect the hell out of people's privacy and show the self-restraint of a goddamn saint. Your modesty and humility are so damn sexy. And trust me. I've had my fair share of guys, and there's no comparison, no emotional intimacy or connection of souls like when I'm with you. I can feel your presence from across the room even if you can't put it into words. And if that isn't evidence of us being two parts of a whole, I don't know what is."

Well, damn.

I worked my throat a few times, overwhelmed by all he'd proclaimed. Drake had given me more than I could have ever dreamed up in my fantasies of a declaration of love. "Do you...think it's selfish to put ourselves above our parents? Because this will tear them apart if you're wrong about Jacqueline."

"Should we hinder our own happiness because of someone else's bitterness and inability to forgive?" Drake shot back but without anger in his tone. "My dad said that love is worth the risk. I have to believe him because I don't want to live without you. Fucking can't."

Twin tears slid down my cheeks as heartache and happiness warred for prominence in my chest.

"Fuck, baby." Drake set aside his empty beer bottle and hopped up, crossing the living room in sure strides. Dropping to his knees in front of me, he clasped my face in his warm hands. "I'm sorry if this is all too much."

"N-No." I blinked the wetness from my eyes, my pulse settling into a steady rhythm at his gentle touch. "It's okay. I mean, we needed this conversation, right?" A smile wobbled to life on my lips.

Drake's gaze dipped to my mouth, and he swallowed hard. "I thought I could be patient, but tell me you love me or order me to leave, Preston," he whispered, dragging his focus back to my eyes. "End this agony in my heart. *Please.*"

The two paths hadn't converged like I'd hoped for, but I couldn't deny the perfect chords of harmony he and I created whenever we came together.

Drake *was* everything I had ever dreamed about, the one I would need if the world crumbled down around us. If I only had five minutes left to live, it wouldn't be Jacqueline or even Nancy I wanted holding me.

It was Drake.

"I love you," I whispered as another tear slid down my cheek. "Always have."

His gaze softened as he swiped the wetness from my face with his thumbs. "Come here, baby."

I leaned forward, surrendering to the rightness of *us* as his lips pressed against mine. We shared a chaste kiss, one full of promise. Forehead against his, I closed my eyes and rested for a quiet moment as contentment settled in my soul.

"You always show me how much you love me," I murmured, pulling back enough I could see his beautiful blue eyes full of emotion I no longer had any wish to run from. "Will you let me do the same for you?"

A slow smirk curled the corner of his lips. "You want to worship my body?"

"Fuck yes," I rushed to answer, breathless with sudden need. "Wannalickeveryinch."

Drake barked a laugh and stood, yanking me up against him.

My breath punched from my lungs at the contact.

"Take me to your bed, Preston." His low voice vibrated against my chest. "Show me how much you love me."

Insides shaking, I clasped his hand and led him toward my bedroom. Wanting to see him, study every dip and valley of the muscle and bone beneath his skin, I flicked the lights on and didn't bother dimming them.

"Strip for me," I demanded, my voice an octave lower from desire.

"Anything for you, baby."

I stood breathless as he slowly unbuttoned his shirt, whimpering a little as he shoved it off his shoulders. Drake Hemmings was a god among men chiseled from the hardest stone. An instrument composed to bring the greatest pleasure. My mouth watered as he made short work of his button and zipper.

"G-Good God," I whispered as he shoved his jeans down those thick thighs. He'd gone commando.

"You're drooling, baby."

I rubbed a hand over my aching cock, and his hard length twitched beneath my gaze. "Can you blame me?" I was breathless with need. "I mean, look at you."

Drake kicked off his shoes and rid himself of his jeans.

He took himself in hand, one slow stroke up to the head causing a bead of pre-cum to well at his slit.

"Fuck," I whispered, starved and staring.

"You gonna get naked with me?"

"Shit." I tore my focus from him and yanked my shirt off overhead with shaking hands.

Drake chuckled as I tripped while trying to free myself from my pants that got caught around my ankles. "Take your time, baby. I'm not going anywhere."

I exhaled slowly, reining in my haste. If I wasn't careful, I was going to shoot my load all over the floor before I even got my hands on Drake. Squeezing the base of my aching cock, I nodded toward the bed.

"On the bed," I rasped. "Face down."

Drake raised an eyebrow but didn't argue.

"God, that ass." I climbed onto the bed behind him, straddled his thighs, and grabbed hold of two handfuls of asscheeks. He flexed, and I chuckled. "Shit, there's nothing to jiggle back here." I kneaded once he relaxed again, smiling as he laughed.

I spread his cheeks, and he quieted instantly. "You wax," I said, surprised by the sight of his hairless, pink hole.

"Like to keep things tidy," he explained while shifting his arms up to slide his hands beneath my pillow.

I'd noted his trimmed pubes, which I appreciated, but hadn't expected this. "Can I taste you?" I whispered, my pulse thrumming and cock bucking at the thought of rimming a man for the first time.

"Preston, you can do whatever the fuck you want to me. My body is yours, baby."

Best. Declaration. Ever.

Jitters erupted in my stomach, making me shaky.

I leaned down and inhaled deeply, filling my lungs with

the scent of soap and Drake's natural musk. My mouth watered. "Smell so good."

Drake groaned and lifted his hips, offering himself for the taking.

I nosed up through his crack, swiping my tongue over his pucker.

"Jesus." Drake cursed a few more times as I licked and probed. "Put it in me, baby."

My abs contracted in a rush of lust, and I pushed against his hole. He bore down, and my tongue slid into tight heat.

"Ah, fuck, yeah."

I grasped his cheeks, keeping him open so I could reach deeper. "Fuck," I breathed when I backed away, his hole winking at me. "So fucking hot." I grazed my thumb over the puckered flesh, but rather than fingering him, I hauled off and slapped his relaxed ass cheek.

"Fuck!" He jolted.

Snickering, I rubbed up over his globes with both of my hands. "Guess there *is* a little jiggle in these babies."

Drake huffed a laugh, and I ran my hands up alongside his spine, shifting forward so my hard length rested against his crack. "Mmm," he groaned in approval, swiveling his hips to tease my dick.

"Lay still and let me touch you," I muttered. "I'm not ready to shoot off all over your back."

The way he sprawled with his hands beneath the pillow made his lats and shoulder muscles pop.

"Goddamn," I whispered, leaning even farther forward to reach his traps. I focused on mapping out the expanse of his upper body while rutting against his ass.

He groaned as I ran my hands over every inch I could, slowly settling onto my haunches to caress down his sides.

One kiss to the slight hint of red my slap had gifted him, and I slid off his legs. Sighing, I spread my fingers wide over his thighs, amazed by the definition of his hamstrings even at rest.

"Your body is exquisite, Drake." I scooted toward the end of my bed and enjoyed the tickle of his wiry hair over my palms as I smoothed over his amazing calf muscles toward his ankle.

"Gonna suck on my toes, baby?"

I snorted. "Not really my kink, but they're definitely as cute as the rest of you."

"Cute." He huffed.

I wiggled his pinkie before giving it a little kiss and nibble since it was a part of Drake—and I loved every inch of him. "Flip over."

Drake obeyed, hands behind his head, eyes darkened by lust, his dick reaching for his belly button.

I drank my fill, studying the contours of his body, the ripple of muscles I could never gain no matter how many hours I spent at the gym. A sigh heaved my chest, and I started my worship of his front, which was just as gorgeous as his backside—better even, because I had access to the cock I wanted to finally ride.

Chapter 30

Drake

I had no intentions of sex when I'd come to Preston's, not even the hope of him finally admitting to how he truly felt for me. But I wasn't about to complain where our conversation had led, the answer he'd given me, and the words I'd been waiting to hear.

He'd made my day—my fucking year, happiness bursting through every cell in my body.

And goddamn, was it hard to lay still while he studied and examined me with his elegant fingers, soft lips, and slick tongue. He licked up the back of my dick but only offered that single tease of where I wanted him most.

"Your body is sick," he whispered, fingertips then lips worshiping my abs. "Who the hell has an actual eight pack?" He hadn't asked me a question, so I stayed quiet, my ego inflated and a grin on my face.

"And these pecs." Preston grabbed hold of them squeezing. "Jesus—they're like rocks."

I flexed on instinct, and Preston cursed again, his cock bucking against mine. Lifting my hips ground us together, and he whimpered, running his hands up my neck to my hair.

Our eyes finally met, and the lust and longing between us made breathing difficult. I clutched at the back of my head to keep from reaching for him and rolling so he lay trapped beneath me.

He'd wanted to memorize my body, and with how he'd finally gifted me his heart and trusted me with his love, I was determined to give him control for however long he wished.

But fuck, staying still was torture with him studying my face, mapping my eyebrows then jawline beneath my beard.

"So gorgeous." He shifted down again, tonguing my tight nipples. His nose nuzzled in my armpit. Sighs and soft needy noises leaked from his lips as they trailed over my skin when he finally sprawled fully atop me so we touched from chest to feet.

"Fuck, baby, you're killing me." I groaned, eyes clenched shut as he frotted against my dick. Pre-cum from both of us slickened the glide, and I shifted, restless beneath him. "Preston."

"Can I be on top? Ride you like this?" His request sounded packed with need, his breath hot against my mouth.

"Fuck yeah."

"I have lube in the bedside table."

So goddamned desperate for him, I moved quicker than he could, clasping his hip to keep him right the fuck there while half-rolling toward that drawer. A few toys lay tucked away too, but I only grabbed what we needed.

But we'd sure as fuck be visiting those another day.

Once more on my back, I slapped the bottle into his

hand. "Get me nice and wet then turn around so I can watch you open yourself up for my dick."

"Oh fuck." Preston gulped, the green of his eyes practically gone with lust.

He spun reverse cowboy a bit clumsily, but I didn't laugh. Preston sat on my abs so he could handle my aching cock, and all other thoughts fled. It'd been over three weeks since I'd had him. Countless days since I'd been one with the man who'd claimed my heart.

My dick ached for him. Dripped in anticipation of owning his hole again.

I hissed as he lubed me up, my hips thrusting, seeking friction in his too-light grip.

Freckles spread over his shoulders down to his slender waist. I grabbed hold of his pale ass cheeks and spread him wide, wishing I could feast on him.

Later.

"Shove some lube up this sweet hole, baby," I ordered, thumbing over his pucker. "Nice and deep."

He reached around, three of his fingertips dripping with slickness.

"One at a time," I said, grabbing his wrist to keep him from hurrying a sight I wanted to etch into my memory forever. "And don't rush. Tease the fuck outta me until I'm begging for you to end my misery."

Preston whimpered while pushing his index inside, shuddering when he buried to the knuckle.

"How do you feel?"

"Hot." He swallowed audibly. "Tight."

"Mmm." I watched as he stroked himself, the wet sounds of finger fucking making my dick drool pre-cum. "Can't wait for your hole to be wrapped around my dick, baby. I'm so fucking hard for you."

He worked in a second, and I praised how his pink pucker stretched around his probing fingers.

"So fucking pretty." I tightened my hold on his plump cheeks, trying to spread him wider. "Three."

Preston hissed while pressing the final finger in deep like I'd told him too.

"Just like that—fuck yourself for me. Show me how badly you want my cock up your needy ass."

"D-Drake." His whine coursed satisfaction through me. Loved talking dirty to him.

My balls firmed up, and I couldn't fucking wait any longer. "Turn around, baby. Sit on my dick and make us both come."

Face flushed, Preston shifted around to face me, his fingers wrapping around the base of my dick. I kept my hands lightly atop his thighs, allowing him to control the moment and fulfill whatever fantasy he wanted played out.

Trembling, he lifted onto his knees and rubbed the head of my cock along his crack until I notched slightly.

"Show me your eyes, baby."

Eyelids fluttering open, those beautiful emerald orbs focused on my face as his hands rested on my chest. I couldn't give two fucks the fingers he'd had knuckles deep in his hole smeared lube over my left pec.

"You okay?" I caressed him from his knees to his waist.

"Mmm hmm," he hummed.

"Then take what you want from me."

He bit his lower lip and sank down, stuffing a few inches of my length up his ass.

"Jesus, Preston," I grunted through clenched teeth, my abs flexing in the need to fuck deeper past his clenching ring. "You're so fucking tight."

He whimpered, lifted until his heat only sucked at my frenum, and lowered, accepting a little more.

"Jesus fuck—again."

It required a fourth lift and descent for him to finally rest against my groin, my cock fully buried, encased in wet heat.

Pre-cum leaked down the side of his rigid cock, but I kept my hands on his upper legs, gently soothing him. "You good?"

"More than," he promised, his voice breathless and reedy thin.

"My dick is all yours to ride however the hell you want."

"Y-You're just gonna lay there?"

"Do you want me to take over?"

He sucked on his lower lip but eventually shook his head. "Not yet."

"Then have at it, baby. Fuck your perfect hole on my cock."

Preston let out another one of those sexy whimpers and began moving over me. Up and down, grinding on my dick then shifting his hips forward and back.

"You ever ride a man like this before?"

"Nuh uh," he whispered between pants for air, and fuck *yes*, did my possessive side rage with glee.

I growled, my fingertips digging into his waist.

"Drake," he gasped while shifting his hips in a circle.

"That's it—make yourself feel good on my dick."

Preston eventually found his rhythm, and I'd never seen anything so goddamned beautiful. Flushed, freckled skin glistening with sweat. His cock so damn hard it barely moved away from where it strained up toward his belly when he bounced on me. His balls, all smooth and tight against his base...his taut stomach flashing hints of abs with every contract of his core while dancing on my rigid cock.

And he was so fucking soft.

I glided my fingers over every inch of his skin I could reach, desperate to fuck up into his body rather than letting him drive. "Love touching you, baby. Can't keep my hands off you."

He whined, face tipping toward the ceiling.

"Lean back, hold my thighs."

Preston listened, gasping at the new angle.

"All right, baby?"

"God, yes," he whispered, breathless and sexy as fuck. "Oh, shit. So good."

Those goddamned noises I couldn't get enough of spilled from his parted lips, his heavy panted breaths, the pulse thrumming in his neck—fuck, did I love him.

"I'm gonna come." He gulped, eyes flying wide open as though surprised. "Holy fuck—I'm gonna come like this. Never knew..." Preston slammed down onto me, causing his cock to jerk. Cum erupted like a geyser from his slit, and I grabbed his hips, letting loose to fuck up into his hole. Every stab into his hot ass jolted his body, bouncing his dick and spraying his cum all the fuck over both of us.

"So goddamn sexy," I hissed through gritted teeth, my own balls seizing. "Give it to me, baby. Every goddamn drop you have in you. Jesus, what a load...and your *ass*." I groaned, caught up in the slick heat of him, the beautiful sounds spilling from his lips.

"L-Love. You," he cried out between my attempts to bury deep inside his guts.

Clutching his waist in a bruising grip, I unleashed with a shout, gasping and groaning as my hips stuttered with every spurt of seed I emptied inside him. "Ah, fuck." I convulsed, grabbing hold of his shoulders and yanking him down onto my chest. "Jesus, baby." I clutched him closer, both of us sweaty and cum-covered, our hearts racing as we writhed together, drawing out every last ounce of pleasure from each other.

I could die a happy man.

Chapter 31

Preston

Three fantasies had come to life.

I smiled against Drake's collarbone where my mouth rested. We were a sweat and cum-covered lump of sated limbs, and I couldn't move.

I'd finally gotten to take my time looking at and touching Drake's muscles. It was over a half hour until I'd mapped him out, licked, and kissed every crevice of his body. I would definitely go back for seconds and thirds in the future.

Could *not* get enough of the man.

He'd also let me ride him, and I got to experience fucking myself on his dick like I'd dreamed about doing. Dildos had given me a workout before, but they were nothing compared to real flesh and blood filling me with every move I made atop it.

Leaning on my thighs had allowed for the perfect angle for him to milk my prostate. I'd never been taken to the edge so quickly, my orgasm slamming into me unexpectedly out of nowhere.

Then the spray of my cum erupting hands-free all over the place like live porn...

A shudder ripped through me over that final fantasy, and Drake clutched me closer against his furnace-like heat.

"Okay?" he murmured against my hair, and I sighed, snuggling in closer.

"Yeah."

Drake rubbed up and down my back, touching me nonstop like he'd done while I'd brought us both to climax.

"Love your hands on me," I admitted with a satisfied sigh.

"Mmm." He squeezed my ass and tried to bury his semi deeper into my body. "Love touching you."

A contented smile once more rested on my face, and we lay in silence, sharing space and breath. My heart slowed, beating in harmony with his. The sweat cooled, and still we lay glued together.

Drake's chest rose high, and a heavy exhale relaxed him beneath me. "Never felt so complete, Preston. Ever," he murmured, his voice a low, sexy rumble.

This was right.

What I wanted for the rest of my life.

Neediness welled up inside me, and I dragged my head off his shoulder so I could see him and assure myself I wasn't dreaming.

Sated, sleepy eyes the color of a cloudless sky peered at me. I shifted forward to reach his mouth, causing his soft dick to slide from my body. He groaned, and I whimpered at the sense of loss but pressed my lips to his.

He cradled my face in his calloused palms, gentle and loving as we kissed in a languid fashion. Our tongues caressed, and we tasted each other, no longer in a hurry to devour.

"Love you so fucking much, baby," he murmured.

"Love you more," I whispered back with a smile.

"Not possible."

I laughed, causing his cum to drip from my hole. "Shit—sorry," I muttered, pushing upright to climb off him, but he clasped my thighs, keeping me in place. "I-I'm leaking cum on your stomach."

"Love that too," he declared, a satisfied grin making his eyes twinkle.

"You're a caveman." I flicked his nipple.

"Damn right I am," he stated, palming my sensitive, spent dick.

I hissed as he fondled my messy, flaccid length, his other hand reaching behind me to rub over my slick hole.

"You're so sexy," he murmured, shoving his cum back into my body. "Seeing and feeling the evidence of our coming together makes me want to do it all over again."

"Shower first?" I suggested, the drying cum splotches on some parts of my skin starting to itch.

"Mmm." Drake stroked his fingers into my relaxed hole a few more times then pulled out to swat my ass cheek. "Let's go." He rolled off the bed onto steady feet.

"Jelly legs," I muttered when I tried to stand beside him.

Drake snickered before yanking me up into his arms.

Grinning, I clung to his neck as he carried me bridal style into my bathroom.

He set me in front of the sink. "Bend over and let me see your hole, baby."

Heat rushed to my face, but I did as told, leaning on my forearms and widening my legs when he nudged them.

Drake spread my cheeks. "You're so pink and puffy, baby. Even more pretty from being wrecked by my dick." He rubbed over my pucker with his thumb, tapping the stickiness a few times. "Bear down and push the rest of my cum out."

"Oh God." My eyelids slammed shut, and I rested my forehead against my arms, wishing the floor would swallow me whole.

"Come on, baby," Drake coaxed with that low timbre that always revved my engine. "Give me what I want."

Flooded by embarrassment, I did as told, expelling the rest of his load.

"There it is. Fuck, that's hot." He used his thumb to gather up the cum leaking over my taint and pushed it into my body again. "Jesus, Preston. You're so fucking perfect."

Two kisses, one to each ass cheek, and Drake pulled me upright against his chest. He pressed his lips to my temple. "I'm going to wash you up, tuck you into bed, and spoon the hell out of you."

"Okay," I murmured, thoroughly on board with being taken care of.

I shivered at the loss of his heat along my back when he made for the shower.

My eyes drank him in as he bent slightly to turn on the water.

That. Ass.

"You're staring," he stated without looking at me.

I huffed. "Of course I am. Your backside is so damn fine."

"Want my ass?" He attempted to twerk his cheeks while glancing over his shoulder at me, but those two lumps of muscle really didn't move much.

I snorted. "Touch, bite, and lick, yes. Fuck? Not unless you can't live without it."

"I can do without," Drake said, turning toward me once more, studying my face.

"Sounds like a perfect match to me."

His blue eyes lit with the kind of happiness that made my chest ache. "Come on, baby." He grasped my hand and led me into the hot spray. "It's my turn to worship you."

We spooned beneath my blankets, Drake's arms caging me against his chest, one of his hairy legs shoved between mine. Our hands clasped atop my sternum, Drake's thumb in constant motion stroking over my skin.

Now that the lust had been sated, my mind wandered to the discussion we'd had and my decision to be with him.

"I think we should tell our parents we're together before letting anyone else know just in case word gets around," I said.

"Want to wait until they're home, or would you rather do it over the phone so it's over with? Any confrontation will be more easily shut down that way if needed."

I really wasn't sure how Jacqueline was going to react to the news I was not only gay but dating my stepbrother, but part of me leaned toward a quieter conversation rather than an explosion. At least, her attitude the previous few weeks suggested I might get a little lucky.

"I want to talk to her in person," I finally settled on, "but that means our relationship stays behind closed doors for another two-plus months since I trust Jacqueline's ability to find out things secondhand. Are you okay hiding it from your friends? Keeping your hands to yourself if we go out in public?"

"I can date you here at home since I can't stop myself from touching you." At least he didn't sound the least bit bothered by my asking him to stay closeted up with me for that length of time.

Needing to see him, I rolled over.

He cuddled me close against his chest, smoothing my hair off my forehead, nothing but contentment in his eyes.

"You're sure?"

"I thought I could wait for you forever but couldn't, which is why I pushed for an answer tonight. But on this? As long as I have access to you, your smile, your laughter, and your kisses, I'm fine holding off on telling anyone else. But like I said, I'm pretty sure our parents already know."

I sighed and pressed my cheek against his chest, snuggling into my favorite spot in the whole wide world.

My cell sounded from my bedside table, shooting adrenaline into my bloodstream, since it could only be one person. Jacqueline had never been a day late in calling me, but she'd been surprising me with change since retiring.

"If that ringtone reminded me of horror and death, I'd think Jacqueline knew we were talking about her," Drake joked, but I didn't laugh.

"I, uh, switched it to default after our talk last Friday." I started to shift away, but Drake kept me close.

"Ignore it for tonight. It's late."

Tension riddled my body, but the cell went quiet. I exhaled loudly but didn't bother relaxing against Drake.

It went off again as expected.

"She won't stop until I pick up."

"Fuck," he muttered the word in my head and loosened his hold on me as I moved from his warmth.

Rolling to my opposite side, I reached for my cell.

"Is it her?" Drake asked when I didn't answer right away.

"No," I said, surprised. "It's a New York area code though."

The phone went silent, and I moved to set it back down.

It rang a third time.

"Shit." I swiped to answer. "Hello?"

"Is this Preston Casswell?" A voice I didn't recognize asked, all official and calm.

Regardless of his steady tone, hairs raised on my nape, and I sat up, swinging my legs off the edge of the bed.

"Yes?" I suggested even though I no longer considered myself as such. I'd been a Gibbons for over two years. My heart beat in my throat, the rush of adrenaline-laced blood whooshing in my ears.

"Who is it?" Drake rolled closer, placing his hand on my back, but for the first time, his touch didn't keep me grounded.

I didn't believe in premonitions or even a sixth sense, but suddenly, I *knew*.

I caught the man's name and that he claimed to be one of Jacqueline's lawyers. The rest of his words echoed in my head until I made sense of them.

Your mother and her husband Devlin were killed in a helicopter crash yesterday afternoon.

My lungs emptied with a rush, and I sagged, reality sweeping over me like a tidal wave—yanking me under.

"Preston!" Drake grabbed the cell from my falling hand. "What the fuck—who the hell is this?" he barked, but I blocked out his voice, curling into a fetal position on the edge of the bed, my eyes dry as the undertow dragged me into a raging sea.

Chapter 32

Drake

One week after the most horrific news delivered to us over a goddamned cell line by Jacqueline's lawyer, and my throat *still* ached.

I'd lost my father. My best fucking friend. The man I'd looked up to and had worshiped as a kid.

Gone without a goodbye, one last hug, or a word of thanks for all he'd done for me. I managed to go through the motions, even hitting the gym to release some of my anger and aggression, but Preston didn't fare as well.

He'd escaped into his mind, shutting me out immediately after the call. I couldn't rouse him to converse with more than grunts or nods. The worst part? Preston didn't cry. Didn't lean into me when I pulled him in my arms, didn't let go of the emotions he bottled up inside him. For once, I couldn't read his face, and his eyes were dim and empty.

I tried to be patient while he worked through the tragic grief we'd been slammed with, and it fucking hurt like hell that I couldn't comfort him.

Dad didn't have a lawyer or a will as far as I was aware, but I didn't care about anything he'd left behind.

I just wanted him back.

Twice, I broke down in Preston's bathroom, choking on sobs to keep silent. I'd moved into his condo without a discussion, knowing he would eventually need me, but I hadn't realized how much *I* needed *him*. The distance he put between us even though I stayed close by his side lanced pain through my chest twenty-four-seven atop my grief.

I was powerless, a sense of hopelessness shrouding me with dark heaviness that barely allowed me to sleep at night.

Jacqueline's lawyers contacted us—Mr. Agosti and Mr. Barone of Agosti & Associates—then travelled to Boston at my request, since Preston refused to go anywhere. They arrived looking like mob bosses, the fine cuts of their suits, polished dress shoes, and expensive watches reminding me of the Casswell name and its value. It had been Mr. Agosti himself who had dropped the bomb of death on us the night Preston had finally admitted to loving me.

Talk about a goddamned upheaval of emotions from one extreme to the other.

The four of us sat at the dining room table in strained stillness regardless of Mr. Agosti beginning to explain Jacqueline's final wishes. I heard every word he said but focused more on the wan, wilted man on the chair close to mine and what the reading of Jacqueline's will would do to him.

Escape his ears completely?

Cause a rent in the wall he'd shoved his emotions behind?

I held his limp hand, praying for the latter, some sign that my lover would return to me.

All legal paperwork over the sale of Casswell Global had been completed. Mr. Agosti assured Preston there would be no issue with the settling of her estate, but he didn't speak or even seem to care about how Preston stared at the edge of the table in front of him.

Jacqueline had owned six properties I hadn't known about that were scattered around the globe, the private jet they'd been using to travel the world, millions in stock and bonds, and life insurance, never mind her offshore accounts and personal property, most notably artwork, antiques, and jewelry.

Preston was already a millionaire on his own, but he was about to become one of the richest men on the face of the earth.

In sweats but at least freshly showered, he remained unmoving. I rubbed my thumb over the back of his hand atop my lap, listening to the lawyer across from us drone on about Jacqueline's assets I could not give two shits about.

He mentioned Dad who'd been set to receive a third of the estate if she passed first, but with him gone too, the entire Casswell fortune would now be split in two.

Half to Preston, her only son.

The other half to...me.

Preston didn't flinch at the unexpected news, but I jerked my focus off his pale fingers to gawk at the lawyer. "*What* did you say?"

"Half of Jacqueline Casswell's fortune now belongs to you, Mr. Hemmings," Mr. Agosti repeated.

"That's not right." I shook my head. "There's got to be a mistake. I'm not—wasn't ever adopted. I'm not—wasn't—her son in any way."

"I assure you, Mr. Hemmings, she was very clear on her wishes when we met with her last weekend."

I stared at the gray haired man as he shuffled through the paperwork in front of him. "Last...*when* did you say?"

"She flew Mr. Barone and I to Greece just this past Sunday and made amendments to her will. Odd timing with her death on the heels of the changes, but they won't be called into question as the helicopter crash has already been declared an accident by the Greek authorities."

Fucking hell.

Scrubbing a hand over my face, I glanced at Preston. He still stared, unmoving, clearly not caring I'd somehow maybe stolen half his inheritance. "I don't want it," I claimed, my voice shaky. "Everything should go to Preston."

"Jacqueline Casswell thought otherwise, and that's all that matters when it comes to her legal will," Mr. Agosti stated firmly, not leaving room for me to argue.

Curses slid through my mind. I didn't desire anything from her.

Not a goddamned thing except for her son to come back to me.

"Mr. Barone and I were still in Greece at the time of their deaths, so as Ms. Casswell's estate planner and executor, Mr. Barone brought their more personal items to the States." He motioned toward the box Mr. Barone had left in the entryway. "Their bodies have been cremated as requested in her will, and I promise we'll make sure their remains are home soon."

Jesus Christ, what a mess.

"We will be transferring ownership of her assets, settling both U.S. and overseas accounts, and tying up other loose ends in the coming weeks," Mr. Barone said, his voice softer than his partner's. "If you have any questions about the process, please don't hesitate to call either me or Mr. Agosti."

I accepted the card he held out, nodding, my thoughts crowded.

Both men stood.

"I changed my name." My love spoke for the first time in days, his voice ragged. "I'm a Gibbons now."

"You are still Jacqueline's son," Mr. Agosti said, less abrupt than he'd been while reading her will. "The surname does not matter."

A heavy exhale sank Preston deeper into his chair.

I kissed his temple and stood, knowing he wouldn't be seeing the lawyers out. I thanked the two men and sent them on their way before returning to the dining room.

Needing to be comfortable and closer to Preston, I gathered him up in my arms and held onto his limp form while stumbling into the living room.

I settled onto the couch, tucking Preston's face against me where he used to feel comforted. "I'm so fucking sorry, Preston. I'll give it all to you. It's not mine—I don't want anything from her."

He whispered something, but I couldn't make out the words.

"What did you say, baby?" I soothed a hand over his hair and down his back, wishing I could coax *everything* from his lips and heart.

"It's my fault." The first hints of grief sounded in his quiet declaration.

The fuck?

I frowned, pulling Preston from my chest so I could see his face.

Pale and lower lip trembling, he wouldn't meet my gaze.

"Give me your eyes," I begged.

He lifted emerald orbs glowing from unshed tears—fucking finally.

My breath left in a rush as I grasped his face in my hands. "Why would you think that, Preston? It was an accident. The Greek authorities determined it was."

Preston swallowed hard, the tears spilling over. "I—I wished her a-away. L-Lots of t-times." He bit on his lower lip to keep a sob from escaping.

"Baby." Throat tight, I pulled him back against me, squeezed the life out of him. "No—it's not your fault, Preston."

"I hadn't r-really meant it," he cried, clutching at my shirt and curling in on himself atop my lap.

Goddamnit.

I stared at the ceiling as tears welled in my eyes. "You're not responsible in any way for their deaths," I managed to croak the words while wishing I could rip away the guilt he admitted to so he wouldn't have to suffer.

"I'm s-so sorry." Preston shuddered and sobbed.

"You have nothing to apologize for." I swallowed against the lump in my throat, but it wouldn't ease.

"She t-took your d-dad with her!" He fully broke down as though deeply ashamed, the guttural cries spilling from his lips tearing my heart in two.

"It was meant to be. You had nothing to do with it, Preston," I whispered and allowed my grief to flow alongside his.

We sat and cried together, the walls finally down where we could find solace in each other. I breathed in the scent of vanilla as my tears dripped onto Preston's hair. His fingers tangled in my shirt, holding on for all he was worth. And I clutched him tight, touching him gently, assuring him with my hands that I didn't blame him for my father's death.

Eventually, the emotions spent themselves, and silence settled over us.

Exhaustion clung to me, every part of my body aching from grief.

I rubbed Preston's back in a soothing gesture, recognizing a sense of thankfulness as well. While I hated to have lost my dad, I was truly glad he'd gone with Jacqueline, so they could be together in whatever afterlife there was.

Fuck knew I wouldn't be able to survive without my other half beside me.

Chapter 33

Preston

It had taken a few days, but we finally went through the box the lawyers had brought back with them from Greece. Devlin's old watch wrapped around Drake's left wrist, and his and Jacqueline's wedding bands hung on a chain around his neck. I hadn't wanted to keep anything of hers, nor did I untie the leather strip that held my mother's journal closed.

I had no clue what I would find written on the cream pages—feared it, even.

But after two meetings with a grief counselor with Drake by my side, I decided I needed to. In typical fashion, I chose to wait for privacy so I could process on my own whatever emotions her written words roused. Drake finally knew everything inside my head and heart, and although I'd come to the realization that I could no longer hide from him, I wanted to be alone with my memories of Jacqueline.

Drake left for the gym, his way of dealing with and working through his own emotions, and I curled up in the corner of my couch, the journal in my shaking hands.

"I've got this," I murmured to myself while struggling to

untie the strap.

The first entry was dated the day they'd left for their tour around the world, and without giving myself another second to chicken out, I dove in.

Devlin suggested I give journaling a try since I have extra time on my hands. It's a good way to reflect over my life now that I'm retired. And while I'm not exactly keen on putting my innermost thoughts where anyone can read them, I'm going to trust my dear husband, as he's never once let me down in the thirteen years that we've been together.

So, to start, I'm willing to admit to myself that there are things in my life I have put aside for far too long. But I'll begin with the incident that planted the seed of change in my heart that made me agree to this writing journey.

She explained the fear and anxiety she'd experienced when I'd been stuck in the elevator with Drake for four hours. Although she knew I would be okay because I had my step-brother with me, who'd always looked out for me, she had been hit with the truth that a sudden turn of events could take loved ones from her life.

That night, she'd been reminded of the child she'd carried, the first time hearing my heartbeat, then the flutterings of movement in her abdomen. She remembered the joy after giving birth but had then suffered from terrible postpartum. Casswell Global had to take a backseat, and she admitted to feeling resentment for the toddler who cried incessantly and followed her around the penthouse, not allowing her a moment of peace.

While I couldn't remember doing what she'd penned on

paper, after being faced with potentially losing her son, she wondered if two-year-old me had only wanted to be seen. Heard. Held and assured of her love she'd been much too busy to give.

Same as her parents had been when dealing with her as a child.

My eyes leaked tears onto the carefully inked pages, but I continued to turn them one after the other, reading over my mother's self-reflection that deepened with every day while on vacation.

Jacqueline wrote that she and Devlin had talked for hours, him coaxing her to share her emotions, something she'd never been good at. They'd watched videos together and read articles about self-reflection, being vulnerable with others, and narcissism, which she admitted to herself she tended toward, as had her father.

My heart broke for Jacqueline's bold descriptions of her own childhood trauma, some of which she had told me over the phone. She promised herself that once she and Devlin returned to the States, she was going to find the best thera-pist in New York and work through her issues so she could be a better mother and hopefully someday grandmother.

She told the story of a gay couple sitting beside them at a restaurant in Madrid the Thursday evening before that phone call that had changed the course of our relationship. Candlelight and soft live music in the background had created a beautiful setting. The gentleman seated had smiled like the sun lit his face, agreeing to marry the one on bended knee beside him.

Rather than focusing on the bitterness of negative memories their engagement roused, Jacqueline had found herself curious. She'd studied the way they hugged and kissed immediately afterward as others in the dining area politely clapped and offered heartfelt congratulations. The two men had spoken to one another, heads together, their words too quiet to hear, but the love in their eyes had struck her deeply.

She recognized the emotions they shared, for she and Devlin experienced the same toward each other. Her heart still continued to beat, she'd claimed, for the man who'd been faithful and loving regardless of how often she lost her cool or lashed out with hurtful words. Devlin had been the second best thing in her life after me, she'd written, and seeing those two men agreeing to commit to each other changed something inside her.

It also brought back a memory from the night she'd been too caught up in her own head to recognize what she had been seeing.

She explained how Drake had hovered over me once we'd been freed from the elevator. His protective nature wasn't new to her, but she realized in that moment while the gay couple got lost in their own little world that the way Drake had looked at me had revealed his heart. Then she recalled his steady gaze on me during brunch, as sure and potent as Devlin's on her. The small touches of reassurance so much like his father's. How Drake had stepped close to me like her husband would whenever he felt the urge to offer affection and comfort.

Jacqueline had come to a conclusion.

The young boy who looked after Preston when they were children has become a man, one who is obviously and help-lessly in love with my son.

And Preston...

· · ·

Her writing trailed off mid-page as though she'd been too troubled to continue. That entry had been dated the Friday morning she had called me and we'd had our first ever heart-to-heart conversation.

I quickly flipped to the next page, my pulse kicking up a bit faster, needy to read her thoughts concerning me—what she'd said about the phone call.

She'd written a new entry later that night.

After some serious soul-searching, I called Preston earlier today and started the discussion by finally apologizing, hoping to open the lines of communication between us. For once, I didn't make excuses for my behavior or blame him for my absence when he was a child. I simply owned up to the fact I had chosen the family business over the innocent little boy who had needed his mother's love. My greatest regret in life is causing him similar trauma to the kind I experienced with my parents.

I hinted at Drake's love for him, but Preston chose to keep his own thoughts close to his heart. My son learned evasion from the best of them, something I'm no longer as proud of as I used to be.

My curiosity was not sated, but perhaps someday he will trust me with his truth.

He mentioned his father, and it felt like Preston tested me to see how much I've truly changed and if I would be open to discussing his growing feelings for Drake.

While I don't understand Nancy's gender and still can't wrap my head around having a male body and claiming to be female, I've realized that I have a lot to learn about sexuality. I'm finally willing to listen and learn. I also need to do better in my thinking and responses in regards to the LGBTQ community.

Preston reminded me of the love I've found that wouldn't have come to fruition had Nancy stayed with us. He then went on to verbally slap my face by offering me forgiveness, regardless of the fact I had hurt him in a similar fashion as Nancy had to me.

For the first time in my life, I broke down in front of my son, trusting him with my emotions, and he said he was willing to move past the hurt for the sake of our relationship. A gift I don't deserve and will never throw away.

The longer I consider when I saw Drake and Preston together as adults, the more I cannot deny the sense of a deeper connection than friendship between them.

I've yet to figure out how I feel about my son perhaps being gay and in love with another man, but all I want is for Preston to finally be happy, something I fear he hasn't experienced due to my expectations. I long to always see a real, uninhibited smile on his face I've seen hints of when he steals glances at my husband's son.

Drake is a younger version of his father, so I can trust him with Preston's fragile heart. I also know he will draw my son out of the shell he hides his more tender emotions behind as Devlin has done with me.

Only once before have I made a rash decision, and it gifted me the kind of love read about in romance novels. Trusting my instincts that led to my happiness once again, I called my lawyer in New York. I'm flying him and his associate to Greece tomorrow to ensure those I care about are always taken care of.

Yes, this is more a matter of the heart than a business transaction, but the only legacy I leave behind that is important is for my child to be provided for—same as the two men who have become his family and I can trust to care for him long after I'm gone.

A few more pages remained, but I paused to gather my thoughts.

Jacqueline had been hinting that morning over the phone, giving me the opportunity to share my feelings for Drake, but fear had kept me from being candid with her as she'd done with me.

Yet another regret to live with.

She would have been fine with my love for Drake, I had no doubt.

Tears threatened, and I closed my eyes, imagining Jacqueline sat with me.

"I've accepted it's truly not my fault that you're gone," I whispered into the stillness, my heart aching, "but guilt is hard to let go. I should have been open with you and given you the words you'd wanted to hear that morning. There's no changing the past, Drake told me just yesterday, only working through the things we face and moving forward. I promise to become the best version of myself as possible." I had to swallow to keep from sobbing. "And when the time comes—because it *will*—I'll make sure my ch-children will know about their g-grandmother and how much you would have adored them."

A low keening sound rose in my chest, and rather than fighting the tears or attempting to ignore the emotion inside me, I gave myself permission to grieve all I had lost and the precious truths I'd found.

Jacqueline—my mom—had loved me and had trusted Drake with my heart.

I hoped wherever she had gone that she rested in the knowledge her son had found the same connection she had shared with Devlin.

We held a celebration of life three weeks later in Manhattan in The Bloomberg's main ballroom.

I would have preferred to get the event over with earlier, but customs held up my mom and Devlin's ashes arrival in New York. Guilt continued to whisper in the back of my mind some days, but with Drake's constant assurance and the therapist we'd begun seeing together, I'd learned how to step forward every single day toward a future I hadn't ever considered.

Jacqueline had already planned the entire affair with her estate manager, Mr. Barone, and for the first time, I was beyond thrilled that she had loved control so much that she took care of everything long before her passing.

I was now a billionaire with a couple of houses scattered around the globe. So was Drake, much to his annoyance. We had both donated millions to charity, supporting various LGBTQ groups and a few politicians devoted to equal rights.

I'd given Nancy and Michael a gift that would allow them to purchase the farm they wanted to buy up in Vermont and then some. My other mom had also been invited to the celebration of life, but that had been my doing rather than Jacqueline's, since there were no last wishes banning Nancy and her husband from attending.

Drake and I had dinner with them the evening before at their house in Queens, a quiet time of tears and hugs.

And now I'm about to face Jacqueline's society—I've got this, I told myself while following Drake onto The Bloomberg's elevator.

There was no sudden jolt during our ride to the ground

floor, no four hours of perfection found prior to our last goodbye to my mother and Devlin. Drake held me from behind, his arms wrapped around me, cheek resting against my temple as the silent metal box around us rushed downward.

Jacqueline's final journal entry had been written the day before the helicopter crash, her words unexpected and ones I'd memorized due to the healing balms they had settled over me like a soft blanket.

If Drake owns Preston's heart as I believe he does, then I will be happy for them both. My son will not find a better partner, one who will love him as his father does me. And in the event my suspicions about their already being together is wrong, when I return home, I will push the two of them into recognizing and accepting what is right in front of their blind eyes —a chance at a happily ever after.

Her words echoed in my head, once more tightening my throat. *It's already been found, Mom.*

"Okay?" Drake checked in with me, his murmured word as warm on my ear as the contentment in my heart.

I searched my feelings, slightly anxious of having to people for a couple of hours, mainly with Mom's friends and old colleagues who would be in attendance. "I'll be fine as long as you stay beside me."

"I'll stick like glue, baby." Drake pressed his lips to my hair as the elevator slowed.

"I'm also introducing you to everyone as my boyfriend."

Drake chuckled and squeezed me tight. "Coming out loud and proud—fucking love it, baby. Love *you*."

As expected, dozens of people interested in brushing elbows with the last living Casswell flocked to me, their feigned empathetic smiles and empty condolences annoying. A few eyes blinked at hearing me call Drake my boyfriend, most of them knowing he'd been my stepbrother.

The stutters and gaping mouths amused me more than anything.

Regardless of what they thought of my sexuality, I still received countless invitations to dinners, parties, upcoming fundraisers, and similar events.

I also graciously declined each and every one.

Yes, I was openly gay, but I was also rich as fuck, and plenty in the upper crust would set aside their bigotry if it meant staying in my good graces. But I had zero interest in lining people's pockets if it wasn't for the good of others, mainly those who didn't have the same opportunities of the mostly straight, white snobs in attendance.

Nancy and Michael arrived a little late, and I had to bite my tongue over the sneers and sniffs sent her way. I hugged them both tight, growing teary-eyed yet again when Nancy did. She held my hand, keeping me close.

When the crew from Elite entered the ballroom a short time later, I insisted Drake go greet those who had come down from Boston to offer their support.

I recognized a few from EEMM's website, two of whom I was...intimately acquainted with.

Nerves lit in my guts, but I gave my focus to Nancy. Eventually, I would have to face both Mason and Kellen, and my palms sweated and heart lost its rhythmic pattern at the thought.

But how my possessive boyfriend behaved would be interesting to say the least.

Chapter 34

Drake

I'd told Sean about the celebration of life when he and I had met for beers a couple weeks earlier, not expecting him to bring so many of my old co-workers along with him, but fuck did I feel a sense of coming home when my people walked into the ballroom.

Leaving Preston in good hands, I hurried to the group who'd arrived in a single party. Sean and Matteo led the way, both dressed in dark suits and ties. We hugged hard, hands clasping backs in bro hugs. Micah hadn't been able to leave his pregnant wife, not that I'd expected him to. Mason and Jasper then Kellen and JJ followed. It was the first I'd been around the two men *my boyfriend* had booked with since he and I had gotten together.

A sense of strangeness twisted my guts, definitely that *mine* feeling that made me want to hover over Preston non-fucking-stop, but these men were my friends and had been for years. Clients had only ever been a business transaction to all of us, and the two who'd pleased my man once upon a time were madly in love and happily tied to their better halves.

Still, I greeted Mason, not sure if he was aware of who Preston was or not.

"How are you, Drake?" he asked, his hazel eyes showing genuine concern.

"Hanging in there, thanks."

"And Preston?"

I cocked an eyebrow, and the hint of a flush rose to his cheeks above his gray whiskers. Guess he knew. "Better every day."

"Glad to hear it," Mason said, entwining his fingers with his husband Jasper, who stood close beside him.

"Thanks for making the trip, Jasper," I said holding out my hand.

"Of course," he said, clasping with a firm grip. "I'm sorry for your loss."

I nodded and turned toward Kellen.

He grabbed me for a tight squeeze before I could say a word, and I couldn't help but chuckle.

"Get off on a little role-play, do you?" I asked, keeping my voice low, close to his ear.

He huffed a laugh but didn't release his hold on me. "He told you?"

"In a little too detailed a tale," I grumbled, surprised by my lack of jealousy.

"I won't apologize."

"Just doing your job, *right?*"

"Whatever the client wants." Kellen repeated what Sean and Micah had demanded of us often enough. "That kid was so damn hungry for you."

"Still is," I said, clasping Kellen's shoulder when pulling away. Thank fuck those two greetings were behind me. "JJ —thanks for coming," I said, greeting the next in line.

Kellen's man nodded, offering condolences before

placing his hand on Kellen's lower back in a possessive touch, which had me glancing over my shoulder.

Preston stood with Nancy and Michael where I'd left him, engrossed in conversation. With him appearing to be okay for the moment, I turned my focus to my group of friends.

Zack greeted me next, then surprisingly EEMM's secretary BetsyAnne. She hugged me tight, not saying a word, her eyes bright with wetness when we stepped away from each other.

"I appreciate all you coming down here," I said, my voice slightly choked.

Sean clasped my shoulder tight, squeezing. "We'll always have your back. I've said it a dozen times, but I'm so fucking sorry about your dad." He swallowed hard, a muscle ticking in his jaw.

Considering how shitty of a relationship he had with his father and had always envied mine, I expected he felt my pain on a deeper level. Dad had treated him like a second son when we'd lived in Boston.

Blinking away tears, I nodded. "Thanks. Come on," I rasped, motioning toward the bar on the left. "Let me get you all a beer."

Bottles in hand mere moments later, we created a close-knit circle.

Zack was the one to lift his drink in toast. "To the future and prosperity in every way."

"And hopefully fulfilling relationships to those of us who want one," BetsyAnne hastened to add, clinking her bottle to his. "God knows I need to find a good man."

I appreciated the off-topic thought, since I was more than ready to put grief and sadness behind me.

"Don't go getting any ideas," Sean grumbled. "Replacing you guys isn't as easy as you think it is."

"Guess that means you're booked almost every night, huh?" I asked Zack.

A crooked smirk curled one side of his mouth. "Won't complain about the money, but I'm tired as fuck and need a break."

"We just had a new client request you for a five-day getaway vacation in paradise," BetsyAnne said, "so maybe you'll have some downtime to sit on the beach and get another type of D."

A few of us chuckled as Zack perked up. "Seriously?"

"Finished the paperwork last night," Sean said.

"Fuck yeah." Zack grinned and took a long pull of his beer. "I definitely won't have any problems pleasing the client in that setting. Even if he keeps me up every damn night with a soda-can girth dick."

Awareness that Preston approached shifted me toward my right as everyone snickered over Zack's declaration.

My lover glanced around the group hesitantly, sliding his palms down his slacks.

My heart ached, and I reached for him with my free hand, noting Nancy and Michael trailing behind him. "Come here, baby."

Preston slid into my personal space right where he belonged, tucked against my side.

"This is my boyfriend Preston," I got to title him as such for the first time tonight—actually, ever. Pride and elation swelled my chest, and I grinned like a goddamned dork.

Everyone took turns stepping in to greet him with handshakes, Mason's face going a shade redder, Kellen attempting and failing to hold back his smirk.

"Glad to see you got the man of your fantasies," he said, and Preston choked on a laugh.

"Uh...yeah. Um, thanks?" Preston's voice shook, his face pink as he focused on the floor.

Goddamn, was my shy man cute as fuck.

Zack and BetsyAnne were the only two glancing around the circle as though unaware of what was going on. Preferring to turn the topic off my embarrassed other half, I introduced Nancy and her husband, no one batting an eye at me calling her Preston's other mom.

Talk about acceptance and support.

My heart felt a little bit lighter, and while I would never get over the sadness of my dad being gone, his and Jacqueline's passing had offered Preston the freedom to be himself. I would have preferred all of us to be happy together on the earth, but it hadn't been meant to be.

We had other family though, truer friends than most people could hope to find—more loyal than the rest of the crowd supposedly celebrating Jacqueline Casswell and her husband's life.

We were only a half hour into the party she'd planned for herself, and already I could sense Preston's weariness.

Jasper initiating conversation with Nancy shifted focus off me and my love where we stood shoulder to shoulder, fingers entwined in a perfect fit. I could still feel hundreds of eyes on us from those outside our small group, but I didn't give two flying fucks what others thought about us being together. If they didn't like it, they could go choke on a goddamned python dick.

Just not Mason's. He was all heart eyes for his younger husband, who daddied the hell out of his needy ass.

A hint of that possessive jealousy roused in my gut, and

I tugged Preston in front of me so he could lean against my chest.

He sagged with relief as I'd expected, and I wrapped my free arm around his stomach, my beer still in the other.

"You okay, baby?" I asked against his temple as he rested his head on my shoulder.

A stuttered inhale expanded his chest before he sighed. "Is it wrong to be thankful we're free to love each other out in the open like this?" he murmured for my ears alone.

I shrugged, my gaze flitting to the two urns on the dais to our right. We would combine our parents' ashes before burying them in New York, where Jacqueline's heart had belonged. Dad wouldn't wish to be anywhere else but by her side, so I didn't mind his grave being so far away from home.

"I honestly don't know," I said, "but I can't help feeling the same. They enjoyed a fulfilling life the past thirteen years and now won't ever have to be alone in their grief. What more could a couple in love ask for?"

"I'll always regret not telling her about us." Lingering sadness strangled the words he so graciously gifted me.

I squeezed him a little tighter and kissed his temple. "Let's live the rest of our days without hiding who we are— every minute to the fullest like they did."

Preston lay his forearm atop mine and entwined our fingers together against his side. "Together?"

"Always."

The Elite crew ended up at The Bloomberg's bar long after the celebration of life ended. Mr. Barone would see to the urns and plans for the following day when Preston and I would take a limo to the gravesite in uptown Manhattan. It was to be a private affair with only the two of us seeing them into their final resting place.

I, for one, was ready for some privacy.

We said goodbye to everyone at the bar, sharing hugs and warm best wishes all around, and I took the opportunity to rag on Zack a bit about his upcoming client he'd lucked out with in getting a five-day vacation.

"Enjoy yourself, man," I said, once more giving him a bro hug.

"I always do."

I grinned in knowing he held a similar attitude as I had in escorting. Easy dick and ass, great pay, without any drama or hassle.

But I wouldn't trade Preston and the future ahead of us for anything in the world and hoped that Zack would find the same someday. He was a great guy and deserved happiness like I'd found.

Since I had a shit ton of free time ahead of me, he quietly insisted when no one paid us attention that I visit the shelter he volunteered at. Zack had always been quiet about his past, and aside from his telling me he'd grown up in Rhode Island, I didn't know much else.

But his eyes when he talked about the run-down building on its last leg, struggling to make ends meet for the hundreds that came through its doors every year?

Yeah.

That place meant a great deal to him, and I'd promised to check it out. Secretly, I would donate whatever money they required to make sure they continued to provide for those who needed a roof over their heads and food in their bellies.

Preston and I took the elevator up to the sixteenth floor alone after saying our goodbyes, our hands clasped, shoulders pressed tightly together. Silence once more filled the mental box, but we were both talked out. It had been a long six hours between the party then downtime at the bar with our friends, and I was ready to collapse. I couldn't imagine how beat Preston must be.

"Shower?" I asked once I locked ourselves in our suite.

"Yeah, then I want to pass out in your arms."

"Sounds like a good plan to me."

Preston stood still as I undressed him, black Tom Ford suit in a heap where it landed. Stripped to his freckled, pale skin, he watched me as I yanked off my clothes, tossing each item atop his on the bathroom's floor.

He sighed, the appreciation in his gaze swelling my ego and my dick.

"He might be up for it," I said assuring him, "but I'm not. I just want to shower to rid the stench of rich snobs off my skin and fall asleep beside you."

"Thank fuck," he muttered, taking my hand when I held it out.

I led him into the shower and cared for him, making quick work of washing myself afterward.

Less than ten minutes later, we spooned in bed, his warm back pressed to my chest. I hummed in contentment, closing my eyes and breathing in the sweet scent of vanilla and spice.

"Thank you for being my rock," he murmured, already on the verge of sleep.

"Thank you for loving me," I responded, smiling against his damp hair.

"Easily done."

"Same," I whispered and kissed the top of his head.

Preston drifted off within seconds, and I allowed my thoughts to roam in the past.

My first trip into Manhattan, the chaos it had created in my mind regardless of Dad's assurance that everything would be okay, then meeting the young kid who would end up proving Dad's words correct.

I was going to miss the fuck out of my old man, but I had plenty of memories to tide me over until we met again in whatever afterlife there might be.

In the meantime, I would focus on pleasing my lover resting in my arms as we walked the path before us.

I prayed it would be a long and fruitful one, because like Preston, I still had plenty of dreams and fantasies to fulfill.

Epilogue

Two Years Later

The private waiting room pressed in on us, attempting to steal the oxygen from my lungs. For once, Preston was the calm one while I rubbed damp palms down my thighs.

He snickered, and I shot him a glowering frown. "What? It's kind of funny."

"Is not," I muttered, glancing at the door, sick and tired of the delay. It'd been twelve hours already. How much longer could it possibly take?

Preston grabbed my hand and slotted our fingers together, gazing at the ring on my left hand. He fiddled with it a bit, a contented smile on his lips.

A rush of happiness welled up inside me, and I yanked him off the chair he sat in, settling him atop my lap.

Sighing, he snuggled in.

"Better," I grunted, caressing my husband's soft, warm skin to soothe myself.

I'd dreamed endless times about the life we had together —the house with the picket fence and how I'd swept my husband into my arms to carry him over the threshold exactly as Preston had told me he'd always fantasized about.

And now our son was soon to arrive.

My throat went thick at the thought of my dad missing out on meeting his grandson. But some days, I swore I could feel him close by in spirit. An occasional Aerosmith song would tear me up with longing for the old days of being carefree and not having responsibilities, but I wouldn't trade the past for the future ahead of us.

The door pushed inward on silent hinges, and Preston scrambled off my lap at the sight of the nurse holding a bundle swaddled in blue.

"He's finally here and healthy," she said, and I slowly stood, my voice choked off and eyes watery as my husband reached for our son, his elegant fingers grabby with excitement.

I swallowed a sob as Preston gathered the boy into his arms with the sweetest gentleness, cooing noises spilling from his lips.

The nurse slipped back out, leaving us alone as a new family of three.

Tears coursed down my cheeks as Preston lifted his bright eyes to me. "Come meet your son, Papa."

I sniffed and moved closer on unsteady feet, for the first time in my life unsure and hesitant. More than anything I'd wanted my kryptonite by my side and to have babies together.

My dream stood before me in living color. My greatest wishes had come true.

I wrapped my arms around them both, afraid to squeeze as hard as I wanted to.

Murky eyes blinked up from the bundle of blankets. He was tiny. Pale as his daddy, hints of red hair peeking beneath the knitted cap on his little head. I hoped his eyes would be as emerald green as Preston's but had learned from all the books we'd read together that it would be a while before that happened.

"You are so precious to us," Preston murmured, stroking the infant's plump cheek with a trembling fingertip. "Papa and I will accept you for whoever you become as you grow up. We're going to love you forever and ever no matter what."

"I'll remind you said that when he's screaming at three in the morning for a bottle or needs his diaper changed," I said with a shaky chuckle before kissing Preston's temple.

"Even then, I'll adore everything about you," he said, leaning down to kiss our son's nose.

The bundle squirmed in his arms, the tiny mouth parting and letting out a shriek.

Damn.

I blinked, straightening a bit but still keeping my arms around them both.

Preston laughed, his face glowing as bright as his eyes in a confidence I suddenly envied. "We've got this."

"Fucking love you," I rasped, overrun with a slew of emotions.

"Love you more," he said, leaning up to plant a kiss on my mouth. "Hmm," he said, eyeing my beard as he pulled back.

"What?"

"You might need to shave this off so you don't scratch our boy's sensitive skin."

"Normally, I'd agree to whatever you say, husband of mine," I stated, ready to stand my ground for a change with the man I couldn't say no to, "but this?" I rubbed a hand along my jaw and trimmed whiskers I'd had since college. "It's staying."

"Mmm hmm." Preston's little noise reached me through our boy's shrieks, as did his *we'll see* he didn't bother voicing.

Ten days later, I sat on the rocking chair in the dark, humming an Aerosmith song to my son who'd finished his bottle and had finally fallen back to sleep. It was after two in the morning, and I'd fed, burped, and changed a disgusting diaper that had me gagging while Preston finally got some rest.

But regardless of my exhaustion, I was in heaven.

The slight weight in my arms was as far from a burden as could be. Sure, our lives had been flipped on its head, the upheaval far beyond what I'd expected. But it was perfect— little Devlin was everything to me, right alongside his father.

"You have the best daddy," I whispered to him, lifting him up to sniff the baby smell I couldn't get enough of. Powder and pure deliciousness. Sniffing, I rubbed my smooth-shaven cheek along his, grinning like a damned fool. "He's so unselfish and dotes on you so much I'm starting to feel a little jealous."

True words, but I would never regret our decision to find a surrogate and start the family we'd both wanted.

"Someday, you'll have another brother or sister," I promised. "But there will be plenty of love to go around. We're going to go fishing, and I'll tell you all about your grandpop and how we used to spend weekends camping up in New Hampshire. We'll take you to Granny and Granddad's farm in Vermont in the spring and learn how to make maple syrup. We'll have to head down to Rhode Island on occasion too to see Mimi and Grandpa Bob, but we won't stay long because your two aunties will probably drive you nuts like they do to me."

I kissed my son on his fuzzy head, loving the soft tickle of his red hair.

A sigh sounded from the doorway, and I turned to see my love leaning against the frame, his eyes sleepy, hair tousled, but a beautiful smile on his lips. "I never expected to find this much happiness, Drake."

I motioned him over then handed son to him when he stood before me. As always, Preston cocooned Devlin in his arms, smooching all over his face. I guided him onto my lap, leaned my head back, and rested my eyes.

"Maybe we should let him sleep in our bed—"

"Nope," I cut Preston off, having had this conversation a dozen times since we'd gotten home from the hospital. "Our bed is sacred, baby. That's the one space I'm unwilling to share with anyone but you. It's the only place I get to have you all to myself."

Preston snickered, and I realized he'd teased me rather than pushing the topic again. "I love your possessiveness."

I grumbled and hugged him tighter. "I don't mind our kids having your affection, but sometimes I just need you. Alone."

Preston pressed his lips to mine, and I could feel his smile. "I'm going to put Devlin back in his crib." He climbed off my lap, and I immediately missed him. "How about you go strip, climb into bed, and get your dick hard so I can ride you."

My eyelids shot up to find Preston's bubble butt turned my way as he lay our son on his back. Tingles woke in my groin regardless of the late hour and the lack of sleep we'd been getting. "You aren't too tired?"

"It's been almost two weeks, Drake. I want you inside me."

"Fuck yeah," I whispered, hopping up with a lot more energy than I thought I had.

Quick as fuck, I lay sprawled on our bed, hard cock in hand stroking upward to bead pre-cum at the tip.

Preston had left the dimmers on overhead, so I could enjoy every move he made in shucking his sleep shorts and T-shirt, revealing all his gorgeous, freckled skin I longed to mark up.

"So damn beautiful," I whispered, and he crawled over me, those emerald eyes on mine, unwavering and lustful. Tucking my hands behind my head to show off my muscles in the way that always had him drooling, I smirked. "Gonna sit on my dick and make me fill you up with a few days' worth of cum?"

He licked up the back of my length, humming over the taste of my pre-cum on his tongue. "If you wouldn't mind eating my ass and getting me ready?"

Groaning, I grabbed hold of his hips and swung him around like he weighed next to nothing. "Suck on my dick while I love on your hole, baby."

"Jesus, Drake."

I filled my palms with his ass cheeks and spread him wide. "Goddamn," I murmured and dove in, burying my face in his crack.

"D-Drake," he stuttered, closing his hand around the base of my dick. "Fuck, your cheeks...so smooth. Oh my God—so good."

I shoved my tongue past his ring, reaching as deep as I could go.

His head sagged, his hot breath ghosting over my throbbing cockhead.

As though hearing my plea, he wrapped his lips around my girth and suckled, causing my hips to jolt upward.

"Ung," I grunted an apology, too busy eating his ass and shoving saliva up inside him to vocalize the actual words.

Preston didn't care—he took me deep, straight into his throat.

Holy fucking hell, this man.

I bruised his ass cheeks with my fingertips before I was done readying him for my dick, but he didn't make a complaint. A quick nip of my teeth on his plump flesh promised another bruise, his whimper satisfying that kinky part of me that enjoyed seeing my marks on his body.

He spun back around when we both neared the edge but paused, glancing over at the bedside table where we kept the baby's monitor.

"He's fine," I said, holding his ass and rutting my aching, sopping wet dick up through his spit-slickened crack.

"I know." He gave me his full attention, the hint of a twinkle in his eyes. "We're about to fulfill another fantasy of mine."

I raised an eyebrow, lifting his hips so I could notch against his pucker. "What's that?"

"Fucking my husband while our child sleeps." He shoved down, filling himself with my dick.

"Preston," I choked on his name, grabbing his face and yanking him against my chest. "Jesus—fucking love you so goddamn much."

"You made all my dreams come true," he whispered against my mouth, moving in a way that was going to have me blowing my load in under sixty seconds. "It's always been you."

"Same, baby—fuck I'm gonna come already."

"Good." He clenched his ring around me and nipped at my lower lip. "I want every drop."

"Need you to come," I thrust upward, my pulse thrumming in time with the throb in my balls.

"After you finish in my ass, I'm going to straddle your thick chest and feed you my dick."

"Fuck!" I stabbed upward into his tight ass, my teeth gritted to keep from shouting.

"I can feel you—fuck, Drake." Preston gasped, rutting away on my dick. "I can feel you pulsing inside me. Oh fuck, I'm gonna—"

Wet heat spurted between our stomachs, and Preston shuddered, his ass milking me dry.

We both heaved for breath, and he huffed a laugh. "Well shit, there goes that fantasy."

"We have a lifetime, baby," I murmured, my body ready to crash, but I stroked my hands up and down his back as euphoric tingles continued to race beneath my skin.

Sighing, Preston snuggled against my chest, not caring about the spunk between us and leaking around my dick still buried in his sweet ass.

"Could die a happy man," he muttered, his voice on the verge of sleep.

"Let me take care of you first," I whispered, kissing his hair.

He hummed an agreement and didn't argue when I slid him off me. Sprawled on his back, eyes closed, he smiled with satisfied. Pink flushed his freckled cheeks, down his neck, and across his chest.

So. Goddamned. Beautiful.

My eyes stung from the overwhelming love I felt for him, but I forced myself to turn away and grab a wet towel from the bathroom.

He hadn't moved by the time I returned, nor did he made a noise when I cleaned him up.

My husband had fucked himself into a quick coma on my dick.

Grinning like a fool, I climbed onto the bed behind him, covered us up, and cradled him against me. A heavy exhale sagged me into the mattress, and I glanced at the monitor.

"Give us a few hours, hmm?" I whispered even though Devlin couldn't hear where he slept in his crib.

The little angel must have heard because I opened my eyes to sunlight filtering through our blinds, my husband snuggled in my arms in the same position as when I'd fallen asleep.

Preston stirred, grinding his ass against my morning wood.

"Mmm. Love waking up like this," I murmured, kissing all the fuck over his neck and shoulder.

"Shit!" He jolted to awareness, jerking from my hold.

Chuckling, I rolled to my back, hands behind my head, the sheet tented at my groin as Preston stumbled butt naked from our room.

His sigh of relief sounded clear through the monitor beside me.

He returned a minute later, rubbing a hand over his face. "How is he still sleeping?"

"Don't know—don't care. Get your ass over here, sit on my chest, and feed me your dick like you wanted to last night."

Arousal darkened his eyes, but I'd only palmed his thighs when a familiar shriek rent the air.

We both laughed.

"Later," I said, and he gave me a quick, hard kiss, his eyes promising me what I wanted. "Now go get our son and assure him we aren't upset with his cockblocking us while I make you some French toast with real maple syrup."

A sentimental, sad smile lifted my husband's lips as he glanced over his shoulder. "You're perfect for me."

"I know—now go get our son and tell him the same."

Preston pulled on sweats before disappearing, and I listened as he cooed to our son, soothing him with words of affirmation and love.

Years of therapy he'd been adamant about continuing had stitched up a lot of the wounds in his heart. The last thing he'd wanted was to keep on with the Casswell generational curse. But with our ridiculous wealth allowing us to simply volunteer and host fundraisers for various LGBTQ groups rather than slaving away at a job twenty-four-seven and him taking my name when we married, he had nothing to fear.

He'd put in the work and had made all his—and my—dreams come true.

About the Author

USA Today bestselling author Lynn Burke is a CrossFit and coffee addict. Her three spawn dictate how often she can be found hunched over her Mac, typing as fast as her fickle muse cooks up hot stories.

You can find more about Lynn at her website: www.authorlynnburke.com

Also By Lynn Burke

Abel's Obsession

Divulging Secrets

Healing Storms

In Between

Reluctant Lumberjack

Resisting his Mate

Billion Dollar Love Anthology

Blood Born Series

Bonds of Worship Series

Dark Leopards MC

Darkest Desires Series

Devil's Outlaws MC

Elite Escort Series

Elite Escorts MM Series

Fallen Gliders MC

Forbidden Obsession Duet

Found by Fate Series

Midnight Sun Series

Missing Link Series

Risso Family Series

Sandy Ridge Series

Sinful Nature Series

Vicious Vipers MC

The Road to Madhapur

DAVID WHITTET

ISBN 978-1-99-116742-2 (Paperback – printed))
ISBN 978-1-99-116749-1 (Paperback – print-on-demand)
ISBN 978-1-99-116743-9 (Epub)
ISBN 978-1-99-116744-6 (Kindle)

Published by Copy Press Books, Nelson, New Zealand 2022
Copy Press Books, 141 Pascoe Street, Nelson, New Zealand

www.davidwhittet.com

Book cover design by Holly Dunn

Designed and distributed in New Zealand by
The Copy Press, Nelson, New Zealand.
www.copypress.co.nz

For Dr Derek Allen.

*Your tireless work amongst the most disadvantaged people on
our planet is a constant inspiration.*

CHAPTER ONE

University of Otago Medical School,
Dunedin, New Zealand, July 1986

Professor Goulding rapped his cane on my desk. 'Wake up, Mr Malone!'

I sat up with a jolt.

The professor leant over me. 'What are the pathological changes in pulmonary tuberculosis?'

Why did he always pick on me? Hands shot up all around me. Was I the only one who didn't know the answer?

'This isn't the first time I've caught you drifting.' Professor Goulding pointed to the screen with his cane. 'Look at this slide and tell me what you see.'

'It's … um … a section of a lung,' I mumbled. 'With … er … tuberculosis.'

Professor Goulding snorted. 'I should have thought that was obvious.'

Everyone laughed. Especially those show-offs in the front row.

Professor Goulding's eyes drilled into mine. 'It's called a granuloma.' He put another slide up on the screen. 'Name this structure.'

I hadn't a clue what it was called and didn't care either. Modern antibiotics had eliminated tuberculosis and learning about it in such minute detail wouldn't prepare us for the challenges of medicine in the outside world.

'It's um …' I dribbled to a standstill. 'I'm not sure, sir.'

More hands went up.

'It's the interlobular vein,' one student said.

'Subsegmental branch,' another added.

Professor Goulding glared at me through tortoiseshell-rimmed glasses that must have been at least as old as he was. 'You just don't know your anatomy, Mr Malone. You need to buck up your ideas if you're to get through your fourth-year exams.'

It was all I could do to stop myself from bolting out of the lecture theatre. Hadn't Professor Goulding heard about AIDS and the new viruses that threatened the future of humanity?

What was I doing here? Why had I chosen to study medicine? It seemed a distant memory now—that day during my last year at school when a Ugandan refugee visited our class.

It hadn't meant much when our teacher explained Akiki was the sole survivor of an entire community wiped out by AIDS. Everything changed when his foster mother led him into the classroom, and I caught sight of the fourteen-year-old's fractured eyes.

Miss Kershaw, our teacher, sat Akiki on a stool in front of the class. His foster mother stood beside him with her hand on his back.

'Welcome to Remutaka College,' Miss Kershaw said. 'We've been learning about your country, Akiki. Some of our students have got together to sponsor children in Uganda.' She pointed to a giant map of Africa on the wall. 'You came from Kuluba, didn't you?'

Akiki shuffled in his seat and half nodded.

'We'd like to hear about your life in Uganda,' Miss Kershaw said. 'I understand you used to help your mum take care of your little sisters.'

Akiki glanced up at the class, then hid his face. Perhaps he couldn't speak English. Trust Miss Kershaw to embarrass him.

Akiki's foster mother stroked his shoulder. 'Remember what I said? Deep breaths.'

Akiki raised his head, his lip twitching. 'You want to know about Abbo and Afiya?'

'They were your sisters?' Miss Kershaw asked.

Akiki nodded. I spotted a tear in the corner of his eye. It was all too much for the poor kid. I just wanted Miss Kershaw to stop interrogating him.

'Our village didn't have a well,' Akiki said. 'Every morning, I took Abbo and Afiya to get water from a pipe in the wall of the council building.'

'Extraordinary,' Miss Kershaw said. 'We're all so used to just turning on the tap to get water. So tell us, how did you get the water from the pipe?'

    David Whittet

Akiki gestured with his hands. 'The pipe jutted out of the concrete wall and had a tap on the end. So we turned it on. Just like you do at home.'

'I guess it must have been a rainwater tank?' Miss Kershaw asked. 'Or did it come from a reservoir?'

Akiki shrugged. 'Not sure. We just filled our buckets and then carried them home on our heads.'

My jaw dropped. Akiki spoke so fluently—not the broken English I was expecting.

'It wasn't all work, was it?' Akiki's foster mother said. 'Tell the class what you did after you'd finished your chores.'

Akiki grinned. 'We played football with some other kids. Kicking a ball made from rags and bits of old tyres.'

'What?' Miss Kershaw said. 'Didn't the scraps go all over the place?'

'We tied them together with string,' Akiki replied. 'Our feet got cut and bruised from all the garbage on the ground—'

Miss Kershaw raised an eyebrow. 'You played barefooted?'

'We didn't care,' Akiki said. 'Sometimes, we'd help Uncle Ejau chase his pigs back into their pen. Then we'd take turns to ride his bike as a reward.'

Akiki's foster mother held up a picture of the village. I pictured Akiki and his mates kicking the homemade football around and imagined the cheers when they scored a goal. Miss Kershaw put more photos of the village on the blackboard. Riding a bike along those blood-red dirt roads through the crowded street markets must have been thrilling.

Akiki dabbed his eyes. 'We were happy until …'

'Until your mum and dad got sick?' Miss Kershaw said.

'Yes.' Akiki's voice broke, and he covered his head with his arms.

'You were so brave.' Akiki's foster mother put her arms around him. 'Tell everyone how you looked after the family.'

Akiki took his hands away from his face and steadied himself on the stool. 'My aunt Mugisa taught me how to cook.'

I could almost smell the spices as Akiki described his aunt's roadside stall.

'Abbo and Afiya were always hungry,' he said. 'Curried cabbage was their favourite.'

Nick, the class smartarse, sniggered. 'Curried cabbage? Yuk! No wonder they died.'

You bastard! I glared at Nick. I'd gladly have wrung his neck.

'Any more from you, Nick, and you can stand outside,' Miss Kershaw said, then turned back to Akiki. 'I bet it was delicious.'

Akiki eyed Nick. 'Curried cabbage is much tastier than the burgers you eat out here.'

Brilliant! I had to stop myself jumping up to give Akiki a round of applause.

'And doubtless more nutritious.' Miss Kershaw paused and took a deep breath. 'I can't imagine how you coped after your parents died.'

I cursed Miss Kershaw under my breath. Why did she say that?

Akiki wiped his face with his sleeve. 'Aunt Mugisa helped me look after Abbo and Afiya. Until they got sick as well and had to go to the sanatorium.'

I had tears in my eyes, too, when Akiki described the sanatorium, and how he defied the village elders by staying to comfort his sisters in their final hours.

'After your sisters … died,' Miss Kershaw said, 'the elders sent you to a refugee camp, didn't they?'

Akiki nodded. 'There were hundreds of us in that camp, all crammed into shacks with plastic roofs.'

'How long were you in the camp?' Miss Kershaw asked. 'Tell us how you came to New Zealand.'

No more! Can't you see he's had enough?

'It's all a blur,' Akiki replied. 'I got a fever, too. They thought I'd caught what my sisters had and moved me into a shack on my own. Next thing I knew, I was in the back of a jeep with this Kiwi bloke.'

'That was Pastor Campbell,' Akiki's foster mother said, 'from the Ugandan mission.'

Akiki hugged his foster mother. 'Whoever he was, he found me a new mum.'

'That's wonderful,' Miss Kershaw said. 'Now, who's got a question for Akiki?'

Silence. Then Nick yawned noisily. I hesitated—there was so much I wanted to ask, but that would stir up more painful memories for Akiki.

Miss Kershaw eyed the class. 'No takers?' She clasped her hands together. 'Well, Akiki is joining us for lunch, so that will give you all a chance to get to know him. Now, can I have a volunteer to look after Akiki? I have matters to discuss with his foster mother.'

I was first with my hand up.

'Thank you, Theo,' Miss Kershaw said. 'Make Akiki feel at home. Now, if you'll excuse us.'

Miss Kershaw and Akiki's foster mother left for the staffroom. Typical. No overcooked beef goulash for them.

We filed into the school canteen, and I handed Akiki a plate at the counter.

Nick was right behind us. 'Did you see that? Theo touched him.'

'Theo's got the clap now,' another boy added.

The rest of the class joined in, pointing and holding their noses.

'Don't come near me. We don't want your filthy germs.'

'Don't let him into the changing rooms,' another boy added. 'Or the toilets!'

I turned and gave them the finger. 'Piss off!'

Akiki's hand shook as I ladled some stew onto his plate.

'Don't take any notice of them,' I said. 'They're retards.'

Akiki sighed. 'I'm used to it. I had to see loads of doctors and have heaps of tests before they let me into New Zealand. And still people think they can catch something from me.'

We sat down at an empty table. 'School lunches here aren't much cop,' I said. 'No curried cabbage, I'm afraid.'

'Can't be worse than the food at the refugee camp,' Akiki said.

I screwed up my nose. 'Don't be so sure.'

Akiki took a spoonful of stew. 'It's okay!'

I smiled. 'You don't have to pretend.' What else could I say to make him feel at home? 'I bet schools in Uganda are different from those in New Zealand.'

'I went to school when I was tiny,' Akiki said. 'But I left to look after my family. Aunt Mugisa gave me some lessons before she got sick. I couldn't read or write when I left Africa.'

I put my hand on Akiki's. 'So who taught you to speak English so well?'

'My foster mum found me a tutor once we got to New Zealand,' Akiki said. 'But she says that's not enough now, and she wants me to come to school here.'

'Brilliant,' I said. 'When will you start?'

Akiki shrugged. 'Not sure.'

He glanced over his shoulder at the other kids.

'Don't worry about them,' I said. 'I'll look after you.'

The bell rang for afternoon classes, and Akiki's foster mother came to collect him.

'I'm glad you've made a friend here, Akiki,' she said. 'Miss Kershaw says you can enrol next term.'

I walked with them out to their car.

'Was there nothing the doctors could do for your mum and dad?' I asked Akiki. 'And your little sisters?'

'We had a medicine man in our village. He tried some herbal remedies and danced around our house to ward off the evil spirits.'

I stared at him. 'But didn't you have any proper doctors? Or a hospital?'

'Doctors were for the rich. Besides, the nearest hospital was kilometres away, and we'd no way of getting there.'

I hadn't thought about what I'd do after completing school. Now, I was sure. I would be a doctor and work in Uganda. Miss Kershaw had told us about international medical aid agencies and how they were always looking for recruits. She'd shown us a film featuring their work in developing countries. Perfect. I couldn't wait to sign up.

The afternoon dragged. I wanted to catch Mr Moseley, the school's career adviser, and made for his office when the final bell rang.

'What subjects do I need for medical school?' I said in a rush.

Mr Moseley stared at me over his bifocals. 'I hope this isn't some knee-jerk reaction. You'll need top grades in biology, physics and chemistry. Are you sure you're up to it? Science has never been your strong point.'

I met his gaze. 'I know. But you don't understand. My heart's set on being a doctor and making a difference. Starting in Uganda.'

Mr Moseley took a handkerchief from his pocket and cleaned his glasses. 'Medicine is a six-year course. It takes dedication and hard study. And have you thought about the cost?'

My heart missed a beat. *The cost?* I shook my head.

Mr Moseley leant forward. 'If you're absolutely sure, I'll help you apply for a scholarship for the University of Otago. Just don't let me down.'

Four years later, and here I was at uni with my head slumped over a desk, struggling to keep my eyes open during another endless lecture on tuberculosis from a professor whose hair was as white as his lab coat. I came to medical school to change the world, not to listen to some old fart describing the microscopic changes in a disease that no longer existed.

CHAPTER TWO

Four years at medical school and I ached for some real-life medicine. I'd done enough of cutting up dead bodies in the anatomy lab and examining diseased remains in giant pots. Just one more week of Professor Goulding rambling on about tuberculosis, then it was my general practice attachment. Yay! An entire month away from that claustrophobic lecture theatre. I pinned a calendar to my bedroom wall and crossed off the days each evening when I got back from lectures.

Nine o'clock on the first morning of my GP attachment, and I was ready and waiting for my briefing with James Rutherford, the professor of general practice.

'We've assigned you to Dr Ralph Greenslade,' Professor Rutherford said with a twitch of his moustache. 'He's one of our most senior GP tutors, and his is the oldest practice in South Dunedin. You'll find Dr Greenslade's approach to medicine is—different.'

A senior GP tutor. I'd hoped for someone young and dynamic. And his approach was different? What did that mean?

Professor Rutherford must have seen the confusion in my eyes. 'Let's just say Dr Greenslade is a little unconventional. You'll see another side to medicine. Who knows? It might give you a new perspective. Professor Goulding said you need a good kick up the backside.'

Bloody Goulding. Trust him to snitch. Still, I refused to let that spoil my morning. I'd been looking forward to general practice for so long. I just hoped Ralph Greenslade wasn't another old-school doctor living in a bygone age.

I pressed my head against the window as the taxi navigated the morning traffic in the cold, damp streets of South Dunedin. Broken shop windows, run-down housing estates. Kids on their way to school, kicking footballs across wasteland. A busker with a mouth organ and an empty cap at his feet. My pulse quickened—this *was* the real world and, for me, the start of a life-changing adventure.

 David Whittet

The Castle Hill Medical Centre was an old and shabby converted maisonette in dire need of decoration. Very sixties. But that didn't matter. It matched the suburbs the practice served and judging by the packed waiting room when I arrived, it made the patients feel at home.

There was scarcely time for introductions. Dr Greenslade looked as dishevelled as the building. His loose tie and tweed jacket were positively pre-sixties and complemented by an unruly shock of long grey hair along the sides of his otherwise bald head.

'You must be Theo Malone,' he said. 'Take a seat in my room.'

Everything about Dr Greenslade and his practice was quirky and not what I expected in a GP's surgery—from the William Blake etchings hanging on his office walls to the patterned wallpaper in a William Morris design.

Dr Greenslade ushered a young woman into the consulting room. She must have been in her mid-twenties. I'd noticed her in the waiting room, shuffling in her seat and continually crossing and uncrossing her legs.

'Come in, Amanda,' Dr Greenslade said. 'I've got a medical student with me today. Do you mind if he sits in on the consultation?'

'That's okay,' she said.

I don't know who looked more uncomfortable. Amanda perched on a chair in front of Dr Greenslade's desk, or me crouched behind it.

'How can I help you today?' Dr Greenslade said. 'How's married life treating you?'

'It's over a year since Jimmy and I got married,' Amanda said. 'Married life's great. Or at least it was until Jimmy lost his job. But that's not why I'm here.' She rolled up her sleeves. 'I just need something to get rid of this. It's driving me crazy.'

Dr Greenslade examined the fiery red rash on both her arms. When he'd finished, he leant back in his chair and cleared his throat. 'Do you mind if my student takes a look?'

Amanda nodded her consent.

Dr Greenslade turned to me. 'Tell me what you see.'

I lurched forward to study Amanda's arms, cringing as my stool squeaked on the floorboards.

'It's raised and erythematous,' I said, desperately trying to remember the correct way to describe a skin eruption. 'There's no sign of infection or cellulitis, and it blanches to touch.'

'So, what's your diagnosis?' Dr Greenslade asked.

The rash was identical to a picture in my dermatology textbook. Thank goodness for a straightforward case for my first general practice patient.

'Eczema,' I said.

Ralph Greenslade shook his head.

I took another look at Amanda's arms. Ran my fingers over the rash. 'Contact dermatitis? Possibly from a new product?'

Amanda shrugged and pulled backwards. 'I can't afford any new products. Not with my Jimmy out of work. In fact, we've had to use a cheaper brand of washing powder—'

'That's it!' I said. 'It *is* contact dermatitis. From the new detergent!'

Dr Greenslade frowned at me. 'No. It's neurodermatitis.'

Amanda eyed him dubiously. 'Neuro *what*?'

'It's a nervous rash.' Ralph Greenslade reached for his pipe. Then, thinking better of it, fiddled with a paperclip instead. 'It can't be easy with Jimmy at home all day. And no money coming in.'

Amanda suddenly burst into tears. Everything came out. How an industrial accident rendered Jimmy unemployable. Redundancy. Living off accident compensation. Struggling to make ends meet. With their mortgage in arrears, they fell victim to loan sharks.

As Amanda told her story, I watched Dr Greenslade unwind the paperclip until it was straight. Then he put it back together while he decided what he could do for her.

'I'm going to arrange counselling for you,' he said. 'With Diane. She's lovely and very experienced. I'm also going to put you in touch with a financial adviser.'

The consultation must have lasted at least half an hour. Maybe more. But Amanda definitely seemed more relaxed when she left, clutching a prescription for hydrocortisone cream.

'There are two ways to practise medicine,' Dr Greenslade told me before calling the next patient. 'You can treat the illness or treat the patient.'

     David Whittet

'But how did you know it was a nervous rash?' I asked. 'It looked like a classic allergy.'

'Body language,' he said. 'Knowing your patient. Didn't you pick up the non-verbal clues as she came into the room?'

I shrugged. 'I could see she was anxious.'

Dr Greenslade studied me. 'If you're going to be a GP, you need to think outside the square.' He stood up and fetched another patient from the waiting room. 'Watch and learn.'

Body language. Non-verbal cues. Thinking outside the square. Hallelujah—a doctor who cared more about people's behaviour than their anatomy. Dr Greenslade was a kindred spirit, and definitely *not* a stuffy academic.

Each patient brought their own story. The young woman with multiple sclerosis, struggling to come to terms with her illness and a husband who threatened to leave whenever she had a relapse. Callous bastard.

Then the jazz pianist, forced to quit his job at a nightclub when shaky fingers stopped him performing.

'He looked uneasy,' I said after the patient left, keen to impress with my observations. 'I watched the way he sat on the edge of the seat. And I saw you gave him propranolol. Is it just anxiety that's stopping him from playing?'

'A neurologist diagnosed him with an essential tremor,' Dr Greenslade said. 'My diagnosis is chronic frustration. He wants to be a concert pianist, performing in concert halls in the big cities, not a seedy nightclub.'

Next up, a couple fighting over which one of them was responsible for their sexually transmitted disease. I hadn't realised GPs needed to be referees.

Dr Greenslade even had his own take on the stream of screaming children with sore throats and earache.

'Children get sick when their mothers are stressed,' he told me.

Proving his point, once he'd written their child's antibiotic prescription, the mothers invariably complained they were 'tired all the time'.

'Do you think I need some vitamins, Doctor?'

'Maybe I'm low on iron. Or magnesium.'

'Could you give me a tonic, Doctor?'

'You don't need supplements,' Dr Greenslade would reply, 'we need to sort out what's going on in your life.'

Fifteen minutes of counselling, and they all felt better, and their kids had stopped crying too.

I was *watching*, and I was *learning*.

Dr Greenslade leant back in his chair and grinned at me. 'Not like that in the textbooks, is it?'

It certainly wasn't. Before I could reply, the receptionist brought in two cups of coffee and a plate of biscuits.

'That's it for morning surgery,' she said, 'but you've got four house calls.'

Ralph Greenslade lit his pipe and dragged on it hungrily, filling the room with smoke.

'Don't forget to sign the repeat prescriptions,' the receptionist added before leaving. 'Mrs McConnell's been on the phone already.'

Dr Greenslade sighed and began signing the scripts. 'General practice isn't all high drama, I'm afraid.' He looked at the list of house calls and smiled. 'But this afternoon, you'll learn what general practice is really all about.'

He was right. Up until then, damp homes were just something I'd heard about on the news. Scurvy and rickets were just pictures in a textbook. Those four house calls brought me face to face with the hardships ordinary New Zealanders battled every single day. Poverty, deprivation and malnourishment—all in one afternoon.

Maude was our first visit, a middle-aged woman struggling to breathe in a flat so cold it turned my fingers blue. We almost tripped over the empty gin bottles scattered across the floor in a rush to get to her. She rolled over on the threadbare mattress and heaved up some thick yellow phlegm.

Dr Greenslade scarcely needed a stethoscope to listen to Maude's chest. I could hear the wheeze from where I stood.

'When does Bert get home?' Dr Greenslade wrote a prescription for antibiotics and tore it off his pad. 'He needs to take time off work to look after you.'

'You know he can't,' Maude spluttered. Was it the infection or the alcohol that made her voice so thick and garbled? 'We're already a couple of months behind on the rent. The landlord's threatened to boot us out.'

'Then we need to get you to hospital,' Dr Greenslade said. 'Just for a few days until you're over the worst of the infection.'

Maude grasped her chest. 'No hospital, please!' The effort brought on another bout of coughing, and she grabbed her inhaler. 'I'll get my aunt Tammi to come in.'

'Make sure you do,' Dr Greenslade said. 'I'll be back to see you tomorrow.'

Maude puffed frantically on her inhaler. 'I can't afford another call-out fee.'

Her ribs heaved so hard I thought her chest muscles were going to give up the fight.

Dr Greenslade paused and rubbed his chin. He put his stethoscope and prescription pad back in his Gladstone bag and closed it deliberately. 'Don't worry. I won't charge you.'

For a second, the rasping stopped, replaced by a gentle sob. A tear trickled down Maude's cheek. 'Thank you, Doctor.'

Dr Greenslade kicked a stone down the pavement and muttered to himself as we walked back to the car. 'Damn … damn … damn …'

'Will she be okay?' I asked. 'Why was she so scared of going to hospital?'

'The landlord will repossess the flat if it's empty. Even for a day.' Dr Greenslade unlocked the car and threw his bag on the back seat. 'Mind you, that might not be such a bad thing. If she were homeless, I could get social services to find her somewhere half-decent to live. And as for Bert—he's a complete waste of space.'

My hands had just about come back to life when we visited a four-year-old with asthma.

'She's been wheezing all morning, Doctor,' the mother said. 'And she went this funny colour. I thought we were going to lose her.'

'Fetch the nebuliser from the car.' Dr Greenslade threw me the keys. 'Quick. It's in that orange box.'

My heart raced as I grabbed the portable nebuliser from the vehicle and rushed back inside.

'Do you know how to use it?' Dr Greenslade asked.

I felt a surge of adrenaline in my gut. 'I've practised in a lab, but not in real life—'

'Time for some hands-on experience,' Dr Greenslade said. 'You nebulise while I draw up the injection.'

I fumbled to get the face mask to fit onto the tubing. My hand shook as I held the mask to the girl's dusky blue face. The fear in her frantic eyes opened mine to the reality of coping in a medical emergency. Would I ever be able to manage a critical case like this on my own?

I let out a huge breath as the girl's cheeks turned pink. Dr Greenslade was talking to the mother, but I wasn't listening. The little girl was getting better—we'd saved her life. And I'd found my true vocation.

'Help me to get her into the car,' Dr Greenslade said. 'We're taking her to hospital. You'll need to keep up the nebulisation till we get there.'

Maybe it was the vapour escaping from the girl's mask, but I felt light-headed. The mask slipped as we clambered into the back of the car, and she began wheezing again.

'Careful,' Dr Greenslade said. 'We're not out of the woods yet.'

Pull yourself together. How had I let that happen? I held the face mask tight over the girl's mouth and nose until we arrived at the Dunedin Hospital.

'Thank you.' The mother hugged me when we left them on the ward. 'I'll never forget you. Never.'

Dr Greenslade grinned as we drove back to the practice. 'I told you I'd show you some real medicine this afternoon. Do you still want to be a GP?'

'More than ever.' I wanted to say more. That afternoon changed my life. How could I put that into words without sounding corny?

When we got back to the medical centre, Judy, the receptionist, dumped a pile of folders on Dr Greenslade's desk. 'Just ten patients this afternoon, Doctor. But they're all your *special* patients.'

'You can't judge how busy you're going to be by the number of patients who have booked,' Dr Greenslade said, picking up a huge file. 'Look at this one. It's a ton in weight. That means it's going to be a *long* consultation.' He winked at the receptionist. 'Judy knows to allow my patients fifteen minutes for every kilogram of their notes.'

'Sonya's your last patient of the day,' Judy said. 'As usual, she threatened to take all her clothes off in the waiting room if we didn't fit her in.'

Sonya was a schizophrenic striptease artist. Dr Greenslade spent over an hour going through her messed-up relationships and trying to unravel the hopeless knots she'd tied herself into. Unlike this morning's cases, the web got more tangled by the minute.

Dr Greenslade sighed when we finally turned out the lights in the medical centre.

'Dinner time,' he said. 'Let's hope Rosemary hasn't given up on us. Listening to Sonya is hungry work.'

Ralph and his wife Rosemary's guest room was a step up from my student accommodation. So was Rosemary's cooking.

'Make yourself at home,' Rosemary said as we sat at the table. 'Robert and Rachel have gone to bed. They got sick of waiting for their dad to come home. I hope you like pasta.'

What did psychologically-minded doctors talk about over dinner? Was Ralph examining the way I was eating? This morning, he'd told me he never lit his pipe at a meeting because he didn't want anyone analysing his 'oral dependency needs'. So what did he make of my clumsy table manners?

Thankfully, Rosemary kept up the conversation. 'Ralph, I can't understand why you've brought more of that clotted cream home. Haven't you told Mrs Bennett it's bad for the heart?'

Patricia Bennett had been our last house visit of the afternoon. She had insisted we stay for afternoon tea, complete with scones and lashings of cream.

'You need to watch your cholesterol,' Ralph had told the plump seventy-year-old. 'Your last blood test was very high.'

Mrs Bennett put down her scone. 'My niece is a dairy farmer in Taranaki, and she sends me an enormous tub of clotted cream every month.'

Ralph frowned. 'It could give you a heart attack or a stroke. You'll have to tell her to stop.'

'She'd be mortified.' Mrs Bennett disappeared into the kitchen and came back with a massive pot of cream. 'You take it, Doctor. If I can't have it, you enjoy it.'

Rosemary brought in the dessert.

Ralph ladled the cream onto his apple crumble and gave her a wicked smile. 'This is true dedication to general practice. Sacrificing my coronary arteries for the sake of my patients.'

Rosemary pointed a spoon at him. 'You're incorrigible.'

I helped Rosemary clear the dishes when we'd finished.

'What are you going to do when you're qualified?' she asked.

'I want to work overseas,' I said.

'Really?'

'Yes.' I caught Rosemary's eye. 'Ever since a Ugandan boy came to our school. His entire family died from AIDS.'

Rosemary smiled. 'So that's what inspired you to go in for medicine?'

'I wanted to start work that day, so I contacted every voluntary organisation I could find. But they said I had to go to medical school first.'

'And now you're here.' Rosemary rinsed the last of the dishes. 'Ralph took a year out to be a ship's doctor when he graduated.'

Ralph brought a coffee percolator into the kitchen. 'That was the life,' he said. 'I'll never forget Tahiti. The closest place to heaven on earth.'

Rosemary rolled her eyes. 'I bet you had a girl in every port—or maybe a nurse.'

Ralph put the percolator on the stove and grinned. 'You're only young once.' He fetched an old photograph album and proudly showed off the pictures of his world trip. 'My God, I was handsome back then.'

Rosemary poked him in the belly. 'Yes, and look what's happened since.' She turned to me. 'Ralph will retire in a few years, and we need some fresh blood around here. So, once you've had your overseas experience, why don't you come back and take over his practice?'

What? Me? Settle down in a suburban practice and start a family? No way. Uganda waited, and it wasn't just a holiday job after qualifying. I'd be there for the long term. I'd promised Akiki—and myself.

'One day, maybe. But not yet. I wouldn't have the patience to deal with Ralph's special patients.'

 David Whittet

I cringed at my feeble excuse. Why hadn't I told Rosemary the truth? For me, Ralph's legacy would be far more significant than simply inheriting a practice. Ralph reignited the fire in my belly. His ability to listen cut through the barriers that stood between the patients and their happiness. An influence that would last a lifetime and an example I was determined to follow.

During my last week at the practice, I had to undertake a case study for my general practice assessment. My first opportunity to manage a patient on my own. I could barely sit still while Ralph briefed me.

'Old Mr Evans has a chronic cough, and he's started bringing up blood. He lives on a farm out in the sticks.' Ralph pulled the case notes out of a filing cabinet. 'His daughter came to see me last week. She's worried about him taking in a Filipino girl as his housekeeper.'

'Why?' I asked. 'Does she think her father's caught something from the girl?'

'That's about it.' Ralph tapped the stale tobacco out of his pipe and grinned. 'Watch these farmers—dirty dogs, some of them!' He handed me the keys to the practice vehicle. 'I want you to take a comprehensive history, then workup a management plan with your differential diagnosis and proposed investigations. Good luck!'

The farm loomed on the horizon, dark and foreboding, like something out of a horror movie. I half expected Norman Bates' mother to appear in the large upstairs window. The dirt track to the yard challenged the rugged four-wheel-drive vehicle, the engine choking, spluttering and smoking as if it didn't want to get there. With a crash of the gearbox, I eventually pulled up outside the entrance.

Ugh! The farmyard stank. I held my breath and waded through the mud to the battered front door. I could hear coughing coming from inside as I stood on the doorstep. Clutching my Gladstone bag, I grasped the Gothic-style door knocker and gave it a hearty thump.

An Asian girl, who couldn't have been much over twenty, opened the door and announced herself as Lilibeth. As she led me down a cold, damp passageway, the sound of coughing grew louder. An old grandfather clock ticked in the hall, punctuating the wheeze emanating from the corridor. Lilibeth marched swiftly towards Mr Evans' room, looking over her shoulder with a frown as if to chide me for dawdling.

The musty atmosphere in the bedroom almost made me gag. As I approached the broken-down four-poster bed, the stench of urine from the mattress was unbearable. I reached for a handkerchief from my pocket and covered my mouth. Lilibeth clearly noticed my repulsion and scowled at me sourly. Accompanying Dr Greenslade on his rounds had opened my eyes to squalor—but not this wide.

I bit my lip, inwardly ashamed that my emotions had overridden my professionalism. But before I could stop myself, I staggered back and confronted Lilibeth. 'How could you let Mr Evans languish like this? It's a disgrace.'

Lilibeth jumped up and slapped me hard on the face. Bloody hell! What had I walked into?

'You rude man,' she said. 'You *very* rude man! Are you a real doctor?' She turned to Mr Evans. 'I'm going to call Dr Greenslade and ask him to come.'

'No, Lili.' The old man shuffled up on his threadbare pillow. 'Wait.'

'This boy's just a student. You need a proper doctor!'

'And he needs to learn. We're going to give him a chance.' Mr Evans beckoned me over. 'Go on, young man, do your damnedest.'

Lilibeth gave me the evil eye while I questioned Evans about his symptoms. She watched in silence when I conducted my examination.

'So, what have I got, Doc?' Evans asked, his voice quaking when I finished the physical.

'We must do some investigations,' I replied, the history still filtering through my brain. 'Starting with some blood tests.'

'Bad, isn't it?' he spluttered, grabbing Lilibeth's arm and pulling her towards him. 'She's got a sharp tongue, this one—and a temper—but I don't know what I would have done without my Lili these past few months.'

I glanced down at the notes I had scribbled while taking the history and rubbed my forehead. Suddenly, all the pieces of the jigsaw came together. Mr Evans was losing weight. Cachectic. His skin was erupting and riddled with staphylococcal infection. They were all cardinal signs of a compromised immune system.

I watched Lilibeth climb onto the bed and perch herself on his lap. Cogs ticked in my brain. I'd read about the spread of HIV in the Philippines in medical journals.

I took a deep breath and addressed Lilibeth with a stammer in my voice. 'I'll have to check you over, too. You'll need a blood test as well. I think you both have AIDS.'

Lilibeth jumped off the bed and smacked me viciously on the other cheek. 'You *bad* man. *Very* bad man!'

The moment I parked the practice vehicle in the doctor's bay back at the medical centre, I knew there was trouble. A middle-aged woman stormed out of the surgery, glared at me and waved her fist. My mouth went dry. She got into her car and slammed the door shut.

Ralph Greenslade came out into the car park. 'That was Mr Evans' daughter. She's not happy.'

'I can see that.' I watched her rev her car engine and drive away at speed. 'She's going to find it difficult to cope when she has to confront her father's diagnosis.'

'I think you'd better come inside. What's happened to your face? You look like the walking wounded, not the doctor!'

'The housemaid sure knows how to land a punch.' I rubbed my cheeks, which had swollen and stung like hell. 'Sometimes, the truth hurts.'

Dr Greenslade wasn't his usual affable self as he steered me into his consulting room. Perhaps he was just testing me. Regardless, I was supremely confident of my assessment. Bracing myself, I took a seat and launched into my case presentation.

While I spoke, Dr Greenslade unwound a paperclip until it was straight. But he didn't put it back together.

'So that's the only diagnosis you've considered, is it? AIDS. Can you think of another reason why a man living in poverty might start coughing up blood?'

I stared back blankly, still entirely sure of my diagnosis.

Dr Greenslade cleared his throat. His eyes locked on to mine. 'A nasty disease is rearing its ugly head again. Making a resurgence amongst the malnourished and debilitated. You'll have had lectures about it.' A momentary pause that lasted forever. 'Actually, Mr Evans has pulmonary tuberculosis.'

Three days later, Professor Rutherford summoned me to his office.

'What were you thinking?' He stood behind his desk, towering over me, his voluminous moustache twitching. 'Telling a pillar of the farming community he's got AIDS. Insinuating he's been sleeping with his maid and accusing the poor girl of being a prostitute. Are you asking to get thrown out of medical school?'

'It wasn't like that, sir. Honestly. I was only trying to help. Dr Greenslade told me the man's daughter was worried he'd caught something from the girl—'

'Dr Greenslade expected you to act professionally. And what did you do? Make absurd assumptions and scare them to death about AIDS.' Professor Rutherford shook his head and sat down at his desk. 'Were you asleep during my lecture on communication and confidentiality?'

'No, sir.' It was true. That was one of the few lectures where I'd taken notes. No use trying to explain. Professor Rutherford wasn't listening and continued laying into me.

'I've just spent the last couple of hours trying to persuade them not to make a formal complaint. You can thank your lucky stars that I've saved your place at the university. Believe me, it wasn't easy.' He looked me straight in the eye. 'You'll never make a GP. A pathologist, perhaps, but not a general practitioner. If you're that obsessed with AIDS, perhaps you should consider a career as a virologist. Work on a cure. But you can't work with people. That's definite.' He hammered the desk with his hand. 'As for missing tuberculosis in a debilitated patient coughing up blood. Well, Professor Goulding tells me you seldom paid attention in his lectures.'

Could I possibly have felt any worse? When I got up to leave the room, Professor Rutherford called after me. 'Dr Greenslade is so upset by the whole affair that he won't take any more students. You've deprived future medical students of one of our best GP teachers.'

I had let down my guru. How could I live with myself?

You will never make a GP. A pathologist, perhaps, but not a general practitioner.

If that was the case, I might as well give up now. Continuing my medical studies was a waste of time and money. Mine and everyone else's.

CHAPTER THREE

Gold Coast, Queensland, Australia, January 1986

Elisha

'A Sunday school teacher? In *India?*' Elisha spat the words back at her father. 'Christ! You've got to be bloody kidding!'

'Go to your room at once,' he said. 'You will not take the Lord's name in vain in this house. You're grounded!'

'Go easy on her,' Elisha's mother, Melissa, intervened. 'This is a huge adjustment for the family.'

'If we're going to India, I might as well be grounded for the rest of my life!' Elisha gave her father the finger and stormed out of the room.

A Sunday school teacher in some goddamn backwater? No frigging way! Elisha slammed her bedroom door shut, threw herself on the bed and beat the mattress with her fist. *Damn you! I'll be eighteen next year. You can't make me go.*

She knew her father was becoming restless. His preaching always went up a notch when another overseas mission was imminent, and last Sunday's sermon was a giveaway. But he usually went alone. Taking the entire family to rural India—that was beyond her worst nightmare.

Growing up in a missionary's family felt like a constant bad dream, and it was bloody unfair. Bible study classes while the other kids hung out with their mates. They had their freedom. She had church every Sunday and endless teasing at school.

'Preacher's daughter! Preacher's daughter!'

Elisha endured the same barrage each day at break time. The girls would surround her in a circle and take turns to hurl insults.

'So we're all going to Hell, are we? Your old man's full of crap!'

'Hell sounds way more fun than Heaven.'

'Say your prayers every night, do you?'

Even Elisha's so-called friend Jackie had joined in. 'Want to come for a sleepover at the weekend, Lee? Oh no. Of course. You can't. You've got church on Sunday morning.'

It hadn't helped that her father had been the target of the Australian media's campaign against missionaries. Elisha had cringed at the front-page stories, plastered on billboards everywhere.

Wesley Martin—saviour or troublemaker?

White Christian missionary Wesley Martin tells the Indian people how to live their lives.

The piss-taking would only worsen when her classmates found out she was going to India to be a Sunday school teacher. Elisha shuddered and rolled over on her bed. There'd been better times. Her eyes fixed on an old newspaper cutting pinned to her cork noticeboard.

Australian missionary Wesley Martin brings new hope to a flood-ridden village in Orissa state.

The starving children's faces in the fading photograph under the headline still brought a lump to her throat. Elisha had been close to her dad back then. She *wanted* to be proud of her father, but how could a man who cared so much for other people's children be so unthinking with his own daughter?

Elisha glanced at another cutting on her noticeboard.

Renowned missionary Wesley Martin adopts an Indian half-caste from a leper colony.

Everything was so much easier for her adopted brother, Isaac. He'd become a legend in Australia on the day he arrived. Elisha couldn't help smiling when she remembered the stories she'd heard about her father's altercation with the immigration service at the border. Hot on theology, but less adept with bureaucracy, he hadn't got the necessary documentation for Isaac to enter Australia as a bona fide refugee.

Isaac had told her how the customs officers had taken them into an interview room for questioning.

'Can't you see the poor boy's exhausted?' Wesley had said. 'We've been travelling for over twenty-four hours. Show some compassion, please.'

'I can see that,' the officer had replied, 'but we have to establish the legitimacy of your adoption.'

Wesley had tapped the desktop. 'He needs a bed, not more hanging around.'

According to Isaac, the customs officer wasn't that impressed. 'We cannot let him through until we have checked your credentials, sir. You must understand. There's been a rise in the trafficking of children across our borders.'

Wesley hadn't given in without a fight. 'Do I look like a people smuggler?' Elisha could just imagine her father's self-righteous tone. 'Isaac's mother and father, and his brother and sister, were all wiped out by malaria. He has nobody. Do you want to deny him a decent home?'

'Of course we don't,' the officer said. 'But we still have to be sure that your intentions towards this boy are honourable, and that his refugee status is genuine.'

Elisha had laughed when Isaac described the look on her father's face when the police took them to an immigration detention centre. The Reverend Wesley Martin was not used to having his integrity questioned. The press had got hold of the story, and the next day they splashed it across the nation's newspapers. Isaac became a cause célèbre in the media. Public pressure forced the authorities to expedite his entry clearance.

Elisha had watched the kids treat Isaac like a film star on his first day at school.

'You're cool, bro!' The boys took turns to give him a high five. 'We saw you on the telly. You socked it to the bastards! Power to the people!'

More irritating for Elisha was the way Isaac's passion for sport made him a hero. Back home, Isaac had captained the local cricket team in Orissa and had led them to the top in the regional championships. Now he coached the school's team and revived their flagging reputation in the inter-school tournaments. His skills extended beyond his beloved cricket. He proved an ace at rugby too. For the first time in years, with Isaac's charisma and leadership, their school thrashed the opposition. All the kids loved him. 'Zac' was their hero.

'Bloody sport,' Elisha muttered to herself. *Why does he get all the kudos and I get all the shit?*

Zac's broad grin did nothing for Elisha's mood when she sat down at the breakfast table the next morning.

'There's a fantastic cricket team in Baripada,' Zac said. 'I can't wait to get back.'

'You and your bloody cricket.' Elisha banged her cereal bowl on the table. 'I'm not in the mood for this!'

'But sis, it's going to be great!' Zac said.

Elisha scowled at her brother. 'Piss off. Jesus! It's going to be hell for me.'

Wesley threw down his newspaper. 'Elisha! What did I tell you yesterday about blasphemy?'

Elisha glared back at him. She hadn't heard a swear word before she'd gone to school. Now, shocking her father was a sure way to get back at him. She was about to come out with another choice expletive when her mother stepped in.

'Give her a break, Wes,' Melissa said. 'We've turned her world upside down.'

Wesley rapped his newspaper on the table. 'Nothing excuses that kind of language.'

'All kids talk like that these days,' Melissa said. 'It means nothing.'

'She is disrespecting the Almighty,' Wesley said. 'I will not have it.'

Melissa reached across the table and took Wesley's arm. 'She needs time to adjust.'

'Nothing will change my mind about India,' Elisha said.

Zac grinned. 'Don't be like that, sis. We could have fun. There's an ace women's hockey team in Baripada. You should join it.'

'*Fun?*' Elisha choked on her toast. '*Women's hockey?* No chance!'

Zac pulled a face. 'Sis!'

'Leave it, Zac,' Melissa said. 'It's all right for you—you're going home. We're taking your sister away from everything she knows.'

'Suppose so,' Zac said. 'But she'll make lots of new friends in Madhapur.'

Elisha snorted. 'I don't need new friends.'

'Come on, sis,' Zac said. 'That's not like you—'

'It is,' Elisha said. 'How many times do I have to tell you? I'm not going.'

Wesley eyeballed Elisha. 'Yes, you are.' He got up from the breakfast table and frowned at his children. 'And stop bickering, both of you. I need some quiet to write my final sermon. It's going to be hard saying goodbye to our brothers and sisters in Christ at the church.'

'So you don't want to leave either,' Elisha said. 'We don't have to go. It's an absolute no-brainer.'

'Don't be silly,' Melissa said, taking Elisha's arm. 'You know we're committed to the mission. We need to have a talk.'

Elisha pulled away. 'Talking about it won't make any difference.'

'It's not easy for me either,' Melissa said, ushering Elisha to her bedroom, 'giving up everything. I've got a life here, too, you know.'

Elisha slumped on her bed. 'So why don't you tell Dad where to get off?'

Melissa shut the bedroom door. 'Don't be so selfish.'

'Selfish?' Elisha said. 'I just want a life. Is that too much to ask?'

Melissa sat down beside her daughter. 'Your dad needs our support. He's passionate about this mission.' She gently stroked Elisha's hair. 'It's our chance to make a difference. To do something for people who haven't had the opportunities we've got.'

Elisha looked down and fiddled with her bracelet. Did they have to go there to make a difference? Couldn't they just send a donation?

Melissa edged closer. 'It won't be forever.'

Elisha pulled away. 'Yes, it will! I've heard Dad talking—'

'Elisha!' Melissa straightened her back and scratched her head. 'Please!'

'Why can't he just go on his own?' Elisha said. 'He doesn't have to take us with him.'

Melissa shuffled up again and put an arm around Elisha. 'We want to keep the family together. Besides, it will be great for Zac.'

Elisha rolled her eyes. 'Zac and Dad can go on their own if they're so bloody keen.'

'No, Elisha.' Melissa shrugged and got up from the bed. 'We're going to make this work as a family.' She paused at the bedroom door. 'Why don't you talk to Joanna?'

Joanna! Why hadn't she thought of Jo before? Elisha jumped off the bed and aimed a high five at her mother. 'That's it! I can stay with Jo while you lot bugger off to India.'

Elisha paid little attention to school that day. She was far too busy rehearsing

　　　　　David Whittet

what she'd say to get Joanna on side. Elisha was first out of the classroom when the bell rang. Minutes later, she burst into the vestry of St Stephen's Church.

'Jo! You've got to help me! Can I stay with you? I'm not leaving Australia.'

A kind face emerged from beneath a stack of religious books and a raft of parish papers. Joanna Johnston, an elder of the church, smiled sympathetically and gestured for Elisha to sit in one of the old leather chairs in the dark and otherwise barren room.

'I've been expecting you,' Joanna said. 'Your mother told me you weren't best pleased about the move to India.'

'Let me stay with you,' Elisha pleaded. 'Please!'

'I wish I could,' Joanna said. 'But you know I can't go against your father.'

'Please! He'll listen to you.' Elisha leant forward, extending an arm towards her old mentor. 'You're the only one I can turn to. My life is over if I have to go to India!'

An awkward silence. Elisha stared at Joanna's confused eyes and watched her fiddle with the crucifix she wore around her neck. The soft light from the stained-glass window emphasised her sallow complexion, giving her an almost ethereal appearance. Elisha had often wondered how old Joanna was. Her conventional dress said she must be at least fifty. Her wrinkles suggested she could be older.

Joanna cleared her throat. 'I'm sorry, Elisha.'

What? Surely Joanna—the woman who had seen her through so many teenage crises—wouldn't let her down when it mattered most?

'Jo!' Elisha said. 'You have to!'

Joanna sighed. 'This time you're asking too much.'

Elisha slumped back in her chair. 'Too much? You've worked miracles before. You're a lifesaver.'

'I wish I was.' Joanna got up and hugged Elisha. 'This must be hard on you.'

Elisha pulled away. 'Hard? It's a bloody death sentence.'

'Can't you see this as a challenge? Think of it as your big overseas experience.'

Elisha made a face. Joanna returned to her desk and picked up some photographs from her pile of papers.

'I was writing an article on the mission for the next edition of the *Parish News* when you came in,' Joanna said, showing Elisha a picture of an outdoor doctors' clinic. 'We're building a field hospital. It's going to be a tremendous adventure.'

Elisha snorted. 'If you're that keen, you can take my place!'

'Actually,' Joanna said, 'I would love to go to Madhapur.'

Elisha shook her head. 'I can't imagine why anyone would want to go to such a backwater.'

'I have a special reason,' Joanna said.

Elisha was used to batting words back and forth with Joanna. She was about to up the ante when she noticed a tear in the corner of Joanna's eye.

'What is it?' Elisha said.

Joanna picked up another photograph and stared at it. 'Rajani,' she whispered, 'my little girl.'

What was she on about? *Jo doesn't have kids. Or does she?*

'Who?' Elisha tried to get a look at the photo. She glimpsed a little Indian girl helping her mother to get water from a pump.

Joanna put the picture down. 'A girl I've been sponsoring at the mission. I'd give anything to see her.'

'So why don't you?'

'If only I could.'

Elisha ran her hand through her hair. Something wasn't right. Why couldn't Joanna go to India if she wanted to? The rest of the church elders did as they pleased. Another tear appeared in Joanna's eye. Maybe Elisha should back off. Give Joanna some space.

Elisha sighed. *I can't give up now. Somehow, I have to get Jo on my side.* It was time for a fresh approach. 'They used to make fun of me at school because of my father. Banged on about him meddling in affairs that had nothing to do with him.'

'That's not fair on your father,' Joanna said.

'But it's true. And it's not right. Barging into their country and telling them what to believe.'

 David Whittet

Joanna's voice hardened. 'Your father has given his life to helping some of the most disadvantaged people on the planet.'

Elisha lowered her head. 'I know that. It's just … everyone's been so mean to me. You've no idea the shit I've had to put up with, all because of my father …' She broke off as her eyes caught Joanna's.

'I know,' Joanna said, 'but that's not his fault.'

'I've had to work so hard to make friends. And just when I've established myself, he wants to drag me away.' Elisha pulled her chair up close. 'Listen, Jo. I'm old enough to decide my own future.'

'Please don't ask me,' Joanna said. 'Your father's been so good to me. He was there when there was nobody else.'

Elisha snapped her fingers. 'I'm eighteen in November. My father can't make me do anything then.' She leant forward and flicked through the draft *Parish News* articles on the desktop. 'If you let me stay with you, I'll help at St Stephen's. I could edit the newsletter for you. I'd even teach at the Sunday school here.'

'No, Elisha. The wider Church needs your help now. India's need is much greater than ours.' Joanna put her hand on Elisha's. 'I know it's not what you want, but the experience will enrich your life. Help you find God.'

'I don't need to find God,' Elisha said. 'He's been rammed down my throat since the day I was born.'

A tense pause. Joanna shook her head and tutted.

Elisha sat bolt upright. 'I'm not a good person. They'd be better off without me.'

'That's not true.'

'It is.' Elisha blinked back a tear. 'I've had to be horrible to survive, what with the other girls ganging up on me. Take Jess. She *knew* I wanted to take Laurie to the ball. I was head over heels. So what did she do? The bitch stole him from under my nose. But I got my own back on the cow. I pinched her dress from her locker and dyed it black. Damn near got me thrown out of school, but it was worth it to see the look on her face!'

'Two wrongs don't make a right,' Joanna said.

'Now you sound like my father,' Elisha replied. 'Turn the other cheek. I never believed it.'

Joanna got up and walked over to the vestry window. She stood motionless, staring into the distance.

What was she thinking? Elisha swallowed. Had she gone too far? Was Joanna cross with her?

At last, Joanna spoke. 'We've all done things we're not proud of.'

'Bet *you* haven't.'

Joanna returned to her seat. She opened her mouth to answer, then covered her face with her hands.

'Don't tell me you're not a saint, like everyone else around here,' Elisha said. It just wasn't possible for Joanna—the woman she'd looked up to for so long—to have some sordid secret. Or was it?

Joanna hung her head. 'I killed someone. My little sister.'

'You killed your sister?' Elisha felt her muscles tense. 'If that's meant to be funny, it's in bloody poor taste.'

'It's not a joke. She had her life in front of her, and I took it away in an instant.'

Elisha stood up. 'I don't believe it! You're lying!'

'I'm not!' Joanna pleaded. 'Listen to me, Elisha. I can explain.'

Elisha covered her ears. 'I'm sorry, Jo. I have to get out.'

Joanna was crying now. 'Please don't leave like this.'

The walls of the vestry closed in on Elisha. She couldn't look at the woman who had been her rock for so many years. Was Joanna really a killer? Could there be a plausible explanation? Too wound up to stay and listen, Elisha bolted from the church.

The more Elisha pounded the streets, the less she understood. Her life was in turmoil when she went into the church, but in the last five minutes, Joanna had made everything infinitely worse.

CHAPTER FOUR

Elisha had no idea where she was going. She glanced over her shoulder and quickened her pace. Joanna was still following, begging her to stop. Elisha didn't want to know. Was everyone in the frigging Church just there to atone for some hideous crime? Repent, and it didn't matter any more? What a load of hypocrites and shysters!

Joanna caught up and grabbed Elisha's arm. 'Come back! It was an accident! I didn't mean to kill my sister.'

Elisha carried on walking. 'You expect me to believe that?'

'We've been friends all these years,' Joanna said. 'Surely you want to hear the whole story?'

Elisha stopped. Joanna was usually so calm, in control of every situation. Tonight, she'd aged twenty years in the past half hour. They sat down together on a park bench.

'I'll hear you out on one condition,' Elisha said. 'None of your "it was God's will" crap. Promise?'

'Promise,' Joanna said. 'But first, shouldn't we let your parents know where you are? They'll be worried.'

Elisha shrugged. 'They won't. I told Mum I was going to see you.'

'I still think we should let them know,' Joanna said. 'It's getting late.'

'I often hang out with my friends till much later than this,' Elisha said. 'Anyway, my father said he would be up half the night writing his farewell sermon. He'll be glad of the peace and quiet. All I want to do at the moment is scream, shout and stamp my feet.'

'At least let me call your mother,' Joanna said. 'Let's go back to the church. I can make some coffee, and we can talk. You must have come straight from school. How about I rustle up some supper?'

'I'm not hungry,' Elisha said, 'and I need something much stronger than coffee. But it is bloody cold out here.'

Joanna took Elisha's hand. 'You're shivering. We need to get you warm.'

Back in the vestry, Joanna put on the kettle and phoned Melissa.

'Your mother was worried about you,' Joanna said. 'She says you were in quite a state when you left for school this morning.'

Elisha took a swig of coffee. 'That's nothing to how I'm feeling now.'

Joanna sat down beside her, took a deep breath, and exhaled slowly. 'I was just sixteen when it happened. Angie, my sister, was fourteen.'

Elisha's eyes met Joanna's, which were all puffy and bloodshot.

'Angie had argued with our parents for weeks,' Joanna continued. 'She wanted to go to a party at her friend Harry's place. Our dad said they were a bad lot, and there would be boys at the party. That was the end of it. Angie couldn't go.'

Elisha noticed a drop of perspiration on Joanna's forehead. 'Go on.'

'I lied to Mum,' Joanna said. 'Promised I'd take Angie to Bible study with me. But I let her go to the party.'

'So, what happened?' Elisha asked. 'You said you killed her.'

'I knew Angie was in trouble,' Joanna said. 'We had this kind of sixth sense between us. Someone at the party was hurting her. I was sure of it. I had to get her home. Keep her safe. I made an excuse at the Bible class. Ran back, took my dad's car, and went to pick her up.'

Elisha caught her breath. 'So you were trying to save your little sister—not kill her.'

'Turned out she was alright,' Joanna said. 'Angie was the life and soul of the party. But I'd lost my nerve and insisted she come home. I dragged her away, kicking and screaming. She said she'd never forgive me for the embarrassment.'

'I can understand that,' Elisha said.

Joanna sobbed uncontrollably. 'She never got the chance to forgive me. We argued all the way home, and I swerved on a corner and crashed into a truck. The impact killed Angie instantly.'

Elisha flung her arms around Joanna. 'I'm so sorry.'

'I was only on a learner's licence,' Joanna said. 'I shouldn't have been driving on my own. The police charged me. I did time, but none of that brought back my beloved sister.'

The two women held on to each other for what felt like an eternity.

'I'm sorry I ran out on you,' Elisha said. 'I should have listened.'

 David Whittet

Joanna sighed and squeezed her hand. 'You came back and you're here now.'

Something else puzzled Elisha. 'You said my father helped you through the bad times. How? What did he do?'

'My family disowned me,' Joanna said. 'No compassion. I wasn't their daughter any more. So I left the Church. Lost my faith. How could a loving God have let that happen to my little sister?' She paused for a moment and eyed Elisha. 'But I read in the newspaper about what your father had done in India. I went to his church and heard him preach about forgiveness.'

Elisha cringed. She'd torn up press cuttings about her father in a fit of temper the previous night.

'Your dad taught me about redemption.' Joanna picked up a photo from her desk and gave it to Elisha. 'He told me about this little girl in India. Her name's Rajani. Your father persuaded me to sponsor her. Adopt her as part of my family.'

Elisha looked at the photograph. 'She's beautiful—if a bit thin. Have you been to see her?'

Joanna's head dropped again. 'I've wanted to. You can't imagine how much. But with a manslaughter conviction, the authorities wouldn't give me a visa.'

'Jo!' Elisha hugged her again.

'But she's still the daughter I never had and the sister I lost, rolled into one.' Joanna fixed her eyes on Elisha. 'I know you don't see eye to eye with your father. But he's a good man. I wouldn't have survived without him.'

Elisha returned her gaze. 'I know.'

Joanna wiped her face with a handkerchief. 'I need to ask you a favour.'

Elisha smiled. 'Don't push your luck.'

Joanna smiled back. 'Okay. Perhaps not tonight. It's late. How about I take you out for tea after school tomorrow? My shout.'

The lights were still on when Elisha got home. Her parents never stayed up this late. Was her father really still working on his sermon? Elisha sighed. They were in for a mighty long service on Sunday.

Melissa had fallen asleep on the sofa, reading a book. Elisha strode up to her father and kissed him on the cheek.

'I heard what you did for Jo,' Elisha said. 'You were a legend. I'm so proud of you.'

Wesley blushed. 'She told you about her accident?'

'She did.' Elisha gave him another kiss. 'And about Rajani.'

Melissa stirred. 'You'll meet Rajani when we get to the mission. I bet you'll be good friends before long.'

Elisha took a step back from her father. 'Don't think this lets you off the hook. I'm still mad about India.'

Wesley took off his glasses. Elisha saw a softness in his eyes that she hadn't noticed before.

'We never wanted to upset you,' he said. 'It's not easy, sometimes. Doing the right thing. And believe me, this mission in India *is* the right thing. We're going to set up a hospital and help some of the neediest of God's children. Little ones are dying because they can't get medicine. We'll change that.'

Elisha put her arms around her father and hugged him. Then she ran off to her bedroom before she started to cry.

School dragged even more than usual the next day. What was the point of concentrating on her lessons, anyway? Elisha was leaving in a couple of weeks.

'Looking forward to living in a mud hut?' Jess whispered during class. 'Sooner you than me. Crapping outside. Yuk!'

That didn't sting any more. Elisha had more important things on her mind. Would that final bell ever ring? What was the favour Joanna needed? It had to have something to do with Rajani.

Joanna was waiting at the crowded espresso bar, and they queued up behind a bunch of tourists to place their order.

'I brought you some photos from the mission,' Joanna said.

Elisha looked at the photographs and pulled a face. 'Don't tell me that's where we're going to live!' Perhaps the kids at school were right after all. The houses were made of clay and thatch.

'No need to panic,' Joanna said. 'There's a small guest house just outside the village.' Joanna sifted through the pile to find a picture of the establishment. 'Look. You'll be staying there.'

Elisha rolled her eyes. 'Not exactly the Ritz, is it?'

Once sat at a table, Joanna showed Elisha pictures of the leper colony. 'Both of Rajani's parents died there. Rajani would have died, too, if it wasn't for your father.'

Elisha felt warm inside, and glad she'd made peace with her dad last night.

Joanna selected a photo of Rajani from the pile. Elisha noticed Jo fiddle with her crucifix again.

'Promise me,' Joanna said, 'you'll visit Rajani once you settle in.'

'Course I will!' Elisha picked up the picture of Rajani. 'I'll need a friend when I get to that godforsaken place. She looks so cute.'

'Mind you,' Joanna said, 'that picture's a couple of years out of date now. She'll have grown—at least I hope she has. I'm relying on you to send me an up-to-date photograph.'

'I've always wanted a little sister.' Elisha took a sip of her long black and paused. 'Perhaps a needy girl in India is the next best thing. I'll look after her for you.'

'That would make me so happy.' Joanna beamed. 'And it'll bring you good karma. I promise!'

Elisha's father shook hands with his congregation as they filed out of the church on the last Sunday before their departure. The flock showered him and his family with good wishes, flowers, gifts, and some generous donations for the mission.

Elisha's hands ached from all the greetings. Zac excused himself and disappeared with some of his mates for a farewell game of football. Elisha looked for Joanna and spotted her collecting the prayer books and placing them back on the shelf.

'I've had enough emotion in the last couple of days to last me a lifetime,' Elisha said.

Joanna laughed. 'Your life is just beginning. There'll be plenty more adventures for you, my girl.' They walked down the churchyard path, arm in arm. 'Now tell me, are you all set for the journey?'

'Ready as I'll ever be,' Elisha said. 'My arm hurts like hell from all those inoculations.' She squeezed Joanna's hand. 'I wish you were coming with us.'

Joanna sighed. 'So do I. You know I'd love to see Rajani.'

Elisha squeezed Joanna's hand harder. 'Why don't you come? I'm sure they'd give you a visa now.'

'I doubt it,' Joanna said. 'You don't know Indian red tape. Anyway, someone has to look after everything here while you're all away. You know I promised your father.'

'Why do you have to do whatever my old man says?' Elisha gazed back at her father, who was still talking to the churchgoers. All of them doubtless hanging on his every word. 'Come to that, why does everyone do what he says?'

Joanna paused before replying, 'Because we respect him.'

Elisha glanced across from her dad outside the church to the neighbouring paddock, where Zac scored the decisive goal in his match. 'Lucky sod. Why does he always win?' she mumbled to herself while he did a victorious lap of honour with his teammates.

Joanna patted her on the shoulder. 'Isaac must be really excited. I bet he's longing to get back to Madhapur.'

'The cheeky bugger told me to join the local hockey team!'

'Why don't you?' Joanna said. 'You're tall, slender and athletic. You'd be great.'

Elisha snorted. 'Me? Athletic? You've got to be joking!'

When they reached the stone arch at the entrance to the churchyard, Joanna stopped abruptly and frowned. 'You won't forget about Rajani, will you?'

Elisha smiled. 'Of course not. I won't let you down.' She gazed into Joanna's eyes. 'I've decided. Rajani's going to be my little sister.'

'Yes!' Joanna grabbed Elisha's arm, and they began an impromptu dance. '*Thank you*, from the bottom of my heart.'

They continued to twirl, to the delight of the parishioners who strolled past.

     David Whittet

'Oh my,' Joanna added, catching her breath. 'Don't forget, I want that photo of Rajani. As soon as you can.'

'You know I will,' Joanna said.

'And one of you and Rajani together.'

'That too.' Elisha waved her hand in the air. 'We'll be like a new sisterhood!'

'How beautiful.' Joanna flung her arms around Elisha, and the pair hugged each other for several minutes.

Joanna eventually pulled back and dabbed her eyes. 'Now, go and finish your packing. I've got presents to wrap for Rajani.'

Two days later, Elisha and Joanna embraced again on Brisbane International Airport's departure level, tears streaming down their cheeks.

'I'm going to miss you,' Joanna said, holding on to Elisha's hand.

'I'll miss you too,' Elisha replied. 'Who's going to listen to my ranting now when my life turns to crap? And it *will* turn to shit in India!'

'Now then,' Joanna tutted with a pretend scowl. 'What did we agree about being positive? You'll find someone new to talk to. When God closes a door—'

'Don't tell me,' Elisha said with a hoot, 'He opens a window.'

'That's right!' Joanna threw her head back and smiled. 'And India is one almighty window of opportunity.'

'Don't start that again.'

With a final cuddle, Joanna pushed Elisha towards her family and the inevitable 'Passengers Only Beyond This Point' sign.

'Off you go,' Joanna said. 'Remember to give Rajani a kiss from me and don't eat her food hamper yourself. At least, not all of it!'

Elisha's father stood at the head of the passport control queue. Isaac was at his side, jumping up and down with excitement, and Melissa plodded a few paces behind. As Elisha disappeared into the throng of passengers, Joanna called after her.

'I'll pray for you, Elisha!'

With a wicked laugh, Elisha turned back to wave at Joanna. 'It'll take more than frigging prayer if I'm going to survive in the backwaters of bloody India!'

CHAPTER FIVE

University of Otago Medical School, New Zealand, August 1988

Theo

You will never make a GP. A pathologist, perhaps, but not a general practitioner.
Two years on, and in my last year at medical school, Professor Rutherford's
words still haunted me. Was he right? Had I chosen the wrong profession,
making a decision based on emotion? Absolutely not. I was going to make
a difference. And there was no way I would let that miserable professor ruin
my career. The other students in my year sucked up to their consultants.
All they cared about was landing a plum house-job. I set my heart on my
forthcoming student elective in Uganda.

'What happens to all the old medicines once they've passed their expiry
date?' I asked Marian Taylor, a staff nurse on the surgical ward. 'Every week,
the orderly collects them. Where do they go after that?'

'They end up in a landfill, I guess,' Marian answered. 'Why do you
ask?'

'I'm doing my elective in Uganda,' I said. 'They're desperately short of
medicines over there. Particularly antibiotics. Instead of throwing them
out, could you collect them for me? Nobody else need know.'

Marian stepped back. 'I'm not so sure. I've heard of students doing this
before, and it always ends in trouble.'

'Chill!' I said, 'I've got it all worked out!'

'Maybe it's not such a good idea, anyway.' Marian scratched her head.
'They get rid of old drugs for a reason.'

My eyes drilled into Marian's. We'd spent hours together on the night
shift and regularly set the world right over coffee at four in the morning.
I knew exactly how to get around her. 'Children die every day in Uganda
because they can't get the antibiotics they need. Is that what you want? Are
you going to help me or not?'

That had to convince her. Didn't it? Marian's expression gave nothing away.

At last a tentative nod. 'Just be careful.'

I hugged her. 'Thank you.'

The next morning, Marian handed me a couple of penicillin vials under the counter in the nursing station.

'Come on, Marian,' I said. 'You can do better than this. I was hoping for a bin liner full of antibiotics.'

'Not with Sister Abbott on night duty,' Marian said. 'I swear that woman has eyes in the back of her head.'

'But you're smarter than her,' I said. 'So we have to go underground.'

We met in the locker room the following day. Marian looked over her shoulder and gave me a carrier bag full of medicines.

'That's more like it,' I said. 'I knew you could do it.'

'I'm still not happy about this,' she said. 'What if we get caught?'

I waved my hand dismissively. 'We won't. Besides, I read a paper in the *New Zealand Medical Journal* last week. Medicines aren't being properly treated before they're dumped on the tip. It's a national disgrace. Refuse companies are just after a quick buck, and it's causing untold damage to the environment.'

Marian hesitated. 'I suppose.'

'So,' I added with a cheeky grin, 'we're not just saving kids in Uganda, we're keeping New Zealand clean and green at the same time.'

By the end of my surgical run, I had two giant trunks full of life-saving drugs. Dozens upon dozens of glistening ampoules that would spare Ugandan children the agony that Akiki had suffered.

Getting the medicines was a breeze compared with battling the Ugandan Medical Board and their endless questions. The university provided me with a letter of introduction outlining the mutual advantages of medical students spending time overseas during their training. That clearly wasn't enough for the Ugandan authorities. I got an airmail letter back asking why I wanted to go to Uganda. 'Don't you have enough teaching facilities in your own country? Perhaps there's another reason for your visit?' I wrote back, assuring them it was purely an educational trip. Another airmail letter arrived. 'Have you ever been in trouble with the police? Do you have a criminal record? Have you been refused entry or deported from any country?'

Strewth. What made them think I would cause trouble? I'd read about the coup two years ago, when Museveni's forces toppled the previous regime. But I wasn't a terrorist. Or an anarchist out to make trouble. I was a final-year medical student who wanted to experience medicine in the raw and to volunteer to help those in need.

Months passed with yet more letters going backwards and forwards, delays with the Ugandan postal system adding to my frustration. Mentioning Akiki was a mistake. The Ugandan immigration minister demanded to know if I was trying to smuggle his family out.

'No,' I wrote back. 'Akiki hasn't got a family. They're all dead.'

I'd all but given up when a well-worn envelope with some exotic stamps arrived on the ward.

Marian watched me fidget with the letter. 'Aren't you going to open it?'

I stuffed the letter into the pocket of my white coat, next to my stethoscope. 'It'll just be a refusal.'

'You don't know that,' Marian said. 'Come on. Open it.'

'No.' I walked away. 'It's the sixth letter I've had from them this month. All of them full of excuses and telling me why I can't go.'

'If you won't open it, I will.' Marian chased after me and snatched the letter from my pocket.

'Give that back!'

Too late. Marian tore the envelope open. *Wahoo!* They've given you the go-ahead!'

I froze. 'For real?'

'Yes!' Marian handed me the letter. 'You're going to Uganda!'

I held the letter up in the air. 'This is for you, Akiki.' Then I hugged Marian and twirled her around the nursing station.

At last, I could honour my promise to Akiki and do something for his people and their country.

A month later, Marian dropped me off at Dunedin Airport. I hadn't slept for the past few nights. What would it be like? Akiki had warned me that

 David Whittet

in Uganda rural hospitals were grim. Overcrowded, understaffed and in dire need of repair. Would I survive? Confronting poverty head-on differed from reading about it in books and looking at pictures. It was one thing having high ideas about making a difference; following through on them was something else. Perhaps I should have just sent the medicines by cargo and hoped they got to where they were most needed. No. I wasn't a quitter, and this was the adventure of a lifetime.

'Good luck!' Marian's chirpy voice brought me back to earth. 'Follow your dreams! Send me a postcard as soon as you arrive.'

A kiss and a cuddle, and she left. I was on my own with two large suitcases and their precious contents. I took a deep, satisfying breath as I lugged them onto the scales at the check-in desk.

The Air New Zealand check-in agent weighed the two cases. 'Did you pack the bags yourself, sir?'

I drew back. 'Yes.'

'Are there any prohibited or dangerous items in your luggage?'

'Nothing dangerous.' Had she noticed the croak in my voice? Did I look guilty?

'Nothing flammable?' she asked.

'No.'

My heart missed a beat. *Please don't open them to have a look.*

'I've checked your bags through to Entebbe,' she said, attaching the baggage tags. I could have hugged her when she loaded the cases onto the conveyor belt. 'Here are your boarding passes. It's Gate Five for the Auckland flight. You must cross to the international terminal at Auckland for your onward flights through Sydney and Dubai.'

Exhausted after more than thirty hours of travel, I pressed my head against the window as the aircraft descended. Glimpses of the vast expanse of lush green bush, punctuated by lakes, rivers and waterfalls, appeared through the clouds. Tall pawpaw trees. Snow-capped mountains, almost close enough to touch. How could there be so much suffering in such a beautiful country?

My heart pounded as the aircraft touched down at Entebbe International Airport. I'd seen TV shows about gung-ho border police in Africa, interrogating foreigners down the barrel of a rifle. I just hoped the Lugandan phrases I'd been practising for months would help.

'Hello. *Ki kati*,' I began. 'Good morning. *Wasuze otya nno.*'

The customs officer, in full military uniform, eyeballed me. 'Why so many bags for a short visit?'

He indicated I should lift them onto the bench. At least his gun was still in its holster.

'I'm a medical student. Come to work at Kalanjala Hospital.' I paused. No use lying. His hand was edging towards his weapon. 'I've brought some medical supplies.'

His finger toyed with the trigger. 'You have permit?'

I fumbled in my pocket. 'I have a student visa and a letter of authorisation from the Ugandan Medical Board.'

He snatched the documents. Meanwhile, the police arrested another passenger and lead him away in handcuffs. Would that be me in a few minutes?

The customs officer showed my letter to his sidekick.

'You from New Zealand?' The second officer twirled his gun in one hand and his moustache in the other. 'And you want to go to Kalanjala?'

Why was that so hard to believe? 'Yes. I want to learn about medicine in your country.'

He rested his gun on the bench. 'You serious?'

'Absolutely.'

Their stony faces cracked. The first officer handed back my papers with a knowing grin.

'*Tukusanyukidde!* Welcome!' he said. 'Good luck. You'll need it at Kalanjala.'

'*Weebale nnyo!* Thank you very much!' My trolley veered in all directions, my cases toppling off as I made for the exit.

Which way was the taxi rank? Dazzled by the midday sun and drenched by the oppressive heat, I struggled to make myself heard over the cacophony.

'Taxi! Taxi! *Takisi!*'

Young drivers honked their horns and beckoned me over with a welcoming smile. Until I told them where I was going. Why would none of them take me to the Kalanjala Hospital?

Across the block, a driver sat in a clapped-out yellow-and-white minibus. He looked like he hadn't eaten for days. Surely he wouldn't turn me down.

'I have to get to Kalanjala Hospital,' I said.

'You want to go to Kalanjala?' The man scratched his balding head. '*Ogambye ki?* Pardon? You sick? I can take you to much better hospital.'

I shook my head. 'I'm not sick. I'm going to work at Kalanjala Hospital.'

The driver frowned at me. 'You are doctor, *ssebo?*' he asked, calling me 'sir' to be polite.

'Medical student.'

'You don't want to work there, *ssebo*. Very bad place.'

Give me strength. I tapped my foot on the kerb. 'Will you take me there or not?'

'It'll cost you, *ssebo*.' He rubbed his chin. 'Long way. *Very* long way. Over two hours.'

Five minutes of haggling and he shook my hand.

'You have deal, *ssebo*,' he said. 'My name Sanyu.'

He loaded my bags on the minibus. After a few false starts with the engine spluttering and stalling, we began the 110-kilometre journey. I discreetly crossed my fingers under the disintegrating dashboard. Sanyu honked his horn as beggars and hustlers competed with chauffeurs and their limousines for space on the road. Mothers pleading for food for their babies. Children covered in bites and sores. Wealthy businessmen pushing them out of the way. The picture was every bit as bad as Akiki had painted, and worse. I closed my eyes as we left the airport complex. Self-doubt resurfaced. My general practice attachment in Dunedin had shown me run-down housing estates and leaking roofs that made them a breeding ground for all manner of bugs. But no starvation—at least not on this scale. How would I cope with what Uganda had in store for me?

I opened my eyes. A bunch of girls in tight leather minidresses and fishnet stockings filled the street. It must be Kampala's notorious red-light district.

'You want me find you girl?' Sanyu said. 'Women here no good. Nasty diseases. I take you to nightclub. Nice girls there.'

'No, thank you,' I said. 'Kalanjala Hospital.'

Sanyu ignored my protests and continued to drive past the local bars. He must have been on commission.

'You have good time here,' he said, pulling up outside a seedy massage parlour.

How could I convince Sanyu I didn't give a stuff about the nightlife? 'I said no. Now, will you take me to Kalanjala Hospital?'

Far more interesting to me was the kaleidoscope of life in front of my eyes as the minibus clattered over the potholes. The squalor of the mud-built houses, kids playing football on the wasteland just as Akiki had described it, the stark beauty of the landscape as we headed out of town.

With no air conditioning in the van and sweat pouring down my face, I wound down the window and inhaled a lungful of burnt rubber. Children lined the roads, arms held out, grasping for food. When we stopped at traffic lights, a multitude of little hands poked through the open window.

'*Owange*. Excuse me,' a little boy cried. '*Mwattu nnyamba!* Please help! *Enjala ennuma!* I am hungry!'

I took some Ugandan coins out of my pocket and shared them amongst the children. 'Here, take this. Get yourselves something to eat.'

'*Weebale*. Thank you,' the children chorused. '*Siiba bulungi!* Have a nice day!'

Sanyu spat out of the window and growled at me. '*Never* give money to kids!'

'Didn't you see their faces?' I asked. 'Those smiles were worth a million dollars!'

'*Kasasiro!* Rubbish! You will not survive in our country!' Sanyu blasted his horn as the traffic lights turned green, and the children ran away.

My jaw dropped when we approached a prefabricated building with a broken roof and crumbling walls. I swallowed hard. 'Is this the hospital?'

Sanyu grinned. 'I told you it was bad place, *ssebo*. Now maybe you believe me.' He parked the van outside the entrance and held out his hand. 'Sixty thousand shillings.'

'We agreed forty,' I said.

'Sixty with tip.' Sanyu clenched his fist and didn't loosen it until I'd got my wallet out and paid him.

 David Whittet

A tall Indian man with a white coat over his brightly coloured waistcoat emerged from the infirmary.

'Mr Malone, I presume,' he said. 'Welcome to Kalanjala Hospital. I'm Mukasa Lall.'

I recognised the name from the signature on my authority. Dr Lall, the medical superintendent.

'Pleased to meet you, sir,' I said.

I was about to shake his hand when a white van pulled up.

'That's our ambulance,' Dr Lall said.

An ambulance? It looked even less roadworthy than the minibus that brought me from the airport. A nurse and an orderly took an elderly man with a rattling chest from the back of the van and laid him on a rickety old gurney.

'Mr Naigaga is one of our regulars,' Dr Lall said.

'He doesn't sound too good,' I said. 'What's wrong with his chest?'

Dr Lall frowned. 'Surely you recognise the signs? He's got chronic obstructive pulmonary disease. Don't they teach you anything in New Zealand?'

This wasn't the first impression I'd hoped for. How was I to know the diagnosis? I'd scarcely laid eyes on the poor man. I kicked the gravel and followed Dr Lall to the emergency department.

'Nebulise Mr Naigaga with salbutamol,' Dr Lall instructed the nurse. 'I'll take the student to his room, then I'll be back.'

Dr Lall led me past wards with broken, rusty beds and urine-stained mattresses. 'We've only got a hundred beds, but some days we see several thousand patients in casualty. Students take part in the roster. So it's straight down to work for you. There's no slacking here.'

I tensed my shoulders. 'I've come to work.'

Two porters trailed behind us, carting my suitcases through the dingy corridors to the staff quarters. Dr Lall watched them struggle to fit the enormous trunks into my tiny room.

'What on earth have you got in those bags?' he asked.

I opened one of my cases. 'I know how difficult it is to get medicines over here, so I've brought some medical supplies.'

Dr Lall inspected each vial of medicine and every bottle of tablets. 'They're all expired,' he growled, thrusting an ampoule under my nose. 'Don't our people deserve proper medicine?'

I hid my face. 'Of course they do, but I heard you were critically short of antibiotics. They're only just out of date. They'll still work.'

'Like hell!' Fire blazed in his eyes. 'Bloody overseas students. We don't need your charity.' He kicked the trunks across the floor, spilling the drugs on the ground. 'Get rid of them.'

I sat on the rusty iron bed for ages after Dr Lall stormed out. He'd told me to report for duty, but I couldn't face anyone. I just wanted to get on the next flight back to New Zealand.

A knock on the door. Gentle at first, but louder when I didn't answer.

'*Ki kati*, Mr Malone.' A warm female voice. 'I'm Kizza. One of the nurses. I've bought you some supper.'

I got up and let her in. With a broad smile that showed off her glistening white teeth, Kizza planted a tray of exotic dishes on my lap and sat down beside me on the bed.

'You must be starving,' she said.

I hung my head. 'I'm not hungry.'

'Don't take it to heart.' Kizza ran her fingers over her braided black hair. 'Lall's a bully. He hates students. Most don't last the first day.' She gazed at me with her soft brown eyes. 'But he's a damn good doctor all the same. We're lucky to have him here.' She heaped some of the food on a spoon. 'Come on. Try this. It's a traditional Ugandan *luwombo*.'

Such a fragrant aroma. A *luwombo* turned out to be a spicy stew steamed in banana leaves. I took a bite and savoured the deliciously delicate flavours. '*Webale nnyo*,' I said. 'Thank you.'

Kizza gathered up the medicines from the floor, reeling off their names like poetry. 'Augmentin, ciprofloxacin, doxycycline, metronidazole. Brilliant. Just what we need!'

I stared at my feet. 'Dr Lall told me to get rid of them.'

'Don't you dare!' Kizza held a vial to her face. 'They're far too precious. Even if the great Mukasa Lall is too proud to admit it. I'll get a porter to come and take them to the ward.'

  David Whittet

'Won't Dr Lall go mad?' I asked.

Kizza put her arm around my shoulder. 'Take no notice of Lall's rantings. He's always sounding off, but he soon calms down. Put up with his temper, and you'll learn from him. I promise you.'

Fifteen minutes later, and Kizza was back with a colleague on her arm.

'Meet Jamila,' Kizza said. 'She's going to help me sort through the antibiotics.'

Jamila thrust her hand into mine and shook it enthusiastically. '*Oli otya*. Hello. Welcome to Kalanjala Hospital. This is a wonderful gift you have brought us.'

My eyes watered as the two women recorded each item with such obvious delight. Abdu, the head porter, arrived with a trolley to take the medicines to the ward.

'Now get some rest,' Kizza told me. 'Tomorrow will be full-on. You're to report to Mirembe, our charge nurse, at nine sharp in casualty. She'll show you the ropes.'

Some hope of sleep. To think I used to moan about the student quarters at Dunedin Hospital. They were luxurious compared to this cramped and noisy room with its iron-strung bed and mouldy mattress. The perpetual flow of traffic outside my window continued throughout the night. Car horns blazed and brakes screeched. Clanging ambulance bells and police sirens rang in my ears. Did Kalanjala ever sleep?

After a breakfast of chapatti and strong Ugandan coffee in the staff canteen, I was ready for anything. Stepping over countless bodies in the corridors, lying on makeshift beds and mattresses, on my way to the emergency department, I wasn't so sure. Where was Mirembe? With at least four patients crammed into each cubicle, it was impossible to find anyone.

Dr Lall's claim that they treated several thousand patients each day seemed unbelievable yesterday. With the sick and the wounded piling through the emergency entrance, today it appeared entirely possible. Mothers with feverish babies clutched in their arms. Kids with broken bones. Labourers with severed limbs. Gaping sores. Some hobbled in. Others carried in on stretchers. All demanded the attention of the few nurses on duty.

I spotted Dr Lall suturing a laceration. Should I ask him where to find Mirembe? I caught his unforgiving eyes. Best not.

I hurried over to a nurse who was nebulising an asthmatic boy. 'Excuse me, are you Mirembe?'

'No. I'm Kaikara, a student nurse.' She pointed to an older nurse with a blue stripe on her cap. 'That's Mirembe.'

Across the floor, the grizzle-haired charge nurse struggled to get an intravenous line into a restless boy's arm, her face screwed up with concentration.

Brushing past a girl with her arm in a sling, I approached Mirembe. 'Excuse me,' I began. 'I'm Theodore Malone from New Zealand.'

'Damn!' Mirembe cursed as the needle missed and blood oozed from the vein. She glared at me and reached for another cannula on the trolley. 'Well?'

'I was told to report to you,' I said. 'To learn the ropes.'

'Can't you see I'm busy?' she said. 'Grab a white coat from the laundry and get stuck into seeing patients.'

Kalanjala Hospital confronted me with diseases I'd only heard of through textbooks. Kizza was right—Mukasa Lall was a brilliant physician. He could be an inspiring teacher, too—when he was in the mood. That didn't happen often enough. I wanted to bolt when he asked me to assist him with an appendicectomy on my second day. Would he shout at me and shatter my confidence? I'd heard he was a tyrant in theatre, and I could never live up to his impossibly high standards. I took a deep breath and steadied my hand on the retractor.

'You're learning,' he said. 'We'll make a surgeon of you yet!'

Just as well he couldn't see how much I was sweating behind my surgical mask.

Back home, I took blood, stitched wounds, and practised giving injections during clinical attachments. If I was lucky, I got to lance a boil. Dr Lall taught me to insert chest drains and implant pacemakers. I even removed a cataract—experience I'd never have gained in New Zealand.

'Pay attention,' Lall said whenever he showed me a new procedure. 'Chances are, you'll have to do the next one on your own.'

David Whittet

That was scary. Surely they wouldn't expect me to carry out complex and hazardous operations unsupervised?

Terror and excitement competed for space in my brain when it was time for my first temporal artery biopsy. What if I severed the vessel?

I grabbed Asif, one of the junior doctors. 'You do the biopsy. I'll observe.'

'You're here to learn,' Asif said. 'It's a straightforward procedure. I'll guide you through it.'

A straightforward procedure. Easy for him to say. My hand shook even more than it did when I assisted Lall with the appendicectomy.

Asif's eyes drilled into mine as I picked up the scalpel and made the incision on the sixty-year-old woman's temple.

'You're doing great, man,' he said. 'Just be careful not to hit the facial nerve.'

I rarely saw the sunlight over that first fortnight. Day merged into night, with the endless flow of critical patients continuing twenty-four seven. Outdated equipment led to constant delays. I lost count of how many times I saw the porters carry water to the operating theatre when the plumbing broke down.

Asif kicked the X-ray machine when it crashed for the third time that day. 'Bloody machine! Everything's broken in this godforsaken place. Why can't Lall get us some proper gear?'

'He told me he's always fighting to get funding,' I said.

'Then he's lying.' Asif glared back at me. 'We've had loads of offers to upgrade the facilities. But Lall's such a bullshitter. He loves going to conferences and bragging about what he can accomplish with zero resources. Smug bastard!'

Six hours in theatre and I hadn't eaten in the past twelve. I grabbed a *rolex* from the canteen, having acquired a taste for the local snack of omelette wrapped in chapatti, like a closed pancake. I had just taken my first bite when Asif dragged me away.

'We need you in casualty. Now. There's a sick kid. Looks like meningitis. He needs a lumbar puncture.'

'I'd love to watch,' I said, my mouth still full of food.

'Sorry, mate. You'll have to do this one on your own. Everyone's flat out.'

I almost choked on the spicy pancake and dropped the remains on the floor. 'No way. I've never done a lumbar puncture!'

'You must try. Look.' Asif pointed to the teeming mass of patients waiting to be seen. 'Nobody else is free.'

Beads of sweat broke out on my forehead. 'No, please. I'm not qualified.'

'Don't worry,' Asif said. 'You've seen Lall do it often enough, and Kizza will help you. She's assisted with heaps of lumbar punctures. She could do it herself with her eyes closed.' He grabbed my arm as I pulled away. 'Time to prove yourself.'

Asif led me through a sea of bodies to a ten-year-old boy collapsed on a stretcher. The porters transferred him to a cot in the corner of the emergency department. His parents hung over him, their tears flooding his feverish body.

'This is Dr Malone,' Asif said. 'He'll be looking after Saleh.'

I'm not a doctor. Just a medical student. I wanted to tell them. But with Asif gone, I saw the fear in the parents' eyes. They didn't need to know about the panic in my heart.

I took a deep breath and knelt beside the boy, lowering the cot side. 'Hello, Saleh. Do you mind if I take a look at you?'

Saleh was too sick to answer. His shirt stuck to his chest with a mixture of perspiration and his mother's tears. I gently pulled it away to reveal a dark red rash that didn't blanch when I touched it. Yes, this was meningitis.

I froze. Saleh was the same age as Akiki was when his parents died. I could see Akiki in this mortally ill boy's face. *I'm doing this for you, Akiki.*

'I'll have to do a test to establish the diagnosis,' I told the parents. 'A spinal tap. I'm afraid it will be rather uncomfortable for Saleh.'

His mother, Namazzi, wiped her eyes. 'Do what you have to do, just get my son well again.'

My voice trembled as Kizza wheeled the lumbar puncture trolley to the bedside. 'I'll do my very best.'

I tried to stop my legs shaking while donning the surgical gown, hat, mask and sterile gloves. Kizza positioned Saleh on his left side, his chin on his chest, his legs flexed up towards his head.

Kizza steadied my hand with hers as I injected the local anaesthetic into Saleh's back. 'You can do this,' she said.

If you've assisted during this procedure so often, why aren't you doing it? I wanted to say the words. Instead, I looked up at her and forced a smile. 'I hope so.'

After palpating the bony landmarks on Saleh's spine, I took the needle and punctured the skin. Was that the right place? Oh God, what if it wasn't? What if I damaged his spinal cord? Paralysed him.

Kizza mopped my brow. I was sweating onto Saleh's back, contaminating the procedure.

I heard Professor Rutherford's voice, loud in my head. Chiding me. *You will never make a doctor … never … never … never …*

I thought I was going to faint when, suddenly, the cerebrospinal fluid flowed through the needle.

'You've done it!' Kizza said. 'What did I tell you? Best lumbar puncture I've seen!'

The relief on Namazzi's face was equal to mine. 'Thank you, Doctor. You're going to save him. I know you are!'

Saleh's father, Ojore, jumped up from his seat, bowed and shook my hand vigorously.

I hadn't slept for a couple of nights, but I needed to join Namazzi and Ojore for an all-night vigil at Saleh's bedside.

I took Namazzi's hand. 'We've started him on penicillin. That should keep him safe until we get the lab results in the morning.'

Namazzi wiped the perspiration from Saleh's face and whispered a prayer. 'Please, God, don't take him away from us.'

I looked into her swollen eyes. 'It was a boy, just like your Saleh that inspired me to be a doctor. His name was Akiki. His entire family died when he was just ten, but he was a fighter. And your Saleh is going to be a survivor too!'

'I don't know.' Namazzi gazed at Saleh and shook her head. His breathing remained shallow and laboured. 'There doesn't seem to be much fight left in him now.'

Ojore put his arms around his wife. 'We lost our first three children. Two stillborns. And our last child died in here before his first birthday. Pneumonia. Saleh is very precious.'

We talked throughout the night. Recent floods had hit local farmers and had destroyed Ojore's crops. Now their sole surviving child's life hung in the balance. Life wasn't fair.

I must have fallen asleep. It was daylight, and I woke up with Namazzi shaking me.

'It's not working, is it?' she cried. 'The penicillin?'

I rubbed the sleep from my eyes. 'Don't lose hope.'

I got up and listened to Saleh's chest with my stethoscope.

Namazzi's swollen eyes gazed into mine. 'We're losing him, aren't we?'

'I told you Saleh was a fighter.' I put a hand on her shoulder. 'And together, we're going to defeat this. I need to get hold of the lab results to make sure he's getting the right antibiotic.'

Despite my assurances, Saleh had deteriorated overnight.

I called the laboratory. 'We need the result on the spinal tap. *Now*.'

'You'll have them as soon as they're done,' the technician said.

'Can't you hurry it up?' I asked. 'This is urgent.'

'We'll fax it to you when it's ready.'

Was that the best they could do? And I had loads of new patients to see. I returned to the decrepit fax machine in the nursing station whenever I could. When it failed to deliver the result by lunchtime, I gave it a thump and stormed off to the laboratory.

Bacterial meningitis. With the confirmation in my hand, I searched for Mukasa Lall. 'It's a methicillin-resistant strain of *Staphylococcus aureus*.'

Dr Lall grabbed the report. 'What are the sensitivities?'

'We need to start him on vancomycin,' I said. 'Immediately.'

Lall tugged at his collar. What was wrong with him? 'We haven't got any,' he said. 'We've run out. There've been so many resistant bugs.'

'Yes, we have!' Kizza's voice. She was standing right behind me. 'Thanks to you, Theo.'

Thank God I brought vancomycin. Watching Kizza add the life-saving drug to the intravenous line was the proudest moment of my life.

Casualty was crazy that afternoon, and it was evening before I got to the ward to see Saleh.

Namazzi was beside herself. 'He's not getting any better. Your superdrug isn't working.'

Saleh's skin was a dusky blue and his breathing erratic.

Tears streamed down Ojore's face. 'He's going to die, isn't he, Doc?'

'No.' I tried to sound convincing, but my voice cracked. 'Give the antibiotics a chance. It's only six hours since we started the infusion.'

Another long night at Saleh's side. This time, we sat in silence. Three in the morning and still no response. I bumped up the dose of vancomycin. Still, Saleh slipped into an even more profound coma. I couldn't look Namazzi or Ojore in the eye.

Hope faded as the new day began. Saleh died at nine o'clock.

Minutes later and Mukasa Lall burst into the ward. 'It's your bloody expired drugs,' he exploded. 'I told you to get rid of them.'

Kizza followed behind him. 'That's not fair!'

Everyone on the ward watched Lall wave his fists at me. 'I hope you're bloody proud of yourself!'

'Please, Dr Lall,' Kizza said. 'Not here.'

I hung my head. Namazzi and Ojore wept uncontrollably. Why wasn't it them shouting at me?

Namazzi dabbed her eyes. 'Don't take it out on the young doctor,' she said. 'It wasn't his fault. He gave us hope.'

Lall snorted. 'False hope.'

How could Namazzi be so forgiving? Ojore too. They'd just lost the last of their children.

Jamila came to comfort Namazzi and Ojore.

'If the boy's mother can understand, why can't you?' Kizza asked Dr Lall, ushering us into the staff room. 'We didn't have any vancomycin. Saleh would have died anyway.'

Lall cut her down with his eyes. 'Better that than building up their expectations only to have them destroyed.'

Kizza glared back at him. 'Besides, we don't know it was the drug that failed Saleh. I checked each vial of vancomycin before administering it. The batch was only just out of date. They don't go off that quickly.'

'Bullshit,' Lall said. 'Stop trying to defend him. You're no pharmacologist.'

'I bet it was one of these superbugs,' Kizza said. 'They're resistant to all known antibiotics.'

'Crap.' Lall turned on me. 'It was your damn useless drugs.'

Kizza stood between Lall and me. 'You don't know that.'

'I do know this.' He shoved her aside and pointed a finger at me. 'Saleh's blood is on your hands.'

I fled from the hospital. Kizza chased after me.

'Come back! It isn't your fault!'

I didn't stop. I couldn't handle sympathy. Not now. I had to be alone. And anywhere but the Kalanjala Hospital.

I took the next flight back to New Zealand. *Saleh's blood is on your hands.* Professor Rutherford was right—I would never make a doctor.

The last thing I needed when I arrived back at Dunedin Airport was a lecture from Marian Taylor.

'There are thousands of kids out there who need your help,' she said. 'You can't abandon all of them because of one child you couldn't save. They need you. You mustn't give up. I won't let you.'

Jet-lagged, disorientated and disillusioned, I barely had the energy to fight back.

'You didn't see his parents' faces when he died,' I said. 'I had to look into his mother's eyes.'

Marian's lecturing continued as we loaded my bags into her car, and she drove me to my flat. Her overbearing tone made me wish I hadn't asked her to meet me. Or told her about Saleh. I tried not to listen, but she knew how to wind me up. If she meant it as a pep talk, it wasn't working.

'Theo,' Marian persisted. 'I know that boy's death wasn't your fault. *You* know it wasn't your fault. And if some pig-headed consultant in Uganda can't see that, he doesn't deserve you.'

Would she ever stop? 'Of course it was my fault. I gave the kid expired drugs.'

'I bet there was nothing wrong with the drugs,' Marian said. 'They last for ages after their official expiry date.'

'You've changed your tune, haven't you?' I snapped. 'It was you who told me they throw away expired drugs for a good reason.'

'And you persuaded me otherwise,' Marian said. 'You were right. It's a criminal waste, life-saving drugs filling landfills. You gave that boy a fighting chance of survival.'

I turned my head away and watched the familiar grey Dunedin skyline come into view. 'I don't want to talk about it any more. You said it would end badly, and it did.'

It was almost a relief to get back to the dreary routine of medical school. Four weeks attached to the dermatology unit ought to have been torture, but instead proved oddly cathartic. I needed a channel for my pent-up anger, and this was the perfect target. Rich people wanting facelifts. Wealthy consultants making a fortune out of their insecurities. This wasn't dermatology, it was appearance medicine. I wished they could see the disfigured faces I'd seen in Uganda, ravaged by disease.

My tutor brushed his palms together at the end of another clinic full of neurotics. 'The beauty of dermatology,' he said, 'is that your patients never get fully better. They always come back for more. And if they're private patients, so much the better.'

I could see the dollar signs in his eyes.

Worse was to come—a month of plastic surgery under the most supercilious consultant of them all. From his immaculate Italian three-piece suit to the shiny tiepin doubtless intended to reflect his glory, Dr Matthew Levi was everything I despised in medicine. Anything for a fast buck. Botox. Tummy tucks. Liposuction. Nothing was off limits for this super-smooth operator.

You bastard! I bit my tongue as Levi seduced yet another socialite into a nose job. I couldn't say anything. After my brush with the university authorities over the tuberculosis case last year, I had to appear the model of an eager and attentive medical student.

Dermatology and plastic surgery and their nine-to-five routines—bliss after twenty-four seven on call. But back at my flat in the evenings, a task loomed that I couldn't put off any longer. The report on my elective was due in on Monday. Every night I sat at the desk in my pokey bedsit. My pen hovered over the blank sheet of paper, images of Saleh's final breath flashing through my mind. Reliving the despair on his parents' faces was too much. I put down my pen and paced around the room.

What would Professor Rutherford say? And what would the dean say about my doing a lumbar puncture without adequate training or supervision?

Next to the empty pad on my desk lay an unread letter from Akiki. How could I face the gushing words of the boy I had so let down? In failing Saleh, I had betrayed Akiki and the promise to make a difference to his people. I stuffed the envelope into the pocket of my white coat and carried

     David Whittet

it around with me every day on my rounds. It felt like a ton of lead pulling me down, day after day. Maybe it wasn't my drugs that killed Saleh, but I still couldn't forgive myself. My heart told me I was guilty.

That's it. I'm not going back to Uganda—or any other developing country.

Perhaps I should make Matthew Levi my role model instead. Civilised working hours and a fat pay cheque every month. A far superior option to slaving your guts out for a perpetual guilt trip.

Get a grip on yourself! How could you even think that?

But the plastic surgery attachment *had* changed me. Maybe it was the weight of Akiki's unread missive on my conscience, but my contempt for Dr Levi thawed. The speed at which my idealism evaporated alarmed me. After a morning of unnecessary breast augmentations, I ought to have spat blood. Incomprehensibly, I didn't.

Sunday night and the deadline for my report was less than twelve hours away. The academic staff told us to concentrate on the positives in our assignments. What had Uganda taught me? Chewing the end of my pen, I wrote about the opportunity to experience a new facet of medicine. How I'd learnt new skills and procedures. That was bull. I tore up the page and threw it in the trash. My heart still bled for all the diseased and dying—and my part in it. I had achieved nothing in Uganda except weeks of misery and a death on my conscience.

My mind made up, I marched into the faculty office the next morning and handed my folder to the secretary.

'Is this the report on your elective in Uganda?' she said. 'I bet it's fascinating. Will you be going back? I could give you some forms to apply for a scholarship.'

'No.' I pushed Akiki's letter further down in my pocket. 'I've decided on a career in dermatology or plastic medicine.'

It wasn't just Akiki. What would Dr Greenslade think of my change of heart? It didn't matter. I'd let him down already.

Matthew Levi leant back on the leather chair in his consulting room—the largest in the outpatient suite—at the end of clinic on the last day of my attachment.

'So, what have you learnt?' he asked.

How to make money. I was about to list all the procedures he'd taught me when the nurse came back in.

'Excuse me, Dr Levi,' she said, 'but there's one more patient to see. A little boy from Africa.'

I turned away as the nurse brought the boy and his mother into the room. I didn't want to know.

'This is Bwanbale,' she said. 'He's an eight-year-old refugee from Uganda. Back home in Kampala, he had a mole removed from his face.'

Matthew Levi looked up. 'A mole? It looks like they took away half of his face.'

'Unfortunately, the wound turned septic,' the nurse continued. 'That's why he's left with this huge keloid scar.'

'All the kids at school make fun of him,' Bwanbale's mother, Hanifah Zuluka, added. 'Is there anything you can do for him, Dr Levi?'

I kept my head down. No way was I going to get emotionally involved with this case and let it weaken my resolve.

'Let's look, shall we?' There was a gentleness in Levi's voice that I hadn't heard before. 'Hop up on the bed. Don't worry—I won't hurt you.'

Hanifah helped Bwanbale onto the examination couch. 'Do as the doctor tells you. He's going to help you.'

The nurse removed the bandaging from Bwanbale's face and focused the light.

'Good God,' Matthew Levi exclaimed. 'How did this happen?'

I'd never heard Levi sound so shocked before. What had taken this supercool specialist's breath away? I forced myself to look at Bwanbale's head and promptly wished I hadn't. Mountains of thick fungating lesions and scar tissue eroded the right side of his face, and a vast crater replaced his chin.

Hanifah wiped her eyes as she told Bwanbale's story. 'The doc in Uganda told us it was skin cancer. He said we had to get it removed fast. The waiting list was too long at the public hospital. Couldn't afford to go private. So we had to go to a backstreet clinic in Kampala.'

'And this is the result.' Matthew Levi groaned and glanced across at me.

'What do you make of this, Mr Malone? I believe you did your elective in Uganda.'

'Yes, I did.' Close up, the mass of necrotic and ulcerated flesh looked and smelled even worse. 'It's a hypertrophic scar—' I tried to sound professional, but my anger broke out. 'No, it's a botched job by some incompetent charlatan!'

'No.' Hanifah put her arm around her son. 'It wasn't the surgeon's fault. There were floods back home. We had to wade through filthy water, and the wound got infected. They couldn't get enough of the right antibiotics, and the ones we had didn't work.'

I clutched Akiki's letter, my knuckles turning white.

Matthew Levi turned to Hanifah. 'Tell me, Mrs Zuluka, has the scarring got worse since the operation?'

Hanifah nodded.

'I'm afraid that's probably because they've left some cancer cells behind,' Levi said. 'That's why it's breaking out and ulcerating.'

Hanifah clung to her son. 'Don't tell me he's going to die?'

'Not on my watch!' Levi said. 'Don't worry, Mrs Zuluka. I've worked miracles on worse scars than this.' He turned to Bwanbale. 'I'm going to make you handsome again!'

Even if he could eliminate the cancer, I knew in my heart that no amount of surgery would make those hideous scars disappear. Levi was a competent doctor, but he wasn't a magician. And now he raised their expectations. That was cruel.

I cursed myself for getting emotionally involved. Just when I'd mapped out a more comfortable future. I tore open Akiki's letter as soon as I got home. It was full of praise for what I was doing for his people. *I don't deserve it—I failed you and your people!*

How do I break it to Akiki that I wasn't going back? And that if I did, I'd only end up making an even bigger mess? I copped out and sent him a three-line letter to say circumstances had changed and I was going to stay in New Zealand and work in plastic surgery.

Although my attachment had finished, Matthew Levi allowed me to observe Bwanbale's surgery. I watched in awe as flaps of grafted skin gradually smoothed over those gross, cavernous eruptions. Perhaps Levi truly could work miracles—four hours of reconstruction, and he'd transformed Bwanbale's face beyond recognition.

I sat with Hanifah at the bedside as Bwanbale came round from the surgery.

'Dr Levi's done a brilliant job,' I said. 'You won't recognise your son when the bandages come off. And he's certain he's got rid of all the cancer.'

'Thank God,' Hanifah said. 'Dr Levi's a good man. Operating privately like this—and in his own time. He won't charge a fee, either.'

He's rich as Croesus—he can afford to be generous! I pinched myself. 'He's definitely one of the top plastic surgeons in the country, if not the world.'

Hanifah leant towards me. 'Dr Levi said you worked in Uganda.'

My face fell. 'I did, Mrs Zuluka. At the Kalanjala Hospital.'

'Then you're a brave young man,' Hanifah said. 'Tell me about it.'

I tried to avoid her soft brown eyes. 'It wasn't a happy time. I was looking after this boy with meningitis, and he died because the antibiotics I gave him didn't work.'

Hanifah gave me a hug when I finished telling her about Saleh.

'So, will you go back to Uganda when you're qualified?' she asked.

'I had such ambitious plans,' I said. 'Thought I could change the world. Saleh taught me I couldn't.'

'So you've given up?' Hanifah said.

I shrugged. 'Pretty much. Once I've got through my finals, I'm going to specialise in plastics, like Dr Levi.'

'We need plastic surgeons in Uganda,' Hanifah said. 'Just think. If there'd been a surgeon in Kampala to operate on Bwanbale, he wouldn't have had to go through all this.'

'I know that,' I said. 'Listen, I'd love to go back to Uganda, but I can't. I'm staying in New Zealand.'

Bwanbale left the hospital a week later. The boyish smile on his newly sculpted face tugged at my heartstrings once more. Why couldn't I move on and go where I was most needed?

Hanifah must have seen the confusion in my eyes. 'Dr Levi has

 David Whittet

transformed my son's face. You could make an even bigger difference to people's lives back in my homeland.'

Walking home, I wished I hadn't sent Akiki such a blunt letter. Perhaps I should write to him and explain. Tell him I was thinking of—

I froze when I reached my flat. Akiki was sitting on the doorstep.

'I won't let you down again,' I said. 'I'm sorry—'

'Enough of the guilt trip,' Akiki said. 'It's time to believe in yourself. Follow your own path. Whether that's here, in Uganda, or somewhere else.'

I put the kettle on and made some coffee.

'What about you?' I asked. 'Have you found your true vocation?'

'I've got a scholarship to study engineering at Otago University,' Akiki said. 'I'm going to be a civil engineer. I've always wanted to build bridges, construct dams, create an infrastructure for future generations.'

'Congratulations,' I said. 'They could use those talents in Uganda.'

Akiki shook his head. 'New Zealand is my home now. It's given me a new beginning and I want to give something back in return. I'm going to work on projects here.'

I couldn't help smiling. 'It's funny, isn't it? You want to help my country, and I'm desperate to go back and do something for yours.'

'So you *are* going back to Uganda?' Akiki said.

'Of course I am.'

Akiki stared at me with his bulging eyes. 'What made you change your mind?'

'Mrs Zuluka,' I said. 'The mother of a Ugandan boy we operated on. She shamed me into it.' I shot Akiki a grin. 'And you, of course.'

'When will you leave?'

'I've still got to get through my final exams and my house doctor jobs. But after that—just try to stop me.' I rapped my knuckles on the table. 'And this time I'll be taking some *real* antibiotics. Believe me!'

CHAPTER SEVEN

'Three more months and you'll be away! We've booked your flights, and your visa's approved. The team at Kampala are looking forward to meeting you!'

How long I'd waited for that phone call! It seemed a lifetime since I'd signed on with Kiwi Doctors for Change, a New Zealand-based international medical aid organisation. I'd begun to wonder if they'd ever get back to me. Now, my hand shook as Mike Bailey, my contact at the organisation, ran through the details. I held the receiver close to my chest long after the call had ended. This was the reason I'd sat through all those mind-numbing lectures. At last, my *real* medical career was about to start!

My stint as a paediatric house officer in Dunedin was nearly over. I'd enjoyed the attachment—most of the time. It was just that I couldn't stop thinking how much worse off the children were in Uganda, and I longed to get back. I'd almost erased the horror of Kalanjala Hospital from my mind. This trip would be different. I had the support of an international medical aid organisation backing me.

I couldn't wait to tell Marian about the job in Uganda and caught up with her for a quick cappuccino in the hospital canteen.

'There'll be no more expired drugs,' I said, 'thanks to the MPSO scheme.'

Marian raised her eyebrows. 'What?'

'Medical Practitioner Supply Order,' I replied. 'Now that I'm qualified, I can order medicines from a pharmacy for emergency use. I'm going to stock up with antibiotics to take to Uganda.'

Marian slurped her coffee. 'Are you sure that's allowed?'

'They're supposed to be for use in New Zealand,' I said, 'but nobody's going to know.'

'Are you sure? I don't want you getting into trouble.'

I put down my coffee cup with a thump. 'That's a risk I have to take. I never want to look a mother in the eye again and tell her that out-of-date drugs killed her child.' I stood up and glared at Marian. 'Never again. I'm getting those drugs, and I'm taking them to Uganda.'

I strode out of the canteen and made straight for the hospital office to get hold of an MPSO requisition form. Trust Marian to put a damper on things. I thought she'd be as excited as I was. Never mind. The thrill I got from completing the order form more than made up for that. My heart beat even faster when I took the application slip to a local pharmacy the next morning.

The pharmacist ran a finger down my list. 'Why do you need so many drugs?'

Why did she need to know? True, I'd requested the maximum number of items allowed on the Ministry of Health's programmes. But what had that got to do with her?

'I'm going to be working in a rural area,' I said.

'Even so. This is excessive.' She stared at me through thick-rimmed glasses that made her eyes even more menacing. 'Besides, I haven't got all of these in stock. I'll need to order them in.' She put the paper on the bench. 'You'll have to come back tomorrow.'

In a rush to get out of the shop, I knocked over a display stand. Cosmetics toppled over the floor. I should have stayed to pick them up, but I didn't.

Why had I chosen that pharmacy? I lay awake that night wondering if all pharmacists were busybodies like her. One thought got me through: I wouldn't have to see her again after I got the drugs in the morning.

Stay calm. I paced around the shop, waiting for her to emerge from the dispensary. What the hell was she doing? Was she keeping me waiting on purpose? Perhaps if I knocked over another display, that would bring her out.

When she did finally appear, I wished she hadn't.

'Dr Malone.' That same fastidious voice. 'I'm afraid I can't complete this order. You must contact your employer for the supplies you need.'

I took a step back. 'My employer?'

'You said you were going to work for a rural practice, didn't you?'

'Yes, I um … but … I need …' I ground to a halt as she continued to eyeball me.

'The practice will supply you with all the medicines you need. I cannot.'

'Yes, but I thought with the MPSO form, I could …'

Why was I even arguing? Her sour expression said it all. She'd decided. 'Goodbye, Dr Malone. Good luck with that rural practice.'

Busted. She knew I was lying. Angry and embarrassed in equal measure, I shuffled towards the door and escaped as fast as I could.

I persuaded myself it wasn't the end of the world. Time for Plan B. I spent the following week writing to pharmaceutical companies, begging them to donate antibiotics. Marian bombarded me with questions, but I brushed her off. There was no way I would tell her about my altercation with the pharmacist. That would be too humiliating. Besides, the drug firms' positive responses meant I could get the supplies I needed legitimately.

Things were looking up—until my last day on the paediatric ward.

The morning started well. I checked the case notes for my last ward round on the unit. All good. Then the porter handed me a flat package.

'Courier delivery for you, Dr Malone,' he said. 'Looks important.'

I clutched the courier envelope. My heart thumped. *Strictly Private and Confidential. To be opened by the addressee only.* I flipped it over. It was from the Medical Council of New Zealand.

Dr Jenkins, the consultant, arrived with the rest of the team.

The staff nurse gave me a gentle nudge. 'You're as white as a sheet, Dr Malone. What's up?' She broke into a playful giggle. 'Don't tell me. You're upset about leaving us.'

The round lasted forever. Dr Jenkins rambled on as usual. Every case reminded him of some obscure diagnosis he'd clinched. All the time that malignant package with the letter inside remained unopened in my pocket. A cancer eating at my soul.

I hoped to get away early, but the staff laid on farewell drinks. Still, any excuse to delay reading the letter that could finish my career before it started.

Smiles, handshakes, laughter. Could everyone see through my fake smiles? Was it obvious my mind was elsewhere?

'Uganda. You went there as a student, didn't you?'

'What an adventure, Theo. I envy you!'

'Don't forget to send us a postcard!'

The ward sister shook my hand vigorously. 'Goodbye and good luck! We'll be thinking about you, halfway around the world in Uganda.'

David Whittet

Marian dropped in on the party after finishing her shift in the surgical unit.

She pulled me to one side. 'Whatever's the matter? You look dreadful.'

I drew the courier package out of my pocket just far enough to reveal the Medical Council emblem.

'Come on,' Marian said. 'Let's get you out of here. We'll face this together.' She turned to the staff. 'It's time to take our leave. Theo's got a lot of packing to do for the big trip.'

Several more excruciating hugs, and we were out of the ward.

Back at my flat, I placed the courier package on the kitchen table.

'I want to open it on my own,' I told Marian.

'Are you sure?'

I nodded.

Marian shrugged. 'Okay. I'll get us a takeaway. Then I'll be back. You need to eat, whatever it says.'

I doubted that. Once Marian left, shaking all over, I tore open the package.

Dear Dr Malone,

Council has received information from Ms Anne Nelson, Community Pharmacist. She alleges that you attempted to obtain medicines on the Medical Practitioners Supply Order to which you were not entitled. Ms Nelson states you informed her you were going to work in a rural practice. Our investigations confirm no such employment has been arranged, and we understand you are planning to work overseas. As you are aware, the MPSO scheme is solely to enable the dispensing of emergency treatment to New Zealanders.

At its meeting on 20 August 1989, Council referred the matter to its Conduct Committee for further investigation. They will be in touch with you shortly and invite your comments.

Council appreciates that such matters are stressful, and we suggest you discuss this matter with a trusted colleague for collegial support.

Yours sincerely,

James Bell

Registrar

I was curled up on the floor when Marian returned with an Indian takeaway. Even a hot madras couldn't raise my spirits. I gagged on the first mouthful.

Marian picked up the letter. I looked up as she read it.

'Don't say it,' I muttered. 'I know. You warned me.'

Marian frowned. 'Did you definitely tell the pharmacist you were taking the medicines abroad?'

'I just said I was going to work in a rural area.'

'So you didn't actually lie to her.' Marian tilted her head. 'You just didn't say that the rural area was in Africa.'

'That's not the point.' I stared down at my feet. 'It's a fair cop. I meant to deceive her.'

'But it wasn't for personal gain.'

'Leave it, Marian. It doesn't matter. I'll be out of the country in a couple of weeks.'

'You don't want a slur hanging over your reputation,' Marian said. 'We need to fight this.'

I was too weary to fight. 'I just want to get some sleep.'

Marian drew her eyebrows together. 'I don't like to leave you alone like this.'

'I'll be okay,' I said. 'Honest.'

At last, Marian put on her coat. Relief. I sat in silence for hours after she left. *Bugger Ms Nelson. The Medical Council, too. Bugger them all.*

The phone rang early the next morning.

'Hi, Theo. Mike Bailey here. All set to go? I just need one more thing from you. Your CGS.'

I almost dropped the telephone. 'My *what*?'

'Certificate of Good Standing. You need to get it from the Medical Council. We can't register you in Uganda without it.'

'Okay. Don't worry,' I stammered. 'I'll get it to you ASAP.'

But could I? My fingers fumbled on the dial as I called the Medical Council.

A terse voice answered the call. 'We can't issue you with a Certificate of Good Standing while you're under investigation.'

'How long will that take?'

 David Whittet

'The conduct committee meets at the end of next month,' she said. 'They'll decide then how they wish to proceed with the case.'

I could have wept. '*Next month?*'

'If it goes to the disciplinary tribunal, it will take much longer.'

'I was only trying to help children in desperate need.'

'You'll have the chance to put your side of the case to the committee in due course.'

It was pointless prolonging the call. I cursed under my breath, waiting for her to finish.

'In the meantime, Dr Malone, I suggest you contact your medical defence lawyer.'

Forget medical defence. I had to convince Mike Bailey that he still needed me in Uganda. After all, the CGS was just a piece of paper. What did that matter when there were kids' lives at stake?

'I'm sorry, mate,' Mike said, 'but no CGS, no job. It's unfortunate, but we've no choice but to cancel your contract.'

I dropped the phone onto the floor while Mike was still talking.

'I wish things could be different. You'd have been a perfect fit for us, Theo.'

How could I tell Akiki I wasn't going back to Uganda? Bwanbale and his mother, too. What would they think of me?

I didn't leave my room for days. The same nightmare haunted me when I managed to sleep. Dying kids, begging for help, and I was in a straitjacket, unable to reach them.

I awoke to someone hammering on the door. *Go away.*

'Theo! Are you okay?'

I knew it was Marian before she spoke. I picked myself up off the floor and limped into the hallway. I didn't want to let her in, but I knew she wouldn't leave till I did.

The fussing began the moment she set eyes on me. 'You look dreadful. I bet you haven't been eating. It's more important than ever that you look after yourself.'

Bugger the niceties. 'Leave it, Marian,' I said. 'Nothing matters any more. I can't go to Uganda.'

'Why not?'

'Because I can't get a bloody Certificate of Good Standing from the Medical Council.'

Marian stared at me. 'Surely that doesn't make any difference to working in Uganda?'

I told her about my telephone conversation with Mike Bailey and how it could be months before the Medical Council reached a decision.

'Shame on Mike Bailey,' Marian said. 'Dumping you like that.'

I slumped into a chair. 'Mike had no choice.'

Marian remained on her feet. 'I told you it was a mistake signing up with a Kiwi outfit. You should have gone with one of the international agencies like Médecins Sans Frontières.'

'It wouldn't have made any difference.' I slid further down in the seat. 'I'm no good to anyone if I can't get registration.'

Marian stamped her foot. 'We have to fight this. Preventing a doctor from working where he's really needed. The public need to know.'

'No, Marian. Please. It'll only make things worse.'

'Theo! You can't just give up!'

'Didn't say I was.' I avoided Marian's probing eyes. The last thing I needed was publicity. Besides, I was about ready to throw everything in. Not that I could breathe a word of that to Marian. I'd have to let her down gently. 'Maybe I'll just go as a general volunteer. Doctors aren't the only lifesavers.'

'They need your medical skills,' Marian shot back. 'Buck up. You're not a quitter!'

'Sometimes, I wish I was. It must make life much easier.' I looked up and wilted under Marian's disapproving glare. 'Alright. I'll call my medical defence society tomorrow and make an appointment with one of their lawyers.'

'That's more like it. Do you want me to come with you?'

I sighed. 'No, I can stand up for myself.'

'You'd better. I'll be on your case if you don't.'

I'd seen that scheming look in her eyes before. What was Marian up to? She left without another word.

David Whittet

The phone rang the next morning. Not Marian again. I rubbed the sleep from my eyes and picked up the handpiece.

'Marian, I don't know what's got into you, but if you're thinking of pulling off a stunt, forget it—'

An assertive voice cut me off. 'Nicky Harper here. *Otago Daily News.* Would you like to comment on the lead story in today's *Dominion*? Put your side of the story?'

I slammed down the receiver and cursed. *Bloody Marian!* She'd been to the press. I didn't want to believe it, but there was no other explanation. I thumped the bedside table. How could she do this to me?

I snuck out of the flat. *Please, God, don't let anyone see me.* My heart stopped when I saw the billboard outside the local newsagent.

Doctor faces disciplinary action over a drugs scandal.

Hiding my face, I stumbled into the shop and grabbed a copy of *The Dominion* from the pile. My picture was on the front page.

'A dollar fifty, sir.'

The shopkeeper recognised me. That awkward look in his eye gave him away. I lowered my head even further, flung a couple of coins on the counter, and without waiting for the change, I was out the door. Back in the security of my flat, I swore I'd never go out again.

Dunedin doctor Theodore Malone cheats the system by ordering vast quantities of antibiotics at taxpayers' expense. My hands shook as I scanned the article. *Contrary to the rules for medical supplies, Dr Malone intended to export the drugs for a private overseas project.* No mention that the medicines were to save lives in the developing world. Bloody journalists. I threw the paper onto the floor.

The telephone rang. Again and again. *Bugger off!* I wasn't giving reporters more ammunition to use against me. Perhaps it was Marian. I took the phone off the hook. I didn't want to talk to her either.

My heart thumped every time I heard footsteps outside. I put on some old headphones. Even heavy rock at full volume couldn't clear my head. I tore off the headset and flung it to the floor.

Marian's voice. Shouting in the passageway. 'I know you're in there, Theo. Open up!'

Why had I taken the headphones off? 'Go away, Marian. I've nothing to say to you.'

'Don't be like that,' she said. 'I'm your friend.'

I yanked the door open and glared at her. 'Friends don't humiliate their mates in public.'

'I'm sorry about *The Dominion*. They twisted what I said.'

That was a piss-poor excuse. 'Why the hell didn't you ask me first?'

Marian raised her eyebrows. 'I knew you'd say no.'

'Damn right.'

She inched forward. 'Stand up for what you believe in. The piece in *The Dominion* is a setback, but we're going to get public opinion on your side.'

'You still don't see what you've done, do you?' I threw my hands in the air. 'I dare not step out of the flat. Reporters accosting me wherever I go, everyone staring at me as if I'm a pariah.'

'That'll soon change.' Marian pushed past me into the flat. 'You're going to be a hero. We can turn this to your advantage. I've got you an interview on Paul Holmes' show.'

'You've done what?' My heart missed a beat. 'Please tell me you're joking!'

The look on her face told me she was not. I collapsed into a chair, unable to speak.

Renowned New Zealand broadcaster Paul Holmes had his own nightly current affairs show, *Holmes,* following the six o'clock news on TV One. He had a reputation for vilifying professionals. A disgraced doctor would be perfect fodder.

Marian sat opposite me. 'This is an opportunity of a lifetime. It's your chance to set the record straight and get support for the project.'

I couldn't look at her. I buried my head in my hands. 'Why are you doing this? Do you get some sadistic pleasure from crushing me?'

Marian frowned. 'How could you say that? This isn't about me—or you, for that matter. We're fighting for those children in Uganda. Shout their stories from the rooftops. Tell people what you saw. Kiwis are generous. They'll be on your side.'

'You know I'm crap at speaking. I've heard about Holmes. He'll make mincemeat of me.'

     David Whittet

'Only if you let him,' Marian said. 'Just be yourself. Tell your story. It'll strike a chord with the public.'

'I'm no good at that sort of thing.'

Marian edged closer. 'If you don't show for the interview, everyone will think you're guilty.'

I pulled away as she put her arm around me. *Damn you, Marian!* She'd left me no choice. Boycotting the *Holmes* show would be an admission of guilt. Imagine what they'd say. *We invited Dr Malone to come on the programme and defend his actions, but he declined our request.*

'Cheer up,' Marian said. 'You've nothing to hide. Go into battle for the cause!'

I shook my head. How dare she play Russian roulette with my career? 'You win, Marian. Either way, I'll be toast.'

I was in no mood to meet with my medical defence society the following morning. The last thing I needed was someone else telling me what to do. I'd almost cancelled the appointment. Five minutes in and I wished I had.

Anne Baxter, the medico-legal lawyer, leant across her desk, her deep hazel eyes desperately trying to engage with mine. 'Is there anything I can say to dissuade you? Going on Paul Holmes' show is professional suicide.'

'Maybe it is.' My eyes darted away. 'But if I don't front, he can say what he likes about me. If I'm there, I can fight back.'

Ms Baxter frowned. 'That's what I'm afraid of. You're a loose cannon. Paul Holmes will twist you around his little finger.' She flicked through my file. 'Communication skills have been your downfall before. Jumping to conclusions on a student assignment. Taking things into your own hands. Pity they didn't teach you how to manage your emotions.'

For a moment I couldn't breathe. Professor Rutherford's voice reverberated through my head. *You will never make a GP. A pathologist, perhaps, but not a general practitioner.*

Pull yourself together. I sat bolt upright and glared at Anne Baxter. 'Don't talk to me about emotions. I watched a kid die because we didn't have antibiotics that worked.'

'I can't imagine what that's like,' Ms Baxter said. 'But you're letting your feelings run away with you again. We could arrange mentoring for you.'

'I don't need counselling,' I shot back. 'I need you to get me off this charge. Then I can get back to Uganda and save children's lives.'

'There's no shame in having a mentor,' she said. 'You need a clear head if you're going to help those kids.'

'A clear head?' I rolled my eyes. 'That goes out of the window when a child dies.'

'I know. I understand.' Ms Baxter shook her head. 'Nobody's questioning your clinical skills. It's your judgement. You need distance. You're too involved.'

'The day I stop caring is the day I give up medicine.'

'I didn't mean you should stop caring … it's just …' Ms Baxter scribbled some notes on a pad. 'I'll draft a response to the Medical Council. You will apologise, make it clear that you have learnt your lesson and we will plead mitigating circumstances.'

I looked down at my feet as she cobbled the words together. None of them true. I couldn't wait to get out of the office.

Ms Baxter shook my hand. 'Think about what I've said. It's not too late to back out of the *Holmes* show.'

If only I could. 'I told you. A no-show is as good as a guilty plea.'

Six years at medical school followed by punishing house surgeon jobs. Where had it got me? Crouched in the back of a taxi on the way to a public lynching. The cab crawled through the Auckland traffic to the TVNZ studios. Marian insisted on accompanying me and rattled off her usual motivational prattle. I wasn't listening. Stuck at traffic lights, I stared out of the window. Everyday people going about their daily routines. Lucky sods. Why did I have to be different?

The media scrum lay in wait at the studio door.

'Dr Malone will not be answering questions before the interview,' Marian said.

I'd got used to hiding my head in public. I didn't need a minder.

Marian loved every minute. Coaxing me in the green room and ingratiating herself with the producer. I wasn't a star arriving for a chat show.

The director arrived and scowled at Marian. 'I'll take over from here.'
That told her.

The floor manager ushered me into the interviewee's chair.

'Don't forget we go out live,' the director said. 'So there are no second chances.'

'Thanks.' Blinded by the studio lights, I tried to settle in the seat.

'Good eye contact with Paul will make you look more genuine,' the director said. 'And you need to do something with your hands.'

'What?'

Before I got a reply, a neon sign lit up. *On Air.* The cameras were rolling. Paul Holmes was in my face and firing questions.

'Why did you do it, Dr Malone? That's what everyone's asking. Are you trying to tell us it was for some higher cause? Or were you just trying to fleece the taxpayer to feather your own nest?'

'Absolutely not. This isn't for me. Thousands of children are dying every day in the developing world because they've no antibiotics. I've held children's hands in Uganda and watched them die, knowing that I could have saved them with the right drugs.'

'That's a highly emotive argument.' Paul Holmes clasped his hands together. 'I agree the Medical Council has been a little disingenuous, but surely charity should begin at home. What if a New Zealand doctor has to hold a dying Kiwi kid's hand because you stole their medicine?'

'Nonsense! No New Zealand child has suffered because of what I've done—'

'That's because they caught you in the act. Before you smuggled the drugs out of the country.'

'There's no shortage of antibiotics here. But over there—it's a humanitarian crisis on a scale you can't imagine.'

'But there are charities to help with this. Many New Zealanders sponsor children through World Vision.'

'That's fantastic. But it's not enough. If you'd been to Uganda, Mr Holmes, and seen children die in front of your eyes, surely you'd want to help them?'

'Of course. But should the taxpayer be forced to pay the bill?'

'I agree that what I did was foolhardy.' I bit my tongue and looked straight at Paul Holmes. 'And I regret my actions. I should have gone about things differently. Worked on fundraising activities. Pestered the pharmaceutical companies to donate supplies. In fact, that's what I'm doing now. If any of your viewers would like to support this vital work, we'll be grateful for any donations.'

'I'm sure there will be a lot of support out there for what you're doing. Good luck with the fundraising and thank you for coming in and being so frank.'

Suddenly it was all over. I was out of the limelight and back in the green room.

'Congratulations! Brilliant interview!' Marian hugged me so tight that I could scarcely breathe. 'You're a star.'

'I'm no star.' I extricated myself from her arms. 'And I don't *want* to be a star.'

'You were a natural in front of the camera,' Marian said.

'Really? That was the most *unnatural* thing I have ever done.'

We continued to argue in the taxi we took to the hotel Marian had booked for the night. I'd had enough.

'Leave it, Marian. Me going on television doesn't save children's lives. Nothing's changed.'

'You're wrong,' Marian said. 'The Medical Council will have to back down now. Public pressure will force them to go easy on you.'

I waved a hand at her. 'As if! Anyway, they're right. I cheated the taxpayer. Professional misconduct. I deserve what I get.'

Marian had that forlorn look she used when she wanted to get around me. 'You don't mean that.'

'I do. The Council is just doing its job. Protecting the public of New Zealand. From people like me.'

'You can't give up now,' Marian said. 'You're a celebrity!'

I turned my head away. 'I want to be a doctor, not a cause célèbre.'

Marian insisted we have dinner together in the hotel restaurant. I would much rather have eaten alone, ordering room service.

'Let's not fall out over this,' Marian said. 'We need to support each other.'

     David Whittet

She fidgeted with her fork. 'Especially as we're going to be working together.'

'Working together?' I said. 'What do you mean?'

Marian took a gulp of water. 'I've done a lot of thinking these last few weeks, and I've decided. I'm going to quit my job on surgical and come with you to Uganda.'

'Are you sure?' I said. 'We don't even know if they'll allow me back.'

'They will,' Marian said. 'I told you, after tonight's performance—'

I almost choked on my soup. 'Tonight doesn't change anything. The Medical Council is still going to throw the book at me.'

'They won't.' Marian put a hand on mine and gave it a stroke. 'Think what we can achieve as a team.'

I pulled back. Had she engineered everything—the leak to *The Dominion* and the *Holmes* show—just to bring us together? Surely not. We'd been mates, but there'd been nothing romantic. At least, not on my part.

'Marian …' I paused and took a deep breath. 'I hope you're not expecting more than a working relationship.'

Marian blushed. 'Of course not.'

The look in her eyes said otherwise.

I should have been mad after all she'd put me through. Dragging my name through the mud. Her hand trembled as she took another sip of water, and her lip quivered as she tried to explain.

'I'm sorry, Theo. I should never have gone to the press. Or the television media.'

'No, you shouldn't.' I stared straight into her eyes. Despite everything, it saddened me to see her so deflated. I heaved a deep sigh. 'Don't worry. I guess I had it coming to me when I broke the rules. I just wish it hadn't been so public.' I stood up and steadied myself on the table. 'It's been a long day and I'm knackered. If you don't mind, I'll go to my room and hit the sack.'

Nothing was quite the same with Marian after that night. She didn't come round to my flat again. She didn't call me. The one time in my life when I really needed a friend and I'd just lost my best mate.

Would the nightmare ever end? The next three months were an endless blur of unremitting briefings with my medical defence society and hearings at the Medical Council. A perpetual fog of writing and rewriting letters and submissions.

Shame forced me into self-imposed exile. I was sick of reporters following me, and people gawking at me in the street. I only left my flat when absolutely necessary. I'd nowhere to go, anyway. And if the paparazzi had their way, no future either.

My life was a train wreck. The bitter Dunedin winter didn't help the isolation, either. Huddled in a corner and unable to eat or sleep, I missed Marian. Perhaps I needed a dose of her relentless positivity. I dialled her number but put down the receiver before it rang. What would I say to her? And could I trust her again?

No. I was on my own.

Even Anne Baxter had all but written me off. I'd put my foot down when she demanded yet another revision to my deposition.

'Not again!' I threw my pen on the table. 'Can't you do it for me?'

'*You* have to present it to Council.' She picked up the pen and handed it back to me. 'Concentrate. Don't you care about the outcome?'

I shook my head. 'I just want it to be over.'

'I thought you wanted to get back to Uganda?'

I shrugged. 'I do. But that's not going to happen, is it? The Medical Council will hang me out to dry. We both know that.'

A fortnight later, Anne Baxter met me at Wellington Airport on the morning of the Professional Conduct Committee hearing. We took a taxi to the Medical Council offices. It was the ride to the TV studio all over again. Rush hour traffic and an unwelcome pep talk. Like Marian, Anne kept telling me what to say and how to behave in front of the panel. Why couldn't she leave me alone?

Following Ms Baxter into the chamber, I should have been shaking all over. I wasn't. The committee had already decided. I could see it in their faces. My heart was numb and my mind indifferent.

'We have considered your submission,' Dr Sue Chapman, the committee chair, began, 'and we acknowledge your offending was not for personal benefit.'

I'd grown to respect Dr Chapman during the investigation. Unlike the others on the panel, something in her eyes said she understood why I took such drastic action. Even today, she seemed a little uneasy reprimanding me.

She cleared her throat and continued, 'We have also considered the submission made on your behalf by Dr Ralph Greenslade.'

Ralph Greenslade stood up for me?

Dr Chapman noticed my surprise. 'Yes, Dr Greenslade's character reference convinced us your intentions were honourable. Dr Greenslade was hoping to attend the hearing in person. Unfortunately, his recent stroke prevented him from making the journey.'

A stroke? Was he alright? My mind was in such turmoil that I scarcely heard the verdict. Dr Chapman continued her summing up of the committee's decision. 'We may sympathise. Indeed, we may admire your commitment to supporting colleagues in the Third World. But however worthy the cause, we cannot ignore or condone such blatant dishonesty, which amounts to professional misconduct.'

The next thing I remember was Anne Baxter patting me on the back.

'Excellent result, Theo,' she said. 'Two years working under supervision. You couldn't have hoped for better than that. They've also waved the fine they would normally impose, since your motives were entirely altruistic.'

I stared at her. 'You don't understand. Ralph Greenslade's had a stroke. That's far more important than what's happening to me. I have to get the next flight back to Dunedin.'

The plane was late landing in Dunedin. I made straight for a payphone.

'Rosemary? Is that you? It's Theo Malone here. I heard Ralph had a stroke. Please tell me he's okay. Can I come and see him?'

'Of course you can,' Rosemary said. 'But be prepared. You'll see an enormous change in Ralph.'

It was a miserable night. I tried to make sense of everything while driving to the Greenslade's house through the pouring rain. Why had Ralph stood up for me? I'd let him down, ended his career as a GP tutor. Had the stress brought on the stroke? Was I responsible for another disaster?

Rosemary had warned me about the change in Ralph, but what about her? I barely recognised Rosemary when she opened the door. It wasn't just the extra lines on her face and the lank hair. Or her rumpled clothes. The spark had gone from her eyes.

What could I say? 'I'm so sorry, Rosemary. When did it happen?'

'A couple of months back. Poor Ralph. It's hit him hard.' She took my raincoat and hung it on a peg. 'He wanted to go to Wellington and speak up for you. But he's just out of rehab.'

I stepped back. 'He shouldn't have been worrying about me.'

'Ralph always had a soft spot for you,' Rosemary said. 'He would have gone to the hearing if the doctors had let him.'

'After all the grief I've caused him?' I said. 'He shouldn't have bothered. I hope it wasn't me who caused the stroke.'

'No,' Rosemary said. 'I blame too much of Mrs Bennett's clotted cream.' She took my arm and led me into the living room.

My mouth fell open when I caught sight of Ralph slumped in his armchair. A dense left hemiparesis contorted his body. With a grimace, he raised his right arm to shake my hand. I grasped his limp palm in mine.

'It's so good to see you again,' I said.

'The prodigal son has returned!' His slurred voice was almost unrecognisable. With another wince, he gestured to Rosemary. 'Bring a chair for my star pupil!'

I sat on the edge of the seat. 'I'm sorry you had to give up teaching because of me. I know I stuffed up with that farmer and his housemaid, but I never meant it to reflect so horribly on you.' I rested my hand on his writhing limbs. 'Can you ever forgive me?'

There, I'd said it. The confession that had given me so many sleepless nights.

Ralph managed a lopsided smile. 'It wasn't just that. Rutherford had been trying to get rid of me for ages. He hated the psychological approach. I was a thorn in his side.'

'Professor Rutherford told me I'd never make a GP.'

Ralph almost choked on his spittle. 'Rutherford should never have been a GP. Let alone a professor of general practice.'

Rosemary came in with a tray of afternoon tea. 'You're talking about

 David Whittet

old farmer Evans and his Filipino maid. The dirty bugger!'

She put the tray on the table and fed Ralph a mug of tea through a straw.

'Still, I hope you've learnt your lesson,' Ralph spluttered between mouthfuls. 'You'll need to be on the lookout for TB when you go back to Uganda.'

'I won't be going back,' I said.

'Oh.' Rosemary finished feeding Ralph, then thrust a cup of tea into my hand. 'So you're going into practice in New Zealand?'

The teacup shook in my hand. 'No, I'm not cut out to be a doctor.'

'Nonsense,' Rosemary said.

'I'm sorry.' The disappointment in both their faces was unbearable, and I hung my head.

Rosemary pressed her lips together. 'I thought you'd be over the moon with the Medical Council case out of the way. Look, you're burnt out. Take a holiday. You'll soon come around.'

I put my cup down before I spilt the tea. 'I don't think so. Actually, I'm thinking about a career change. Maybe I'll retrain as a lawyer. Or possibly an accountant. Failing that, a used-car salesman. Yes, that's it. A used-car salesman.'

'Theo!' Ralph gagged on his drink. 'A used-car salesman? How could you?' Rosemary mopped his face, but he hadn't finished. 'You'd better watch it. The blasphemy laws haven't been repealed yet!'

I couldn't help grinning. The stroke hadn't blunted Ralph's sharp wit.

'Maybe a salesman is a bit extreme,' I said. 'My father was an airline pilot. Perhaps I should try that.'

Rosemary frowned. Her reproachful eyes locked on to mine.

'Maybe that's not such a good idea,' I said. 'My old man had a girl in every port—or should I say airport. And a lover in every flight crew. He left us when I was four. My mother never recovered.'

Rosemary leant forward and put her hand on my shoulder. 'I'm sorry about your mother. But you're a doctor, Theo. That's who you are. You can't change that.'

'You *mustn't* change that,' Ralph added, his body jerking forward. 'I won't let you!'

I threw my head back. What could I say? Every bone in my body wanted to quit. But how could I let my guru down a second time?

Rosemary cleared away the tea things. Ralph and I sat in silence. When Rosemary came back from the kitchen, she had a tell-tale smile and stood in front of me with her arms folded.

'The perfect solution is under our noses. We've struggled to get locums since Ralph's stroke. Why don't you come and work for us?'

'I don't know.' I looked down at my feet and held my breath. 'Don't forget, I have to work under supervision for the next two years.'

'JP!' Ralph croaked, his face suddenly animated. 'Call John Parry!'

Before I had time to think of an excuse, Ralph and Rosemary arranged a meeting with Dr John Parry, a senior Dunedin GP, affectionately known to all as JP.

'So, you are the famous—or should I say infamous—Dr Malone.' He shook my hands with a firm grip. 'I admire your guts. Going head-to-head with Paul Holmes. That must have taken some nerve.'

'Not really.' I stepped backwards. 'I was … kind of forced into it.'

'Well, you survived, and that's something to be proud of. I'm delighted to be your supervisor.'

A few phone calls and a myriad of forms, all completed in triplicate, and the arrangements satisfied the Medical Council. My rehabilitation had begun.

On my first morning, I called in to see Ralph on my way to the medical centre.

'Thank you for believing in me,' I said. 'Even when I didn't believe in myself.'

Ralph smiled, his face appearing less distorted than before. 'John Parry's a good man. If anyone can put the fire back in your belly, it's JP.'

Working in Dr Greenslade's old practice *did* renew my enthusiasm for medicine. Working under supervision had definite benefits. Weekly feedback sessions with JP always energised me.

The leaky homes were still there and just as cold, damp and degrading.

So was asthma, scurvy and rickets. Nothing had changed since my student attachment. Perhaps Paul Holmes was right. Charity should start at home.

Annette, a thirty-year-old account manager, burst into my consulting room and threw herself onto the chair.

'I want you to write this down,' she began. 'The stress at work is killing me. I'm a wreck. I blame my employers—they're responsible. When I die of a heart attack, I want my family to sue them.'

Despite her dramatic show of angst, I noticed a tremor in her hands.

'Okay,' I said. 'I've got all that. But I'd like to take a look at you.'

'Don't waste your time, Doc. I've lost count of the number of GPs I've seen. They all agree it's my work.'

'I need to examine you, all the same.' I took her pulse. It was 120 beats per minute. 'Tell me, have you felt your heart beating fast?'

'All the time. And I sweat like a pig.'

Her skin felt warm and moist. Her eyes bulged, and her eyelids lagged. She had a discrete mass at the front of her neck.

'We need some tests to confirm the diagnosis,' I said when I finished the examination. 'But I think you have an overactive thyroid gland. I want you to take this form to the laboratory. They'll take some blood. I'm also ordering a thyroid scan, and you may need to see a specialist.'

I couldn't wait to present the case to JP at our next meeting.

'It *was* thyrotoxicosis,' I said. 'Annette's a new woman now she's on carbimazole. She's happy at work. Says I changed her life.'

JP beamed. 'Well done! It's not just the developing world that needs your diagnostic skills. There's a place for you here!'

I gazed straight back at him. 'I'm going back to Uganda. As soon as I'm allowed.'

JP frowned. 'And there's nothing I can do to change your mind?'

I smiled. 'No. Another three months and I can get a Certificate of Good Standing.'

That afternoon, I wondered what Marian was doing. Strangely, I wanted to tell her about Annette. She'd seen my failures, so she ought to share my successes. I picked up the telephone after my last patient of the day.

'Is that surgical? I'm trying to get hold of Marian Taylor. Does she still work in your ward? What? She's left? Gone where? To work overseas? You don't know where?'

I felt a lump in my throat as I put down the receiver. How could Marian just disappear and leave so many unanswered questions? Why did she leak the story to the press? Was it for her sake or mine? That still did my head in. Maybe she was right all along—perhaps my appearance on the *Holmes* show forced the Medical Council's hand. Did I owe her an apology? Or even a vote of thanks? Now I would never know.

With a sigh, I reached for my jacket and left the consulting room. Whatever our differences, I wished we hadn't parted on such bad terms.

I was on the phone to Mike Bailey the moment my supervision was over. 'When can I start work? I've got my CGS, and I can't wait to get back to Uganda.'

'Theo! Good to hear from you! Great to have you back on board.'

The line went dead for a moment.

'Are you still there, Mike?'

'Yes … it's just … I'm afraid we're fully staffed in Uganda now.' His voice trailed off momentarily. 'Actually, your nurse Marian Taylor took the last place out there. She's doing a fantastic job. As good as any of the doctors. If not better.'

'Yes. Marian's an exceptional nurse.' I tried to hide the disappointment in my voice. 'It's just … I particularly wanted to go back to Uganda. For personal reasons.'

'I know, Theo.' Mike sounded like he understood. 'You have a connection with Uganda. But not an entirely happy one.' I heard him rustle through some papers. 'Perhaps it's all for the best. We need your skills—and your passion—for another project. I want you to go to Madhapur. With your experience at the Kalanjala Hospital, you're the ideal person to help the locals get their infirmary up and running.'

'*Madhapur?* Where's that?'

'Orissa state, India. We've got a great team out there. They'll make sure you're supported. You'll love Madhapur—and the community. This is the opportunity you've been waiting for. The chance to make a real difference.' He broke off, perhaps sensing a lack of enthusiasm on my part. 'And you're guaranteed an authentic curry. Every day!'

As I put the phone down and pondered for a few minutes, I knew that far more than a good vindaloo awaited me in Madhapur.

CHAPTER EIGHT

India, February 1986

Elisha

It'll take more than frigging prayer if I'm going to survive in the backwaters of bloody India! Elisha recalled saying.

Damn right! Joanna had warned her that arrival in India was an assault on the senses. Zac teased her about the sewers the entire flight to Calcutta.

'The drains get pretty ripe in the hot season,' he said. 'But you'll get used to it.'

'Bugger off, Zac,' Elisha said.

The stench of effluent struck the moment they stepped off the plane in Calcutta.

Elisha held a handkerchief over her nose in one hand and clutched a sick bag with the other. 'I'm going to puke!'

Zac smirked. 'Sis! You've turned green.'

Melissa scowled at Zac. 'Back off.' She massaged Elisha's back as they lined up in the immigration hall. 'Just take some deep breaths. You'll feel better when we get out in the fresh air.'

I'd feel better if we'd never left Australia. It was just as pungent outside the terminal, if not worse. The smell of the drains competed with the fragrant aroma of the spices on the roadside stalls.

Elisha could have cried when she saw the enormous queue for taxis. 'It's going to take forever.'

'It won't. Look.' Melissa pointed to the sea of yellow-and-black Morris Oxfords. 'There're loads of cabs.'

A busker worked his way down the line, playing a tune on his bamboo flute. His sidekick beat the rhythm on a pair of tabla drums, while a kid rattled a tambourine.

Zac clapped his hands in time with the drummer and grinned at Elisha. 'Get with the beat, sis!'

Elisha pulled a face. 'It's not exactly heavy rock.'

'Rupee, sir. Rupee, madam,' the boy said. 'We play your favourite song.' Melissa tossed him a coin.

Zac gave Elisha a playful dig in the ribs. 'What about "The Green, Green Grass of Home"?'

Elisha shot him a dirty look. *Bloody Zac.* Had he no idea how she was feeling?

A man in a bright orange shirt with a matching turban approached Elisha.

'I take your picture with snake.' He took a cobra out of a basket and began draping it over Elisha's shoulders.

Elisha tripped on the kerb in a desperate attempt to push him away. 'Get off me!'

The man shook his head. 'You not want? Never mind. Watch snake dance when I play tune.'

Zac bounced from foot to foot. 'My uncle used to take me to see a snake charmer when I was a kid.' He pointed to the ornately carved musical instrument the man pulled from his case. 'That's a pungi. Isn't it cool?'

Elisha covered her ears. Cool or not, the instrument, shaped like a balloon on the end of a stick, made a hideous droning noise. She took a further step back when the snake rose up from its basket, and she grabbed her father's arm. 'Make him take it away.'

'Leave my daughter alone,' Wesley said. 'Snake charmers are illegal. Do you want me to report you?'

The man waved his fist and spat on the ground. Elisha screwed up her eyes. Was he going to punch her father? Or worse?

Perhaps someone was watching over them because at that very moment, a taxicab pulled up, and the driver honked the horn. 'Where to, sir?'

Wesley wiped the perspiration off his forehead. 'Howrah Railway Station. Quick as you can.'

Elisha's eyes darted from the hawkers peddling their goods to the amputees on the roadside. Families huddled together on tarpaulins laid on the pavement. Did people really live like this?

Whenever the taxi stopped in the traffic, beggars hammered on the cab window. 'Rupee for the child! Please! No food! No home!'

A crack appeared on the windscreen.

Elisha grabbed hold of her mother. 'They're going to get in!'

'They won't harm us.' Melissa nestled Elisha in her arms and turned to Wesley. 'How much further?'

'Not far.' Wesley tapped the taxi driver on the shoulder. 'Try to avoid the Chandni Chowk area.'

The cab lurched in a new direction, swinging from side to side. Horns blazing. Teaming streets. Everywhere.

Elisha buried her head in her hands and sobbed. 'I can't take any more of this. I want to go home.'

'My darling!' Melissa ran her fingers through Elisha's hair. 'We'll be out of Calcutta soon. It'll be different when we get to Madhapur. I promise.'

'Dad! Look!' Zac pointed to a billboard. 'East Bengal FC won the Calcutta Football League!'

'I heard they'd lifted their game this season,' Wesley said.

Zac grinned. 'I can't wait to get training again.'

How can you talk about bloody soccer at a time like this?

Elisha grabbed the sick bag again. A fresh wave of nausea struck when the taxi careered around a corner and pulled up at Howrah Station.

Wesley opened the cab door. A boy in a monkey suit poked his head inside and made a face at Elisha.

'Clear off!' Wesley said.

Elisha clung to the cab's armrest. 'I'm not getting out!'

Wesley glanced at his watch. 'Come on. He's gone now. We'll miss the train if we don't hurry. Then we'll have to stay the night here.'

What? Stay the night in this godawful place?

Elisha edged close to the taxi door.

'Hold on to my hand and don't let go,' Melissa said.

I won't. Elisha's fingers dug into her mother so hard they almost drew blood. More buskers. More beggars. All vying for a spare banknote.

          David Whittet

Wesley hailed a porter who loaded their cases onto a trolley.

Zac charged ahead and pointed to a train crossing the Howrah Bridge, an enormous cantilever suspension bridge, linking the cities of Howrah and Calcutta across the Hooghly River. Hordes of kids clung to the outside of the carriages while others jostled for space on the roof.

'Wow!' Zac said. 'You don't see anything like that in Australia!'

'Stupid boys.' Wesley watched a young lad lose his grip and fall to the trackside. 'Risking their lives like that.'

A guard chased some kids away from the carriage when they boarded the train. Why didn't Elisha find that reassuring? She looked up. More boys were climbing onto the engine.

Wesley and Zac played I spy as the train rattled across the plains towards the Mayurbhanj district. Elisha pressed her head against the grimy window, staring at the endless paddy fields that stretched to the horizon. Women labourers waded through the waist-high water from the recent Orissa floods.

Zac bounced a football on the carriage floor, the repetitive thud merging with the clickety-clack of the train's wheels.

Elisha dozed. Her eyes were almost closed when a face appeared in the window. She jumped bolt upright. 'What the—'

'Don't panic, sis!' Zac briefly stopped playing with the football. 'It's just another hitchhiker climbing along the train.'

Wesley glanced up from the notes for his introductory sermon. 'I told you train surfers were a menace. I don't know why the railway board doesn't put a stop to it.'

Elisha turned away from the window and nuzzled up to her mother.

Only eight hours in the country and already I'm a nervous wreck.

Every time the train pulled up at a station, Elisha wanted to get out of that horrid, stuffy carriage and away from the prying eyes of the other passengers.

'Not this one, darling,' Melissa said.

Elisha rocked on her seat and rubbed her aching legs. 'I've got cramp.'

'Just two more stops and we're there,' Melissa said. 'Deepesh Banerjee is coming to meet us.'

Elisha stared into the distance. Perhaps arrival at Madhapur would be even scarier than the train ride.

Another hour and they finally arrived at Rairakhol Railway Station. Elisha's stomach churned when she caught sight of the welcoming committee on the platform. A tall man in a white silk suit opened the carriage door the moment the train stopped. That must be Deepesh Banerjee, the head of the Church's Indian mission. He grasped her father's hand and helped him onto the platform.

'Welcome back to the Mayurbhanj, Pastor Martin!' Deepesh grasped Wesley's hands and shook them vigorously. 'I trust you had a comfortable journey.'

'Yes,' Wesley said. 'We did. God has brought us safely back to you.'

'And this is your beautiful family,' Deepesh said. 'I've heard so much about you.' He brought his hands together in front of his chest, saluting Melissa with a traditional greeting. 'Namaste!'

He stepped forward and ruffled Zac's hair. 'You must be Isaac. I see you've brought your football.'

Zac bounced the ball on the platform. 'I can't wait to train with the team again.'

'Glad you're so keen,' Deepesh said. 'The season's just getting underway.'

Elisha sighed. 'Don't encourage him.'

'And you must be Elisha,' Deepesh said. 'Namaste. There's someone here who's dying to meet you.'

Elisha had already worked out that the fifteen-year-old girl jumping up and down behind the church dignitaries had to be Rajani. A grey-haired woman brought the girl forward.

'Meet Rajani,' the woman said. 'I'm her great-aunt.'

The two girls stared at each other. Elisha gripped her hands together. Who should make the first move? She took an uneven stride and then rushed ahead and hugged Rajani.

Everyone cheered.

'Jo has told me so much about you,' Elisha said. 'You're even more beautiful than the photograph.'

 David Whittet

Rajani laughed and ran her fingers through her silky black hair. 'You're joking. I'm not beautiful.'

Elisha gave her a gentle prod. 'Want to bet?'

Rajani frowned. 'My great-aunt Nisha says gambling's evil. Work of the devil.'

Elisha scratched her head. 'I didn't mean it literally. Your great-aunt sounds like my old man.'

Elisha was going to say more when Deepesh Banerjee clapped his hands.

'Brothers and sisters in Christ,' he began. 'We must unite in prayer to dedicate this mission. We will come together in the Rairakhol church hall before we drive to Madhapur.'

Elisha tugged on her father's arm. 'Please, Dad, let me stay outside with Rajani while you're praying. We've so much to talk about.'

'Very well,' Wesley said. 'It's good that you have a friend. But not too noisy, mind. You mustn't disturb the blessing.'

'We won't.'

Elisha *meant* to keep her voice down. Sat on the grass with Rajani outside the church, she couldn't help herself. With their heads close together, they giggled like little girls.

Elisha winked. 'I don't suppose you get any rock concerts out here?'

Rajani sighed. 'No. Life's quiet. My great-aunt says that's good. Gives us time to think about God's blessings.'

Elisha rolled her eyes. 'So, what on earth do you do in the evenings?'

'We have prayer meetings and Bible study,' Rajani said.

Elisha shrugged. 'Back home, we have parties and discos. I know which I prefer.'

'Don't be like that,' Rajani said.

'Does your great-aunt let you have *any* fun?'

'We have socials at the church.'

Elisha pulled a clump of grass out of the ground. 'You must be bored as hell.'

'Not at all. Life's good.'

Elisha shook her head. 'Sooner you than me.' But what if this was to be her life from now on? Her father always preached about being content with little. Elisha never believed it.

Rajani glanced across at the church. 'Looks like they've finished the blessing.'

Elisha got up and brushed the grass off her jeans. 'So how long does it take to get to Madhapur?'

'About an hour,' Rajani said. 'Jai, one of our volunteers, is taking us in his van.'

Elisha gazed at the vista of lakes and rivers as the minivan clattered along the gravel road, the landscape dotted with the occasional temple and isolated hamlet. 'This really is the back of beyond. Not a department store in sight. I bet there's not even a cinema in Madhapur.'

'I'm afraid not,' Rajani said. 'But my uncle has a sixteen-millimetre projector and sometimes he shows us some inspirational films.'

Elisha screwed up her face. 'Great.'

More paddy plantations flashed past. A sea of green rice-plants, their tiny inflorescent flowers swaying in the breeze.

Elisha groaned. 'Fields, paddocks, meadows. Is there nothing else in this awful place?'

Rajani grinned. 'I thought you would be used to wide-open spaces coming from Australia. Joanna sent me a photograph of the outback.'

'A photo! Yes!' Elisha fumbled in her rucksack and pulled out her trusty Olympus Trip 35 mm pocket camera. 'I promised Jo I'd send her a picture of you. And us.'

Elisha took so many shots of Rajani that she had to load another roll of film. When she held the camera at arm's length to capture both of them together, she accidentally bumped the driver's seat.

Jai swerved to miss a pothole. 'Hey, watch it back there. You're ruining my suspension!'

'Sorry.' Elisha settled back in her seat. 'I'm dying to get the film developed. Is there a good photo store in Madhapur?'

Rajani shook her head. 'There's a pharmacy in Baripada that does film. But it'll take a couple of weeks or more.'

Elisha groaned. 'Back in Aussie, the Kodak Express shop does it in a couple of hours.'

 David Whittet

Elisha's first glimpse of Madhapur wasn't promising. The main street was just what she'd dreaded—a succession of old and dilapidated buildings as far as she could see. The church looked boring, just like they did back home. But the temple, with its dome and glistening white marble, reminded her of a mystical shrine in a fantasy movie she'd seen.

At least it had a secondary school. That meant there had to be some young people around to liven things up.

'You don't want to mess with the high school kids,' Rajani said. 'They're a rough lot. Much better bunch at the church school. That's where I go. My great-aunt says you're going to be helping out at our Sunday school.'

Elisha nodded and pulled a face.

Rajani gazed back with a sparkle in her eyes. 'Never mind. We get volunteers at the mission from all over the world. Some of the guys have been handsome—'

Elisha grinned. 'Now you're talking.'

'And they're all devout churchgoing boys. Maybe you'll fall in love, and we'll have a wedding!'

Elisha threw her arms in the air. Was there nobody in this wretched place who wasn't some pious evangelist? 'Not bloody likely! I'm seventeen and I intend to live.'

Is that our house? Jai dropped them off outside a lime-green concrete house with a corrugated iron roof. Elisha blinked. It was even worse than the photo Joanna had shown her.

Wesley turned the key in the front door. 'God bless our new home.'

'Amen,' Melissa said. 'Let's pray we'll all be happy here.'

Some hope. Elisha looked in the lounge. Then in all the other rooms. 'Where's the telly?'

'There's no television out here,' Wesley said. 'There's a local radio station, but that's about it.'

Elisha rolled her eyes. 'No TV. No cinema. No parties. No nothing. Why have you brought me here?'

Wesley continued unloading the trunks. 'To revitalise the Sunday school.'

Melissa put her arm around Elisha. 'At least you've got a new friend.'

Elisha shrugged. 'Yes, but Rajani will be at school all day.'

'So will you,' Wesley said. 'I want you to teach at the church school during the week as well as on Sunday.'

Zac burst in from outside. 'Far out! There's even a backyard for cricket practice. Can we put up a net?'

Trust Zac. Elisha wandered through to the bedrooms. 'Dibs this one.' At least it had a dressing table, albeit broken.

Rajani's great-aunt Nisha brought round some biryani for their supper.

Melissa set the table. 'It's been an exhausting day. We'll all feel better when we've had something to eat.'

That was her mother's answer for everything. And biryani? She'd had that once before from an Indian takeaway back home and it gave her stomach ache.

Elisha sat at the table and eyed her parents. 'You two have God. Zac has his sport. Mum could do the teaching. You don't need me out here.'

'No, dear,' Melissa said while serving the rice. 'I'm going back to nursing. I'll be helping out at the sanatorium, so I won't have time to teach at the school.'

'Besides,' Wesley said, 'we need fresh blood in the school. A young person with bright ideas.'

Elisha waved her fork at her father. 'I'm right out of inspiration.'

'Why don't you do some drawing?' Melissa said. 'You used to be so good at it.'

'Yeh, sis,' Zac said. 'Shame to let your talent go to waste.'

Melissa smiled. 'You could illustrate Bible stories for the children. They'd love it.'

'I do dark fantasy,' Elisha said. 'Not Bible stories.'

'There's your challenge,' Wesley said. 'Adapt your pictures for the scriptures. I told you we needed smart new thinking.'

Melissa put her hand on Elisha's. 'So you're not left out. You're a vital part of the mission.'

What a load of bollocks. Had they really dragged her halfway around the world to draw pictures for a bunch of kids who probably hated Sunday school as much as she'd done? Deliciously surreal art was Elisha's only escape. Turn her drawings into religious propaganda? That was rich. Her father told her off for blasphemy. *You will not take the Lord's name in vain!* Now he expected her to defile her work. *Sacrilege! I won't do it.*

Elisha lay on her bed that night, fidgeting and staring at the bug crawling across the cracked ceiling. *Dammit.* Maybe she could try a fresh take on all those far too reverential Bible pictures. After all, she'd nothing else to do. She pulled a pencil and a sketchpad out of her suitcase and doodled. A punk Angel Gabriel? Perhaps not. What about three Goth kings following a freakishly phantasmagorical Star of Bethlehem? She settled on a rockstar David and gangster Goliath. That didn't work either. Elisha tore the page off the pad, screwed it up and dragged the bedclothes over her head.

What the hell was all that noise? Elisha rubbed the sleep from her eyes, then peered through her bedroom window at Zac and the local cricket team practising in the yard.

Zac clean bowled the batsman and shouted '*Howzat!*' at the top of his voice.

Elisha picked up her pencil again and began sketching. Not an angel this time. More like a demon. Zac playing cricket. With a giggle, she added some horns. That would teach him to wake her up at such an ungodly hour.

Should she show it to her mother? With a glint in her eye, Elisha strode into the kitchen, sketch in hand.

'For heaven's sake,' Melissa said, 'rub out those horns before your father sees them.'

Zac burst in from the yard, lathered in sweat. 'I'll soon knock them back in shape, and we'll be in the Orissa championships.' He leant over Elisha's shoulder. 'Is that me? Cool! I should grow some horns. Scare off the opposition.'

Elisha hid the picture when Wesley came into the room for breakfast.

'You should draw Rajani,' Melissa told Elisha. 'Send Joanna her portrait.'

What a terrific idea. Elisha was due to meet Rajani that morning for a tour of the Madhapur Christian School. Boring. Sketching Rajani would be much more fun.

'I have to show you around the school first,' Rajani insisted. 'I guess schools in Australia are different.'

You call these mud huts a school? 'Too right.' Elisha picked up a book in one of the classrooms. *Preaching the Gospel in Foreign Lands.* 'In Aussie, we wouldn't tolerate a bunch of foreigners coming over and telling us how to live our lives. I don't know why you put up with it.'

'Many Hindus don't like it,' Rajani said. 'Some of them get mighty angry with your father.'

Elisha stomped her foot. 'If I had my way, we'd clear out and go home.'

'Don't say that.' Rajani squeezed Elisha's hand. 'I've only just got to know you. You *can't* leave!'

Elisha sighed. 'My father wouldn't let me, anyway. Don't think I haven't tried.'

Rajani's entreating brown eyes focused on Elisha. 'The children need a role model. Maybe that's why God sent you here.'

Elisha snorted. 'Don't you start. Now, can I draw you? I'm going to send the picture to Jo.'

'Alright,' Rajani said, 'provided you promise to help me with the kids on Sunday.'

Elisha bit her lip as the children filed out of the service during the second hymn, 'Guide Me, O Thou Great Redeemer'. That stirring Welsh tune with its rousing chorus always brought a lump to her throat.

Rajani gathered the boys and girls around them in the church hall. 'I want you all to make Elisha welcome. She's come all the way from Australia to be with us. And today she's going to tell us about a shepherd and his lost sheep.'

Elisha opened her sketchbook. Why was her hand shaking as she held up the drawing of the shepherd watching over his flocks that she'd done last night? *Pull yourself together. They're just kids.*

'Did you do that, miss?' a boy asked.

'She sure did,' Rajani said. 'Isn't she clever?'

Elisha cleared her throat, and read from Luke, Chapter 15, to the children: '"Which of you, if you had a hundred sheep, and lost one of them, wouldn't leave the ninety-nine in the field, and go after the one that was lost, searching until you found it?"'

Jayesh, a bright-eyed four-year-old, gazed up at Elisha, a tear in his eye. 'I'd do anything to find Siya, my pet dog, if he got lost.'

Rajani stroked Jayesh's hair. 'I know you would. Because you're an absolute sweetie!'

'Do you want to sit on my lap, Jayesh?' Elisha couldn't believe she'd just said that. 'You too, Kali.' The children all huddled tightly as she continued the story, '"When he found the lost sheep, the good shepherd was overjoyed."' Elisha held up another of her drawings, with the shepherd carrying the sheep home over his shoulder. '"He called his friends, his family and his neighbours, saying to them, 'Rejoice with me, for I have found my sheep which was lost!' I tell you, there will be more joy in Heaven over one sinner who repents, than over ninety-nine righteous people who need no forgiveness."'

The children clapped when Elisha showed them the last picture of the celebrations.

'What does "rejoice" mean?' Hiran asked.

Elisha thought for a moment. 'To be happy and thankful.'

Jayesh smiled. 'I'm happy the shepherd found his lost sheep.'

Rajani patted Elisha's shoulder. 'You're a born storyteller. I've never seen the children so engrossed in a Bible story before!'

After the church service finished, Elisha noticed Melissa and Wesley at the back of the hall. With the children crowding around her and chattering, Elisha strained to hear what her parents were saying.

'See how children love her'—that was her mother's voice—'I'm so proud of her.'

'Me too.' Did her father really say that?

Elisha stared at him over the children's heads. *Dad!* He stood with his chin up and his chest out. There was love in his eyes.

'Excuse me a moment, kids,' Elisha said.

She got up, ran across to her father and kissed him on the cheek.

Next Sunday, Elisha told the children about the prodigal son, with more pencil drawings to illustrate the story. The kids booed when the younger son left home and squandered his money and cheered when he came to his senses and returned to his father.

'It's not fair,' Rohan, a precocious eleven-year-old, remarked. 'The older boy stayed home and supported his dad. The young boy was a total loser, yet he got all the praise. Where's the justice in that?'

'I don't think I'd like a fatted calf, anyway.' Kali wrinkled his nose. 'It sounds horrible.'

Rajani took Rohan aside after the class. 'It's a parable.'

Rohan screwed up his face. 'A *what?*'

'A story to illustrate something important,' Rajani explained. 'It's about forgiveness. A loving father will forgive his son no matter what. God will forgive us if we are truly sorry.'

Every week there were new pictures and a fresh and exciting take on the familiar Bible stories. The children cooed at the discovery of baby Moses floating downriver in a basket and gasped when Noah built the Ark.

'Imagine all those animals in one boat,' Jayesh said. 'I wish I could've been there.'

Best of all, they loved the Good Samaritan.

'What's a Samaritan?' Hiran asked.

'Someone who does good for others,' Rajani said. 'Just like Elisha's dad. Pastor Martin is our Good Samaritan. He's worked miracles for our community.'

Rohan studied the picture of the Samaritan tending to the injured man's wounds. 'I wish I could draw like that.'

Elisha's eyes sparkled. 'Would you like to?'

'I'd love to,' Rohan said. 'Your pictures are so cool.'

Elisha eyed Rajani. 'We could start an art class at the school.'

'Brilliant,' Rajani said. 'Let's do it.'

A few weeks later, the children brought their own sketches to Sunday school and jostled to be the first to show them to Elisha.

'My goodness, Rohan,' Elisha said. 'That's beautiful. You've really captured the sower planting his seed. You too, Harin. Gorgeous. Well done. You're all so clever. Next week's story is the parable of the faithful servant. Let's see what fantastic pictures you can make to illustrate that.'

Teaching the children new brushstrokes gave Elisha an energy she hadn't felt since she left Australia.

'Do you still want to go home?' Rajani asked as they cleared up the paints after the class finished.

'Guess not.' Elisha paused as she rinsed the brushes. 'I love the kids. They're great. And doing my art again. It's been a lifesaver.'

'I meant what I said about your father,' Rajani said. 'He *is* our Good Samaritan.'

Elisha shrugged. 'He means well.'

'It's much more than that.' Rajani placed a stack of canvases on the shelf and swung around to face Elisha. 'He's been pestering the local government minister to increase the local housing grant—'

'Interfering in other people's business as usual,' Elisha said.

'No.' Rajani grabbed Elisha's hand and pulled her closer. 'Government here is corrupt. We need someone to shake them up.'

The girls continued to talk while preparing the classroom for the next lesson.

'Everyone complains about the Christians.' Rajani ran the duster over the blackboard. 'But they're the ones who actually do something. Nobody else has made such a difference to our lives. This school, rebuilding the village after the floods. That's all down to your father.'

Elisha dumped a pile of exercise books on the desk. 'I suppose.'

'I wouldn't have survived without Joanna, either. We lived on the street after the flood destroyed our home. It was Joanna who gave great-aunt Nisha the money for a new house, and it's thanks to her we have food on our table.'

'Yes,' Elisha agreed. 'Jo's a saint.'

Rajani put down the duster and looked straight into Elisha's eyes. 'So is your father.'

'I must write to Jo again,' Elisha said. 'I owe her a letter and some more pics.'

'Wait until tomorrow,' Rajani said. 'It's the first of April. Orissa Day. I've made a costume for the street parade. I want you to take my photo and send it to Joanna.'

'Brilliant,' Elisha said. 'I'm longing to see some Hindu culture.'

'I could always take you to see Krishna,' Rajani said. 'He's a spiritual guru to the Hindi people.'

'Yes, please,' Elisha said. 'That would be fantastic.'

Rajani hesitated. 'But your father wouldn't approve. I don't want to get you into trouble.'

'Forget about my old man,' Elisha said. 'I want to see the real India.'

Elisha wasn't long out of bed when Rajani burst into Elisha's room the next morning.

'Got your camera?' Rajani said.

Elisha moaned. 'What time do you call this?'

'It's half past seven,' Rajani said. 'We need to get going if you want a good view of the parade.'

Elisha rubbed her eyes, dazzled by the sparkling sequins that embellished Rajani's sari.

'Did you really make that dress yourself?' Elisha asked. 'You're so clever.'

Rajani smiled. 'My great-aunt helped with the embroidery.'

'You look beautiful,' Elisha said. With the gold brocade on the deep red silk, Rajani was stunning.

Elisha couldn't stop clicking her camera, and she'd gone through three rolls of film by the end of the parade.

'Jo's going to love these,' she said to Rajani. 'She'll be thrilled to see you on that float. If there was a Miss Madhapur contest, you'd be the winner. No competition.'

Rajani blushed. 'Stop it.'

'No kidding,' Elisha said. 'You could be the next Miss India. Now, you promised you'd take me to see Krishna.'

Elisha and Rajani took off their shoes at the entrance to the Madhapur temple.

Dressed in yellow satin robes, Krishna sat on a golden cushion. Elisha blinked as the revered leader mesmerised them with his hypnotic eyes. Without a word, Krishna reached out for Rajani's hand and held it in his, running his finger over the creases in her palm.

 David Whittet

'You, Rajani, are an old soul,' Krishna said. 'You have been here many times before.'

'An old soul?' Elisha exclaimed. 'Rajani is only fifteen.'

'Krishna uses the expression in its Hindu sense,' Rajani explained.

'Life is a wheel with many spokes,' Krishna said. 'A continuous cycle of birth, life, death, and rebirth until we attain Nirvana.'

Elisha screwed up her face. 'So, let me get this right. You're saying Rajani is a reincarnation?'

'Indeed she is,' Krishna answered. 'A wise and learned spirit. You will do well to heed her words.'

Elisha raised her eyebrows and gazed at Rajani. 'Here's me thinking I was older than you. Turns out you're older than me. Well, what do you know?' Elisha bowed her head for a moment, then thrust her hands at Krishna. 'Have I had a previous life too?'

Instead of looking at her hands, Krishna turned to her shadow on the wall. The dying rays of the setting sun shone through the shrine, casting a large silhouette on the stone.

'Look at your reflection. It is tall, is it not? A long shadow means you have far to travel before you reach Nirvana.' Krishna ran his fingers across her palm, firmly pressing her skin. 'You have many lives ahead.' He released Elisha's hands and stroked his long grey beard. 'But I fear your present incarnation is troubled.'

Elisha gasped. 'What do you mean?'

'Look after those you love,' Krishna said, 'and all will be well.'

Their eyes met. His pupils dilated. She could almost *feel* him read her soul with those sparkling eyes, as incandescent as the white Ambaji marble that adorned the temple.

It was too intense for Elisha. She turned her face away and shook. 'I think we should leave.' She jumped to her feet and tugged on Rajani's arm. 'Come on, Rajani. I want to go home.'

'Take care of your mother!' Krishna called after them as the girls scurried away. '*Your mother!*'

My mother. What did he mean?

'He was just telling you to look after her,' Rajani said as they walked home. 'What was it he said? *Look after those you love.* I don't think it was anything more than that.'

Elisha wasn't so sure. But when she got back to the house, her mother was in the kitchen cooking the dinner as she always did. And she was as stroppy as usual, moaning about Zac's muddy football boots and the state of Elisha's bedroom. Nothing had changed.

David Whittet

CHAPTER NINE

Elisha awoke to the sound of the garbage truck and the street sweeping machine the following morning. Through her bedroom window, she watched the workmen clean up the debris from the Orissa Day celebrations.

When they moved on to the next street, Elisha rummaged through her bedside table and pulled out a notepad. Lying on the bed, she fanned herself with the pad, picked up her pen and fiddled with it for a minute. Then she began furiously scribbling a letter.

My dearest Jo,

I'll tell you the weirdest thing. Rajani took me to see this spiritual guru, Krishna. He said Rajani has been reborn. She's lived before as a different being. I've been thinking. What if Rajani is a reincarnation of your dead sister, Angie? Perhaps God really does move in mysterious ways. Maybe when you adopted Rajani, you brought Angie back to life in a new body. I can see you in her smile—and in her laugh. Dad says that's rubbish. Not scriptural. 'Don't listen to those false prophets!' I suppose you'd agree with him, but I believe it. You were right, India has changed me. I am becoming more spiritual. Even if it's not scriptural!

Elisha put her pen down. Should she mention what Krishna had said about her mother? No. Rajani was probably right. Krishna just wanted her to take care of her mum. No sense in worrying Jo about something that would never happen.

The house was quiet. Her mother was on the early shift at the field hospital, and her father would be at the mission. Elisha grabbed a samosa from the kitchen bench for her breakfast. She'd just about got over her addiction to fast food. Taking a bite, Elisha had to admit samosas were far tastier than hamburgers. She peered out of the window. Zac and his mates were playing cricket in the backyard. As usual. Elisha went into her father's study to hunt for an airmail stamp. Where did he keep them?

She looked under his paperweight. No. She picked up a pile of books. There they were. Elisha was about to take a stamp when she heard a scream from outside.

What the hell was that? Elisha dropped the books onto the floor and rushed out of the back door.

Zac was collapsed on the ground. What was wrong with him? He was clasping his right knee, and he'd gone a pale green. She'd never seen him look like that before. He was rolling around on the ground and shrieking. That wasn't like Zac, either.

'Don't just stand there,' Elisha shouted at the other boys. 'Help him! I'm going to call Mum.'

Elisha rushed back inside and picked up the phone. 'Mum! You've got to come home quickly! Zac's had an accident. I think he's broken his knee.'

Zac looked like he was about to pass out when Elisha got back in the yard. Had Krishna got it all wrong? Was it Zac she had to look after and not her mother?

'Can one of you please tell me what happened?' Elisha said, helping the boys to prop Zac up against the backyard wall.

'We were just practising,' one of the teammates said. 'Zac missed the shot, and the ball hit him on the knee.'

Ashok, a lanky sixteen-year-old, stepped forward. 'It was me. I was bowling. This is my fault. I'm so sorry.'

Elisha could see the tears in his eyes. 'Don't beat yourself up,' she said. 'It was an accident.'

Where was her mother? Elisha glanced at her watch. It was five minutes since she called Melissa, and the hospital was just down the road. Every second felt like a lifetime. What would her mother be doing if she were here?

'I think we should get him inside,' Elisha said to the boys, 'and fetch me a towel and some ice from the fridge.'

The boys carried Zac inside and sat him on a chair in the kitchen. Ashok handed Elisha a sponge, and she cleaned the blood off Zac's leg.

Elisha breathed a sigh of relief when her mother arrived and knelt beside Zac.

'It's buggered, isn't it?' Zac groaned.

'Shush, darling. Let me look.' Melissa examined the knee. 'It's certainly very swollen. I'll have to take you to the hospital for an X-ray.'

'Damn!' Tears welled in Zac's eyes. 'The championship trials are next week. I'm never going to make it.'

Elisha put an arm around Zac. She understood how important making the premier football league was to her brother.

Melissa gave Elisha a nudge. 'Call your father. Tell him to get the van. We need to take Zac to the hospital.'

Elisha had never seen her father look so distraught as he did when he saw Zac. His hands were shaking.

'Wes! Thank God you're here,' Melissa said. 'Help me get Isaac into the van.'

Wesley lifted Zac off the chair. 'Hold on to me, son. You're going to be alright.'

Elisha followed them out to the van. Why did parents always promise everything was going to be okay? Zac looked positively dreadful.

'Will they be able to deal with it here?' Elisha asked her mother.

'Arjun is on duty today,' Melissa said. 'He'll know what to do.'

Dr Arjun Basar, a middle-aged physician with a shock of grey hair, was waiting at the gate when they arrived at the field hospital.

'Namaste, Mel. Namaste, Pastor Martin.' Dr Basar bowed and pressed his fingers together in the traditional greeting. 'What's your boy been up to? A cricketing injury, is it? Wheel him through into casualty.'

Elisha helped Zac into the wheelchair. Movement made him wince. She could feel his pain and supported his leg as best she could. A porter pushed the wheelchair through the swing doors into the assessment cubicle.

'Your mother's a fine nurse,' Arjun told Zac. 'Now, our X-ray machine is not the most up to date in the world, but it does the job.'

Elisha held Zac's hand while the radiographer slid a plate under his knee. She felt the doctor's eyes watching her.

'Looks like your sister would make a great nurse too,' Arjun added. 'You're lucky to have two such lovely ladies looking after you.'

'Hold still, Isaac,' the radiographer said. 'Everyone else, behind the screen, please.'

Elisha continued to squeeze her brother's hand while they waited for the films to be developed.

'It's buggered,' Zac kept muttering. 'Buggered. Buggered. Buggered.'

'Shush,' Elisha said. 'You don't know that.'

She heard Arjun talking to her mother. He had the X-rays on the viewing box.

'This is a job for the orthopods in Baripada,' Arjun said. 'I'll call and let them know you're coming.' He knelt down beside Zac. 'I think you've torn a cartilage.'

'A cartilage?' Zac groaned. 'That's the entire season gone.'

'Your mother tells me you're a keen sportsman,' Arjun said.

Zac nodded.

'Then you'll understand it's vital we get this fixed,' Arjun continued. 'My colleagues in Baripada will do an operation to remove the damaged meniscus, and we'll have you back on the cricket pitch as soon as we can.'

Elisha watched Zac writhe in agony during the three-hour ride to the charity hospital in Baripada, bouncing up and down in the back of the mission's makeshift ambulance.

'How much further?' he moaned each time they went over a bump in the road.

Dark thoughts flashed through Elisha's mind. A torn cartilage didn't sound too serious. But was it really something more serious? The doctor's expression had suggested it could be. *Will he still have a leg by the time we get to the hospital? I've heard they specialise in amputations at Baripada.*

The grim look on the orthopaedic surgeon's face when they arrived, escalated her fear. Nawab Patel, flanked by students on either side, stood in the ambulance bay as they pulled up. He grabbed the X-rays and held them up to the light before handing them to his students.

'What's the diagnosis?' Without waiting for an answer, Patel bent down and examined Zac's knee in the back of the ambulance. When he'd finished, he turned to the students. 'What do you see on the films? Come on, haven't you worked it out yet?'

'What are they talking about?' Zac said. 'What's he seen on the X-rays?'

'Don't worry,' Melissa said. 'They're just deciding on the best treatment. They'll soon have you right.'

Elisha gripped Zac's hand even tighter. She knew Zac didn't believe their mother's platitude any more than she did.

A nurse in a starched blue uniform arrived.

'Sister,' Patel said. 'Prep him for theatre. He's shattered the patella and torn the lateral meniscus.'

'That's the football season written off as well,' Zac groaned as the porters wheeled him towards the anaesthetic room.

'He's going to be alright, isn't he?' Melissa asked.

'You're a nurse, Mrs Martin,' Patel said. 'You know the stakes. There are no guarantees. The internal damage is severe. Now, I need you to sign the consent form.'

'Can I stay with Zac while he has his operation?' Elisha asked. 'He's so frightened.'

'No,' Melissa said. 'The operating theatre is a sterile area. We have to stay here and let the doctors get on with their work.'

Melissa signed the papers and Zac disappeared into the anaesthetic room.

Sitting with her parents in the waiting room, more black thoughts entered Elisha's head. What if Zac could *never* play sport again? It would destroy him. What if he couldn't *walk* again? She'd heard about sportsmen having personality changes after injuries that finished their careers. Elisha couldn't bear to see Zac becoming bitter and twisted.

A nurse arrived with three cups of sweet chai. 'Drink this,' she said. 'Sugar is good for shock.'

It didn't help. Elisha watched her mother grasp her father's hand. Melissa was obviously panicking as much as she was.

'Cricket, football, rugby. They're Zac's life,' Melissa said. 'What's he going to do? What can we say to him?'

Wesley rubbed his chin. 'God will speak to Zac. Whatever the outcome of the surgery, God will bring purpose to Zac's life.'

Elisha stared at her father. 'Do you really believe that?'

Wesley didn't hesitate. 'Yes, I do.'

Elisha stood up and paced around the cramped waiting room. How could her father have such blind faith at such a dreadful time? Elisha had begun to see a higher purpose in her own life, what with the children at the Sunday school and Rajani. But now—resentment at having to come to India flooded back.

Melissa got up and held Elisha's hand. 'We should pray for Zac. That's all we can do now.'

An hour later, the theatre doors swung open and Nawab Patel emerged, still in his scrubs. He looked more approachable without his bow tie.

Elisha rushed up to him. 'You haven't taken Zac's leg off, have you?'

'Good heavens, no,' Patel said. 'Your brother's in recovery.'

'How is he?' Elisha asked. 'Will he walk again? Will he be able to play cricket?'

Patel resumed his smooth, professional voice. 'It's early days. But the surgery went as well as we could have hoped or expected.'

Melissa and Patel talked about the operation. Elisha listened, but it was all medical speak, and she couldn't understand a word of it.

As well as they hoped or expected. That was doctor talk, too. At least Zac still had both his legs. Did that mean he had a fighting chance of playing sport again?

'Can I see him?' Elisha asked.

'Not until he's on the ward,' Patel said. 'Now, if you'll excuse me, I have other patients to check up on.'

Why was he so long in the recovery room? Had something gone wrong?

Elisha still couldn't get near Zac when he got back to the ward. Her mother was fussing over him even more than the hospital nurses, continually checking his pulse and wiping his brow.

Her father was hovering too. He tapped Zac on the shoulder. 'It's bad luck, son. But there'll be new opportunities. When God closes a door—'

Not that again! What a dumb thing to say. And from his pained expression, it didn't cheer Zac up one bit.

At last, Melissa and Wesley left to get some chai and Elisha could get close to her brother. Zac looked a lot better than she expected.

 David Whittet

'Sis,' he mumbled.

'Zac!' There was a drip in his hand, so Elisha stroked his arm instead. 'We're going to get through this together. I'll coach you. We'll get you back at the wicket, and the football pitch.'

Zac managed a smile. 'You? Coach me? You don't even like cricket or football. In fact, you hate all forms of sport!'

Elisha grinned back. 'At least I made you laugh.'

They were still enjoying the moment when Melissa and Wesley returned to the ward.

'I'm going to stay in the relatives' room at the hospital,' Melissa said. 'You'll go home with your father.'

'Oh, Mum!' Elisha said. 'Can't I stay here with you?'

'No,' Melissa said. 'Rajani needs your help at the school.'

'Rajani doesn't need me,' Elisha protested. 'She's much better at everything than I am.'

'Nonsense,' Melissa said. 'She was just saying the other day how much she relies on you. Now, say goodbye to Zac.'

Wesley put his arm on Elisha's shoulder. 'Don't worry. Zac's going to be okay. We need to get going. Bibha is on her way back from an outreach clinic, and she's going to give us a ride home.'

Elisha kissed her brother on the cheek. 'I'll be back tomorrow, promise.'

'We'll see,' Melissa said. 'If you can get a ride after you've finished at the school—'

Just try to stop me!

Elisha had an idea on the way home. Bibha, a nurse at the mission, went out to remote clinics most days.

'Bibha,' Elisha said, leaning forward from the back of the car. 'Where's your clinic tomorrow?'

'I'm at Naranpur in the morning and Sirisbani in the afternoon,' Bibha said. 'Why?'

'When you've finished at Naranpur,' Elisha said, 'I wondered if you could pick me up and take me to Baripada to see Zac.'

'That must be at least twenty kilometres out of her way,' Wesley said.

'Dad! I want to see my brother!'

'I'll take you,' Bibha said. 'It's no trouble.'

Elisha hurried Rajani through the classes in the morning.

'I want you to come with me to see Zac,' Elisha said when they cleared up the classroom. 'I need some moral support.'

'Why?' Rajani asked. 'What is it?'

'I've been talking to Zac's teammates,' Elisha said. 'They want Zac to do them a favour. I'm not sure how he's going to take it.'

Elisha braced herself when they reached the hospital. She clutched Rajani's hand as they got out of the car and climbed the steps to the imposing entrance.

'Zac will be delighted to see you,' Rajani said. 'Nothing else matters.'

Didn't it? Sport meant everything to Zac. Elisha's heart beat faster with each step through the endless corridors. She stopped at the door outside the ward and whispered in Rajani's ear, 'Wish me luck.'

Rajani opened the swing door. 'You can do this.'

Elisha took a deep breath and strode up to Zac's bed. 'Zac!'

'Sis!' Zac sat up on his pillow. 'Thank you for coming! You too, Rajani. Great to see you both!'

Zac looked so much better. Elisha feared her news might tip him over the edge.

'Your mates are all asking after you,' Elisha said.

'I bet they are,' Zac replied. 'They'll all be vying to see who can replace me as captain of the football team.'

'Since you can't play next season,' Elisha began, the words coming out in a garbled flurry, 'the team wondered if …' She flinched, anticipating his reaction. 'If you would be their official photographer for the year.'

'What? Team photographer?' Zac spewed the words back. 'You're joking!'

'No,' Elisha said. 'You could use my Olympus camera.'

Zac made a face. 'Is that a consolation prize?'

Rajani drew up a chair and sat next to Elisha at the bedside. 'Honestly, Zac, think about it. You won't lose touch with your mates on the team.'

'And as a photographer,' Elisha said, thinking fast on her feet, 'you can analyse the players' strengths and weaknesses. That way, when you're back next year, you'll be even better than before.'

Zac smiled. Relief. Did that mean he'd bought her story?

'You've got it all worked out, haven't you, sis?' he said. 'You hate sport, now you're talking like a coach.' His grin disappeared when he looked down at his leg. 'But I'm not sure I'm going to be fit for next year. Or the year after that.'

Elisha blinked back a tear. 'Don't say that.'

She stared at the blood seeping through the bandaging and knew Zac was right. What would become of her happy-go-lucky brother if he could never play again? Would he turn into an angry young man? There was nothing else she could say to make him feel better. She just put her hand on his and held it tight.

Melissa came onto the ward and examined the charts at the end of the bed. She felt Zac's forehead. 'You're spiking a fever. When did you last see a doctor?'

'Not since the operation,' Zac replied. 'The ward sister's been around a few times. They're very short-staffed.'

'That's no excuse,' Melissa said. 'Is there nobody on duty?'

Zac pointed to a patient in traction across the ward. 'That poor guy had to wait an hour to get his pain relievers.'

'It's not good enough!' Melissa said. 'I'm going to take your temperature now.' She grabbed the thermometer at the bedside and stuck it in Zac's mouth.

'I heard the nurses talking when we came in,' Elisha said. 'Something about a cholera epidemic and the staff going down like flies.'

'A parent at the school said there was cholera in Baripada,' Rajani added.

Melissa took the thermometer out of Zac's mouth. 'Forty point five. You're burning up!' She put her hand on his forehead again. 'I'm going to fetch a doctor.'

What? Zac's temperature was 40.5? Elisha shuddered. That must be serious. Her mother had freaked out and called the doctor when Elisha's temperature was just 39.0 with tonsillitis.

Minutes later, her mother was back on the ward with Nawab Patel. Another shudder swept through Elisha's body as she heard them talk. Osteomyelitis. What was that?

'Once the infection gets into the bone …' Patel broke off and threw his hands in the air. 'I'm sorry, Mrs Martin, but the prognosis is poor. I may be able to save the leg if I can clear all that necrotic tissue, but I'm not making any promises.'

Before Elisha could ask questions, Patel was gone, and Zac was back in surgery. Zac *would* be bitter and angry after this.

Elisha turned to her mother. 'I'm not going home until Zac's out of theatre.'

'Neither am I,' Rajani said.

Melissa frowned. 'I'm not sure. If there's cholera in the hospital, you'd be safer at home.'

Elisha glared back. 'I had the vaccine before we left Australia. And it bloody well hurt.'

'I've had a cholera jab too,' Rajani said. 'So we'll both be okay.'

Elisha stamped her foot. 'I am *not* leaving until I know Zac's okay.'

Four hours and Zac was still not back on the ward. Elisha and Rajani sat together in silence on a bench in the waiting area. An orderly arrived with a trolley and offered them some chai. Rajani took a cup, but Elisha had drunk enough sweet tea for a lifetime and knew she'd throw up.

A porter rolled up for his tea break, and the orderly gave him a mug of chai and a chapatti.

'What happens if we all get cholera?' the porter said. 'There'll be nobody left to look after the patients.'

'The hospital will close,' the orderly answered. 'And the patients will die.'

Elisha clasped Rajani's hand. 'Thank God you came with me. I couldn't have survived this on my own.'

Rajani didn't reply. She just snuggled closer to Elisha.

Another half hour and at last the swing doors opened, and the theatre staff wheeled Zac back to the ward. Elisha jumped to her feet. She could hardly see Zac for the mass of traction equipment tethered to his bed.

Patel removed his face mask and used it to wipe the sweat off his face.

 David Whittet

'I'm sorry it took so long,' he said. 'Sister is off sick, and I had to debride the wound on my own. But I saved his leg.'

Elisha could have kissed him. 'Thank you, Doctor! Thank you!'

'We're not out of the woods yet,' Patel said. 'But cleaning out the dead tissue is a big step forward. Hopefully, the antibiotics will do the rest.'

Elisha watched Zac sleep off the anaesthetic. The tubes in his mouth made his breathing noisy, but his face looked remarkably peaceful. Part of her didn't want him to wake up and see the mass of apparatus on his knee.

Wesley came in, and they all gathered around the bed.

Zac opened his eyes and sobbed. 'I'll never be able to play sport again.'

Elisha wanted to say something but couldn't find the words. She just stared at him and hoped he could see the love in her eyes.

'At least you'll walk again,' Melissa said. 'The physio says she'll soon have you back on your feet.'

Zac snorted. 'What good is walking if I can't play cricket or football?'

Wesley put his hand on the bed. 'Cheer up, son. Count your blessings.'

'*Blessings?*' Zac spat the word back in his father's face.

Wesley frowned. 'Yes, Isaac. God has a plan for you.'

'Dad!' Elisha glared at her father. 'Give him a break.'

'Leave it, Wes,' Melissa said. 'Now's not the time.'

Wesley took a deep breath. 'I just want Isaac to know that God will reward him in Heaven.'

'Stop it, Dad!' Zac pulled himself upright in the bed, tears rolling down his cheeks. 'I don't care about God or Heaven. For once in your life, can't you understand it's the present that matters?'

'That's enough, both of you,' Melissa said. 'I think you should go home now, Wes. Take Elisha and Rajani back with you.'

Elisha drew back from her father. 'I'm not going back with him. I'm staying here tonight with Zac.'

Rajani took Wesley's arm. 'I'll go back with Wes. I'll look after the school tomorrow so Elisha can stay with Zac.'

Elisha held Zac's hand throughout the night, periodically wiping the sweat off his face while he slept. Her mother went off to get some sleep and came back at breakfast time.

'This place is like a mausoleum with so many staff off sick,' Melissa said. 'I can't understand why all the staff aren't vaccinated against cholera.'

The staff nurse overheard her. 'Money. Supply. Same old story.'

Melissa eyed the nurse. 'If I hadn't checked Isaac's temperature last night, he'd have died of septicaemia. That's not good enough.'

'No, it's not,' the staff nurse agreed. 'I only wish there was something we could do about it.'

'Well, there is something I can do about it,' Melissa said and marched off the ward.

Elisha sighed. What was her mother getting herself into this time?

Thirty minutes later, Melissa was back.

Elisha's mouth fell open. 'You've volunteered for *what*?'

'They're desperate for nurses vaccinated against cholera,' Melissa said. 'And I don't want to see another boy suffer from neglect like our Isaac.'

'I've got a bad feeling about this, Mum,' Elisha said. 'You don't have to work here.'

'I don't *have* to,' Melissa said, 'but I *want* to. People will die if they can't get the staff to look after them. I start work tomorrow in the emergency department.'

'What about Zac?' Elisha said. 'He needs you.'

Melissa put her arm around Elisha. 'Zac's got you and Rajani. You're both doing a great job keeping his spirits up.'

'What if you catch some nasty disease?' Elisha said. 'Like the other nurses.'

'Don't worry,' Melissa said. 'I've had shots for all the illnesses I could possibly get out here, including cholera. With the current epidemic, that makes me the perfect person to work here. And I *will* work here.'

Take care of your mother. Krishna's words took on a new and urgent meaning. Elisha had to stop her mother from working at the hospital. But how? During the long hours they sat at Zac's bedside, Elisha studied her mother's face. Melissa had always been stubborn, and today she looked more determined than ever. Once her mother made up her mind, there

David Whittet

was no going back. Elisha knew that from bitter experience.

Elisha stood and paced up and down the ward. Perhaps Krishna was wrong. Maybe he didn't know what he was talking about, and he was just a fraud like her father said. Elisha scratched her head. She trusted Krishna. Those piercing eyes, so direct they had to be telling the truth. Besides, Elisha wasn't taking any chances with her mother.

Elisha sat down again at the bedside. Should she tell her mother about Krishna and his warning? Would her mother listen? Probably not. And as for her father, he'd go mad if he knew she'd gone against him and been to see Krishna.

After two days of intensive care, Nawab Patel declared Zac out of immediate danger.

Tears streamed down Elisha's cheeks. She jumped up off her chair and clapped her hands.

'Now you know your brother's safe,' Melissa said. 'It's time for you to go home.'

Elisha slumped back in her seat and glared at her mother. 'Must I?'

'Yes,' Melissa said. 'I've asked Bibha to take you home.'

Elisha desperately needed someone to share her burden. What about Bibha? She was a nurse. Surely she'd understand Melissa was putting herself at unnecessary risk when the family needed her most.

'Bibha,' Elisha began, 'have you heard my mum wants to volunteer at the hospital?'

Bibha's eyes gleamed. 'Yes. I think it's a wonderful thing your mother's doing. So brave. So selfless.'

Elisha didn't listen to the rest. Did nobody understand how she felt? If only she could talk to Joanna. Jo would know what to do. Wait a minute— they had a phone at home. Elisha couldn't wait to get home and call Joanna.

Her fingers trembled as she dialled the number. Had she got the international dialling code right? Would her father overhear the call from his study? What if he did? Elisha didn't care. She just wanted to talk to her old mentor.

An automated voice cracked in the distance. 'Overseas calls are not permitted on this line.'

Elisha dropped the phone. There was nothing else for it. She took a deep breath and went to her father's study. What was another telling off when her mother's life was at stake?

'Dad,' she said, 'I'm worried about Mum working at the charity hospital in Baripada.'

Wesley looked up from his papers. 'Why?'

'We've been through so much with Zac,' Elisha said. 'I couldn't bear anything to happen to Mum.'

'Isaac is much better,' Wesley said. 'He's coming home at the weekend. I don't know what you're so worried about. Your mother is looking forward to working at the hospital and making a difference to so many lives.'

Elisha shuffled her feet. 'Please don't be angry, but Rajani and I went to see Krishna, and he warned me something would happen to Mum.'

Wesley frowned. 'Didn't I tell you to stay away from that old rogue?'

Elisha crossed her arms. 'Rajani says he's very wise.'

Wesley tapped his fingers on the table. 'He's a heretic. And you should set Rajani a good example.'

'I'm trying to embrace Indian culture,' Elisha said, 'and Krishna specifically told me I had to look after my mother.'

Wesley snorted. 'What would that heathen know?'

More than you'd ever give him credit for. 'He's not a heathen,' Elisha said, 'and whatever you think about Krishna, we've got to stop Mum working in Baripada.'

'Rubbish. I tell you, that man is a false prophet.'

Why was her father so narrow-minded? 'Listen, Dad. Even if you don't believe Krishna, Mum's taking an awful risk. It's not safe.'

'Your mother believes God is calling her to work at that hospital,' Wesley said, 'and so do I. We must go wherever God sends us.'

'Even if it sends her to her death?' Elisha took a step forward and placed a hand on her father's desk. 'Zac needs her now more than ever. So do I.'

'God will protect her.' Wesley took off his glasses and examined her with those condescending eyes that made her feel like a baby. 'Have you finished preparing for this week's Sunday school?'

Elisha wanted to swear but held back. *Finished?* I haven't started.'

    David Whittet

'Then go and do it,' Wesley said.

Elisha walked towards the door, then stopped. 'You know, Dad, I was just beginning to believe in your mission and all it stands for. I'd felt I could be a part of it. But now—' She broke off and stormed out of the room.

Lying on her bed, Elisha pulled out an exercise book with her Sunday school notes and immediately stuffed them back in the drawer. *Who the hell does he think he is? Ordering me about like I am still a child.*

If only she'd been able to talk to Joanna. But would it have helped? Joanna was into self-sacrifice and would probably think Melissa was doing the right thing.

Elisha got up, her hands steepled. *If Mum's hell-bent on working at the hospital, then so am I. I'll sign up as a volunteer. They can't turn me away—I've had all my jabs.* Elisha felt a flush of heat in her face. Her mother would be furious. *Tough. If it's safe enough for her, it's safe enough for me. I'm going to watch over her, and there's nothing she can do about it.*

Elisha grabbed a pen and some notepaper from her bedside table and began writing Joanna another letter.

You said you'd pray for me. Well, I need that prayer now—more than ever before.

CHAPTER TEN

How will we get through the night? Elisha's stomach churned as she followed her mother from case to case, each more heart-wrenching than the last. *Pull yourself together. Concentrate. You're here for your mother.* Elisha watched her mother's breathing quicken as she assisted the casualty officer to suture a ten-year-old girl's scalp laceration.

Elisha felt a lump in her throat as Melissa did her best to comfort the girl.

'Squeeze my hand as tight as you can, my sweet,' Melissa said. 'It'll be over in a minute.'

From the look on her mother's face and the way her hand trembled, Melissa needed just as much emotional support herself. Elisha could do with someone to hold her hand too. She never imagined casualty would be such a minefield. But she couldn't let the poor kid see that they were both as scared as she was.

'What's your name?' Elisha asked.

The girl flinched as the next stitch went in. 'Aanya.'

'That's such a pretty name,' Elisha said. 'Where's your mummy?'

Another suture. Aanya cringed. 'I haven't got a mummy.'

'So who looks after you?' Melissa asked. 'And how did you cut your head?'

'My aunty,' Aanya said. 'She fell down while we were having our tea. I banged my head on the table, trying to get her up.'

'That must have been so frightening,' Elisha said. She wanted to hug Aanya, but her mother pushed her back.

'Careful,' Melissa said. 'We haven't finished stitching the wound.'

'Where's your aunty now?' Elisha said.

Aanya pointed to a woman on a bed. Tears welled up in the girl's eyes. 'I thought she was dead at first. She just didn't move.'

Melissa took out a handkerchief and dried Aanya's eyes. 'You were very brave to help her.'

Dr Chaudhry, the casualty officer, put in the last suture. 'We think your aunty's had a stroke.'

'What's that?' Aanya asked.

How do you explain a stroke to a ten-year-old? Elisha found it difficult enough to understand herself.

'I think it means your aunty's not very well,' Elisha said. 'But the doctors are going to make her better.'

'All done,' Dr Chaudhry said. 'Now, run along, Aanya. The orderly will look after you. Nurse Martin has other kids to see.'

Aanya embraced Elisha and clung to her.

'I want to stay with you,' Aanya said. 'Please.'

Elisha would have loved to hug Aanya for the rest of the night—the poor kid certainly needed it. But Elisha had to keep a close eye on her mother, and all around phones rang, pagers bleeped, monitors blinked, and alarms blazed. The stone floors echoed with scurrying feet as the staff raced from one emergency to the next.

'This nice lady is going to look after you.' Elisha struggled to get the words out as she handed Aanya over to the orderly. 'Your aunty will be well again soon. You'll see.'

Chaos continued in the casualty department throughout the night, with the skeleton staff rushed off their feet. Elisha's head spun as she chased around after her mother.

The charge nurse's voice rang out over the tannoy: 'Code Red. Motor vehicle accident on Udala Road. Multiple casualties. ETA four minutes.'

More announcements moments later.

'Industrial accident in the Betanoti Forest. Spinal injury and fractured femur.'

'Patient in cubicle three in respiratory distress.'

Every time Elisha heard a distressed patient scream, she wondered if it was Aanya or her aunt. She kept looking out for Aanya but didn't see her again. She must have gone with her aunt when they moved her to the ward.

'Who'll look after Aanya if they keep her aunt in hospital?' Elisha asked her mother.

Melissa shrugged. 'The social worker will sort something out.'

'What if they can't?' Elisha said. 'I want to help her. Can we take her home?'

'I wish we could,' Melissa said. 'But that's how it is, working in casualty. You just get involved with one person's story, and it's time to move on to another.'

Melissa was right. With so much going on all around, Elisha scarcely had another moment to think about Aanya.

'Cardiac arrest,' the loudspeaker blazed. 'Paramedics resuscitating in the ambulance. All available staff to assist.'

Sweat poured off Melissa's face as she struggled with CPR in the sweltering heat. Elisha's heart thumped in time with her mother's chest compressions. No sooner had Melissa finished assisting with the resuscitation than she had to dress a four-year-old's burns. Elisha shook her head. Her mum would be a wreck if she carried on at this rate.

'You need to take a break,' Elisha said. 'I'm going to tell the doctor.'

The matron came over. 'No need,' she said. 'Take a fifteen-minute break, Nurse Martin. You look like you need it. Nurse Gupta will take over here.'

'Thanks.' Melissa handed over the dressing of the four-year-old burns victim to the new nurse. 'You're right. I was beginning to—'

'Get something to eat,' Elisha interrupted. 'And a drink of water.'

'You look about finished as well, Miss Martin,' the matron said. 'You need some food, too. We don't want you fainting on the job.'

'I won't,' Elisha said.

Melissa put her hand on Elisha's shoulder then turned to the matron. 'I told Elisha it would be too much for her, but she wouldn't listen.'

Elisha screwed up her face. *And you wouldn't have stopped for a break if I wasn't here.*

Melissa had just taken her first bite of chapatti when Dr Chaudhry tapped her on the shoulder.

'Sorry to cut your break short,' he said, 'but we need you.'

Elisha glared at him. 'Can't you see she's exhausted? She hasn't had a break all night.'

'I'm sorry,' Dr Chaudhry said, 'but there's been a shooting in Kuchei. I need your mother to nurse a victim with severe bleeding.'

     David Whittet

Melissa took another mouthful of chapatti and washed it down with a swig from her water bottle. She turned to Elisha without making eye contact. 'It's okay. I'll manage.'

It's not okay. Elisha followed her mother and Dr Chaudhry, stepping over the sea of patients camped out on the floor, waiting to be seen. The place was more of a battleground than ever. She listened to Dr Chaudhry briefing her mother. *This is going to kill Mum.*

'Kaamil is the victim of a local gang shooting,' Dr Chaudhry said. 'You'll be looking after him until we can get a surgeon in from Calcutta to remove the bullet from his leg.'

'Isn't there a surgeon here who could do it?' Melissa asked.

Dr Chaudhry pointed to the makeshift operating tables in the emergency cubicles. 'They're all flat out.'

Elisha caught up. 'What about Nawab Patel?' she said. 'He could do it. He operated on my brother.'

'Nawab's an orthopaedic surgeon,' Melissa replied. 'We need a general surgeon.'

'Besides,' Dr Chaudhry said, 'Nawab's gone down with cholera.'

Elisha grabbed her mother's arm. Did they expect her to do everything in this hospital? She held on to her mother as the porters wheeled Kaamil into the unit. How had this boy—who didn't look much older than Zac—got involved with a gang? Elisha tried not to look at his blood-splattered torso and avoided his bloodshot eyes.

'You'll have to let go of my arm,' Melissa said. 'I have to attend to the boy's wound.'

'For heaven's sake put some gloves on,' Elisha said. 'Or you'll be the next one off sick.'

Melissa grabbed some gloves off the trolley while the porters lifted Kaamil onto the bed.

'Have you called the police?' Melissa asked one of the paramedics who had brought Kaamil in.

'No,' the paramedic replied. 'He wouldn't let us.'

'We must report this,' Melissa said, turning to Kaamil. 'Who did this to you?'

Kaamil jerked up off the bed, the effort winding him. 'No! No police!'

Elisha sat down beside him and held his hand. 'Why are you so scared?'

Kaamil slumped back on the pillow and closed his eyes.

Melissa took off the makeshift bandage and began cleaning the wound. 'I've got a son,' she said. 'He's a bit younger than you. Your mother must be beside herself with worry. Would you like me to call her?'

'No, please,' Kaamil said. 'Just leave me alone.'

'What is it?' Elisha said. 'You're safe in here.'

'I'm not safe anywhere,' Kaamil said.

Elisha saw the terror on his face and gave his hand another squeeze. 'Do you have any brothers or sisters?'

Kaamil shook his head. Elisha watched him raise his eyes, continually scanning the emergency ward.

Melissa finished the dressing and caught her breath. 'Tell me who did this to you.'

Kaamil shied away. 'I can't.'

Melissa glared at him. 'You must.'

'Mum! Give him a break.' Elisha scowled at her mother then grinned at Kaamil. 'Looks like we've got a long night ahead of us. So, if you don't want to talk about your family, why don't I tell you about mine? My brother Zac's a sports fanatic, and he can be a right pain in the arse, but—'

Elisha stopped abruptly when Kaamil began to shake. His body convulsed, and he went so pale his face was almost as white as hers. She followed his panic-stricken gaze. Two mean-looking gangsters had pushed their way past the throng of waiting patients. Both had guns. They raised their fists in the air in what Elisha assumed was a gang salute.

Melissa was already on her feet. 'Help! Security! Quick!'

The gangsters pushed the other patients out of the way as they drew closer.

'Don't let them get me!' Kaamil spluttered in between rasping breaths.

Elisha gulped. 'What do they want with you?'

Melissa stood in front of Kaamil, holding her hands up against the gangsters. 'Do you owe them money? We can help.'

Kaamil hid under the sheets. 'No. Nothing like that.'

David Whittet

'What then?' Melissa said.

Kaamil didn't answer. Elisha's heart thumped. She wanted to hide under the bedclothes, too.

The matron arrived with two porters.

'Where the hell is security?' Melissa screamed. 'Don't just stand there, get that mob out of here. They're armed, and they're scaring the patients.'

'Security's on the way,' the matron said. 'They're ex-Indian Army. They'll soon deal with these thugs.'

'About time,' Melissa said. 'Kaamil almost died of fright.'

Elisha covered her mouth with her hand. The security guards disarmed the gangsters and escorted the men off the premises.

'Thank you, Nurse Martin,' the matron said. 'You handled that well.'

Elisha cuddled her mother. 'Well? She was brilliant!'

Her mother was always magnificent when she was fired up.

Elisha pulled back the blanket from Kaamil's face. 'You can come out now. They've gone.'

The matron stood over Kaamil's bed. 'Like it or not,' she said, 'I'm going to call your parents. They need to be here.'

'You're wasting your time,' Kaamil said. 'They won't come.'

'If my son was in the state you're in,' Melissa said, 'I'd want to be there at his side.'

Kaamil covered his face with his shaking hands. 'Your son's not a …'

Elisha stared into his flickering eyes. 'What?'

'A queer … a homosexual …' Kaamil sobbed. 'My parents won't have anything to do with me.'

Melissa flung her arms around him. 'My poor child. Is that why the gang is after you? Because you're—*different?*'

Melissa broke off. Elisha looked up and saw Dr Chaudhry standing behind her mother.

'A word, please, Melissa,' Dr Chaudhry said.

He took Melissa aside, and Elisha struggled to make out what they were saying. Something about wearing full protective gear, now they knew Kaamil was homosexual. She heard her mother groan.

'But he's only a boy,' she heard her mother say. 'He won't have …'

Chaudhry raised his voice. 'A high-risk boy. Now off you go and get gowned up. Your daughter should wear protective equipment too. It's just until we establish Kaamil's HIV status.'

Elisha shuddered. She glanced at Kaamil and then across to Chaudhry and her mother.

Take care of your mother. Elisha had almost forgotten Krishna's warning amid the turmoil of the night. Now his words came flooding back. Why hadn't she done more to stop her mother working at the hospital? Why hadn't her father listened when she told him about the risks? *I told you something disastrous would happen.*

An orderly fetched their protective suits, and Elisha followed her mother to the changing rooms in silence.

Melissa grinned. 'Bet you never thought we'd end the night looking like astronauts.'

How could her mother make light of the situation? HIV was a death sentence. Her mother was a nurse—she had to know that. And behind that cheery face, her mother would be as terrified as she was.

You're here to support your mother. Elisha forced a smile. 'They do look like spacesuits, don't they?'

'Elisha,' Melissa said. 'You're tired. Why don't you go home? I'll be fine.'

'I'm staying here with you, Mum,' Elisha said.

Melissa stopped changing for a moment. 'I'm so glad you came with me. You've been wonderful with the patients. But you need to get some rest—'

Elisha zipped up the protective suit. 'I'm not leaving.'

Putting on the gear made the danger feel even more immediate. Elisha struggled to breathe through the mask and Perspex headwear. She'd always been claustrophobic. How would she survive the night?

Back in casualty, Dr Chaudhry gave Melissa her instructions. 'I want you to do Kaamil's observations every half hour,' he said. 'We can't do his surgery until morning.'

Melissa pointed to the *Nil by mouth* sign on his bed. 'Can I at least get him something to eat? He looks half-starved.'

Dr Chaudhry nodded. 'Nothing after three in the morning, though. Now, I must get a protective suit, too. Then I'll be back to take some blood.'

　　　　　David Whittet

Melissa stroked Kaamil's arm with her gloved hand. 'I'm going to get you some soup. That'll make you feel better.' She turned to Elisha. 'Why don't you sit with him while I nip to the canteen?'

Elisha drew up a chair. 'Okay, Mum.'

'You can sit a bit closer,' Melissa said. 'We're safe with all this protective gear.'

Are we? Elisha swallowed hard and edged towards Kaamil's bedside.

'That's better,' Melissa said. 'I'll be back in a jiffy.'

Elisha raised her head to meet Kaamil's eyes. 'Those men were mighty scary. How did you get involved with them?'

Kaamil closed his eyes. 'You don't want to know.'

'I do.' Elisha wanted to hold Kaamil's hand the way her mother had but lost her nerve. Were those latex gloves really safe? 'Tell me about it.'

At last, Kaamil opened his eyes again. 'It's not a pretty story. I'd nowhere to go after my dad threw me out. I ended up in a hostel.'

'At least that's better than living on the street,' Elisha said.

'They were kind to me at that hostel,' Kaamil said. 'At least—until they found out I was gay.'

Elisha bit her lip. 'What happened then?'

Kaamil sighed. 'They booted me out. Story of my life.'

Melissa arrived back with a bowl of mulligatawny soup. 'I hope you like it hot,' she said.

'It sure smells good,' Kaamil said.

Elisha drew up her chair. 'Kaamil was just telling me how he was thrown out of a hostel just for being gay.'

Melissa spoon-fed Kaamil the spicy broth. 'So what did you do?'

Kaamil slurped the soup and looked around. 'I've said enough.'

Melissa pressed another spoonful of soup to Kaamil's lips. 'No more excuses. We can't help you if we don't know the whole story.'

'Alright.' Kaamil swallowed the next mouthful. 'There was nothing left for me here. I climbed on top of a train going to Calcutta—'

'You were on the roof?' Elisha exclaimed. 'We saw kids clinging for their lives on to the carriage when we came here. Weren't you scared of falling off?'

Kaamil shuddered. 'More frightened of getting mugged if I didn't get away. I reckoned I'd have a better chance of survival in Calcutta.'

Melissa scooped the last of the soup from the bowl. 'Calcutta looked pretty rough to me when we went through its streets in the taxi.'

'You learn to be streetwise—fast,' Kaamil said. 'I headed for Sonagachi. There'd be somewhere I could doss down in a ghetto.'

Melissa shook her head. 'Sonagachi? That's the notorious red-light district, isn't it?'

Kaamil nodded. 'It was rough, alright, but … it was a new beginning.'

Elisha watched a faint smile creep across Kaamil's face. After a moment's hesitation, she rested her gloved hand on his. 'How so?'

Kaamil sat up. 'I met this boy, begging on the street. Ramesh. We became lovers. We had nothing—except each other. But we were happy for a few glorious months.'

Elisha saw the gleam in Kaamil's eyes fade. 'So, what went wrong?'

'Ramesh's brother tracked him down.' Kaamil's head fell back onto the pillow. 'Turned out he came from a family of gangsters. Our affair brought shame to the gang. We've been on the run from them ever since.'

'So where's Ramesh now?' Elisha asked.

Kaamil turned his head away. 'We thought we'd found a safe haven out in a shelter. But they soon found us. Shot at me. And Ramesh's brother dragged him off. God knows what they'll do to him.'

Elisha tilted her head. 'Surely they won't harm their own flesh and blood?'

'He's disgraced them. You don't understand what shame means to an Indian family.' Kaamil yanked at the intravenous drip in his arm. 'You should leave me to die. I'd rather die here than let the gang get their hands on me.'

'Stop that!' Melissa lunged across the bed to stop him removing the intravenous line. In the struggle, she inadvertently pulled the sheet off his body. Blood poured from the gunshot wound on his leg.

'Help!' Melissa pushed the emergency call button on the bed and waved her arms in the air. 'He's haemorrhaging!'

The crash team arrived in seconds. Elisha stood back. A surge of

     David Whittet

adrenaline pumped through her body as she watched the doctors. If only there was something she could do to help.

'We need an urgent cross-match,' Dr Chaudhry shouted, tightening a tourniquet on Kaamil's leg to stem the blood flow. 'And get at least ten units of packed RBCs for immediate transfusion.'

'His blood pressure's dropping,' Melissa warned, her hand shaking as she released the cuff from Kaamil's arm. 'We're losing him.'

'At last!' Chaudhry exclaimed when the porter arrived with the blood. 'We need to get this into him fast.'

'No!' Kaamil jerked his arm away. 'I don't want it!'

Chaudhry made another attempt to connect the life-saving blood to the intravenous line. Kaamil pulled away once more.

'Melissa!' Chaudhry yelled. 'For God's sake, hold his arm steady.'

Elisha stepped forward and glared at Dr Chaudhry. 'Can't you see my mother's doing her best?'

'It's alright, Elisha,' Melissa said. 'We're all doing our best.' She grabbed Kaamil's arm again. 'Please, Kaamil … calm down … you don't know what you're doing!'

With a last cry of despair, Kaamil yanked the drip out of his vein. Blood spurted from his arm, turning the crash team's white protective suits a deep red. Elisha froze. Blood covered her face shield, obscuring her view. It was like a scene from a horror movie playing in slow motion. Except it was painfully and horribly real.

'Damn!' Melissa cried.

Elisha wiped the blood off her headgear. 'What is it, Mum?'

'It's nothing, dear. It's just …' Melissa broke off, holding her thumb. 'I've …'

'Quick!' Chaudhry shouted. 'Get that glove off and get your hand under a tap.'

Almost falling over the drip stand, Elisha chased after Dr Chaudhry and her mother as they disappeared into the sluice room. Melissa stood in front of the sink, squeezing her thumb and running it under the tap.

'Will someone please tell me what's going on?' Elisha demanded.

Dr Chaudhry pulled off his protective headwear and met Elisha's eyes.

'I'm afraid your mother punctured her thumb on Kaamil's intravenous line.'

Elisha's heart missed a beat. 'You mean she's got AIDS?'

'Of course not.' Dr Chaudhry put a hand on Elisha's shoulder. 'We just need to take some routine measures to keep your mother safe.'

Keep her safe? You're bloody kidding! It's too late for that. Elisha rushed across to the sink and flung her arms around her mother.

 David Whittet

CHAPTER ELEVEN

Three days later, Elisha sat alone in a drab, windowless waiting room at the charity hospital in Baripada. She glanced up at the stains on the ceiling and down at the lizard crawling across the floor. How much longer? She looked at her watch. Her parents had been in with the consultant for almost an hour. Professor Mallick, the eminent virologist from the University of Calcutta, had come 250 kilometres to see her mother. It had to be serious when such a distinguished man travelled all that way.

Elisha picked up a magazine and gazed at the model's beautiful face. With immaculate make-up and perfect hair, the model looked stunning. Lucky brat. Elisha hadn't washed her face or combed her hair since the night in casualty. She threw the magazine back onto the pile. It was all in Hindi anyway.

Raised voices. What were they saying? Elisha strained her ears. All she could hear was her father proclaiming how the Lord would protect them. Typical. *God didn't stop Mum from getting a needle-stick injury.*

It was another quarter of an hour before the door opened, and Professor Mallick showed Melissa and Wesley out of the consulting room. When Elisha saw the solemn look on the immaculately dressed professor's face, she half wished they'd disappear back into the office. It was bad news. She was sure of it.

'Sir …' Elisha jumped up to speak to the professor. So many questions raced through her head. She needed answers, but with the professor peering at her over his bifocals, her mind went blank.

'You must be Melissa's daughter,' he said.

Elisha nodded.

The professor stroked his beard. 'Look after your mother.' He shook Elisha's hand and made off down the corridor.

Elisha called after him. 'Professor Mallick—'

Too late. The professor was through the swing doors and out of the hospital.

Elisha turned to her mother. 'What did he say? You're shaking!'

'It's been a long day,' Melissa said. 'Let's not talk in the corridor.'

'Your mother's tired,' Wesley interrupted. 'We need to get home. No more questions.'

'I need to know,' Elisha said. 'I heard you say Mum needs God's help. She's got AIDS, hasn't she?'

'Of course she hasn't,' Wesley said. 'We all need God's protection every day. Now, you heard your mother. She's exhausted. Let's get her home.'

Melissa put her arm around Elisha. 'My darling! Everything's going to be alright. You'll see.'

Was it? Elisha knew her mother was hiding something.

Look after your mother. First Krishna, now Professor Mallick. How could she help her mother if nobody would tell her the truth?

Wesley drove them home. How could he be so calm? Didn't he care? Despite the arguments and conflict between them, Elisha envied her father's faith, his absolute conviction that God would see them through.

Sat next to her mother in silence on the back seat, Elisha tried to piece everything together. If her father was telling the truth—and she'd never known him to lie—her mother hadn't got AIDS. At least, not yet. She wished she'd paid more attention during biology lessons at school. One thing she did remember—you can't get a test for six weeks after a needle-stick injury. Was that what Professor Mallick was telling them? But why had their consultation with him taken so long?

Elisha studied her mother's face in the darkness. Melissa looked so pale and tired, her gaunt features highlighted by the flickering headlights of passing cars.

After a sleepless night, Elisha had to know the truth. She got up early, hoping to catch her mother alone before breakfast. Damn. Her father was there already and Zac not far behind. That meant at least half an hour listening to her father trumpeting about the mission and Zac moaning about not being able to play football. Would they ever stop talking and go away?

At last, Wesley left for his office, and Zac took off to find a friend who'd listen to his grumbling. Melissa began clearing the breakfast dishes, and Elisha followed her mother to the kitchen sink.

'Mum,' Elisha said, 'you'd tell me if you've got AIDS, wouldn't you? I mean … I know you can't get a test straight away … so what were you and Dad talking about with the professor? And why did it take so long?'

'You'd better sit down.' Melissa led Elisha back to the kitchen table, and they sat opposite each other. 'Professor Mallick told us Kaamil is HIV positive.'

Elisha felt her eyes welling up. 'Oh, God! So you *will* get AIDS.'

'No.' Melissa reached across the table and put her hand on Elisha's. 'The professor said the chances of my catching aids from that accidental prick on my thumb are very low.'

Elisha blinked back a tear. 'How low?'

'I have to have blood tests over the next few months.' Melissa tightened her grip on Elisha's hand. 'But the professor told us that only three in a thousand needle-stick injuries result in HIV infection.'

Why didn't that sound reassuring? Elisha couldn't look at her mother. 'I told you working at that hospital would end in disaster.'

Melissa squeezed Elisha's hand even harder. 'You saw how much they needed me in casualty that night. Remember Aanya and her aunt?'

Elisha got up from the table and paced around the room. She hadn't forgotten Aanya or any of the desperately sick and injured souls she'd seen in casualty. The agony in their faces still haunted her.

'Come back and sit down,' Melissa said. 'Kaamil was alone in the world and terrified. He needed me—us. I'm glad we were there for him, and I'd do the same again.'

'I know you would.' Elisha sat next to her mother. 'Have you told Zac?'

Melissa shook her head. 'He's got enough going on, coming to terms with his knee injury and having to give up his beloved sport.'

'Don't you think he should know?' Elisha said. 'He needs his mother now more than ever before. So do I.'

'And I'll be here for both of you,' Melissa said. 'I'm going to be absolutely fine. I promise.'

But would she? Elisha took in a deep breath. Would life ever be the same again?

The monsoon broke later that week. Torrential rain, overflowing drains and gutters, thunder and lightning—they all reflected Elisha's turbulent mood. She watched the local women paddling through the puddles as they went about their errands. The rains swept away the dirt and sand that had accumulated over the hot season. If only they could wash away the troubles tormenting Elisha.

Instead, they brought fresh concerns. Melissa disappeared each afternoon and refused to tell Elisha where she was going. Was it to the doctor? And if it was, did it mean she was going downhill? Had she developed full-blown AIDS?

Whatever the reason for her outings, she came home drenched.

'This has to stop,' Elisha said. 'You're soaked to the skin! You promised you'd take care of yourself.'

Melissa took off her wet clothes and slumped over the kitchen table. 'Don't fuss.'

'Where have you been?' Elisha demanded. 'Tell me. Were you at the hospital for a check-up? Is it bad news?'

'No, silly,' Melissa said. 'I went to see Kaamil.'

What? Elisha stared at her mother. 'Hasn't that boy done us enough damage?' The words came out before Elisha could stop them, and she immediately hated herself. She wanted to feel compassion for Kaamil, but instead, a wave of resentment swept over her.

'Kaamil needs me,' Melissa said. 'He's got nobody—you heard his story. I thought you'd understand.'

'I do … I mean …' Elisha ought to have understood. She was an outsider at school and knew how it felt to be ostracised. But her playground teasing was nothing compared to the hatred Kaamil had experienced. 'I've been worried sick. Why didn't you tell me where you were going?'

Melissa shrugged. 'Because I knew you'd try to talk me out of it.'

'Damn right I would,' Elisha shot back.

 David Whittet

'Don't be like that,' Melissa said. 'It's a miracle Kaamil survived. I've been tending his wounds.'

Elisha flinched. Hadn't her mother learnt anything from her experience at the hospital? 'So if you haven't got AIDS already, you'll get it now.'

'Nonsense,' Melissa said. 'I'm perfectly safe. I've been wearing protective gear like we had at the hospital.'

Elisha glared at her mother. 'That didn't stop you getting a needle-stick injury, did it?'

'That won't happen again.'

'You don't know that.'

'I'm very careful,' Melissa said. 'Remember, I used to be a district nurse back in Australia.'

'Can't he go to a clinic? Don't they have district nurses out here?'

Melissa smiled. 'No. We're not in Australia now.'

If only we were. Then none of this would have happened. 'It was you and Dad who insisted that we came to this godforsaken place. I never wanted to.'

Melissa got up and faced Elisha. 'I'm just trying to do what I think's right. I only wish I could help him reconcile with his parents.'

'You'll never do that,' Elisha said. 'Rajani's told me about the stigma of homosexuality in Indian communities.'

'You may be right.' Melissa paused and took a deep breath. 'Why don't you come with me tomorrow? Kaamil would love to see you again.'

'What?' Elisha swallowed hard. Deep down, she would like to see Kaamil again too. But the risks … Didn't her mother understand the danger?

'I wish you'd let me talk to Zac,' Elisha said after a long pause.

'There's no sense in worrying him just now,' Melissa replied. 'I told you, he's got enough on his mind.'

That was true. Elisha was growing sick of her brother's constant moaning. He was so wrapped up in his own misery, he probably wouldn't want to know, anyway.

'Why don't you talk to Rajani?' Melissa asked.

'It'll get back to Zac if I do,' Elisha said. 'Those two are getting mighty close.'

'I'm sure Rajani will respect our privacy if you ask her,' Melissa said. 'Think about it. Now, I'm going to take a shower and go to bed. I'm exhausted.'

Elisha hadn't been back to the school in weeks. She avoided the children's eyes as she stepped into the dingy classroom. Rajani was writing on the blackboard and didn't see her at first. When their eyes finally met, Rajani dropped the chalk and raced to embrace Elisha.

Rajani sent the children off for an early break and listened to Elisha's story with tears in her eyes.

'Your poor mother,' Rajani said. 'Always helping people and this happens.'

'Please don't tell me it's God's will,' Elisha said.

Rajani frowned. 'You know me better than that.'

'So, do I go with my mother to see Kaamil?' Elisha asked.

'You need someone wiser than me to advise you.' Rajani paused and rubbed her chin. 'I think you should go back to Krishna.'

Elisha froze. *Krishna!* That ill-fated visit just a couple of months back had triggered the disastrous chain reaction. How could she face him again?

'What good would that do?' Elisha said. 'Maybe my father was right all along, and he's just a charlatan.'

'No!' Rajani eyed her intently. 'He'll help you.'

Half an hour later, Elisha took off her shoes at the temple entrance and then took a step back. It wasn't too late—she could still make a run for it. No, she'd promised Rajani.

Elisha looked down at her bare feet as she walked towards Krishna. He sat on his golden cushion, draped in his yellow satin robes, just as he'd been on her last visit.

'You told me to take care of my mother,' Elisha said. 'Please, Krishna, tell me what you meant.'

'Namaste!' Krishna stood up and gave Elisha the traditional Hindu greeting. 'I have been waiting for you to come back.'

     David Whittet

Elisha almost slipped over on the polished mosaic floor of the temple. 'You knew I was coming?'

Krishna nodded.

'You saw something that day, didn't you?' Elisha gazed at Krishna. He seemed even more other-worldly than before, his satin robes almost incandescent in the morning sun. 'How did you know Mum was going to get sick?'

'Your mother has a generous spirit,' Krishna said. 'I have seen her tending to our lepers when I have been out on my religious duties. It was inevitable that she would eventually sacrifice her life for the sake of another.'

Sacrifice her life? Elisha baulked. 'So, she is going to die?'

'Remember,' Krishna said, 'I told you about the wheel and its many spokes. How we are all part of that continuous cycle of birth, life and death. Your mother is a step closer to Nirvana.'

Tears rolled down Elisha's cheeks. 'There must be something we can do to stop this. You're wise, Krishna. Can't you help her?'

'I cannot interfere with the Almighty's plans. Don't be sad. God will be with you—and your mother.' Krishna reached out and held Elisha's hand. 'Come and pray with me.'

'Pray?' Elisha pulled away. 'That's exactly what my father would say. You're two of a kind.'

Krishna smiled. 'Indeed. Pastor Martin and I are fellow travellers. Both seeking God.'

Elisha grunted. 'Yes, but not the same one.'

Krishna reached out to Elisha again. 'Don't be angry, my child. Cherish every moment with your mother while you still have her.'

Elisha dried her eyes on her sleeve. 'Mum wants me to go back with her to this boy, Kaamil. The one that's given her …' She couldn't bring herself to finish the sentence.

'Then you should go,' Krishna said. 'If anything can cure your mother, it's karma.'

'Karma,' Elisha repeated the word. Could that be the secret to restoring her mother's health? 'Thank you, Krishna.'

Elisha raced home. Her mother was just finishing a plate of vegetable biryani when she burst into the kitchen.

'I'm coming with you!' Elisha flung her arms around her mother. 'To see Kaamil!'

'You're just in time,' Melissa said. 'I was about to leave. Grab some food for yourself and we'll be off.'

Armed with a bowl of the biryani, Elisha climbed into the van her mother had borrowed from the mission.

'I didn't think you'd come,' Melissa said. 'What made you change your mind?'

Elisha hesitated. What should she say? Would her mother understand? 'Don't tell Dad, but I went to see this revered spiritual guru—'

'You mean Krishna?' Melissa started the engine and pulled out onto the road. 'At the temple?'

'Yes,' Elisha said. 'You're not cross with me?'

'Of course not,' Melissa said. 'I like Krishna.'

'Dad doesn't.'

'No.' Melissa laughed. 'So tell me, what did Krishna say to you?'

'He told me that you needed as much good karma as you could get,' Elisha said. 'So I figured if we could do something for Kaamil, it might stop you getting AIDS.'

Melissa took her hand off the steering wheel for a moment to pat her daughter's arm. 'God bless you, my darling. And bless Krishna too.'

After a half-hour drive, they pulled up at a ghetto on the outskirts of Baripada. A row of shacks stretched along the side of the railway line, each swamped with slum dwellers. Babies cried. Kids played on the train track. The smell reminded Elisha of the moment she'd stepped off the plane in Calcutta.

'Kaamil lives here?' Elisha asked.

'I wouldn't call it living. But he dosses down here every night.' Melissa took her nurse's bag out of the van. 'The wound on his leg is going to go septic if he stays here much longer. That's why I wanted to get him back with his family.'

Elisha followed her mother. They must have walked a good half mile down the track. Elisha couldn't look at the teeming mass of humanity or the children that jostled around her, each hoping for a spare rupee. However hard Elisha screwed her eyes shut, the images didn't go away.

Eventually, they arrived at a small hovel, isolated from the rest of the community.

A voice. So faint and husky it was scarcely recognisable.

'Elisha! Is it really you?'

'Kaamil!' Elisha opened her eyes. His shrunken body looked even more wasted than it had done in casualty. But his eyes shone brighter.

'How wonderful,' Kaamil said. 'I didn't think I'd see you again.'

Melissa opened her nurse's bag and put on her protective gear. She sat Kaamil down on the earthen bank outside the hovel and took off his dirty dressings.

'Your mother's an absolute angel,' Kaamil said.

'I know she is.' Elisha drew back when she saw the pus oozing from Kaamil's leg. 'I couldn't do what she's doing. Not in a million years.'

'Of course you could,' Melissa said. 'You'd make a wonderful nurse. You were great in casualty.'

Kaamil flinched as Melissa cleaned his wound with disinfectant. 'Ouch! That stings!'

Elisha watched her mother painstakingly remove the dead tissue from the wound with a pair of tweezers. 'You're right, Kaamil. She *is* an angel.'

Elisha accompanied her mother to the ghetto almost each day over the next month. Karma was working. Kaamil's leg was healing. Melissa looked healthier—and happier.

'Will you stop coming to see me when my leg's better?' Kaamil asked with a frown.

'Of course not,' Melissa replied. 'And today, Elisha and I have some good news for you. We've been talking to our friends at the mission. We've found a couple who will take you in and give you a new home.'

Kaamil's mouth fell open and his head jerked back. Elisha held his shoulder to stop him falling over.

'You mean I can leave this awful place?' he said.

'That's right,' Melissa replied, putting her wound care kit back in her bag. 'We'll take you to meet your new parents tomorrow.'

Kaamil got up and did a dance along the railway track. 'I don't know what to say!'

'Just be careful with that leg,' Melissa said. 'Come and sit down.'

Elisha grinned as Kaamil squatted beside them. 'You don't need to say anything. Your smile says it all.'

'Have you told them …' Kaamil's smile disappeared, and he shook. 'Do they know … that I'm … homosexual? And HIV positive?'

'They do,' Melissa said. 'And they're fine about it.'

Kaamil's smile returned. 'Thank you! I said you were an angel!'

Elisha gazed at Kaamil and then Melissa. Yes, her mother was one extraordinary human being.

CHAPTER TWELVE

It's Kaamil's big day! Elisha was surprised at just how excited she felt when she woke the next morning. She flung on her clothes and rushed to the kitchen. Her mother had told her they'd be leaving after an early breakfast. So where was her mother? And why was her father making breakfast?

'What's Mum doing?' Elisha asked. 'She told me to be up early. We're taking Kaamil to meet his new family.'

'Your mother isn't feeling very well,' Wesley said. 'She's caught a cold. I'll be taking you to—'

Elisha didn't wait for the rest of the sentence. She charged out of the kitchen and made for her mother's bedroom.

'Mum!' Elisha stopped and covered her mouth with her hand. Her mother looked dreadful. Pale, haggard and drawn. Sores festered under her nose. Her cheeks drawn in and wasted. 'What's happened to you?'

'I've got a shocking cold,' Melissa said. 'That's all.'

It's no ordinary cold. Elisha's mind went back to those biology lessons at school. Her mother had all the signs of seroconversion. It was as if the lifeblood had drained from Melissa's body.

'What about Kaamil?' Elisha asked.

'Your father's going to take you,' Melissa said. 'Zac's going with you too.' She lifted her head for a moment. 'Mind you don't say anything to Zac about … my … what happened at the hospital.'

'I wish you'd let me …' Elisha was desperate to talk to her brother and more convinced than ever that he had a right to know what was happening to his mother. But now wasn't the time to argue. 'Alright, Mum. I won't say anything.'

Melissa sank back onto the pillow. 'Thank you.'

Elisha sat on the bed. 'I won't go with Dad and Zac. I'm staying here to look after you.'

'No, darling,' Melissa said. 'You must go. Kaamil will be so disappointed if neither of us go.'

'I know.' Elisha watched her mother cough and try to hide the blood-stained mucous in a tissue. 'But I can't leave you here on your own.'

'I'll be fine. Dr Basar is coming to see me.' Melissa caught her breath. 'I want you to do this for me. Give Kaamil my love. Tell him I'll be with him in spirit today.'

'I will.' Elisha put a hand on her mother's. She wanted to say more, tell her mother how much she loved her and all those other things that were so difficult to express. Instead, Elisha squeezed her mother's hand and left the bedroom before bursting into tears.

The half-hour drive to the ghetto where Kaamil lived had passed in a flash when it was Elisha and her mother in the van. Today it lasted forever.

'What's up with Mum?' Zac asked his father. 'I heard you call the doctor before we left.'

'It's nothing,' Wesley said. 'She's got a cold. That's all.'

Liar! It was just as well Zac was in the front with his father. If he'd been in the back with Elisha, she'd have whispered something in his ear.

Kaamil was waiting for them, his few worldly possessions in a plastic bag.

'Where's Melissa?' Kaamil peered into the van, then turned to Elisha. 'Where's your mother?'

'I'm sorry, Kaamil,' Elisha said, 'but she's not well.'

Kaamil took a step back. 'What's wrong?'

Wesley put a hand on Kaamil's shoulder. 'It's just a cold. She'll be better in no time, and she'll be out to see you in your new home as soon as she can.'

'She'll be with you in spirit today,' Elisha said. 'She asked me to give you her love.'

'This is my fault, isn't it?' Kaamil said. 'She's caught something from me, hasn't she?'

Wesley patted Kaamil on the back. 'Of course not.'

'I think it's the change of season,' Elisha said. 'She got soaked in the heavy rain.'

'That's my fault too. She only came out in the rain because of me.' Kaamil glanced around the ghetto. 'There's so much sickness here. I bet she did catch something here.'

Wesley followed Kaamil's eyes. 'It's a truly awful place, that's for sure.' He gave Kaamil another pat on the back. 'That's why we're here. To get you out of this dreadful situation. There's a new home waiting for you just a few kilometres down the road, and an entirely new life.'

Elisha wiped a tear off her cheek as Wesley took Kaamil's hand and helped him into the van. How could her father be so kind to Kaamil but so insensitive to his own family?

Zac sat next to Kaamil in the van. With the ghetto far behind them, the two boys exchanged stories about their leg injuries. Like Zac, Kaamil had once hoped to be a sportsman. Elisha sat behind them and smiled to herself, unexpectedly thankful that Zac had come with them. She'd never seen Kaamil so alive. Perhaps it would do her brother good to see that there were those worse off than him.

The boys were so engrossed in conversation that they hardly noticed the van pull up at a smart town house outside Baripada.

'Out you get,' Wesley said. 'Your new life awaits.'

Kaamil shook as he climbed out of the van. 'I'm scared.'

'Don't be,' Wesley said. 'Mr and Mrs Kumar are lovely people and they're longing to meet you.'

They were wonderful people. Elisha saw the love in Lajita Kumar's eyes the moment she opened the door and embraced Kaamil.

'Namaste,' Lajita said. 'Welcome to our home. I want you to call me Mummy.'

'Mummy!' Tears rolled down Kaamil's cheeks. 'My mummy. You've no idea how good that sounds.'

'And you can call me Dad,' Ravinder Kumar said. 'Now, come inside and have some chai.'

It warmed Elisha's heart to see the sparkle in Kaamil's eyes as they all sat cross-legged around a low wooden table in the front room.

'Make yourselves at home,' Lajita said.

'We will,' Zac said, helping himself to a bowl of *bhuja* snacks. 'Did I see a games room when we came in?'

Once they'd all finished their chai, Elisha followed Zac and Kaamil through to the games room.

'Wow!' Zac said. 'They've got a billiards table.' He handed Kaamil a cue stick. 'This is going to be fun.'

Elisha watched them play. Zac, competitive as ever, hobbled around the table, shouting gleefully whenever he scored. Kaamil limped on his injured leg and just smiled when he won any points. They'd both earned a break, and here was something they could do together. Kaamil, in particular, deserved all the happiness he could get. Elisha's stomach churned. She wanted Kaamil to be happy—but was it really worth the sacrifice her mother had made?

Elisha spent the ride home wondering how she would feel about Kaamil if her mother didn't recover. Would she resent him? Would she hate him? It wasn't Kaamil's fault that her mother was working in casualty that night. How could she hold him responsible?

Dr Arjun Basar was just leaving the house when they got back.

'Sahib!' Dr Basar shook Wesley's hand. 'I've just given Melissa another antibiotic injection. I'll be back to see her in the morning.'

'Is she alright?' Elisha asked. 'She looked dreadful this morning.'

'As well as can be expected,' Dr Basar said. 'We need to give the antibiotics another twenty-four hours.'

As well as can be expected. Why did doctors always use that meaningless phrase? Elisha rushed inside to her mother's bedroom.

Melissa raised her head off the pillow, perspiration pouring down her face. 'Darling! You're back. How did it go?'

Elisha sat down on the edge of the bed. She wanted to cry when she saw the bloodstains on the sheets. *Be brave for your mother.* 'Yes. I wish you could have seen Kaamil's eyes when he met Lajita and Ravinder.'

'I'd have given anything to have been there. So Kaamil settled in?' Melissa broke off with a fit of coughing. 'Tell me all about it.'

Give me strength. Elisha did her best to sound cheerful as she recounted the day's events. All the time watching her mother's erratic breathing.

'It's wonderful Zac and Kaamil got on so well together,' Melissa said. 'Kaamil needs a friend.'

Elisha slipped out of the bedroom when her mother fell asleep. She paused for a moment outside her father's study, rehearsing what she was going to say. How could she make him understand?

'Dad,' she began, 'Mum looks terrible. You must realise how sick she is.'

Wesley looked up from behind his desk. 'She's certainly caught a nasty chill.'

'It's more than a chill,' Elisha said. 'We learnt about seroconversion at school. She's got AIDS, and the sooner we face up to it, the better.'

Wesley put down his pen and took off his glasses. 'If she has …' He stopped and wiped his eyes. 'What more can we do? Except pray.'

'We need to get her back to Australia,' Elisha said. 'They're trialling some new drugs at the Royal Brisbane Hospital.'

Wesley met her eyes then quickly looked away. 'There's no cure for AIDS. Not here, not in Australia or anywhere else. Your mother's in God's hands now.'

Not that again. 'Can't you see? She'd have a much better chance of survival back home—'

Wesley tidied the papers on his desk. 'Orissa is our home now.'

Elisha glared at her father. 'India will *never* be my home.'

'And anyway,' Wesley said, 'the healthcare here is as good as anywhere in the world.'

'You cannot be serious. They buggered up Zac's knee, and they didn't give Mum the right protective equipment.'

Wesley stood up. 'That's not true. A needle-stick injury can happen anywhere. Even in Australia.'

Elisha had been so proud of her father during the day. He'd shown such kindness to Kaamil. Now—why wasn't he as choked up about Mum as she was?

'Zac has a right to know what's going on,' Elisha said, 'and if you don't tell him, I will.'

She made for the door and bolted.

Dr Basar visited regularly over the next few days and declared the antibiotics were working. Elisha couldn't see it. Her mother looked more exhausted than ever. And although she did her best to hide it, Melissa was still coughing up blood.

I can't just stand by and watch. But what could Elisha do? Despite getting weaker each day, her mother insisted she was going to see Kaamil and his new family.

'Please, Mum,' Elisha begged. 'You're not strong enough yet. Kaamil wouldn't want to see you like this.'

'I'm feeling better,' Melissa said. 'You know how much I was looking forward to seeing the look on Kaamil's face when he met his new parents. Nothing will stop me seeing how he's getting on with his new family.'

Elisha cornered Dr Basar on his next visit.

'Tell Mum she's not well enough to visit Kaamil,' Elisha pleaded. 'Please, Doctor.'

Dr Basar scratched his chin. 'I think a trip to Baripada and seeing Kaamil will do your mother a power of good.' He put his stethoscope back in his Gladstone bag. 'You know how much she's been looking forward to it.'

Was Dr Basar trying to tell her that this was her mother's dying wish?

Wesley fixed a date for the trip. Elisha decided she wasn't going. But as the day grew closer, her mother was definitely getting stronger. Was it just the excitement? Would she relapse once she'd seen Kaamil? Or worse still, while she was there?

Elisha had to talk to someone who wouldn't go all religious on her. Thank God for Zac. And thank God she'd had the guts to tell him what was happening to their mother.

'I want you to look after Mum tomorrow,' Elisha said, grabbing Zac's arm. 'I'm not going.'

'Sis!' Zac stared at her. 'You have to. Mum needs you more than ever before.'

'I can't bear it,' Elisha said. 'I had a nightmare last night. Mum collapsed and died in front of Kaamil.'

'All the more reason to go. You'll regret it if you don't and something happens.' He hugged his sister. 'Don't worry. Mum's getting better. It's going to be okay. You'll see.'

     David Whittet

Zac was right. Whatever her doubts about the trip, Elisha couldn't let her mother down.

Elisha's heart thumped all the way to Kaamil's new home.

'What a lovely district,' Melissa said, brushing away a tear as they got closer. 'I'm so glad we could do this for Kaamil.'

Elisha closed her eyes when they arrived and her mother flung her arms around Kaamil. Was this the moment her mum would crash, just as she'd done in the dream?

'God bless you, Kaamil,' Melissa said. 'You don't know how much this means to me. Seeing you here so happy and settled.'

Elisha glanced up. Far from falling apart, there was new life in her mother's eyes.

Zac nudged Elisha. 'What did I tell you? She's a new woman.'

Really? A new woman? Elisha had to admit that her mother hadn't been so alive in weeks. Was she genuinely getting stronger? Or was it just bravado?

The fresh burst of energy seemed to last well beyond the visit to Kaamil. But was Melissa ready to take on a more active role with the mission? Elisha despaired when her mother insisted on leading prayer groups and giving talks about her experience as a casualty nurse. Did she have to set herself such a punishing schedule? Elisha saw the tell-tale signs that everyone else ignored. Her mother's yawns and groans. The pained expressions when nobody was looking.

Elisha watched her mother get ready for another gospel meeting. Make-up couldn't hide the weariness in her face. At least, not from Elisha.

'Listen to me, Mum.' Elisha swallowed. 'You're doing too much. Why don't you have a rest today? You need it.'

'No, darling,' Melissa said. 'There's work to be done. Souls to be saved.'

'You'll do yourself in if you go on at this rate.'

Melissa shrugged and continued putting on her make-up. 'If my days are numbered, then it's even more important that I get out there and spread the word while I still can.'

A burning rage flamed in Elisha's belly as she watched her mother deteriorate each day while her father paraded her around the mission like a celebrity.

'You've got to stop her, Dad,' Elisha pleaded. 'It's killing her.'

'We've got a special service at St Anne's in Baripada on Sunday,' Wesley said. 'It's dedicated to healing, and I've asked your mother to preach the sermon.'

You must be kidding. She can't even heal herself, let alone anyone else. Elisha could have slapped him. 'She isn't up to it, Dad. I don't think she'll make it.'

'Your mother's stronger than you think,' Wesley said, 'and this will be an opportunity to show how God protects his own.'

If only He did. Elisha covered her face. *Mum's dying.*

Every bump on the road to Baripada deepened Elisha's fear that something would go horribly wrong at the service at St Anne's Convent School Church. Huddled up to her in the back of the car, she could feel her mother's bare bones jutting out and pressing into her. Melissa wouldn't last the day. Why couldn't her father see that?

Elisha took a deep breath. 'Dad, I think we should turn back.'

Wesley glanced over his shoulder from the driver's seat. 'We can't. Everyone's expecting us.'

'I don't care,' Elisha said. 'Look at Mum. She won't last the day.'

'She will,' Wesley said.

Melissa pressed her fingers to her mouth. 'Shush, darling. Don't make a scene. I'm going to be alright. I want to do this.'

Wesley hit the accelerator. 'She'll be fine.'

She won't. Elisha buried her head in her hands. She dare not look at her mother for the rest of the journey.

A host of dignitaries from the Indian mission greeted them when they arrived at St Anne's. Could none of them see her mother was sick? Elisha's legs shook even more than her mother's when they entered the church. She couldn't bear to look when Wesley led Melissa to the pulpit to begin her sermon.

The congregation hushed in expectation. Melissa cleared her throat. 'Good morning … brothers and sisters … in Christ …' Elisha cringed as her mother spluttered and struggled with the words. Why didn't Wesley stop her? Surely even he could see this was a disaster.

Melissa started again, her words even more slurred and disjointed. 'Brothers … and … sisters … in … Christ … welcome … to … this special … service …'

Elisha covered her face. How could everyone sit there and watch her mother embarrass herself? *If Dad won't do anything, then I will.* Elisha stood up and marched to the front of the church. She felt the stir in the congregation as she climbed the stairs to the pulpit and joined her mother.

How could she do this without humiliating her mother any further?

Elisha took Melissa's hand. 'You can all see my mother is gravely ill. She is an amazing woman who has sacrificed her life for the good of others.'

'She's a saint,' an official called out. Others in the congregation nodded in agreement.

Elisha went on to describe how Melissa had been there for Kaamil in his hour of need at the hospital, wiping away a tear when she got to the needle-stick injury that stole her mother's future. Elisha held her head up high when she told them how her mother had travelled to the ghetto every day to dress Kaamil's wound.

'That tragic accident on a chaotic night in casualty could have made her bitter and resentful.' Elisha cuddled her mother. 'I know I would have been. But not my mother. The love she showed that boy has taught me so much about what really matters in life.'

The congregation broke out in spontaneous applause and chanted blessings. 'Hallelujah! Praise the Lord! Amen!'

Some officials stood up and recited verses of scripture. 'Yea, though I walk through the valley of the shadow of death, I will fear no evil.'

Still shaking, Melissa whispered in Elisha's ear. 'Thank you, my darling. That was beautiful. Now, I'd like to go home.'

Elisha freaked out when her mother's eyes darted in all directions. *She's going to black out.* 'Hold on to me, Mum.' Where was her father? 'Dad! Come quickly!'

Melissa's face turned a pale green and she let out a loud belch.

Elisha massaged her mother's back. 'Deep breaths, Mum. That's right. You can do this.'

Melissa continued to heave. The belching got louder. Elisha hardly noticed the commotion in the church. She just wished she could see her father.

Elisha gripped her mother. 'I'm going to take you outside. You need some air.'

Melissa was a dead weight, and Elisha struggled to get her down from the pulpit.

'Help me! Please! Dad! Anyone!'

Too late. Melissa lurched out of Elisha's arms and threw up, showering the officials in the front row in blood and vomit.

This was the end. Elisha knew it in her heart. She collapsed to the floor with her mother in her arms.

'Mummy. My mummy. Don't leave me.'

Elisha didn't let go until her mother gasped her last breath.

CHAPTER THIRTEEN

Gold Coast, Queensland, Australia, August 1987

'It was horrible. Beyond belief.' Elisha sat down beside Joanna. 'The authorities insisted we burn all of Mum's possessions along with her body. They're paranoid about spreading AIDS. I had to get tested, along with all the bigwigs she splattered with blood and puke when she died. And as for the funeral, I've never seen so much weeping and wailing. Pastors speaking in tongues. I thought my head was going to explode.'

Joanna rested her hand on Elisha's. 'I can't imagine how bad it was for you.'

Elisha glanced up at Joanna. 'So you understand why I had to get out?'

'I just wish you hadn't left your father when he was so vulnerable.' Joanna lowered her face. 'Rajani too. Your mother's death hit her hard as well.'

'I know.' Elisha saw the disappointment in Joanna's eyes. 'It broke my heart to leave her. She'd have given anything to come with me and meet you.'

Joanna frowned. 'If only she could.'

Elisha drew back her chair. The memory of abandoning Rajani and the Sunday school remained raw. She couldn't get Rajani's pleading voice out of her head …

'You can't go,' Rajani had said as they tidied up the classroom after the children had left. 'I won't let you. We need each other more than ever now. Please—'

'I'm sorry.' There were no words to express how Elisha felt. 'But there's nothing left for me here. I have to get out of India.'

'What about the children?' Rajani said. 'They need you too. Don't you care about them?'

'I do.' Elisha bit her lip. 'It's just … I can't go on telling Bible stories. Not if I don't believe it any more.' She glanced up at Rajani. 'You can do it now.'

Rajani shook her head and sobbed. 'I can't. Not without you.'

Elisha tried to embrace Rajani, but she backed away.

'The children love you,' Elisha said. 'They'll soon forget about me.'

Rajani dabbed her eyes. 'No, they won't.'

Elisha wanted to cry, too, but she hadn't any tears left.

Rajani was right. The kids were devastated when Elisha told them she was leaving. They'd just had their first Sunday school lesson without her when she burst into the church to break the news.

'Please tell me it's not true,' Rohan cried. 'You can't leave us!'

'Just when it was starting to be fun,' Jayesh groaned.

'Who's going to show us how to draw now?' Harin asked.

Elisha avoided the children's eyes. 'Rajani will. You don't need me.'

'Yes, we do,' Kali begged. 'Your stories are the only decent thing about Sunday school. It'll be boring without you.'

'Blame my father,' Elisha snapped and strode out of the church. 'I'm sorry, Rajani. I have to go.'

Elisha *did* blame her father. He'd sent her mother to her death. The fights with her father were even more heart-wrenching than her arguments with Rajani.

'How can you still pretend this is God's will?' Elisha paced up and down her father's study while he shrank behind the desk. 'God didn't save her. Didn't answer your prayers, did He?'

Wesley rubbed his chin. 'His ways are not our ways.'

Elisha snorted. 'Crap. That's what you always say.'

'Because it's true,' Wesley said. 'God has called your mother home.'

'Is that the best you can do?' Elisha walked away. 'I'm going back to Australia. I want nothing more to do with your mission.'

Wesley stood up. 'No, Elisha.'

'You can't stop me. I'm eighteen. I'm not a child any more!'

'Don't leave me. Not now.'

There were tears in her father's eyes. She'd never seen him cry before. 'Dad!'

'It's a terrible thing to doubt everything you've ever believed.' Wesley flung his arms around Elisha. 'We have to make this mission work. Give your mother's death some meaning. Otherwise—what's the point of anything?'

Elisha hugged him. 'I'm sorry. I don't belong here. I have to get out.' She glanced up at his dark face and bewildered eyes. 'You've still got Zac. He's a good boy. He'll take my place and help with the Sunday school.'

Wesley sighed. 'Isaac's mad at me, too. He thinks I've destroyed his career as a sportsman.'

'He'll come round.' Elisha smiled. 'He's much more forgiving than me.'

'Will you ever forgive me?'

'I will.' Elisha kissed her father on the cheek. 'I have already. But I'm still going home.'

Even now, clearing away the tea things at Joanna's house a fortnight later, Elisha could still see her father's broken face in her mind.

'I've let you down, haven't I, Jo?' Elisha said. 'You look as miserable as Dad and Rajani did when I left them at the railway station.'

Joanna shrugged. 'You did what you had to do.'

'Everyone wanted me to stay on and build a legacy for Mum. You think I should have done, don't you?'

'Perhaps you'll go back one day. It's what your mother would have wanted.'

Elisha threw her tea towel on the draining board. 'I will *never* go back to India.'

Over the next three months, Elisha hardly left her bedroom. She'd hoped living with Joanna would be a miracle cure. It wasn't. Why did Joanna make her feel like a quitter? Maybe she had done the wrong thing, leaving her father like that. But she had the right to grieve for her mother in peace.

Elisha never emerged for breakfast before mid-morning.

Joanna sat next to her at the kitchen table. 'Listen, Elisha. You can't go on like this.'

Elisha scowled at Joanna. 'Why not?'

Joanna shuffled and started again. 'Because it's not healthy. It would help if you got out. Burn off some of that pent-up anger.'

'What's the point?'

'Don't you have some old friends you could catch up with?'

Elisha screwed up her face and pushed her untouched cereal bowl away. 'They'd only ask me about India and my mother. I don't want to talk about it.'

Joanna put her hand on Elisha's. 'Have you heard from your father?'

Elisha shook her head.

'What about Zac?' Joanna said.

'Not a word.'

Joanna pinched her lips. 'Surely you've written to your father. He'll be worried about you.'

Elisha shrugged. 'Don't know what to say.'

'You could write to Rajani. She'd understand how you're feeling.'

'She wouldn't.'

Joanna squeezed Elisha's hand. 'Of course she would. She's written to me several times. She misses you. Asks me what you're doing every time she writes.'

Elisha raised her eyes. 'Really?'

'Yes.' Joanna let out a forceful breath. 'Listen, I'm not stupid. I've seen you taking airmail letters from the letter box. I know you've heard from them.'

'I haven't.' Elisha hid her face. 'They were just … some newsletters about the mission. Nothing important. I threw them out.'

Elisha slunk off to her bedroom and shut the door. *Guess I've stuffed up again.*

For more than an hour she sat on her bed, contemplating the bundle of unopened letters in her bedside drawer. They looked so colourful with their pictorial Indian stamps and vibrant postmarks. Dare she look inside?

Her hands trembling, Elisha sorted them into date order, picked up her nail file and used it to open the envelopes. She read the ones from Rajani first.

Dearest Elisha,

I miss you so much! My dear friend! Life hasn't been the same since you left. Zac has been helping at Sunday school. Can you believe it? He's had the kids roaring with laughter when he's acted out some of the Bible stories.

 David Whittet

Elisha put down the letter for a second. She could imagine Zac playing the fool and the children loving it.

> *Of course, the kids miss your beautiful drawings. They all want to know if you're coming back. I've been doing my best, trying to keep the art classes going. Zac's helped with that, too.*

Zac helping with art? That was a first.

> *Zac and I have been getting close. He invited me to the football on Saturday. Poor Zac. He's still unhappy about being reduced to the team photographer when he dreamt about being their star player. But he doesn't bear a grudge about the injury. He's so brave—he even joked about Ashok being the next Maradona.*
> *I wore that gold shawl to the match—remember, the one you said made me look more grown-up. I was Zac's assistant. He's into video now. If he can't be a sportsman, he's going to be a film-maker. You should have seen the two of us. Zac limping along the sideline, camera in hand. Me following behind with a video recorder slung over my shoulder.*

Elisha smiled for the first time since her mother died. She could imagine Zac hobbling up and down the field, attached to Rajani by the video cable.

> *I think Zac wants to ask me out, but he's too shy. Did he have any girlfriends back in Australia?*

Zac was always popular with the girls at school. Elisha couldn't resist another giggle. She remembered when a cheerleader had a crush on him—and how her father exploded when he found out.

> *I'm so glad you're spending time with Joanna. But please, Elisha, just let me know you're okay. No need for a long letter. Just a couple of lines will do.*
> *Forever friends,*
> *Rajani*

Elisha put the letter back in its envelope. What must Rajani think of her? Almost three months on and no reply. Should she write back now? What would she say after so long? Maybe it was too late.

Her fingers still trembling, Elisha opened Rajani's next letter. It was all about the mission's leper colony, and how Zac was helping her with that, too. Elisha stuffed the letter back in the drawer. She didn't want to be reminded about the mission and its work.

After another hour lying on her bed, Elisha crept into the living room. Joanna had dozed off reading a book.

'Jo.' Elisha knelt down beside her. 'I'm sorry. I shouldn't have lied to you about the letters. It's just—my head's all over the place.'

Joanna opened her eyes. 'I understand. It will get easier. I promise.'

'I hope so.' Elisha forced a smile. 'Zac and Rajani are getting close. They'll soon be an item. He's been helping her at the leper colony.'

'Yes,' Joanna said. 'Rajani was full of it in her letters to me. I'm so pleased she's carrying on the work. It was your mother's passion.'

Elisha hid her face. 'I know.'

Joanna edged closer and took an envelope from her pocket. 'This is the last letter your mother wrote to me before she died. She was so proud of the work you were doing with the children at the Sunday school—'

'Stop!' Elisha thumped the table. 'I don't want to know.'

Joanna put an arm on Elisha's shoulder. 'She hoped you would train as a nurse and carry on her work—'

'No!' Elisha jumped to her feet and glared at Joanna. 'Leave me alone.'

'You could make such a difference to other people's lives.'

'And die of AIDS or some other ghastly disease like my mother?' Elisha made for the door, still eyeballing Joanna. 'No, thank you.'

'Wait.' Joanna grabbed her arm. 'Surely doing something worthwhile has to beat moping around here all day?'

Elisha pulled away. 'I'm not ready to die yet.'

'Then do something with your life,' Joanna called after her as Elisha slammed her bedroom door.

Joanna had always been Elisha's rock. The person she turned to when her world caved in. But now? *She wants me to be a nurse? After everything that's happened? What planet is she on?*

Elisha spent the rest of the day—and night—curled up in bed, sulking and looking for excuses. Of course she wanted to make something of her life, but to follow in her mother's footsteps? How could Joanna be so thoughtless as to suggest it at such a time?

Elisha didn't want to sleep. Every night she dreamt about her mother vomiting blood and dying in her arms. She pulled Rajani's letters out of the drawer again, took a deep breath and began to read.

Zac's been brilliant. He's got his mates from the football team to come and help me feed the lepers. Mealtimes have been so much fun. Zac's always joking with the lepers, asking them how it feels to have a football team waiting on them.

Not more gushing praise for Zac! Was this her brother she was reading about? He was no saint. Elisha sighed—Rajani must be besotted with Zac if she thought he was an angel. And Zac must be pretty keen on Rajani to get him working at the leper colony.

Rajani went on to explain how she made the soup extra hot for the lepers.

Every day I ask them if they enjoyed the soup. They always say it was perfect, but I know they can't taste it with the nerve damage in their mouths. But I still make the broth extra spicy. I can only hope adding a few more chillies might bring a morsel of flavour to brighten their colourless existence.

Elisha held the letter to her chest. Rajani was such a darling.

Submerged under the sheets, Elisha drifted off to sleep. She dreamt about her mother again. But tonight was different—Melissa wasn't dying. She was alive and urging Elisha to do the right thing: *You'll make a wonderful nurse. I saw you with the patients in casualty—you were brilliant. You can do it, my darling. You must do it.*

Elisha was up early for breakfast the next morning. The first time since she'd returned to Australia.

'Alright, Jo,' she said. 'You win. I'll get a prospectus for nursing college. But this doesn't mean I'm going back to India.'

CHAPTER FOURTEEN

Elisha glanced around the waiting room at James Cook University in Brisbane. *Why am I here?* The other students all looked like they'd found their vocation. Elisha remained ambivalent about hers.

The receptionist ushered her into the interview room. 'This way, please, Miss Martin.'

Prying eyes. Staring at her. Elisha lowered her head and stumbled into a chair opposite the panel.

The dean, a distinguished-looking man in his late fifties, removed his glasses and stared into her eyes. 'Tell us why you want to be a nurse.'

'I want to … I mean … um …' Elisha dribbled to a standstill. What had Joanna told her to say? 'I want to help people when they need it most.'

The professor of nursing science, a smartly dressed woman with sharp eyes, leant forward. 'I read about your family in the papers. Tragic business. Are you planning to take over from your mother? I must say, you're brave to train and continue her work—'

'No!' Elisha shrank back. She couldn't breathe. She had to get air. 'You'll have to excuse me.'

Elisha was out of the door and running down the corridor.

Two hours later, Elisha collapsed in a chair back home and buried her head in her arms.

'I blew it, Jo.'

Joanna sat down beside her. 'They'll understand.'

'They won't,' Elisha said. 'You should have seen their faces when I walked out.'

'They know what you've been through,' Joanna said. 'They'll give you another chance.'

Elisha dabbed her eyes. 'It was a dumb idea, anyway. Nursing's not for me.'

'We'll see.' Joanna got up and fetched a letter. 'This arrived while you were out.'

Another letter from Rajani. Elisha wasn't sure she was ready for this, but she opened it anyway. At least she'd replied to the last one.

My dearest Elisha,

What fantastic news—you're going to be a nurse! Best news I've heard in ages! You'll be absolutely wonderful. Think what good you could do out here—

Elisha threw down the letter. 'I can't read this.'

Joanna picked it up. 'Rajani would have given anything for the opportunity to train as a nurse.'

Elisha covered her face. 'Don't.'

'You need to hear this.' Joanna began reading Rajani's letter out loud: '"Do you remember Azad and Davinda?"'

Elisha did remember them. An elderly couple at the leper colony, their skin so ravaged by the disease that Elisha had scarcely been able to look at them.

Joanna continued reading Rajani's letter: '"When I was a baby, Davinda used to feed me. And when I was a little girl, Azad always brought me treats from the market when he went into town. Now they've just got stumps for hands, and I have to spoon-feed them."'

'How come Davinda was feeding Rajani?' Elisha asked.

'Davinda and Azad were dear friends with Rajani's parents, Vijay and Jaya,' Joanna said. 'Davinda looked after Rajani's brother Rajiv, too. That was before they all got sick, and Rajani's family died.'

Elisha looked up. 'I didn't know Rajani had a brother.'

Joanna read more of Rajani's letter: '"I used to sit on Azad's lap, and he would read me a story. Now he's almost blind, his kind eyes covered in blisters and hidden behind his thick glasses. But he still holds his head up high."'

Elisha shook her head. *Does she really think this will make me go back?*

'"Davinda taught me at primary school,"' Joanna continued. '"She used to look so elegant. These days she covers herself in a dirty red shawl, too proud to let anyone see the ugly sores underneath."'

'Why is she telling me this?' Elisha asked. 'I'm not going back.'

Joanna put down the letter. 'When Davinda and Azad caught leprosy, they were terrified they'd be sent to an asylum. Rajani's parents hid them away in their house. That was before your father built the sanctuary at Madhapur.'

Elisha shrugged. 'So?'

'Rajani's parents caught leprosy from them. First Vijay, then Jaya. Rajiv too. Davinda caught a chill, and they all went down with pneumonia. Davinda and Azad survived. Rajani's family didn't. It's a miracle Rajani survived.'

Elisha blinked back a tear. 'Rajani's forgiven them? And she still looks after them?'

'Rajani has a loving heart,' Joanna said. 'She'd forgive anyone.'

'She would.' Elisha paused and rubbed her chin. 'I wonder if she's forgiven me for leaving India?'

Joanna paused and pulled another letter out of her apron pocket. 'This came from your father. He's hurting. He wishes he'd listened to you and stopped your mother from working at the hospital.' Joanna put a hand on Elisha's. 'Most of all, he hopes you're happy and finding peace.'

Elisha pushed Joanna aside and made for the telephone. She picked up the receiver and dialled the university. 'I need to speak to the dean of nursing.'

'Hold the line, please.'

Elisha played with the phone cord as she waited to be connected. What could she say?

'Miss Martin.' It was the dean's assertive voice. 'I didn't expect to hear from you again.'

Elisha stumbled to find the right words. 'I shouldn't have walked out of the interview … I'm sorry … It's just … when the professor started to talk about my mother …'

'We understood.'

'You did?'

Minutes later, Elisha put down the phone and hugged Joanna. 'They're going to give me another chance. I've got a fresh interview next week.'

Joanna beamed. 'I told you they'd make allowances after all you've been through.'

'I'm still not going back to India,' Elisha said. 'So don't start getting ideas.'

'Maybe not to work,' Joanna said, 'but you could always go back for a visit. Catch up with Rajani, Zac and your dad.'

'They'd all gang up on me and talk me into staying on.' Elisha stood back from Joanna and crossed her arms. 'No. I'm staying in Australia. There are plenty of deprived places here and sick people who need help.'

Over the next four years, Elisha lost count of the number of times she told Joanna she was quitting.

'You can't,' Joanna would say. 'I won't let you.'

'Why do I have to know the names of all those blood vessels?' Elisha used to complain. 'How will that help to make me a better nurse?'

Other times she would just complain about the sheer volume of study.

'It's all for a purpose,' Joanna had insisted.

'Yes,' Elisha would reply. 'Stopping me from getting my degree.'

No one was more surprised than Elisha when she graduated with honours.

'You look so smart in your gown,' Joanna beamed as the photographers gathered after the graduation ceremony.

'I want you in the photographs,' Elisha said. 'If it wasn't for you pushing me, I'd have quit long ago.'

'Thank God I did,' Joanna said as the photographer lined up the shot. 'With this qualification, you've got the tools to change the world.'

Not quite. Elisha smiled for the photograph. It was just a bachelor of nursing science. Still, the pride in Joanna's eyes made all those years of gruelling study seem worthwhile. *And I am going to make something of my life.*

Over the next few days, Elisha scanned the classifieds in the nursing journals. Her tutors had told her they were crying out for nurses in the outback. She'd always wanted to see Ayers Rock. What was it they called it now? Yes, Uluru. Elisha shot off a job application to Alice Springs. This was her chance to do good for the community. Make that difference Joanna was always on about.

Elisha went running in the park each morning. How would she cope in the outback with so little support? Had she made the right choice? *Get a grip, girl! Alice Springs is just the challenge you need.*

Elisha walked through the door, covered in perspiration after her run.

Joanna waved an envelope in the air. 'There's a telegram for you.'

Elisha gasped. 'Is it from Alice Springs? Have I got the job?'

Joanna fidgeted with her crucifix. 'No. It's from India.'

Elisha snatched the telegram and tore it open. 'It's from Zac.'

Joanna smiled. 'What is it? Has he proposed to Rajani at last? Have they invited you to their wedding?'

'No.' Elisha's hand shook as she read the telegram. 'Rajani's sick. She's in a coma. Her life's on the line.'

Joanna turned pale. 'A coma? No! Whatever's happened to her?'

Elisha thought Joanna was going to collapse. 'She caught a cold. It turned to pneumonia, and now she's on a respirator.'

'You must go to her,' Joanna said, tears streaming down her cheeks.

Elisha flung her arms around Joanna. She'd never seen Joanna cry before.

'I'm so sorry, Jo. I'd go if I could. You know I would. But—'

Joanna pulled away from Elisha. 'But what?'

'The job in Alice Springs. My heart's set on it.'

Joanna dabbed her eyes. 'Rajani is your friend. She needs you.'

Elisha felt a lump in her throat. How could she be so selfish? Joanna was right. Of course she was. Elisha went into the hall, picked up the telephone and dialled a travel agent. 'I need a seat on the next flight to Calcutta.'

   David Whittet

CHAPTER FIFTEEN

A three-hour delay leaving Brisbane and a missed connection in Bangkok. Would Rajani still be alive by the time Elisha got to the hospital in Baripada?

It had taken Elisha three days to organise the flights to Calcutta and renew her visa. And it took three long-distance phone calls to Zac to persuade him to leave Rajani's bedside and come and meet her at Calcutta International Airport. No way was Elisha facing those beggars thumping on the taxi window on her own. Not to mention the snake charmers and street pedlars who had terrified her when she first arrived in India. And the kids hanging off the train roof. Elisha shuddered at the memory. Back then, she thought her world was ending. Now her head was more messed up than ever.

Joanna had seen her off at Brisbane International Airport, just as she'd done six years earlier.

'God be with you,' Joanna said with a final hug.

Last time, Elisha had left with a cheeky grin and a throwaway line. *It'll take more than frigging prayer if I'm going to survive in the backwaters of bloody India!* There were no jokes today. Elisha wasn't sure what she believed any more, but she was thankful for Joanna's blessing.

The flights dragged. Trashy movies. Inedible food. Elisha tried to get some sleep, but her mind went back to an earful from Zac on the telephone the previous night.

'Rajani wrote to you every week,' he'd said. 'Why didn't you reply?'

The exasperation in Zac's voice ricocheted down the phone line. What would it be like when she had to confront him face to face?

'I'm sorry,' she'd mumbled. 'I just … I couldn't bear to open them. I was hurting.'

'Rajani was hurting too,' Zac had hit back, 'and so was I. Sometimes, sis, I could wring your neck.'

Elisha flicked through the pages of the in-flight magazine. Zac thought she was a selfish bitch. Rajani probably felt the same. And with Rajani in a coma, would she get the chance to apologise to her best friend? Elisha stuffed the magazine back into the seat pocket. Zac was right—she had been wallowing in her own grief. But things were going to change.

The stink was exactly the same as before when Elisha stepped off the aeroplane at Calcutta International Airport. She remembered how Zac had teased her about the drains being high in the hot season. Crowds jostled for a place in the immigration queue. They were all tired and grumpy from the flight and as evil-smelling as the drains.

It took Elisha more than an hour to get through immigration. Would Zac be waiting for her in the arrivals hall? Would he still be cross with her?

The customs officer stamped her passport. She picked up her suitcase, took a deep breath, and stepped through the sliding doors. And there was Zac with the same cocky smile on his face.

'You don't look quite as green as you did last time you arrived in India,' he said, flinging his arms around her. 'And at least you've left the sick bag on the plane.'

Elisha dropped her case. 'Oh, Zac. It's so good to see you.'

'Here, let me take that.' Zac picked up her suitcase and fetched a trolley. 'Dad's outside getting us a taxi.'

Dad's here? Elisha gulped. She knew she'd have to face her father again— but not now. She wasn't ready. Not by a long shot.

'Elisha!' It was her father's voice, and he was standing at the terminal door. 'Thank you … Bless you … Thank you for coming back.'

Elisha froze. The stammer in her father's voice told her he was as unsure of himself as she was of herself. A moment's pause and they ran into each other's arms.

'My daddy!' Elisha felt the wet of her father's tears on her face as he hugged her even tighter than her brother had done.

'I've missed you so much,' her father said. 'We've all missed you.'

He didn't let go of her until they had sidestepped the street traders and were safely inside a taxi.

Beggars hammering on the windows when they stopped at traffic lights, terrified Elisha just as much as they'd done before. But there was something even scarier on her mind. She scarcely dared to ask.

'How's Rajani? Is she still in a coma?'

The grief in Zac's eyes said it all. 'She's been on life support for more than a week.' He turned and looked out of the window. 'Not a glimmer.'

'That's not quite true,' Elisha's father said. 'The doctors said there've been some positive signs in the last couple of days.' He put his arm around Elisha. 'They're hoping that she might recognise your voice, and it might spark a reaction.'

Elisha hardly noticed the teeming masses at Howrah Railway Station. She charged down the platform ahead of Zac and her father. It was a six-hour train ride to Baripada, and Elisha had to get to Rajani before it was too late.

A jolt and they were away. Elisha watched her father drift off to sleep as the train crossed the Howrah Bridge. Zac looked exhausted, too. Elisha had been travelling for the best part of two days, but she was wide awake, and she wanted answers from Zac.

'Rajani persuaded me to make a film about the leper colony,' Zac said. 'She invited me to tea at her great-aunt Nisha's house after football one Saturday. I told her I wanted to be a film director now that I couldn't play sport.'

'Rajani told me you were into movies,' Elisha said.

Zac frowned. 'I thought you hadn't opened any of Rajani's letters.'

'I read that one,' Elisha said. 'She said you were a budding Steven Spielberg.'

'Satyajit Ray, please,' Zac said.

'Who?'

Zac raised his eyebrows. 'Satyajit Ray. Only the most famous Indian film-maker of all time.'

'Never heard of him.'

Zac sighed. 'Neither had Rajani. Mind you, I'm surprised she'd heard of Steven Spielberg. She told me she'd only been to the cinema a couple of times when her great-aunt took her to the Children's Film Society.'

'Tell me about the film you made for the leper colony,' Elisha said.

'I was stoked when Rajani asked me,' Zac said. 'Hoped it would be my big break. Satyajit Ray made his name with a film about a boy called Apu in a small Bengal village, and he used amateur actors—'

'Cut the crap,' Elisha snapped. 'I don't want a history of Indian cinema. I want to hear about Rajani.'

'We had some differences over the content of the film,' Zac said. 'I wanted an exposé of the health service. Rajani wanted something to attract sponsors. We argued. She didn't want it sensationalised. I told her great art shouldn't be afraid of controversy.'

Elisha rolled her eyes. 'I'm with Rajani.'

'Anyway, we agreed to tell some of the residents' stories. Rajani interviewed Davinda and Azad—a couple who'd known her parents.'

'Yes,' Elisha said. 'Jo told me about Davinda and Azad.'

'Rajani was a natural in front of the camera. She got down on her knees with Aashi, a widow whose four children all had leprosy. With the kids on her lap, Rajani recited her lines about leprosy being a curable disease. She made a plea for the authorities to fund the drugs with such simple dignity that I was in tears behind the camera.'

Elisha felt her eyes well up. That was so like Rajani.

Zac's eyes were brimming too. He wiped away a tear and put on a brave face. 'Of course, it wasn't all plain sailing. I wanted to show Aashi crying. But she couldn't because her ulcerated eyes were as dry as a bone. Rajani wouldn't let me use artificial tears. I can't think why.'

'I can.'

'Anyway, it gave me a good line for the voice-over: "Leprosy is cruel—it makes you want to cry but stops you being able to do so."' Zac blinked back another tear. 'When we'd finished the film, Rajani thanked me for doing the film and said nobody could have done a better job. Not even Satyajit Ray. She remembered his name!'

'So how did you feel, helping Rajani to look after the lepers?' Elisha asked.

'I wasn't keen at first,' Zac said. 'I thought it would be gross. Bring back memories of my own childhood. My birth parents both had leprosy.'

'I know. Dad said.' Elisha leant across the carriage and put a hand on his knee. 'But it didn't upset you?'

               David Whittet

'No.' Zac paused. 'If anyone had told me I'd find joy amongst lepers, I'd have said they were crazy. But that place—it wasn't a shelter or a colony or any of those other names people use. It was a house of hope. And that's what we called our film. *House of Hope.*'

Elisha smiled. She'd never heard her brother talk like this before. He must have grown up while she'd been away. That, or Rajani had brought out his feminine side.

The train rattled across the plains. Elisha glanced out of the window. Women trudged through the mud in an endless expanse of paddy fields— that meant they were getting closer.

'So when did Rajani get sick?' Elisha asked.

Her father stirred and opened his eyes. 'It was just after you finished the film, wasn't it, Isaac?'

'Rajani looked tired at the wrap party,' Zac said.

Elisha pulled a face. 'The *what*?'

'It's a celebration when the film's in the can,' Zac said. 'I mean—when the shooting's complete. We had supper with the residents. They were all stoked about being celebrities. Davinda was a hoot. "Who'd have thought it?" she said. "Us lot becoming movie stars." She waved her stump at Azad and grinned. "I'd dance you round the floor if I could."' Zac broke off for a moment. 'At least, it would have been a grin if only her muscles worked.'

'Surely that must have warmed Rajani's heart,' Elisha said.

Zac stiffened. 'I could tell Rajani wasn't enjoying the party. She kept disappearing, and I could hear her coughing. When I asked her what was wrong, she said it was just a cold.' He looked down at his shoes. 'If I hadn't been so engrossed editing the film, I'd have seen she wasn't herself sooner. I should have taken better care of her.'

Elisha watched her father put his arm around Zac. 'Don't blame yourself,' he said. 'It wasn't your fault.'

Zac pulled away. 'But it was. I kept pestering her. Begged her to sit in on the editing sessions. I wanted to show her the sequences I was working on and how I'd captured the residents' personalities.

'"Seems like you're doing a great job," Rajani would say. "You don't need me."

'But I wanted her there to share my excitement. And above all, she had to be there for the gala premiere.'

'A premiere?' Elisha said. 'There isn't even a cinema in Madhapur.'

'I talked the schoolmaster into lending us his prized video projector,' Zac said. 'And I went down on my knees to persuade the secretary to let us use the village hall.' He bit a fingernail. 'Now I wish I hadn't bothered.'

Elisha noticed a flush creep across her father's cheeks. 'It was my fault,' he said. 'I encouraged Isaac to put on a show. News of the film had spread, and we wanted to show it to the local government officials and our friends at the mission.' His eyes met Elisha's. 'I would never have suggested such a grand event if I'd known Rajani was so sick.'

Was her father thinking about that dreadful day at St Anne's too? 'I know that, Dad,' she said.

'I couldn't understand why Rajani wasn't as excited as I was,' Zac said. 'Until the morning of the premiere. She was sitting on her bed when I called around, her one smart party frock laid out beside her. And she was crying.

'"I'm sorry, Zac," she said, "I'm not going to make it tonight."

'She looked dreadful. But it still didn't occur to me that she was really sick.

'"Why don't you stay in bed today?" I said. "Get some rest. That way, you might feel better by tonight."

'"Maybe," she said and closed her eyes.

'When I called for her an hour before the performance was due to start, her great-aunt Nisha wouldn't let me in.

'"She's not well," Nisha said. "She won't be coming to your film show."

'Rajani stumbled into the hallway, her nightdress soaked in sweat.

'"It's alright," I said. "We'll cancel the premiere. It can wait until you're better."

'Rajani wouldn't hear of it. "What? With all those people coming? No way. You go and enjoy yourself. It's your film. Your baby."'

Elisha smiled. That was typical of Rajani.

'I told her it was her film too,' Zac continued. 'She just told me to convince everyone to donate to the cause. And I did—for her. We raised a small fortune. I was so excited, and I rushed round to tell Rajani. There was an ambulance outside when I arrived. I scarcely dared go inside. Dr Basar sat on the edge of Rajani's bed, listening to her chest. Nisha paced up and down the bedroom, praying out loud. Then Rajani started coughing up blood.

'Everything was a blur after that. I remember the paramedics helped Dr Basar get Rajani into the ambulance. Nisha wanted me to stay behind, but I wasn't abandoning Rajani. I clung to one of Rajani's hands, and Nisha held the other all the way to the hospital.'

Elisha pressed her hands against her cheeks. *I should have been there too.*

Her father must have guessed what she was thinking. He raised his eyes toward her. 'You couldn't have done any more even if you'd been here.'

Elisha met his gaze. 'I should never have left India. I'll never forgive myself if Rajani doesn't make it.'

Zac shot bolt upright. 'Doesn't make it? She *has* to make it!'

Elisha bit her tongue. Why had she said that? 'I'm sorry, Zac, I didn't mean—of course she's going to make it.'

But would Rajani make it? At least her father hadn't piped up about it all being in God's hands. They sat in silence until the train drew up at Baripada Station.

An uneasy hush continued on the taxi ride to the hospital. Elisha barely noticed the once-familiar streets. Perhaps it was just as well her eyes were so bleary. Every corner held a terrible memory.

Elisha shuddered as her father helped her out of the taxi. How she hated that hospital. Starting with Zac's knee, it had brought them nothing but bad luck. They'd allowed her mother to get a needle-stick injury. What hope was there for Rajani?

The endless corridors had that same overpowering hospital smell Elisha remembered from the first time they'd arrived with Zac in an ambulance.

Her father gave her hand a squeeze. 'Don't be too alarmed when you first see Rajani and all the monitors. It just means they're taking good care of her.' He let go of Elisha's hand and gave her a pat on the back. 'You go in. I'll wait outside. They don't like too many visitors at a time in intensive care.'

Zac had already gowned up. Elisha had noticed how his limp got worse when he became stressed.

'You have to wear this gear in intensive care,' he said. 'I suppose you know all about that, now you're a nurse.'

Elisha sighed. 'That doesn't make it any easier.'

'I guess not.'

Elisha put on her gown and face mask. After racing to get to the hospital, she scarcely dared to follow Zac into the unit. She froze at the entrance, confronted by a wall of cardiac monitors, all bleeping like mad. Was that really her best friend on the bed, pale and wasted, with tubes in her mouth and nose? Elisha had only seen one person that sick before. And that was her mother.

'Come and sit beside her,' Zac said. 'Talk to her. Remember, we're relying on you.'

Elisha fought the urge to run. She couldn't sit and watch someone else she loved die. Besides, nothing she could do would make any difference to Rajani.

Zac pulled up a chair for her. 'Sis, please.'

Elisha sat down and rested her hand on Rajani's heavily bandaged arm. What could she say? Elisha cleared her throat and began to ramble. 'You made life bearable when we first arrived in India. I never wanted to leave Australia, and I was anti-everything. Remember? No discos, no parties, no cinema. Church and Sunday school. I'd have gone mad if it wasn't for you. We had fun teaching the kids how to paint, didn't we? I'll never forget that beautiful dress you wore for the parade on Orissa Day. That was when you took me to see Krishna.'

Did Rajani stir when Elisha mentioned Krishna's name? Or was it just Elisha's imagination?

The nurse came in to take Rajani's observations. Elisha stepped out of the unit to get a glass of water. She sat down beside her father, who was still reading in the reception area.

'I will sit with Rajani for a few minutes and pray for her,' he said. 'Then I'm going back to Madhapur.' He stood up and put on a gown. 'You don't know how much it means to me—all of us—that you're here.'

Elisha kept talking to Rajani throughout the night, long after her father had left, and Zac had fallen asleep. The erratic trace on Rajani's cardiac monitor seemed to settle when Elisha recalled some of the fun they'd had together.

'Remember the Sunday you got the hymns mixed up? You gave Mira the organist the wrong hymn numbers. Everyone started singing the wrong words to the wrong tune.'

Rajani opened her eyes for a moment.

'It cracked me up,' Elisha continued. 'I hadn't laughed so much since the time my dad forgot to take his glasses to church and had to make up the sermon as he went along.'

Rajani raised her head and pulled the tube out of her mouth. 'Where am I? What's happened to me?' She gazed at the bank of cardiac monitors and then at Elisha. 'What are you doing here?'

Elisha stroked Rajani's hand. 'You're in hospital at Baripada, and I'm here because I care about you.'

Rajani stared into Elisha's eyes. 'You've come to say goodbye, haven't you? Because I'm going to die, aren't I?'

Elisha shook her head. 'Don't talk like that.'

Rajani sank back on her pillow and closed her eyes again.

Elisha bit her tongue. 'They just need to find the right antibiotic. Then you'll be okay. I promise.'

But she couldn't promise. Why had she just said that? There was a critical shortage of antibiotics throughout Orissa. What if Rajani didn't make it? Elisha couldn't bear to think about it and held on to Rajani's tiny hand.

Rajani stirred again. 'What'll happen to the lepers when I'm gone? Who'll take care of them?'

'I will,' Elisha said. 'I'm a qualified nurse now.' She pointed to Zac, who was still sound asleep on a chair. 'And Zac's promised to help.'

Rajani drifted in and out of a coma for the rest of the night. Elisha didn't leave her bedside and tried to ignore the erratic tracings on the cardiac monitor.

'You're the best friend I've ever had,' Elisha said, holding Rajani in her arms. 'Don't leave me.'

'Best friends forever.' Rajani gasped for air, struggling to get the words out. 'Except—maybe forever isn't really forever. Krishna said I'm an old soul. It looks like I'm about to start a new life.'

Tears ran down Elisha's cheeks. 'Krishna told me I have a long shadow. So I have years ahead of me. How can I bear them without you?'

CHAPTER SIXTEEN

Baripada, India, September 1992

Theo

The volunteer's welcoming smile at Baripada Railway Station almost made up for the exhaustion I felt after travelling thirty plus hours. An eager young man in his early twenties, Devender shook my hand vigorously and helped unload my trunks from the train.

'I've only got a small van from the mission,' he said. 'I hope we can fit everything in. I've never seen a doctor with so much luggage.'

'I come well prepared,' I said. 'I've brought some medical supplies from home.'

Devender looked more worried than pleased.

'Medical supplies?' he said. 'Where did they come from? I hope you haven't been up to your old tricks, Dr Malone.'

Extraordinary—halfway around the globe and they'd still heard about my brush with the authorities.

'Gee, news travels fast,' I said. 'Even to the remotest corner of the world.'

'You got half an inch in *The Times of India*,' Devender said. 'But only a couple of lines in the *Baripada Gazette*.'

'What did they say about me?' I asked.

'Mostly negative stuff,' Devender replied, 'about white men thinking they have all the answers to Third World problems.'

'I can understand that,' I said. 'I hope you don't think I've come to—'

Devender interrupted me. 'Of course not. None of us believe what we read in the newspapers.'

As we loaded the last of my suitcases into the back of the van, I saw a sadness in Devender's eyes that I hadn't noticed before.

'I hope they're full of antibiotics,' he said, 'because we need them.'

'Take a look,' I replied.

'Wow!' Devender's eyes gleamed at the vast array of ampoules and medicine bottles, which sparkled in the afternoon sun. 'Where did you get these? Are they all genuine?'

I grinned. 'Don't worry. They're all above board and not past their expiry date. I've been fundraising for months.'

Devender picked up a vial. 'Thank God for that. We've got a very sick girl in intensive care at Baripada. Rajani. She's a lovely kid. Nothing the doctors here have tried has worked. Perhaps these might help.'

'Take me to her,' I said. 'Sounds like there's no time to lose. Tell me about her condition on the way.'

We jumped into the van, and Devender went through Rajani's history, struggling to make himself heard above the blazing horns as we negotiated the Baripada traffic.

'She just had a cold to start with,' Devender said. 'Next thing we knew, she was in hospital with pneumonia. Now she's on a machine to help her breathe.' He stared at me while we stopped at some traffic lights. 'You're going to make her better, with your experience and all those fancy medicines.'

I couldn't meet his eyes. He obviously hadn't heard about Saleh and my exploits in Uganda.

'My drugs aren't a miracle cure,' I said. 'But I promise you, I'll do my very best for Rajani.'

The stench of disease and decay hit me as we entered the charity hospital at Baripada. The putrid atmosphere at Kalanjala Hospital had been overpowering, but this was worse. Devender hurried us through the throng of waiting patients. It seemed almost impossible, but there were even more makeshift beds in the corridors than at Kalanjala.

Rajani was on a ventilator in intensive care. I stared at her through the cubicle window. She had that look of death about her I'd seen so often in Uganda. A Caucasian girl sat at the bedside, clinging to Rajani's hand.

'That's Elisha, Rajani's friend,' Devender said as we gowned up. 'Elisha and her brother, Isaac, have been taking turns to keep vigil at Rajani's bed all the time she's been in intensive care.'

    David Whittet

Elisha looked up as Devender led me to Rajani's bedside.

'Meet Dr Malone,' Devender said to Elisha. 'He's our new doctor. I've just picked him up from the railway station, and he's got a truckload of antibiotics.'

Elisha looked up at me. 'You're a doctor?' she said. 'And you've got new antibiotics?'

Her imploring eyes reminded me of Saleh's mother, Namazzi.

I took a deep breath. 'Yes, I've brought antibiotics, but—'

'Say there's something you can do for her,' Elisha pleaded. 'Please.'

I reached for the stethoscope hanging at the end of the bed. 'I need to examine Rajani first, then we'll have a talk.' My heart pounded as I listened to Rajani's chest. 'She's got a pneumothorax—'

'A pneumothorax?' Elisha clutched the bedrail. 'That's a collapsed lung, isn't it? We covered it in my nursing training.'

'You're a nurse?' I said. 'Then you'll know that sometimes happens when a patient is on a ventilator. We need to re-inflate her lung.'

I was about to press the call button at the end of the bed when the intensive care nurse came in to do Rajani's observations.

'Nurse—' I glanced at her name badge '—Nurse Verma, I'm worried about Rajani.'

'Pulse ninety-six, blood pressure one-forty over seventy.' Unperturbed, Nurse Verma continued recording the numbers on the chart. She looked at me when she'd finished. 'Rajani is stable.'

'Stable?' I said. 'She's got a pneumothorax, and we need to act fast. Who's the doctor in charge?'

'Dr Suresh is the registrar,' Nurse Verma replied.

'You need to fetch him now,' I said.

'He's in theatre. Assisting the consultant, Dr Prabhakar, with a bronchoscopy.'

Damn. 'Call them,' I said. 'Tell them I'm the new Madhapur doctor, and I've diagnosed a tension pneumothorax. This is urgent.' As if to echo my words, the buzzer on Rajani's cardiac monitor started bleeping. 'She's gone into tachycardia. Quick, one of them needs to get here fast.'

I checked Rajani's heart rate while Nurse Verma phoned the doctors.

A hundred and sixty beats per minute and thready, and Rajani's face had gone that awful purple colour that inevitably precedes—

'Neither of them can leave theatre,' Nurse Verma said, interrupting my thought process. 'The other doctors are all tied up too. Dr Suresh says as you're a doctor, you'll have to do it yourself.'

I gulped. 'I'm not sure I can.'

Elisha turned to face me. Her eyes were still pleading.

'You can do it,' she said. 'I've just lost my mother. I can't lose my best friend as well.'

Why did I always land in trouble wherever I went? I'd no experience with chest decompression. What if I failed?

'Get me a sixteen-gauge needle,' I said to Nurse Verma, 'and a tube thoracostomy set.'

Quickly scrubbing up and donning a gown and gloves, I palpated Rajani's chest to find the second intercostal space. Nurse Verma disinfected Rajani's skin and handed me the needle. Had she noticed my hand was trembling? Elisha and Devender were watching me like hawks, too. Did any of them realise I was absolutely terrified?

Rajani was so thin and emaciated. Her ribs stuck out, and it was easy to identify the point where I had to go in. I held the needle in position and took a deep breath.

A mental image flashed through my mind. Saleh's dying gasp.

You will never make a doctor. Would Professor Rutherford haunt me for the rest of my life?

Pull yourself together. You can do this. It's a straightforward textbook procedure.

I plunged the needle into Rajani's chest. The gush of air that came out was the most welcome sound I had ever heard. It meant success.

Elisha must have seen the relief on my face. 'You've done it, Doctor!' She let out a huge breath, just as Namazzi had done after Saleh's lumbar puncture. 'Thank you, from the bottom of my heart.'

I think she'd have hugged me if Nurse Verma hadn't stopped her from touching my surgical gown.

'We're not there yet,' I said. 'We can't relax until we've got the chest tube in place.'

I'd just made the incision to introduce the drain when I heard voices in the corridor.

'That'll be Dr Suresh and Dr Prabhakar,' Nurse Verma said. 'They must have finished in theatre.'

I listened to their conversation while inserting the tube into Rajani's chest. My hands shook again.

'It pisses me off'—I guessed that was the consultant speaking—'foreign doctors marching into our hospitals as if they owned them. How dare he carry out procedures on our patients?'

'I told him to'—that must have been the registrar—'there was no choice. It was an emergency, and he's a qualified doctor—'

And she was going to die. I finished the sentence for him in my mind.

I'd got the tube in place and sealed when the door burst open, and the two doctors came in.

'He's saved her life,' Elisha said.

Dr Suresh stepped forward. 'She's certainly a much better colour than I've seen her.' Rajani opened her eyes as he listened to her chest. 'Well done, Dr … um …'

'Dr Malone,' I said. 'Call me Theo.'

'Well, Theo,' Dr Suresh said. 'I believe you *have* saved her life.'

This time Nurse Verma couldn't stop Elisha from hugging me. Dr Prabhakar left the room without a word.

Dr Suresh stayed behind. 'The old grump's worried you're going to blame our ventilator for giving her the pneumothorax.'

'It's an unavoidable complication of ventilation,' I said. 'I've seen it happen in hospitals in New Zealand. Now, we must get Rajani on some IV antibiotics.'

Dr Suresh looked down at his feet. 'Sputum cultures showed an MRSA. Vancomycin is the only hope. And we haven't got any.'

'I've got vancomycin in my trunk,' I said. 'Come on, Dev. Let's get it.'

Vancomycin. Another mental image of Saleh. Surely history wouldn't repeat itself?

Devender unlocked the van, and I rifled through my case to find the vancomycin ampoules. *These drugs will work. They're within the expiry date, and there's nothing wrong with them.* I kept repeating the words to myself as we went back through the corridors to intensive care.

Dr Suresh injected the antibiotic into Rajani's IV line. 'She's looking better already.' He turned to me. 'Best not tell Prabhakar we've used your drugs. I'll say we got it from a supplier in Calcutta.'

'I have to tell Zac,' Elisha said. 'He's not coming in till six. I can't wait till then. Can you pick him up, Dev?'

'I ought to get Theo to the mission first,' Devender said. 'He looks exhausted.'

'It won't take long,' Elisha said. 'Twenty minutes tops.'

I'd been living on adrenaline for the past few hours, and with the drama over, I was ready to collapse. But how could I resist Elisha's beseeching eyes?

'It's okay,' I said. 'I can keep going a bit longer. Let's go and fetch Zac.'

Elisha kissed me on the cheek. 'Thank you. I won't forget this.'

Devender drove us through the teeming streets of downtown Baripada. Fruit and vegetable stalls lined the streets, while merchants, shoeshiners, and barbers all vied for space and trade. All of life was here, but somehow, I couldn't take my eyes off Elisha.

'Zac's been out of his mind with worry,' she said. 'He's been staying at this hostel all the time Rajani's been in hospital. I don't know what he'll do if she …' Elisha broke off and brushed away a tear. 'I don't know what I'll do either.'

The hostel was dark and barren, just like the student accommodation back home in Dunedin. Coming in from the bright sunlight made it feel even dingier.

Elisha hammered on Zac's door. 'Open up! Rajani's going to be okay!'

My heart missed a beat. What if Rajani relapsed? It was still early days. Before I could say anything, Zac flung the door open. 'She is?'

'She had a collapsed lung,' Elisha said. 'That's why she wasn't getting better.'

Zac shook his head. 'A collapsed lung? Then she won't be okay.'

'She will.' Elisha dragged me into the room. 'This brilliant doctor put a drain in her chest and saved her life.'

 David Whittet

Zac's eyes lit up the room. 'Hallelujah!'

'Hold on,' I said. 'She's still critical.'

'But she's got a fighting chance now,' Zac said.

'And Rajani's a fighter,' Elisha added.

Zac stumbled towards me. What was wrong with his knee? Before I could make a spot diagnosis, he gave me a hug like none other. 'God bless you,' he said. 'You're a friend for life.'

'More than just a friend,' Elisha added. 'He's our saviour!'

'Give the poor man a break,' Devender said. 'He's blushing. And I bet he saves lives every day of the week.'

'No.' My cheeks *were* burning. 'I just carried out a procedure any doctor could do.'

'But they didn't do it,' Elisha said, 'and you did.'

'We must get going,' Devender said. 'Get your things together, Zac, and I'll take you and Elisha to the hospital. Then I really must get Theo to his house in Madhapur. I don't know how he can keep his eyes open.'

'I do need some sleep,' I admitted. 'It's been one extraordinary day.'

I couldn't make Elisha and Zac out. An Australian girl and an Indian boy—were they half-brother and half-sister? They squabbled all the way back to the hospital about the most trivial things—football, movies and suchlike—but behind the banter, I could feel the warmth and attachment between them. As an only child, I'd often wondered what it would be like to have a brother or sister. Whatever their birth relationship, Elisha and Zac were closer than any other siblings I'd met. And the joy in their faces when we got back to the hospital and saw Rajani sitting up in bed, made me glad I'd come to India.

It was dark when we finally got away from the hospital, and then only after more hugs and a promise to return the next day to check on Rajani.

'Are all your entrances as dramatic as this?' Devender asked as we set off for Madhapur. 'Your feet have hardly touched the ground, and you're a hero already.'

'Dr Prabhakar didn't think so,' I replied. 'Did you see the way he looked at me?'

'Don't take any notice of Prabhakar,' Devender said. 'It wasn't personal. All the consultants here fiercely protect their territory.'

'I can see how they feel,' I said. 'White doctors invading their turf.'

'It's not just because you're white,' Devender said. 'They've had it in for all the doctors we've had at the mission. Indians and foreigners.'

'Then they must doubly hate me,' I said. 'A white man *and* working for the mission.'

'Don't take it to heart,' Devender said.

'I won't,' I replied with a grin. 'I'm used to it. I have a knack for upsetting people wherever I work.'

Devender swerved to miss an ox on the road. 'I hope you're not going to stir up trouble at the mission.'

I laughed. 'Tell me about Isaac and Elisha. Are they really brother and sister?'

'Elisha is our pastor's daughter. Zac is her adopted brother. Pastor Martin rescued him when his family all died from malaria.'

'Your pastor must be one in a million.'

Devender smiled. 'He is.'

'What's wrong with Zac's knee?' I asked.

'He got hit by a cricket ball,' Devender said. 'It should have been a simple operation to fix it. But the wound turned septic. That happens all the time out here.'

'Poor kid. He's got a dreadful limp.'

'He was hoping to be an ace footballer,' Devender said. 'Now he wants to be a movie director.'

So that's what they were arguing about on the way to the hospital.

'Elisha said she'd just lost her mother,' I said. 'What happened?'

Devender pulled the van to the side of the road. There were tears in his eyes as he told me about Melissa's needle-stick injury and death from AIDS. 'None of us have got over it,' he said. 'I don't think we ever will.'

'I'm amazed your pastor stayed on,' I said. 'How do you carry on after something like that?'

'Pastor Martin's an extraordinary man,' Devender replied. 'We just have to believe God has some higher purpose.'

David Whittet

I stared at Devender. 'I'm not sure I could do that.'

Devender restarted the engine, and we continued the drive to Madhapur. 'Elisha broke down after her mother died. She returned to Australia and only came back here because Rajani's sick.'

I bit my lip. 'Then we've got to make sure Rajani gets better.'

'She will,' Devender said. 'With your medicine and God's help.'

But would she? Antibiotics had let me down before. Please, not another tragedy like Saleh. I'd hardly ever prayed before, but that night I did. 'Please, God. If you're there, and if you're listening, let Rajani live.'

I awoke with a start the next morning when Devender brought me a cup of chai.

'Once you're up and dressed,' he said, 'I'll take you to meet the team at the field hospital.'

I rubbed the sleep out of my eyes. 'I want to go back to Baripada and see how Rajani's doing. The antibiotics should be kicking in by now.'

'I'll drive you over,' Devender said. 'But have breakfast with Pastor Martin and the crew first.'

'Okay.'

I couldn't work out why I was so nervous about meeting Pastor Martin, but I was. What did you say to a man who'd just lost his wife in such tragic circumstances but still believed it was God's will?

'Dr Malone!' The pastor shook my hand vigorously. 'We're so happy you've come to join us.'

'I'm glad to be here,' I said. 'Call me Theo, please.'

'And I'm Wesley,' he said. 'Named after the great evangelist. Won't you have some breakfast while we bring you up to speed on the work we're doing here?'

Over a spread of roti, bhaji and pakora—so much tastier than Indian food back home—plus an endless supply of chai, Wesley told me about the outreach programme to promote health education in the community. I could tell he was incredibly proud of their work at the leper colony.

'Isaac and Rajani had just finished making a film about the lepers when she got sick,' he said. 'They called it *House of Hope*.'

There was kindness in his eyes, but sadness too. And an unexpected vulnerability. Especially when he talked about Elisha. He grabbed my hand as we got up from the table.

'Elisha's thinking about staying on as a nurse in the field hospital. Can you talk to her, Theo? Tell her how much she's needed. I couldn't bear to lose her again.'

'I'm not sure she'll listen to me,' I said. 'We only met yesterday.'

Wesley smiled. 'Devender says there was a definite spark between you.'

'I'm not sure about that ...'

Devender returned after taking a phone call. 'And you've saved her best friend's life. I've just heard from the hospital. Rajani's made a miraculous recovery overnight.'

Was Rajani really better? I didn't have time to think on the drive to Baripada. Devender invited Rajani's great-aunt Nisha to come with us to the hospital. Nisha spent the entire journey urging me to persuade Elisha to stay on.

'She's such a lovely girl,' Nisha repeated, time after time. 'And so good for my Rajani.'

Nisha's hands shook as we donned our gowns and face masks at the intensive care unit.

'Here, let me help you,' I said, determined not to let her see that my palms were sweating. 'Don't worry. Everything's going to be fine.' I glanced up and saw Rajani through the glass window. 'Look! Rajani's off the ventilator.'

'Thank God!' Nisha said. 'Our prayers have been answered!'

We stood for a moment and watched Elisha sponge Rajani's hair.

'See what I mean?' Nisha said. 'Elisha's a born nurse. She *has* to stay.'

My stomach fluttered as Elisha gently brushed Rajani's hair. Elisha had Kizza's loving eyes—and perhaps a hint of Marian's subterfuge. I knew then she *would* make a fantastic nurse.

Our eyes met through the window, and Elisha beckoned us into the unit.

'Theo! Nisha!' Elisha beamed at us both.

Nisha put her arms around Rajani. 'My darling. I never thought I'd see you again.'

		David Whittet

'It's a miracle, isn't it?' Elisha said. 'How can we ever thank Theo for this?'

'There is something you could do,' I said.

Elisha waved a hand. 'Anything.'

I took a deep breath. 'Your dad wants you to stay and work for the mission. And so do I.'

Elisha turned from me to Nisha. 'Have you two been ganging up on me?'

'We all want you to stay,' Nisha said. 'You told me you took up nursing to honour your mother. Staying on here would be a fitting tribute to both your mother and to Rajani's miraculous recovery.'

'Too right.' Rajani raised her head from the pillow and eyed Elisha. 'No way are you leaving me again.'

Elisha sighed and squeezed Rajani's hand. 'Looks like I'm stuck here.'

Nisha and I stepped out of the unit when Zac arrived. His deep brown eyes welled up when Elisha told him she'd decided to stay on in India. And I got another bear hug when Dr Suresh announced Rajani would soon be out of intensive care and onto the ward.

Devender drove Nisha and me back to Madhapur.

'So the pair of you talked Elisha into staying,' Devender said. 'How did you do it?'

I shrugged. 'I think she'd already decided.'

'It broke Rajani's heart when Elisha went back to Australia,' Nisha said. 'Mine too. But to see the two of them together today! Rajani's face was a picture when Elisha agreed to stay. I wish I had a camera.'

'Zac looked stoked too,' I said. 'He was almost in tears.'

'Pastor Martin will be thrilled as well,' Devender added. 'So, Theo, you and Elisha will work together at the field hospital. We'll expect great things from both of you.'

Working with Elisha. Why did my heart rate quicken at the thought? And why couldn't I get Elisha out of my mind?

CHAPTER SEVENTEEN

Diwali. The Festival of Lights. I wasn't sure what to expect. Everyone in Madhapur had been talking about it for the past few weeks. Occupational therapy sessions at the field hospital had never been busier, with all the patients making decorations.

Elisha knelt beside an older man with a wheezy chest. 'You can do this, Mr Shah,' she said, guiding his fingers to mould a small clay pot. 'There, that's beautiful. All we have to do now is persuade the doctor to let you out of hospital for the celebrations.' Elisha stood up and eyed me. 'Well, Theo. What about it?'

'I'm not sure,' I said. 'Mr Shah has emphysema.'

'Devender's offered to look after him,' Elisha said, 'and a night at Diwali will do him far more good than being cooped up in here.'

One look at Mr Shah's pleading eyes and I knew she was right. 'Okay,' I said. 'But make sure Devender knows how to help Mr Shah use his inhalers, and he has to come back to the hospital straight away if there are any problems.'

My clinic was almost empty in the lead up to the festival. Everyone was far too busy to visit the doctor. I watched the townsfolk deck their houses with coloured fairy lights and line the streets with garlands. What were the women doing on the tarmac in the middle of town? I wondered.

'We're making a mosaic,' Nisha told me. 'It's called a rangoli.'

They worked on it for days, using coloured sand, rice and rose petals.

'We'll decorate it with candles on the night,' Nisha said. 'It'll look spectacular.'

It did. The rush of energy when I stepped out on the street was overwhelming. Fireworks went off everywhere. Children with sparklers. The women carried brass pots wafting a tantalising, spicy aroma and arranged them around the mosaic. Everyone in the village had contributed at least one dish for the gigantic feast.

Elisha arrived with some helpers from the field hospital, all of them carrying small clay lamps. 'Make room for these!'

I could scarcely believe my eyes. Elisha had worked around the clock for weeks in occupational therapy, and the exquisite collection of lamps was extraordinary.

'Did the patients make all of them?' I asked.

'Sure did,' Elisha said, directing the helpers to place a lamp between each of the brass pots. 'They're called diyas.'

Roman candles filled the air with a thrilling blaze of light and colour while rockets soared in the sky.

'Wow!' I staggered to avoid a firecracker that danced at our feet. 'We've nothing like this in New Zealand.'

Elisha laughed. 'Nor do we. Australia Day could do with livening up.'

Rajani rolled up with Zac and gave Elisha a playful dig in the ribs.

'I don't believe it,' Rajani said. 'You've just admitted we've got something in India that's better than in Australia.'

'Not fair,' Elisha shot back. 'I loved Orissa Day. Remember?'

We squatted on the ground to eat the magnificent dinner, carefully avoiding the firecrackers that were still everywhere.

'I'm so glad I got to be here,' Rajani said.

'You nearly didn't make it,' Zac said.

'I know.' Rajani glanced around at the crowd. 'I love Diwali.'

Zac gave her a mischievous grin. 'Even though it's a Hindu celebration?'

'Diwali is for everyone,' Rajani said. 'It represents the victory of light over darkness and the triumph of good over evil.'

'And knowledge over ignorance,' Elisha added. 'Isn't that what Krishna told us?'

Rajani nodded.

'It's time I got you home,' Zac said to Rajani. 'You look tired.'

Rajani took a last mouthful of mithai, an Indian sweet. 'Spoilsport.'

'Your great-aunt wanted you to stay in bed,' Zac said. 'You've no idea the fight I had to bring you here.'

Rajani stood up and brushed the crumbs off her sari. 'Okay, I'm coming.'

It was only two months since I'd arrived in India and put that drain in Rajani's chest. That was just the beginning. Mike Bailey at Kiwi Doctors for Change had told me Madhapur would be a challenge, and he wasn't kidding. The under-resourced field hospital at Madhapur made the war on infectious diseases even more formidable than it was at Kalanjala Hospital. An influenza outbreak left many of the old and debilitated with pneumonia, and my trunkful of antibiotics was almost empty. What would I do when they ran out?

I watched Zac lead Rajani away through the crowd. Like everyone else, Rajani had put on her best traditional clothes for the occasion. Although still thin and pale, her recovery had been remarkable. Within weeks, she was back helping at the school. Perhaps it really was a miracle.

Elisha and I wandered along the main street, continually side-stepping over the candles that carpeted the ground.

'Rajani's amazing, isn't she?' I said. 'I can't believe how quickly she's got back on her feet.'

Elisha put an arm over my shoulder. 'Thanks to you.'

'And thanks to a lot of generous Kiwis who helped me raise the money for the medicines,' I said. 'She'd have died without the antibiotics.'

Elisha shuddered. 'I know. I'd hate to see anyone else suffer like Rajani did.'

'We can't let it happen to anyone else.'

'How can we stop it?' Elisha said. 'You told me last week your drugs are almost gone. You can't keep running back to New Zealand for help.'

'No.' I stopped walking and turned to face Elisha. 'But we could fundraise here. Take today, for instance. Such an incredible community atmosphere. We should organise events, getting local businesses on board and asking for donations.'

'That won't be as easy as you think,' Elisha said. 'For a start, nobody here has any money. And forget about local companies. They're in survival mode.'

I looked around. People were still feasting. The sky was ablaze as fireworks continued into the night. 'So who's paying for all this?'

'The local authority supports Diwali,' Elisha said. 'But they won't help

David Whittet

you. In fact, you need to be careful. Some people here get furious about outsiders meddling in their affairs.'

'Yes, Dev warned me about that,' I said. 'But then, I'm used to making enemies.'

I told Elisha how my previous attempt to get essential drugs to take overseas landed me on prime-time television to defend myself.

Elisha laughed. 'It sounds like the kind of crazy thing my father would do. He's always getting into trouble.'

'Did I do right?' I asked.

'You did right,' Elisha said with a sigh. 'So you've been on TV. Zac was on the telly as well when he first came to Australia. That was a hoot. Now that he can't play football, he wants to be a film director.'

'Yes. I heard Zac helped Rajani make a film about the leper colony.'

'They did. And believe it or not, it was really professional.'

I gave Elisha a gentle nudge. 'Don't run your brother down. He could be useful to us if we need someone to make the campaign videos.'

The aromatic smell of ghee filled the air as the diyas burnt out, and I walked Elisha home.

'I'm with you,' Elisha said. 'I'll talk to Zac. He'll be thrilled at the opportunity.'

There was a warmth in Elisha's eyes as we said goodnight. Did she feel the same way about me as I felt about her?

A measles epidemic swept through the community shortly after the Diwali celebrations. Children piled into the waiting room at the field hospital, each covered in a fiery red rash. I made a mental tally of the numbers and rushed into the ward to find Elisha.

'There are at least a dozen kids needing admission,' I said. 'All with measles.'

'We've no more beds,' Elisha said. 'And even if we had, we don't want to bring infectious children in here.'

'No.' I glanced around the ward at the sick and debilitated patients. 'We need an isolation unit. Isn't there a Medical Officer of Health we can go to for help?'

'That's Dr Reddy,' Elisha said. 'My father says he's—'

'We need to call him straight away,' I interrupted. 'There's no time to lose.'

Arjun Basar, our most senior doctor at the field hospital, walked past us. 'Good luck with that. In the twenty years I've been here, I've only seen him a couple of times.'

I shook my head. 'Back home, measles is a notifiable disease.'

Elisha took my arm. She must have realised I was about to explode. 'I'll ask my father if we can use the church as a makeshift isolation unit.'

Faraj, a medical student on attachment to us from Calcutta, burst into the ward. 'Come quick, Theo! One of the kids … I think he's going to …'

I didn't need Faraj to finish the sentence. A sudden sense of dread overwhelmed me the moment I took little Nadim from his mother's arms. The four-year-old was burning up and fighting for breath.

'Fetch me a paediatric ET tube,' I shouted. 'And call an ambulance. We need to get him to intensive care at Baripada.'

Tears streamed down the mother's face. 'He's going to be alright, isn't he?'

Was he? Before I could get the tube into his airway, Nadim convulsed and gave a last gasp. His body went limp and that awful blue colour I'd seen before in Uganda.

'I'm so sorry, Mrs Gupta,' I stammered. 'He's gone.'

The anguish on the mother's face took me straight back to Kalanjala Hospital and Saleh. What could I say to her? I wanted to weep, too.

Elisha took Mrs Gupta aside and comforted her with the usual platitudes about how we'd done our best to stop the spread of measles. But we hadn't. We should have acted faster, closed the school, and isolated the kids at the first sign of the outbreak. A volunteer brought Mrs Gupta a cup of chai. Tea, the women's answer to all Madhapur's ills. I had a different solution. Immunisation was the only way to prevent this disaster from happening again.

Three weeks on from Nadim's death, and the rest of the children had recovered. The church had proved a surprisingly functional isolation unit.

I sat down on a pew next to Elisha after we'd sent the last child home.

 David Whittet

'Nadim didn't need to die,' I said. 'And he wouldn't have if we'd done things better and closed the school earlier.'

'That wasn't our call,' Elisha said. 'Stop blaming yourself. It wasn't your fault.'

My eyes met Elisha's. 'Nadim's death shouldn't be in vain. I won't let it. We need to campaign for an immunisation programme.'

'I told you fundraising's a non-starter out here,' Elisha said. 'Nobody has two rupees to rub together.'

Faraj had been clearing up some of the makeshift beds in the vestry and came over. 'My father works for a pharmaceutical company. I bet he could get us a good deal on vaccines.'

'That's fantastic!' I jumped up and patted Faraj on the back. 'We're a step closer already.'

'Be careful,' Elisha said. 'People around here don't trust pharmaceutical companies. You should talk to Harish.'

I raised my eyebrows. 'If I must.' Harish was a young doctor from Kerala. I'd no idea why he came to work with us. He acted like he knew it all and disparaged everything we did. I sat down next to Elisha again. 'We'll have a staff meeting after tomorrow's ward round.'

News of the meeting met with groans from everyone.

'Surely you don't need me,' Harish moaned. 'I'm studying for a fellowship exam.'

'You must come,' I said. 'We need your input.'

'Don't worry,' Elisha added. 'There'll be food.'

'I'll be late,' Arjun Basar said, 'and if there's spare cash floating around, how about a new X-ray machine?'

Give me strength! Did none of them care that an innocent child had lost his life?

'Thank you for coming,' Elisha said as the team drifted into the staff room after the ward round. 'Help yourself to the food.'

Devender wheeled in a trolley with platefuls of samosas, bargees and pakoras. An orderly followed with an urn of chai.

'Good luck,' Elisha whispered in my ear.

'I'll need it,' I whispered back.

'You'll be fine,' Elisha said.

'Of course he will,' Faraj said, sitting down beside us. 'I called my father last night, and he's keen to help.'

The nurses grabbed some food and squatted on the floor. Harish stood at the back with his arms crossed.

'This has been a stressful time for us all,' I said. 'Thank you all for the work you've done to see us through this epidemic. It's to your credit that we only lost one life.'

Arjun slipped in. 'Apologies. I hope I'm not too late for the food.'

I cleared my throat and continued, 'But one life lost is one too many. Nadim's death is a stark reminder of the need for an effective immunisation programme in our community. I propose we start a fund to buy vaccines and call it the Nadim Gupta Trust.'

Harish shook his head. 'You'll never get it past the local authorities. Prasad's dead against outsiders coming in and vaccinating children on his patch.'

Who the hell was Prasad? Before I could get a word in, Prem, a local woman and a volunteer nurse with the mission, took over.

'Harish's right,' she said. 'I went to one of Mr Prasad's rallies before the last election. He went on about white Christians poisoning our children. Giving them drugs they wouldn't give to their own children.'

'That's nonsense,' I said. 'All kids in New Zealand get the measles vaccine.'

Elisha nudged me. 'Calm down.'

I took a deep breath. 'Who is Prasad, anyway? I thought Dr Reddy was the Medical Officer of Health for the district.'

'He is,' Harish said. 'Prasad's the District Collector.'

'The *what*?' I asked.

'The local government administrator,' Harish explained. 'You don't understand politics out here like we do.'

Damn right. Part of me wanted to go straight back to New Zealand.

'Hold on,' Faraj said. 'These aren't vaccines made overseas. They're made by an Indian firm. My father's company.'

 David Whittet

'Yes,' Harish shot back. 'A multinational corporation with headquarters in Switzerland and owned by white Christians.'

The bastard was enjoying this. I glared at Harish. 'Whose side are you on?'

'I'm just telling you how it is,' Harish said. 'No good getting the vaccines then not being able to use them.'

'I still say the money would be better spent on a new X-ray machine,' Arjun said.

Arjun and his bloody X-ray machine. I glanced at Elisha and took another deep breath.

'X-rays don't save lives,' I said. 'Vaccines do. We're lucky we only lost one life in this outbreak. We had a measles epidemic in New Zealand a couple of years back. Hundreds of children died, all because some mothers wouldn't immunise their children.'

'We've lost far too many children to measles in Australia, as well,' Elisha said. 'The next outbreak could be a whole lot worse. Think about it. That's all we ask.'

Everyone got up and put their cup and plates back on the trolley. Would they think about it? And if they did, would it do any good?

Elisha followed me into my office.

'That was a waste of time,' I said, slumping into my chair. 'Trust Harish to sabotage our plans.'

Elisha sat on the edge of my desk. 'That's not fair. We need someone on the team who's politically savvy.' She put a hand on my arm. 'Get Harish on side, and he'll be our strongest ally.'

I looked up at her. 'You really think so?'

'I do,' Elisha said, picking up a pen and a notepad from my desk. 'Enough talk. Let's make plans.'

Over the next few months, we pursued every conceivable avenue to get the money. We wrote begging letters to anyone we thought would take any notice. Elisha badgered her father's contacts at the mission headquarters while Rajani recorded an advert that went out on local radio. Zac made a short video, which we distributed to the local Rotary Club and other charities. By mid-March, with a generous price reduction from Faraj's father, we had enough cash to buy the vaccines.

Harish shook my hand when the delivery truck arrived. 'You don't give up, do you?' he said. 'I never thought you'd do it.'

'I knew we would,' Elisha said, 'with Theo leading us.'

She kissed me on the cheek. Was it just professional solidarity, or did her feelings run deeper? Should I kiss her back? Or hug her? Too late. Her father arrived to bless the vaccines.

'Splendid work, Theo,' he said. 'You and Elisha make a great team.'

Had he seen Elisha kiss me? How would he feel if we were more than professional colleagues?

Pull yourself together. There's work to be done.

'We need to get the vaccines in the fridge,' I said. 'We can't afford to break the cold chain.'

'Here, let me help you,' Harish said.

An army of volunteers from the mission joined us to load the precious vaccines into the huge refrigerator we'd bought for the field hospital.

'Think how many lives these are going to save,' I said when the last box was safely in the fridge. 'I can't wait to get started jabbing the kids.'

'Me too,' Elisha said. 'This is so exciting.'

'Hold on,' Harish said. 'We need to set up a meeting with Dr Reddy. Get his approval.'

'What?' I tapped my fingers on the fridge door. 'You mean we have to put the children's lives on hold?'

Harish eyed me. 'Remember what I told you? We need to do this right.'

'Yes, but …'

'Don't worry,' Harish said. 'I'll tell you what to say.'

Elisha put a hand on my shoulder. 'Harish is right. We've put so much into this. What's another couple of days?'

A couple of days? I groaned. Knowing Indian red tape, the vaccines would be past their expiry date before we got permission.

It was a fortnight before we heard from Dr Reddy. All that time, the vaccines waited idly in the fridge. It made my blood boil. How many kids could we

David Whittet

have immunised while we hung around? Two hundred, at least.

'About bloody time,' I said when the summons to the local government office eventually arrived.

'Remember what I told you,' Harish urged as Elisha and I set off. 'Stay calm. Make it sound like it was their idea. And whatever you do, don't start lecturing them.'

'I'll make sure he doesn't,' Elisha said.

The government offices were the most palatial buildings in the district. Dr Reddy sat behind an enormous mahogany desk, surrounded by an entourage of officials. The esteemed Medical Officer of Health was a short, stocky man with a moustache that reminded me of Professor Rutherford.

Dr Reddy got up and shook my hand. 'Pleased to meet you, Dr Malone. You too, Miss Martin. I've heard good things about what you've been doing for Madhapur.'

My heart thumped as he indicated we should sit on the other side of the table. The whir of the overhead fan broke the uncomfortable silence while they all waited for my reply.

'Thank you, sir,' I said. 'We're passionate about making a difference to your community.'

'Of course,' Dr Reddy began, 'we're all delighted that you care so much about our people, but—'

One of the public servants finished the sentence. 'We were wondering why you're not putting your energy into the healthcare issues back home in New Zealand. Don't you care about the kids in your own country?'

Harish had warned me they'd bring this up. I caught Elisha's eye. *Don't worry. I won't lose my cool.*

'I love my country,' I said. 'New Zealand is my home, and yes, we have our own health problems and inequalities back home.'

Dr Reddy scratched his moustache. 'So why don't you go back and fix them?'

'I will. One day.' I glanced around at the officials, hoping to make a connection. 'It's just … we have doctors doing a fantastic job in some of the poorer communities in New Zealand. I want to do the same for you here.'

I knew I'd said the wrong thing the instant the words left my mouth.

'Did it not occur to you that we have enough doctors of our own in India?' Dr Reddy said. 'Or maybe you don't think we're up to the job. Is that it?'

How could I make them understand? 'No. Not at all. I'm in awe of what your doctors are achieving here in impossible conditions.'

'Then maybe you should go home and let us get on with our work,' Dr Reddy said.

'You're a doctor—you *know* these vaccines will save lives.' I caught my breath. What had Harish told me? *Make them think it's their idea.* 'Of course, we're only going to use vaccines manufactured in India. I'm sure you've been looking into this too.'

Dr Reddy gave his moustache another twitch. 'The final decision's not mine. That's up to Mr Prasad, and I believe he has some questions for you.'

'Indeed, I do. Thank you, Dr Reddy.' A burly man who looked like he'd had too many government-funded dinners for his own good, rose from the table and glared at me. 'Indian-produced vaccines, you say? Allow me to correct you. European-made vaccines packed by exploited and underpaid Indian workers. All to line the pockets of some white Swiss bankers.'

Bloody hell! I cursed under my breath. Faraj hadn't said anything about that. 'That's unfortunate,' I said, 'but it doesn't matter where they've come from. These vaccines will save lives. Indian children's lives. Hundreds and thousands of them.'

'Or kill them,' Prasad said. 'I've heard enough. I forbid the use of these vaccines.' He signed an official-looking document and gave it a stamp. 'You have seven days to get rid of the vaccines. My men will supervise their destruction.' His eyes fixed on mine. 'Or you can take them back to New Zealand. Go on, poison your own kids.'

Elisha couldn't stop me this time. I lunged forward and shouted across the table.

'What is it with you? Do you want your children to die?'

'That's enough,' Elisha said. 'You're only making things worse.'

Things couldn't be any worse. I pushed Elisha aside and continued yelling. 'Is it because you don't want poor people to get healthy? And become powerful enough to stand up to you? Threaten your grip on power, do they?'

'Stop it, Theo!' Elisha pulled me back into my chair. 'I'm so sorry, Mr

Prasad. Dr Malone gets carried away … he's passionate about what he believes in.'

'I know,' Prasad said. 'I read about him in *The Times of India*. And the *Baripada Gazette*.'

Why did Elisha apologise for me? I meant every word I said. She dragged me out of the office like I was the guilty party, and that hurt.

We walked home in silence. It was the first serious falling-out I'd had with Elisha, and I didn't like it.

Harish was waiting for us when we got back. 'How did it go?'

I pumped a fist. 'I socked it to the bastards.'

Harish almost fell over. 'Please tell me you're joking.'

Elisha sighed. 'He's not.'

Did Elisha really think I'd gone too far? Maybe she was right. I couldn't let go when it was something I believed in. Was that a virtue or a vice? Either way, I had to sort things out with Elisha. I walked up and down the street that evening, rehearsing what I was going to say, before I dared knock on her door.

'Are you still mad at me?' I asked.

'No. Come in.' Elisha gestured for me to follow her into the room. 'Insulting Prasad wasn't the wisest move—'

'I know,' I interrupted. 'I'm sorry.'

'But I was going to say,' Elisha continued, 'everything you said is true. It breaks my heart to think we've got to destroy all those precious vaccines.'

I sat down next to her on the bed. 'We haven't.'

'What?'

'Prasad said we had a week to get rid of the shots. So we'd better get vaccinating. Can we get all the kids jabbed in a week?'

Elisha went pale. 'What about the order forbidding us?'

'That'll take ages,' I said. 'Sometimes Indian red tape works in our favour.'

'I'm not sure,' Elisha said. 'It's taking an awful risk.'

'We're doing this for the children,' I said. 'And they're worth it.'

Elisha hesitated. 'I know they are.' She looked me in the eye. 'When do we start?'

CHAPTER EIGHTEEN

Two hours before daylight and thirty more kids to jab.

'You're next, Saeed,' Elisha said. 'Then you, Salena, followed by Nadia, Mishka, Samir and Suvarna.'

'Will it hurt?' Saeed asked as he eyed the vaccine.

'Just a little scratch,' I said. 'But how cool is this, being out with your mates in the middle of the night?'

'Pretty cool, I guess.' Saeed gave a yelp as the needle went in.

'That wasn't too bad, was it?' I said.

Saeed shook his head and ran off to rejoin the other children.

One of his mates gave him a nudge. 'I heard you squeal.'

'I did not,' Saeed said. 'I thought you were going to cry when you got yours.'

Judging by the teasing and rivalry, the kids were just as thrilled as we were at this extraordinary undercover operation.

'Keep your voices down,' Elisha urged, ushering the children to the entrance of the small field hospital. 'Just sit quietly until your parents come to pick you up. We don't want anyone else to know you're here.'

'Why not?' Anika, one of the youngest of the children, asked.

'This is *our* secret,' Elisha said. 'You mustn't tell anyone else.'

'You mean, I can't tell my uncle how brave I've been?' Chandra asked.

'Definitely not,' I butted in. Chandra's uncle worked for the district council.

Rajani and Zac stood guard, escorting the children to their waiting parents.

Looking up to watch them leave, I noticed it was getting light. There was still a line of children to immunise. Were we going to get them all done in time?

Elisha must have read my mind. 'Nearly there,' she said. 'Come on, Zaina. You too, Aadesh. No time to waste.'

I took a deep breath and delivered the final shot. 'You're the lucky last,'

 David Whittet

I said to Sahana, a shy five-year-old. 'That makes you special.'

Elisha put down her clipboard. 'Run along now, Sahana. Your mum's waiting for you.'

Sahana skipped off to her mother. I grabbed hold of Elisha and twirled her around the floor.

'Yay! We've done it! Together, we've done it!' I beckoned to Rajani to join the dance. 'Come on. No slacking. You too, Zac, if your knee's not too sore.'

'Just try to stop me,' Zac said.

We all joined hands and cavorted around in circles.

'I can't do this without music,' Elisha said. 'There's no beat.'

'Okay then,' Zac said, 'let's have a chorus of "We Are The Champions".'

After another lap, with some diabolical singing, we all ended up giggling in a heap on the floor.

'That was fun,' I said. 'Thank you all for what you've done this morning. You know how much it means to me.'

Rajani sat up. 'Thank you, Theo. And you, Elisha. This is my home. My community. I can't thank you enough for what you've done for us.'

Elisha put her arm around Rajani. 'It's our home now, too.'

'That's so sweet.' Rajani hugged Elisha, then jumped to her feet. 'Off the floor, all of you. You're coming back with me for a celebratory breakfast.'

Rajani's great-aunt Nisha must have been up all night as well. The spread was stupendous. Silver platters and shining copper bowls filled with Indian delicacies neatly arranged on a red silk tablecloth. Pakoras, bhaji, biryani, korma, masala—aromatic spices filled the air as we squatted around the table.

'Delicious,' I said, dipping my naan bread in the tarka daal. 'I wouldn't have missed this for the world.'

Nisha laughed. 'Jabbing children must be hungry work.'

I returned her smile. 'Sure is.'

'Controlling that many kids is hard work too,' Zac added. He was on his third helping of murg makhani already.

'Do you eat like this every day?' I asked Rajani. 'Because if you do, I'm coming to live with your aunt Nisha.'

'Not quite,' Rajani said. 'This is special. For you, Theo.'

'You see,' Nisha said, 'I never had the chance to thank you for saving Rajani's life.'

'There's no need,' I said. 'I only did what any doctor would have done.'

Nisha poured me a cup of chai from her brass teapot. 'You did more than the other doctors.' She paused and gave Rajani a hug. 'This girl is precious.'

'She certainly is,' Zac added. 'I thought we'd lost her before you arrived.'

I felt my cheeks flush. 'Well, I hope we've saved a lot more lives with the work we've done to get those vaccines.'

'And the brass nerve to defy the authorities,' Elisha said.

I took a spoonful of the sweet saffron rice dessert. 'I think we can all give ourselves a pat on the pack.'

'I hope no one finds out what you were doing last night,' Nisha said. 'I shouldn't think that little field hospital has seen so much activity since the old days when it was a TB sanatorium.'

I almost choked on my chai. 'It used to be for tuberculosis patients?'

Nisha nodded. That brought me down to earth. Why did everything have to remind me of the first monumental mistake of my career?

'I don't know about the rest of you,' Elisha said, 'but I'm knackered. I need my bed.'

'I'll walk you home,' I said.

I could see she was tired, but there was something I needed to run past her.

'I've been thinking,' I said as we wandered down the street. 'I want to write a paper for the *Indian Medical Journal*. Tell the world how we raised money for the immunisations and had the balls to administer them.'

Elisha stopped dead. 'Are you mad? We've just risked everything to give the children these vaccines in secret. Now you want to tell everyone?'

I grinned. 'That's just the point. We've given the kids their vaccinations. They can't take them back.'

Elisha glared at me. 'But they can stop us immunising any more children, and there are so many other kids who need our help.'

I lowered my head. Elisha was right, as usual. Publicity could jeopardise our ability to reach other communities that were equally desperate.

'Besides,' Elisha continued, 'they could lock us up. I bet Prasad is dying for the chance to arrest us.'

She wasn't wrong there, either. Prasad wouldn't hesitate to have me clapped in irons.

'You win,' I said. 'It's just—I'd love to shame those bastards. Show them what we can do with a bit of ingenuity and determination.'

'You will, one day. Just not now.' Elisha kissed me on the cheek and ran inside her house.

The following week, Elisha's father visited me at the field hospital.

'Pastor Martin! Good to see you.' I'd have shaken his hand but didn't have a free arm with all the case files from the morning round.

He glanced down the ward. 'You've been a breath of fresh air here at our little hospital.'

'Thanks, but it's not just me.' I led him into my office and dumped the records on my desk. 'We've got a great team here.'

'Teams need leadership, and you're a great motivator.' Pastor Martin sat down, clutching his hands together. 'We're all eternally grateful for what you did for Rajani—'

Why did I sense a 'but' was coming? He went on to tell me how I'd been such a positive influence on Elisha. It was another fifteen minutes before he came out with the real reason for his visit.

He shuffled his chair closer to mine. 'We have to be careful. The slightest mistake could threaten the entire mission. We've survived by keeping a low profile.'

'Then maybe I'm not the right man for you,' I said. 'I have a knack for getting into trouble wherever I go.'

Pastor Martin leant forward, his keen eyes appraising me. 'I heard about your altercation with our District Collector, Mr Prasad.'

Yes, I told the bastard where to get off. I bit my tongue. How could I say it more subtly? 'I just don't understand how he could deny those kids the vaccine. It made me so angry. Reddy, too. And he dares to call himself a doctor.'

'It's difficult for Dr Reddy,' Pastor Martin said. 'He treads a fine line—'

I drew back. 'Are you asking me to feel sorry for him?'

'No. Just to understand.' Pastor Martin fiddled with his glasses. 'Dr Reddy's on your side.'

I shook my head. 'It didn't sound like that to me. He went along with everything Prasad said.'

'Because he had to. Dr Reddy's not the enemy, and Prasad's just a puppet.'

What? 'Prasad acts like he's God.'

Pastor Martin moved even closer and lowered his voice. 'The militants have spies in local government. Prasad knew everything he said to you would get back to the ringleaders. He had to make a show of rebuking you and getting rid of the vaccines. Otherwise, they'd have hounded him from office and lynched him.'

I hesitated. 'There were spies amongst the men that came with Prasad?'

Pastor Martin nodded. 'So, he forced you undercover. If he hadn't wanted you to use the vaccines, he wouldn't have given you a week—he'd have confiscated them then and there.'

My mouth fell open. 'Prasad knew we were giving the children the shots?'

Pastor Martin gave me one of his all-knowing smiles. 'Theo! Did you really think you could keep it secret? Mothers talk. Kids talk. It's big news. Everyone's going on about it.'

My jaw dropped even further. I suppose I should have figured it out for myself.

Pastor Martin rested his hands on the desk. 'The local authorities may condemn us in public, but they've been good to us. Like most of the Hindu community, they appreciate what we're doing. But the extremists—they'll do anything to destroy our work. We had a bomb scare at the school the other week.'

I froze. *A bomb.* I'd heard Elisha and Rajani talking about Hindu activists targeting the Christian community but hadn't taken much notice up till now. I hung my head. The thought of me putting lives at risk by barging ahead with the vaccinations made me feel physically sick.

Pastor Martin must have read my mind. 'It wasn't your fault. We

     David Whittet

think Akbar Zahin was behind it. He's fanatically anti-Christian and anti-white, too. His mob has threatened us before. Up in Sundergarh, they've been torching churches. It's thanks to Prasad and the police that it hasn't happened here.'

I didn't care about danger. But Elisha, Zac and Rajani …

'The last thing you need here is a stirrer like me,' I said. 'I should leave.'

'No.' Pastor Martin stood up and put his hand on my shoulder. 'Just be careful. Don't invite trouble.' He walked towards the door and paused. 'We'll get through this. You're making an enormous difference to the people here. Don't let anyone stop that.'

Did Elisha know about the bomb scare? I scratched the back of my neck. She'd have said something if she knew. I went straight to the ward to find Elisha after her father left. My hand was still trembling when I opened the door to the nursing station. She was sitting there on her own, writing up her case notes. I pulled up a chair and sat beside her.

'Your father's told me about the bomb scare.' I put my hand on her shoulder. 'You need a bodyguard. So does your father. Zac and Rajani too.'

Elisha looked up from her case notes. 'I've been trying to persuade Dad to get a minder for ages, but he won't hear of it.'

'What?' I pulled back and stared at her. 'Why not?'

'He doesn't want anyone coming between him and the people.' Elisha put down her pen and gave a half-hearted shrug. 'He believes God will save him whatever happens.'

I wasn't sure if that was brave or just plain stupid. If these guys burnt down churches, who could tell what they might do to the pastor. 'I hope he doesn't live to regret it.'

'So do I. God didn't save my mother.' Elisha blinked back a tear. 'You've no idea how much sleep I've lost.'

I put my arm around Elisha again. 'It's not just your dad I'm worried about. It's you.'

Elisha dried her eyes on her sleeve. 'We'll be okay. Deepesh Banerjee has talked to the local police—'

'Who's Deepesh Banerjee?' I asked. 'And what's he got to do with it?'

'The head of the Indian mission,' Elisha said. 'The police have been watching the militants and keeping an eye on us, too. Acting as unofficial bodyguards.'

'That's not good enough.' I reached for the telephone. 'We need proper bodyguards. Trained marksmen—'

'Wait.' Elisha led me through the ward and pointed at the window. 'Look.'

Armed police stood discreetly positioned at either side of the hospital entrance. They reminded me of the customs officials at Entebbe Airport with their fingers on the trigger.

'They won't stand any nonsense,' Elisha said. 'Relax, Theo. We're safe.'

An elderly patient called out as we walked back through the ward. 'Nurse!'

'What is it, Mr Kapadia?' Elisha said.

'What's up with the doc?'

Elisha went over to his bedside. 'Nothing.'

'He looks mighty upset about something. Has he killed one of his patients?'

Elisha giggled. 'Of course not. Don't take any notice of Dr Malone. He's from New Zealand.' She patted the old man's arm. 'I'll be back in a minute to take your blood pressure.'

Elisha fetched the blood pressure cuff and her stethoscope from the nursing station. 'When I said we're safe,' she whispered in my ear, 'I meant as long as you don't get up to your old tricks and stir up trouble.'

I looked down at my feet. I'd written that paper for the *Indian Medical Journal* and had posted it to the editor that morning.

I couldn't bring myself to tell Elisha what I'd done. Maybe they wouldn't publish my work, anyway. I just kept my head down and concentrated on finding another project. Surely there was something I could do that would make a difference to the community and not get up anyone's nose.

When Rajani took me to the leper colony, I felt the fire in my belly ignite once more.

     David Whittet

'Zac made a film,' Rajani said. 'I was hoping to use it for fundraising so we could get some of those new medicines they're using for leprosy. But then I became sick, and I never got to see the finished production.'

'I'd love to see the movie,' I said. 'But what about Faraj's father? He could help us source the drugs.'

That night, Elisha, Rajani, Zac and I huddled around an old television set and watched the video.

'That was brilliant,' I said. 'You've got an eye for camera angles, Zac. You're going to be the next …' I racked my brains for the name of a famous Indian film director.

Rajani came to my rescue. 'Satyajit Ray.'

Zac jumped up and kissed Rajani on the cheek. 'You remembered!'

'You were mighty special in the film too, Rajani,' Elisha said. 'You could be a news anchor on the telly.'

Rajani pulled a face. 'That's not me.'

'But what about a documentary presenter?' I said. 'Rajani could ace that. We could start with some health promotion films.'

'Enough about me,' Rajani said. 'Let's get down to business. How are we going to get the money for the drugs?'

The team was back in gear. We'd perfected the begging letter during the immunisation campaign. Faraj took the missive to his father and came back with even more names to canvass. We pestered them, bombarding them mercilessly with pleas for support. Would this venture upset the authorities? We were still intruding on their turf. And what about the militants? Strangely, it didn't seem to matter any more. Everywhere we went, I could see a police officer with a gun tailing us.

'We've done it!' Rajani burst onto the ward, brandishing a letter. 'The first batch of drugs will be here by the end of the week.'

Excitement built as the big day approached. Zac was there with his video camera when the consignment arrived and shot an emotional scene with Faraj and his father handing over the medicines to Rajani.

'Your brother's a real pro,' I whispered in Elisha's ear. 'A movie mogul in the making.'

'He's doing this for Rajani,' Elisha said. 'Can't you see?'

Zac and Rajani were busy discussing the next shot as we followed them into the leper colony. A band of helpers set up some lights and Zac filmed Rajani giving the first dose of medicine to a young leper boy.

'Now, that really is a wrap,' Zac announced proudly. 'I'm going to make a new director's cut of the film and we're going to have another gala premiere.' He turned to Rajani. 'And this time, you're not missing it. I won't let you.'

The entire community poured into the village hall for the film screening. It was standing room only for many.

'Great to see everyone supporting Zac and Rajani,' Elisha said.

I was about to reply when my heart missed a beat. Mr Prasad and a contingent from the local authority walked through the door.

'What the hell are they doing here?' I said. 'Have they come to shut us down?'

'Calm down,' Elisha replied. 'I expect he's come to watch the film. Dad says underneath all that officialdom, he's a decent guy.'

I still wasn't convinced. 'The bastard's got it in for me,' I said. 'He's up to something.'

'Don't be so silly!' Elisha pointed across the room. 'Look!'

Pastor Martin shook Prasad's hand, and they chatted amiably. My heart missed another beat when they came over to see me.

'You've met our new doctor,' Pastor Martin said.

'Indeed.' Prasad shook my hand. 'We meet again, Dr Malone.'

How weird was that? What should I say? 'Thank you for coming to see our film, Mr Prasad.' That was the best I could do.

I'd just got over the shock of Prasad's appearance when Dr Reddy arrived with a bouquet for Rajani.

'I hear you're the star of the show,' he said. 'Congratulations! These are from me and my wife.'

Rajani blushed. 'I'm just the presenter. The lepers are the true stars.'

'Then share the flowers with them,' Mrs Reddy said.

'I will,' Rajani said. 'What a lovely thought. I'll take them in tomorrow morning. It'll brighten their day. Thank you.'

At the end of the film, Zac received a three-minute standing ovation.

'Bravo!' I shouted at the top of my voice. 'Here's to the next …' What the hell was the name of that Indian film director?

Rajani rescued me for the second time. 'Satyajit Ray. Zac's going to be as great as Satyajit Ray.'

Even Prasad clapped. The women cheered and festooned us with garlands.

Pastor Martin addressed the crowd. 'Isaac and Rajani have called their film *House of Hope*. I'm sure we'd all agree that's a more appropriate name for the Madhapur leper colony. Some of you may not know that both Isaac and Rajani have been personally affected by leprosy. Isaac can only have been two when his mother caught leprosy, and Rajani was not much older when her father got the disease. Severely debilitated and confined to a leper colony, a malaria outbreak amongst the residents wiped out their entire families. I'm sure you appreciate that this makes Isaac and Rajani's achievement with the film even more poignant. To Isaac and Rajani—Elisha and Theo, too—I say this: You haven't just made a movie, you've turned that old asylum into a genuine *house of hope*. I'm proud of all of you.'

Another round of applause. Pastor Martin sat down. I saw Elisha whisper something in his ear, and he was back on his feet.

'I know you're all looking forward to the buffet the ladies have laid on for us, but before we start, I'd like to say a few words about our new doctor, Theodore Malone.'

Had Elisha put him up to this? I covered my face with my hands as the pastor continued.

'In just nine months, Theo has set up community programmes, rejuvenated our little hospital and energised the team. No other doctor here has done that.'

I looked up to see Prasad pocket a bunch of samosas from the table, and he and his entourage were out of the door. Typical. They were only here for the food. Still, I breathed a sigh of relief to see the back of them.

The guests continued to lavish praise on Zac over the buffet dinner. With his suit and bow tie, he looked the part. Rajani would grace a red carpet anywhere in the world. I should have been enjoying the party as much as they were, but I had something to tell Elisha, and I wasn't sure how she'd take it. Perhaps the success of the evening would soften her reaction.

'Elisha, darling.' I took a deep breath. 'You remember I told you I wanted to write a paper for the *Indian Medical Journal*?'

'Yes,' Elisha said, 'and I told you not to. Far too dangerous.'

That wasn't a good start. I cleared my throat and began again. 'Don't be angry with me, but—'

Elisha cut me off. 'You did it anyway. I might have known.'

'I never thought they'd publish it,' I said.

'But I'm guessing they did.'

'Not just that. The editor commended our work in his editorial.' I grasped Elisha's arm. It was all or nothing. 'They've asked me to present the paper to the World Organization of Family Doctors at their conference in Calcutta next month, and I want you to come with me.'

No answer. Elisha's eyes gave nothing away. She strode to the front of the hall. The crowd hushed. What was she going to say? Surely she wouldn't berate me in front of all these people.

'My dear friends,' she began. 'Earlier this evening, my father told you how, in less than a year, Theo Malone has transformed the healthcare of this community. I am proud to announce that the prestigious *Indian Medical Journal* has published Theo's work to great acclaim. He's going to give a lecture at an international medical conference in Calcutta, and I'm going with him.' Amid the resounding applause, she thrust an arm in the air. 'Together we can take on the world!'

That night, I really believed we *could* take on the world. And win.

CHAPTER NINETEEN

World Family Doctors' Conference in Calcutta, May 1993

Throughout the world, four million children die unnecessarily every year from vaccine-preventable illnesses. Thirty million infants in India are not protected by routine immunisations.

I kept repeating those words to myself on the train to Calcutta. It was my new mantra, the message I had to get across when I delivered the opening keynote to an audience of the most influential family doctors from around the globe. Presenting at such a pre-eminent conference was my one chance to make an impression on the world stage, and I couldn't afford to blow it. Not with senior officials from the World Health Organization in attendance. They had the power to implement change, and I knew exactly what I wanted to say to them.

'Four million kids a year.' I turned to Elisha, who sat opposite me in the carriage. 'That's like the entire population of New Zealand being wiped out every single year. I just can't get my head around it. Can you imagine the human suffering?'

Elisha looked up from the *Indian Women's Weekly*. 'It's not me you have to convince. Or the authorities come to that. There's a piece in here about the anti-vax brigade.' She handed me her magazine. 'They're a powerful movement in Calcutta.'

I scanned the article and felt my blood pressure skyrocket. Same old conspiracy theories. Doctors and pharmaceutical companies colluding and making money from unsafe and experimental treatments. 'Bollocks! Have the idiots any idea of the harm they're doing, printing such total bullshit?'

Elisha sighed. 'No. They just want to sell their magazine.'

I tossed the magazine back to Elisha. 'Don't the bastards realise kids' lives are at stake?'

'Hold on,' Elisha said, stuffing the magazine away in her bag. 'I'm on your side!'

'Sorry. I didn't mean to take it out on you.' I reached out for her hand. 'It's just … I've taken on these shysters before. And won.'

I was still fuming when the train pulled into Howrah Station, and we jostled with the masses to get a taxi to our hotel. We'd hit Calcutta's rush hour, and the blazing horns and irate drivers echoed my mood. My mind went back to my first brush with the anti-vaccination movement back in New Zealand. A public health nurse in a rural community used her position to indoctrinate mothers on the evils of immunisation. I remember reading a flyer in the waiting room at her clinic, claiming that vaccinating children was tantamount to child abuse. Could there be any worse abuse than four million children dying of vaccine-preventable illness every year?

Why hadn't I thought of that before? I put my arm around Elisha in the back of the cab. 'I've just thought of a brilliant closing line for my presentation tomorrow.'

The taxi pulled up at the Andhra Palace Hotel. 'Tell me over dinner,' Elisha said, 'I'm starving.'

The Andhra Palace Hotel wasn't the least palatial. It was decidedly seedy, but it was the best I could afford on my pay from the mission. I certainly hadn't made a cent out of immunisation, whatever those trashy magazines said about doctors lining their pockets.

'Sorry about the hotel,' I said as we sat down in the dingy dining room.

'I wasn't expecting the Ritz,' Elisha said.

The waiter recommended the channa masala. 'House speciality,' he said.

'It's funny,' Elisha said, 'when we first came to India, I hated the food. Now—anything else tastes bland.'

I almost choked on a chilli. 'Blimey! This is hot!'

'Try some of the chutney,' Elisha said. 'We can't have you going down with Delhi belly before your presentation tomorrow.'

'I won't. Nothing will stop me from giving that lecture.'

'So, what was the idea you were on about in the taxi?' Elisha asked.

 David Whittet

I took a sip of water and cleared my throat. 'Remember how I told you about the public health nurse in New Zealand who said immunisation was child abuse?'

Elisha pointed her fork at me. 'As if you'd let me forget.'

I clenched my fist around my fork. 'Refusing children life-saving vaccines *is* child abuse, and of the very worst kind.'

'Tell them about Nadim,' Elisha said. 'You've brought a slide with his photograph, haven't you? Make it personal. Our children are our future.'

'Even better!' I beamed at Elisha. 'I've got loads of pictures of vulnerable kids. This is going to be fantastic!'

I was feeling high when I said goodnight to Elisha. We had separate rooms at the hotel—I'd agonised about booking a double room. But she was the pastor's daughter and sharing a room would be off limits. Wouldn't it? We'd worked closely together over the past few months, but apart from a few hugs and kisses on the cheek, we hadn't been intimate. Anyway, this trip wasn't about us. It was for all those kids dying of vaccine-preventable illnesses.

That hadn't stopped me from asking Zac for advice before we left. He knew Elisha better than anyone. I'd cornered him when we were clearing the hall after the film show. I'd tried to sound matter-of-fact, but I could feel my cheeks were burning. 'Has Elisha had many boyfriends?'

Zac was dismantling the projector and looked up at me with one of his mischievous grins. 'She had the hots for this weirdo kid Jackson. Can't think why. He was a total jerk.'

'That was back in Australia?' I asked.

'Yeh.' Zac put the lens cap on the projector and winked. 'Then there was Jonno. She fancied him like crazy. Couldn't stop talking about him.'

Was he winding me up? He must have known how I felt about Elisha. 'What about in India?' I'd asked. 'Any boyfriends here?'

Zac shook his head. 'You've got it bad, mate, haven't you?'

My entire face must have been on fire by now. I talked about matters of the heart with my patients all the time. Why was it so hard when it came to myself?

'Zac,' I said, helping him put the projector back in its case, 'have you ever … done it with … I mean … have you ever slept with Rajani?'

Zac pulled a face. 'God, no! She's far too religious for that. No sex before marriage with Rajani. More's the pity.' He gave me a poke. 'But Elisha's no saint. You're in with a chance there. Are you going to make your move on her when you're in Calcutta?'

I flapped a hand in his direction. *Cheeky bastard.* 'Of course not. This is a serious conference. About saving kids' lives.'

Zac had winked. 'Alright! I believe you!'

I'd put all romantic thoughts behind me after that. Things had got messy with Marian Taylor when I sensed she was developing feelings for me. She wanted to take things further, and I backed away. I'd always put work first—until I met Elisha.

The beds at the Andhra Palace Hotel were undersized and exceedingly uncomfortable. As I struggled to find a bearable position, I kept thinking about Elisha curled up alone in the adjacent room. Was she still awake? And if so—was she thinking about me? *Don't even go there. We're here for the kids.*

Unable to sleep, I spent most of the night rearranging my slides and rehearsing what I was going to say in my lecture. By four in the morning, I was almost word-perfect.

Elisha's hands were shaking when we helped ourselves to the hotel's buffet breakfast the following morning. Mine were, too—but then, I'd been up all night. Hadn't she slept, either?

'Those beds were mighty uncomfortable, weren't they?' I said.

I thought Elisha was going to drop her plate of samosas. 'I had the radio on while I was getting dressed,' she said. 'A group of anti-vaccine campaigners have got wind the conference is opening with your talk on global immunisation, and they're planning to picket the conference centre.'

I was ready to explode again, but I saw the panic in Elisha's eyes and instead took a deep breath. 'Bring it on. I told you, I've taken on the bastards before and won.'

Elisha didn't look at all reassured as we sat down at the breakfast table. 'That's what I'm afraid of. You need to keep a cool head for the presentation.'

I took a bite of naan bread. 'I will.'

'I know you,' Elisha said. 'You mustn't let them rattle you.'

 David Whittet

'I'll do my best.' I met Elisha's uneasy gaze. 'Don't worry. Everything will be fine.'

But would it? Demonstrators were there handing out flyers when we arrived at the Calcutta Convention Centre. Doubtless thinking I was a delegate, one of the protesters stuffed a paper in my hand. I tore it up in front of his eyes.

'That's Dr Malone.' Another picket marched up and spat on me. 'I saw his picture in the paper.'

'Get him!' The protesters had me cornered, and before I could duck, they shoved a clump of mud in my face. 'Take that!'

I gagged on the mud. It tasted like shit—and probably was. I swallowed a chunk and it suck in my throat. Brushing the dirt out of my eyes, I saw Elisha trying to pull the men off me.

'Leave him alone,' she yelled. 'Is this your idea of a rational debate on the issue?'

The ring leader turned on Elisha with his fists clenched.

'Don't hurt her!' I got the words out before more dung hit my mouth. Where the hell was security? I spat out as much of the muck as I could. 'Help! Somebody!'

I'd swallowed another mouthful before the security guards arrived and broke up the protesters.

'I'm so sorry, Dr Malone,' one of the conference officials said. 'Let me take you to the restroom and get you cleaned up.'

'I just want to wash my mouth out,' I said. 'I think I'm going to be sick.'

Elisha had made me buy a new suit for the presentation. 'You need to look smart,' she kept telling me. 'Everybody will be looking at you. You need a decent suit.'

'I never wear suits,' I'd protested.

Elisha had the last word—as usual. 'Well, you're going to wear one in Calcutta. I'm not having you standing up in front of all those professors dressed in cast-offs.'

I couldn't stop myself laughing as the usher helped me sponge the mud off the pinstriped jacket and the silk tie. The stains wouldn't have looked nearly as bad on my usual casual wear.

'That's better,' the usher said. 'Now, I need to get you to the speakers' preparation room.'

Elisha was waiting outside the gentlemen's washroom. 'It might sound strange,' she said, 'but I think the protesters have done you a favour. Listen. Everyone's talking about it.'

She pointed to a group of delegates who were sounding off about one of the anti-vax flyers. I caught snippets of their conversation.

'Bloody nonsense!'

'A white Christian discovered penicillin!'

'Same old arguments. All debunked years ago.'

'How dare they invade our conference!'

Elisha tugged on my arm. 'See? They're all fired up. They'll be hanging on your every word.'

'Let's hope you're right.' I wished I hadn't washed my face. My address would have been much more dramatic if I'd gone on stage showing what the mob had done to me.

I unwound as we made our way through the crowd. The centre buzzed with anticipation. Delegates from all over the world renewed their acquaintance and caught up with each other's stories. When we arrived at the speakers' preparation room, the projectionist loaded my slides into his machine and gave me a remote to advance them. He fitted me up with a microphone, and we did a test run.

'Professor Lindberg is waiting to meet you,' the usher said. 'I'll take you to the green room.'

Perhaps it was just as well I'd cleaned myself up. Elisha straightened my tie. She knew how excited I was to meet Michael Lindberg, the president of the World Organization of Family Doctors.

I felt a surge of adrenaline in my gut. It was the first time I'd been inside a green room since that disastrous interview with Paul Holmes.

'You'll be okay,' Elisha whispered in my ear. She must have seen my forehead glistening with sweat.

Dressed in the Swedish GP College's tie and blazer, Professor Lindberg shook my hand heartily. 'Dr Malone! Delighted to meet you!'

I hoped he didn't notice my palm was wet. 'Delighted to meet you, too.'

'I can only apologise for the hecklers,' Professor Lindberg said. 'I trust you're not hurt?'

I shook my head.

'He's a bit shaken up,' Elisha said. 'I hope they won't give us any more trouble.'

'They won't,' Professor Lindberg said. 'I've given security a good talking-to, and we'll soon have the troublemakers out of the building.' He turned to the colleague who stood next to him. 'I'd like you to meet Professor Giovanni from the World Health Organization. Between the two of us, we'll do our best to make it up to you.'

Professor Giovanni's handshake was even more vigorous. 'I read your paper, Dr Malone, and I've heard about the work you've been doing down in Madhapur.'

He was a stocky man with a thin, well-kept moustache, immaculately turned out in a three-piece suit—exactly how I imagined a director of the World Health Organization.

'We've been trying to get immunisation rates up in the Mayurbhanj for years,' Professor Giovanni said, 'particularly for measles, diphtheria, polio, pertussis, and tetanus. We never had much success until you came along.'

'Thank you, sir,' I said. 'It's been a challenge, I can tell you.'

'Once Theo sets his mind on something,' Elisha said, 'there's no stopping him. He had us up all night vaccinating the kids.'

'Yes, I read about it in the *Indian Medical Journal*,' Professor Giovanni said. 'With your permission, I want to make a special announcement before you begin your presentation.'

My heart pounded as I waited in the wings a few minutes later. What was Professor Giovanni going to say that was so momentous?

'Good luck,' Elisha whispered, taking her seat in the front row of the auditorium.

Michael Lindberg took his place on the stage. The lights went down, and the delegates' chatter muffled abruptly. I thought my chest would burst in the expectant hush.

'It is with great pleasure that I welcome Dr Theo Malone as our opening keynote speaker. Dr Malone is no stranger to controversy. You will have read how he stood up to the local authorities and immunised all the children in Madhapur for measles. You may have noticed that he looks a little dishevelled at present. The reason? A group of anti-vaccination protesters assaulted him on his way into the building this morning. Now, I know you're all eager to hear what Dr Malone has to say, but bear with me a moment longer. My good friend and colleague, Professor Alessandro Giovanni from the World Health Organization, has an important announcement to make.'

'Thank you, Michael.' Professor Giovanni cleared his throat. 'As you all know, Theo Malone is a New Zealander who has brought Orissa some much-needed Kiwi ingenuity. Whatever the obstacles, he gets things done. In recognition of this and with the WHO's commitment to improving the health of remote rural communities, we have made a resolution. The recent World Health Assembly passed a motion to provide Dr Malone and his team with funding to immunise all the children in the entire Mayurbhanj district for measles.'

I could have kissed him in front of all those people, and I wouldn't have been ashamed. I caught Elisha's eye in the front row, and we shared the moment.

'Thank you so much, Professor Giovanni.' I shook his hand as energetically as he'd shaken mine when we'd met. 'Your generous donation will save lives, change futures and empower communities.' And it would. I shot Elisha another glance.

'It's a pleasure to support such a dedicated team.' Professor Giovanni extracted his hand from mine and addressed the audience. 'And now I hand you over to Theo Malone to deliver his address.'

I felt more like dancing around the stage than delivering a keynote—and I couldn't dance to save myself. *Concentrate. You've been waiting for this opportunity your entire career.* I pinched myself and stumbled across to the podium. I fiddled with the remote, praying the first slide would come up without a glitch. And there was Nadim, up there on the screen. He'd never made it to Calcutta while he was alive. Now his soulful eyes stared at a lecture theatre full of the world's most influential doctors and policymakers.

'This is Nadim Gupta,' I began. 'He is one of the four million children

 David Whittet

globally, who died unnecessarily over the past year from vaccine-preventable illnesses.'

I glanced at the audience for their reaction. Everyone's eyes were fixed on the screen. Elisha gave me a thumbs up. I mouthed her a 'thank you'—starting with Nadim's image was a brilliant idea.

'Look at his face,' I continued. 'Look at his eyes. If he'd had the measles jab, he'd still be alive.' I took a sip of water from the glass on the lectern. 'Four million children. Dead. Can you imagine the scale of human misery that represents? It's the entire population of New Zealand, my home country. And here in India, thirty million infants don't get their routine immunisations. So why are so many people—many of them in prominent positions—hell-bent on stopping us in this vital work? Professor Lindberg told you the demonstrators accosted me this morning.' I forced a smile. 'I can still taste the muck they shoved in my mouth.' And I could—that lingering faecal taste just wouldn't go away. I waited for the ripple of amusement to settle before carrying on. 'But it's no joke. You will have seen the flyers plastered around the hall. Some of you will have found their malicious leaflets on your seats. I wish security hadn't thrown them out. I'd like them to see the pictures I'm going to show you now. All these children had promising lives ahead of them until disease stole their futures.' I kept my finger on the remote, displaying a montage of the children's faces. Image after image of the most adorable kids. I'd seen the slides so many times, but on that giant screen, they still brought a lump to my throat. 'Every one of these kids would be alive if they'd received their immunisations. This is not some evil conspiracy by the pharmaceutical companies and the medical profession. Our children are our future. And we're letting them die.'

Elisha had urged me to be positive, so I focused on recent advances in vaccine technology. Inoculation against viral diarrhoea, the biggest killer in rural India, was on the horizon. To illustrate what we could do, I showed a video Zac had taken of our all-night session jabbing the Madhapur children.

I finished with the story of the public health nurse in New Zealand and her anti-vaccination campaign. 'She claimed that childhood immunisation was the most extreme and shameful example of child abuse in modern times.' I paused for a moment to take in the wave of widening eyes and dropped jaws amongst the delegates. 'I beg to differ.' I stood tall over the lectern and stared straight at the audience. 'In my view, there could be no greater child abuse than allowing four million children to die from vaccine-preventable diseases. I make no apology for coming back to this statistic and the human tragedy it represents for mothers, fathers, families and communities. We can prevent this disaster from continuing. Immunisation saves two and a half million children's lives each year, and that is a fraction of what we could achieve.'

Applause rang out throughout the auditorium. Many of the professors gave a standing ovation with cries of 'Bravo!'

I'd done it. I'd got my message across, and judging by their response, they'd taken it to their hearts.

Professor Lindberg returned to the stage. 'We all knew Dr Malone was passionate,' he said, 'but that took my breath away. In fact, it's one of the most inspiring keynotes I've ever heard.'

I pointed to Elisha. 'I couldn't have done any of this without this extraordinary young woman. She's the one you should applaud.'

Elisha stood up and waved to the audience. More shouts of 'Bravo!'

Professor Lindberg hushed the crowd and opened the session to questions from the audience.

An American man got up. 'If I gave you a million US dollars for your project, how would you spend it?'

I scratched my head. 'Well, Professor Giovanni has told us that the WHO will fund our immunisation programme throughout the region. So, supposing you offered me a million dollars—I'd want to make sure we put every cent to good use.' After a moment's pause, the answer came to me. 'I'd use that million dollars as baksheesh to bribe the authorities, and the protesters, to let us administer the vaccines.'

The crowd roared with laughter. Cameras clicked. Delegates came up to the podium and shook my hand. I wished Ralph Greenslade could have been there with me to share the moment. If it wasn't for him, I'd have given up long ago.

Sat at the top table for the conference banquet, Michael Lindberg eyed me quizzically.

'What would you really do if someone gave you a million dollars?'

Before I could collect my thoughts, Elisha answered.

'We should spend it on building a well for the people of Madhapur,' she said. 'Clean water is as important as immunisation. There've been cholera epidemics in the district. That's what killed my mother—indirectly.'

Elisha had told me about her mother's needle-stick injury. How cholera wiped out the regular hospital staff, and that Melissa had volunteered to take their place, with disastrous consequences.

'A well will be our next project,' I said. 'We'll build it in memory of your mother.'

'I can't promise you a million bucks,' Alessandro Giovanni chipped in. 'But I assure you, the WHO would back the venture.'

It was almost midnight when we got to Howrah Station for the night train home. Teaming masses continued to converge on the concourse and jostle for space on the platforms. Where the hell was our train? Elisha clung to my arm as we battled our way past the beggars, buskers and street vendors.

'How much further?' Elisha moaned.

'We're nearly there,' I said. 'It's that blue train over there.'

Elisha ducked to miss a man's spit. 'Doesn't anyone in Calcutta go to sleep?'

I pointed to a bunch of vagrants settling down for the night at the trackside.

Elisha's hand tightened on my arm. 'My mother looked after a boy who lived by the railway. We found him a new home. I never heard what became of Kaamil after that.' She gazed at the sea of itinerant families, each claiming their patch on the tarpaulin. 'If we did have a million bucks, we should buy a home for all these people.'

'It'll take more than a million to sort out India's homelessness,' I said with a sigh. 'One project at a time. Immunise the kids. Build the well. Then we can start building houses.'

'Promise?' Elisha said. 'I'll hold you to it.'

'I'm sure you will.' I helped Elisha into the carriage. 'Jump in. I just need a quick word with the guard.'

This was going to cost. 'Excuse me. How much for a private berth?'

The guard shook his head. 'Only one berth left. And reserved for important passenger.'

I'm sure it is. I handed him a wadge of notes.

The guard licked his finger and counted them. 'VIP pay more than this.'

I gave him more money.

'Fifty more rupees,' the guard insisted.

I emptied my pockets. Thank God I had enough. I needed that private berth. There was something I had to ask Elisha before I lost my nerve.

Elisha nestled her head against my shoulder as we sat on the bunk.

'We make a great team, don't we?' I said. 'These past few days have been brilliant—the happiest of my life.'

Elisha snuggled up closer. 'Mine too.'

I hesitated. 'Are we more than a team?'

Elisha raised her eyes to meet mine. 'You tell me.'

Even after my talk with Zac, I was no better at expressing myself. 'I think we are. We're soulmates.' I stared back at her all-consuming lilac blue eyes and took a deep breath. 'What I'm trying to say is … I love you.'

Elisha nudged me playfully. 'You want to date?' She raised an eyebrow. 'At last! I thought you'd never ask.'

'I've been meaning to say something …' I stumbled to find the right words. 'It's just … we've been so wrapped up preparing for the conference.'

Elisha frowned. 'Are you sure it's a girlfriend you want and not just a colleague?'

'I want *you.*' My lip quivered. 'I'm not just asking you out. I want you to marry me.'

Elisha pulled back. 'What? Marry you?'

I nodded. 'I love you, Elisha. Do you want me to get down on one knee?'

Elisha grinned. 'Not much space for that in a railway compartment.' Her grin disappeared. 'So, you want *me.* When you booked separate rooms at the hotel in Calcutta, I convinced myself you didn't fancy me. I thought we'd sleep together.'

How could I have got it so wrong? Had I blown it? 'I wanted to share

David Whittet

a room with you … I did …' My voice broke as I struggled to explain. 'I wanted us to make love, but—'

Elisha finished the sentence for me. 'But you were afraid to ask because of my dad.' She rolled her eyes. 'Having a preacher for a father is a pain in the bloody arse. Boys run a mile when they find out my old man's a missionary.'

'I'm not like that,' I said. 'You know that. I admire your father. He's made a difference to so many lives. Take Zac and Rajani.'

Elisha gave a half-hearted shrug. 'I know. It's just difficult living with such saintly people.'

Should I tell her I'd confided in Zac? What the hell. I'd nothing to lose. 'Zac told me you were a rebel, and you definitely weren't an angel—'

'Bloody cheek,' Elisha interrupted. 'He's no saint either. I could tell you stories about him that would—'

This time, I stopped her. 'Zac told me I should make my move on you while we were in Calcutta.'

'Then why the hell didn't you?' Elisha glared at me for a full minute, then laughed. 'You can be such a fool, Theo Malone.' She flung her arms around me. 'Come here!'

Her lips brushed against mine. Her breath caressed my cheeks with the sweet smell of jasmine. Her intoxicating taste as our mouths locked together took me to an enchanted garden full of exotic flowers, far above that rattling train and the plains of the Mayurbhanj.

I needed to take a breath and was back in that cramped berth. Our lips parted for a moment before Elisha pulled our heads back together.

The train pulled into a siding and stopped.

'Looks like it's going to be a long night,' Elisha said with a seductive grin. 'Why don't we make up for lost time?'

'What?' I almost fell off the bunk. 'In here?'

She started unbuttoning my shirt. 'Why not? It's a private berth, isn't it?'

'Shouldn't we plan the vaccine roll-out? And decide how we're going to build the well?'

'Tomorrow. Tonight is for us.' Elisha wriggled out of her dress and glanced up at the window. 'You'd better pull down the blinds. We don't want any of the freeloaders on the roof looking in.'

Damn right. After fixing the ragged blinds that insisted on rewinding themselves, I fumbled with the remainder of my buttons. What a relief to get out of that uncomfortable suit.

The train jolted back into motion and thrust our bodies together. Elisha clenched my back and pulled me even closer.

'I want to feel you inside me,' Elisha breathed. 'Right now.'

Our bodies lurched from side to side, writhing in sync with the train's movements. The carriage shook when an express rattled past in the opposite direction, and we almost bounced off the bunk.

Elisha's eyes twinkled with mischief. 'Get back here!'

We both laughed as I climbed back on top of her.

'You don't get away that easily,' she said.

The vibrations grew more intense as the train gathered momentum.

My back arched when the train jerked across a junction, thrusting me deeper inside her.

Elisha gasped. 'Don't stop!'

I never wanted that train journey to end.

The engine's horn blazed through the darkness as if announcing to the world that we were about to climax. My back arched, and my body convulsed. Elisha groaned and shuddered underneath me, her skin glowing in the dim light of the carriage.

I held Elisha tight. I would have to let go when we arrived at our station. I prayed the train would slow down or pull into another siding and stop. I never wanted to let go.

Did it mean as much to Elisha as it did to me? I gently wiped the sweat off her forehead. Had sex diminished the overwhelming success of the conference? I loved her now more than ever, and I wanted to spend the rest of my life with her.

The train slowed down. The loud screech of the brakes brought a lump to my throat. I squinted through the gap between the blind and the window frame and recognised the familiar lights. We were almost there.

Elisha giggled and reached for her dress. 'Better get some clothes on.'

  David Whittet

She laughed even louder as I struggled to put on that wretched suit. Why wouldn't my legs go in those trousers? And as for fastening that belt …

'Here, let me help you,' Elisha said. 'You need a woman to look after you.' She stared straight into my eyes. 'Yes, Theo, I will marry you. And like I said at the film night, together we *will* take on the world.'

CHAPTER TWENTY

Madhapur, the Following Day

Tomorrow. The mission can wait till tomorrow, tonight is for us. That's what Elisha had said on the train. Day broke, and keen as I was to get going on the immunisation campaign and building the well, my heart was still racing. The tingle that surged through my body refused to go away.

I'd taken loads of photographs at the conference, and since Zac had set up his own darkroom, I rushed over to his place to get my pictures developed. But that wasn't the real reason I wanted to see Zac. I just had to see his face when I told him about last night.

My grin must have given it away. He gave me a monumental dig in the ribs before I had the chance to open my mouth.

'You've done it, haven't you?' he said. 'Lucky sod! Spill. I want to hear all the sordid details.'

I'd been looking forward to gloating, but last night was far too precious for cheap point-scoring. I glanced up at the sky. 'It was like … we were on the night train to Heaven.'

Zac frowned. 'Don't get all starry-eyed on me. What was it *really* like?'

Surely the gleam in my eyes said it all. 'Like I said. It was as if that train took us to another place … green pastures, such fields … and just Elisha and me.'

Zac rolled his eyes. 'Blimey! You *have* got it bad.'

'I'm just telling you how it was. A meeting of souls.'

'I never thought I'd see you go so soppy,' Zac said. 'You've changed, Theo.'

I handed Zac a bag with the rolls of film for developing. 'Maybe I have, and it's all down to your sister.'

Zac inspected the rolls of film and smirked. 'No dirty pictures on these, I hope?'

It was my turn to give *him* a poke. 'You should hurry up and get your wedding day fixed up. Who knows? Rajani may do the same for you.'

Zac put down the films on his bench. 'She already has—changed me, that is.' His smugness disappeared, and his eyes widened. 'I love her, and I'll wait as long as it takes. I respect her far too much to push her before she's ready.'

Back at the field hospital, I thought about what Zac had said. Elisha *had* changed me—I hadn't realised quite how much before Calcutta. But the goal remained the same. We would change the world or die trying. There was no going back, and I threw myself into working on the broader vaccine roll-out and drawing up plans for the well. The hospital was full too. There'd been a recent outbreak of salmonella.

Perhaps it was as well I was so busy. It was a chance to escape the constant attention of the Madhapur matchmakers. As far as I could remember—not that I had much experience of such matters—back home in New Zealand, engagements were relatively low key. The women would get together and shout a bridal shower. That was about it. Clearly, the etiquette here was different. The entire Madhapur township partied, with fairy lights and marigolds again lining the streets as they had for Diwali. Like all their celebrations, the festivities lasted for days on end.

Rajani was as excited about the engagement as she was about building the well and insisted on making traditional Indian wedding costumes for Elisha and me.

'My great-aunt used to be a dressmaker,' Rajani told us. 'We'll make you both look absolutely stunning.'

'I don't want to be of too much trouble to Nisha,' Elisha said. 'I was thinking of something simpler.'

Rajani pulled a face. 'Nonsense! You're not in Aussie now!'

Elisha and Rajani spent a lot of time alone together. They claimed it was just to get all the measurements and fittings right. *Yeah, right.* There would be girl talk. What had Elisha told Rajani about our night of passion on the train? Maybe nothing. Fat chance. Elisha couldn't resist sharing it any more than I could with Zac.

I'd stopped worrying about it when Elisha put her head around my office door.

'Time for your measuring session,' she said.

It was the first time she'd been in the hospital that week.

'Must I?' I pointed to the mass of papers on my desk. 'I've a heap of lab results to get through.'

'You can do that tonight,' Elisha said. 'I'm not having you showing me up at the wedding.'

I put down my pen and sighed. 'The last time you got me kitted out in a fancy suit, I got plastered in mud.'

'The locals here are much more friendly.' Elisha grinned. 'I'll expect you at Nisha's house at two. Don't be late.'

When I arrived, Rajani was there in Nisha's front room, needle and thread in her hands, working with Elisha on the bridal gown.

'Sit down,' Nisha said. 'Make yourself comfortable. I'll make some chai. But first, I want to see how these look.' She studied me and sifted through a collection of silk fabrics, holding the samples against my face. 'Hmm—I think these darker colours will suit your skin tone.'

Elisha glanced up. 'And his darker nature.'

I shot her a dark look.

'Sorry,' she said. 'Couldn't resist it.'

'You'll both be magnificent,' Nisha said. 'Won't they, Rajani?'

Rajani sewed a sequin onto Elisha's dress. 'Of course they will.'

Nisha fetched a magazine with pictures of Indian bridegrooms in traditional dress and handed it to me. 'You look at this while I make the chai.'

I leafed through the magazine. The models looked splendid in their lavish Indian costumes. But was it me? Would it be as uncomfortable as that awful pinstripe suit?

Zac arrived the moment Nisha came back in from the kitchen with the tray and a plateful of Indian sweets. Did all would-be film-makers have such a finely tuned nose for food?

Rajani stepped back to inspect her progress on Elisha's dress. 'How's it looking, Aunty?' she asked Nisha.

'Gorgeous.' Nisha put the tray down on a table. 'It'll be your turn soon, Rajani.'

Rajani blushed. 'When I get married, I want a true Bollywood-style romance.'

'Did you hear that, Zac?' I said. 'You'd better watch out. Could be mighty expensive.'

Zac snapped a finger in my direction.

Rajani went an even deeper red. 'Stop that!'

'Why?' Elisha said. 'Everyone knows you two are going to be next.'

Rajani undid her stitching and started again. 'Don't be silly. We're just good friends.'

Elisha grinned. 'That's what they all say. Admit it, you're crazy about him.'

Rajani dropped her sewing kit. 'Now look what you made me do.'

I glanced over my shoulder at Zac. He had a cake in one hand and his video camera in the other. He'd been avidly filming the wedding preparations but hit the pause button whenever the subject turned to him and Rajani. I couldn't stop myself teasing him.

'What about it, Zac?' I said. 'An up-and-coming film director in India needs a large-scale wedding. You could hire a studio in Bombay for the reception. Get you noticed. Might even get your picture in the *Bollywood Reporter*.'

Zac turned as crimson as Rajani. 'Shut it, Theo.'

'Anyway,' Elisha said, 'with all the celebrations the folk here are planning, my wedding's going to be even bigger than Bollywood.'

Rajani giggled. 'A doctor and a nurse. Working together in a remote village. That's not Bollywood. It's pure Mills and Boon!'

I'd read somewhere that the Hindi versions of Mills and Boon novels were best sellers. That was doubtless true, but never in my wildest dreams did I imagine anyone would compare my life to one of those soppy stories.

Elisha insisted I dress up for the gala banquet—the culmination of the engagement celebrations.

'I'm *not* wearing that suit,' I said.

'At least put on a decent shirt,' she said. '*Everyone*'s going to be there.'

And they were. A small musical ensemble, led by the town's bandmaster on his sitar, played a ceremonial march. Elisha and I paraded down the street, the adults cheering and the children waving colourful flags they'd made at school. It must have taken the children forever—there were pictures of brides, grooms and wedding ceremonies on the flags.

The crowd showered us with incense. My eyes met Elisha's.

'Sure beats getting deluged in mud and poo,' I whispered.

Leading the parade got us to the front of the queue for the enormous buffet. I took in a lungful of the spicy aroma.

'We should get hitched more often if they put on a spread like this,' I said.

Elisha laughed. 'Any excuse to party. The women love to cook. Whenever there's a special event, they all try to outdo one another.' She paused for a moment. 'I guess they've got nothing else to look forward to.'

'You're right.' I looked around. So much food on the trestle tables, but so many hungry people waiting and clutching their plates. 'When you live in poverty, any opportunity to live it up must be precious.'

'You're overthinking again,' Elisha said. 'Relax. We should enjoy the day like everyone else.'

An elderly lady with a shock of grizzled hair came up and greeted us. 'You two are a perfect match,' she said. 'You will have a long and happy life together. I have seen it in the stars.'

'Who's that?' I whispered in Elisha's ear.

'It's Indali,' Elisha said. 'Madhapur's official matchmaker. You remember. I told you about her.'

Of course. I'd steered clear of the village's fortune tellers and marriage brokers. Until now. Indali pulled me aside. I wanted to tell her that my love for Elisha had nothing to do with the stars. We were kindred spirits. Soulmates. But then—perhaps that *was* written in the heavens.

I smiled back at her. 'Destiny intended us to meet. Right here in Madhapur.'

Indali dazzled me with her hypnotic eyes. 'Yes, I believe you were. You must tell us about it when you make your speech.'

		David Whittet

Speech? What was the old woman on about? 'I wasn't planning on saying anything.'

'You must,' Indali said. 'Why else do you think everyone is here?'

I pointed to the array of delightfully fragrant dishes on the table. 'For the food.'

'No. To listen to you.' Indali's eyes continued to mess with my head. 'Karma requires you to speak.'

There was no way I was going to get out of it. I sighed. 'When?'

'As soon as we finish our repast.' With that, Indali picked up a plate of vegetable biryani and joined the other women elders.

'What do you say to an audience of incurable romantics?' I muttered. 'I suppose I should give them what they want.' I took a bite of chapatti. Perhaps a heart-warming medical romance was just what the townsfolk needed. 'How about a sentimental story about a doctor and a nurse who were meant for each other—'

Elisha was on her third pakora, and I thought she was going to choke on it. 'Don't you dare!'

'There has to be a reason Mills and Boon novels are so popular out here.' I dipped some naan bread in a bowl of daal. 'Besides, can you come up with a better idea?'

Zac and Rajani joined us and sat on the grass beside us. True to form, Zac's plate was overflowing.

'Don't worry,' Rajani said. 'You'll be fine. Elisha went on about how brilliant you were in front of all those doctors in Calcutta.'

'That was easy.' How did I explain that addressing the locals terrified me far more than a conference hall full of professors? 'I had something specific to tell them.'

Rajani frowned. 'And you've nothing to say to our village?'

Elisha stared at me, her eyes wide open. 'You do *have* something to say to Madhapur. Tell them we plan to build a well for the village.'

'Brilliant!' Rajani said. 'Elisha's hardly stopped talking about it since you got back from the conference.'

'I'm not sure,' I said. 'I thought we'd agreed to keep it under wraps until we'd got the funding.'

'Go on,' Elisha said. 'We've got the WHO backing us.'

'I know … it's just …' Why was I hesitating? 'You're right. It's great news for everyone.'

Rajani put down her plate and hugged both Elisha and me. 'Madhapur needs clean water more than anything else. Linking your marriage to giving the people a well *will* bring you good karma.'

Zac got up to get a second helping. He came back with his plate stacked even higher. I couldn't even finish mine.

'You'd better sort out what you're going to say,' he said in between mouthfuls. 'You're centre stage once everyone's finished eating.' He glanced around the crowd. 'And that won't be long.' He patted his tummy. 'Don't worry. I'll be there filming you.'

Twenty minutes later, and I was on my feet in front of the crowd.

'When Elisha and I were in Calcutta,' I began, 'an American doctor asked me what I'd do if he gave me a million dollars towards our work—'

'I'm only marrying him for the million bucks,' Elisha interrupted.

Everyone laughed.

'You think she's joking?' Zac said. 'You don't know my sister. She's just after your money.'

'Then I'm afraid she'll be bitterly disappointed.' I turned back to address the townsfolk. 'He didn't actually give us any money, but it got us thinking. Elisha told me about the far-reaching effects of the cholera outbreaks. Her mother was working at the hospital because they were so short-staffed due to cholera. And if she hadn't been on duty in casualty that night, she wouldn't have got the needle-stick injury.'

I was about to add, *and she wouldn't have died of AIDS*, when I caught sight of Pastor Martin in the crowd and bit my lip. How was he coping? Perhaps I shouldn't have said anything about Melissa's death and stirred up painful memories. There were tears in his eyes as he stepped forward and sat beside Elisha.

I looked down at the notes I'd scribbled on a serviette, and continued, 'Elisha's dream is to build a well to bring clean drinking water to our village. Just before I proposed to Elisha, I promised her we'd build it together.'

The crowd erupted in a wave of applause. The women waved their resplendently dyed scarves in the air—so much more vivid and arresting than the party hats we had back home. The men cheered and stamped their feet, and the children continued to wave their homemade flags. An eight-year-old girl proudly showed me the picture she'd drawn on her flag.

'That's you,' she said. 'That's Elisha, and that's the wedding cake.'

'Did you do it all yourself?' I asked.

'No, Rajani helped me,' she said and skipped away.

Pastor Martin rose to his feet. The crowd fell silent as he made his way to the front.

'It is five years since my dear wife, Melissa, passed away,' he said. 'There's not a day goes by that I don't miss her.' He wiped his eyes. 'Not a single day.'

Elisha rushed to her father and embraced him. 'Oh, Daddy!'

Pastor Martin brushed away a tear. 'If Melissa were here today, she would be so proud of her daughter and her soon-to-be son-in-law.'

'She *is* here, Dad,' Elisha said. 'I can feel her with us.'

Once the speeches concluded, the band struck up a triumphant melody. The womenfolk danced in the street, their brightly coloured saris creating a sea of colour that enveloped every corner of the settlement.

'We must bless the site where we will build the well,' Rajani said. 'You should do it, Pastor Martin.'

Pastor Martin paused and scratched his forehead. 'Krishna should make the dedication. He represents the people of Madhapur.'

I could read the confusion in Elisha's eyes.

'Dad!' Elisha stared at him. 'You must do it. For Mum.'

'Then we'll do it together,' Pastor Martin said.

That evening, Krishna and Pastor Martin stood side by side at the location we had chosen for the new well. I watched the tears stream down Elisha's cheeks as the two men held the same trenching shovel and jointly made a cross on the ground.

The Christians sang a hymn:

God bless this Holy land,
Hallowed by Thy almighty hand.

The Hindus chanted:

Om shanti, shanti, shanti.
Om shanti, shanti, shanti.

Rajani had told me that was an invocation of peace in Hindu and Buddhist traditions.

I didn't have a singing voice, but I couldn't stop myself joining in—first with a verse of the hymn and then with a chorus of 'Om Shanti'. The melodies blended together beautifully into a glorious anthem. An ode to peace and unity. Maybe I was becoming a poet like Zac had jested. Regardless, for one night at least, a cause close to everyone's heart united us all.

Elisha hummed the tunes as we walked home together, arm in arm. Her eyes shone as brightly as the stars that lit the evening sky.

'I never thought I'd see the day my father would acknowledge Krishna's role in the community,' she said. 'Let alone share a consecration with him.'

'I'm so pleased you're sorting things out with your father,' I said.

'So am I,' Elisha replied. 'And tonight I feel closer to my father than I have done since …'

'Since your mother died?'

'No. I haven't felt this way about my dad since I was a little girl.'

Some women walked past us, carrying their empty brass pots home, their saris still radiant in the fading light. Elisha stopped and gazed up at the heavens.

'But tonight,' Elisha said, 'something has changed. It feels like an entirely new beginning.'

We both stood for a moment studying the stars, then continued walking home.

'I'll never forget tonight either,' I said. 'I was ready to make a run for it when Indali told me I had to make a speech. I even thought of pretending to be sick.'

Elisha smiled. 'I'm glad you didn't.'

'So am I,' I said. 'I'm not sentimental, but listening to the Christians and Hindus singing together—'

 David Whittet

'There were some Sikhs and Buddhists there too,' Elisha said. 'And Abdel Nour is a Muslim.'

'And they all joined in.' I took another look up at the sky. 'If only every day could be like that—throughout the world.'

The sparkle had left Elisha's eyes when we arrived home.

'What is it?' I asked.

'Thursday is the fifth anniversary of Mum's death,' she said. 'Remember? I told you my dad is taking me to lay flowers at the church where Mum died.'

'Perhaps it'll be a bit easier after tonight,' I said, putting my arms around her. 'Would you like me to go with you?'

Elisha held me tighter than she'd ever done before. 'I wish you could. But there's more father and daughter stuff we need to sort out on our own.'

'That's okay.' I ran my fingers through her hair. 'I'll be here for you when you come back.'

CHAPTER TWENTY-ONE

The Road to Baripada

Elisha

Why was her parting from Theo so emotional? Elisha was only going away for the day, and it was just to Baripada, not the other side of the world. She kissed him so urgently and cuddled him so powerfully that she could hardly breathe.

'Take care,' Theo said. 'You'll be okay.'

His eyes said it all. *He understands—he knows this is something I have to do.* Even if the very thought of going back to that dreaded church brought Elisha out in a cold sweat.

'I'll be with you in spirit,' Theo said, 'and you know I'll be here for you when you get back.'

'I know you will.'

With a last kiss, Elisha let go of Theo and climbed into the van. When her father started the engine, Elisha fought the urge to bolt from the van straight back into Theo's arms.

Theo waved like a madman as they drove off. 'Don't be late home!' he called after them.

Elisha put her head out of the window and blew Theo a kiss. 'We won't.' She pulled her head back inside the van and glanced at her father. 'Will we?'

'Some of our friends from the wider mission are joining us at the church,' her father replied. 'So we can't rush off. They want to pay their respects to your mother too.'

Elisha sighed and turned away from her father. She gazed back down the street. Was leaving Theo for the day so painful just because they were young and in love? Elisha convinced herself it was only that. Yet her heart stood still when Theo disappeared from view out of the back of the van.

The road looked as bleak as it had done on that dark day five years earlier when they'd driven her mother to St Anne's Convent School—and to her death. Elisha had been so angry with her father that morning. Today, she didn't know what to feel.

Her father's eyes remained fixed on the road, and his hands clenched the steering wheel. The twitch on his face told her he was suffering, too.

What should she say? Who should speak first? There was so much she wanted to say about her mother. Was this the right moment? Would there ever be an appropriate time?

'Dad.' Elisha stopped and took a deep breath. 'Did you know Mum was going to die in the church that morning?'

Wesley turned his head towards her. 'Of course I didn't. What made you think that?'

'I'm not sure,' Elisha said. 'I thought maybe you were taking her to her last resting place.'

'I was so caught up with the mission, I didn't see what was going on around me,' Wesley said. 'If I'd realised how sick she was, I would never have pushed her to do that sermon.'

Elisha noticed another nervous tic on her father's face. Did he really mean that? Back then, he'd been so determined that her mother would proclaim the power of healing that day. When she'd challenged him, he'd gone on about God looking after His own.

Wesley lowered his head. 'I should have listened to you,' he said. 'I'll never forgive myself.'

Elisha would have hugged him if he wasn't driving the van. She'd never seen him so vulnerable before. 'Mum went out fighting. That's what she'd have wanted. And to die in a church.'

'You were there for her. Holding her. Comforting her. While the rest of us just stood there like idiots.' Wesley pulled the van to the side of the road, tears in his eyes. 'I should have been there with you, sharing those last precious moments.'

Elisha put her hand on her father's. 'Don't beat yourself up, Dad. You were in shock.'

It had taken her five years to forgive him. Five years of bitterness and recriminations. Now she could let go of all that anger. Elisha had her father again.

She gave his hand a squeeze. 'Thank you for asking Krishna to take part in the dedication ceremony. What made you change your mind about him?'

'It's what your mother would have wanted.' Wesley took off his glasses and dabbed his eyes. 'She liked Krishna. Persuaded me we're all fellow spirits, and that Heaven and Nirvana are really both the same place.'

'That's Mum. She'd have been so happy to see you come together.' Elisha leant across and kissed her father on the cheek. 'You did the right thing. I'm so proud of you.'

Wesley put his glasses back on and restarted the engine. 'You're right. Clean water is more important than anything else. I want to make it up to you. I'll help with the fundraising. Preach about it on Sunday and get the Church on board.'

There was an immediacy in his voice that Elisha hadn't heard before. She really had got her father back.

'Thank you, Dad,' she said. 'It'll be Mum's legacy.'

'It's the least I can do for you and for your poor mother.'

'Zac's making another film,' Elisha said. 'He's doing a promotional video for the well.'

'That's fantastic,' her father said. 'If it's as successful as his film about the lepers—there'll be no stopping you.'

'We'll send it to the local charities,' Elisha said. 'There's nobody quite like Theo for twisting people's arms. He's pestering all the contacts we made in Calcutta already. With the Church on board as well—we're going to do this.'

Baripada was as chaotic as ever. Everybody going about their business as if it was just another day. Lucky sods. After almost an hour stuck in traffic, her father found a parking space.

'I'm afraid we'll have to walk the rest of the way,' he said.

'That's alright,' Elisha said. 'I need some air.' She took her father's arm as they got out of the van. 'It means so much to me, having you involved in a project that's so close to my heart.'

'It means the world to me, too,' her father said. 'The well *will* be your mother's legacy.'

The moment she saw the dusky grey stone of St Anne's, Elisha backed away, taking quick, jerky steps. The church looked as cold and uninviting as it had on that terrifying day five years ago.

'Don't be frightened,' her father said, reaching out for her hand. 'God will help us through today.'

Elisha's immediate reaction was to hit back. God hadn't helped her mother on that dreadful day. But she'd just made her peace with her father. And besides, his palm was sweating too. He was just as frightened as she was.

'Wesley!' Deepesh Banerjee shook her father's hand. 'Thank you so much for coming.'

Elisha had barely noticed the contingent from the mission headquarters gathered in the foyer to meet them. Hugs, greetings, prayers—they all faded into the distance. Back at nursing college, she'd learnt about post-traumatic stress disorder and the healing power of returning to the scene of the trauma. That meant nothing now. Elisha remained locked five years in the past.

An official opened the church door. Elisha thought her heart would explode when she glanced inside.

Deepesh took her aside and spoke to her softly. 'You're so brave to come with your father. I pray you will find some peace and closure.'

Elisha took a deep breath and let her father lead her into the church. Her knees shook as much today as they had five years back when her mother staggered to the pulpit to deliver her last words.

Images flooded back. Her mother spluttering in the pulpit—a vision as painful today as it was unbearable then. The echo of her mother's dying words: '*Thank you, my darling. That was beautiful. Now I'd like to go home.*'

Mummy never made it home!

Elisha clutched a bouquet of crimson lilies she'd picked first thing that morning. She laid the flowers on the floor at the exact spot where her mother had fallen. Her tutors were wrong. None of this was healing.

Her father and the other missionaries got down on their knees in front of the altar. Elisha was about to join them when she spotted some dark stains on the ornately polished mosaic floor. Her throat closed as she bent down for a closer look.

'It's Mummy's blood,' she cried. 'Why's my mummy's blood still here? Why haven't they cleaned it up?'

'Elisha, my darling!' Her father got up off his knees and rested a hand on her shoulder. 'That's not your mummy's blood.'

She felt his hand tremble. 'If it's not Mummy's blood, what is it?'

He lifted his hand off her shoulder and took a handkerchief from his pocket to dry her eyes. 'They're just bleach marks …'

Elisha looked up at her father. 'I don't understand.'

There were tears in her father's eyes. 'When God called your beloved mother home …' He wiped his face and started again. 'Once your dear mother was with God … they had to … um … cleanse the church … because …'

Mummy had AIDS. Elisha still struggled to breathe. The cleaners must have scrubbed the floor for days—weeks even—to have made such a mess of the floor. They'd gouged a chunk of the mosaic. Five years on and nobody had done anything about it.

Elisha glared at the missionaries, all of them except her father still kneeling in front of the altar. 'So why haven't you fixed it?'

Pastor Sanjay Kapoor, the leader of the Baripada mission, stood up and took over. 'We were going to repair the floor, but—'

'What?'

Pastor Kapoor bit his lip. 'Finding a skilled craftsman able to do the work was difficult, especially with such an intricate mosaic. And our funds were low.'

Elisha brushed away her tears. 'It's alright. My mother wouldn't have wanted money spent on a mosaic. She'd have much rather seen it used for something more worthwhile than a floor. Something that would benefit other people.'

'Like the well we're going to build,' her father said.

'You're building a well?' Deepesh asked. 'In Madhapur? That's wonderful news!'

'It's my daughter's idea,' her father said. 'She and her fiancé have got the WHO on board. I told Elisha the mission would support them, too.'

'We sure will,' Deepesh said. 'God bless you, Elisha. You must be so proud of her, Wes.'

'I am.'

Elisha watched her father blink back another tear.

'Melissa would also have been so proud,' he said. 'Why don't we use those lilies you picked to make a memorial?'

Her father took her hand and helped Elisha to gather the lilies that she'd laid on the floor. They rearranged them so that their blood-red petals covered the broken mosaic.

'They were Mum's favourite flowers,' Elisha said.

'Come and pray with us,' Deepesh said.

Elisha stumbled to her feet, and her father helped her return to the altar. As they all knelt together, she glanced back at the lily petals. The sun shone through the stained-glass window, emphasising their deep crimson colour. Her mother would have been delighted. Elisha could breathe again, and she snuggled up to her father as he began to pray.

'Heavenly Father,' her father said, 'we give thanks for Melissa. In her brief life, my beloved wife enriched the lives of all who knew her. She gave me love, understanding, joy—and a beautiful daughter. She was a mother to Isaac when his natural mother was taken from us. Now Melissa is with God in everlasting peace.'

'Amen,' they all chanted.

'Amen,' Elisha repeated. Her mind remained a blur. She wasn't sure what she believed any more. But she hoped—and prayed—that what her father said was true.

Elisha took a last look at the petals as they left the church. *I'll never forget you, Mum. You'll always be in my heart.* She shielded her eyes as they stepped out into the sunlight. *It's over. I've done it.* She grasped her father's arm. *We've done it.*

'You must stay for tea,' Pastor Kapoor said. 'Come and meet my family.'

Must we? Elisha eyed her father, desperately willing him to say no. Yes, he'd told her they'd have to spend some time with the mission staff, but couldn't he see she just needed to get home?

Her father put a hand on Pastor Kapoor's shoulder. 'We'd be delighted.'

'Shouldn't we get back?' Elisha said. 'Theo will be waiting for me.'

Her father looked at his watch. 'I'd like to get home before dark if we can. But—' He paused for a moment and turned back to Pastor Kapoor. 'Of course we'll come. Such a pity Zahira couldn't get to the service with her new baby.'

The idea of tea with a devout church family was torture when all Elisha wanted was to get back to Theo. She'd endured enough well-intended but meaningless sympathy for a lifetime. Theo understood her. He didn't go on about some higher plan or suggest her mother died for a reason. Theo just held her tight in his loving arms. And right now, that's exactly what she needed—to rant and rave about the injustice of everything.

Pastor Kapoor must have read her mind. 'Don't worry,' he said. 'We won't keep you long. My wife Zahira is longing to meet you.'

Elisha trudged a couple of paces behind her father as they made their way to the Kapoor's house on foot. She regretted not asking Theo to come with her. No. She needed that time alone with her father in the van. They'd sorted so much out and reached a new-found harmony. Elisha noticed the way Pastor Kapoor comforted her father while they walked. Not just the words, but the sympathetic gestures and the caring glances. Her father needed support just as much as she did, and she was selfish to even think about denying it to him by rushing home. Theo had said he'd be waiting for her when she got home. Nobody would be waiting for her father.

Ten minutes' walk, and they arrived at a small yellow clay-and-cement house with a thatched roof. Not much from the outside, but the homely atmosphere in the Kapoor's household took Elisha by surprise. Her experience of missionary families had often been less than ideal, but the Kapoors were not in the least sanctimonious. And Zahir—she was delightful. A beautiful, petite lady, Elisha imagined she was how Rajani might look in ten years.

'I hear you're getting married,' Zahira said. 'Sanjay has told me about the fantastic work you are doing with your new man.'

'Theo's a genius at twisting people's arms and getting funding,' Elisha said. 'Have you heard about the well we're going to build?'

'Sanjay's just told me,' Zahira said. 'What a tremendous thing to do for the community.'

     David Whittet

'The well is just the start. There's so much else to be done.' Elisha watched Zahira feed her baby. 'What's her name?'

'Januja,' Zahira said. 'It means creation—it comes from the Sanskrit word *janu*, meaning "soul".'

Elisha felt her stomach flutter. It had never done that before. 'How old is she?'

'Six months old today.' Zahira finished breastfeeding and winded Januja, who obliged with a prize burp. 'Good girl!'

Elisha laughed. She'd never had maternal instincts, but today—she felt a warm glow inside that refused to go away.

'Would you like to hold her?' Zahira asked.

'Can I?'

'Of course you can.'

'She's so tiny!' Elisha said. 'And absolutely gorgeous.'

Elisha handed the baby back to Zahira before the stirrings got too intense.

'You'll have a baby of your own before long,' Zahira said.

Elisha took a step back. 'Maybe.'

Zahira laid Januja in a straw crib and rocked her gently. 'Sleep tight, my angel.'

Elisha suddenly wanted to share her newly discovered instincts with Theo. She glanced out of the window. The sun was low in the sky—it would soon be dark. 'I'll put the kettle on,' she said.

'Good thinking,' Zahira said as Januja fell asleep. 'Sanjay will be dying for a cup of tea. I expect your father will be too, and Deepesh.'

Five minutes later, carrying a large pot of tea and a tray full of savouries, they joined the men. They all sat around a circular table in the front room.

'I've been hearing more about this well you're going to build,' Pastor Kapoor said. 'It seems when you and your fiancé get your teeth into something, things happen fast.'

Elisha smiled. 'Theo's certainly got fire in his belly.'

'Sounds like you have too,' Pastor Kapoor said.

'I do.' Elisha paused for a moment. 'It's just … sometimes I have to bring Theo back to earth.'

Zahira poured the tea. 'So, you're the brains behind the operation.'

Elisha shuffled on her stool. 'I wouldn't say that. But we make a great team.'

'We heard how you immunised all those kids in secret,' Pastor Kapoor said. 'I hope this isn't as risky.'

Elisha waved a hand dismissively. 'Surely nobody can complain about providing the people with safe drinking water.'

Zahira passed around the tray of food. 'The militants object to everything we do.'

Deepesh took a sip of tea. 'They sure do.'

'Has there been more trouble?' Elisha asked. 'Are you listening, Dad?'

'There've been some more churches torched up in Sundergarh,' Sanjay said. 'I keep telling you, Wes, you need a bodyguard. Everyone else in the mission has a police guard.'

'God is my protector,' Wesley said.

Elisha sighed. *Typical.*

'We worry about you, Wes,' Zahira said. 'Can't you talk some sense into him, Elisha?'

'I wish I could.' Elisha cast her father a sceptical gaze. Perhaps with the truce they'd achieved that morning, she could persuade him otherwise. She'd talk to him on the drive home.

Wesley avoided her glare. 'Let's get back to fundraising for the well.' He eyed Deepesh. 'Hasn't the mission worked with other communities on similar projects?'

'We have,' Deepesh said. 'I'll talk to our outreach team tomorrow. We'll put a letter together and send it out to our sponsors. They love to support this kind of venture.'

'I can also put you in touch with a reliable building contractor,' Pastor Kapoor added. 'He does community work like this at cost.'

Elisha beamed at them. 'This is brilliant! Thank you all so much!'

'Our pleasure,' Deepesh said. 'That's what the mission is all about—or should be all about. How would you feel about an article for the mission's magazine, covering the work you and Dr Malone are doing?'

'Sure,' Elisha said. 'Anything that raises awareness of the living conditions in villages like ours.'

'I'll get one of our staffers and a photographer down to get the story,' Deepesh said.

'No problem.' Elisha looked at her watch and nudged her father. 'We ought to get going. I promised Theo we'd be home before ten.'

'Your father looks tired,' Zahira said. 'Why not stay the night with us? I can make up a couple of beds, and you can ring Theo and let him know.'

'I'm fine,' Wesley said. 'Thanks for the offer, but I need to be at the mission first thing in the morning.'

Elisha kissed baby Januja and hugged Zahira as they left. She'd only spent a couple of hours with the family but felt an immediate kinship with Zahira and her baby. And with the mission's resources behind them, building the well would be a reality. Some good had come from the day that had given her so many sleepless nights. Perhaps her tutors at nursing school had been right after all. Possibly, facing the scene of the tragedy and moving on really was cathartic. Her father appeared happier, too. The pained expression of this morning and the nervous twitch had disappeared. She felt closer to him than she'd done for a long time. Perhaps her mother was up there somewhere, drawing them together.

The release of tension combined with the darkness and the hum of the vehicle's engine, and Elisha fought to keep her eyes open. She'd promised herself she'd talk to her father about a bodyguard. Somehow, the moment just didn't seem right, and she wasn't up for another argument. Not when they were getting on so well.

With a yawn, Elisha allowed herself to drift off to sleep. The odd jerk when a dog strayed onto the road brought her around, but she soon closed her eyes again.

A sudden screeching of tyres. Shouting. That wasn't a stray dog. Elisha sat bolt upright. A truck with a mob of angry youths in the back was running them off the road. Her father's hands shook as he pulled the van onto the verge.

'Who are they?' Elisha gasped. 'You don't think they're—'

Wesley shook his head. 'They're just kids. Probably on their way home from a party.'

Elisha watched them wave their fists as the truck disappeared into the distance. 'They looked pretty mean to me.'

Her father was still trembling, and there was nothing Elisha could do to help. Perhaps they should have stayed the night with the Kapoors.

'They've given you a nasty shock,' she said. 'Are you going to be okay?'

'Give me a minute and I'll be fine,' her father said.

Elisha sighed. 'I dared to think we'd had a good day—at least, as positive as it could be in the circumstances.'

'And we have. Don't let a crowd of drunken lads spoil it.' Her father reached across and put his arm around her. 'You don't know how much it means to me, having you taking such an active part in the mission. When your mother died, and you went back to Australia—'

Elisha saw the tears well up in his eyes and looked down at her feet. 'Don't get all gloomy and teary-eyed on me.'

Her father swallowed hard. 'It needs to be said. I knew you blamed me for your mother's death, and that's why you left. I told you then it was a terrible thing to doubt everything you'd ever believed in. You said God hadn't answered my prayers. And you got so angry when I said His ways were not our ways.'

His eyes looked so sad. Tormented. Elisha hid her face. 'Dad! Don't.'

'After you'd gone, I questioned everything. My life. My faith, everything ...'

'Dad! You don't have to do this. I understand.'

'If it wasn't for Zac and Rajani, I think I might have given up. Rajani kept telling me the lepers needed our care. Reminded me what our work is really all about.' Wesley pulled himself up in his seat. 'Then God brought you back to me.'

Elisha felt a lump in her throat. 'I'm sorry I left you. Jo told me it was wrong. I was just so wrapped up in my own grief.' She leant over and hugged him. 'I'm sorry I haven't always given you the respect you deserve.'

'I'm sorry, too. I always put the mission first. Instead of thinking about what it was doing to you. I should never have dragged you out here to India.'

Elisha raised a palm. 'Stop! I'm happy to be here. I learnt so much from

     David Whittet

what Mum did for that poor kid, Kaamil.' She paused and gave him a dig in the ribs. 'And if we hadn't come to India, I'd never have met Theo.'

'I know how much you both care about the people of Madhapur,' her father said. 'Promise me, if anything happens to me, you'll carry on with the work? You and Theo?'

'Of course we will.' Elisha hugged him again. 'But nothing's going to happen to you, because like it or not, when we get home, I'm going to see Mr Prasad and get you a police guard.'

Wesley smiled. 'Alright. You win.'

Elisha shifted back into the passenger seat. 'Now, don't you think it's time we got home?'

Her father started the engine. Elisha settled herself in the seat, resting her head on the headrest. Now she could take a nap with a clear conscience. She'd said what she had to say, and her father had agreed.

Elisha closed her eyes. She'd have so much to tell Theo when they got home. She heard the indicator making that clicking noise as her father pulled out. A bright light shone through her closed eyelids. Obviously, the glare from oncoming headlights, and Elisha put her arms over her eyes to shield them from the light.

The van stopped. Why has her father done that? Perhaps the van had just stalled. She took her arms away from her face and peered up through the windscreen. It took a second to take in the scene in front of her.

'Get your head down,' her father screamed.

Elisha's heart pumped against her chest as a truck hurtled towards them. *What do they want with us?*

The last thing Elisha saw as she curled up in the footwell was a mob jumping off the truck, wielding burning torches and hurling abuse at them.

'Filthy Christian pigs!'

'Scum!'

'Get out of our country! Parasites!'

The truck rammed into their van and sent them skidding into a ditch. A sudden crash, and Elisha was upside down. The van must have rolled over.

Was her father okay? He'd hit his head on the roof. Was he alive? Dazzled by the mob and their blazing torches, she couldn't see.

The van burst into flames. Shards of burning upholstery struck her face. She barely noticed the pain in her desperate bid to force open the door and escape, and to save her father. *Damn.* The impact and the heat had buckled the door, and there was no way she could get it open.

Her father smashed the windscreen with his fists. He was still alive. *Thank God!* She fought for air as her father pleaded with the attackers.

'It's me you want!' he begged. 'Do what you want with me, but let my daughter go!'

The gang had them surrounded. Elisha shrank at their cold, hard eyes—they wouldn't show any mercy. Her father must have seen that, too, but he didn't give up.

'Leave me to die, burn me alive if you must—but save my daughter! Get her out! Before it's too late! Please!'

The ringleader poked a flaming torch in her father's face. 'Why don't you ask God to save you and your precious daughter, Pastor Martin? What? He's not listening?'

Another mobster threw his flare into the van. 'Looks like you're both going to burn in Hell!'

Elisha's hair was on fire. The skin blistered on her hand. Was this really the end? Would she die without the chance to say goodbye to Theo?

The flames raged, but strangely, Elisha's mind slowed down. She'd heard one's entire life flashed past in the moments before death, but for her, just a few thoughts survived amid the furnace. What would happen to the mission and field hospital if she and her father died? Would Theo stay on without her? Would he build the well? And what about the lepers? Who would look after them?

Another lungful of acrid smoke and Elisha suddenly became defiant. The mission *had* to survive. No way would these thugs win. The mission had been successful before her father joined the missionaries, and it would continue working for the community after he died. Elisha gasped for another breath. And the lepers—they had Zac and Rajani and a host of dedicated workers. They'd managed when she went back to Australia. What about the well? If there truly was an afterlife, she'd be up there giving Theo a hard time if he didn't get his finger out and build that well.

 David Whittet

The mob's chanting grew louder, each taking a turn to throw their burning torches into the blaze.

Coughing and spluttering, her father continued pleading for her. 'Show some mercy! For pity's sake! She's got her life in front of her! She doesn't deserve this!'

Another shaft of fiery debris hit Elisha's head. She clung to her father, hardly daring to look at his burning clothes and smouldering skin.

'I love you, Dad,' she whispered, rubbing her face against his scorching cheeks.

Elisha just wanted to die in his arms. Soon they would both be with her mother—five years to the day after she'd left them.

CHAPTER TWENTY-TWO

Theo

Almost midnight and still no sign of them. Elisha promised me they'd be back by ten at the latest. Where were they? And why was my heart beating so fast that my chest hurt?

Zac would know. My hand shook as I picked up the telephone. I'd dialled the number so often, but tonight it took me half a dozen attempts to get it right. When I did get through, Zac was his usual laid-back self, but there was an edge to his voice.

'Sorry, mate,' Zac said. 'Not a word.'

'Nothing?' I held the handpiece to my chest for a moment. *Something's wrong. I know it is.* I took a deep breath and lifted the receiver back to my mouth. 'Listen, Zac, I'm worried—'

'So's Rajani,' Zac said, interrupting me. 'I told her to chill. You both know what my sister's like. She's probably up to something in Baripada.'

My stomach churned. 'Not with her father with her.'

'You're as bad as Rajani,' Zac said. 'She's been on about the rebels torching churches. Got it into her head they might burn down St Anne's while Elisha and Dad were there praying.'

My heart beat even faster. *That's exactly what I'm thinking.*

'I told her not to be so silly,' Zac said. 'We'd have heard by now if anything nasty had happened.'

The phone went dead for a moment, then Zac's voice again, this time even more clipped. 'Hang on a minute. There's someone at the door. If it's Elisha and Dad, I'll give them a rollicking for worrying us like this.'

Muffled voices on the other end of the phone. Not Elisha's or her father's. Then my pounding heart almost stopped beating altogether. I heard Rajani sobbing in the background.

David Whittet

Zac's voice trembled when he came back on the phone. 'Theo—mate—the police have just arrived. There's been an accident outside Baripada.'

My throat closed up. 'Is she alright? Elisha? And your dad?'

'Mate—I don't know.'

I slammed down the receiver and ran to the Martins' house. Adrenaline drove my still shaky legs, almost tripping on the rubble in my panic to get there. Turning the corner, I suddenly stopped. The harsh blue flashing light of the police car parked outside the Martins' house cast a cold shadow over the street—and my heart.

Zac ran up and flung his arms around me, sobbing. 'He's dead! My dad!'

I held him in a bear hug. 'Oh, Zac, I'm so sorry. What happened?'

'They got him,' Zac cried. 'They said they would, and now they've done it!'

'Who? The militants? And Elisha?' I could scarcely get the words out. 'What's happened to Elisha? Where is she?'

'The mob … they burnt both of them alive,' Zac wailed.

I let go of Zac and collapsed onto a fence. My heart caved in. I fought for breath and scarcely dared think the words, let alone utter them out loud. 'Elisha's dead too?'

Zac clenched his fists. 'She might as well be.' He grasped the sides of his head and turned to the policeman. 'She's going to die, isn't she?'

'I think you'd better come inside and sit down,' the police officer said.

Rajani was in the front room with her head in her arms. She embraced both Zac and me, and the three of us collapsed in a huddle.

'We're sure it was Akbar Zahin and his gang,' the police officer continued. 'He's been biding his time, stirring up hatred against Christians. They must have followed Pastor Martin and Elisha, ran them off the road and set fire to their van.'

I gasped for air. 'Elisha's still alive?'

'She was still breathing when we found her at the side of the road,' the police officer said. 'It seems someone pulled her out of the wreckage. They're rushing her to the government hospital at Baripada.'

'Then what are we waiting for?' Another burst of adrenaline propelled me to my feet. 'I'll fetch the van. Who's coming with me to the hospital?'

'Hold on,' the police officer said. 'You're in no fit state to drive.'

I glared back. 'Try stopping me.'

Zac put his arm on my shoulder. 'Theo! We don't want another accident.'

'We'll get you a police escort,' the officer said. 'Just give me a minute.'

We don't have a minute! 'How long's that going to take?'

The officer drew in a long breath. 'You need to prepare yourself, Dr Malone. Miss Martin is severely burnt. Almost her entire skin—'

'I've worked in a burns unit and seen total body burns.' I didn't care what Elisha looked like as long as she was still alive. Couldn't the officer see that? 'Please—just get us to the hospital as fast as you can.'

Twenty minutes later, crammed together with Zac and Rajani in the back seat, my mind ran riot as the police car sped along the road to Baripada. *Please, Elisha—be alive when we get to the hospital.* I didn't care what she looked like—I just wanted to hold her again. This had to be a ghastly nightmare, and I would soon wake up. I hit my face hard. Maybe that would wake me up, and it would all be over. It didn't. I hit myself again. Even harder. I was still wide awake and huddled up in the back of that police car. But my stinging face numbed the pain of the trauma for a few seconds.

Anger took over. If only I could get my hands on those bloody militants. I clenched my fists, imagining what I would do to them. Elisha's father, too! Why the hell hadn't he listened to what everyone was saying and got himself a bodyguard?

Zac held Rajani tight in his arms. None of us spoke. Rajani sobbed. Otherwise, silence.

The police driver slowed down. I looked up. What was going on? Floodlights lit a line of police cars at the roadside. Then I saw it. Behind the police cordon. The upturned, burnt-out wreck of Pastor Martin's van.

I leant forward to speak to the police driver. 'Stop the car, please. I want to get out and look.'

'Are you sure?' the driver asked. 'I don't think that's a—'

'Just stop the car,' I said, cutting him off. 'I'm feeling sick. I need to get some air.'

 David Whittet

The driver pulled up onto the verge. 'If you're sure.'

I did feel like throwing up, but that wasn't the reason I needed to get out. While I couldn't explain it to myself, let alone anyone else, I had to see where Elisha had suffered such horror. It was part of sharing the pain—we were kindred spirits. If only I could have been with her. And for a moment, in my mind, I was. I felt the heat of the flames on my face and the fire consume my body, the way it must have done to hers. Why hadn't she let me go with her and her father to the church?

I watched the police comb the debris for clues. I took a step forward and froze. Could anyone possibly have survived such an inferno? No way. Elisha hadn't made it—they were just humouring me. Perhaps the driver was right, and I shouldn't have got out of the car. Because in minutes, I had convinced myself that somewhere amongst the carnage, in that mangled heap of charred metal, were the mortal remains of Elisha and her father.

Zac held on to Rajani. It must have been even worse for him than it was for me. I wanted to say something, but words wouldn't make any difference. I couldn't think past my own pain, anyway.

'Mate,' Zac said, 'we should get going to the hospital.'

I kicked a piece of burnt-out metal. 'What's the point?' I pointed to the smouldering wreck. 'Are you trying to tell me Elisha got out of that?'

'She did!' Zac said. 'Didn't you hear what the policeman said?'

I kicked some more burnt rubble. 'He's lying.'

Tears streamed down Rajani's face. 'You're not lying, are you?' she asked the police driver.

'We wouldn't do that,' the driver replied. 'Excuse me a moment. That's HQ trying to get hold of us.'

I strained to hear the message over the police radio. No use. Instead, Elisha's voice rang in my ears. *I'm alive, Theo. I'm alive—and I need you with me ... now.*

Moments later, the driver was back. 'They're airlifting Elisha to Calcutta for urgent surgery.'

'I'm going with her,' I said.

'Then we'd better get moving,' the driver said.

She's alive! But for how much longer? The image of the wreckage had blasted a hole in my brain. The driver *was* right—I should never have got out of the police car. And we'd wasted precious time. Would we get to the hospital in time?

Back in the police car, the driver turned on the blue flashing light.

'As fast as you can, please,' I urged.

How I hated that road to Baripada! The blue flashing light cast an eerie flare across the bleak night landscape. A landscape as barren as my soul.

'I'm coming to Calcutta too,' Zac said.

Rajani rubbed her eyes. 'So am I.'

The driver looked over his shoulder at us and frowned. 'There won't be enough room for all of you in the helicopter.'

I glanced at Zac and Rajani. Zac should be the one to go. He was Elisha's brother—well, at least, her half-brother. But she was my fiancée, the love of my life …

Zac met my gaze. 'You go, Theo. It's you she'll want to see when she comes round.'

Rajani gave a half-hearted shrug. 'We'll come to Calcutta on the train tomorrow.' She clasped her hands together, her eyes dull. 'I'll have to go back to Madhapur anyway and sort out the school.'

'Can't Madhu or one of the other girls do that?' Zac asked.

Rajani shook her head. 'It has to be me. I want the kids to hear about Elisha and Pastor Martin from me.'

'Okay,' Zac said, holding Rajani close. 'I understand. But I want to see my sister first.'

It took another fifteen agonising minutes before we arrived at the government hospital. Fifteen more minutes cursing under my breath. Railing against the militants, the authorities, religion—everyone who'd let this happen.

I was out of the door the moment the police car pulled up at the hospital. Minutes later, chasing down the corridor behind the gurney, I caught my first glimpse of Elisha, her entire body swathed in bandages. Only her forlorn, frightened eyes were visible, staring blankly at the ceiling through the dressings.

 David Whittet

'My daddy! My daddy! Where is he?' she mumbled as the porters wheeled her into the lift.

Zac rushed forward, tears streaming down his cheeks. 'He's gone, sis, he's gone.'

'Gone? Gone where?' Elisha began to shake. 'Into the burning fires of Hell?'

'No, sis,' Zac said. 'He's at peace.'

Elisha closed her eyes as we reached the roof. I glanced at the monitors—her heart rate had dropped, and she'd slipped back into a coma. *Don't leave me!* With her body wrapped up in a shroud of bandages, I couldn't even touch her skin. I just grasped her bandaged hand. Held it. Squeezed it. Hoped—prayed—that she could feel something.

Zac and Rajani followed us to the rooftop heliport. Rajani clung to the gurney and refused to let go when the intensive care crew attempted to load Elisha into the helicopter.

Zac gently pulled Rajani back. 'You'll see Elisha tomorrow. Remember what you said about talking to the children in the morning?'

'We won't get to see her for a couple of days,' Rajani said. 'I wasn't thinking how long it'll take to get a train to Calcutta. Who knows if she'll still …?' Rajani broke off in tears.

I finished the sentence for her in my mind. *Who knows if she'll still be alive in a couple of days?*

Zac's eyes were watering too. He must have been thinking the same, but he held it together for Rajani. 'She's going to be okay. She's got her own personal doctor with her.'

'Thanks, mate.' I took in a deep breath and patted Zac on the back. 'I'll make sure they take care of her.'

Her own personal doctor. What use was I to Elisha in the state I was in?

I bent down to face Rajani. 'Zac's right,' I said. 'Elisha's a fighter. She's going to pull through.'

But would she? I hugged both Zac and Rajani, overcome with guilt that I was going with Elisha, and they were staying behind.

'Time to go,' the intensive care specialist said.

'Okay.' I clambered on board the helicopter before I completely broke down. The rotor blade began to whirl.

Elisha opened her eyes. The noise must have roused her.

'Where's Zac?' she said. 'Why isn't he coming?'

'He is,' I said. 'He'll see you tomorrow. Rajani too.'

'Tomorrow? I want to see them now.'

I felt even more ashamed of taking the place on the helicopter. 'Rajani has to go back to Madhapur to sort things out at the school.'

'Promise they'll be here tomorrow?'

I swallowed hard. 'Well, in a couple of days tops.' I peered out the helicopter window. 'Look, Zac and Rajani are waving at you.'

Perhaps if I could raise Elisha's head, she could see them waving and it would bring her some comfort.

'Try not to overexcite her,' the specialist said, checking Elisha's monitor.

I glanced out of the window again. Zac and Rajani clung to each other as the turbulence from the rotor blade almost blew them off their feet. I waved back at them as the helicopter took off and they disappeared from view, along with the drab lights of Baripada.

Elisha lapsed in and out of consciousness during the flight, rambling incoherently when she came round.

'Daddy! Daddy! What's happening to us? I thought you said we'd go to Heaven when we died. Why are we burning in Hell?'

What could I say or do to make her feel better? I tried fanning her skin with my hand. The helicopter was stifling, and maybe she thought she was still on fire.

'You're safe now, my darling,' I said. 'I won't let anything else happen to you, I promise.'

The burns unit at the Calcutta Medical College and Hospital had that familiar smell of despair. Bodies so hideously scarred they were scarcely human. I tried not to look at them as the orderlies wheeled Elisha through the ward. Thank God she was still delirious and couldn't see the other patients' grotesque faces.

Elisha stirred when the nurses lifted her onto the hospital bed in the intensive care unit. The sister shone a light in her eyes.

 David Whittet

'Fire! Fire!' Elisha fought the nurses and attempted to get off the bed. 'Get me out of here! Where's Daddy? We're burning in Hell!'

The burns registrar came in and gave her an injection to sedate her. When he pulled back the dressings and foil to listen to her heart and lungs, I got my first glimpse of the charred black mass that used to be her chest.

'We need to intubate,' the registrar said. 'She's got some upper airway oedema.'

I watched the doctor, who must have been around my age, perform the procedure that I'd done so often in emergency situations. I mirrored his actions with my hands, feeling his pain as he struggled to get the endotracheal tube past the swelling. We both took a deep breath when it was safely in place.

'She must stay on the ventilator overnight,' the registrar told the sister. 'And keep the fluids up. At least seven hundred millilitres per hour.'

'How bad is she?' I asked, as if I didn't know already. 'Will you be able to graft the burns?'

The registrar hesitated. 'She's got sixty to seventy per cent burns. And they're sixth degree. We're contacting our skin bank to see what we can do.'

The next forty-eight hours were the longest of my life. I spent the night watching the fluid trickle down the IV line drop by drop and agonised about what her skin would look like under the bandages.

And so it went on through the following day. By mid-afternoon, Elisha was off the ventilator and breathing normally, but she remained comatose.

The police came, wanting to take a statement. They'd be lucky. I felt like giving them a piece of my mind. Why couldn't they have been there and stopped the disaster from happening? Why hadn't they insisted on providing Pastor Martin with police protection?

'Have you caught the bastards?' I asked, bracing myself.

'We've got Akbar Zahin in custody,' the detective said. 'Actually, it was one of Zahin's men who gave him up. A young lad called Salim. He was so appalled at what the men did, he risked his life to pull your fiancée out of the fire.'

Elisha opened her eyes. 'Salim! Salim!'

'Yes, Salim,' the detective said. 'He saved your life, Miss Martin.'

Elisha showed even more signs of life when Zac and Rajani arrived that evening. She talked about the boy who rescued her.

'I was holding on to Dad. We were both burning. I just wanted to die in his arms. Then I felt this arm grip my shoulder.' Elisha sank back on the pillow. 'I wish he'd left me there. Then I'd be with Mum and Dad.'

'Sis!' Zac said. 'Don't say that.'

'But it's true.' Elisha gazed at the array of monitors and equipment that surrounded her. 'What future is there for me?'

Rajani brushed back a tear and took Elisha's arm. 'Remember what Krishna told you? He said you had a long shadow. That means you have a long life ahead of you.'

Elisha groaned. 'I don't know how I'm going to endure another day, let alone a lifetime.'

I squeezed Elisha's other arm. 'You will. Because we're all here for you.'

The nurse came in to check Elisha's pulse and blood pressure. 'It's good to see you perking up, Elisha,' she said. 'Wonderful what a bit of company can do for you.'

But were our empty words enough? Elisha's eyes still peered through the bandages, her expression like that of a lost child.

'My father should have survived, not me,' Elisha said. 'He was a good man.'

Rajani pulled her chair close to the bedside. 'He was. And you're a good—'

'I'm not,' Elisha interrupted. 'I was mean to my father. Remember how I used to blame him for trying to convert people to Christianity? That wasn't it at all. He just wanted to make people's lives better.'

'And he did,' Rajani said. 'He turned lepers from being outcasts into humans with dignity. He gave them hope. You should be proud of your father's memory.'

'I am,' Elisha said. 'Before the mob attacked us, I promised my dad I'd carry on his work.'

'Then you must,' Rajani said.

Elisha glanced around at all the scarred faces in the intensive care unit. 'How can I, looking like an ogre? I'll frighten everyone away.'

'Nonsense,' Rajani shot back. 'Think about those lepers. You said yourself they were beautiful.'

'On the inside, maybe,' Elisha said.

'On the inside and the outside,' Rajani insisted.

I couldn't listen to any more. *Beautiful on the inside and the outside.* I could have wept; I wanted to. Excusing myself, I slipped off the ward and paced up and down the corridor. I hated myself for being so superficial, but I couldn't bear the thought of Elisha looking like something out of a horror film. I'd heard one orderly call her Molasar, a giant rubber monster with glowing red eyes from the movie *The Keep,* which was popular at the time.

Dr Anand, the consultant, was sitting in his office, and he beckoned me in. Why was I so sure this meant more bad news?

'Take a seat, Dr Malone,' he began. 'I'm sure I don't need to tell you Miss Martin's burns are severe and extensive. And I'm sure you'll appreciate we have a limited amount of white skin in our tissue bank. The cosmetic result we're able to achieve may be less than ideal.'

I didn't sit down. I'd made my mind up. 'I'm taking Elisha back with me to New Zealand.'

The backlash was inevitable—and not just from the hospital staff. I'd mentally prepared for the storm when Zac and Rajani burst into the visitor's room the following day.

'What's all this about taking Elisha away?' Rajani said, her bewildered eyes gazing into mine.

'You can't,' Zac said. 'I won't let you.'

'Listen to me.' I stared at Zac's resentful face. 'They haven't got the facilities here. Dr Anand admitted it. I'm not having them doing a botched skin graft on Elisha.'

'The quality of care at this hospital is as good as anywhere in the world,' Zac said. 'If not better.'

I couldn't believe what I was about to say. 'If it wasn't for me, Rajani, you'd be dead, thanks to the medical care out here.'

Rajani burst into tears.

Zac cut me down with his eyes. 'That was cruel.'

It was the wrong thing to say—but it was also true. I bit my lip and tried to explain. 'I'm sorry, Rajani, I didn't mean to upset you.' I sat down beside her and put my arm on her shoulder. 'Put it down to lack of sleep. We're all exhausted and overemotional.' How could I explain this to them? I cleared my throat and started again. 'I know you don't want to hear this, but there's this brilliant doctor back home in New Zealand. He operated on a Ugandan boy and did a fantastic job. Matthew Levi's the man to fix Elisha.'

I'd called Matthew Levi the previous night. He'd done well for himself, moving to Auckland and an even more lucrative private practice.

'You can come with us,' I added hastily.

'I can't,' Rajani said. 'Even if I could get a visa, my place is here. Working with the lepers, carrying on Pastor Martin's work at the mission.'

'What about you, Zac?' I said. 'Won't you come and support your sister?'

Zac's hands tightened into fists. 'I belong here, too, with Rajani. I told you, I won't allow you to take Elisha away from me.'

'Have you asked Elisha what she wants?' I said. 'I have.'

Zac tapped his fingers on the waiting room table. 'And what's that?'

I looked him straight in the eye. 'Your sister wants her skin back.'

'Are you sure that's not because you're pestering her?' Zac said.

'Ask her yourself,' I replied.

'I will,' Zac said. 'But at the moment, she's preoccupied with Dad's funeral. The doctors won't let her go. And just when I thought it couldn't get any worse, some uncle we haven't heard from in ages is kicking up a stink about sending Dad's remains back to Australia.'

'Pastor Martin would have wanted his ashes scattered in the Mayurbhanj,' Rajani added. 'His soul was—*is*—here.'

I never wanted to fall out with Zac. He'd been such a good mate—one of the best I'd ever had. Perhaps it was inevitable we'd clash over Elisha—we both loved her dearly and wanted what was best for her. We were both under enormous stress, and our hearts continued to pull us in opposite directions.

The atmosphere remained equally tense when we travelled back by train to Madhapur for the funeral a couple of days later. I sat opposite Zac and

     David Whittet

Rajani in the cramped carriage. There was still not the slightest doubt in my mind that taking Elisha back to New Zealand was the right thing to do.

Preachers from across India and mission staff packed the train, all making the journey to pay their respects to Pastor Martin. I was still mad at the mission. Why hadn't they protected Elisha and her father? Listening to them go on about Pastor Martin's good works, and his faith that God would protect him, drove me to distraction. I was about to say something when Zac caught my attention. Why was he loading a new cassette into his video camera? Surely he wasn't—

'You're never going to film the wake,' I said, almost spitting the words at him.

'I'm doing it for Elisha,' Zac said.

Like hell! 'What?'

Zac continued fiddling with his video camera. 'Since they wouldn't let her come with us, Elisha wants me to video the ceremony so she can watch it later.'

I still didn't believe him. My mind was beyond all reason. I convinced myself Zac had his eyes on Bollywood and was only videoing the ceremony to get material for some ghoulish horror film.

Rajani must have seen the doubt in my eyes.

'It's true,' she said. 'Elisha asked him to make a video.'

The funeral rite was worse than a horror film. How could you light a pyre for someone who's already been cremated alive? Deepesh Banerjee and his minions carried a muslin sheath to the river's edge, chanting prayers, singing hymns, and speaking in tongues. Were Elisha's father's mortal remains really wrapped up in that sheath? Or was it all just an act? And how dare they sing praises to a God who'd allowed this atrocity! I wanted to stand up and scream. Ask them what God was doing when the thugs set fire to the van. That would have made a spectacular scene for Zac's video.

Deepesh Banerjee prepared to light the pyre. More speaking in tongues. More gibberish. Zac edged forward to get a better shot. I could have kicked the camera out of his hand.

'Is that sensational enough for you?' I screamed at him. 'Why don't you film Elisha's burns as well, in close-up and glorious technicolour?'

'Maybe I should,' Zac said. 'Make a documentary about the human spirit. Show that whatever those evil monsters do to us, hate never wins.'

'Hate never wins?' I shot him a furious glance. 'What planet are you on, Zac? Your father's dead, your sister's maimed for life, and you have the gall to say hate never wins? Well, I tell you, mate, it just has.'

And I meant it. Those thugs had destroyed all our lives.

I have to get out of this country, and I am taking Elisha with me to New Zealand.

     David Whittet

CHAPTER TWENTY-THREE

Rajani pushed Elisha's wheelchair towards the departure gate. We'd remained silent during the hour-long ambulance ride from the hospital to the airport.

'So, this is it, sis,' Zac said when we reached passport control. 'It's not too late to change your mind.'

'Don't say that,' Elisha said. 'I need you to tell me I'm doing the right thing.'

'You are,' Rajani said, giving the wheelchair a last shove towards the departure gate. 'Theo's a good man. He'll take care of you.'

Over the past couple of weeks, Rajani had acted as a referee while Zac and I pulled Elisha's heartstrings in opposite directions. I never wanted to fight with Zac or Rajani, but I had to do what was best for Elisha.

'You'd better look after her,' Zac said, shifting his angry glare to me. 'Or you'll have me to answer to.'

Was I doing the right thing? The hugs, kisses and tears at the airport that morning made me think. It was the first time I'd doubted myself since that meeting with Dr Anand. I had to sign a mass of papers, taking responsibility for Elisha during the flight and absolving the hospital of any blame for her early discharge against medical advice. We had to get on the aeroplane before I lost my nerve.

I felt a lump in my throat as I took the wheelchair from Rajani. 'Come on. It's time to go.'

Rajani put her arms around Elisha. 'I can't even give you a decent hug without hurting you.'

'Never mind that,' Elisha said. 'Come here.'

Elisha's wounds were giving her grief. I could feel her pain as the two girls embraced.

'Will I ever see you again?' Rajani said.

Tears stained Elisha's bandages. 'I deserted you once before. I promise I'll be back. As soon as I'm better.'

'Damn right you're coming back,' Zac said. 'Even if I have to come and get you myself.'

Zac's expression was unforgiving. He wasn't just angry—he was worried about his sister. I understood that. Of course I did. I only wished he appreciated how I felt. I couldn't even look at Rajani. The depth of feeling was taking its toll on Elisha—I could tell from the way her body shook and her voice quavered.

I wheeled Elisha through to security and dared not look back.

They boarded us before the other passengers. As a gesture of goodwill, the airline gave us a private area in first class, separated by a curtain and usually reserved for celebrities. Perhaps they just didn't want their other premium customers to see Elisha's burns. The Calcutta Medical College's early grafts had made her scars even worse, a hideous mottled mosaic of mismatched skin colours.

The cabin crew helped me to transfer Elisha from the wheelchair to her seat and strap her in.

'My father always promised he'd take us to New Zealand for a holiday,' Elisha said, settling into the seat. 'But he never did. Perhaps there weren't enough preachers over there—he had to have fellowship wherever he went.'

The flight attendants smiled. 'I thought New Zealand was God's own country,' one of them said. 'Now, can I get you a drink, Miss Martin?'

'Just some water, please,' Elisha said. 'The doctors told me I need to keep my fluids up on the flight.'

The journey back to New Zealand felt like even more of a marathon than when I'd first flown to India. I guess I was full of hope back then. The movies were all Bollywood romances—Elisha became maudlin when she was tired, and that was the last thing she needed.

Midway through the first leg of the trip, the flight to Singapore, Elisha started fiddling with her water bottle and muttering. 'Why did I live and my father die? Why did God spare me?'

   David Whittet

I sighed. We'd been through this a thousand times. 'You survived because one of the boys came to their senses and pulled you out of the wreckage.'

Elisha managed a half-smile through her scarred lips. 'My father would have said God planned it that way.'

I raised my eyebrows. 'Don't tell me you think this was all an act of God. I thought you were the sceptic of the family.'

'Experiences like this change you,' Elisha said. 'It's almost as if Dad knew what was going to happen. We'd parked at the side of the road. Just before they set fire to the car, he asked me to carry on his work if anything should happen to him.' She suddenly burst into tears. 'And now I can't. Because *you're* taking me away from Madhapur. I want to go back! *Take me back!*'

The flight attendant popped her head around the curtain. 'Is everything alright?'

'Yes,' I said. 'She's just a bit upset. It's been a tough time for her.'

I'd got used to Elisha's fragile emotions following the attack—crying one minute, laughing the next. She always directed her anger at me. Maybe I deserved it.

Elisha raised her muddled eyes to mine. 'Rajani said you were a good man. Are you?'

Was I? I sure didn't know any more. Before I could think of an appropriate reply, Elisha was off again.

'This is your fault, Theo. If you hadn't upset so many local government officials, then the Hindu militants might not have set the van on fire.'

What could I say? There was so much I wanted to tell her. Had she forgotten that I was the one who pushed for her and her father to have bodyguards? I'd never wanted them to take that trip to Baripada alone. But speaking up would only inflame things. Instead, I cradled her disfigured hand.

'We have the chance to make a difference in New Zealand,' I said. 'I've got a job offer in a remote practice in the Far North.'

Elisha jerked her head backwards. 'What? You're going to leave me in hospital and push off to do your own thing?'

'Don't be silly. I won't take up the position until you've had your surgery and you've had time to recover.' I stroked her forehead softly. 'We're going to do this together. It's a Māori settlement with high health-needs. Poverty, diabetes, heart disease. We'll have our work cut out.'

Elisha's puckered face brightened. 'A Māori community? I'd like that. I was going to work for an aboriginal provider in Alice Springs when I first got my nursing degree. Then Rajani got sick, and I had to leave Australia … Well, you know the rest.'

Thank God she was happy with the idea. I kissed her lips. 'We've always made a great team, haven't we? It'll be just like it was when we first met.'

Except it wouldn't. At least not yet. Elisha had major surgery to get through first.

     David Whittet

CHAPTER TWENTY-FOUR

Belvedere Private Hospital, Auckland,
New Zealand, the Following Day

When we arrived at the Belvedere Hospital, Bwanbale and his mother, Hanifah Zuluka, were there to greet us.

'Bwanbale!' I shook his hand. 'How you've grown!'

'He's quite the handsome young man now, isn't he?' Hanifah said. 'Thanks to Dr Levi.' She turned to Elisha. 'He's a fantastic surgeon. He did a wonderful job on my boy, and I'm sure he'll do the same for you.'

'I hope so.' Elisha moved some bandages covering her head to reveal the extent of her burns. 'But I think Dr Levi has his work cut out with my face.'

'That man can work miracles,' Hanifah said, 'and we've got the photos to prove it.'

Once the nurses had settled Elisha in her hospital bed, Hanifah rummaged in her handbag and pulled out some photographs.

'That's Bwanbale before the surgery.' Hanifah passed the photo to Elisha. 'You wouldn't believe it was the same boy, would you?'

I noticed Elisha's hand shaking as she held the picture, and I put my arm around her. 'Matthew Levi did an awesome job, didn't he? Bwanbale's face looked even worse than it does in the pictures. I almost passed out the first time I saw that fungating lesion in the outpatient clinic.'

Elisha handed the picture back to Hanifah. 'Can he really make that much difference to me?'

'Of course he can,' Hanifah said. 'I told you, Dr Levi is a magician!'

Matthew Levi must have seemed like a saint to Bwanbale and his mother. The superb cosmetic result had changed the boy's life, and Matthew had done it all without charging a cent.

'I'm not sure that Dr Levi has magical powers,' I said, 'but I do know he's a first-rate surgeon.' I gave Elisha another cuddle. 'And that's what we need.'

'You couldn't be in better hands.' Hanifah kissed Elisha's hand as they got up to leave. 'You must come down to Dunedin to see us when you're feeling better. I want to see for myself how beautiful you look after the operation.'

Once we'd farewelled Bwanbale and Hanifah, an immaculately dressed young woman, a 'Patient Services Assistant' according to her name badge, brought in a pot of Earl Grey tea on a tray arranged with the finest Royal Doulton china.

'Who's paying for all this?' Elisha asked. 'Paramedics meeting us on board the plane. The medical escort to the hospital. And places like this don't come cheap. Not to mention the cost of the surgery. Can we afford it?'

I waved my hand dismissively. 'Matthew Levi has refused to take a fee. Just like he did for Bwanbale.' I didn't tell her about the bank loan I'd taken out to cover the hospital costs.

Elisha sipped the tea. 'When we first moved to India, my mother used to say she'd sell her soul for a cup of Earl Grey after all that sweet chai they served us over there. Now I know what she meant.'

The moment Elisha put her cup down, Matthew Levi burst into the private room, surrounded by his registrar, house doctor, and a group of medical students.

'Dr Malone!' Levi greeted me with a hearty handshake. 'Good to see you back in civilisation. Never quite understood why you took off and left us.'

My hand stung from the handshake. 'Turned out plastic surgery just wasn't my vocation.'

'Pity,' Levi said as he approached Elisha. 'This would never have happened if you'd stayed in New Zealand.'

I caught Elisha's eyes, and they weren't happy.

'We wouldn't have met if I hadn't gone to India,' I said.

Levi picked up the case file from the trolley and flicked through it. 'Well, let's see what the natives have done to you,' he said, summoning a nurse to undo Elisha's bandages. 'My goodness. They really wished you ill.'

I could have hit him. How could he be so insensitive? Even his students looked embarrassed by his inappropriate choice of words. Was his crass behaviour just because it was me? Levi was never politically correct, but his bedside manner was always super smooth, especially when dealing with private patients.

I bristled in sympathy as Levi examined Elisha. She pulled away whenever he touched her skin.

'Seventy per cent burns,' Levi said. 'I'm afraid your modelling days are over.'

'They never began,' Elisha said.

Levi turned to his students. 'She may not be gracing the catwalks, but we can certainly make her look a lot more presentable. I want you all in theatre tomorrow morning. Watch and learn.'

'Natives indeed!' Elisha spat the words in my face after Levi and his entourage had left. 'What the hell does he know about India?'

'Nothing,' I said. 'I think he was just trying to make light of a difficult situation. Put you at your ease.'

'Well, it didn't work,' Elisha said. 'Catwalk! How dare he!'

'Don't take any notice of his manner,' I said. 'Levi's a fine surgeon and that's what matters.'

'He's a bigot,' Elisha said, 'and that matters to me.'

I squeezed her hand. 'You don't have to like him. Once he's worked his magic on your scars, you'll never have to see him again.'

I knew Elisha didn't buy my lame excuses for Matthew Levi's behaviour. He had been unbelievably thoughtless. But I meant what I said, Levi was a brilliant surgeon. Elisha would understand why I chose him when she looked in the mirror after the surgery.

Matthew Levi invited me to observe the operation from the gallery. I'd watched him operate before—the last time I was in that theatre was for Bwanbale's surgery. Watching Levi perform was like witnessing a master illusionist at work. Skin grafts seemed to appear from his sleeves like a conjuring trick. He then juggled the flaps of tissue until they miraculously fell into place. Perhaps he really was a magician.

But today was personal. Elisha was under the knife. The woman I loved. I held my breath every time he raised a flap of skin and breathed a sigh of relief when he stitched it back in place. I'd bitten my nails to the quick by the end of the six-hour operation.

The students in the gallery applauded when Levi finally laid down his scalpel. I felt strangely light-headed as I made for the changing room to thank Levi. He took off his mask and head covering, sweat pouring from his face. This time, it was me who made the powerful handshake.

'I won't forget this,' I said. 'I owe you.'

Levi wiped his forehead. 'Then come and work with me.'

I stepped back. 'I can't. I've signed up to a GP practice in Northland.'

Levi shook his head. 'Just don't go off to some other danger zone and get yourself into trouble.' He pulled off his theatre scrubs, which had stuck to his body with perspiration. 'Promise me that.'

Matthew Levi could be a jerk, but he was a genius too. Today had proved that. I'd made the right choice. The trauma of leaving India and wrenching Elisha away from Zac and Rajani faded from my consciousness. The cost of the private hospital, the uncertainty of our future—none of that mattered any more. Elisha was going to get better.

She *was* getting better. The nurses removed some of her bandages over the following days, and the excellence of Matthew Levi's work shone through. The skin on Elisha's face was still raw, but it was smoother and a uniform colour. After hours of persuasion, she at last agreed to look in the mirror.

'My eyebrows are all lopsided,' Elisha said.

'It's only because your face is still swollen,' I said. 'It'll come right.'

Elisha ran her fingers over her cheeks. 'They're still very lumpy.'

'The grafts need time to take,' I said. 'But look, you can hardly see the scars.'

'I suppose they do look better,' Elisha said.

'Believe me, they do.'

Elisha put the mirror down. 'I guess so.'

There was something I had to ask. I gazed into Elisha's eyes. 'Did I do

David Whittet

the right thing to bring you here and ask Matthew Levi to do the operation?'

My heart missed several beats while I waited for her to answer.

'You did.' She picked up the mirror and studied her face again. 'I just wish we hadn't left Zac and Rajani behind.'

Three weeks later, Elisha was up and about and almost ready to be discharged from hospital.

'I had a call from Hanifah last night,' I said. 'She asked how the surgery went. We said we'd go and see them in Dunedin when you were feeling better.'

'Not now,' Elisha said. 'I'm not ready to face the world.'

'I was thinking … maybe the weekend after next. Maybe you'll feel up to it by then. Hanifah and Bwanbale are longing to see how you look.'

'Maybe they can come and see us when we're settled up north.' Elisha laid back on her bed and pulled up the sheets until they almost covered her face. 'Besides, I've heard it's freezing down in Dunedin.'

A nurse came in to take Elisha's blood pressure.

'What's this I hear?' the nurse said. 'A trip to Dunedin?' She rescued Elisha's arm from under the sheet and pumped up the blood pressure cuff. 'I'd say that would do you a power of good.'

Elisha shook her head. 'You go, Theo. I'm staying here. I'll be fine.' She smiled at the nurse. 'Everyone here's taking such good care of me.'

'I'm not leaving you, Elisha,' I said.

The nurse recorded Elisha's blood pressure on the chart at the end of the bed and left the room.

'Actually …' Elisha sat up on the bed. 'I was thinking of asking Joanna to come and see me.'

Joanna! Why hadn't I thought of getting her over to support Elisha? I'd heard so much about Joanna, from both Elisha and Rajani. How she'd sponsored Rajani when her family died, and helped Elisha turn her life around after her mother's tragic death. Joanna was just the person to pull Elisha through this crisis.

'That's a wonderful idea,' I said.

'You really mean that?' Elisha said.

'I do.'

Elisha leant forward and kissed me. It was definitely the happiest I'd seen her since we arrived in New Zealand.

I hesitated for a moment. 'I still think I should stay here and make sure you're okay.'

'Nonsense,' Elisha said. 'You go to Dunedin. Jo and I need some girl time together. Without you hovering.'

David Whittet

CHAPTER TWENTY-FIVE

Belvedere Private Hospital, Four Days Later

Elisha

'Jo!' Elisha jumped off her bed and flung her arms around Joanna. 'I thought I'd never see you again.'

'Elisha!' Joanna freed an arm to wipe away a tear. 'My darling Elisha!'

The two women sat on the edge of the bed in each other's arms. Elisha had longed to spill her heart to Joanna. Now that Joanna was here, she couldn't find the words. Why couldn't they talk the way they used to?

Only an occasional snivel broke the uneasy silence. As Elisha clung to Joanna, she felt the dampness of Joanna's tears seeping through her bandages and onto her cheeks.

'Oh, Jo!' Elisha said. 'How I've wanted to see you … talk to you …'

Joanna blew her nose. 'I've been praying for you … we've held all-night vigils at the church … I know that probably doesn't mean much to you … but …'

'It does.' Elisha raised her eyes to meet Joanna's. 'I'm not sure why, but it does.'

Joanna gave another sob and suddenly pulled back. 'What am I doing? The nurse told me not to touch your bandages. And here am I, crying into them.'

'Bugger that,' Elisha said. 'Give me another hug before matron comes back!'

'We didn't get the whole story at first … just scraps of news on the radio.' Joanna's croaking voice trailed off. 'First that some extremists had torched your father's van. When I heard you were in the van, too, I thought you'd both been burnt alive …' She dried her eyes and started again. 'I felt so guilty. It was me who persuaded you to go back to India.'

Elisha felt Joanna's body tremble as they embraced. 'It wasn't you, Jo. It was those thugs.'

Joanna dried her eyes on her sleeve. 'I just can't get my head around it. Why did God allow such a senseless act of hatred?'

You don't know? Then what hope is there for me? Elisha kept her eyes fixed on Joanna. 'The mob went on about us being white Christians. Just days before they killed him, Dad had joined forces with Krishna. They laid the foundations for a well to bring safe drinking water to everyone in Madhapur.' Elisha almost choked on her words as she continued, 'I'll never understand why my father had to die. Didn't God want him to continue his work?'

Joanna dabbed her eyes again. 'I don't have any answers.' She lowered her head. 'God must be weeping when he sees what a bloody awful mess we've made of His world.'

Elisha had never heard Joanna swear before, even though they'd been through some tough times together. Elisha remembered Joanna had talked about losing her faith when her sister, Angie, died. The sorrow in Joanna's eyes was as intense now as it had been then.

'Oh, Jo,' Elisha said. 'I didn't even think how bad this has been for you.'

'Enough about me. I'm here for you.' Joanna got up from the bed. 'Why don't we go for a walk?'

Elisha froze. 'Go for a walk?'

'Yes,' Joanna said. 'Then we can get a coffee. There's a nice little café down the road.'

'They make perfectly good coffee here,' Elisha said.

'It'll do you good to get out.' Joanna pointed to the window. 'The sun's shining outside.'

Elisha gripped the end of the bed. 'No. Please, Jo.'

Joanna held out a hand to Elisha. 'Come on.'

Elisha shrank back. 'I can't go out. Matthew Levi wouldn't allow it. He's paranoid about the wounds getting infected.'

'I thought you were almost ready to leave hospital?'

'I am but …' How could Elisha explain her dread of facing the world again? 'I'm not ready. And if the wounds get infected, I won't be able to leave.'

'I know you're scared,' Joanna said, 'but you can't hide away forever.'

 David Whittet

Elisha took a sharp intake of breath. 'I told you. Matthew Levi will go ballistic if I undo all his work.'

'Will he?' Joanna sat on a chair and crossed her arms. 'We'll see about that.'

They'd both fallen asleep when Matthew Levi arrived with his students on a ward round an hour later.

'Good afternoon,' he said. 'How's my star patient today?'

Elisha awoke with a start. 'I'm … um …'

'Missing Theo, are you?' Levi said. 'Well, let's take a look at you.' He stepped forward to examine Elisha's face. 'Excellent.' He peeled away the bandages from her nose and beckoned his students to look. 'See how well those grafts have healed. That flap's near-perfect.'

Elisha closed her eyes as the students crowded around, gawking at her with their sweaty faces.

'Nurse,' Levi continued, 'I want these bandages off her face. They've served their purpose.'

'Yes, Doctor.' The nurse carefully removed the remainder of Elisha's bandages.

Elisha thrust out her hand and grabbed the bandaging. How could they take away her mask, her only defence against the outside world?

'Give those to me,' the nurse said, 'they're dirty.'

'Yes,' Levi said. 'We don't want you getting an infection and spoiling my handiwork.'

Elisha sank back on the bed. They would never understand how she felt.

Joanna got up and introduced herself. 'I'm one of Elisha's oldest and closest friends. I want to thank you from the bottom of my heart for everything you've done for her.'

Elisha shook her head. She didn't need Joanna sucking up to Levi.

'It's been my pleasure,' Levi said. 'She's done brilliantly. Physically, at least. But mentally—she seems to have got herself into a rut.'

'I think she needs some fresh air,' Joanna said. 'I want to take her out for a coffee, but she says you wouldn't let her. Something about the wounds getting infected.'

Levi frowned at Elisha. 'I never said that.'

Elisha grabbed a sheet from the bed and hid behind it.

'Keep that contaminated sheet away from your face,' Levi said. 'That's how you *will* get an infection.'

'So I can take her out?' Joanna asked.

'A short trip out will be fine,' Levi replied.

Jo! Whose side are you on? Elisha wanted to say the words out loud. She'd asked Joanna to come and support her, not make things worse. But in her heart, she knew Joanna was right. Elisha couldn't hide away forever, and she was done with fighting.

'I'll take good care of her,' Joanna said. 'I promise.'

'Excellent,' Levi said as he left with his students. 'Not too long at first mind. We don't want to overtire her.'

The nurse cleared away the old bandages. Elisha watched the last piece of her armour disappear.

'No time like the present,' Joanna said. 'Up you get. We'll wrap you up warm. Here, you can borrow my coat.'

'Jo …' Elisha's lips trembled. 'I've scarcely been outside a hospital since … you know … when the thugs set fire to the van.'

'You've got to get used to people seeing you.' Joanna helped Elisha into the coat. 'Remember, I'm with you. We're going to fight this together.'

Dazzled by the bright sunlight, Elisha held on to Joanna's arm as she took her first tentative steps outside the Belvedere Private Hospital. The crowded street, the buzz and chatter, the clinking of cups in the café—Elisha's heart pounded, and she gripped Joanna even tighter.

'Everyone's looking at me,' Elisha whispered.

'No, they're not,' Joanna said. 'You sit down, and I'll order the coffees.'

Elisha had to admit that she felt more alive amidst the bustling atmosphere of the café. More alive than she had since … *don't even go there.* Elisha glanced around at the patrons. As usual, Joanna was right. They were all far too involved with their own gossip to take any notice of her scarred face.

Joanna arrived with two coffees and a plate of cakes to die for. 'I bet they don't make cappuccinos like that at the hospital,' she said.

Elisha took a sip. Burns to her mouth had diminished her sense of taste and reduced her enjoyment of food.

'Rajani told me she made the lepers' dinner extra spicy in the hope they might taste it,' Elisha said. 'Now I know how the lepers felt. But … I can taste this coffee.'

'I asked them to give you an extra shot,' Joanna said. 'Talking of Rajani, I had a letter from her before I left home. I'm so proud of the work she's doing, keeping everyone's spirits up and holding the mission together. Have you heard from her?'

Elisha took another sip of coffee. 'Last week. She says Zac's helping her run the leper colony.'

'I heard Zac and Rajani made a film,' Joanna said. 'What was it they called it?'

Elisha thought back to that massive pile of letters it had taken her so long to open. '*House of Hope.*'

'So,' Joanna said, 'are Rajani and Zac an item?'

'There'll be wedding bells before long.' Elisha put down her coffee cup and wiped away a tear. 'And I won't be there for their big day.'

'I'm so sorry.' Joanna put a hand on Elisha's. 'Perhaps you'll be able to go back.'

'I should be there *now*,' Elisha said, 'helping with the mission. Working with the lepers. I promised my father I would, minutes before he died. I've let him down.'

Joanna took a handkerchief from her pocket and handed it to Elisha. 'Of course you haven't. Your dad would understand. He'd be proud of you.'

'I never wanted to come to New Zealand,' Elisha said. 'Theo had me on a flight here before I knew what was going on.'

Joanna lowered her eyebrows. 'Theo told me it was because they didn't have enough white skin in India for your graft.'

'I'm not sure I believe him,' Elisha said. 'He was desperate to get out of India.'

'Elisha!' Joanna leant forward and squeezed Elisha's hand. 'Theo's got your best interests at heart. He loves you. I've only just met him, but I can see that. He's stuck by you through all this, and he got a top surgeon to look after you.'

Elisha snorted. 'He got me a pig-headed brute.'

Joanna shook her head. 'What have you got against Matthew Levi? He seemed like a perfect gentleman to me. From what I've heard, he's the best plastic surgeon in New Zealand.'

'The most obnoxious,' Elisha said. 'You should have heard what he said to me. Went on about the natives wishing me ill.'

Joanna pursed her lips. 'That was inappropriate. But it must have been difficult for him to know what to say. Especially to a colleague's fiancée.'

'Levi's a professional. Don't make excuses for him.' Elisha scowled at Joanna. 'I don't want Theo spending too much time with him.'

'Why ever not?'

'Theo's changed.' Elisha pushed her empty cup aside. 'He's after a private practice and a six-figure income. I can see it in his eyes. He'll be in partnership with Levi given half a chance.'

'I thought you were going up north to a Māori practice?'

Elisha shrugged. 'We are. If Theo can drag himself away from Auckland.'

'He was full of the job in Northland when he met me at the airport,' Joanna said. 'His heart's set on it.'

'I hope so. It's just … I miss Zac and Rajani so much it hurts … The women at the mission too … I didn't realise how much they meant to me … I told Rajani that Madhapur was my home now. It still is …' Elisha broke off. Why was it so hard to explain to Joanna how lonely and confused she'd been? 'You see, I've no friends over here.'

Joanna pulled her chair closer and put an arm on Elisha's shoulder. 'You've got me now, and the Northland practice to look forward to. Remember how you were going to work with an indigenous community in Alice Springs?'

Elisha opened her mouth to reply, but only another sob came out. She'd been full of hope when she applied for that post in Alice Springs. It seemed a lifetime ago now—and that time in her life was beset with tragedy too. Memories of her mother's death flooded back.

     David Whittet

'It's all too much, isn't it?' Joanna said. 'Perhaps Zac could come to New Zealand and visit you.'

Elisha shook her head. 'He won't leave Rajani. And even if he did come, he'd only fight with Theo.'

Joanna scratched her head. 'I thought Theo and Zac were best mates.'

'They were, but stuff happened after the attack.' Elisha stopped to think. She'd been barely conscious most of the time, and she'd never really understood what had gone on between Theo and Zac. She just wondered why the two most important men in her life had to fall out when she needed them both to support her.

'Rajani didn't say anything about it in her letter,' Joanna said. 'Except how hard Zac's taken his father's death.'

Elisha dried her eyes. 'I don't think Theo realises what Zac's been through. Both of Zac's parents died when he was very young. Now he's lost both his adoptive parents. Dad did so much for Zac. Gave him a new life when he had nothing. Zac loved our dad so much.'

'I'm sure Theo does understand,' Joanna said. 'I guess Zac and Theo express their grief in different ways.'

'Maybe.' Elisha's voice softened. 'Zac's been suffering since we went to India. He never really adjusted to his knee injury.'

Joanna raised her eyebrows. 'I thought you said he'd embraced a new career as a film-maker.'

'That's what he wanted everyone to think,' Elisha said. 'But he was hurting on the inside. Rajani saw it first. Then one night I caught him out boozing with his mates. He was drunk and kept going on about being a bloody cripple. I had to sober him up before he got home. Dad would have been devastated to see him like that.'

'Poor Zac,' Joanna said. 'I didn't realise. I must write to him and pray for him.'

'At least he's got Rajani,' Elisha said.

'And you've got Theo.' Joanna stood up. 'We'd better get you back to the hospital. I promised Matthew Levi I wouldn't overtire you.'

The receptionist beckoned to them when they returned to the Belvedere.

'There's a phone call for you, Elisha,' she said. 'It's Dr Malone. Would you like to take it in your room?'

'Yes … I mean …' Elisha's mouth went dry. Why did Theo have to pick that moment to call? She wanted to talk to him. So why was her heart racing?

'I'll give you a minute to get to your room,' the receptionist said, 'then I'll put the call through.'

'Okay.' Elisha glanced at Joanna. 'Do you mind—'

'I'll wait outside,' Joanna said, patting Elisha on the back. 'Go on! Theo's waiting to talk to you!'

Twenty minutes later, Joanna put her head around the door of Elisha's private room.

'So, what did Theo have to say?' Joanna asked. 'Spill.'

'He's visiting a Ugandan boy and his family,' Elisha said. 'He's also going to see his old mentor Ralph Greenslade while he's down in Dunedin.'

'Theo told me about Bwanbale,' Joanna said. 'Matthew Levi operated on him out of the goodness of his heart, didn't he?'

Elisha met Joanna's eyes. 'Yes.'

'Just like he did for you,' Joanna said. 'I still don't see what you've got against him.'

'He's a …' Elisha clasped her hands together. What could she say that she hadn't already? Maybe she had misjudged Levi, but she still didn't trust him. 'It's just … like I said … Theo's easily influenced. I don't want him turning into an arrogant surgeon.'

Joanna waved her hand. 'Come on. Theo's a better man than that. He's got integrity. You know he has.'

'I hope so.' Elisha smiled and leant back on her bed. 'On the phone, Theo was full of what he hopes to achieve up in Northland.'

'What did I tell you?' Joanna said. 'I'm going to leave you to get some rest. Dream about your new life in—what was the name of the place?'

'It's near Kerikeri in the Bay of Islands.'

'I've seen pictures of the Bay of Islands,' Joanna said. 'It's a paradise.' She hugged Elisha again. 'I'll be back in the morning. Try and get some sleep.'

David Whittet

Elisha lay awake all night. Was she worrying about nothing? The new practice would take Theo away from Matthew Levi's influence, and Theo would be back doing the work he loved. He wanted her to join him at the medical centre and work as a practice nurse. The thought was both thrilling and terrifying. She longed to do something useful again and give her life some meaning. But first, she had to manage life in a new community with a face that made her look like an ogre.

CHAPTER TWENTY-SIX

Air New Zealand Flight, Auckland to Dunedin

Theo

Why had Elisha taken such a dislike to Matthew Levi? And why couldn't she see what an excellent job he'd made of her surgery? I settled into my seat on the Boeing 737 and did up the seatbelt. I knew the answer. Those crass bedside comments. But if you were as good a surgeon as Levi, did it matter if you were a thoughtless jerk at times?

The engines roared, and we soared above the Auckland skyline. I thought how different my life would have been if I had been seduced into a career in plastic surgery. Would I have ended up making the same inappropriate gaffs as Levi? Surely not. As a medical student, I'd looked down on plastic surgery and appearance medicine as money-making scams for lazy consultants. I was wrong. Plastic surgery was every bit as valuable as any other branch of medicine. Just look at the difference surgery had made to Bwanbale's life—and the difference it was *going* to make for Elisha's future.

I spotted Bwanbale from the aircraft window as the 737 taxied in at Dunedin Airport. He was there at the gate with his mother, waving madly.

'You haven't brought your lovely fiancée,' Hanifah said. 'We were looking forward to seeing what Dr Levi had done for her.'

'She has an old friend from Australia visiting her,' I said. 'My ears have been burning all the way down from Auckland. I'm sure they've been sounding off about me.'

Hanifah grinned. 'Only good things, I'll bet.'

'I'm not so sure,' I replied. 'Anyway, you must come and see us when we're settled in at the practice in the Bay of Islands.'

'When are you getting married?' Hanifah asked. 'We'll expect an invitation to the wedding.'

 David Whittet

'Soon, I hope.' I picked up my overnight bag from the carousel. 'Of course, we'd love to have you there.'

'I'm coming too!' Bwanbale said.

I ruffled his hair. 'Of course you are.'

Hanifah led us to their car, a run-down old Toyota Corolla, and chatted all the way to their town house in South Dunedin. She told me about their early days as refugees in New Zealand and how proud she was when her husband got a job at Cadbury's.

Bwanbale bounced up and down on the back seat. 'My dad works at the chocolate factory, and sometimes he brings some home!'

'When we took Bwanbale back to see Dr Levi at the follow-up clinic,' Hanifah said, 'we met a nurse called Marian who said she knew you. She told us she was going to work in Uganda.'

'Yes,' I said. 'I knew Marian Taylor.'

'Have you heard from her?' Hanifah asked. 'She was so kind to Bwanbale.'

I lowered my head. 'Last I heard, Marian was still working in Uganda.'

Marian Taylor. We'd had our differences, but we'd been close—once. Was she still in Uganda? I'd called Mike Bailey at the agency to tell him I was leaving India. I suddenly wished I'd asked him about Marian.

'Yes,' I said. 'Marian was—is—a lovely nurse.'

As we approached the Zuluka's house, we passed Ralph Greenslade's old practice. Was JP still working there? We'd swung around the corner before I could get a look at the sign. What had become of Ralph? I had to find out before I left Dunedin.

Their house could easily have been any one of those leaky homes I'd visited with Ralph Greenslade during my student attachment. When we arrived, Bwanbale dragged me to his bedroom. Inside was a terrific collection of model aircraft.

'Wow,' I said. 'You must love planes.'

'I do.' Bwanbale handed me a beautifully detailed model of a Sikorsky S-92 helicopter. 'This one's my favourite.'

'My father was an airline pilot,' I said. 'Perhaps you'll be a captain one day, too.'

'I want to be a helicopter pilot,' Bwanbale said. 'Actually, I really wanted to be a doctor like you and Dr Levi, but I'm no good at studying. I'd never get through all those exams.'

'I wasn't much good at learning from books either,' I said. 'In fact, one professor told me I'd never make a doctor.'

'But you did,' Bwanbale said. 'And I bet you love it.'

I scratched the back of my neck. 'Most of the time. So why a helicopter pilot?'

Bwanbale pulled a photograph of the Westpac Rescue Helicopter out of a drawer. 'I thought the next best thing to being a doctor would be flying a rescue helicopter. That way, I can still help Kiwis in their hour of need. I've applied for a scholarship.'

I felt a lump in my throat. People loved to complain about refugees being a drain on our resources. But Bwanbale, like Akiki, was determined to give something back to the community his family now called home.

Hanifah cooked us a traditional Ugandan dinner of *luwombo*, a stew made from vegetables steamed in banana leaves, with a side of *simsim*, a roasted bean and sesame paste. Just when I thought I couldn't eat anything else, she brought out a plate of *kikomando*, a chapatti cut into pieces and served with fried beans.

'I haven't had a *kikomando* since I left Uganda,' I said.

Hanifah smiled. 'Perhaps you should go back.'

I sighed. 'I'd love to see Uganda again. It's an extraordinary country. All those fabulous sights, sounds and tastes.' I helped myself to another piece of *kikomando*. 'I'd be back in a flash. But not to work.' I glanced up at Hanifah. 'Bwanbale and I had a chat this afternoon, and we both decided that New Zealand's our home.'

To finish, Bwanbale's father, Mukisa, brought in a cafetière of thick, strong Ugandan coffee, together with a very Kiwi treat—a chocolate fish.

'Could I use your phone?' I asked. 'There's someone I'd rather like to catch up with.'

'Of course.' Mukisa led me into the hall.

My fingers trembled as I dialled the Greenslade's number. 'Is that you, Rosemary? It's Theo Malone … What? … Ralph's in a rest home?'

I put down the receiver and went back into the living room. 'I need to

David Whittet

ask you a huge favour. When you take me back to the airport, could we make a stop at the Pinehaven Nursing Home, please? I want to see my old GP tutor from my student days.'

'No problem,' Hanifah said. 'But we'd better get moving. We don't want you to miss your flight.'

Walking into the rest home, I didn't know what to expect. It had shocked me when I first saw Ralph after his stroke. He must be much worse now. It would have been the last resort for Rosemary to put him into care. At least I still recognised him when the caregiver took me to his room.

I put my hand on his. 'It's so good to see you again.'

'Rosemary tells me you're going to work in the Bay of Islands,' Ralph said. 'So, you resisted the urge to be a used-car salesman?'

I laughed. Ralph's voice sounded much less slurred than a couple of years ago. He hadn't lost his dry sense of humour, either.

'Maybe I should have done,' I said. 'Perhaps I'd have done less harm selling cars. I often wonder if Professor Rutherford was right all along.'

'Nonsense!' Ralph pulled himself up in his chair. 'Forget about Rutherford. That pompous old fart has retired. Good riddance. JP says the new professor's a breath of fresh air.'

'Well, that's good news,' I said. 'But I always manage to upset people wherever I go. Things didn't end well in India.'

Ralph put an arm on my shoulder. 'I know. Rosemary read about the attack on your fiancée and her father. I'm so sorry. I could have cried when she told me. And you were doing such great work out there. There was a piece about you in the *New Zealand Medical Journal*.'

I covered my face with my hands. 'I should have just kept my head down. Maybe if I hadn't been so antagonistic, the militants wouldn't have torched the van.'

'It wasn't your fault,' Ralph said. 'It's time to put the past behind you. Your fiancée survived. You've got each other. Go and make a new life for yourselves up north.'

Good old Ralph Greenslade. He always helped me to see things in perspective. Elisha and I *would* have a new beginning in Northland. But first, there was a vital task on my mind that I had to complete before I could move on. I bought a roll of film at Auckland Airport on my way back to the hospital.

Joanna was packing up her things when I arrived.

'Perfect,' I said. 'I can get you both in the picture.'

Elisha watched me load the film into the camera. 'What are you doing?'

I squinted through the viewfinder. 'I'm taking a photo for Zac and Rajani.'

Joanna beamed. 'What a lovely idea.'

Elisha hid her face. 'I don't want any photos of me.'

I put the camera down for a moment and sat beside Elisha on the bed. 'If Zac can see the difference surgery has made to your face, then maybe he'll forgive me for taking you away from him.'

'Please,' Joanna said. 'Do it for Zac and for Rajani.'

'Go on!' I gently stroked Elisha's back. 'You can do this.'

Elisha swallowed and moved one of her hands away from her face. 'Oh, all right. But I want to see the photos before you send them to Zac.'

'No problem,' I said. 'Big smile.'

Elisha slowly removed her other hand and gave a cautious smile. I picked up the camera and took a couple of shots before she changed her mind.

'Get back,' Elisha said, pulling her hair over her cheeks. 'I don't want any hideous close-ups of my scars.'

'Okay.' I stepped further away and took some more photos. 'Now, let's get the film to a photo shop,' I said. 'Then Joanna can see the photos before she goes home.'

'That would be fantastic,' Joanna said. 'Don't look so worried, Elisha. You were great.'

We collected the prints on our way to the airport the following day.

'They're gorgeous,' Joanna said. 'Zac and Rajani will be thrilled to see them.'

'Let me see.' Elisha grabbed the photos. 'Ugh! Don't send that one, it's ghastly.' She flicked through a few more. 'That one's okay. And that one too. Actually, this one's quite nice.'

Thank God there were a few she liked. I'd been careful to hide Elisha's scars in the shadows when I took the photos.

'We'll send those ones then,' I said, separating the photos that met with Elisha's approval from the rest. 'I'll write to Zac and Rajani tonight and post the photos with the letter in the morning.'

'I'm going to write to them too,' Elisha said. 'You might have to help me, though. My hand's still shaky.'

'That's lovely,' Joanna said. 'They'll be thrilled.' She glanced at her watch. 'They'll be calling my flight any minute.'

I eyed Elisha as Joanna edged towards passport control. I'd spent a restless night worrying that Joanna's departure might send Elisha over the top. Instead, Elisha's expression softened, and she hugged Joanna.

'Thank you, Jo,' Elisha said. 'Thank you for everything.'

Joanna blinked back a tear. 'I'm sorry I pushed you so hard, but I had to get you out of that hospital room and into the world.'

'It's what I needed,' Elisha said. 'I feel alive again, for the first time since … well … you know …'

Joanna held Elisha tight. 'I do.'

'You've been terrific, Joanna,' I said. 'I can't thank you enough. It's like … since you came … I've got Elisha back.'

But had I? Would Elisha ever be the same again?

The fragile gleam I'd seen in Elisha's eye at the airport disappeared when, two days later, Matron announced it was time to leave hospital.

I helped Elisha gather her things together. 'I'm looking forward to Northland,' I said. 'Aren't you? It's going to be an adventure.'

'I suppose so,' Elisha said and continued packing.

Matthew Levi looked in before we left.

'I'll be sorry to lose my star patient,' he said, inspecting Elisha's face. 'These grafts have taken beautifully.'

'They have,' I said. 'I took these photos for Elisha's brother in India.'

Elisha scowled as I handed some reprints to Levi.

Levi looked through the photographs and grinned. 'I'd love to get some copies for my collection. They're great to reassure clients before their surgery.' He handed the photos back to me. 'So, it's Northland next for you two, is it? At least—I suppose that's better than India.'

'I'll be working for a Māori community clinic in the Bay of Islands,' I said.

'You're on a hiding to nothing,' Levi said. 'I've heard how those Māori providers treat their doctors.'

'It's what we both want,' Elisha said.

Levi raised an eyebrow.

'It *is* what we want,' I said. 'It's going to be a challenge, but we're both up for that.' I put a hand on Elisha's shoulder. 'Elisha's going to work as a practice nurse once she's feeling better.'

Levi sighed. 'I can see I'm never going to persuade you to come and join my plastic surgery practice.' He shook my hand then Elisha's. 'Good luck to you both up north. You're going to need it.'

I followed Levi out into the corridor. 'Please don't think we're not grateful for everything you've done,' I said. 'Because we are. You've done a fantastic job. Elisha doesn't mean to be rude. It's just—her head's still all over the place, but she'll thank you once her scars have fully healed.'

'She's got a tough time ahead,' Levi said. 'Even with the best outcome from her surgery, she's got huge adjustments to make. Are you sure taking her to the back of beyond is a smart move?'

'I know Elisha,' I said. 'She needs to feel she's making a difference and working in a rural practice will give her that.'

Levi rolled his eyes. 'I hope you know what you're getting yourselves into.' He strode off down the corridor. 'Come back to me when you get fed up and need a new job. I'll be waiting for you.'

I thought about Matthew Levi's warning while Elisha and I packed our belongings into the camper van I'd hired and set off for the Far North. Was I really on a hiding to nothing? Whatever the new practice had in store for us, part of me felt envious of Levi's comfortable and secure lifestyle.

CHAPTER TWENTY-SEVEN

Bay of Islands, Northland, New Zealand

Patients queued down the street. It was standing room only in the waiting room. Three or four sick people booked into each fifteen-minute appointment slot. Would every day be as crazy as my first morning at the Kahurangi Medical Centre?

'They've been waiting for you,' Ngaire, the practice nurse, said. 'We haven't had a permanent doctor for ages. Just a string of locums. None of them stay very long.'

No wonder! Only a fool would work here. On top of the patient workload, there were all the repeat prescriptions, sick certificates, and social welfare forms to complete. Perhaps Matthew Levi was right after all. I was on a hiding to nothing.

A call-out to a motor vehicle accident meant there was no chance of a lunch break. I'd hoped to pop home and check on Elisha. How was she coping alone in the house? She'd refused my efforts to persuade her to work at the medical centre as a practice nurse, claiming her scars would frighten off the patients. I'd assured her it wouldn't matter. The patients would understand. Knowing how much she'd suffered would bring them closer together and establish a bond. Elisha wasn't convinced and grew even more determined to stay at home.

By half past five, I hadn't stopped long enough to take a breath, and I could feel my blood glucose dropping. If I didn't get something to eat soon, I would faint. I had to get back to Elisha as well. Just when I thought I might get away, Ngaire poked her head around the consulting room door. 'I'm sorry,' she said, 'I've had to squeeze in another patient. This is Ariana. She's beside herself.'

Ariana Parata, a young Māori woman in her late teens, sat down and burst into tears.

'What is it?' I reached for a box of tissues and handed them to her.

'Everything!' She took a tissue and continued to sob.

I gave her a minute to compose herself before pressing any further. Experience had taught me a brief silence could be cathartic. Eventually, Ariana dried her eyes.

'Tell me about it,' I said.

'Everyone told me it was a mistake,' she said. 'I swore I'd prove them wrong. But …'

'But you couldn't?' I said. 'Who's everyone? And what was the mistake?'

'My family,' Ariana said. 'All my friends, too. They all told me I'd never survive teachers training college.'

'It doesn't sound like your whānau were very supportive.' I leant forward and tried to engage with her. 'So, what went wrong?'

'They said I wouldn't cope, and I didn't.' Ariana took another tissue. 'I'd set my heart on being a teacher. I wanted to work at our village school. But not any more.' She dabbed her eyes again. 'All I need from you, Doc, is a medical certificate to say I can't go back.'

I unwound a paper clip as she talked—a habit I'd acquired from Ralph Greenslade.

'Are you sure?' I asked. 'Why not take some time out? You don't have to decide straight away.'

'I'm not going back.'

'I could arrange counselling for you,' I said. 'That'll help you develop strategies to deal with the stress.'

'It's not just stress.' Ariana raised her eyes to mine. 'I'm tired, and I've lost interest in everything. Even my horse.'

'You're a keen equestrian?'

'I love my horse.' Ariana looked down and stared at her hands. 'But I haven't had the energy to ride her for weeks.'

I bent the paperclip back into shape. 'Have you been feeling low in your spirits?'

'That's the funny thing,' Ariana said. 'I *want* to ride, but these days I just haven't got the get-up-and-go.'

This didn't sound like straightforward depression—or simple stress either. Something else was going on.

    David Whittet

'Do you mind if I take a look at you?' I asked. 'You look very pale.'

Apart from the pallor, the examination was normal. Outwardly, Ariana was a healthy nineteen-year-old.

'How about I write you a certificate for two weeks?' I suggested. 'That'll give you some breathing space. The nurse will take some blood from you, and we'll see if we can find out why you've been so tired. Maybe we'll get you back on that horse before long.'

Ariana took the certificate. 'I doubt it.' She turned back to me as she left the consulting room. 'But thanks.'

I scribbled some notes in the case file. Probably illegible to anyone but me, but never mind. At last, I could go home and see Elisha, and get something to eat.

Ngaire was spinning down the blood samples as I left. 'What are all these for?' she said. 'Surely she just needed some antidepressants.'

'I'm not convinced she is depressed,' I said. 'At least, I think there may be more to it. I want to rule out anything organic.'

Ngaire shrugged. 'I should have thought it was obvious she was depressed. But you're the doctor.'

Although I'd been longing to get home all day to see Elisha, I stood outside the front door for a full minute before I went in. What would I find? After a day on her own in an unfamiliar place, she'd have every right to be wallowing in self-pity.

The living room was empty. So was the kitchen. I stepped into the bedroom. Elisha was sat in front of the dressing table mirror, draping her head with a shawl.

'What do you think?' she said. 'Quite fetching, isn't it?'

My jaw dropped. For a moment—to my eyes, at least—she *did* look like an oriental princess.

Elisha continued rearranging the shawl over her face. 'Perhaps I could be like those purdah women in India and go around with my face covered all the time.'

'Maybe,' I said. 'Just be careful about getting an infection. Remember what Matthew Levi said? Those grafts are still vulnerable. Make sure anything you put next to your face is clean.'

'Okay, don't fuss.' Elisha put the shawl down on the dressing table. 'Anyway, how was your first day at work?'

'Exhausting,' I said. 'I'm sorry I didn't get home at lunchtime.'

'Don't worry.' Elisha turned to face me. 'Dawn from down the road came to see me. She's lovely.'

Whoever Dawn was, I could have hugged her then and there. Friendship and acceptance by the locals—that was exactly what Elisha needed.

'How about I get us a takeaway from the fish and chip shop,' I said. 'I'm absolutely starving. You can tell me all about Dawn and I'll tell you about the medical centre while we eat.'

'No need,' Elisha said. 'Dawn brought us some hāpuka as a welcome present. Her husband's a fisherman.'

Dawn *was* an angel. The local fish and chip shop—the only business in the impoverished community that seemed to be thriving—looked decidedly seedy.

'I haven't done any cooking in ages,' Elisha said. 'I hope I don't ruin it.'

'I'm sure it will be delicious,' I said. 'I haven't eaten all day.'

Elisha turned on the stove and fetched a pan. 'Dawn's invited us to dinner at their place. She's such a sweetie. She didn't even gawp at my scars.'

'What did I tell you?' I said. 'Nobody cares how you look. Why don't you come and work at the medical centre? You don't need to go purdah.'

Elisha took the pan off the stove. 'It's too soon.'

'Ngaire, the practice nurse, could sure do with some help. So could I, come to that.'

'I'm not ready.' Elisha plated the fish, and we sat down at the table. 'Not everyone's kind like Dawn.'

'I don't know,' I said. 'You might be surprised. It's a close-knit community.'

'We'll see.' Elisha watched me take a mouthful of hāpuka. 'Is it alright?'

'Divine,' I said. 'I feel better already. Tell me about Dawn.'

'She told me about the local Women's Institute. They have all sorts of stuff going on. They're fundraising for the school at the moment.'

     David Whittet

'Do you think you might go along?' I said. 'You could certainly teach them a thing or two about fundraising.'

'Maybe.' Elisha raised her head. 'But I would like to take Dawn up on her offer of dinner at their place. What about the weekend?'

'I'd like that,' I said. 'I just hope I don't get called away on an emergency. I'm on call twenty-four seven.'

'They'd understand,' Elisha said. 'You still haven't told me about your day, though.'

I took another helping of hāpuka before answering. 'Pretty crazy. I didn't think my head could take any more when this young woman came in. She'd just failed her first year at teachers training college and wanted a certificate to say she couldn't go back.' I paused for another bite. 'Everyone seems to think she's depressed. But I'm sure something else is going on.'

Elisha looked at me inquisitively. 'Why?'

'She told me she's passionate about her horse,' I said. 'She wants to go riding, but she hasn't the energy. That's not depression.'

'Sounds like it to me,' Elisha said. 'And believe me, I know about depression.'

'When you're depressed,' I said, 'you lose interest in the things you enjoy. Ariana hasn't lost the desire, just the stamina to do it.'

Elisha put down her knife and fork. 'The people here are lucky to have you as their doctor.'

I got up and put my arm around her. 'They're lucky to have you, too. Your nursing skills are going to be great for this community.'

'Ready for the fray?' Ngaire asked when I arrived at the medical centre the next morning. 'We're full-on again.'

Please, not another day like yesterday. 'As much as I'll ever be,' I said.

My first patient, a woman in her late forties with a striking tā moko on her chin, settled herself into the chair. That meant it was going to be a long consultation.

'How did you get on with Ariana yesterday?' she said. 'She's my niece. Poor girl. She was never cut out to be a teacher.'

Did all the patients here—and the staff, too, for that matter—gossip about one another?

'You know I can't talk about other patients,' I said as politely as I could.

Almost every patient that morning seemed to consider it their sworn duty to give me their opinion on Ariana. According to the locals, she was too highly strung and destined to fail. Ariana struck me as a capable young woman held back by a wave of negativity from her extended whānau and the community. I remained convinced she was fighting an as-yet-undiagnosed medical condition.

Ariana's blood tests all came back normal. What was going on? Could it be fibromyalgia or an autoimmune disease? They were notorious for producing a negative laboratory screen. I shot off a letter to the local consultant physician to request further investigation.

Three weeks later, and for the first time since I'd started, I got a tea break. I'd just taken my first sip when Ngaire answered the phone.

'It's Dr Pemberton for you,' she said, 'and he sounds mad.'

'What the hell are you playing at?' Dr Damian Pemberton shouted down the telephone line so loud that I was sure Ngaire and the rest of the medical centre could hear what he was saying. 'Wasting my time with a neurotic girl with absolutely no physical signs and normal blood results. Don't you know the difference between medicine and psychiatry? Anyone with half an eye could see she was depressed. I've referred her to the psychiatrists.'

Ngaire smirked as I put the receiver down. 'I hate to rub it in,' she said, 'but I told you so.'

Ariana was almost as angry with me as Dr Pemberton when she came in for a renewal of her sickness certificate the following day.

'Why did you send me to such an obnoxious man?' she said. 'He made me feel like a bludger.'

'I'm sorry,' I said. 'I'm new here, and I didn't know what he was like.'

'Well, he can stuff it,' Ariana said. 'I won't see a shrink.'

I watched her drinking compulsively from her water bottle while I completed her medical certificate.

'Do you always drink that much water?' I asked.

    David Whittet

'Yes. I prefer it icy cold. I always keep a few bottles in the fridge.' She managed a smile. 'My dad gets up in the night to pass water. I get up to drink water. And I'm peeing all the time, too.'

I squiggled my signature on the form and handed it to her. 'I think I know what's wrong with you. I'm going to order some more tests.'

I couldn't wait to get back home to Elisha and run my idea past her.

'Diabetes insipidus,' I said. 'I'd stake my life on it.'

Elisha was curled up on the sofa, reading. 'Diabetes insipidus? I remember something about it from nursing school.' She put down her book. 'Isn't that the condition where the doctors used to test for it by dipping their fingers in the urine and tasting it?'

'That's right,' I said. 'If the urine had no taste, it was diabetes insipidus; if it tasted sweet, it was sugar diabetes.'

Elisha pulled a face. 'Yuk.'

'Thank God for test strips,' I said. 'Seriously, though, it would explain why Ariana *wants* to do things, but her body won't let her.'

'So what causes it?'

'Most likely a brain tumour. Probably in the pituitary. She needs a CT scan urgently.' I paced up and down the living room. 'If I'm right—and I'm sure I am—I'm going to write it up for the *New Zealand Medical Journal*.'

Elisha picked up her paperback and continued reading. 'I only hope it doesn't cause as much trouble as the paper you published in the Indian journal.'

Getting an urgent CT proved almost impossible. The nearest scanner was in Auckland, and access was at the sole discretion of Dr Damian Pemberton. The arrogant bastard wouldn't even take my calls. Then I remembered another of Ralph Greenslade's tricks. I got Pemberton's registrar on the telephone. Kept going on about the disciplinary action that would follow if they missed a brain tumour in such a young person. All the while, I was fiddling with a paperclip right up against the mouthpiece.

'What the hell is that crackling noise?' the registrar asked.

'I'm recording the conversation,' I said. 'In case it's needed for medico-legal reasons.'

Good old Ralph and his paperclips! They booked the CT for the following week.

Ariana panicked when I called her to go over the arrangements. 'You think I've got cancer? Am I going to die?'

What could I say? I had to be honest. 'Something is going on in your head, and the sooner we find out what it is, the faster we can fix it.'

At home that night, Elisha must have noticed I was playing with my food, chasing it around the plate.

'What's the matter?' she said.

'It's Ariana,' I said. 'She's got her scan next week, and she's terrified.'

Elisha cleared the dishes. 'I know how she feels. I was scared shitless before my surgery.'

'She's going through it on her own,' I said. 'Her whānau are down south at a tangi.'

'Can't they come back from the funeral to support her?' Elisha said. 'What about her friends?'

I shrugged. 'They're still convinced it's all in her mind and the scan's a waste of time.'

'No wonder she's screwed up,' Elisha said. 'I'll go to Auckland with Ariana when she has the scan.'

'You will?' I followed Elisha into the kitchen. 'Are you sure?'

'I can't let the poor kid go alone.' Elisha put on some rubber gloves and started washing up. 'Besides, it's time I got off my backside and did something useful. It'll do me good to get out of the house.'

I felt as nervous as Ariana looked when the taxi arrived to take them to Auckland. My stomach churned as the cab pulled away. The last time I waved Elisha off, the trip ended in disaster. The hours dragged throughout the day. It was a struggle to concentrate on my patients' stories.

Elisha rang me at midday. 'It's all done. Ariana was so brave. The radiologist's looking at the films. He'll fax the report through to you this afternoon.'

 David Whittet

I stood by the fax machine, waiting. What was the delay? It was after three and still no report. Did that mean it was bad news?

Suddenly the fax started making that familiar warbling noise. I tore the page off the machine.

'It's a pituitary adenoma!' I did a victory dance around the medical centre. 'And it's benign! They'll be able to fix it with surgery.'

Ngaire looked sheepish. 'Go on! Say it! I bet you're dying to rub my nose in it. And get your own back on Damian Pemberton.'

'No,' I said with a sigh. I meant it too. They could both wait for the journal article.

I persuaded a colleague in Kerikeri to cover the practice for a few days while I went down to Auckland to join Elisha and Ariana. By the time I arrived, Ariana was in the neurosurgical unit and prepped for theatre. Elisha was at her side, holding her hand.

'I want to scrub up and come into theatre,' I said to the neurosurgical registrar. 'This is my case. I've followed this from the beginning.'

'I suppose you have,' the registrar replied. 'I'll have to ask Mr Vernon, the consultant.'

An hour later, I was in the operating theatre, watching James Vernon remove a four-centimetre macroadenoma from the base of Ariana's brain. It was also her twentieth birthday.

James Vernon put the excised tumour in a bottle and turned to me. 'Just as well you diagnosed it when you did. Otherwise'—he threw his hands in the air—'any longer and even if she survived, she'd have been paralysed.'

When I changed out of my scrubs and joined Elisha on the recovery ward, Ariana's parents had arrived and were at her bedside.

Ariana's mother turned to me. 'I don't know how to thank you, Dr Malone. You saved my daughter's life.'

'It's kind of you to say so, Mrs Parata,' I said, 'but I just did what any doctor would do.'

Ariana's father stood up and shook my hand. 'No, you did much more than that. You're a miracle worker.'

'Don't tell him that,' Elisha said. 'He's got a big enough ego as it is.'

'But it's true!' Ariana said, opening her eyes. 'Nobody else would listen.'

Less than a month after Ariana's surgery, a letter arrived with the New Zealand Medical Association's crest on the envelope. A surge of adrenaline surged through my veins as I tore it open.

'They're going to publish my paper!' I threw my arms around Elisha at the breakfast table. 'It'll be in next week's edition of the journal.'

On the day of publication, my phone buzzed during morning surgery with messages of congratulation. The one that meant most was from JP in Dunedin.

'This beats that case of thyrotoxicosis you diagnosed hands down,' he said. 'Ralph Greenslade sends his congratulations. He's so proud of you.'

Ngaire put through another call immediately after JP's. 'It's Mrs Rutene,' she said.

I leant back in my chair and picked up the receiver. Mrs Rutene, the chair of the trust that owned the Kahurangi Medical Centre, doubtless wanted to acknowledge my achievement. 'Did you see the article in the *New Zealand Medical Journal*?'

'I did.' The coldness in her voice cut through my high spirits. 'We have concerns about your practice and the accuracy of the information in your paper. You went ahead and published without prior consent from the board, in breach of your employment contract. You will attend a disciplinary meeting at our offices at two o'clock tomorrow.'

What the hell? 'A disciplinary hearing? You're joking. My paper was entirely accurate. Nobody told me I had to get permission to publish a case report.'

'This is a serious matter, Dr Malone. You may bring a support person with you tomorrow.'

The phone shook in my hand. 'I can't possibly come tomorrow. I've got patients booked.'

'You *will* be at the trust's office at two.'

Mrs Rutene hung up before I could get another word in.

I couldn't say anything to Elisha when I got home. Not after she'd warned me about submitting the paper. I pretended I was still excited about getting published and told her about all the compliments when all I wanted to do was curl up in a ball and disappear.

Elisha must have noticed how many times I spilt the coffee at breakfast, but she didn't say anything. She kissed me goodbye as usual when I left for work.

How could I concentrate on the morning surgery with this hanging over me? Was telling the truth a disciplinary matter? What had happened to 'open and honest reporting'—the new buzzwords for the profession?

Five to two. I hesitated outside the trust's office in Kerikeri. My heart wanted me to make a run for it. My brain told me I had done nothing wrong, and I had to go in and fight.

Mrs Rutene ushered me into the interview room.

'Dr Malone,' she said, 'I'd like you to meet the board of trustees. Dr Armstrong, Dr Hewitt, Ereti Tuhaka—our iwi representative, Alison Steadman—our legal counsel, and I believe you know Dr Pemberton.'

Damian Pemberton! I might have known. Ngaire had warned me he was a vindictive creep. My legs wobbled as he cut me down with his eyes, and I thought I was going to fall before I reached the chair.

'We've called you here today to address our concerns about your performance,' Mrs Rutene continued. 'We also need to address issues relating to your judgement and intellectual honesty considering your ill-advised case report in the *New Zealand Medical Journal*.'

'I submitted the paper because it has some important educational lessons,' I said. 'That's something you should encourage.'

'Please don't interrupt, Dr Malone.' Mrs Rutene gave me a disdainful look and carried on. 'We have done an audit of your referral letters and found them grossly inadequate. Of particular concern, the information you gave Dr Pemberton on Ariana Parata was misleading in the extreme. Your negligence almost led to the death of a young woman.'

My mouth fell open. '*I* made the diagnosis—'

Damian Pemberton snorted. 'If it wasn't for my prompt action in ordering a CT, the outcome would have been very different.'

I stood up and eyeballed him. 'I got that CT done! You wouldn't even speak to me.'

Pemberton glared back. 'Are you calling me a liar?'

I wanted to punch the smug bastard's face. 'I'm saying the CT only happened because I bulldozed your registrar. He was scared shitless of going against you.'

'This is absurd.' Pemberton flicked through his papers and pulled out a form. 'I have the referral here. Look—signed by *my* registrar on *my* behalf.'

'You don't have to prove anything to us, Dr Pemberton,' Mrs Rutene said. 'It's not your reputation that's in question.'

I slunk back into my chair. Pemberton wasn't just a liar. The prize bullshitter had got them all sucking up to his story. Or had he?

'I think Damian *does* need to justify himself,' Ereti Tuhaka said. 'I would like to see the referral letter that Dr Malone sent to Damian.'

'There's a transcript in the papers we sent you for this meeting if you'd care to take a look,' Mrs Rutene said.

'A transcript, yes,' Ereti Tuhaka replied. 'I want to see the original. Or at the very least, a photocopy. That *should* have been included in the documentation.'

Mrs Rutene turned to Damian Pemberton. 'Do you have it with you?' Pemberton shook his head.

'That's very convenient,' Ereti Tuhaka said, 'because I've got a letter here from Ariana Parata's mother saying Dr Malone was the only one who listened to her daughter. And he saved her life.' She held up a bundle of correspondence. 'And these are the copies of Dr Malone's letters that Mrs Parata obtained from the hospital.'

Checkmate! Thank God for Ereti Tuhaka! I wanted to get up and hug her.

'This is preposterous!' Pemberton glared at each of the board members in turn. 'We agreed we'd require Dr Malone to provide a written apology and ask the *NZMJ* to print a correction crediting me.'

'I think it's Dr Malone who deserves the apology,' Ereti Tuhaka said. 'We should all be very proud of him. Not only did his astute diagnosis save a teenager with her entire life in front of her, but a paper in such a prestigious journal as the *NZMJ* reflects favourably on the trust.'

Mrs Rutene gritted her teeth and packed up her papers. 'It seems we owe you an apology, Dr Malone. But in future, you will obtain written

David Whittet

consent from the board before speaking publicly or publishing on any matter relating to your work for the trust.'

You bitch! You're gagging me! 'Yes, Mrs Rutene.'

Mrs Rutene shot Damian Pemberton a scowl. 'I need a word with you in private.'

I avoided eye contact with Pemberton as he left the office with Mrs Rutene. Why did I make enemies wherever I went? I never set out to upset anyone.

Ereti Tuhaka tapped me on the shoulder. 'You're the best thing that's happened to our community in years. Don't let those buggers get you down. Keep up the good work—I've heard nothing but good about you from the iwi.'

The house was dark when I got home. Silent, too. I was bursting to share my news with Elisha, but where was she? I turned on the light in the living room. Everything was as I'd left it in the morning. It didn't look like she'd been in the kitchen either. Or the bedroom. I called her name repeatedly. No reply. Where else could I look? Surely she wouldn't be in the storeroom. My hand shook as I opened the door.

'Elisha? Are you in here?'

I strained my eyes as the light streamed into the dingy storeroom. Scarcely visible amongst the dusty boxes, Elisha lay curled up on the floor in the foetal position.

'Elisha!'

Elisha raised her head, tears rolling down her cheeks. 'Theo, something's happening to me … my skin … it's … it's … going bad … I daren't look in a mirror any more …'

In the shadows of that storeroom, I saw it. Perhaps I'd seen it before and refused to believe it. Maybe I'd just been too wrapped up in Ariana's case to notice the changes in Elisha's skin. They'd been subtle at first, but the grafts were contracting and changing colour. Elisha had tried to hide it by continuing to cover her face with a headscarf. Now there was nothing to conceal the discolouration and distortion of her face.

CHAPTER TWENTY-EIGHT

The walls of Dr Matthew Levi's upmarket Remuera consulting rooms closed in around me. I'd believed with all my heart that he was the right surgeon for Elisha—and that he'd done a good job. How could everything have gone so wrong and in a matter of less than six months?

Gone was Levi's normal self-confidence. Replaced by a wrinkled brow when he examined Elisha. The repeated grunts said it all.

'You kept the grafts clean, didn't you?' he said.

Elisha flinched.

'Of course she did,' I answered for her.

Levi took a closer look with his dermatoscope. 'It looks like there's been sepsis here. Remember what I said about absolute skin hygiene?'

Elisha didn't answer. She looked down at her feet.

'Listen, Matthew,' I said. 'No excuses. Please. You should have warned us this might happen.'

'I did.' He straightened his bow tie—something he always did when asserting himself. 'We went through all the risks, including tissue contraction. I made that very clear to you.' He waved a piece of paper in front of Elisha. 'And you signed to say you understood.'

'Only because you told me I had to,' Elisha said.

I wasn't sure if Elisha's comment was directed at me or Levi or both of us. Probably me. I did tell her she had to sign. And to be fair, Levi had told us the grafts would contract over time.

'I want a second opinion,' Elisha said.

'No problem,' Levi replied. 'I can arrange that for you—'

'Not with one of your mates,' Elisha shot back. 'I want someone independent.'

'Very well,' Levi said. 'You can get off the bed. I've finished examining you. Come and sit down and we'll have a talk.' He sat us down on the designer leather chairs. 'I'm not sure what you were expecting, but—'

'I wasn't expecting the grafts to change colour,' I said. 'The whole reason we came back to New Zealand was because they didn't have enough white skin in India.'

'I warned you about that, too.' Levi reached across his desk and pointed to another line in the consent form that Elisha had signed. 'Grafts *do* change colour in time.'

'Yes, but not in a matter of months,' I said.

Levi rubbed his chin. 'I must admit that's unusual. Perhaps it was the less-than-optimal work they did in Calcutta before you got to me.'

'That's right,' Elisha snapped. 'Blame someone else.' She glared at me. 'I wish we'd stayed in India. At least the doctors there didn't make promises they couldn't keep.'

'Her burns were clean when we arrived at the Belvedere,' I said.

Levi opened the case file on his desk and studied the photographs he'd taken prior to the surgery. 'You're right, they were. Something's happened—'

'Damn right it has,' Elisha said.

Levi stood up and took another look at the grafts through his dermatoscope. 'I'll swear there's been sepsis. Are you certain you kept them scrupulously clean?'

I squeezed my eyes shut. My mind went back to that first night I'd come home to find Elisha with her face draped in a shawl. I hadn't thought much about it at the time. But she kept covering her face, and always on the rare occasions she left the house. Was this all Elisha's fault? Had she allowed her grafts to get infected? Even if it was Elisha's fault, I couldn't say anything. The shawls were her mask, the only way she could face the outside world.

Then I remembered what Joanna had said before she had left. She'd taken me aside at the airport.

'You need to watch Elisha,' Joanna had whispered in my ear. 'Matthew Levi says she's got to keep those bandages off her face. Otherwise, she'll get a nasty infection and undo all his good work.'

My heart stood still. Levi was talking again but I wasn't listening. None of this was Elisha's fault—or Levi's. It was mine. I should have heeded Joanna's advice. And I was a doctor. Why hadn't I seen the early signs—and done something about it? Had I expected too much of Elisha and pushed her too far and too quickly? I tried to imagine how I would have felt if the roles were reversed. How would I have coped, facing the world with a face so badly scarred as to be unrecognisable? Would I have blamed it all on the surgeon?

Elisha's voice abruptly interrupted my train of thought.

'No way,' she said. 'You're not coming near me again.'

'What was that?' I asked. 'I missed what you said.'

'I was just telling Elisha that I could revise the grafts,' Levi said. 'I'm sure I could get a better cosmetic result. But we'll need to keep you in a sterile chamber for longer this time. Make sure the grafts stay absolutely clean.'

'I told you,' Elisha said, 'I don't want any more surgery. At least, not from you.'

Levi put the photos back in Elisha's case file and closed the folder. 'Then I'm sorry, but there's nothing more to be done.' He caught my eye. 'I'm sorry, Theo. I really wanted to help. But I can't work miracles.' He reached out a hand to Elisha. 'I mean that, I really wanted to help you.' He paused for a moment, his voice croaking. 'I still do.'

Elisha backed away. Why couldn't she see that he cared?

I sighed. 'I'm sorry too, Matthew. I'll talk to Elisha, but—'

'But nothing.' Elisha glared at me. 'We're going.'

Levi buzzed for his secretary. 'Pamela will show you out.'

An immaculately groomed young woman, who'd have been equally at home on the front cover of a glossy fashion magazine, escorted us from the premises.

I'd pinned my hopes on Matthew Levi fixing Elisha's grafts. I still believed he could. We walked back to our motel in silence. There was so much going through my head that I wanted to say out loud. *Did you have to be so mean to Matthew? You could have shown him some respect. He was trying to help you.* Something else weighed on my mind—something even more contentious. Although her grafts had contracted, her skin looked a hell of a lot better than it did before he operated. But Elisha's eyes were cold and voicing any of these thoughts would only inflame the situation.

The silence continued as we sat at opposite ends of the dining table in the motel room, eating an Indian takeaway. Was there *anything* I could do to put things right?

 David Whittet

I took a mouthful of curry. It had to be the blandest apology for Indian food I'd ever tasted.

'Not a patch on the real thing, is it?' I said.

Elisha pushed her plate aside. 'No, it isn't. I told you we shouldn't have left India.' She glared at me across the table. 'And we only did because you promised Levi could work miracles.'

I gave up on the curry, too, and moved my chair around the table to get closer to Elisha. 'Listen,' I said. 'Matthew Levi's not an ogre.'

Elisha pulled away. 'No, Levi's not the ogre.' She pointed to her face. 'I'm the ogress! Levi did this to me.'

I couldn't let that pass. 'No. Those thugs in India did that to you. Matthew's trying to help.'

'I cannot stand that man,' Elisha said. 'I don't want Levi near me again.'

'His name's Matthew,' I said. 'Why can't you use his first name?'

'He's not my friend.'

I edged closer again and put my hand on Elisha's. 'I wasn't sure about Matthew at first. When I was a student, I thought he was just another money-grubbing plastic surgeon.'

Elisha glanced up. 'So what made you change your mind?'

'I saw what Matthew did for Bwanbale.' I paused and took a deep breath. 'You saw it yourself. His mother showed you photos of what Bwanbale looked like before Matthew operated.'

Elisha shrugged. 'Bwanbale was lucky.'

'Complex grafts often take more than one operation,' I said. 'Why won't you give Matthew another chance?'

Elisha backed off again. 'No way. I still want a second opinion, but not from Levi.'

I sighed. This was a fight I would never win. 'Alright, my love. We'll get a second opinion. And a third and a fourth and a fifth. Until we find someone who can fix you.'

Three months later, we were in yet another private doctor's office—the latest in a long string of unsuccessful consultations.

The surgeon inspected Elisha's skin with his dermatoscope. 'What a shame you didn't come to me first,' he said. 'I could have done a much better job than Matthew Levi.'

I bet you could—at a price. One specialist would recommend laser treatment, the next further grafting. The only point of agreement was that none of them would offer a guarantee.

I'd taken a leave of absence from the Northland practice and got a locum job at Auckland's City Medical Clinic. Locuming wasn't me, but the pay was good—and it needed to be with the consultants' exorbitant fees. I didn't mind working my butt off at the downtown clinic and would gladly continue if it was doing Elisha any good. But it wasn't. And I went into medicine to make a difference, not to line the pockets of rich consultants.

Accommodation in Auckland didn't come cheap either—even the pokey one-bedroom flat we'd rented. I dreaded the bank statements arriving. We were damn near bankrupt.

Couldn't Elisha see we were going nowhere? Another disappointing specialist's appointment followed by pot noodles for supper. I had to say something, and it was the smell of those noodles that did it.

'This can't go on.' I got up from the table, paced around for a couple of minutes, then pulled up my chair next to hers. 'All these consultations— they're not helping you, and it's cleaning me out.'

Elisha picked at her noodles. 'I know, but … I hate looking like this.'

'Honestly, darling, you look fine.'

'Crap!' Elisha threw her arms in the air. 'I've got a face—and a body— that only a mother could love.'

I moved closer and cuddled her. 'I love you.'

She eyed me suspiciously. 'You don't have to say that.'

'I mean it.'

And I did. It wasn't the scars that worried me. I'd seen worse when I worked on a burns unit. It was Elisha's eyes. That harsh, unforgiving look. That's what messed with my head. And it would continue to do so, judging by her expression when we got up from the table and threw the noodles into the garbage.

Working at the City Medical Clinic the following day proved even more

David Whittet

punishing than usual. Every single appointment triple booked. Everyone in the clinic breathed a sigh of relief when the last patient left.

'Thank God that's over,' one of the younger doctors said. 'I'm off, going out to the Civic with my girlfriend.'

Lucky sod. I was no socialite, but I'd have given my soul for a night on the town. A slap-up meal and a trip to the theatre or a nightclub. All I had to look forward to was more instant noodles. The tantalising aromas emanating from the restaurants as I trudged down Queen Street drove me wild. I dragged myself up the steps to our flat. The lift had been out of order since we arrived, and I'll swear there were more steps to climb every day.

I was about to turn the key in the lock when Elisha opened the door.

'I've been thinking,' she said, 'I don't want to see any more specialists and I don't want any more surgery.'

Hallelujah! I'd dreaded telling her we just couldn't afford another opinion. 'What's brought this on?' I asked.

'I looked in the mirror this morning,' Elisha said, 'and for the first time since the attack, I didn't cry when I saw my face.'

I hugged Elisha. 'That's wonderful!'

'I swear I'd have hit the next smarmy quack who treats me like a hunk of meat with a dollar sign on it.' Elisha twitched as she raised her eyes to meet mine. 'Are you absolutely sure you don't mind going to bed with an ogress every night? And waking up next to her every morning?'

'Darling! I've told you—you'll always be perfect to me.' I gave her a gentle prod. 'Besides, I was thinking I'd have to go into private practice myself to pay the consultants' fees.'

Elisha screwed up her eyes. 'I don't want you to do that.'

'So what shall we do?' I asked. 'City Medical is driving me crazy.'

'I guess we could …' Elisha broke off.

I knew what she was thinking, and I finished the sentence for her. 'We could go back to Northland.'

There was a gleam in Elisha's eyes I hadn't seen in ages. 'Yes, let's.'

Yay! I felt years younger in an instant. No more City Medical. No more ghastly locums, working till I dropped. I was going back to *real* general practice.

'I'll hand in my notice at City Medical in the morning,' I said. 'But first, we're going out for a decent dinner, even if it costs the last cent I've got.'

The first few months back in the Bay of Islands were brilliant. The autumn colours proved particularly kind to Elisha's complexion, minimising her scars and highlighting her radiant eyes. She went out more, building her confidence. And when she smiled, I had my Elisha back.

Getting my teeth back into some real medicine was a relief, too. Although, I was actually busier than I'd been at City Medical. Poor Ngaire was rushed off her feet, taking blood, dressing wounds, and making a concerted effort to get on top of the diabetes reviews.

'I sure could use an extra pair of hands,' she said at the end of another exhausting week. 'And we start the flu vaccine next week.'

'I'll talk to Elisha tonight,' I said.

Ngaire put the last of the used instruments into the steriliser. 'Are you sure she's ready?'

'She'll be thrilled,' I said. 'Doing the flu vaccines is the perfect opportunity for her to get back to work.'

I rushed home to give Elisha the news—and *yes*, she was delighted.

'It'll be like the old days,' she said. 'Remember that all-night session jabbing the kids in secret?'

I could tell she missed the excitement. 'Yes, well … I hope it won't be that dramatic.' I took off my coat and hung it up. 'Mind you, those goons at the trust are as bad as Prasad and his minions.'

We both laughed and sat down for supper—more fresh hāpuka from our neighbour Dawn. No more pot noodles for us.

'When do I start?' Elisha asked. 'I can't wait. It's going to be *fun*.'

And it was fun—for the first month. I didn't care about the workload when I could see Elisha's smile in between my consultations.

'All done,' Elisha said as she drew up the last of the flu vaccines and jabbed a grateful eighty-year-old. 'Don't forget you have to wait twenty minutes, Mrs Pari.'

'Phew,' Ngaire said. 'We've never got through the flu programme that fast before. Well done, Elisha. You're a lifesaver!'

     David Whittet

If there hadn't been a waiting room full of patients watching, I'd have twirled Elisha around the floor. I had to settle for a modest thumbs up.

When I went back to the waiting room to collect my next patient, Elisha was there, helping Mrs Pari to get up. My throat thickened as Elisha guided the old lady to her mobility scooter. I felt at ease with the world. We had turned the corner and built a new life for ourselves.

'You can go home now, Mrs Pari,' Elisha said. 'That's you, protected against the flu, and all set for winter.'

Winter. Each day grew colder, and every frost brought a fresh slew of bills to our letter box. I didn't care about that. Elisha was happy. She took on more responsibility at the practice and rapidly built up a following of loyal and devoted patients. I tried to ignore her coughing at first.

'It's just a sniffle,' she would say.

'All new staff pick up every bug that's going when they first join the practice,' Ngaire said. 'After that, you build up immunity to the local germs.'

'That's right,' the receptionist chipped in. 'I kept getting colds when I started working here. Now I never get sick.'

Two months on, and Elisha's cough got worse. I couldn't overlook it any longer. When she called me into the treatment room to check an elderly man's wound, Elisha had a coughing fit and spluttered all over the dressing.

Ngaire finished attending to a child with asthma and turned to me. 'I think you should take Elisha home. We can't have her working like this.'

'You're right,' I replied. 'Come on, Elisha. A couple of days' rest and you'll be fine.'

Elisha got up and put on a face mask. 'I'm okay.'

'You're not,' Ngaire said.

Elisha went back to finish the dressing. 'Don't fuss.'

Ngaire put a hand on Elisha's shoulder. 'You need to listen, Elisha. You're no good to anyone like this. Take some time out and get better.'

'But we're so busy,' Elisha said. 'How will you cope on your own?'

'I've done it before,' Ngaire said. 'And believe me, I'll be the first to welcome you back when you're well again.'

Elisha looked up at me with her appealing eyes. 'Theo … please!'

I snapped my fingers. 'Home!'

If only home was warmer. I spent what little cash we had left on firewood, but even that didn't thaw the ice palace they called the doctor's residence.

I tucked Elisha up in bed with a hot-water bottle.

'I'm *not* staying home to stagnate,' she said. 'I'll be back at work next week. You'll see.'

She was, although my heart missed a beat every time she coughed or sneezed. Elisha had such sublime empathy for patients, having experienced major trauma herself. I felt a lump in my throat when she comforted sick children and helped old ladies, like Mrs Pari, with their walking frames.

Winter hit hard, and each successive infection laid Elisha low for longer. It was all so unfair. Elisha was alive again when she was at the medical centre. She refused to slow down, and I couldn't get her to spend more than a couple of days in bed at the most. I hadn't the heart to hold her back. Thank God the worst of winter would soon be behind us. With spring less than a month away, I kept repeating Ngaire's words to myself: *All new staff pick up every bug that's going.* With the days getting warmer, I dared to believe that Ngaire could be right. Elisha began to look stronger. Maybe she was building resistance to the local germs.

'I'm helping Ngaire to set up a diabetes clinic,' Elisha said over breakfast. 'There's so much maturity-onset diabetes in the community ...'

Elisha continued enthusiastically about the new clinic, but I stopped listening. She'd just stuffed a blood-stained handkerchief in her pocket.

Stay calm. Maybe it's just a nose bleed. I knew it wasn't.

I reached out and held her hand. 'How long have you been coughing up blood?'

'It's nothing.' Elisha got up from the breakfast table. 'Hurry up, or we'll be late for work. I can't wait to get started on the diabetes clinic.'

I kept hold of her hand. 'You're not going to work until I've listened to your chest.'

Elisha frowned. 'But the diabetes clinic—'

'But nothing.'

I fetched my stethoscope and we sat down again at the table. My hand shook as I laid the stethoscope on her chest. What would I hear? I was

     David Whittet

almost too frightened to listen. When I did, my breathing was almost as erratic as Elisha's. And it wasn't just my hands shaking when I heard the coarse crackles, reduced air entry, and the pleural rub.

I took a deep breath. Tried to keep control. 'I'm taking you to the hospital in Kerikeri.'

'The diabetes clinic,' Elisha protested. 'That's far more important than me.'

You can't work. You're sick—you've got pneumonia. I couldn't say it out loud and let Elisha see I was scared shitless. 'Ngaire will take care of the clinic. If we get you to hospital now, you'll be back to work far more quickly.'

'How quickly?'

I bit my lip. 'A week or two tops.'

'Promise?'

'Absolutely.' I couldn't meet her eyes. She must have known it was a promise I couldn't guarantee.

I grabbed the telephone and dialled 111. *Come on!* I fiddled with the phone cord, convinced Elisha's breathing was getting shallower while I waited for the operator.

'*What?*' I spat the word into the telephone—the nearest ambulance crew were at least half an hour away. 'No … I can't wait … I'll drive her to the hospital myself.'

The clinic vehicle had a flashing light on the roof, emergency gear in the back and was equipped with a radio transmitter. It was as good as any ambulance.

I gripped Elisha's arm and led her out to the vehicle. 'You're doing great,' I said. 'Just take it one step at a time.'

Elisha gasped for breath. 'Theo … I don't think I'm going to make it.'

'Of course you are,' I said. 'Hold on to me.'

Her tight, frightened eyes as I got her into the vehicle told me she'd realised just how sick she was.

I gave her the most reassuring smile I could. 'We'll have you there in no time.'

I turned on the green flashing light and hit the accelerator, hooting at all the dawdling day trippers who got in the way. I broke all the speed limits when we got onto the open road. So what if I got a speeding ticket? Every second was precious. Elisha drifted in and out of consciousness. I had to get her to the hospital before it was too late.

Elisha stirred when we swerved around a corner.

'We're nearly there,' I said. 'That's Kerikeri just ahead.'

I ran a red light on the way into Kerikeri. Out of nowhere, a police car appeared, lights flashing and siren blazing. Didn't the buggers know a green flashing light on the roof meant it was a doctor on an emergency?

The radio transmitter crackled. I turned up the volume to hear the message.

'Ambulance control told us you were coming through,' the voice said. 'We're giving you a police escort to the hospital.'

An hour later, I sat at Elisha's bedside as the medical registrar set up the intravenous line.

'We've sent off blood cultures and a sputum sample,' he said, 'but it'll be twenty-four hours before we get preliminary results. In the meantime, we'll get her started on a cocktail of antibiotics.'

Keeping vigil at Elisha's bedside gave me time to think. I blamed that cold, damp doctor's residence for making Elisha sick. Things were going to change. If the trust wouldn't provide us with decent accommodation—well, I'd have to make other plans.

Forty-eight hours of intravenous antibiotics and Elisha's breathing improved.

I gave her hand a gentle squeeze. 'You gave me a fright.'

The staff nurse took Elisha's blood pressure. 'She had us all worried, I can tell you.'

'I was scared too,' Elisha said. 'Not being able to breathe.'

I drew my chair closer after the nurse left. 'It's that miserable house that did this to you. We're not going back.'

Elisha sat up. 'They're giving us a new house?'

'No.' I took a deep breath. 'Seeing you like this—it's time for some tough decisions.'

Elisha frowned. 'What do you mean?'

I reached for my briefcase and pulled out some papers. 'I've been offered a new contract.'

Elisha looked at me suspiciously. 'Doing what?'

I lowered my head slightly. 'Appearance medicine.'

Elisha's reaction wasn't as violent as I expected.

'Appearance medicine?' she said. 'You told me you went into medicine to change the world.'

'I did.'

Elisha eyed me intently. 'Don't you care any more?'

'I *do*. You know I do … but now you come first.' I gave her hand another squeeze. 'We've done more in the time we've been together than most achieve in a lifetime.'

'But there's still so much more to do,' Elisha said. 'I promised my father I'd build the well.'

'I know.' How could I make her understand? 'The mission will go on without us. What about that letter you got from Rajani? She and Zac have got work on the well underway.' I gave Elisha an encouraging smile. 'Get yourself well and maybe we can go back for the well's opening.'

Elisha sighed. '*Appearance medicine*. I never thought you'd sell your soul.'

I haven't. I won't. Surely she knew me better than that? 'Appearance medicine doesn't have to be a rip-off. Making people feel better about themselves really matters. It's still making a difference—just in another way.'

Elisha raised her eyebrows. 'And the money has nothing to do with it?'

'We need to get back on our feet.' I closed my eyes for a moment, then focused on Elisha. 'And yes, if I'm honest, I do envy the fortune those specialists make while we survive on pot noodles.'

'So we'll be dining out on caviar from now on, will we?' Elisha said. 'Theo! That's not us.'

'No. But at least it'll get us out of debt.' I waved my new partnership agreement in front of her. 'Take a look at this.'

Elisha slumped back on her pillow. 'Just promise me you won't have anything to do with Matthew Levi. That's all I ask.'

My jaw dropped. I felt my cheeks burning and stuffed the agreement back in my briefcase.

Elisha pulled herself up again. 'Show me that.'

I reluctantly handed over the contract and watched her read the first incriminating lines. If she had the strength and if her arms weren't attached to a drip, I'm sure she would have torn it up.

'You are *not* going into partnership with Matthew Levi,' Elisha said.

'Just till we get ourselves out of this mess.' I pulled some more papers out of my briefcase. Bank statements, overdue accounts, final demands. 'I didn't want to show you these until you were feeling better, but … can't you see? I'm desperate.'

Elisha brushed the papers aside. 'I don't want anything more to do with Levi.'

I picked up the bills and put them back in my briefcase along with the contract. 'Matthew's our only hope of getting our heads above water.'

'We may be in debt,' Elisha said, 'but we've still got our pride.'

'Please!' I'd have gone down on my knees if I thought it would do any good. 'As soon as we can make ends meet, I'll finish with Matthew.'

Elisha glared at me. 'I said no.'

I was never going to win. Part of me wanted to remind her it was all those wasted second opinions that had got us into this trouble, but that would be too unkind.

'Alright,' I said with a sigh, 'but I don't know how we're going to survive.'

'You can open up your own clinic,' Elisha said. 'I can just about manage you doing appearance medicine, but not with Matthew Levi.'

'I've no client base,' I said. 'Goodwill is everything in appearance medicine. You've no idea how difficult it'll be, going alone.'

Elisha's expression softened. 'You can do it, Theo. You've got integrity. You're not a crook like all those money-grubbing consultants. You'll soon build up a practice of local patients.'

Would I? You needed contacts to break into appearance and I had none apart from Matthew. 'I hope you're right.'

'I am.' This time, Elisha squeezed my hand. 'We don't need Levi.'

        David Whittet

CHAPTER TWENTY-NINE

A month later, I had my own private consulting rooms in Auckland's fashionable Remuera suburb. I felt a surge of pride as I walked through the door on my first morning and saw my name emblazoned on a brass plaque:

Dr Theo Malone
Appearance Medicine Specialist

My receptionist, Sabrina, greeted me. 'Good morning, Dr Malone.'

'Call me Theo,' I said. 'Please.'

Although less glamorous than Pamela at Matthew Levi's rooms, Sabrina had a warm smile. I glanced at the empty page in the appointment book on her desk.

'No patients booked in yet?' I asked.

'Not yet,' Sabrina said, 'but I'm sure the phone will be ringing like crazy once word gets around about our brilliant young doctor.'

Would it? The phone was painfully silent right now. I shrugged and tried to sound laid-back. 'That's what my fiancée, Elisha, said.'

Sabrina fiddled with her pen. 'I'm sure she's right. There'll be a waiting list for appointments in no time.'

I desperately wanted Elisha to be right. *You'll soon build up a practice of local patients … we don't need Levi.* Three weeks on and only a trickle of patients, convinced me that I *did* need Matthew. The spring sunshine brought in as many bills as the winter frost had done. And the bank loan I'd taken out to set up the practice—I daren't think about that.

Elisha was wrong about Matthew. He'd understood when I broke the contract with him. Remarkably, he even put in a good word with the landlord for my new rooms.

'Good luck, mate,' he'd said, giving me a hearty handshake. 'My door's still open if you change your mind.'

I'm sure he knew it wasn't *my* mind that needed changing.

The few patients I saw didn't have any money. Overseas visitors left without paying their bills. And then there was the ex-gangster …

Sabrina looked unusually pale when she came into my consulting room. 'There's a rather unpleasant-looking man arrived in reception,' she said. 'Shall I tell him to go away?'

'No, send him in,' I said. 'We can't afford to turn anyone down.'

At first sight, the towering Māori man with his full facial tattoo did look intimidating. Much less so when he sat on the edge of the chair.

'You have to help me, Doc,' he said. 'I've heard you people can do tattoo removal.'

I got up and took a closer look at his tā moko. 'Laser treatment can break down the pigments,' I said. 'But the grooves—they're much more difficult.'

'Do what you can, Doc,' he pleaded. 'I must have a new identity.'

What was I letting myself in for? Would I have the gang on my back? Still, I wasn't in a position to refuse work. Maybe he was on the witness protection scheme, and the police would pay. Perhaps not.

He told me how his father raised him to be a gang leader, with frequent beatings as his teaching method. The scars were still there on his back. As a teenager, he'd gone through a ritual initiation into the gang, which involved receiving a full facial tattoo.

'It's like a gang patch,' he explained. 'Branded for life. You're not meant to leave the gang.'

I asked him why he had. Several versions came out during the countless hours I worked on his face. Something to do with love and a new start away from the gang.

At the end of the course of treatment, his face may not have been perfect, but it was certainly different—and that seemed to be all that mattered to him.

'Thanks a million, Doc,' he said. 'You're a lifesaver.'

'About my fee,' I said. 'We agreed …'

He was out the door before I could finish the sentence. I never saw him again.

How did I break it to Elisha and make her understand the practice wasn't making enough to cover the overheads? She'd made such a brilliant recovery from her pneumonia, and I didn't want to worry her about money. Every night when I got home, she'd dig me in the ribs and ask me how many facelifts I'd done. At first, it was mildly amusing. After a week working on an ex-gangster's tattoo, it was infuriating.

'Chance would be a fine thing,' I said as I put down my briefcase and hung up my jacket in the hallway of our apartment. 'The only patient I've seen all week's an ex-gangster, and the bugger didn't pay.'

'Maybe he didn't have any money,' Elisha said. 'So you did a good turn for someone in need. Isn't that why you went into medicine?'

I wasn't sure if removing a tā moko from an ex-gangster on the run constituted an act of humanitarianism. 'I meant what I said about appearance medicine making a difference, helping people to feel better about themselves. But …' I knew what I wanted to say. *We need a better class of patients to survive. We need Matthew Levi.* Instead, I simply shrugged and slumped onto the sofa.

Elisha sat beside me. 'Don't give up. We've been through worse than this.'

We had—but right now, it didn't feel that way.

Other than an elderly lady wanting her toenails cut, my waiting room was empty the following day. I should have sent her away—she needed a podiatrist, not a doctor. But she was a paying customer, and I was desperate and not too proud to cut toenails.

The phone rang as I saw the elderly lady out. Thank God. Somebody wanting to make an appointment at last.

'It's your bank manager,' Sabrina said. 'Shall I put him through?'

I grasped the door for support. 'Yes,' I said, trying to hide the quake in my voice. 'I'll take it in my office.'

The bank manager definitely agreed I needed a higher class of clientele. 'Remuera is full of rich people,' he said, 'and most of them needing face jobs. So why aren't you attracting them?'

Excuses had never been my strong point. The quake in my voice got even worse, and the words sounded hollow as they left my mouth. 'It takes time to build up a reputation. I've only been open a couple of months.'

'That's as maybe,' the bank manager said, 'but if I don't see some money coming in over the next fortnight, I'll have no option but to foreclose on your loan.'

I fought the urge to slam down the receiver and make a run for it. 'But … please … you can't expect me to turn things around in just two weeks.'

A pause. I could picture the manager in his office shaking his head.

'Dr Malone,' he said at last, 'I'll never understand why you didn't go into practice with Matthew Levi when you had the chance.' Another pause. 'Maybe it's not too late.'

Maybe it wasn't. There were no patients booked for the rest of the afternoon, so I told Sabrina I was going home. I rehearsed what I was going to say to Elisha in my head, time after time. *It's not as if Matthew and I would be partners. We'd just be practising out of the same building. It would save heaps of money, and I'd have much better resources.* Would Elisha buy it? I took a deep breath and put my key in the front door.

Elisha looked up from her book when I sat down on the sofa beside her. 'What is it, darling?' she said.

'I had one patient today,' I said. 'An eighty-year-old who wanted her toenails cut.'

Elisha rested her hand on mine. 'You'll have more tomorrow.'

I raised my eyes to hers. 'There's not going to be a tomorrow. The bank manager called me today. Unless I start making some money, he's going to call in the loan.'

Elisha drew back. 'So what are you going to do?'

I drew another long breath. 'The bank manager had a solution. He suggested I join an established practice. He'll extend my credit if I do. And he has just the practice in mind.'

'That's great,' Elisha said. 'You had me worried for a minute. It'll do you good to have some colleagues.'

'You don't mind if I go in with some other doctors?' I asked.

'Of course not.' Elisha eyed me suspiciously. 'As long as it's not Matthew Levi.'

I gulped. 'But—'

David Whittet

Elisha glared at me. 'You made all this up, didn't you? Just to frighten me into letting you work with that crook Levi.'

'No!' I stared back at her. 'We can go to the bank together tomorrow if you don't believe me.'

'I *want* to believe you,' Elisha said. 'But you've changed since we left India.'

'We've both changed.' I tried to put my arm around Elisha, but she pulled away. 'And that's only natural after everything we've been through.'

'I suppose so,' Elisha said. 'I just don't want us to have anything more to do with Levi.'

'I know you blame him for your surgery …'

What was the use? Elisha shut off whenever I tried to explain it wasn't Matthew's fault her grafts got infected.

I cleared my throat and started again. 'What if it's going in with Matthew or bust?'

'It won't come to that,' Elisha said. 'There are loads of practices out there you could join. We don't need Levi.'

Three weeks searching for an alternative practice, and a dozen more calls from the bank manager, told me that we definitely *did* need Matthew Levi. Auckland's appearance medicine doctors were a closed circle and news of my failed clinic spread fast. I could almost hear them laughing at me. The doctor who cuts toenails. I faced total ruin if I didn't …

The day before the bank was due to call in my loan, I picked up the telephone in my deserted rooms. 'Matthew … you remember saying you'd keep your door open for me? We need to talk …'

I didn't want to deceive Elisha. But I didn't want to go bankrupt either.

I ought to have felt more guilty than I did. The prospect of a secure income put paid to any doubts I might have had. I crept out of the house early that first morning before Elisha was awake. It was easier that way.

I cornered Matthew the minute I arrived at the consulting rooms. 'Remember what I said on the phone? Elisha mustn't know about our arrangement. Promise me you won't tell her.'

Matthew rubbed his chin. 'I hope you know what you're doing, Theo.

I won't breathe a word—but word gets around. Wouldn't it be better to tell her the truth?'

If only I could. I'd never lied to Elisha before, and I didn't want to start now. But what choice did I have? It wasn't just the bank manager giving me grief. Our landlord threatened eviction if I didn't come up with the rent. Without this job, we'd have been out on the streets in days. And with Elisha's fragile lungs … I knew all too well what would happen.

I met Matthew's eyes. 'You're right. I will tell her—as soon as she's ready to hear it.'

'Don't leave it too long,' Matthew said. 'Or you'll regret it.'

'I won't.'

Matthew disappeared into his office. I paused for a moment before going into mine. Could I ever tell Elisha the truth? Admit I was working with Matthew? How long could I keep up the pretence? And would it end in disaster?

Such thoughts vanished when my first patient came through the door. Amy, a sixteen-year-old with severe facial acne, shuffled in with her head bowed. Without looking up, she sat down and burst into tears.

Her mother followed and sat beside her. 'Amy's tried everything. She's even got a part-time job in the evenings to pay for all the creams and lotions. None of them work.'

Amy glanced up. 'If you can't help me, I swear I'll—'

'I'm worried Amy will harm herself,' the mother interrupted.

I examined Amy's face. She'd be an ideal candidate for photodynamic therapy.

'I can't promise you an overnight cure,' I said. 'But give me a couple of months, and your skin will be a whole lot better.'

My next patient was a boy with prominent ears. His mother told me how he played truant from school—the other kids teased him and called him 'Trophy Man' because his ears resembled the handles on a cup. I felt alive again as I explained how a simple procedure would give him a new beginning.

I went home that evening bursting to tell Elisha about everything I'd done. But I couldn't—not without letting it slip that I was working with Matthew. I simply couldn't face another row.

    David Whittet

'You look much brighter tonight,' Elisha said. 'You must have done a ton of facelifts in your new clinic.'

I couldn't look her in the eye. 'It was pretty full-on. Actually, I've got a headache. I'm going to skip dinner and head straight to bed.'

That became the habit. I avoided talking to Elisha whenever I could. We were like two strangers living in the same apartment. Everything felt wrong. Matthew had warned me—the deception couldn't go on.

A month of sleepless nights and the stress took its toll at work as well as at home. Walking the streets at three in the morning, I made my decision. I would go back into general practice. Not in some remote rural place this time. I'd been studying the classifieds in the *New Zealand Medical Journal*. They were crying out for GPs in the smaller provincial towns, and I'd always wanted to see Akaroa. Elisha would love the South Island. And how I longed to be at peace with her again.

I watched the sunrise over the Auckland skyline. This would be a new beginning. I'd get to the clinic early and tell him appearance medicine wasn't for me, and I was leaving. He'd understand.

Matthew was already there when I arrived.

'I need to talk to you,' I said. 'It's important.'

'Okay. But first, there's a case I want you to see.' Matthew led me into his consulting room. 'This is Jamie Beale.'

A young man—he must have been in his early twenties—sat on the edge of Matthew's examination couch. I gasped—I just couldn't stop myself. Multiple bulging tumours that resembled clusters of mushrooms covered every centimetre of his skin. I'd seen pictures of neurofibromatosis in textbooks. None of that prepared me for what was in front of my eyes.

Jamie hid his face.

'I'm sorry,' I said, ashamed of my unprofessionalism. 'I didn't mean to stare.'

Jamie's mother stood beside him and covered his near-naked body with a sheet. She turned to Matthew. 'Can you really help Jamie? You know we can't afford to pay you.'

Matthew waved his hand. 'Don't worry about that, Mrs Beale.' He ran his fingers over Jamie's face. 'We won't be able to get rid of all these growths—at least, not in one go. We'll tackle the biggest first.' He smiled at Jamie. 'Just losing these enormous lumps on your forehead will make a tremendous difference.'

'We're so grateful, Dr Levi,' Mrs Beale said. 'I don't know how to thank you.'

Mathew turned to me. 'Dr Malone is going to help with the operation.'

What? I'd never assisted with anything as advanced as this.

'Are you sure?' I whispered in Matthew's ear. 'You need someone far more experienced than I am.'

'You'll be fine,' Matthew said. 'Now, what was it you wanted to talk to me about?'

I shuffled my feet. 'Nothing. Nothing at all.'

Akaroa would have to wait.

It was time to come clean with Elisha. I'd tell her about Jamie. Surely that would convince her that she was mistaken about Matthew. What did it matter that he was arrogant and often said the wrong thing, when he was so incredibly generous? He'd waved his fee for Bwanbale because the family had no money. Now he was doing the same for Jamie.

Elisha was watching television when I got home. She barely acknowledged my presence.

I felt my confidence evaporate rapidly. 'Can we turn that off for a minute,' I said. 'There's something I need to tell you.'

Without a word, Elisha got up and turned off the television.

If I didn't get it out straight away, I'd bottle it. 'Matthew Levi has asked me to assist him with an operation.'

Silence. It was the first time I'd mentioned Matthew's name to her in over a month. Her eyes told me her attitude towards him hadn't softened.

'Remember Bwanbale?' I said. 'Well, Matthew's doing it again. He's going to operate, without charging a fee, on this poor kid with hideous neurofibromatosis. Nobody else would take them on unless they paid upfront.'

'How come you were talking to Levi anyway?' Elisha asked.

Tell her. Tell her now. I took another look at her unforgiving eyes and lost my nerve. 'The appearance medicine community is very close-knit.' I

David Whittet

bit my tongue and continued. 'We all try to help each other out. Matthew wanted my help.'

'I don't see why he asked you,' Elisha said. 'You're not even a trained surgeon.'

'I guess he knows I'm into philanthropic work,' I said.

Elisha snorted. 'Until you went into appearance medicine and gave up on everything you believed in.'

'That's not fair,' I said. 'Helping kids like Bwanbale and this guy Jamie *is* what I believe in.'

Elisha crossed her arms. 'I only hope Levi does a better job for that boy than he did for me.'

That wasn't fair either. I remained convinced it was a low-grade infection and not Matthew's surgery that had been the problem. Besides, there'd been a slow but definite improvement in Elisha's face over the past three months. Hadn't she looked in the mirror?

'Your skin's great,' I said.

Elisha cut me off with a dismissive wave of her hand. 'Crap! And if you're telling me this because you want to go into practice with Levi—'

'I *am* going to assist Matthew with this operation, whatever you say.'

'Okay. But I'm warning you, Theo …' She pointed to the front door. 'Any more dealings with Levi after the operation, and I'm straight out of that door.'

Elisha got up and turned the television back on.

I meant what I said to Elisha. Nothing would stop me from assisting at Jamie's operation. I'd promised Jamie's mother, but it was more than that. There was no way I would miss out on first-hand experience of surgical treatment for such a rare and extreme case of neurofibromatosis. I'd part with Matthew once Jamie's treatment was complete.

Matthew left Jamie's pre-operative workup to me, and I grew close to both him and his mother. I steadied Jamie's trembling arm when I took a blood sample for the laboratory.

'What if the surgery makes me worse?' Jamie asked. 'I'll top myself if it does.'

I finished taking the blood and held his hand. 'It won't. I promise. Look at these.' I handed Jamie some before and after photos of Bwanbale—and Elisha. 'See what Dr Levi can do.'

'Can I have a look?' Mrs Beale asked. 'Gosh! They're amazing. This is going to change your life, Jamie.'

The wait for the surgery over the next couple of weeks was almost as painful for me as it must have been for them. Hiding the truth from Elisha. Wondering if she'd still be there when I came home from work. This was no way to live.

I asked Elisha if she would meet Jamie and his mother. Maybe that would change her mind.

Elisha just shrugged and carried on watching television. 'If they see what Levi's done to me, they'll cancel the operation.'

They've seen pictures, and they're blown away by what Matthew's done for you. What was the use? Jamie's surgery would be a defining moment in my medical career, and I couldn't share it with the woman closest to my heart.

Had I missed anything? I went through the pre-op checklist on the morning of the operation and listened to Jamie's chest.

'Is everything okay?' Mrs Beale asked.

'Absolutely,' I said. 'Don't worry. We'll take good care of him.'

The porters arrived and wheeled Jamie into the anaesthetic room.

Mrs Beale stayed with Jamie until he was asleep.

'He'll come out a new man,' I told her as we headed into theatre.

Matthew had lost none of his conjuring skills. With a flick of the scalpel, he sliced off the tumours. As if by magic, he replaced them with a flap of skin. Mathew's hands were so nimble, his movements precise. I cursed myself when the forceps slipped between my fingers.

After four gruelling hours in theatre, we followed Jamie into the recovery room. Even with the wounds in their raw state, I could tell Matthew had made an extraordinary transformation.

'That was frigging unbelievable,' I said. 'It's nothing short of a miracle.'

Matthew took off his surgical mask. 'It's gone well. But this is just the first stage. I'm going to tackle those bulges on his neck next time.'

Next time! I couldn't leave the practice now—I had to stay on and see

 David Whittet

Jamie's surgery through, whatever Elisha thought. It was more than just professional interest. I cared about Jamie.

Mrs Beale greeted me when I came out of theatre.

'I'll never forget what you've done for my boy,' she said.

I smiled back. 'It's Dr Levi you should thank. I only assisted.'

'If you hadn't persuaded my Jamie to go through with it, he'd have chickened out.' Mrs Beale put her arm on my shoulder. 'You and Dr Levi make a wonderful team.'

She was right. With Matthew's surgical wizardry and my social conscience, we complimented each other perfectly. If only Elisha hadn't taken such a dislike to him, we could have been great together.

CHAPTER THIRTY

Appearance medicine wasn't just Botox, facelifts, body shaping and laser hair removal. Jamie's surgery proved that. My head was still buzzing when I got home after the operation. To my surprise, Elisha jumped up the moment I arrived.

'How did it go?' she asked.

'Brilliant!' I'd been bursting to tell Elisha about Jamie's operation but didn't think she would listen. 'It's early days, but … When Jamie went into theatre, I promised his mother he'd come out a new man. And you know … I really believe we changed that young man's life today.'

'I'm happy for Jamie,' Elisha said, 'and I'm pleased you helped with the operation.'

What had brought about this change of heart? Dare I say more about working with Matthew?

'Of course, we're not there yet,' I said. 'Jamie's going to need a lot more surgery, and I want to help with that, too.'

'I'm glad you've found yourself again because I'm still lost.' Elisha's eyes met mine. 'It's alright for you. Getting out of the apartment and going to work. I'm stuck here, day in, day out.'

'Oh, my darling!' I put my arm around her and held her tight. Elisha was hurting, and over the past month, I'd done nothing to help her. 'It won't always be like this. I promise.'

'It will.' Elisha lowered her head. 'When we were up north, at least I could work at the practice. But nobody wants to see a grotesque face like mine in an appearance medicine clinic.'

'Nonsense!' I stroked Elisha's hair. 'Actually, I'm thinking of going back into general practice once Jamie's surgery's done. I was thinking of Akaroa. You've always said you wanted to see the South Island. You could work at the practice there.'

Elisha pulled away. 'You've just said Jamie needs loads more surgery. That'll take forever. I'm sorry, Theo. I can't wait that long.'

   David Whittet

Elisha got up and walked away. My heart stood still as I followed her into the bedroom, and my eyes focused on a neatly packed suitcase at the foot of the bed.

'Elisha, you're not—'

She sat on the edge of the bed. 'I'm not leaving you. I just need to get away for a month or two.'

I stared at her blankly. 'Yes, but where?'

'I'm going to Australia,' Elisha said. 'I want to spend some more time with Joanna.'

I sat next to her on the bed. 'That's a great idea. She did you a power of good when she came to see you in hospital.'

Elisha dabbed her eyes. 'Jo was my rock when I was a kid. But now—I don't know, I think she's as miserable as I am. She adored my mother and worshipped my father. The unfairness of everything … it's shaken her faith.'

I rubbed Elisha's back. 'Perhaps you can help each other.'

Elisha fidgeted with the blanket. 'Maybe.'

'Anyway,' I said, 'she'll be amazed at how much better you look than when you were in hospital.'

Elisha put her hands over her face. 'In your dreams.'

I shook my head. 'How many times do I have to tell you? Your face looks better every day.'

Her scars *were* improving. Why couldn't she see that?

I stroked her hand. 'When will you leave?'

'Tomorrow.'

I felt a sinking feeling in my stomach. 'That soon?'

'I rang Jo this afternoon,' Elisha said. 'The Church over there is planning a memorial service for my mum and dad. Jo wants me to be there. I'm not sure I'm up to it, but—'

'You are.' I squeezed Elisha's hand. 'You must go. It'll give you closure, and you need that more than anything.'

Elisha looked down at the floor. 'I know … it's just …'

I gave her hand another squeeze. 'I'll miss you. I'll be waiting for you when you come back.'

After hurriedly cancelling my appointments, I repeated those words to Elisha at the airport the next morning. With a last hug, I watched her disappear, a lost soul in a faceless crowd. Had I driven her away? Would she come back a different person? Would she come back at all?

Of course she will—don't even think that.

The biting autumn wind that swirled around my head when I left the airport continued to chill my heart in the weeks that followed. Before she left, Elisha had asked me if I was happy. Now she was gone, I realised how much I regretted the bad blood between us. We used to share everything. The day before her departure for Australia was the first serious talk we'd had in months.

The next fortnight also underlined how much I missed general practice. Elisha was right about that too—appearance medicine wasn't me. For two entire weeks, I did nothing but pamper the privileged. I just wished Matthew would fix a date for Jamie's operation. Then I could make plans for Akaroa and get back to general practice.

There had to be a way to persuade Matthew to get his arse into gear. I pestered him every morning as soon as he arrived at the rooms.

'You promised Jamie you'd get it done this month,' I said. 'Please don't let him down.'

What excuse would he use today? Matthew put his hand on my shoulder as if we were best mates. We were colleagues, not buddies.

'It's not that simple,' he said. 'Getting an anaesthetist to work for free isn't easy.'

I'd have anaesthetised Jamie myself if I could. Other days, Matthew claimed it was lack of theatre time or nursing staff causing the delay.

Damn him. Matthew could make anything happen if he put his mind to it. He'd lost interest in Jamie. I even found myself wondering if Elisha might have been right about Matthew all along. *Surely not—think what he did for Bwanbale, and what he's done—and is going to do—for Jamie. His heart's in the right place.* But was it? As time dragged on, I saw more of the arrogant prick that enraged me as a student and less of the decent human being who cared about humanity.

David Whittet

Time was getting short. The practice vacancy in Akaroa wouldn't remain open forever, and I wanted to be there when Elisha came back from Australia. But I'd given Mrs Beale my word that I would stay with Matthew until Jamie's surgery was complete.

After an endless morning massaging the egos of Auckland's socialites, I groaned when Veronica Ashton-Forbes strode into my consulting room. Her dazzling Versace suit and purple-tinted hair said it all. After a handshake that almost cut off the circulation to my fingers, she made herself comfortable in a chair. This was going to be a long and tedious consultation.

'I've heard good things about you, Dr Malone,' she began, 'and I've got a proposition to make.'

'A proposition?'

She nodded. 'Indeed. Something that'll change your career. May I call you Theo?'

'I guess so.'

I tried to look away and pretend I wasn't interested, but Veronica Ashton-Forbes' magnetic eyes captivated me.

'I run a modelling agency. Several of my clients have been to see you. They like you.' She leant forward over my desk. 'I want you to take over the contract to look after all my girls.'

I shielded my face. 'Miss Ashton-Forbes—'

She laughed. 'Call me Vron. Or just Vee. That's what everyone does.'

Her flirtatious posturing made me feel acutely uncomfortable. I tried again to disengage from those seductive eyes.

'Listen, Vee—' Why did that sound so wrong? 'What I was going to say was—I appreciate your generous offer and your confidence in me. I'm sure looking after your clients would be a dream job. But I'm afraid in my present situation, I can't possibly accept.'

'Why ever not?'

'I'm moving out of Dr Levi's rooms,' I said. 'I'm going back into general practice.'

Veronica raised her eyebrows. 'I had a boyfriend who was a GP. On call twenty-four seven and always called out when we were in bed making love. He died of a heart attack when he was fifty.' She took a folder out of her briefcase. 'Take a look at this contract. That'll soon change your mind.'

It won't. I pushed the folder back across the desk. 'I told you, I'm giving up appearance medicine.'

Veronica waved the contract in front of my nose. 'You can't be serious.'

'I am.'

'Why?'

I shrugged. 'Personal reasons.'

'Has Matthew given you the boot? Is that what this is all about?' Veronica gave another cocky chuckle. 'Well, you won't be the first, and you're better off without him.'

'Matthew doesn't know I'm leaving. Please don't tell him.'

'I won't.' Veronica threw the contract on my desk. 'You don't know me—yet. I don't give in easily.' She got up, her eyes continuing to mess with my head. 'Offers like mine come along once in a lifetime. Think about it. You'll regret it if you turn me down. I promise you that.'

Veronica reminded me of my aunt Ida. Like Veronica, my aunt was a glamorous woman. She'd been a dancer in her day. I'm sure both women had kind hearts beneath their outsized personalities. My aunt liked everything her own way, which made me apprehensive when I was sent to stay with her as a child. I felt just as uneasy with Veronica.

I *did* think about what Veronica had said. In fact, I didn't think about much else over the next few days. I'd never make the money she was offering in general practice. Not in a lifetime.

As if to twist my arm, Veronica kept booking her clients in to see me. The models were all young hopefuls, determined to make their mark in a cut-throat profession. Helping them to overcome their insecurities was a welcome change from pandering to the rich and famous.

A month on, and I'd paid back my bank loan. If I continued working for Veronica, I'd soon have the deposit for an apartment of my own.

Veronica was true to her word and kept up the pressure. 'It's not too late to sign,' she said. 'Just think, this time next year, you could be in your own consulting suite and having parties in your new penthouse pad.'

 David Whittet

Surely that was too much to throw away. I took another look at the contract and reached for my pen.

Had I really sold my soul? What would Elisha say? Something else troubled me. What would Ralph Greenslade think about what I was doing now?

'No, I'm not signing.' I put the pen back in my pocket. 'I'm going to be a GP in Akaroa.'

'We'll see,' Veronica said, unfazed. 'I haven't finished with you yet, Theo.'

I had to get out of Auckland and away from the temptation. Getting Matthew to fix a date for Jamie's surgery took on even greater urgency.

'Have you found an anaesthetist yet?' I asked Matthew for the umpteenth time. 'I'll ask Dominic Armstrong,' Matthew said. 'I'm playing golf with him this afternoon.'

That meant he hadn't done anything so far. Typical Matthew.

'Can you tell Dr Armstrong it's urgent?' I said. 'Jamie's mother is convinced the bulge on his neck is getting bigger.'

Matthew grunted. 'Alright. If it'll get you off my back.'

I'd noticed a definite cooling in Matthew's attitude towards me. I put it down to my constant pestering, but maybe it was more than that. Had Veronica talked to him? Did he know I was about to abandon him?

None of that mattered when Matthew poked his head into my consulting room the following morning.

'Dominic agreed,' Matthew said. 'Everything's fixed for Jamie's surgery on Saturday week. The theatre staff are coming in on their day off, and Dominic and I are sacrificing a golf match. Happy now?'

I was. More than he'd ever understand.

The phone was ringing when I got home to the apartment. I raced inside and grabbed the receiver.

'Elisha! Brilliant timing!' I couldn't wait to tell her we'd fixed the date for Jamie's surgery. 'I've got some brilliant news—'

'Me first,' Elisha said. 'I want you here for my parents' memorial service. It would mean so much to me.'

'I'd love to come,' I said, and I meant it. 'I never met your mother. But your father—he was a man in a million.'

'He was. And the service will be in his old church.'

'I'll book a flight in the morning,' I said. 'When is the service?'

'Saturday week.'

I almost dropped the receiver. *Saturday week.* How could fate be so cruel? 'Elisha, I can't.'

The line went dead for a minute before Elisha replied. 'Why not?'

'That was going to be my news. We've finally got a date for Jamie's operation, and it's … Saturday week.'

'But I need you here to support me.' I could hear the despair in Elisha's voice.

'I want to be there for you,' I said. 'Believe me, I'd change the operation date if I could, but it's the only date we can manage. So many people are giving up their free time.'

'You're a GP, not a surgeon,' Elisha said. 'You don't need to be there.'

I gave my word to Mrs Beale, and to Jamie. How could I explain that to Elisha over the telephone? 'I know I don't *have* to be there, but I *want* to be there.'

I knew I had said the wrong thing before the words had left my mouth. There was a painful silence on the line before Elisha replied.

'At least now I know where your priorities lie,' she said. 'Zac's coming all the way from India, and you can't make it from New Zealand.'

'Don't say that,' I pleaded. 'You come first. Of course you do. It just— this surgery will transform a young man's life.'

'And it will transform his life just the same if you're not there,' Elisha hit back.

But would it? My instinct told me Matthew had lost interest in the case and regretted promising to do more surgery for free. Would he cancel the operation for good if I pulled out?

'It's not as simple as that,' I said. 'Are you sure you can't change the date of the memorial service? Just by a couple of days?'

'No. It's all arranged. The invitations have gone out. People over here have rearranged their lives to keep the day free. Zac's made sacrifices to get

 David Whittet

here. Pity you can't too.' The finality in Elisha's voice unnerved me. For an awful moment, I thought she was going to hang up. 'I told you, Theo. It's time to make up your mind where your loyalties lie.'

Don't make me choose. 'You're right. I'm sorry, Elisha. Of course I'll be there for the service.'

I could *feel* her relief. 'Thank you, Theo. You've no idea how much that means to me.'

Perhaps I hadn't. I thought about my priorities long after I put the phone down. Did I really appreciate the extent of the post-traumatic stress disorder Elisha was going through? Her mother's death from AIDS, Rajani's near-fatal illness, and the attack by the Hindu militants. I couldn't begin to imagine what it must have been like. Watching her father burn to death and narrowly escaping being burnt alive herself. After that, she'd gone through major surgery and been bitterly disappointed in the result. Elisha's body was scarred on the outside, but the mental anguish must have been a thousand times worse.

Mrs Beale had an appointment to see me in the morning. I'd planned to give her the good news about Jamie's operation. Instead, I'd be making excuses and breaking her heart. Unless I could catch Matthew first and convince him to go ahead with the surgery without me. I made sure I was at the medical centre early and ready to jump on him as soon as he arrived.

'Matthew,' I began. 'Something's cropped up. I can't make Saturday week.'

'What?' Matthew threw his arms in the air. 'This had better be good.'

'It's personal,' I said. 'I have to go to Australia for a memorial service for Elisha's parents.'

Matthew glared at me. 'Why the hell didn't you tell me before?'

'I only found out last night.'

'So, after twisting my colleagues' arms,' Matthew said, 'we have to cancel.'

'Surely you can still go ahead?' I said. 'You don't need me.'

Matthew grunted. 'Where else am I going to get an assistant willing to give up their Saturday without being paid?'

'Can't we reschedule the surgery?' I said. 'I'll only be away a few days.'

'You've no idea how many favours I've called in to make this happen. It's Saturday week, or Jamie goes on the public hospital waiting list.'

I felt a lump in my throat. 'Then he'll never get the operation.'

'So be it.' Matthew walked away. 'Saturday week or I'm out.'

How would I break this to Mrs Beale? I didn't have time to think. Moments after Matthew disappeared into his consulting room, she arrived in reception.

'What have you got to tell me, Doctor?' she asked. 'Is it good news at last?'

'We were all set to go for the surgery on Saturday week, but ...' My mouth dried up.

Mrs Beale's face fell. 'But what? Not another delay.'

'I'm sorry,' I said. 'It's my fault. I have to go to Australia for a few days.'

'Can't Dr Levi operate without you?' Mrs Beale asked. 'Or rearrange it for when you come back?'

'Dr Levi's cross with me for messing him around. He says he won't do the operation unless I'm there that Saturday.' I put my arm on her shoulder. 'I'm sorry, Mrs Beale. I'm afraid Jamie will have to go through the public hospital.'

'No.' Tears ran down her cheeks. 'We've been there before. None of the surgeons will take him on. There must be something you can do.'

I couldn't bring myself to look at her. 'Believe me, Mrs Beale, I wouldn't go if it wasn't important. You see, my fiancée lost her parents in tragic circumstances, and I have to go to support her at the memorial service.'

Mrs Beale wiped the tears off her face with her sleeve. 'I understand. Of course you must go.'

My eyes met hers. What was I to do? How could I bear the responsibility of ruining a young man's life?

Mrs Beale must have seen the turmoil in my face. 'Go,' she said. 'Family comes first. Go and support your fiancée.'

Another look at her eyes and I knew I could not. Elisha meant everything to me, but I'd made a promise that I couldn't break. 'No, I'm staying for Jamie's operation. My fiancée will understand.'

David Whittet

Would Elisha understand? Maybe—if only she'd met Jamie and seen how desperately he needed that surgery.

Listening to patients obsessing over minute imperfections in their bodies was more painful than ever. Especially while I wrestled with what I was going to say to Elisha. I'd tell her she was right about Matthew. The bastard wouldn't budge on the operation date. He *was* a jerk who didn't really care about anyone but himself and his image. On second thought, perhaps I should leave Matthew out of it.

I grabbed the phone as soon as I got back to the apartment and dialled Elisha's number.

'I love you, Elisha,' I began, 'with all my heart. I wouldn't hurt you for the world. But if you'd seen the look in that poor mother's eyes when I told her that her son's surgery would be cancelled, you'd understand. I know you would.'

There was an uncomfortable pause before Elisha replied. 'You must do what you believe is right, Theo,' she said. 'At least I'll have Zac and Jo to support me at the church.'

'You'll have me too,' I said. 'Because although I can't be at the service in person, I'll be with you in spirit.'

I meant every word I said. But I still felt guilty.

There was something I could do to make it up to Elisha. First thing the following morning, I called the Akaroa practice. With Jamie's surgery out of the way, I'd be free to start work there in a fortnight.

'What?' For the second time in the last two days, I almost dropped the telephone receiver. 'You've filled the position … with a young doctor from Canada?'

Perhaps it was for the best. The South Island was cold, and I didn't want Elisha catching pneumonia again. There were other GP vacancies. I took another look at the classifieds in the *New Zealand Medical Journal.* None of them had the same appeal as Akaroa. Veronica's proposal began to look more attractive. A warm home on Auckland's North Shore. That would be great for Elisha's health, and I had no wish to end up in an early grave like Veronica's former boyfriend.

By the end of the week, I had signed the contract.

Saturday week. When Matthew first confirmed the date, those two words filled me with hope. When the day came, I felt nothing but fear and foreboding. It didn't help that Matthew turned up at the operating suite looking less than his usual sartorial elegance. With his bow tie crooked and his shirt half undone, he looked decidedly hungover.

I watched him fumble with the buttons as we changed into our theatre scrubs.

'What were you up to last night?' I said.

'Charity dinner with the Rotary Club,' Matthew said. 'We should put you up for membership.'

I took a deep breath. 'Are you sure you're okay to operate?'

Matthew grunted. 'You're the one who's been haranguing me to operate on him.'

'I know, but …' I couldn't bring myself to say it. Damn Matthew. If we had to reschedule the surgery, I'd have missed the memorial service for nothing. Why wasn't I in Australia, standing at Elisha's side?

Matthew thumped me on the back. 'Don't worry, Theo. It's not as if—'

'—he's one of your rich fee-paying patients!' I'd completed the sentence for him before I could stop myself.

Matthew cut me down with his bloodshot eyes. 'How dare you!'

I stepped back. 'I'm sorry. I shouldn't have said that.'

'Damn right, you shouldn't.' Matthew moved across to the basin and scrubbed his hands so hard he almost drew blood. 'You've no idea what I've given up to be here today.'

A round of golf? Big deal.

He must have read my mind. 'I've covered the cost of hiring this theatre suite out of my own pocket. That didn't come cheap. And I've paid the theatre staff to come on a weekend.'

'There's always tomorrow,' I said.

A nurse came into the scrub room and helped Matthew into his gown. He snapped on his gloves and stormed into the theatre.

What could I do? I'd promised Mrs Beale I'd look after Jamie. Should

David Whittet

I voice my concerns to the anaesthetist? Not that it would do any good with Matthew's mate Dominic Armstrong anaesthetising. They were thick as thieves, and Dominic wouldn't hear a bad word about his golfing buddy.

'You're sweating, Dr Malone,' the scrub nurse said. 'Let me wipe your face before you gown up.'

I was still perspiring into my face mask when I followed Matthew through the swing doors into the operating theatre.

Jamie was already on the table with Matthew stood over him, his scalpel poised for action.

Matthew glanced at Dominic. 'Okay to start?'

Dominic nodded. 'He's all yours.'

I cleared my throat. 'Dr Armstrong.'

He peered at me over the anaesthetic machine. 'Yes, Dr Malone.'

It was no use. Matthew had made his first incision. 'Nothing.'

It was my hand that was shaking and not Matthew's as I pulled on the retractor. His movements were confident, and his fingers rock steady, teasing away the delicate tissues surrounding the blood vessels on Jamie's neck. Perhaps Matthew was the consummate professional who could perform surgery in whatever state he was in.

I held my breath when Matthew separated a giant tumour mass from the jugular vein. His eyes blazed at me like torches.

'Still think we should have postponed the surgery?' Matthew said.

'Of course not,' I replied.

Matthew turned to the theatre sister. 'Dr Malone didn't think I was up to the job.'

I squirmed—thankful the mask hid my red face.

Matthew stood back after removing the four largest tumours from Jamie's neck. 'I'd like to have a go at that lesion over the thyroid while we're in here.'

'That wasn't on the schedule, Dr Levi,' the theatre sister said. She glanced at Dr Armstrong. 'Is that going to be okay?'

'Blood pressure's stable,' Dr Armstrong replied. 'Not too much blood loss so far. You can proceed if you wish, Matthew.'

'We've been in surgery for three hours already,' I said. 'Jamie's body's taken a battering. Don't you think we should leave that until next time?'

Matthew glared at me. 'If I'd listened to you, Jamie would still have a neck like an elephant.'

'I know. You've done a great job.' I stumbled for the right words. 'But that one's going to be tricky. Wouldn't it be better to do it when we're all fresh?'

Matthew ignored me and continued dissecting the deep-seated tumour. Was he doing this to show off? Taking on an additional procedure just to prove to me he was in a fit state to do it?

'Cautery, Sister,' Matthew said. 'Quickly.'

The sister applied the diathermy instrument to the bleeding vessel. 'Careful, Doctor,' she said. 'You're very close to the—'

The operating room turned crimson as blood spurted from Jamie's carotid artery and coated the overhead light.

'Christ!' Matthew screamed. 'Artery forceps, Sister. Now!'

'Blood pressure's falling,' Dr Armstrong said. 'Forty over twenty. We're losing him.'

'Hold on to him,' Matthew cried out. 'I just need to clamp the vessel.'

'Ten over five,' Dr Armstrong said.

My body froze as the scene played out in front of me like a horror movie.

'Shit!' Matthew yelled as the forceps slipped in the sea of blood.

The alarm on Jamie's cardiac monitor rang out above the pandemonium of the operating theatre. Matthew made another attempt to clamp the artery. Blood squirted even faster.

I glanced up at the monitor screen. The tracing was flat. Jamie's heart had stopped beating.

'Fuck!' Matthew threw the forceps on the floor and tore off his blood-sodden mask.

'Matthew!' I shrieked. 'Don't give up on him … please …'

I gabbed some forceps and tried to stop the bleeding myself.

The theatre sister pulled me back. 'It's no use, Theo. Jamie's dead.'

My eyes fixed on Jamie's lifeless body. Blood still poured from his mutilated neck, collecting in a giant puddle on the floor. The theatre sister covered him with a drape and a scrub nurse began cleaning up the blood.

I stood in silence for a minute to pay my last respects to a young man whose one hope of a better future had just been so cruelly and needlessly taken from him. If I wasn't so angry, I would have wept. Matthew had disappeared into the scrub area along with Dr Armstrong. I took off my face mask and followed them.

Dr Armstrong had his hand on Matthew's shoulder. 'I'm sorry, Matt, but we must report this to the coroner. There'll be an investigation.'

I couldn't hold back any longer. 'You were showing off!' I spat the words in Matthew's face. 'Trying to prove to me you were fit to operate. You gambled with Jamie's life, and you lost. I'll tell the coroner you weren't fit to be in theatre.'

Matthew picked up a scalpel and pointed it at me. 'You breathe one word of this, and I'll see it finishes your career. I want you out of my rooms. Now!'

'I was going anyway,' I said. 'I don't want to have anything more to do with you.'

'Mrs Beale is outside,' the theatre sister said. 'She wants to know what's going on.'

'Would you like me to tell her?' Dr Armstrong said to Matthew. 'It might be better coming from me.'

'No,' I interrupted. 'I'll talk to her.'

'You will not,' Matthew retaliated. 'I'm not having you spreading lies about me. I will break the sad news to Mrs Beale.'

The thought of Matthew telling Mrs Beale how he'd done everything he could for Jamie made me want to puke. Would she ever forgive me for being part of the operation that killed her son?

I waited until Matthew had gone before going back to the changing room. Would he destroy my career? I'd made a powerful enemy. With a coroner's inquest, Elisha was bound to find out I'd been in partnership with Matthew all this time. Would she come back? Could she ever forgive me for lying to her and missing the memorial service?

CHAPTER THIRTY-ONE

Elisha

Elisha scanned the sea of faces meeting the passengers in the arrivals hall. Chauffeurs held up placards with their clients' names. Would Joanna still recognise her now the scars had contracted, and her skin had changed colour? These days, Elisha barely recognised herself on the rare occasions she dared to look in a mirror. She had spent the three-and-a-half-hour flight worrying that with her increasingly disfigured face, Joanna might not recognise her.

'Elisha!' Joanna appeared out of the crowd and flung her arms around Elisha. 'I didn't know what to expect after all those miserable letters you sent me. But—you look wonderful.'

Elisha snorted. 'Crap. I look like shit.'

'Nonsense. You look much better than you did in hospital.' Joanna took a step closer and studied Elisha's face. 'The scars have almost disappeared, and that slight puffiness in the cheeks makes you look distinguished.'

Is she blind? Can't she see everyone's staring at me like I'm a female Quasimodo?

Elisha gave Joanna a playful poke. 'You're still full of it, Jo. I'm hideous, and you know it.'

Joanna laughed. 'It's great to see you however you look. And you haven't changed either. Same old cheeky monkey.'

Elisha grinned. She couldn't remember the last time she'd done that. 'Come on, let's get out of here. I'm giving the kids nightmares.'

Did Joanna really believe she looked better than she had in hospital? Although she was far from convinced, Elisha found that surprisingly reassuring. And did Joanna really not care what Elisha looked like? Theo pretended the scars didn't matter to him, but Elisha was sure they did.

Elisha ran her fingers across the flaking paintwork of Joanna's van, an ageing Volkswagen Dormobile.

'Same old motor,' Elisha said. 'Are you sure it'll get us home?'

'Of course,' Joanna replied. 'Same way it takes the old folks to church every Sunday. Now, give me your case, and you hop in.'

Elisha settled into the passenger seat for the thirty-minute drive to Joanna's house. The familiar landscape, the old van, Joanna's Australian accent—it was all too much. Elisha had been away from home too long.

'So,' Joanna said. 'Have you and Theo fixed your wedding day? Remember, you promised me an invitation.'

Elisha shrugged. 'I'm not ready to tie the knot. Perhaps I never will be.'

Joanna almost stalled the engine. 'What? I thought you were—'

'We're still engaged,' Elisha said. 'But I'm not sure now. We don't seem to make each other happy any more.'

'I'm sorry to hear that,' Joanna said. 'You've been through so much together. That has to be worth something.'

'I guess so.' Elisha gazed out of the window at the beachfront condominiums. They hadn't changed since she was a little girl. 'Theo's gone into partnership with Matthew Levi. He thinks I don't know, but I do.'

'And that's a bad thing?' Joanna shook her head. 'I still don't see why you have such a downer on him.'

Elisha pointed to her face. 'Look what the bastard did to me!'

Joanna squinted across at her. 'I'd say he did a brilliant job.'

Elisha pulled a face. If Joanna hadn't been driving, she'd have got a thump. How quickly they'd resumed their old relationship. Much more so than they'd done at the hospital. But was it just on the surface? Did Joanna have any more answers now than she did back then? Or were they still two lost souls, both searching for direction?

Joanna's house hadn't changed either. The same immaculately kept living room, with its basic but comfortable furniture, and adorned with religious ornaments. A cross above the fireplace and an exquisite porcelain figurine of Jesus on the mantelpiece dominated the room. While Joanna busied herself in the kitchen making a pot of tea, Elisha sat on the edge of the settee, crossing and uncrossing her legs. She glanced at the pile of *Parish News* magazines on the table and the shelves overflowing with Christian books.

Joanna came in and poured the tea. 'Everything will feel better after a nice cup of tea.'

Elisha took a deep breath. 'I'm sorry I was so difficult when you came to the hospital. My head was all over the place after the surgery.'

'I was pretty messed up too,' Joanna said. 'And believe me, you weren't difficult.'

'Everything was so raw back then,' Elisha said. 'But now—'

'You want to sort things out,' Joanna said, passing Elisha a cup of tea. 'Well, I'm here to listen whenever you're ready.'

Elisha sighed. *Where do I start?* 'I'm not sure I'll ever be ready. But here goes. You told me God was going to open new doors for me in India. Well, all He's done is slam them in my face.'

'I tried to explain this when you were in the hospital, but I know it didn't come out right.' Joanna put down her teacup and reached for Elisha's hand. 'I really thought India would be a fantastic opportunity for you. Help you to find yourself. Now—I wish I'd taken more notice of what you said.'

Elisha noticed a tear in the corner of Joanna's eye. 'I told you I didn't blame you, remember? It was those thugs.'

Joanna hung her head. 'You begged me to persuade your father you should stay behind. I wish to God I had. I would have done if I had any idea what you'd have to go through.'

'You weren't to know,' Elisha said. 'I was just a grumpy teenager, trying to get out of something I didn't want.'

Joanna took a handkerchief out of her pocket and dried her eyes. 'Anyway, this isn't about me. It's about you and putting your life back together.'

Elisha shrugged. 'My life's beyond repair, and don't you dare tell me this disaster is all part of God's plan.'

Joanna fiddled with the crucifix around her neck. 'Of course not,' she said. 'You know me better than that.'

   David Whittet

Did she? Joanna always played with her crucifix when she was unsure of herself. Perhaps Joanna *did* believe this tragedy was part of some divine strategy.

'It's all such a bloody mess,' Elisha said. 'I wish to God I'd died in the fire with my father. I wanted to die in his arms. Then we'd have all been together, Mum, Dad and I.'

Joanna raised her hands. 'I understand how you feel, but let's not go through that again. You're here now. For Zac and Rajani. And Theo.'

'I'm precious little good to Zac and Rajani, being stuck in New Zealand.'

'What about Theo? He'd have been heartbroken.'

Would he? Elisha thought for a moment before she replied. 'He'd have been sad for a while. But he'd have recovered and moved on.'

Joanna threw her arms in the air. 'You were about to be married! It would have destroyed him.'

'I know,' Elisha said. 'He would have been devastated. But he'd have thrown himself back into his work. Kept on changing the world for the better. Instead, he's left having to look after me.'

'I'm sure that's what he wants,' Joanna said. 'He loves you. I could see that.'

Elisha squared her shoulders. 'Perhaps love isn't enough. The burns have changed everything. I've lost count of all the plastic surgeons we've been to since Levi buggered up my operation. Their fees have bankrupted us. Theo's had to go into private practice as an appearance medicine specialist to earn enough money for us to survive.'

Joanna shook her head. 'Matthew Levi didn't bugger up your surgery. He did a brilliant job. Okay, the scars have contracted a bit, and yes, your skin's changed colour. But—you look great.'

Elisha's body stiffened as her mind wrestled with something she scarcely dared admit to herself. Did she dare admit it to Joanna?

'Jo,' Elisha said, taking in a deep breath, 'you remember when Levi did his ward round at the hospital? How he told me to keep those contaminated bandages away from my face?'

Joanna nodded.

Elisha took another sharp breath and continued, 'Well, when we were in Northland, I didn't want people to see my face … so I found this old shawl …'

Had Joanna worked out the secret that had tortured Elisha for the past few months? Elisha had convinced herself that by contaminating her grafts with a dirty shawl, she had caused the deterioration in her skin herself.

'And you wanted to cover up,' Joanna said. 'That's only natural.'

'I guess so,' Elisha said, unsure if she was relieved or disappointed that Joanna hadn't cottoned on.

Joanna glanced at the clock on the wall and began stacking the teacups on the tray. 'We should get cleared up. I said we'd go to the church. I want you to meet Luke McLoughlin. He's the minister who took over when your father left for India.'

'Today?'

'Luke wants to go over the order of service with you,' Joanna said. 'Everything's organised for the memorial on Saturday week.'

Elisha raised her eyes to Joanna's. 'So soon? I was hoping for more time.'

'Don't worry,' Joanna said. 'Luke's lovely. He'll help you—we'll both help you. Now, help me get cleared up. And I've got some exciting news for you.'

Elisha didn't feel up for any more surprises, exciting or otherwise.

'Don't be cross with me,' Elisha said as they washed the dishes, 'but the more I think about it, the more certain I am that Theo would be better off without me. I want to go back to India and finish my father's work.'

There—she'd said it. Elisha glanced at Joanna tentatively to gauge her response. Sure enough, Joanna frowned the way she always did when she was unhappy with Elisha.

'You *must* sort things out with Theo first,' Joanna said. 'You'll regret it if you don't.'

Elisha turned her head away. 'Maybe I will.'

'You can't keep running away—'

'I'm not!' Elisha turned back to face Joanna. 'I never wanted to leave India. It was Theo who insisted we go to New Zealand.'

'Would he go back to Madhapur with you?'

'I doubt it,' Elisha said. 'He's too wrapped up in his new career.'

Joanna put down the tea towel and wrapped her arms around Elisha. 'I've said it before. Theo's a good man. He's stuck by you and done his best for you.'

'I suppose so.' Elisha rested her head against Joanna's chest. 'It's just—I haven't had a chance to grieve for my father. I keep thinking about what he said just before the mob attacked. He asked me to carry on his work at the mission.'

Joanna stroked Elisha's hair. 'Your dad would understand.'

'Would he? I promised and I've failed him.' Elisha peered up at Joanna. 'This sounds ridiculous, but I keep thinking if we do go to Heaven when we die, I'll have to face my father when I get there. He'll be mad at me for letting him down.'

'He won't. Because you're going to make him proud of you.' Joanna hugged Elisha again. 'The memorial service will be healing. I promise it will.'

'As long as I don't freak out,' Elisha said. 'Anyway, what was the big surprise you were going to tell me about?'

Joanna grinned with a spark in her eye. 'Zac's coming for the service!'

Elisha's heart missed a beat. Had she heard that right? 'What? Zac's coming all the way from India?'

Joanna nodded. 'Sure thing.'

'That's brilliant.' Elisha wanted to pick Joanna up and twirl her around, but afraid that it might bring on a coughing fit, she settled for a kiss on the cheek. 'I've been longing to see Zac again.'

Joanna beamed. 'You won't have to wait much longer. He'll be here in a couple of days.' She paused and eyed Elisha. 'Why don't you ask Theo to come for the service?'

Elisha stifled a cough. 'Do you think I should?'

'Yes, I do,' Joanna said. 'It's a chance to rekindle your relationship away from all your worries.'

'I'll call him now.' Elisha jumped to her feet. 'Can I use your phone?'

'Of course. It's in the hall.'

Elisha turned back to Joanna before she left the room. 'Thank you, Jo. I knew I could count on you to sort me out.'

Why did everything have to be so bloody complicated? Elisha had another bout of coughing when she put down the phone.

'Are you alright?' Joanna called from the living room.

'I'm fine.'

Joanna came out into the hall. 'You don't sound it.'

Elisha didn't feel it either. Nor did she want to explain the disconcerting phone call she'd just had with Theo.

'So, is Theo coming for the service?' Joanna asked.

Elisha sighed. 'Yes. But I had to put the hard word on him.'

'Why? Didn't he want to come?'

'He was meant to be assisting Matthew Levi with an operation,' Elisha said. 'But I told him Levi would have to find someone else.'

'Good for you,' Joanna said. 'I'm glad Theo's going to be here. Now, do you feel up to going to the church and meeting the new pastor?'

'I'm sorry, Jo. I'm tired. Could we do it tomorrow?'

'Of course we can,' Joanna said. 'You've been coughing rather a lot. Are you sure you're okay? Would you like me to call the doctor?'

'No. I just need some rest.' Elisha rubbed her eyes and picked up her suitcase. 'If you don't mind, I'll go to bed. I'll be fine in the morning.'

Elisha lay awake all night, thinking about Theo. She knew he cared about the patient with neurofibromatosis—what was his name? Yes, Jamie. But she needed Theo more than Jamie did. Levi could easily find a replacement for Theo, and someone much better qualified for the job. But for her, nobody could replace Theo.

Elisha struggled to suppress her cough throughout the night. She didn't want Joanna fussing.

The Reverend Luke McLoughlin laid his hands on Elisha's head when she arrived at the church with Joanna. His soft touch proved unexpectedly comforting.

'Merciful Lord,' Reverend McLoughlin said, 'Elisha has suffered, bring peace to her troubled soul.'

Elisha found that simple blessing surprisingly calming.

'We all have treasured memories of your father,' Reverend McLoughlin continued. 'I know many of the parishioners will be sharing their stories.'

'I'd like to say a few words,' Joanna said, 'about how Elisha's father helped me when I was at rock bottom.'

'You're one of many lives our beloved Wesley turned around,' Reverend McLoughlin said. 'But we mustn't forget there were some lighter moments too.' He turned to Elisha and grinned. 'I was at college with your father.'

Elisha almost toppled over when the minister bent down and whispered in her ear. Had she heard him right? Her father would *never* have got himself locked in the girls' dorm at a vicars' retreat.

'You don't mind if I tell that story, do you?' Reverend McLoughlin asked. 'You don't think it's too disrespectful?'

Don't mind? Too disrespectful? Elisha hooted. 'If only I'd known. My dad would never have heard the end of it.' She looked up at the minister's all-knowing eyes. *He understands.* 'A bit of humour will make the service more bearable.'

'I hope so.' Reverend McLoughlin paused. 'Joanna told me your father joined forces with Krishna to lay the foundations for a well in Madhapur. I'm going to conclude my address explaining your father died trying to heal the rift between Christians and Hindus.'

Elisha dabbed her eyes. She noticed Joanna had tears in her eyes, too.

'That's how I'd like my father to be remembered,' Elisha said. 'Thank you, Reverend McLoughlin.'

'Call me Luke,' he said. 'Now, go and think about what you're going to say at the service.'

Elisha felt more alive as she walked back with Joanna, glad she'd come for the memorial. She'd cope with the service with Theo at her side. He was good at writing speeches, and he'd help her compose her eulogy.

Everything was coming together—until the phone call from Theo that evening.

'What is it?' Joanna asked.

Elisha wiped away a tear. 'Theo's not coming.'

Joanna almost dropped the plates she was carrying. 'Why?'

Elisha shrugged. *Perhaps he doesn't think I'm worth it. No, that's not true.*

Elisha pulled herself up in the chair. 'He says Levi can't find anyone else to assist with the operation.'

Joanna continued setting the table for dinner. 'That's so disappointing. Can't they reschedule? Or find someone else?'

Elisha rolled her eyes. 'Apparently not. He claims it must be him.'

Joanna sat down next to Elisha. 'It must be important …'

'Don't make excuses for him. The whole thing sucks. I bet Matthew Levi's behind it. He's got Theo under his thumb.'

'Surely not.' Joanna ladled some homemade mulligatawny soup into a bowl and handed it to Elisha. 'I made it extra spicy for you. I remembered what you said about the burns in your mouth ruining your sense of taste.'

'Just like Rajani and the lepers.' Elisha slurped the soup. 'Thanks.'

Elisha could taste the soup. The exotic flavour made her miss India even more.

After she'd eaten as much as she could, Elisha leant back and wiped her mouth with a serviette. 'I had hoped Theo and Zac might patch up their differences when they met.'

'Maybe it's for the best,' Joanna said. 'We wouldn't want them clashing at the service.'

Elisha frowned. 'Suppose not.'

'I'll have a word with Zac when he arrives,' Joanna said. 'See if I can persuade him to call Theo. At least get them talking to each other.'

A blazing horn awoke Elisha the following morning. She jumped out of bed and rushed to her bedroom window to see a taxi pull up.

'Jo!' she shouted. 'It's Zac! He's here!'

Still in her pyjamas, Elisha grabbed Joanna, who was making breakfast, and they both ran out into the street.

'Zac!' Elisha flung her arms around her brother. 'I've missed you so much.'

'Sis!' Zac gave her his usual roguish grin. 'You look great!'

'Bullshit!' Elisha dug him in the ribs. 'I look horrible.'

'No way!' Zac shot back. 'Tell her, Jo!'

David Whittet

Joanna laughed. 'Don't take any notice of her. She gave me a rollicking, too, for saying she looked good.'

'You're a pair of charmers.' Elisha felt overwhelmed when anyone mentioned her appearance. Theo was always trying to build up her self-esteem. Zac and Joanna were just doing the same. 'But thanks.'

'You're welcome, sis,' Zac said. 'I meant it. Look at you—radiant as ever. The jammies are cool too!'

That got Zac another poke. But Elisha knew he meant it, and that mattered. She'd almost backed out of returning to Australia, worrying about meeting her old friends and what they would think of her face. She embraced him again. 'I love you, Zac!'

Joanna hugged them both. 'It's so good to see the two of you together again. Now, come inside. You're just in time for breakfast, Zac. I'm cooking some bacon and eggs.'

'Actually, Jo,' Zac said. 'Since I met Rajani, I've gone vegetarian.'

'I'll see what I can rustle up for you,' Joanna said. 'I've got some homemade muesli. I'm longing to hear about Rajani. If only she could have come with you.'

'You and me both,' Elisha said. 'I miss Rajani so much.'

'We tried,' Zac said. 'But Indian red tape—it's like hitting your head against a brick wall.'

Theo could have done it if only we hadn't left India. Elisha sighed as they all sat down at the breakfast table. *Theo took on the Indian authorities and didn't let go until he got what he wanted.*

'Don't look so sad,' Zac said. 'Rajani will be here in spirit.'

Elisha caught her breath. 'Theo will be with us in spirit as well.'

'You mean Theo's not coming?' Zac said. 'I thought he'd be here supporting you.'

Elisha lowered her head. 'He wanted to, but he can't. He's assisting with an operation in New Zealand.'

Zac rolled his eyes. 'I didn't know he was a surgeon.'

'He's not,' Elisha said. 'He's doing this as a goodwill gesture for a man with neurofibromatosis.'

'I might have known he'd find some excuse,' Zac said.

'Zac!' Elisha pointed a finger at him. 'That was unfair.'

She'd felt the same about Theo last night. Overnight, she'd had time to think about his dilemma. Besides, she didn't like anyone else criticising Theo. Not even her brother.

'What is it between you and Theo?' Joanna asked.

'Theo changed after the attack,' Zac said.

Joanna shrugged. 'That's hardly surprising.'

'He went all weird on me at Dad's funeral,' Zac said. 'Accused me of being a ghoul because I took some video of the ceremony.' He turned to Elisha. 'I did it for you, sis. You couldn't be there because you were stuck in the hospital.'

Elisha hesitated. 'I would like to watch it. One day. When I'm brave enough.'

'Then,' Zac continued, 'after making all those promises about what he would do for the community, Theo buggers off home to New Zealand. And he took you with him.'

'That's not fair either!' Elisha had lost her appetite and pushed her plate away. 'We went to New Zealand for my sake. They didn't have enough white skin in Calcutta for my grafts.'

'Sorry, sis, I didn't mean that.' Zac extended a hand towards her. 'I just hoped he would bring you back to India after the surgery.'

Elisha had hoped that, too. She still hoped he would one day. Right now, she didn't want to argue with Zac, especially after they'd been apart for so long. There was one sure way to turn the conversation around.

'Remember, Theo saved Rajani's life.' Elisha looked Zac straight in the eyes. 'Rajani—the love of your life.'

'I know, I know,' Zac spluttered. 'I'll always owe him for what he did for Rajani.'

'We're all thankful for that,' Joanna said. 'How is Rajani? I want to hear all the news from Madhapur.'

Zac took a moment to compose himself. 'Rajani's great. We're busy fundraising for the well.'

Elisha shot Zac a playful grin. 'How come you're not married yet?'

Zac smiled back. 'Waiting for you to come back for the wedding, sis.'

 David Whittet

'What else is going on in Madhapur?' Joanna asked.

'Akbar Zahin and the rest of the Hindu militants have been sent to prison.' Zac arched across the table and placed his hand on Elisha's. 'Salim, the boy who pulled you out of the wreckage, testified against them.'

'I'd like to meet Salim,' Elisha said.

'Come back to Madhapur with me, and you will,' Zac said. 'Salim's working for the mission.'

Joanna cleared away the breakfast dishes. 'You must meet our minister, Zac,' she said. 'We'll go to the church once we've done the washing up.'

'Luke McLoughlin's lovely,' Elisha said, picking up a tea towel. 'He even had some funny stories about Dad's antics when he was a young man.'

Elisha still couldn't picture her father locked in a dorm with a bunch of girls.

Before she met Luke McLoughlin, Elisha hadn't decided what she would say at the service. Everything was still too raw, and Elisha couldn't remember how many times she'd torn up her draft eulogy. She knew what the parishioners would want to hear, but somehow that just didn't feel right. Did Elisha dare voice the darker thoughts going through her mind? Luke McLoughlin persuaded her to speak from the heart and not care about what other people thought.

'That's the only way you'll get closure,' he'd told her.

Luke reminded her of this when he greeted her at the church on the morning of the service.

'Be brave, Elisha,' he said, grasping her hands. 'Straight from the heart and you'll find peace.'

Flanked by Joanna and Zac, Elisha stumbled down the aisle, and they took their places on the front pew. The church looked more beautiful than ever. Elisha glanced around the once-familiar setting. The morning sun shone through the stained-glass windows and cast a warm glow over the congregation. She smiled at some of the churchgoers she recognised. But did they recognise her? Would people know who she was when she got up to speak? Her appearance had changed beyond recognition since the last time she attended a service at the church.

Tears welled up in Elisha's eyes when Luke began describing her father's tireless work for the Church in Australia and the community in Madhapur. They trickled down her cheeks when he talked about Melissa's selfless commitment to caring for the lepers and nursing at the hospital. She wiped her face and managed a smile when Luke described her father's student antics and how her mother endlessly teased him about them. When he got to the bit about God calling them both home to Heaven, Elisha thought she was going to collapse.

She held on to Zac's arm when Joanna got up to speak.

'Wesley was there for me in my darkest hour,' Joanna began. 'I'd just lost my beloved sister, Angie, in a tragic accident, which was my fault. Everyone else shut me out, but Wesley helped me find forgiveness from the Lord and rekindle my faith.'

Elisha closed her eyes. Joanna's story was as painful today as it had been the first time she heard it.

Zac's tribute was even more distressing. Elisha cringed as he fought back the tears and stumbled with his words. She'd been too engrossed in her own misery to appreciate how much he was suffering.

'I would have died with the rest of my family if it wasn't for Wes.' Zac dried his eyes. 'He gave me a new life here in Australia. Raised me with love and gave me hope.'

Elisha couldn't bear to listen and buried her head in her hands.

A gentle nudge from Joanna brought her back to earth. 'It's your turn, Elisha. Be strong.'

I can't do this—I must do this. Elisha had found inner strength at the service on the day her mother had died, and she had to do it again today.

Zac helped her up, and Joanna led her to the pulpit.

Elisha wanted to scream about the injustice of everything. Instead, she cleared her throat and took a long, hard breath. 'When my father told me we were going to India, I was furious. I begged my parents to let me stay behind with Jo. I even thought of running away. But Jo persuaded me to rise to the challenge, and to look after Rajani for her. Meeting Rajani is the best thing that came out of my time at Madhapur. We worked together at the Sunday school until my mother died …' Elisha caught Zac's eyes and broke off. 'Our dear mother. I blamed my dad for letting her work at that hospital. I left India and came back to Jo. It broke my father's heart—I know that now. But I eventually returned to India, and later, just before the mob attacked, I made my peace with my father. Thank God I had the chance before he was taken. I promised Dad I would carry on his work at the mission. One day, I'll go back to India again, and I will.'

Elisha felt her throat closing up. Joanna stood, put her arms around Elisha and helped her back to her seat.

When the time came for Zac to return to India, a fresh wave of emotion swept through Elisha.

Zac continued to pester her as they fought their way through the terminal at Brisbane International Airport. 'Sure you won't change your mind and come back with me?'

Elisha had almost given in to the relentless pressure. She'd got used to having Zac around again and listening to him talking about Rajani made her miss her dear friend even more. 'Not yet,' she sighed. 'Everything's still too raw.'

Joanna took Zac's arm. 'I wish I could go with you and see Rajani.'

Something caught Elisha's eye as they passed the newsagent. 'Wait a minute, that's Matthew Levi.' She picked up the newspaper from the stand and took a closer look. Yes, it *was* Levi's photo on the front page. Her heart stood still as she read about a bungled operation resulting in the death of a young man with neurofibromatosis.

'What is it?' Joanna said.

'That's the operation Theo stayed to assist,' Elisha said. 'I'm sure it is.'

Elisha bought the paper, and they read it while queuing for check-in.

'Looks like Theo's got himself in a heap of trouble,' Zac said. 'Why don't you cut him loose and come back to Madhapur?'

Why couldn't he just shut up and read the article? Had Zac forgotten that just a few days earlier, he'd admitted he was indebted to Theo for saving Rajani's life?

'Levi's the one who's in trouble.' Elisha pointed to the small print. 'Look. They're not blaming Theo.'

'I bet he's in it up to his neck,' Zac said.

'Stop it, Zac. Theo really cared about that boy. Just like he did for Rajani. He'll be hurting.' Elisha paused as they reached the front of the queue. 'Zac, please. Let's not part like this. Who knows when I'll see you again?'

'Sorry, sis. It's just …' Zac broke off and put his arms around Elisha. 'I'm going to miss you so much.'

Elisha and Joanna watched Zac disappear into passport control.

Elisha shook her head. 'Am I doing the right thing? Should I be going with him?'

'You need to sort things out with Theo first,' Joanna said. 'You'll regret it if you don't. Besides, you're young. You've got your entire life ahead of you. Plenty of time to go back to India and finish your father's work.'

'That's just it, I haven't.' Elisha grabbed Joanna's hand. 'Theo doesn't know about this, but I went to see a respiratory physician in Auckland. I'd been so short of breath after that bout of pneumonia. Turns out the smoke has irreparably damaged my lungs. I may not have much longer.'

Joanna clutched the security barrier.

Elisha stared at her ashen face. 'Are you alright, Jo?'

'Yes. I'm sorry. That was a shock.' Joanna pulled herself up straight and faced Elisha. 'If time's short'—she blinked back a tear—'it's even more important that you set things right with Theo. Perhaps he'll go back to India with you. After all, he cares as much about the Madhapur community as you do, doesn't he?'

Does he? Elisha wondered if Theo ever gave Madhapur a second thought. And if he did, it was doubtless bitter. She tried to call Theo repeatedly over the next couple of days, but she couldn't get through. Was he okay after the trauma of the operation? Would he keep his promise about leaving appearance medicine? Or was that just a ploy to keep her happy? One question towered above the rest. Would Theo ever be the champion of the underprivileged again? Or had money and power irrevocably changed him?

David Whittet

CHAPTER THIRTY-TWO

Marina Medical Rooms, Auckland Harbour Basin, New Zealand

Theo

Before she left for Australia, I promised Elisha a new life. We'd move to Akaroa, and I'd go back into general practice. She'd smiled for the first time in ages when I said she could work as a practice nurse again. Elisha was due home at the end of the week, and here I was, treating some of the most beautiful girls on the planet in a stylish new office on Auckland's waterfront.

I had to admit that the work proved much more enjoyable—and professionally satisfying—than I expected. Of course, there were the inevitable rejuvenation treatments. Girls with perfect skin wanting to look even more immaculate. Who could blame them in such a competitive world?

Then there was Monique.

'Veronica's giving me the chance to work in the US,' Monique said. 'She's hoping to persuade *Vogue* to come to New Zealand.'

Glossy magazines weren't my thing, but I'd heard of *Vogue*. I might even have seen a well-thumbed copy in a waiting room. 'Isn't it here already?'

'We get the Australian edition,' Monique explained. 'We had our own once. Veronica wants to get it back.'

'Perhaps you'll be on the front cover,' I said.

'Maybe.' Monique pointed to a blemish on her neck. 'Veronica wants me to get rid of this before I leave for America.'

I got out my dermatoscope and took a closer look. 'When did you first notice it?'

'About a month ago,' Monique said. 'It came out of nowhere.'

'Has it got any bigger?'

Monique shook her head. 'God no. It's humungous enough as it is.'

I focused the dermatoscope on the dark spot on her neck. 'Any colour change?'

'I don't think so.' Monique's muscles stiffened. She must have seen the apprehension in my eyes. 'It's not serious, is it?'

I put down the dermatoscope and eyed her directly. 'I'll have to take a biopsy to be sure, but … don't be alarmed, but I'm almost certain it's a melanoma.'

Monique pulled back, the mascara running on her face. 'A melanoma?' She put her hand over the spot on her neck. 'Am I going to die?'

'Everything's going to be fine,' I said. 'By sending you in early, Veronica may very well have saved your life.'

'Veronica has just saved my life?'

'She has. If we excise the melanoma now, before it spreads, you'll be cured.' I glanced at the appointment book on my desk. 'I'll book you in for this afternoon.'

I was right. The biopsy confirmed a superficial melanoma, and a scan two days later showed it hadn't spread. Appearance medicine *did* save lives. I could hold my head up when I collected Elisha at the airport.

I was about to head off for the airport when Monique came in to see my nurse for a change of dressing. I popped into the treatment room to take a look at the wound.

'It's healing beautifully,' I said. 'We can take the sutures out on Monday.'

'The lab report's back, Doctor,' the nurse said, pointing to the desk.

I clutched my car keys. What if I hadn't removed the entire lesion and there were melanoma cells left behind? I took a deep breath and picked up the report.

Eureka! I wanted to shout the word out loud.

'The margins are clear,' I said, rapidly composing myself.

'Does that mean I'm cured?' Monique said.

'Obviously, we'll need to keep an eye on you,' I said. 'But yes, you're cured!'

Monique blinked back a tear. 'If I hadn't been going to America … and I hadn't come to see you when I did … It doesn't bear thinking about.'

'I told you, Veronica saved your life,' I said. '*Vogue*, too, if that's why she's sending you to America.'

Monique dabbed her eyes. She wasn't wearing any mascara today. 'God bless America! God bless Veronica, too!' Monique reached out a hand towards me. 'And God bless you, Doc!'

The buzz began to evaporate on the drive to the airport. How would I break it to Elisha that we weren't going to Akaroa? She'd be devastated. Would she believe that I was equally disappointed to miss out on the position? Stuck in the Auckland traffic, I was sure of one thing: Elisha wouldn't be the least bit impressed that Veronica's advance had set me up and allowed me to put a deposit on an upmarket apartment on the North Shore.

The inquest into Jamie's death weighed on my mind, too. I'd have to come clean with Elisha and admit that she'd been right about Matthew Levi all along. Plus, would she forgive me for missing the memorial service?

The moment I caught sight of Elisha's face amongst the throng of arriving passengers, I knew something was wrong. I'd expected her to be drained after the service, but she was short of breath and struggled with her suitcase. My heart stood still when she got closer. Her scars always looked worse when she was overwrought, but I was certain they'd contracted some more.

Then I saw it. The newspaper in her hand. She knew.

I ran towards her. What should I say? How could I make her understand?

Elisha got in first. 'Why didn't you tell me?'

'Darling, I'm so sorry …'

Elisha batted me away with the newspaper when I reached out to put my arms around her.

'I tried to call you,' she said. 'I was worried about you. I know how much you cared about that kid Jamie. But you never answered.'

'I wasn't home much. Everything went crazy after Jamie died. I had to get out of Matthew Levi's rooms fast …' I bit my lip. I'd just admitted I'd been working with Matthew.

Elisha cut me down with eyes that would burn through any of my excuses. 'Do you think I'm stupid? I've known all along you've been working with Levi.'

I couldn't look at her. Not straight away. 'Why didn't you say something?'

'I was waiting for you to fess up.' Elisha paused as another passenger pushed past her. 'And I couldn't face another argument.'

'Here, let me take your suitcase.' Standing in the middle of the crowded arrivals hall, we were holding everyone up. 'I'm sorry. I should have been honest with you. It's just … I was afraid you might leave me if I told you the truth.'

'Lying was bound to drive me away,' Elisha said. 'Surely you could see that?'

I grabbed her suitcase and we walked to the car. 'We were broke when we left Northland. I just wanted to get us out of the rut.'

'Well, it looks like you've got yourself into a heap of trouble.' Elisha pointed to Matthew's photo in the newspaper. 'Why couldn't you get a decent surgeon to operate on that boy?'

'Nobody else was prepared to take on Jamie.' I unlocked the car and helped Elisha into the passenger seat. 'The poor kid was desperate. You'd understand if you'd seen the massive lumps on his face.' I turned away and put Elisha's case in the boot. My eyes were wet, and I didn't want her to see it. 'Believe me, I never thought it would turn out like this.'

Elisha pulled a face. 'I warned you. Look what he did to me.'

I put the key in the ignition and started the engine. 'You were right about Mathew being an arsehole. But he could be a brilliant surgeon …' I dared not finish the sentence. *If only he hadn't been hungover that morning.* I almost stalled the engine. 'None of this needed to happen.'

Elisha's expression softened as we left the airport and headed home. 'I admired you when you took risks to help others. Don't let Levi's cock-up stop you from doing the right thing.' She glanced across at me. 'We can put all this behind us and make a fresh start in Akaroa.'

I pulled up abruptly at some traffic lights. 'I'm sorry, Elisha. The position in Akaroa … it's been taken …'

I felt my heart shrink as Elisha broke eye contact.

'So, what are we going to do?' she said.

I hesitated, knowing what I was about to say would make her feel a thousand times worse. 'I'm afraid I've got to stick with appearance medicine for a bit longer.'

 David Whittet

Elisha glared at me. 'Please tell me you're not still working with Levi.'

'No. I'm finished with Matthew.'

'Promise?'

'Cross my heart. I've rented rooms at the harbour.'

'Can you afford them?'

'I've got a sponsor. Don't worry, it's all above board.' We arrived home before Elisha could ask too many more questions. I didn't dare think what she would make of Veronica Ashton-Forbes.

Elisha hardly ate any of the sag aloo that I'd specially cooked for her homecoming.

She pushed her plate away. 'Theo, if we're not going to Akaroa, why don't we go back to India? I promised my father I would carry on his work, and you need to get back to some real work. Appearance medicine isn't you.'

I swallowed my last mouthful of curry. 'It's not all facelifts and massaging egos. I took a melanoma off a girl's neck this week and saved her life.'

Elisha shrugged. 'You could save more lives in Madhapur.'

'I can't leave yet,' I said. 'I have to stay for the inquest into Jamie's death, and that could be months away.'

Elisha frowned. 'We can still go to India. You can come back to New Zealand for the inquest.'

'No.' I cleared the table and took the dishes through to the kitchen. 'I need to be here to prepare for the hearing with my lawyer.'

There was another reason. I didn't *want* to go back to India. Not after what those bastards did to Elisha. The image of that roadside carnage still smouldered in my mind and woke me in a cold sweat each night.

Elisha followed me through to the kitchen. 'You need a lawyer?' She eyed me suspiciously. 'Please tell me you're not in trouble. They haven't taken your passport away, have they?'

I took a step back. 'Of course not. I just want to see Matthew Levi nailed for what he did to Jamie.'

'Good. No more secrets.'

Secrets. I'd been about to break the news about the North Shore apartment. This probably wasn't the right time to tell her, but I took a deep breath and went ahead.

'Actually, darling, I have a surprise for you.'

'What?'

'Now I'm earning decent money, it's time we got out of this grotty little flat.' I rolled up my sleeves and started washing the dishes. 'I've seen this apartment. It's got a fantastic view across to the harbour. And it's got a dishwasher.'

'That would have impressed me once.' Elisha picked up a tea towel and started drying the dishes. 'Not now.'

'At least come and see it,' I said. 'I'll pick you up after work tomorrow.'

Elisha looked at me dubiously. 'What if I don't like it?'

I mentally crossed my fingers. 'You will.'

My last patient of the day had a shopping list of problems. All I wanted was to get away and show Elisha the apartment, convinced she'd fall in love with the place once she saw it.

I heard Elisha's voice in reception. That wasn't what we'd arranged.

'Excuse me.' I ushered my patient out of the waiting room and gestured to my receptionist. 'Madeleine, make Serena a follow-up appointment for Monday.' I turned to Elisha. 'Darling! I was about to come and collect you.'

'I thought I'd get in first,' Elisha said. 'See what you were up to.'

Why did that make me nervous? 'Great,' I said. 'Come and see my new office.'

Elisha looked around my consulting room and brushed a hand against the plush leather chairs. 'It looks like you've got all the facilities you could ever want,' she said.

'Pretty much,' I said.

Elisha muttered precisely what I was thinking. 'All the equipment we couldn't even dream of in India.'

Veronica put her head around the door. 'Theo, I was just passing and thought we could catch up on ...' She stopped when she saw Elisha. 'I'm sorry, I didn't realise you still had a patient.'

Elisha glared at her. 'I may look like a patient, but I'm not.'

    David Whittet

'This is my fiancée, Elisha,' I said.

Veronica took a step back. 'I do apologise.' She extended a hand to Elisha. 'I'm so pleased to meet you.'

It was the first time I'd seen Veronica unsure of herself.

'We're just off to see the apartment,' I said, shuffling from one foot to the other.

Veronica beamed at Elisha. 'You're going to love it. Don't forget, I want an invitation to the housewarming party.'

I caught Elisha's eye and began to fidget with the apartment keys I'd got from the real estate agent. 'If you'll excuse us, Veronica, we'd better get going.'

'Of course. Don't let me hold you up.' Veronica made for the door, then turned back. 'Don't forget lunch at the Connoisseurs Club on Friday, Theo. Lovely to meet you, Elisha.'

Caught in the gridlock of Auckland's rush hour traffic, the drive to the apartment was as long as it was uncomfortable.

After a deathly silence, Elisha shot me a sideways glance. 'The Connoisseurs Club. I didn't realise you'd turned into a playboy while I was away.'

'I haven't.' How could she even think that? 'The club's just business. I have to meet Veronica's clients. It's not where I'd choose to spend my time.'

'I bet Levi's a member,' Elisha muttered.

I pulled the car into a bay outside the apartment block. 'Please, for half an hour, can we put everything behind us and concentrate on the apartment? I think you'll be amazed.'

Elisha nodded. 'Guess so.'

The view of the harbour from the panoramic window was spectacular.

'Just look at that,' I said. The crimson sky, the shimmering rays of the setting sun glistening on the water—surely that had to impress Elisha. I pointed to the mass of yachts. 'Perhaps we should get a boat and take up sailing.'

Elisha shrugged. She didn't give anything away as she inspected each room, opening every single cupboard and drawer.

'Well?' I asked.

Elisha paused for a moment before replying. 'It's perfect.'

So why wasn't she smiling?

We stopped to pick up an Indian takeaway on the way back to the flat. Sat on the edge of her chair and fiddling with her fork, she didn't eat much more of it than she had of my sag aloo the previous night. The tormented look in her eyes told me she had something to say that I didn't want to hear.

'I didn't mean to go behind your back,' Elisha said, raising her chin, 'but I've been worried about my breathing, and I went to see a specialist at the hospital.'

You did what? And you gave me a tongue-lashing for not being upfront! I swallowed hard. I'd noticed Elisha was coughing more, and I had planned to take her to see a respiratory physician. 'What did the doctor say?'

'That the fire has permanently damaged my lungs, and I may not have long to live.'

'My darling!' I flung my arms around her. 'Why didn't you tell me?'

Elisha brushed away a tear. 'I needed to get my head around it first.'

My mind catapulted into overdrive. 'There's no time to lose. I'll get you an appointment with Bill Jameson tomorrow. Bill's the top man in Auckland on pulmonary disease.'

'It's no use,' Elisha said. 'I'm stuffed. I've seen the scan of my lungs. They're buggered.'

I stroked Elisha's back. 'Don't give up. Please.'

'I won't.'

I felt Elisha's muscles stiffen as she spoke. 'What is it?' I asked.

'I promised my father I'd carry on his work at the mission.' Elisha turned to face me. 'And that's what I'm going to do. I'm going back to India.'

'You can't. The risk of catching a lethal infection out there in Madhapur is massive.'

'I'm going back. Whatever you say.'

'Elisha! You're throwing away your life.'

'No. I'm making something of it while I've still got the chance.'

Her eyes locked on to mine. I'd never seen them so determined.

 David Whittet

'If my time really is limited,' she continued, 'I want to spend it helping Zac and Rajani to build the well. Come with me. We can do this together.'

I covered my face. 'I can't.'

'Why not? I told you before, you can come back for the inquest.'

'It's not just the inquest. It's India.'

Elisha pulled my hands away from my face. 'Look at me, Theo. This life isn't you. Celebrities with more money than sense. Millionaire penthouse pads. You never cared about any of this before. When you proposed to me on the train, you said we were soulmates.'

My mind went back to that night of unbridled passion on the overnight train from Calcutta. We'd only attempted to make love a few times since Elisha's burns and had to abandon it altogether when it became too painful.

'We *are* soulmates,' I said. 'And I still want to marry you. Let's do it. Fix a date.'

'Only if you come back with me to India.'

'I'm not ready to face Madhapur.' I daren't tell her I never wanted to see that godforsaken place again. 'Maybe one day, but not now.'

'Theo!' Elisha pulled her chair away from me. 'I haven't got long. I can't wait for you.'

Overwhelmed by a surge of adrenaline in my gut, I got up and paced up and down the room. 'I'm sorry. I haven't forgiven those militants yet.'

Elisha ran her fingers across the scars on her face. 'It wasn't the people's fault. They didn't do this to me. The Madhapur community were as sickened as everyone else.'

'I know, but ...'

'Akbar Zahin and the rest of the mob are all in prison. Except for Salim, the boy who pulled me out of the flames. I want to meet him. Zac says Salim's dedicated himself to fighting for religious tolerance.' Elisha paused and fixed her eyes on mine. 'If I've forgiven them, why can't you?'

'One day, I might.' I bit my lip before finishing the sentence. 'But not yet.'

Why couldn't I let go of the hate? I hadn't realised how angry I was. Angry with the militants for destroying our dream. Angry with Matthew

Levi for what he'd done to Jamie. Angry with Veronica for sucking me into her world and tempting me with promises of riches.

I was just as angry with Elisha for being right. Appearance medicine and luxury apartments weren't my style. I wasn't the man I used to be—I knew that in my heart. Most of all, I was angry with myself for not listening to her.

I sat down again, next to Elisha. 'They're better off without me in Madhapur. When I was a medical student, the professor of general practice told me I'd never make a GP. He was right. Everything I've done has ended in disaster. I killed a boy in Uganda because my drugs were out of date. Now I've done the same to Jamie. And if I hadn't kicked up a stink about the immunisations, those militants wouldn't have attacked you.'

'You saved Rajani,' Elisha said. 'And look what you did for that boy, Bwanbale. The rest of that stuff wasn't your fault.'

'Yes, it was.' I wanted to stop myself, but I couldn't. 'I'm sick of living like a pauper out in the sticks. At least as a cosmetic surgeon, I'll make some money for once in my sorry life.'

What had I just said? Without a word, Elisha got up and shut herself in the bedroom. I heard her crying. Should I give her some space or try to comfort her?

I crept in and lay beside her on the bed. 'I'm sorry. I didn't mean that.'

Elisha pushed me away and continued to sob. Was there anything I could say or do that would make any difference, or was this the end?

Three days later, with tears in my eyes, I watched Elisha check-in at Auckland Airport.

'You've got a three-hour stopover in Singapore,' the airline agent said. 'I've checked your bags through to Calcutta.'

Was she really leaving? The reality hit me when she picked up the boarding pass. I'd have got down on my knees and begged her to stay if I thought it would make any difference. Constant apologising didn't seem to matter.

'Is there anything I can say that'll make you change your mind?' I asked.

Elisha shook her head. 'Please, Theo. No more. Don't make this even more difficult than it already is.'

I closed my eyes as Elisha disappeared into the distance. *Go after her, you bloody fool. Tell her how much you love her. Say you'll go to India with her. Then she'll know you mean it.*

Instead, I walked back to my car and drove home through the Auckland traffic, knowing I had just made the worst mistake of my life.

CHAPTER THIRTY-THREE

Coroner's Court, Auckland

Lies! Cover-up! I thought my head would explode. Sitting through three days of crap from Matthew Levi and his lawyers at the inquest made up my mind. Damn the consequences, I was going to ignore my lawyer's advice to be cautious. Day four was my turn, and I would tell the truth about what happened to Jamie Beale in the operating theatre on that dreadful day.

Mrs Beale was up before me. Her hand shook so much I thought she was going to drop the Bible when she took her oath.

She brushed away a tear and cleared her throat. 'There isn't a moment I don't think about Jamie.'

I felt her pain as she turned towards Matthew Levi. How brave of her to confront the man who had destroyed her life. I wanted to jump up and hug her.

'For the past twenty-two years, Jamie brought me more joy than I can bear to think about. I needed him as much as he needed me. Now he's gone and I have nothing. My future died with him.' Mrs Beale shifted her gaze from Matthew to the coroner. 'But I don't blame Dr Levi.'

What? Had she gone crazy? Or had I misheard her?

'Can you explain that, Mrs Beale?' the coroner asked.

Mrs Beale steadied herself on the witness stand. I could scarcely bear to listen to her broken voice as she answered.

'We'd seen several other surgeons before Dr Levi. They told me Jamie had this—I think they called it a shunt—between the tumour on his neck and one of the big blood vessels going to his head.' She broke off to wipe her nose on a handkerchief. 'They told me that operating would risk Jamie bleeding to death.'

Matthew Levi's lawyer leapt to his feet. 'Why didn't you tell Dr Levi before the operation?'

Mrs Beale hung her head. 'Because if I had, he wouldn't have operated.'

Matthew thrust his arms in the air. 'Damn right I wouldn't.'

The coroner peered at her over his bifocals. 'So, Mrs Beale, can you explain to us why you saw fit to put your son's life at such an extraordinary risk?'

'Believe me, it wasn't easy.' Tears rolled down her cheeks. 'Jamie was desperate. He said he would kill himself if he couldn't get rid of that tumour. It wasn't just the looks. The weight made him top-heavy. It was growing so fast he was struggling to stand up.'

'I hear what you're saying, Mrs Beale,' the coroner said, 'but allowing the surgery to go ahead when you knew it could kill him was reckless in the extreme.'

'He'd tried to end his life before. I knew he'd do it if he couldn't get the operation. At least this way he had a fighting chance.'

The coroner scratched his head. 'In light of Mrs Beale's evidence, I don't think we need to hear any more. Is there anything you wish to add, Dr Malone?'

I caught the smug grin on Matthew's face. He wasn't off the hook yet. Why hadn't he gone through Jamie's old records? If he had, he'd have known about the shunt. My train of thought hit a sudden roadblock. I'd done Jamie's pre-operative workup, and there was nothing in the notes about any previous consultations or scan results. How could that be? I glanced across at Mrs Beale. Had she been so desperate that she'd somehow managed to conceal Jamie's identity? Was that even his real name?

I pulled myself up from the chair to address the coroner. 'No, sir. I've nothing to say.'

Mrs Beale caught my arm as I wandered out of the courtroom. I'd been so careful to avoid Matthew that I hadn't noticed her hovering beside me. Not wanting to talk to her any more than I did to Matthew, I pulled away.

'Don't look at me like that,' she said. 'I didn't mean to trick you and Dr Levi.'

'It's okay, Mrs Beale,' I said. 'You had your reasons.'

But I was angry. The image of Jamie bleeding to death on that operating table still brought me out in a cold sweat.

She kept clinging on to me. 'Can we sit down for a minute and let me explain?'

While all I could think of was getting out of that courthouse, a part of me wanted to know how she'd duped us so successfully.

I sighed. 'Alright.'

I followed her outside and we sat on a bench.

'I've had to deal with this on my own,' she said. 'Jamie's father couldn't bear to look at him and left soon after he was born.'

'I still can't work out how you hid Jamie's medical history,' I said. 'I went through all the hospital files before the operation. It's as though he'd never seen a doctor before.'

'Jamie wasn't my first child. I had another boy. His skin was covered in lumps as well. He was so ill he didn't make it to his first birthday. When I took Jamie for his investigations—'

'You used the dead child's name.' Suddenly it all made sense. I blew out my cheeks and stared at her. 'So that's why there were no records.'

Only a desperate mother could have seen it through. Never letting it slip that she was using a false identity. I shook my head, scarcely able to believe she'd got away with it.

'I know what you're thinking.' Her wounded eyes gazed into mine. 'But I had to give Jamie a chance. At least he died with hope. Like I said to the coroner, better that than topping himself.'

Who was I to judge her? Not one, but two children with the same ghastly condition.

I stood up to leave. 'You did what you thought was right, Mrs Beale.'

'You don't blame me?'

'No.' I paused. 'I've done some pretty crazy things myself when I've been up against it.'

'I know you've had it rough too, Doctor,' she said. 'Are you married yet? Your girl was in Australia for a memorial service when Jamie had his operation. It was kind of you to stay behind.'

Was it? Jamie would still be alive if I'd gone to Australia and Matthew had cancelled the surgery the way he'd threatened.

We took a few steps down the road together.

 David Whittet

'Elisha's gone back to India,' I said. 'She's sick. I don't think I'll ever see her again.'

Mrs Beale stopped and pulled me back. 'You still love her, don't you?'

Was it that obvious? I turned my head away.

Mrs Beale's eyes fixed on mine. 'Take my advice. Go after her.'

If only it was as simple as hopping on an aeroplane. I'd only had one reply to the countless letters I'd sent to Elisha. The half-dozen or so lines didn't give me the slightest clue as to how she was feeling or what she was thinking. Except she wasn't ready to hear from me. I got more from Rajani when I wrote to her in desperation. Since she got back, Elisha had thrown herself into fundraising for the well. That didn't surprise me. She had been spending time with Salim, the boy who rescued her from the inferno. That made me jealous.

The drive home took longer than ever in the heavy traffic. I thought more about what Mrs Beale had said. With the inquest over, there was little to keep me in New Zealand. How would Elisha react if I followed her out to Madhapur? I felt a sudden chill. Maybe she wouldn't want to see me at all.

I was still working it out when I reached the apartment. It was more than three months since I moved in, and without Elisha, it felt like a mausoleum. Every footstep echoed as I unlocked the door and disarmed the security system. I fetched a packet of instant noodles from the pantry and boiled the kettle. That was a joke. I'd gone into appearance medicine for a better standard of living, and here I was with junk food for supper yet again.

Elisha and Salim. Why had that upset me so much? Was our engagement off? Did it end when she returned to India? Mrs Beale was right—I did still love Elisha.

I poured myself a glass of wine. Drinking on my own. That was a bad sign. I tipped the alcohol down the sink and made up my mind to confront Veronica in the morning. Tell her I was taking at least a month off to go to India and sort things out.

Veronica demolished my pleas with her eyes. 'You're doing what?' She threw her hands in the air, the exact same way my aunt Ida had done when I was a kid. 'I know you've been stressed, what with the inquest and everything.

But that's over. You need to get your arse back into gear and start giving my clients the service they deserve.'

'I'm losing Elisha,' I said. 'I have to see her before it's too late.'

'At least stay for the Spring Ball.' Veronica leant forward. 'Monique's back from America next week. She wants a dance with the man who saved her life.'

'I don't dance.'

'Then we need to teach you. The ball will be a great photo opportunity.' Veronica picked up a magazine from her desk. 'Look. Monique is going to be on the front cover of *Vogue*.' She handed me the proof copy. 'And with the right publicity, we will get our New Zealand edition again.'

I stared at Monique's flawless face on the cover. 'Elisha could have been on a magazine cover,' I said. 'You should have seen her before the burns. She was beautiful. Still is—Elisha's the same person on the inside.'

But was she? Elisha had changed. Inevitably. With all the patients I'd counselled for PTSD, I should have understood Elisha better. Mental scars ran deeper than any physical disfigurement. I'd been wrong to take her away from Zac and Rajani when she most needed them and to deprive her of her support network. At least she was with them now.

'Alright,' I said. 'I'll stay for the ball. But I'm flying out to India the next day.'

I wrote to Elisha again that night.

I'm coming, my darling. I'm leaving appearance medicine behind. As soon as I can get away.

I'd never been more certain of anything in all my life. Nothing would stop me—except for the letter from Rajani that arrived the day before the Spring Ball. Elisha and Salim were engaged.

A society ball was the last thing I needed. I could have torn every tuxedo to shreds in the exclusive menswear shop Veronica sent me to on the morning of the ball. Why had I let Elisha go back to India alone? If only I'd got over myself and put Elisha's feelings before my own angst. Should I still go after her? But I was the man who had let her down. How could I possibly compete with the boy who had saved her life?

 David Whittet

'You look magnificent,' the obsequious shop assistant said. 'That suit's a perfect fit.'

Magnificent? I glanced in the mirror. Balls. I looked like the sham I was.

Veronica introduced me to her colleagues at the ball as if I were a hero. That made me feel even more of a fake. Maybe I was a good doctor, but I was turning into a lousy human being.

Then there was the photo shoot with Monique, and the obligatory dance. The paparazzi were out in force, with cameras flashing every second. Staying upright while dancing was enough of a challenge without being blinded in the process.

'Bravo!' Veronica shouted when the dance finished. 'You were great.'

'Nonsense,' I said. 'I was rubbish.'

Monique took me aside. 'I want you to meet my friend Clemmie. She's hoping you can get her on the front cover of *Vogue*, too.'

Dressed in a skimpy black number, Clementine had a petite body and heart-stopping eyes. 'Can you, Doc?' she said. 'I've heard so much about you.'

I shook my head. 'Monique getting on the cover of *Vogue* had nothing to do with me.'

'Of course it did!' Monique said. 'You're too modest, Doc.' She pointed to her neck. 'There was a massive mole here that would have killed me.'

I stepped back. 'I only did what any doctor would do.'

'Isn't he cute?' Clementine said.

Monique laughed. 'He's a darling.'

Cute? Darling? If only they knew how messed up I was on the inside.

'Dance with me,' Clementine said.

Monique gave her a nudge. 'He's an ace doctor, but I'm warning you, he's a crap dancer.'

I put down my wine glass. 'Actually, I was about to go home. It's been a long day.'

Before I could get away, Veronica strode over. 'For heaven's sake, Theo, lighten up! Have some fun for a change. Dance with the girl.'

Lighten up. Have fun. I couldn't remember when I last did that.

I took Clementine's hand. 'Okay, but you heard what Monique said about my dancing.'

'Then I'll have to teach you.' Clementine led me onto the dance floor. 'Come on.'

I managed a waltz without treading on Clementine's feet.

'You see,' she said, 'you're a natural.'

But when it came to the polka, my feet couldn't keep up with hers and we collapsed on the floor in fits of laughter.

'I'm going home,' I said.

'Not blood likely!' Clementine grabbed my arm. 'You're not leaving before the samba.'

We danced all night. Each time I tripped over and capsized, Clementine pulled me up.

'Everyone's watching,' I protested.

'Let them,' Clementine said. 'This is *fun*.'

It was. I hadn't enjoyed myself that much in a long time.

CHAPTER THIRTY-FOUR

Veronica's Office, Queen Street, Auckland

After a couple of weeks of agonising, I just wanted to sign the damn contract and be done with it.

'Delighted you're staying on.' Veronica picked up her designer fountain pen and signed the contract with a flourish. 'You won't regret it. Your future belongs with us.' She pushed the contract across her desk to me. 'Your turn.'

I gulped. Did I really want to *belong* to the Ashton-Forbes Modelling Agency?

I'd lost count of how many times I'd tried to call Elisha. When I did get through, she wouldn't talk to me. Zac invariably answered the phone. 'Mate—she's not ready to talk to you,' he'd said. 'She's moved on.'

So Elisha had moved on. Maybe it was time for me to do the same. I took a pen from my pocket and signed Veronica's contract.

'If that's all, I'll be off.' I handed the contract back to Veronica and stood up. 'I've got a patient booked in at eleven.'

Veronica looked at her watch and sank back in her leather chair. 'Plenty of time.' She gestured for me to sit down again. 'I want the goss on you and Clemmie.'

I edged closer to the door. 'Nothing to tell.'

'Come on. You and Clemmie looked pretty intimate at the ball. Talk about dancing cheek to cheek.' Veronica winked at me. 'Lucy said Clemmie's moving in with you.'

Trust Lucy to give away our secret. I shuffled from one foot to the other. 'We're thinking about it.'

Veronica grinned. 'You're blushing, Theo!'

'I'm not!' I was out of the door, knowing full well my cheeks were burning.

'Why don't you celebrate with a housewarming party?' Veronica called after me. 'Four months you've been in that penthouse pad, and we still haven't had an invitation. I thought you'd be dying to show it off.'

Clementine. Exquisite, exasperating, irresistible Clementine. Why had I allowed her sultry eyes to seduce me? Those first few weeks together were a roller coaster of emotion. Maybe I was just on the rebound. Sensual and provocative, Clementine was everything Elisha was not. Nothing worried Clementine. She lived life her way and bugger the consequences.

'Clemmie's a rebel,' Veronica had told me. 'Her folks have a huge estate on Waiheke Island. They had great plans for their daughter and got her a place at an exclusive finishing school. But Clemmie wasn't interested in learning to be a lady. She ran away at sixteen and joined a rock band.'

That didn't surprise me. Veronica had seen Clementine performing with the band at a nightclub and recruited her for the modelling agency.

Perhaps Clementine had more in common with Elisha than I thought. Elisha told me how, as a teenager, she'd rebelled against the Church and her father's mission. She'd threatened to run away from home rather than go to India. But getting involved in her father's work had given Elisha vision and purpose. And that's what Clementine needed now.

'You should join a band again,' I urged Clementine. 'Follow your dream.'

Clementine wrinkled her nose. 'Nah. There's no money in music. But if I could get on the front cover of an international magazine like Monique ...'

I bit my tongue. 'You've got a beautiful voice and a talent for writing songs. Don't throw it away.'

Clementine shrugged and dismissed the idea with a wave of her hand.

I learnt to stop pushing and enjoy the ride. Life with Clementine was an experience, an endless kaleidoscope of discos and late-night parties.

Saturday night and another raucous party at Lucy's place. I was exhausted and desperate to get out of the city. I snuggled up to Clementine in the taxi on the way home.

'We never get any time to ourselves,' I said. 'We're both free tomorrow so why don't we go for a drive in the county?'

Clementine pulled a face. 'The country?'

I laughed. 'Yes. There's life beyond the big smoke, you know. We could take a picnic.'

'*What?* Stale sandwiches while squatting on the ground. It doesn't sound much fun to me.'

Creature comforts were everything to Clementine. 'Come on,' I said. 'Give it a go. Who knows? You might even enjoy yourself.'

Sunday morning and I loaded the hamper into the back of my new BMW convertible. Clementine emerged from the bedroom, rubbing her eyes.

'I didn't know life began this early,' she groaned.

'I thought you'd be used to early-morning shoots,' I said.

'Yes, but this is my day off, and I need my beauty sleep.' She snatched a towel and headed for the shower. 'This had better be good.'

'It will be,' I shouted after her. 'What's not to like? An open-top car. The wind rushing through your hair, and the finest gourmet sandwiches.'

Heading north on the motorway, Clementine put on her Chanel sunglasses, undid her ponytail, and threw her head back.

'I'd almost forgotten what it was like,' she said, 'that blast of air on your face. My first boyfriend was a biker. He had this classic Harley-Davidson, and we used to go on road trips with his mates.' She sighed and turned her head towards me. 'He loved that bike more than he did me.'

An hour on the highway, and at last we were out of the city. Another hour or so along winding lanes and gravel roads, and we were in pristine bush and not another vehicle in sight. I pulled into a clearing in the forest.

Clementine got out of the car and wandered through the thicket. 'I did a glamour shoot in some woods just like these.' She posed with her legs wrapped around a tree. 'It was super raunchy. I was meant to be this sexy wood nymph, and I had to—'

'I don't want to know,' I said, laughing. 'Come and help me unpack.'

We laid a groundsheet on the grass and opened the picnic hamper. I popped the cork on a bottle of champagne.

'Bubbly!' Clementine exclaimed. 'This is way better than I expected. Cheers!'

We raised our glasses and clinked them together. 'Cheers!'

'These sarnies aren't bad either,' Clementine said. 'Where did you get them?'

'That deli in Newmarket you're always going on about.'

'You're learning, Theo.'

When we'd finished eating, Clementine put her arms around me and kissed me on the lips. Her Dior perfume always made my head reel.

'Time for your reward,' she said.

'I wasn't expecting—'

Clementine put a finger to her lips. 'Shush.' She began unbuttoning my shirt.

'Wait.'

'Relax.' She pulled off her top and wriggled out of her jeans.

I could scarcely bring myself to look as she flashed her breasts in front of my face. Such pert nipples and silky, unblemished skin. In the darkness of the bedroom, it wasn't so obvious. Here in the forest, her flawless body glistened in the shafts of sunlight that shone through the trees. Had Clementine any idea how lucky she was? How would she cope if a disaster robbed her of her looks? I closed my eyes as she peeled off her knickers.

'You like doing it with your eyes shut?' she said. 'I'd have brought you a blindfold if I'd known.'

What? I opened my eyes and stared at her.

She grinned. 'I can do the full dominatrix routine if that's what turns you on.' She rolled me over and spanked me.

'Stop it! I'm not into that!'

'I think you are.' She aimed another playful slap. 'Don't pretend.'

'I'm not!' I fought back as she smacked me yet again. 'That hurt!'

Our naked bodies rolled off the mat and into the long grass. This tango was even more ungainly than our performance on the dance floor. It was time to stop overthinking. To hell with guilt. To hell with inhibitions. I pulled her around to face me and thrust into her. My back arched as her fingers dug into my flesh. Her legs wrapped around me, drawing me further inside until the ground shifted beneath us and her body convulsed against mine.

David Whittet

'Holy fuck!' Clementine cried as we slid into a ditch.

Giggling like kids, we climbed out of the undergrowth. Then, still naked, Clementine laid back on the mat, brushing the mud and twigs off her body.

'Why *did* you screw up your eyes when I stripped off?' she said. 'Don't you like my body?'

'Of course I do.'

She cupped her breasts with her hands. 'I guess you must get tired of looking at naked bodies in your line of work.'

'Not all of them are as perfect as yours, I can assure you. In fact, some are absolutely …' I broke off. Did she know about Elisha? I hadn't said anything, but Veronica might have done.

Clementine frowned. 'What is it?'

I sat up and put my hand on her back. 'Nothing.'

The sun disappeared behind the trees. The wind brought a chill, and we started to get dressed.

Clementine pulled her top over her head and pointed to a dimple on her cheek. 'I want you to fix this before the housewarming party and my big shoot next week.'

I buttoned up my shirt. 'I think it makes you look more beautiful.'

'Maybe you do,' Clementine said, 'but fashion editors don't.' She pulled on her jeans and stared into my eyes. 'Listen, Theo. I know you think I'm vain and stupid. Maybe I am just a spoilt child. But my body's my livelihood. It's a cut-throat world in the fashion industry. Ask Vee. And in a few years, when everything begins to sag, nobody will be interested in me.'

There was a vulnerability in Clementine's eyes that I hadn't seen before, and I hugged her tight. 'I'll make sure you look perfect for the housewarming party.'

The adventure with Clementine might have lasted forever if it wasn't for that wretched housewarming party. And for Lucy's interfering. The minute I had told Clementine about the party, she was on the phone to Lucy arranging the most expensive caterer in town and booking a canopy for the deck with a hire company.

'Is that really necessary?' I asked. 'I thought we'd just have a few friends.'

'No, Theo,' Clementine said. 'This is going to be *big*. Anyone who's anyone will be at our party. And nobody can organise a bash like Lucy.'

'This is our party, not Lucy's,' I protested.

'What is it with you and Lucy?' Clementine flicked back her long dark hair. 'Don't you like her?'

Where to start. Clementine was a different person when Lucy was around. 'It's just …' I shrugged, too gutless to say what I was thinking. 'She's just a bit loud. That's all.'

I'd promised Clementine she'd be immaculate for the party, and she looked a million dollars. So did all the guests, with their posh frocks and designer suits. What would Elisha have said about the impeccably coiffured hair and smiles plastered on with make-up? I felt a lump in my throat. I'd seen more genuine emotion on the wrinkled faces in an old people's home and more joy amongst the lepers in Madhapur.

I was fast running out of polite conversation when Veronica cornered me with a woman who'd had one nose job too many.

'I'd like you to meet Lady Penhaligon,' Veronica said. 'She's looking for a personal physician.'

'Pleased to meet you.' I shook her hand while desperately searching for an escape route.

Too late. Lady Penhaligon grabbed my arm. 'I've heard such good things about you from Vee. My last cosmetic surgeon was useless.' She pointed to her swollen cheeks. 'Another botched job.'

So why keep going back for more? 'What a disgrace,' I said. And it was—with her near-perfect bone structure, she must have been beautiful before she went under the knife. 'I tell you, Lady Penhaligon, there are some sharks out there.'

'I know they were just after my money.' She gripped my arm even tighter. 'But you're different. Vee says I can trust you.'

I caught Clementine's eye at the other side of the patio and mouthed, '*Help me*.' She grinned and continued gossiping to her mates.

Lady Penhaligon was just the first of a raft of high society women Veronica had lined up for me. All of them thinking I was their saviour.

David Whittet

'Enough!' I hissed in Veronica's ear.

Veronica grinned. 'You're going to be a busy boy after tonight.'

Midnight and the last of the stragglers still hung out on the porch. Where was Clementine? Instead of hosting with me, she'd buggered off with Lucy and the rest of the girls hours ago. Typical.

Mrs Forsyth, one of Veronica's wealthy patrons, tapped me on the shoulder. 'Be a darling and fetch my coat. Your girlfriend put it in the guest room.'

'With pleasure,' I said. 'I won't be a moment.'

At least that meant she was leaving. Another of Alexandra Forsyth's overblown stories about the prizes she'd won at dog shows the world over, and I'd have thrown up.

What the hell was going on in the guest bedroom?

I heard Clementine shriek from inside. 'I'm not doing that!'

Lucy's voice. 'We get to tickle you all over for two minutes if you don't.'

So that was where the girls were holed up. I opened the door and gasped.

Clementine was doing jumping jacks on the bed wearing Mrs Forsyth's fur coat, and she had nothing on underneath. 'We're playing truth or dare,' she said. 'It's a girls-only game, but you can join us if you like.'

I might have been tempted for a moment, but the malicious glint in Lucy's eyes rapidly turned me off. I took a step back. 'I've come for Mrs Forsyth's coat.'

'Get it off, Clemmie!' the girls chanted. 'Get it off!'

Clementine did a quick flash, then made for the en-suite bathroom.

'What if Mrs Forsyth had come for her coat herself?' I said, trying not to look at Monique in her soaking wet T-shirt or Samantha with her pants on her head.

'Then the old bag would have something to feast her eyes on,' Lucy said. 'Sure beats one of her dog shows.'

The girls clapped and burst into fits of giggles.

'Bloody right!'

'You're wicked, Luce!'

Clementine returned from the bathroom, clad in a towel. 'The girls are staying for a sleepover,' she said, handing me the fur coat. 'Okay?'

Did I have a choice? 'Guess so.'

I grabbed Mrs Forsyth's zillion-dollar fur coat, which now reeked of Clementine's Dior perfume, and retreated into the corridor.

'Here you are, Mrs Forsyth.' I helped her put the coat on, praying she wouldn't notice the perfume.

'You must come to one of my candlelight suppers,' she said. 'And bring that lovely girl of yours, too.'

If only you knew what that 'lovely girl' was doing right now. 'We will. Goodnight, Mrs Forsyth.' I smiled sweetly and shut the door behind her.

Thank God that's over. Mrs Forsyth was the last of the guests to leave. Well, not quite. Would the girls carry on all night?

Lucy was still calling the shots, her voice soaring above the uproar coming from the spare room. 'Your turn, Felicity. Pick one of these toys and show us how you'd use it.'

More raucous laughter. 'You're blushing, Fliss!'

'Go for it, girl!'

'Which is it going to be? The pink one?'

'Have another drink, and let's see what you're made of.'

What was going on behind that door? The stakes had obviously got much higher. I hovered outside. Should I go in? I had my hand on the doorknob when Lucy's voice rang out again.

'That's a lie, Suzie. You have to eat a whole bar of soap!'

Perhaps not. I'd had quite enough for one night and it was time for bed. Besides, I had work in the morning. Not that I got much sleep with the constant racket from the guest room. Clementine went on about *her* beauty sleep. It was just a couple of months since she moved in, and already there were bags under *my* eyes.

My head was throbbing by the early hours. Finally, I got up and wandered into the kitchen to get some paracetamol and a glass of water. The fridge door was open and tomato sauce splattered all over the breakfast bar. Some of the girls had crashed out on the floor, the remains of the canapés daubed over their faces. The dares must have got messy.

 David Whittet

Clementine came in from the deck. She flinched when she saw me. 'I thought you were asleep.'

'I've got a headache,' I said. 'I've come to get some paracetamol.'

'You go back to bed,' Clementine said. 'I'll bring it to you.'

I hesitated.

'Go on.' Clementine nudged me towards the bedroom. 'I'll clear up this mess in the morning. I promise.'

What was she trying to hide? Why was she so keen to get me out of the way?

Lucy called her from the deck. 'Come on, Clemmie. You're missing all the fun.'

I pushed past Clementine. *What the hell?* I blinked repeatedly, but it didn't change anything. Lucy and Felicity were huddled over a table snorting a fine white powder through paper straws.

'Get out!' I glared at Lucy. 'And take that gear with you. We don't do drugs in this house.'

'Chill, Doc!' Lucy handed me a straw. 'Here, have a sniff. It's good stuff.'

'I don't do drugs.' I screwed up the straw and threw it at her. 'What part of that don't you understand?'

'Suit yourself.' Lucy took another snort. Her slurred voice and fractured eyes told me she was already high.

'Get out! And take the gear with you.' I turned to Clementine. 'Don't you realise what this could do to me? My career will be over if we get busted.'

'I'm sorry, Theo.' Clementine hid her face. 'I'd no idea she was bringing drugs.'

Didn't she? Clementine and Lucy were always close.

Lucy scooped the powder into a bag. 'Come on, Fliss. Round to my place. You coming, Clemmie?'

Would she go with them? I watched Clementine squirm.

'No, Luce,' she said. 'You shouldn't have done it.'

'*I didn't know.* How many times do I have to tell you?' Clementine repeated the words endlessly throughout the night. 'Why won't you believe me?'

I stared back at her. 'Look me in the eyes and say it.'

Her bloodshot eyes locked on to mine. 'I didn't know. Honest. Lucy's a law unto herself.'

I believed her. But nothing was quite the same after that night.

Three strong coffees and I still couldn't face work in the morning. Veronica chuckled when I called in sick.

'Hungover, are we?' she asked.

'Something like that.'

'What about Clemmie? Does she have a sore head, too?'

I glanced across at Clementine, who had crashed out on the sofa. 'She won't be coming in today either.'

Three weeks later, Clementine announced she'd signed on with a new modelling agency in Australia. Had I driven her away? The long silences since the party couldn't have helped, and she'd started going out on her own.

'I'll miss you,' I said. 'I'm sorry things got so …'

Clementine cut me off. 'Come with me. We both need a fresh start.'

Did she mean it? Or was she just saying that to make the split easier, knowing I was committed to working for Veronica?

'If only I could. But I've signed a two-year contract with Veronica.'

'She might release you,' Clementine said. 'She's let me go.'

I shook my head. 'Veronica's spent a small fortune on setting up the clinic.' I forced a smile. 'Besides, who else is going to sort out Lady Penhaligon's face?'

Clementine hugged me. 'We've had some good times, haven't we?' There were tears in her eyes. 'I'll never forget you, Theo.'

Perhaps she wouldn't. I knew I would never forget Clementine.

Alone again. Returning to an empty apartment night after night, I had plenty of time to reflect. Was Clementine just a fling that was fun while it lasted? And if so, why couldn't I get her out of my mind?

Clementine was the lucky one, getting out of Veronica's contract.

'I signed up to take care of your models,' I told Veronica at our next briefing. 'Not to pander to rich socialites with more money than sense.'

'You have to take the rough with the smooth,' Veronica said, 'and you've made quite an impression on Lady Penhaligon.'

I scratched my head. 'I can't think why.'

Veronica gave me one of her hard stares. 'Remember, Theo, my money pays your mortgage.'

As if I could forget. I dreaded going home for another endless evening. Forty channels on the new state-of-the-art satellite television and still nothing worth watching. Romances. Trashy soaps. Who watched this garbage, anyway? I flipped through a few more channels. Reality TV. Game shows. *Hell's teeth*—I'd had more than my fill of games from the girls and their antics.

I switched to another station. A fashion show. Even worse. I rummaged through the magazine rack and found the TV guide. Channels thirty-nine and forty were dedicated to documentaries. Thirty-nine was showing *Your Life in Their Hands—Advances in Modern Surgery*. Knowing my luck, Matthew Levi would be the star surgeon. I shuddered and skipped to channel forty.

A documentary on rural India. *Give me a break.* I was about to turn the television off when I saw something that made my heart miss a beat. *That's my old consulting room in Madhapur.* I gripped the side of my chair. Was I seeing things? *There's Elisha, sitting at my old desk!*

Where was that programme guide? My hand shook as I read the synopsis.

Out of the Ashes, a film by Isaac Martin. The story of a community's recovery from disaster. Five years on from a brutal attack, the brave daughter of murdered missionary Wesley Martin is determined to complete his work. And helping her, the boy who saved her life.

Was it really five years since the nightmare began? I stared at the screen until it hurt. Elisha was calm and self-assured—I couldn't believe how great she looked. Her burns were scarcely noticeable, or was that just Zac's clever filming?

My heart missed another beat when Elisha put her arm around an Indian boy and introduced him as her rescuer. I grabbed the remote but couldn't bring myself to press the off button. Salim's engaging smile and the glow on Elisha's face made my eyes water. I bit my tongue. The two of them were made for each other.

I breathed again when the scene changed to the temple. Krishna looked more solemn than ever. I turned up the volume. *What?* They'd chosen the wrong place to build the well? Surely not—the site had been blessed. There was more. The contractor they'd brought in to fix it had done a runner with all the money they'd raised.

Before I could take in the news, Elisha was back on screen, wiping away a tear as she spoke to the camera. 'Unless we can recover a million rupees—that's the amount the lowlife stole from us—our dream of safe, clean drinking water for the people of Madhapur is finished. So we're asking for donations. Please support the Madhapur Well Appeal.'

Elisha sure knew how to turn on the emotion. She'd always been able to tug at the heartstrings. Zac's gift with the camera had flourished, too. Maybe he would be another—what was the name of that famous Indian film director? But would their passionate appeal be enough to raise a million rupees?

Early the following morning, I called the consulting rooms.

'Madeline, I need you to reschedule my first few appointments. I'm going to be late in.'

'You can't,' Madeline said. 'Lady Penhaligon is booked in at nine.'

'Then she'll have to wait or come on another day.' I put down the receiver. There were more important things on my mind.

Nine o'clock and I was first in the queue outside the bank.

'I want to send some money to India,' I told the teller. 'To the Madhapur Well Appeal.'

'How much?' the teller asked.

'A million rupees,' I said. 'How much is that in New Zealand dollars?'

The teller punched the numbers into his calculator. 'Twenty thousand dollars.'

     David Whittet

'There should be enough in my savings account,' I said.

'Let's see.' The teller tapped a few more numbers into his computer. 'Only just. But it'll leave you vulnerable. You've just taken out a huge mortgage.'

'I know.' It would certainly clean me out. What if interest rates went up? Would I survive? I didn't care any more. Worst-case scenario, I'd have to sell the apartment. It had brought me nothing but trouble, anyway.

The teller scratched his head. 'Are you sure you want to proceed? I think you should talk it over with the manager.'

'Just make the donation,' I said. 'I don't need to see the manager. Some things are more important than money.'

'Very well.' The teller grimaced as he typed up the transfer document. 'Do you want to send a message to the recipient?'

I paused for a moment. 'No. Make it anonymous.'

CHAPTER THIRTY-FIVE

Madhapur

Elisha

After the emptiness of the past five years, it felt good to be doing something worthwhile again. Even licking the envelopes for the appeal letters gave Elisha immense satisfaction.

Her return to India had been an emotional roller coaster, starting with hugs from Zac and Rajani the moment she stepped off the train. Beside them on the platform stood an Indian boy. He couldn't have been much more than twenty and had the most heart-stopping eyes Elisha had ever seen.

'Meet Salim,' Zac said.

What did you say to the boy who saved your life? Elisha just flung her arms around him and cried.

With such striking good looks, Elisha wasted no time making Salim the face of the fundraising campaign for the new well. He appeared on all the billboards. His picture was in all the corporate mailings and the flyers they distributed throughout Orissa state and beyond.

It didn't seem long before they raised enough to start work. Elisha just wanted to get going, but she let Zac talk her into another photo—or rather, video—opportunity.

Elisha had almost forgotten how much the townsfolk loved to celebrate. The fairy lights and marigolds were out again, lining the streets. The last time Madhapur had partied like this was for the dedication ceremony for the well. Elisha took a sharp breath. That was at her engagement party with Theo.

The media junket arrived, cameras at the ready. Elisha glanced at her watch. Mr Prasad had promised he'd be there at two to officiate. It wasn't like him to be late. Where was he?

David Whittet

The drilling rig was in place. A tall orange derrick mounted on the back of a lorry held the drill pipe ready for action. The engineer waited with his finger on the button. Kids were getting bored.

When Prasad did show up, Elisha knew something was wrong from the way he strutted towards them, flanked by his band of technical officers.

'You will have seen my men boring some test holes,' Mr Prasad began. 'I have to inform you that the water samples they obtained from this area showed significant contamination with human waste.'

Elisha grabbed Salim's hand and held it tight. Her father had consecrated that site just days before he died. It *couldn't* be wrong. Krishna had blessed it, too.

'Why did the bastard wait for the ceremony to tell us?' Zac hissed in her ear. 'Typical bloody Prasad. He has to be centre stage for everything.'

Prasad held a test bottle in the air as though it were a trophy. 'If it wasn't for our vigilance, we'd all be facing another cholera outbreak.'

The crowd dropped the brightly coloured flags they were waving, like falling dominos. Nobody could face the lavish buffet the women had prepared.

Rajani put her arm around Elisha. 'At least we've found out before we spent all our money drilling. Don't cry. We'll find a new site for the well.'

Elisha couldn't hold back the tears any longer. 'I know, but my father chose that spot. He put a cross on the ground.'

'Pastor Martin wouldn't have given up,' Rajani said.

Divit Bhandari, announcing himself as the council's chief scientific officer, sat down beside them. 'I can fix this for you. We did some testing over by Saradhapur. The water there's clean. No germs and easy to extract.' He leant forward and lowered his voice. 'And don't worry about Prasad. I take care of the drilling consents.'

Two months later, Elisha sat in the tiny mission office, mailing a fresh set of begging letters.

Zac paced up and down in front of her. 'I'm going to expose that bastard Bhandari. Nobody cons me out of a million rupees and gets away with it.'

'Cool it, Zac,' Elisha said. 'You're going to give yourself an ulcer. Bhandari's not worth it.'

'Chief scientific officer, my arse,' Zac said. 'The son of a bitch has been fleecing people all over Orissa. I won't rest until the scumbag's behind bars.'

Elisha sealed the last envelope. 'At least the appeal's going well. The TV programme's starting to bring in some money.'

Zac flung his arms in the air. 'Yes, but it's never going to raise a million rupees.'

Rajani burst into the office. 'It just has.' She waved a bank statement at them. 'Look!'

Elisha took the paper, her hand shaking so much she could hardly read it. 'An anonymous donation from New Zealand.' Her mouth fell open. 'It has to be Theo. Who else in New Zealand knows about our well?'

'It could have been anyone,' Zac said. 'The appeal went out on TVNZ last week.'

'I still think it was Theo,' Elisha said.

'I can't see Theo having that much to spare,' Zac said, 'and if he did, I bet he wouldn't give it to us. No, it'll be some other Kiwi. I've heard they're good buggers.'

'What does it matter who sent it?' Rajani grabbed Zac's arm, and they embraced each other. 'We've got the money we need. Hallelujah!'

Who had sent the donation? It *did* matter to Elisha, and she was going to find out.

Would Zac and Salim ever leave for the match? Elisha wanted some time on her own with Rajani. Sound her out about the donation while the boys were at the football.

'You need to get your skates on,' Elisha said. 'It's Madhapur versus Baripada. It'll be packed.'

Rajani's great-aunt Nisha fussed over the boys in the kitchen, packing them a food basket. 'They can't go without their samosas.'

Great-aunt Nisha. Kind and generous, she'd taken Elisha in when she returned to Madhapur. But she could be equally frustrating. The last thing the lads would be thinking about during the game was their stomachs.

 David Whittet

At last, the boys were out the door, and Nisha was back in the kitchen.

Elisha grabbed Rajani's arm and whispered in her ear. 'Is there any way we can trace where the money came from?'

'I asked the bank,' Rajani said. 'They could only say it came from a New Zealand bank on Auckland's North Shore.'

Elisha's pulse quickened. 'That's where Theo lives.'

Rajani frowned. 'So do a lot of other people, don't they? Isn't Auckland New Zealand's biggest city?'

Elisha nodded. 'But whatever you or Zac say, I'm sure it was Theo.'

Nisha came back into the room with a pot of chai. Elisha slumped on a chair. More tiresome chatter.

Nisha took a sip of tea and smiled at Rajani. 'You look pleased with yourself.'

Rajani put her arms around her great-aunt. 'We've just had some great news. Someone's given us the money to build the well.'

'That's fantastic!' Nisha said. 'We should celebrate!'

'Elisha thinks it was Theo who sent the money,' Rajani said.

'Dr Malone?' Nisha rubbed her chin. 'What makes you think that?'

Elisha shrugged. 'I don't know. It's just a feeling.'

Nisha reached out and stroked Elisha's arm with her wrinkled hand. 'Tell me about it.'

Elisha often felt the need for someone Nisha's age to confide in. But somehow, she couldn't talk to Nisha the way she had to Joanna. How she missed those heart-to-heart chats with Joanna. They would often argue and sometimes fight, but nothing was off limits. If overseas phone calls weren't so expensive, there were many times Elisha would have loved to ring Joanna.

'I can't explain,' Elisha said. 'It just seems too much of a coincidence that the money came from the very place where Theo lives in New Zealand.'

Nisha stood up and cleared away the cups. 'I'm off to see Raveena,' she said. 'We've got a party to organise.'

Elisha sighed. Not another jamboree. The last one ended in tears.

'You want it to be Theo, don't you?' Rajani said. 'Do you still love him?'

'I love who he used to be before …' Elisha broke off. It was too painful to admit how she felt to herself, let alone anyone else—even her best friend.

'Let's go for a walk,' Rajani said. 'We can meet the boys at the football ground.'

The two girls wandered down the street, arm in arm.

'I guess you're right,' Elisha said. 'It doesn't matter who sent the money. Theo's doubtless found himself some rich woman by now. I bet he's forgotten all about me.'

Rajani squeezed her hand. 'Of course he hasn't. What about all those letters he sent you?'

'He's stopped writing now,' Elisha said.

Rajani stopped abruptly. 'That's because I told him you and Salim were engaged.'

'You did what?' Elisha bit her lip. Why did she care?

'He had a right to know,' Rajani said. 'I don't know why you couldn't tell him yourself.'

'I wanted to, it's just …' Elisha shook her head. She used to be able to open her heart to Rajani. So why was it so difficult now?

'Write to him,' Rajani said. 'That's the only way you'll know for certain if he made the donation.'

The distant chanting reached a crescendo as Elisha and Rajani arrived outside the stadium.

'*Go, Madhapur! Go! Go! Go! We are the champions!*'

Rajani raced towards the pitch. 'We're winning! Sock it to them, Madhapur! You can do it! Knock Baripada out of town!'

Another deafening cheer. '*Goal!*'

Elisha didn't care who'd just scored. She watched Rajani jumping up and down. Why did everyone get so worked up over a game of soccer?

The whistle blew and the crowd erupted.

'*We reign supreme! Madhapur forever, Baripada never! We reign supreme!*'

Zac burst onto the pitch, dragging Salim behind him.

'Man of the match!' Zac cried. 'No contest. You're man of the match, Ashok!'

Zac hoisted Ashok over his shoulders. The fans followed them for a victory lap around the grounds, waving their banners in the air.

'Get a photo!' Zac said, tossing his camera to Salim. 'This is going on the front cover of next week's *Madhapur Gazette*.'

Elisha winced. Shouldn't news of the donation be the top story?

Salim walked her home. 'Can't wait for the party,' he said. 'Zac's going to be the DJ. That'll be a laugh. Pick you up at seven?'

'I'm not going,' Elisha said. 'I need an early night.'

Salim stared at her with his soulful brown eyes. 'But everyone will be there. It's the first time we've won in years.'

'Everyone but me,' Elisha said. 'You go and enjoy yourself.'

Was it you, Theo? I have to know. Elisha started writing to Theo. After scribbling a few lines, she screwed up the letter and threw it in the bin. No words could express the conflict that raged in her head—or how she felt about Theo.

Elisha collapsed on her bed. She didn't need a letter—her heart told her Theo had made the donation. Was he deliberately messing with her head by sending the money anonymously? Regardless, the funds were manna from Heaven for the community. Theo must have been doing well for himself if he could afford to give away a million rupees.

The football team's after-party raged in the village hall down the road. Elisha buried her head under the bedclothes and covered her ears to block the noise. Why couldn't she get Theo out of her mind? They'd been so close—once. She remembered the good times, like the thrill of the night they immunised the kids in secret. Then there was the high of the conference in Calcutta—and the train ride home.

Did she still love Theo? And where did that leave Salim?

Elisha spent the next few days in bed. She'd escaped the football after-party, and she was equally determined to steer clear of the community event to celebrate the resumption of work on the well. Most of all, she wasn't ready to face Salim. Elisha peered through her bedroom window on the morning of the celebrations. There was Nisha, out in the street, organising everyone. Why did such brightly coloured flags and decorations look so drab?

A knock on the door. Rajani's voice. 'What's up with you? I've just seen Salim. He's gutted that you're not joining in the festivities.'

'I just want to get on with building the well,' Elisha said. 'We don't need any more parties. This ridiculous pantomime has held us up for a week already.'

'Lighten up, girl!' Rajani sat down next to Elisha on the bed and rubbed her back. 'What's the rush? We've got the money now.'

Elisha took a blood-stained handkerchief out of her pocket and showed it to Rajani. 'I haven't got long.'

'You're coughing up blood again?'

Elisha nodded. 'Every morning.'

'Why didn't you tell me? We need to get you to the hospital.'

'No,' Elisha said. 'No doctors. No hospital. If I can only live to see the well completed, I'll die happy.'

'Don't say that.' Rajani brushed the tears from her eyes. 'Does Salim know? You have to tell him.'

'I will.' Elisha flinched. Hiding her deteriorating health was unfair to Salim, and to everyone else at the mission. 'It's just … I have to find the right moment.' She sighed and got up off the bed. 'Come on. Let's join the others and party.'

Elisha wasn't sure how she did it, but with Salim at her side, she had a smile for everyone throughout the day-long celebrations. She thanked all the people who told her how good she looked. If only they knew how she really felt. Elisha even managed to hold herself together when Krishna blessed the new location they'd chosen for the well.

'How do we know this isn't going to be another disaster?' one of the villagers shouted.

'That won't happen again,' Zac said. 'This time, we've got a reputable engineering firm from Calcutta on the project. They've built waterways, dams and wells throughout India.'

Elisha staggered to her feet. Salim helped her to the front and held her arm as she addressed the crowd.

'As you all know, we can only continue work on the well due to a donation from a very generous New Zealander. I'm sure many of you have

   David Whittet

worked out that our mysterious benefactor is someone known to us all. The man who immunised your children. The man who wasn't afraid to stand up to the authorities.' Elisha's head swooned, but she had to finish. 'I ask you to join me in a vote of thanks to Dr Theo Malone.'

The crowd cheered.

Salim's grip on her hand tightened. 'Help me! She's going to fall!'

Rajani grabbed her other arm. 'I've got her.'

Elisha couldn't make sense of the jumbled-up images before her eyes. She could just distinguish Krishna's face. Was he giving her the last rites? Was this the end?

For a moment, Elisha was back in the burning wreckage with her father. Panic set in as the flames burnt her flesh once more. Then peace. Her mother and father were calling her home.

Zac's voice echoed in the distance. 'Sis! Stay with us!'

Another voice. 'You can't leave us.'

Was that Rajani? Or was it Salim? Elisha couldn't be sure.

'Call Dr Basar.' That was Zac again. 'We've got to get her to the hospital.'

'No!' Elisha cried. 'Take me home.'

It didn't feel like her own bed when she opened her eyes. There were monitors bleeping and wires attached to her chest. Elisha wasn't ready to die. Much as she wanted to join her mother and father, there was something she had to do first.

Zac, Rajani and Salim kept vigil at her bedside. But Elisha's mind was elsewhere. She'd prayed for the chance to put things right with Theo. She *had* to persuade him to give up his private practice and do something meaningful again. Was she too late?

CHAPTER THIRTY-SIX

Marina Medical Rooms, Auckland Harbour Basin

Theo

Veronica burst into my office after the last patient of the morning.

'What the hell are you playing at, Theo?' she demanded. 'Keeping Lady Penhaligon waiting for over an hour, then refusing to do her surgery. You'll apologise to her and fix a date for the operation.'

I felt like a scolded child. Veronica's flapping hands reminded me of the tongue-lashings from my aunt Ida when I'd been naughty as a boy.

'No. I'm not operating on Lady Penhaligon.' I tapped my fingers on the desk. 'From now on, I'm only doing stuff that's really necessary.'

Veronica's eyes drilled into mine. 'If Mrs Penhaligon thinks it's necessary, then it *is* necessary.'

I rapped the desk even more ferociously. 'That's bullshit. And you know it.'

Veronica lunged forward. 'I made you what you are. I can just as easily take you down.'

I glared back at her. 'Go on then. I don't care.'

Veronica's expression softened. The way my aunt Ida's used to after she'd given me a telling off. 'Let's not fall out over this. If you don't do the surgery, someone else will, and they won't do it half as well as you.'

'That doesn't make it right.'

'Maybe not.' Veronica drew back. 'But it's far better that she sees you than the unscrupulous surgeons she's been to before. She will go back to them if you don't treat her.'

I wanted to stand up and scream. Instead, I shrugged half-heartedly. 'Okay. I'll see her.'

'Smart move,' Veronica said. 'I'll tell Lady Penhaligon you'll see her this afternoon. Make sure you don't keep her waiting.'

David Whittet

I swallowed hard. 'I won't.'

I couldn't look at Veronica. A sinking feeling in my gut told me I'd just made a dreadful mistake. By backing down, I'd committed myself to a lifetime of facelifts and tummy tucks. But what choice did I have? With a hike in interest rates and a fall in property values on the North Shore, I'd stopped opening letters from the bank. I'd never escape appearance medicine.

Two o'clock precisely, and Lady Penhaligon entered my consulting room. She raised her false eyebrows at me. 'I'm prepared to overlook your conduct this once, Dr Malone.' Could she possibly be more patronising if she tried? 'But don't let it happen again.' She pulled her chair forward and took a photo out of her Dior handbag. 'My nose is too big. I want it to look like this.'

I glanced at the photo. A model in her twenties. Lady Penhaligon might have looked like that once. She probably still would if it wasn't for the botched surgery on her cheeks.

'I could try a rhinoplasty,' I said. 'That could improve the appearance, but no promises.'

'Don't get technical with me,' she said. 'Just make it smaller.'

I shrugged. 'Are you sure that's what you want?'

'Most definitely,' Lady Penhaligon said. 'And while you're at it, my lips need some attention. They could do with some fillers to plump them up.'

Really? Don't ruin your best feature. I sighed. 'Alright, Lady Penhaligon. You're the boss.'

And she was. Lady Penhaligon never missed an opportunity to remind me that she was in command. However many procedures I did for her, she wanted more. Did she care about the outcome, or was she just addicted to cosmetic surgery?

'One more thing,' Lady Penhaligon said after the latest treatment. 'My daughter is after a facelift. I've booked her an appointment for tomorrow. Nat wants the works. No expense spared.'

Natasha Penhaligon was beautiful, with her long blonde hair, flawless skin and all-consuming eyes. Her mother must have been equally striking before she went under the knife.

'You don't need me,' I said when Natasha arrived the next day.

Natasha's eyelashes swept up as she blinked at me. 'Oh, but I do.' She ran her fingers over her cheeks. 'I'm only thirty-five, and already my face is sagging. And look at my eyes.'

I shook my head. 'They look perfect to me.'

'See those wrinkles?' Natasha pointed to her eyelids. 'I've heard eyelid surgery can work wonders for this drooping skin and get rid of these hideous bags—'

'Very well. I'll take a look.' I couldn't see a single wrinkle through the dermatoscope. 'Seriously, you look great. There's nothing I can do for you.'

Natasha frowned. 'I've seen what you've done for Veronica's models. I want to look as incredible as they do.'

I clasped my hands. 'You do already.' If I allowed my rage to erupt, it would be unstoppable—and it would end my career. 'Why can't you just be thankful for what you've got?'

'Because I want to look perfect. Like my mother.'

Perfect? Had she looked at her mother recently? 'Lady Penhaligon must have been as beautiful as you—once,' I said. 'Now, her face is a train wreck. So's the rest of her body, come to that. I won't let it happen to you.'

Natasha's mouth fell open. Clearly, nobody had talked to her like that before. I wanted to say more. Tell her about Elisha. *How would you cope with seventy per cent burns?* Or about Bwanbale and Jamie Beale. *What if you were born covered in lumps?*

The fire in Natasha's eyes warned me I'd gone too far already.

'How dare you insult my mother!' she said. 'If she's not looking terrific, that's your fault. She's paid you enough money.'

'This isn't about money.' I put my dermatoscope back on its stand. 'It's about doing the right thing. And in your case, that means not doing unnecessary procedures.'

Natasha sprang to her feet. 'Screw you! My cousin Lucy said you were a stuck-up git.'

You're Lucy's cousin? Before I could say anything, Natasha gave me the finger and she was out the door.

I'd just got my breath back when Madeleine, the receptionist, ushered in a woman wanting liposuction.

I put the woman on the scales.

'You don't need it,' I said. 'Your BMI is in the normal range.'

'But I *feel* gross,' she said. 'What about some water tablets? Or some weight-loss pills? I hear they make you feel good, too.'

Athletes wanting steroids. Actresses wanting breast augmentations. I'd had enough of the lot of them.

Five o'clock and the last patient left, cursing at me, and slamming the door as they went. I'd been expecting a visit from Veronica all afternoon. Doubtless, she'd have heard from Natalie and her mother by now, and I'd be in for an almighty rollicking.

Half an hour later and I still hadn't heard from Veronica. The silence was almost as scary as the inevitable confrontation. After finishing my case notes, I put the folders away and grabbed my jacket. I was about to leave when the phone rang.

'Listen, Veronica.' I was determined to get in first. 'You've every right to be mad at me. I just can't go on like this. It's wrong. Exploiting wealthy misfits, charging them a fortune for surgery they don't need.'

'I'm not mad.' Veronica's voice was extraordinarily calm. 'But Natasha is, and her cousin Lucy's baying for your blood.'

'Lucy's one of your girls,' I said. 'Can't you rein her in?'

'No chance,' Veronica said. 'I sacked her when she turned up for work under the influence of drugs. Lucy's a loose cannon. Watch yourself, Theo.'

'Don't worry about me,' I said. 'I can look after myself.'

Back at my car, I wasn't so sure. I drove around the city for a couple of hours, going through it in my head. What could Lucy do to me? Bloody hell—she was the one snorting coke. And as for Natasha—what if she did report me? The Medical Council constantly warned doctors against taking advantage of vulnerable patients. I was right to refuse Natasha inappropriate surgery. So why was I worried?

Maybe a sugar fix would help me face the empty apartment. I headed to a fast-food drive-through. At least it would make a change from pot noodles. A slurp of cola and a bite of burger, and I almost threw up. Back home, I collapsed on the bed. I'd had enough for one day.

Seven in the morning. I reached for the alarm clock to stop the awful din. But the noise didn't go when I pressed the button. Damn. It was the telephone.

I wiped the sleep from my eyes and picked up the receiver. 'Hello.'

'Is that you, Dr Malone? Are you okay?'

It was Mrs Beale's voice. I hadn't heard from her in ages. Why was she calling me at this hour?

'I'm alright,' I said, suppressing a yawn. 'Why shouldn't I be?'

'Haven't you seen the paper?' she asked.

'No. I don't have one delivered.'

'You're all over the front page.'

I held my breath as Mrs Beale read the headline.

'"*Prominent North Shore doctor Theodore Malone hosts wild drug parties at his penthouse apartment.*"' Mrs Beale paused and sighed sympathetically. 'Of course, I don't believe a word of it. There's even worse further down. "*These drug-fuelled binges are funded through Dr Malone's lucrative private practice, seducing insecure women into unnecessary surgery.*"'

I dropped the handpiece. Bloody Lucy. I might have known the evil bitch would lie through her teeth. Mrs Beale was still on the end of the phone reading the newspaper, but my mind had shut down. I fumbled to retrieve the handpiece with my shaking hand.

'I'm sorry, Mrs Beale,' I said. 'I can't listen to any more.'

'Don't you want to know what they're saying?'

'No.'

The line went quiet for a few moments. I watched the first rays of sunlight shine through the curtain of my bedroom window. Another day. Why couldn't the dawn just go away?

'Are you still there, Doc?' Mrs Beale asked.

'Yes.'

'I didn't mean to upset you,' she said. 'I just called to make sure you weren't taking the news to heart.'

'I'll manage somehow,' I said. But would I?

 David Whittet

'If you need a character witness—'

'Thank you,' I said as politely as I could. 'I really appreciate you calling.'

'You're welcome, Doctor. If there's anything more I can do, you've only to ask.'

'Goodbye, Mrs Beale.' I put down the receiver and buried my head under the bedclothes.

Moments later, the phone rang again.

'TVNZ News. Have you anything to say, Dr Malone? Is it true the girls at your drug-snorting raves were all your patients? Are you going to resign?'

Radio New Zealand was next. 'Are you going to apologise to all the women you've fleeced? Will you be repaying the exorbitant fees you charged them?'

Newstalk ZB wasn't any kinder. 'When are you going to front up, Dr Malone? Our phone lines are jammed with listeners demanding answers. How can we trust our doctors when they make a fortune out of women's insecurities then spend it leading young girls into substance abuse?'

Why wouldn't they believe me? I repeated time and again that I'd never had drugs in the apartment, and as soon as I found the girls using, I'd turned them out. None of them would listen. I should have known—after all, I'd been on the wrong end of the media before, and this promised to be even more degrading.

I was about to take the phone off the hook when it rang again.

'Paul Holmes here.'

I threw the handset across the floor. How could I possibly survive the shame a second time? While I had nothing to do with the drugs, I had made money from cosmetic procedures. My four-poster bed, with its luxurious gravity-defying mattress and sumptuous sheets, suddenly felt acutely uncomfortable.

No use languishing at home. I had to keep working. Hold my head up high and prove the media sharks wrong. I wasn't going to sit and wait for the inevitable letter from the Medical Council: *Strictly Private and Confidential. To be opened by addressee only*.

I took a shower and put on my best suit. Appearances mattered. After forcing myself to eat some breakfast, I set off for work.

There was no escape driving to the medical centre. The talkback show on my car radio was all about me. I almost crashed into the vehicle in front of me when someone I didn't know and who didn't know me called me a filthy scumbag.

'I didn't think you'd be coming in,' Madeleine said as I stepped into the empty waiting room. 'All your patients have cancelled. I tried to call you, but your phone just gave the engaged tone.'

'Let my patients know it's business as usual,' I said. 'Tell them everything they've heard about me is a pack of lies, and I'm going to prove it.'

'Okay.' Madeleine scratched her head. 'There is one more thing. Lester Birt called.'

The landlord for the medical rooms. 'What did he want?'

'His rent.' Madeleine looked down. 'And to tell you he's terminating the lease. He wants you out by the end of the week.'

'He can't do that!'

Madeleine handed me the contract. 'I'm afraid he can.'

My world collapsed before my eyes. Bills mounted up, and with my practising certificate suspended, there was no possibility of getting back to work. Cheques bounced. Letters from the bank remained unopened until the manager called, threatening foreclosure.

The incessant media calls continued. Maybe the reporters were right. Perhaps I was just a miserable bugger only interested in myself.

I disconnected the phone from its socket when I wasn't talking to Anne Baxter at my medical protection society. Poor Ms Baxter. She tried so hard to buck me up, but I knew I was finished.

Yes, I'd been here before. But last time I was in trouble, my career was in front of me. I had something worth fighting for. Now I had nothing, and I no longer cared.

David Whittet

CHAPTER THIRTY-SEVEN

Two years ago, Gary Wilkes of Citywide Real Estate persuaded me the development on Auckland's North Shore was the opportunity of a lifetime.

'You can't go wrong,' he'd insisted, waving the brochure in front of my face. 'But you'll have to get in now. These apartments are selling like hot cakes.'

I hadn't taken much convincing. Gary told me I wouldn't regret it when we shook hands on the deal.

Today was a different story.

'With the downturn in the economy, we've seen a distinct lowering in demand for luxury apartments.' Gary punched some numbers into his calculator. 'You'll lose at least a hundred grand if you sell now. Are you sure you can't wait until the market picks up?'

He knew damn well I was facing a mortgagee sale.

I shrugged. 'It's only money. Put it on the market.'

'Very well.' Gary scribbled some notes on his clipboard. 'So, what's next for you, Theo?'

'Blocked sinks and peeling wallpaper,' I said. 'I'm renting in South Auckland.'

Gary pulled a face. 'That's not going to help rebuild your career.'

Patronising bastard. 'Maybe not. But it's close to the community clinic where I'm going to work.'

I had to get out of the office before Gary made another snide comment. What did he know about anything? My cramped bedsit on the wrong side of the tracks felt more like home than that lavish penthouse ever did.

And I *was* getting my life back together. Unable to prove any illicit drug use or inappropriate practice, the Medical Council had let me off with a warning. While work at the community clinic wasn't cutting-edge medicine, it was good to be doing something worthwhile again. With free treatment for everyone, the overflow in the waiting room reminded me of the Northland practice. Some days it was just treating an endless stream of children with colds or school sores, but then I'd see a kid with a streptococcal throat. Preventing rheumatic fever with a course of penicillin was much more satisfying than a needless facelift.

I was about to pack up after another full day when the receptionist put her head around my consulting room door.

'There's someone here to see you, Doctor. She says it's personal.'

Personal? I clasped my hands together, praying it wasn't a journalist who'd tracked me down. 'Okay. Show her in.'

The receptionist beckoned to the woman in the waiting room. 'Come through, Miss Parata.'

What? Miss Parata? Surely it couldn't be Ariana. I almost tripped over my chair in the race to find out.

'Doc!' Ariana Parata flung her arms around me. 'It *is* you!'

'It's so good to see you again,' I said. 'But how did you know I was here?'

'I've been doing an attachment at Girls High,' Ariana said. 'I heard the staff talking about this lovely doctor called Theo coming to the school to teach the kids about hygiene. It had to be you.'

'So you made it to teachers training college,' I said. 'I knew you would.'

'I owe that to you, Doc!' Ariana hugged me even tighter. 'But what about you? I've been so worried about you, what with all that horrible stuff in the newspapers.'

'You saw that?' I drew back. 'It wasn't true, you know. At least, not all of it.'

Ariana stood tall. 'I didn't believe a word of it. In fact, I gave those reporters a piece of my mind.'

'You did what?'

'Well, I couldn't have them slagging off the doctor who saved my life.' She moved towards the door. 'I'll tell you all about it over a coffee. My shout. Have you been to Doreen's Diner?'

I hadn't been to a café since leaving private practice. 'No.'

'Come on then.'

       David Whittet

Ariana led me down the street. We dodged when some kids kicked a football across the road.

'Funny, isn't it?' Ariana said. 'Every house has a satellite dish but none of the kids have decent school lunches.'

Doreen's Diner was a pokey tearoom. Still, a cup of instant there with Ariana was way more appealing than an espresso with Veronica at a chic café in Ponsonby.

'I begged the journos to tell my story,' Ariana said. 'How you fought the specialists to get me that scan. But none of the buggers would go with it.'

I took a slurp of coffee. 'Maybe it was all for the best. Going into cosmetic surgery was a mistake. Sucking up to rich jet-setters. That's not why I went into medicine. I deserved some of the things the paparazzi said about me.'

'I don't believe that,' Ariana said. 'Anyway, you're making a difference to people's lives now.' Her eyes met mine. 'So, where's Elisha?'

I fidgeted with my coffee cup. 'She's gone back to India.'

'On her own?'

I nodded. 'She went to finish building the well that we started.'

'That was brave. Especially after …' Ariana broke off and ran her fingers through her hair. 'Elisha was so kind. She understood how I felt. I guess she'd been through so much with her burns.' Ariana turned to me. 'Why didn't you go with her?'

'I wish I had—now.' And I meant it.

Ariana shook her head. 'So why don't you go after her?'

I took a last mouthful of coffee. 'It's too late. She's found someone else.'

Ariana reached out across the table with her hand. 'I'm so sorry.'

Why hadn't I gone back to India with Elisha? How many times had I asked myself that question and come to the same answer?

'Letting Elisha go was the biggest mistake of my life,' I said. 'Still, I've got work to do here. Teaching those kids of yours how to stop getting school sores.'

Wandering home from the tearoom after Ariana had left, I wondered how work on the well in Madhapur was progressing. Had my donation made a difference? With no television in my bedsit, I'd no way of knowing.

At least Elisha would be proud of the work I was doing now at the community clinic.

I ignored the phone when it rang at midnight. Doubtless another reporter trying to harass me. I thought the bastards had given up. When it rang for the third time, something made me pick up.

'Hello.'

'Theo, is that you?' It was Zac, and his voice was trembling. 'You need to get on an aeroplane and get here fast.'

'What?'

'Elisha's taken a turn for the worse, and she wants to see you.'

She wants to see me? My hand shook so hard I almost dropped the receiver. 'Are you sure? I let her down. I wasn't there for her when she needed me.'

'I don't understand it either,' Zac said. 'But Elisha insists she loves you.'

How could she still love me? Elisha had a large, forgiving heart, but I was a miserable bugger, and she had someone else now.

'What about Salim?' I said.

'He's gone to uni,' Zac replied. 'Mate, it's you she wants.'

'She's not …' The words stuck in my throat and a chill crept over my body. 'I mean, she's not dying, is she?'

Tears trickled down my cheeks as I waited for Zac to reply.

'She collapsed making a speech,' he said at last. 'Actually, she was speaking about you.'

'About me?'

'She figured it was you who sent the money for the well we're building, and she wanted the townsfolk to know.' Zac paused. I heard a sniffle. 'We thought we'd lost her when she passed out, but my sister's a tough nut, and she rallied round.'

Yes, that was Elisha. She was a fighter and she'd never give in.

'Listen, Theo,' Zac continued, 'the doctor says she's not in immediate danger. But please don't leave it too long.'

'I won't.' And I meant what I said. 'Tell Elisha I'll be there as soon as I can get on a flight.'

I spent the rest of the night planning. Technically, I was still a locum at the community clinic, so I didn't have to give notice. They'd understand, anyway. My biggest fear when I rang the Air New Zealand call centre was my credit card being declined.

'I need to get to Calcutta as soon as possible,' I told the agent.

'Flights are filling up,' she said. 'I can get you to Singapore on Thursday with a connection to Calcutta the following morning.'

'Wait a minute,' I said. There *was* something I could do to make amends. 'Scrap that. Can you route me through Brisbane? I need a couple of days there on the way.'

It was a long shot, but if my plan worked, it would definitely put more than a smile on Elisha's face.

CHAPTER THIRTY-EIGHT

Orissa State, India, One Week Later

Five minutes and we'd be there. The familiar rolling plains of the Mayurbhanj flashed past the window as the train approached Rairakhol Railway Station. Some things never changed—the women labourers knee-deep in water in the paddy fields and the sickly-sweet chai served on Indian trains.

Joanna sat next to me in the carriage. I'd spent the entire journey picturing Elisha's face the moment she glimpsed her old mentor and confidante. Rajani would be over the moon as well. I just hoped it wouldn't be too much for Elisha's fragile state of health. What if she had a heart attack?

The platform came into view, and I glimpsed the welcoming party. Mission staff and local government officials all lined up. Rajani and her great-aunt Nisha were at the front waving their hands. But where was Elisha? I strained to see through the dirty carriage window. She wasn't there.

I screwed my eyes shut and prayed. *Please, God, tell me she didn't pass away before I've got here.*

Joanna's gentle hand stroked my shoulder. 'Don't worry, Theo. Everything's going to work out.'

My chest tightened. I could scarcely breathe as I forced myself to take another look at the platform. Was that Zac pushing through the crowd? My heart pounded even faster. It was—and he was escorting Elisha in a wheelchair. She looked pale and wasted, a shadow of the dynamic woman on that documentary programme less than a year back. None of that mattered. Elisha was alive.

I grabbed Joanna's arm, and we rushed through the carriage. Before the train came to a halt, I'd thrown the door open and thrust my hands in the air. 'Elisha!'

'Theo!' Tears streamed down Elisha's face. 'You've come back to me.'

'And I've brought someone to see you.'

I led Joanna out of the carriage.

'Jo! It can't be!' Elisha rubbed her eyes and stared at Joanna. 'Is it really you?'

Joanna stepped onto the platform. 'It is.'

Zac helped Elisha up from her wheelchair, and she stumbled towards us. Joanna held out her arms, and the two women embraced.

'I never thought I'd see you again!' Elisha said.

'Nor did I,' Joanna said, pulling me into the huddle. 'It's all thanks to your friend here.'

Elisha's frail hand grasped mine. 'Theo! You're a saint!'

'No, I'm not,' I said. 'I've been a selfish bastard. I deserted you when you needed me most, and I wanted to make it up to you.'

I stepped back as Rajani raced forward and flung her arms around Joanna.

The raw emotion as Rajani and Joanna clung to each other was so intense and so private that I closed my eyes for a moment.

It was a full minute before either of them could speak.

'I've been waiting for this moment my entire life,' Rajani said, her head still nuzzled in Joanna's bosom.

'Me too,' Joanna murmured.

Watching the three women closest to my heart—Elisha, Rajani and Joanna—hugging each other, brought me almost more joy than I could bear.

Zac dug me in the ribs. 'You kept that mighty quiet. How the hell did you get a visa for Joanna? We've been trying for years.'

I approached the line-up of government officials and put my hand on Mr Prasad's shoulder.

'This is the man we have to thank,' I said. 'He steamrollered the red tape and got Joanna a visa in record time.'

Prasad stepped forward and addressed the crowd. 'Dr Malone's a persistent bugger. He wouldn't let go until I stamped the visa.'

That was the first time I'd seen my old adversary smile. Throwing myself at Prasad's mercy to get Joanna's visa had been a high-risk strategy. I had no money to offer him baksheesh. Instead, I bombarded Prasad with endless phone calls at all hours of the day and night. Once I got through his bureaucratic facade, he opened up. Turned out he blamed himself for not insisting that Pastor Martin have a bodyguard on that ill-fated trip to Baripada. He told me that Dr Reddy was carrying on the immunisation programme. I'd have kissed him if he hadn't been twelve thousand kilometres away on the end of a telephone.

Now he was standing right beside me on the platform at Rairakhol Station.

'Yes,' I said, 'Mr Prasad is responsible for the joyous reunion of these lovely ladies.'

Prasad posed for a photo opportunity with Joanna, Elisha and Rajani.

'But there's more,' I continued. 'Mr Prasad has pledged his support and committed local government resources to complete work on our well.' I raised my arm. 'Three cheers for Mr Prasad!'

We cheered, and the crowd broke out in riotous applause.

Zac pulled me aside. 'Are you sure we can trust Prasad? You should have seen him gloat when everything fell apart a few months back.'

'Don't worry,' I said. 'Prasad can't go back on his word now. Not after all this public adulation.'

Zac thumped me on the back. 'You always were a sneaky bastard, Theo Malone! You're two of a kind, you and Prasad. Praising him was just a trap to keep him sweet, wasn't it?'

'So what if it was?' I said. 'He's done worse to us.' The crowd were still showering Prasad with hugs and handshakes. 'Besides, we need all the help we can get. There's no time to lose.' I eyed Zac directly and blinked back a tear. 'You told me Elisha didn't have long. I can see that for myself now. We have to finish the well while she's still alive. We owe it to her.'

Zac looked close to tears, too. 'We do.'

'We owe her something else.' I put my hand on his shoulder. 'Can we be friends again? I'm sorry about all the bad blood and taking Elisha away from you—'

'You're here for her now,' Zac said, 'and that's what matters.'

Those generous words meant so much. So did the hug that followed.

On the days that we made positive progress with the well, Elisha grew visibly stronger. When there were setbacks with poor quality concrete and supply chain issues, she languished. Fortunately, with Prasad's men working alongside the engineering firm Zac had engaged, we were able to overcome the obstacles. I wheeled Elisha out to the site each day. We brought the workmen mouth-watering snacks that Elisha had made with Rajani—and a little help from great-aunt Nisha. Being in a wheelchair didn't stop Elisha from taking an active part in the construction. She reviewed the work with a keen eye and constantly challenged the workmen to go the extra mile for the community.

Three weeks later, we had the news we'd been waiting for.

'At this rate,' the foreman said, 'we'll finish by the end of the month.'

For a moment, I thought Elisha was going to rise up from her wheelchair and kiss the foreman. Instead, she wiped the tears from her eyes.

'Clean drinking water for everyone,' she said. 'It's been a dream for so long. I can't believe it's happening.'

'Neither can I. But this dream is definitely coming true.' I took her hand in mine and helped her to stand. 'Come and see.'

I guided her across the gravel to the newly cemented circular wall surrounding the well. We sat on that wall long after the workmen had left.

'Promise me this, Theo,' Elisha said. 'When I'm gone, you'll carry on the work we started together … before—'

I squeezed her hand and finished the sentence for her. 'Before our lives were torn apart.' I turned to face her head-on. 'You're not going anywhere. Trust me, I'm a doctor.'

'And I'm a nurse,' Elisha said, the serenity in her eyes catching me off guard. 'Be serious, Theo. We both know I don't have long.'

'You're looking better than you have in ages,' I said. 'But if an elephant trampled you underfoot, I swear I'll dedicate the rest of my life to the health of this community.'

'You're not just saying that?'

I wasn't. 'I'll never let you down again.'

Elisha beamed. 'You'd better not'—she pointed to the sky—'because I'll be watching you from up there.'

Her scars relaxed so much when she smiled that they were scarcely noticeable. She moved closer, her warm breath caressing my skin. We hadn't been intimate for so long, and so much had happened since the last time. The gentle touch of her lips sent goosebumps down my spine as she kissed my cheek. I'd almost forgotten what that felt like.

Elisha leant back, suddenly serious again. 'We need to get more Indian doctors involved if our service is going to survive. Harish has left, and Arjun Basar is retiring.'

'We have to improve our facilities and make it an attractive career choice,' I said, rapidly composing myself. 'It's hard enough recruiting doctors to the larger centres, let alone out in the sticks.'

'I know that,' Elisha said. 'But there's one bit of good news. Salim's gone to medical school in Calcutta. He's promised to come back and work here when he's qualified.'

My toes curled. That was the first time she'd mentioned Salim since I'd arrived. 'Rajani told me you two were engaged.'

Elisha looked down at the ground. 'My head was all over the place, and Salim had saved my life.'

I bit my tongue. Why had I brought up their engagement? It was obviously still raw.

'You don't have to explain,' I said.

'Salim is a great kid,' Elisha said, 'but I could never love him the way I love you.'

An irresistible force drew our heads together again. This time our lips met. Would it feel the same? Was Elisha ready for this? I almost slipped off the wall when she kissed me full on the lips.

'Thank you for bringing Jo,' Elisha said. 'You've no idea how much that means to me and to Rajani.'

I ran my fingers through her hair. 'I think I do.'

A bead of perspiration trickled from my forehead into my eye. God! Had Elisha noticed I was sweating? Could I brush it away without her seeing?

She pulled me closer. Her mouth found mine once more, and our lips joined so tightly I could scarcely breathe.

'I love you,' she said, prizing her lips away long enough to speak.

'I love you too,' I said. 'With all my heart.'

If only a kiss could last forever. I never wanted to let Elisha out of my arms, and I wouldn't have done so if a loud voice hadn't destroyed the moment.

'Watch out! You'll fall down the well if you carry on like that!'

Who the hell was it? I turned my head to see Zac grinning and waving a paper in the air.

'Sorry to interrupt your sexy tryst,' he said, 'but we've got some terrific news.'

'Zac!' Elisha steadied herself on the parapet. 'What is it?'

He handed her the paper. 'We've done it! The water samples are clean!'

'That's brilliant,' Elisha said. 'Now we can arrange the consecration.'

'I'll get on to the mission headquarters and fix the date,' Zac said. 'We've been waiting for this for so long.'

'I want Krishna there too,' Elisha said. 'Building the well is about healing divisions. This is going to be a joint Christian–Hindu ceremony.'

There was someone else who should be at the consecration. I took a deep breath. 'You should invite Salim. We have to make sure he feels part of the community if we want him to work with us when he graduates.'

The heavenly aroma of fragrant spices filled the air. How much I'd missed Indian cooking while back in New Zealand! Could the women of Madhapur possibly have exceeded the feast they'd provided for the Diwali celebrations when I first met Elisha all those years ago? I wouldn't have believed it before today.

'Look!' I wheeled Elisha out onto the street to watch the townsfolk carrying tray after tray full of mouth-watering delicacies to the banqueting table in the centre of the village. 'I can't wait to tuck into all that beautiful food.'

Elisha smiled. 'You've got to sit through all the speeches first.'

Nisha joined us, wafting a dish of channa masala under my nose.

'That's torture,' I said.

Elisha gazed at the brightly coloured flags and banners as I pushed her down the road in her wheelchair. Fairy lights and garlands of marigolds once again lined the streets.

'I do love the way Indian communities celebrate,' Elisha said. 'Everyone's so happy. Just look at those kids.' She waved at the children who were busy painting their faces outside the school. 'That's beautiful, Anushka. Makes you look like a princess, a *rani*.'

'I can do your face too, Elisha,' the schoolmaster said.

'Much as I'd like to take you up on your offer,' Elisha said, 'I have to look sombre for the ceremony.'

The village band paraded down the street, playing a medley of gospel songs and Hindu mantras. 'Onward Christian Soldiers' and 'Nāsadīya Sūkta', the Hindu hymn of creation, went surprisingly well together.

'I told you today would bring Hindus and Christians together,' Elisha said.

The young drummer gave me a wink as they marched past us. It was Chandra. How he'd grown since we immunised him all those years ago!

The entire village gathered around the well. I wheeled Elisha through the multitude of women, so elegant in their saris, and the men equally handsome in their traditional red-and-gold coats. On a platform at the front, Krishna stood tall, his golden robes gleaming in the sunlight. Next to him, dressed in a white silk suit, Pastor Deepesh Banerjee—the head of the mission in India, and Pastor Sanjay Kapoor with a contingent from the Baripada office.

I beckoned to a young man in the crowd. 'Salim! Come and help me!'

Salim and I lifted Elisha from her wheelchair and onto the stage, where we helped her into the ceremonial chair. It was draped with a satin sash and had a deep crimson cushion.

'Hold it there!' Zac appeared with his fancy new camera. 'I have to get a picture of this.'

Once Zac had his shot, Salim and I stepped off the stage.

'Don't go,' Elisha said. 'I want my two men beside me.'

How weird was that? I patted Salim on the back, then we drew up a couple of chairs and sat on either side of her.

Pastor Banerjee and Krishna joined hands for a blessing.

'Heavenly Father,' Pastor Banerjee began, 'we give thanks for your multitudinous blessings and praise you for bestowing on us the gift of

David Whittet

fresh, clean water. Bless this well, and may it bring health to all the people of Madhapur.'

Elisha reached out for my hand when Pastor Banerjee recalled the sacrifices made on the journey.

'Our dear brother Wesley Martin gave his life for this community, and Elisha has battled extraordinary odds to complete her father's work.'

Elisha pulled on my arm. 'Help me up.'

She'd promised me she wouldn't make another emotional speech. I didn't want her passing out again like last time. I caught Joanna's eye in the crowd. Rajani gave me a wink too. We all knew nothing would stop Elisha once she'd decided on something. I dutifully supported her onto her feet.

Elisha shot me a defiant glance before she started. 'I've been told to sit quietly and behave myself. Theo said I could draw the first bucket of water from the well, but nothing more. Well, I'm sorry, Theo, but you ought to know by now that's not me.'

The crowd cheered. Everyone was close to tears when Elisha spoke of peace and reconciliation and how love conquered hatred.

'I bear no hatred or animosity towards the men who attacked our van on that dreadful night,' she said. 'I forgive them and pray with all my heart that they will let go of the hatred and let love into their souls.'

A lump stuck in my throat. I couldn't decide if I was more proud of Elisha for those words or frightened for her safety as she teetered closer to the edge of the stage.

Elisha turned to Salim. 'As for this young man, he dared to stand up to the gang. He pulled me out of the blazing wreckage, knowing full well he risked lynching by the mob.'

I tried to make myself heard over the applause. 'What's more,' I said, 'Salim's training to be a doctor. When he's qualified, he'll be coming back to work with us.'

'I may have tried to tell you this before,' Elisha continued, with a mischievous grin, 'but I'll repeat it, and this time I promise not to pass out. Without Theo's generous donation, there would be no well.' She raised her hand to quieten the crowd. 'So, without further ado, I'm going to ask Theo and Salim to help me raise the first pail of water from our new well.'

The crowd chanted as we hauled up the inaugural bucket:

Om shanti, shanti, shanti.
Om shanti, shanti, shanti.

I remembered that chant from the blessing ceremony all those years ago.

A schoolboy pulled on Krishna's satin robes. 'What does it mean?'

'Peace,' Krishna said. 'When you chant *Shanti* three times, you bring peace in body, mind and spirit.'

Elisha fell back onto the chair and peeked at me through her half-closed eyes. 'I'm sorry, Theo. I won't make it for the banquet. I need to go home.'

'Don't worry,' I said. 'We thought it might be too much for you, so Nisha kept some food for us at her place. We'll have our own personal feast.'

Rajani and Joanna strolled across to the stage.

'A private party?' Rajani asked. 'Are we invited?'

'Of course you are,' I said.

Zac arrived lugging his film-making gear. 'Not you, Salim. I want to shoot an interview with you before you go back to Calcutta, and you can help me film the banquet.'

Nisha laid out a myriad of exotic dishes on an ornate mat on her living room floor. All the treats from the banquet were there, with little clay oil lamps illuminating each of the cast-iron bowls full of delicacies. We sat in a circle, Joanna and Rajani on one side, Elisha and I on the other, Nisha fussing over us.

I'd noticed how much Elisha's skin deteriorated when she was exhausted. Tonight, it was a mottled yellow. She'd lived for today for so long. Would she go downhill fast now it was over?

I raised a spoonful of tarka daal to her mouth. 'Try to eat something. This is nice and easy to swallow.'

Elisha managed half a plate of daal before flagging and resting her head on my lap.

'Theo,' she whispered, 'I want you to marry me.'

David Whittet

CHAPTER THIRTY-NINE

'What's this I hear? A midnight proposal?' I opened my eyes to see Nisha hovering over me. 'Rajani says you're getting married at last, so I thought you'd need this.'

Nisha held out the traditional Indian groom's costume she'd made for me when Elisha and I had first got engaged.

Elisha was still asleep on my lap. We must have crashed out on the mat last night after we'd finished eating.

I gazed at the dazzling gold sequins and the elegant embroidery.

'You've kept it all these years?' I said.

Nisha smiled. 'I knew you two would get it together one day.'

Rajani followed her great-aunt, carrying the Indian bridal gown she'd created for Elisha.

Elisha stirred. 'Where am I?' She rubbed her eyes. 'Wow! My wedding dress!' She ran her fingers over the silk and the beads. 'I'd forgotten it was this beautiful!'

Joanna bustled in from the kitchen with a plate of breakfast samosas.

'Did you make that dress yourself?' Joanna asked.

'I did most of it,' Rajani said, 'with a little help from Aunty Nisha.'

'You're such a clever girl,' Joanna said, patting Rajani on the back and putting the samosas on the table. 'Help yourselves to breakfast.'

Rajani and I helped Elisha to her feet.

'Why don't you try the dress on?' Rajani asked Elisha.

'It'll probably hang off me now,' Elisha said. 'I've lost so much weight.'

'Don't worry,' Nisha said. 'We can make alterations.'

Needle and thread in hand, Nisha and Rajani took Elisha to a bedroom.

Joanna squatted on the floor next to me. 'Have you decided on a date? Don't leave it too long, in case—'

I stared at the ground, unable to bear the end of her sentence. The last thing I needed was a reminder that it would be a race to arrange the wedding before Elisha's passing.

I took a deep breath. 'It's all happened so quickly. When I woke this morning, I wondered if I'd dreamt Elisha's proposal.' I looked up at Joanna. 'Worse still, I thought she might have changed her mind in the cold light of day.'

Joanna rubbed my shoulder. 'She'd never do that. Not now.'

Rajani opened the door and dragged Elisha back into the living room. 'Doesn't she look fantastic?' Rajani said.

Nisha followed them in, flapping her arms. 'Cover your eyes, Theo. I've heard Westerners believe it's bad luck to see the bride in her wedding dress before the ceremony.'

'I'm not superstitious,' I said. 'At least, not about that sort of thing.'

It was too late anyway. I'd seen Elisha, and she looked stunning in the Indian bridal gown. The traditional red-and-gold *lehenga*—a full, ankle-length skirt—with its long panels embellished with golden thread and crystals, added a fullness that hid her wasted muscles. The exquisitely embroidered *dupatta,* a shawl-like scarf, concealed her gaunt features and highlighted her soulful eyes.

'I'm going to find Zac,' Rajani said. 'We have to get a photo!'

'Who's going to make *your* wedding dress, Rajani?' Joanna called after her. 'Why don't you and Zac make this a double wedding?'

Nisha disappeared for a moment and returned with an exquisite crimson bridal sari as perfect as Elisha's gown. 'I've made this for Rajani, in anticipation.'

'It's gorgeous,' Joanna said. 'I can just picture Rajani walking up the aisle in it. She'd look sensational. Now, all we need is for Zac to pop the question.'

Nisha sighed. 'I've been waiting long enough. I'm beginning to despair that Zac will ever pluck up the courage to ask her.'

'I can't think why,' Elisha said. 'He's crazy about her. Perhaps we should ask Rajani for him.'

Joanna raised her eyebrows. 'How about a joint wedding, Elisha? I can just see you and Rajani walking down the aisle together.'

'I've thought about that,' Elisha said. 'But—'

     David Whittet

Before Elisha could finish the sentence, Rajani returned, dragging Zac along with her.

'Wow!' Zac's eyes widened. 'Sis! You look amazing!' He fetched his video camera and started shooting. 'A wedding will make a perfect end for my film about the well.'

'We were just thinking,' Joanna said, 'wouldn't it be lovely if you and Rajani got married in a joint ceremony with Theo and Elisha?'

Zac blushed. It was the first time I'd seen him utterly speechless.

'What are you waiting for?' Nisha said. 'Ask her!'

'Go on,' Elisha teased. 'The suspense is driving us mad.'

'Okay.' Zac's cheeks turned even redder. 'What about it, Rajani?'

Joanna shook her head. 'Zac! That's not how you propose to a girl!'

'Yeh, Zac,' I said. 'Get down on your knees and ask her properly.'

Zac put his video camera down and knelt on the floor.

'That's more like it,' I said, picking up his camera and pressing the record button. 'Now, how about some passion?'

'Piss off, Theo!' Zac shuffled awkwardly. 'Will you marry me, Rajani?'

'Of course I will.' Rajani beamed at him, relief in her eyes. 'You've no idea how long I've waited for this moment.'

'Better watch out, Zac,' I said, zooming in with the camera. It felt good to be able to tease Zac again without any animosity. 'Rajani's upstaging you.'

'You don't hold the camera like that,' he said. 'You'd never make it as a film director.'

'I don't know,' I said. 'A learned professor once told me I'd never make a doctor.'

Elisha tugged on my arm. 'I'm not sure I'm up to a big wedding. I want Krishna to marry us quietly at the temple.'

I stroked Elisha's hand. 'That's fine by me. We can do whatever you wish.'

Elisha glanced up at Rajani. 'I'm sorry. I know you want to get married in a church. You should have the wedding of your dreams. You've waited long enough.'

'I know,' Rajani said, 'but a joint wedding would mean so much to me.'

'Me too,' Zac said.

Rajani put her arm around Zac and sighed. 'But we have to be married in the eyes of God.'

'Are you sure about the temple, sis?' Zac said. 'Mum and Dad would have wanted you to marry in a church.'

'They'd have understood,' Elisha said. 'Remember, Dad did that joint blessing with Krishna for the well.'

'I'm not so sure,' Joanna said. 'Your father's spirit won't rest easy unless you have a church wedding.'

Nisha brought in another plate of samosas from the kitchen. 'I agree. Pastor Martin would have wanted his daughter married in a church.'

'A church or a temple,' Elisha said. 'Heaven or Nirvana. We're all aiming for the same place. We've just got a different way of getting there. It's the same God.'

'Why don't we have a Christian *and* a Hindu wedding?' I said. 'We could have a service at the church and a blessing at the temple.'

'How about it, sis?' Zac said. 'It would be so cool, you and me getting hitched together.'

Elisha kissed my cheek. 'Thank you. That's a beautiful idea.'

I felt her muscles relax. She turned to Zac and kissed him, too.

Nisha bustled off to the kitchen again. 'I'd better brew some more chai. We can't plan a joint wedding without refreshment.'

'We should have a *roce* ceremony,' Rajani said.

Zac sat up. 'A *what*?'

'Don't look so worried,' Rajani said with a mischievous smile. 'It'll be fun. Everyone will pour coconut juice over us.'

Zac pulled a face. 'You're kidding.'

I laughed. 'Don't worry, Zac. We'll find someone to film it.'

Nisha returned with the morning's third pot of chai. 'We've never had a *roce* ceremony in Madhapur. It's popular down in Mangalore.' She winked at Rajani. 'Let's do it.'

Zac bit a fingernail. 'So what the hell is it?'

Nisha explained that the word *roce,* meaning 'juice', symbolises purity, like the pure white milk of a coconut. The ceremony celebrates the last day of bachelorhood and spinsterhood for the bride and groom, signifying the

David Whittet

transition to married life. The custom of anointing the bride and groom with oil and coconut juice is an adaptation of the *haldi* ceremony held on the eve of Hindu weddings, and it symbolises the washing away of sins, purifying the soul for marriage. 'Like Rajani said, we all get to douse you in a load of goo.' Nisha stopped and glanced at Elisha. 'I'm sorry—I guess that's out of the question in your condition.'

'Oil's good for my skin,' Elisha said. 'At least, that's what the surgeons told me. Besides, if it's both a Hindu and a Christian tradition, then I'm up for it.'

Less than a week later, Elisha and I knelt together on a wooden platform in front of the townsfolk. Rajani and Zac were on their knees next to us. Candles flickered in the twilight, children waved sparklers in the air, the women carried baskets of fruit and sweets. We seemed oddly out of place, dressed in T-shirts and jeans, while everyone else wore their traditional costumes. But then, Nisha had warned us this would be a messy business.

Pastor Deepesh Banerjee opened with a prayer. 'Dearly beloved, we are gathered in the presence of God to give thanks to our Heavenly Father who, in His graciousness, has united these two couples through love. Bless Elisha and Theodore. Bless Rajani and Isaac. Guide them, dear Lord, guard them and keep them strong in their love, from this day forward and forevermore. Amen.'

'Amen,' the crowd repeated, their heads bowed.

'Are you okay?' I whispered in Elisha's ear.

She nodded. 'Look. Those kids are having such fun with the sparklers!'

A tear in the corner of her eye told me she wasn't doing all that well. Elisha loved children. Watching them play and knowing she couldn't have a family of her own must have hurt.

Nisha stood before the gathering and held an iron bowl high above her head. 'Hallelujah! Thanks be to God!'

When she lowered the bowl, Pastor Banerjee stepped forward and dipped a finger in the oil.

I took a deep breath and squeezed Elisha's hand. She closed her eyes when Pastor Banerjee approached us. I felt her shudder. Was this ceremony a mistake? Why hadn't we stuck to the quiet service in the temple she'd wanted?

Pastor Banerjee drew a cross on our foreheads with the oil. 'God bless you, Elisha. God bless you, Theo.'

I hardly dared look at Elisha. When I did, her face looked the most serene I'd seen it since returning to India.

The cross on our foreheads was just the beginning. The women descended on us, pouring oil on our ears and over our heads. Next came the coconut juice, rubbed on our heads, faces, hands and feet.

'I wouldn't have missed this for the world,' Elisha said.

Considering how happy she looked, neither would I.

Something else caught my attention. Ashok had got hold of Zac's video camera. To my delight, he was up close and personal, shooting Zac's obvious mortification at being plastered in gunge.

'Good on you, Ashok!' I shouted. 'Get in there and make Zac squirm!'

After a shower, we all met up at the village hall for dinner. The women festooned us with garlands as we entered. Elisha and Rajani were breathtaking in their purple-and-gold saris. Tradition required Zac and me to wear Indian kurta pyjamas.

'You boys look super cute,' Rajani said. 'Quick Ashok, get a picture.'

Zac shielded his face. 'No! Go away!'

I grabbed Zac's arm and pulled it away from his head. 'Come on, we may as well do a decent pose.'

The women arranged the wedding costumes on a table. Pastor Banerjee laid his hands on Elisha and Rajani's bridal dresses and the sherwani coats Zac and I would wear.

When he finished the blessing, Pastor Banerjee turned to Elisha. 'Your mother and father would be so proud of you. I can feel Pastor Martin's presence with us today.'

'So can I,' Elisha said.

Nisha came up and put her arm around Elisha. 'You've been so brave. Now, let's get you home. You need some rest before the big day tomorrow.'

What was going on? I was halfway through getting dressed when I heard horses neighing in the street. I glanced through my bedroom window. Half the village was outside with two ornately decorated horses.

David Whittet

Bugger! A button came off my tight-fitting sherwani as I rushed to the door. I'd been struggling for at least half an hour to get the costume on without damaging the delicately woven brocade. Too late for repairs now. I pulled the sash across so the missing button didn't show.

No sooner was I out of the door when one of the woman elders accosted me with a needle and thread. Did she carry that everywhere? Or just to weddings?

'You men are hopeless,' she said. 'Here, let me fix it for you.'

Zac arrived looking almost as confused as I was.

'Have you any idea what's happening?' I asked him. 'I thought we were meeting at the church.'

'So did I,' Zac said. 'Then Rajani told me we were having a wedding barat.'

I caught my breath. 'A *what?*

The woman finished sewing my button. 'Never heard of a barat?' she said. 'Well, you're about to find out.'

More of the women elders gathered around me. One of them held a bowl filled with a fragrant red paste and she daubed it on my forehead.

I'd never ridden on horseback before, and my heart stood still when I worked out what was going to happen. Before I could protest, the men hoisted me onto one of the horses and Zac onto the other. What if I fell off? That *would* ruin my wedding outfit.

'Just relax,' one of the local farmers said, 'then the horse will, too.'

Relax? You've got to be kidding!

The band struck up a wedding march, and they paraded down the street alongside us, escorting us along in a celebratory procession.

'In the movies, they have elephants,' Zac said. 'Not horses.'

Elephants. That would have been even scarier.

More people waited at the church to greet us. One of the women handed me a handkerchief to wipe the perspiration off my face while they helped me down from the horse.

'What a splendid entrance,' she said. 'You and Isaac looked so handsome riding in on horseback. Just wait and see what we've got lined up for Elisha and Rajani.'

Surely they wouldn't expect Elisha to ride in on horseback?

I gave the handkerchief back to the woman. 'Elisha's sick. I hope you're not pushing her too far.'

The woman smiled. 'Just watch.'

A horn sounded in the distance. A cloud of dust spread from the end of the street. The band picked up their instruments again and began a rendition of 'Here Comes the Bride'.

Then, appearing through the haze like a mirage—could it be? I blinked and took another hard look. Was that a tractor? It was almost unrecognisable underneath all the flowers and decorations. It was towing a trailer carrying Elisha and Rajani, madly waving to the crowds.

Zac groaned. 'I don't believe it. Ranjeev and his clapped-out tractor. This definitely isn't like the movies.'

Elisha beamed as the women lifted her out of the trailer. The traditions hadn't worried her one bit. It was me they'd spooked.

The Madhapur church wasn't in itself particularly striking, with no stained-glass windows or ornate carvings on the pews. A plain wooden cross stood above a simple, unpretentious altar. But today, decked with wall-to-wall flowers and aglow in the candlelight, the little chapel was stunning.

Rajani had chosen 'Lord of All Hopefulness' for the opening hymn. The local bandmaster introduced the haunting Irish melody on a solo clarinet. I gave up my fight to restrain the tears when the voices united.

Pastor Banerjee sprinkled incense and began the introductory prayer. 'Almighty God, we gather to celebrate Your gift of love and its presence amongst us. We rejoice that these two couples have committed themselves to a life of loving faithfulness to one another.'

If only we had a lifetime ahead of us. If only I'd been more understanding—and more faithful—in the short time we'd had together.

Elisha looked radiant in her gorgeous red-and-gold bridal gown as we stood in front of the altar.

'Before God and this congregation,' Pastor Banerjee continued, 'I ask that you affirm your commitment to the covenant of marriage. To share your joys and sorrows, whatever the future may hold.'

I met Elisha's eyes. We each knew what the other was thinking.

Pastor Banerjee turned to me. 'Theodore, will you take Elisha to be your lawful wedded wife? Will you love her, comfort her, honour and protect her, and, forsaking all others, be faithful to her as long as you both shall live?'

There was an enormous lump in my throat as I responded. 'I will.'

'Elisha, will you take Theodore to be your lawful wedded husband?'

My mind drifted as Pastor Banerjee repeated the vows for Elisha. How different the service might have been if the mob hadn't torched the van with Elisha and her father in it. She'd have had her dad walk her up the aisle. And what if her mother hadn't caught AIDS? I forced myself back to Pastor Banerjee and Elisha's oath.

'Will you love him, comfort him, honour and protect him, and, forsaking all others, be faithful to him as long as you both shall live?'

Elisha was so much more confident than I was with her answer: 'I will.'

Pastor Banerjee asked Zac and Rajani the same questions. Was I wrong to envy them? I watched Zac stare childlike into Rajani's eyes as he confirmed his vow. For them, this was a fairy-tale wedding. Zac had just been offered a job as assistant director on a major Bollywood production. They had a world of opportunity and discovery before them. If only we had the same.

Elisha steadied my shaking hand as I placed the ring on her finger. It should be me supporting her, not the other way around.

'Theodore and Elisha, Isaac and Rajani,' Pastor Banerjee said, 'you have declared your marriages by the joining of hands and by the giving and receiving of rings. I therefore proclaim that you are husband and wife. Those whom God has joined, let no man put asunder.'

Elisha had chosen the closing hymn, 'Dear Lord and Father of Mankind'. I held it together through the first three verses. After that, I was too choked up to join in the singing.

Drop Thy still dews of quietness,
Till all our strivings cease.
Take from our souls the strain and stress,
And let our ordered lives confess
The beauty of Thy peace.

I hadn't been in a church more than a handful of times in the past few years. It had never meant that much until now. But today—something stirred inside me that I'd never felt before, and likewise, I prayed like never before. Prayed for the strength to make Elisha's final days on this planet as happy as I possibly could.

Pastor Banerjee gestured for us to follow him down the aisle as everyone sang the last and most heart-wrenching verse of the hymn.

> *Breathe through the heats of our desire*
> *Thy coolness and Thy balm;*
> *Let sense be dumb, let flesh retire;*
> *Speak through the earthquake, wind, and fire,*
> *O still, small voice of calm.*

I held on to Elisha's arm as we left the church. How brave of her to choose a hymn with 'fire' in its words. She was crying, too, but they weren't tears of despair. I could see that. They were tears of hope, and yes—joy.

The sun was low in the sky when we reached the temple. Dressed in his traditional yellow satin robes, Krishna sat cross-legged on his golden cushion. My heart and my mind were still all over the place. Elisha tipped her head back, her eyes half-closed as we knelt on the marble floor.

Krishna leant forward and rested a hand on Elisha's shoulder. 'Your earthly journey is almost complete.' He embraced me with his other arm. 'Your time as husband and wife is but a moment in life's continuum. Remember, Elisha, what I told you about the many spokes of the wheel?'

Elisha nodded.

Krishna pointed to the wall. 'Look.'

We both followed Krishna's hand to see our long shadows projected by the last rays of sunlight.

'Your shadows are touching each other,' Krishna said. 'That means you will work together in future lives on your journey towards Nirvana.' A smile crept over his imposing features. 'Or towards Heaven, as our Christian friends call it.'

Elisha clasped her fingers together. 'So this isn't the end for Theo and me?'

'It is just the beginning,' Krishna said. 'From this day onwards, your souls are bound together for eternity.'

'Eternity.' Elisha repeated the word and took a deep breath. 'That's beautiful.'

Krishna's words echoed through my mind as I pushed Elisha home in her wheelchair and carried her across the threshold for the first time as husband and wife. I prayed from the bottom of my heart that our souls *would* be bound together for eternity.

CHAPTER FORTY

The Road to Madhapur, Three Weeks Later

Dark clouds gathered over the plains of the Mayurbhanj. A flash of lightning lit up the bleak horizon. Distant thunder rumbled. The rising storm swept a blanket of dust across the terrain and into my face. I didn't want to let go, but it was time to say goodbye. I gripped the urn and held it high above my head. Another gust of wind, stronger than the last, carried with it the ashes of the woman I loved.

The end had come quickly. Elisha and I had only twelve days together as husband and wife. Twelve short days. The most precious in all my life.

Each morning I took Elisha to the well. She loved to watch the women drawing water and carrying the pails on their heads. Nisha was invariably the first there, and she always poured Elisha a cup of water.

'Here, drink this,' Nisha said. 'Who knows? It might cure you.'

Elisha grinned. 'If only it could.' She gulped the water and wiped her lips. 'But I'm thankful to God I've lived to see the well completed, and all you lovely people using it.'

On the twelfth day, Elisha asked me to take her to the site of the mob's attack on the road to Baripada.

'Are you sure you're up for it?' I asked.

Elisha nodded. 'There's something I have to do.' She picked up a simple wooden cross. 'I made this for my father.'

We set out early. The last few days had been sweltering, and the midday sun would be too much for Elisha. As we approached the location, my mind went back to that dreadful night when the police car stopped, and I saw the burnt-out wreckage at the roadside. What was going through Elisha's head? It was hard enough for me to bear, and I hadn't even been there—at least not until a few hours after the atrocity.

I parked the car on the verge and went to get Elisha's wheelchair out of the back.

 David Whittet

'I don't need that today,' she said. 'Just help me to walk.'

Holding on to my arm, Elisha clambered out of the vehicle and knelt down on the grass. She dug a small hole in the mud with her bare hands and positioned the cross in the ground.

'God bless you, Dad,' she whispered.

I helped Elisha up onto her feet. 'We'd better get back,' I said. 'It's getting hot.'

'I want you to take me out into the fields,' Elisha said. 'I need to feel the wind in my hair one last time.'

The day was muggy, and there wasn't even a hint of a breeze. But it was what Elisha wanted.

'Okay,' I said. 'As long as you're not too tired.'

We drove out past the paddy fields to the lowlands. The blistering heat had me sweating, but it didn't seem to bother Elisha. Even the rice pickers had taken refuge in the shade.

'These fields were flooded when I first came to India,' Elisha said. 'I remember looking at them through the train window.'

We sat down on the long grass in a field. Elisha pointed to a purple cloud on the horizon.

'See that?' she said. 'The monsoon is coming. It's coming for me. I'll go out with the rains.'

I swallowed. 'Don't say that.'

'But it's true,' Elisha said. 'They say the flooding's going to be worse this year than ever before.' She turned to face me, alarm in her eyes. 'If the floods strike Madhapur, you'll help the people, won't you? And don't forget the lepers. They'll need someone to take them to safety.'

I put my hand on hers and gave it a gentle squeeze. 'You know I will. Remember what I promised you when we were sitting on the wall beside the well?'

'That's right,' Elisha said, 'and then Zac caught us kissing.'

'He thought we were going to fall into the well,' I said. 'Cheeky bugger!'

'I love you, Theo.' Elisha sank back into my arms. 'Krishna said our souls are bound together for eternity.' She smiled and closed her eyes. 'Don't you forget that.' She never opened her eyes again.

Please, God, not now! My heart stood still. I've no idea how long I sat there, cradling her, willing her to live just a few minutes longer. It was too soon to let go.

The sun disappeared behind the dark, forbidding clouds. A drop of rain landed on my head, and I raised a first to the monsoon. *You can't have her! I won't let you take her away from me!*

Less than a fortnight after carrying Elisha over the threshold, I hoisted her lifeless body over my shoulder and took her to the car. She often told me Madhapur was her spiritual home. I drove her back there for the last time.

Joanna was there for me when I got back. She took care of the little things that meant so much, such as discreetly removing Elisha's wheelchair from the back of the car. I couldn't have faced that. And it was Joanna who held my hand at the blazing funeral pyre.

'Dust to dust. Ashes to ashes,' Pastor Banerjee proclaimed.

Flames. Ashes. Fire had killed Elisha's father. Fire had destroyed Elisha's life and brought it to a premature end. And now, it was consuming what remained of her body.

Pastor Banerjee asked me to speak at the funeral breakfast. I was in no fit state to make a speech. Zac was braver than me and stood up to say a few words.

'Back in Australia,' Zac began, 'my sister and I always argued about sport. Elisha hated any kind of sport with a passion. When my father announced we were moving to India, I teased her about joining the women's hockey team in Baripada. You should have seen the look on her face!'

'They need all the help they can get in that hockey team,' one woman said. 'They've lost every game this season.'

'I'm afraid my sister wouldn't have been much help to them,' Zac replied. 'Every time I told her to sign up with a sports team, it used to drive her wild. She'd start swearing, and then she'd get a telling off from Dad.'

That was Elisha. I could just hear her cursing at Zac and her father giving her a rollicking. I wanted to laugh. I wanted to cry. Most of all, I wanted to see her face again. The pent-up emotions of the last few days burst out, tears of sorrow, grief and regret streaming down my face.

Joanna walked me home after the wake. 'What will you do now?' she asked. 'Will you stay on?'

'I promised Elisha I'd carry on our work,' I said, 'and I won't let her down again.'

Joanna smiled. 'You're a good man, Theo.'

'I've no choice. Elisha said she'd be watching me from above. And believe me, she will be.' I looked up at the sky. 'She was convinced the monsoon would bring widespread flooding this year. She asked me to look after the townsfolk. Especially the lepers.'

'I wish I could stay and help,' Joanna said. 'I'd love to play some small part in carrying on Pastor Martin's work.'

'You and Elisha's father go back a long way, don't you?' I said.

'Pastor Martin was there when I was at rock bottom,' Joanna said. 'You know it was Wes who arranged for me to sponsor Rajani?'

I nodded. 'Elisha told me.'

Joanna paused and took a deep breath. 'You've no idea how I longed to meet Rajani. Or how many times I applied for a visa. I used to cry when they turned me down. Year after year, it was always the same story. I'd given up hope. Then you turned up.' Joanna took another long breath. 'Now I'm just getting to know Rajani, and I don't want to leave.'

'So why don't you stay?' I asked. 'Rajani's going to need all the support she can get when she moves to Bombay with Zac.'

Joanna sighed. 'My visa runs out in a fortnight.'

I raised an eyebrow. 'Give me five minutes with Prasad, and I'll soon fix that.'

Joanna was helping Rajani and Zac to pack up when I burst into Nisha's front room a couple of days later. I held up Joanna's passport, displaying the freshly stamped visa. 'I've done it!'

It hadn't been as easy as I'd hoped. Prasad could be a stubborn bugger. Just as well I'd found out about the baksheesh he'd paid to get his agricultural bill passed.

'So, how does it feel being married to a hotshot film director?' I asked

Rajani. 'At least you'll have Joanna with you to help you to settle into your new life in Bombay.'

'It's called Mumbai now,' Zac said.

'Film can be a powerful force for good,' Rajani said. 'It was a screening of Zac's documentary about the well, at a film festival, that attracted a top producer's attention and got him the job. I'm just worried about the field hospital, and the lepers. Who's going to look after them after we're gone?'

'Me,' I said. 'I promised Elisha.'

Rajani hugged me. 'Thank you. You're an angel.'

'I'm no saint,' I said. 'But I'm going to do right by Elisha.'

A cloudburst the following morning sent me scurrying to find Joanna.

'Elisha was right about the monsoon,' I said. 'Are you ready to go? What about Zac and Rajani?'

'Come in,' Joanna said, the downpour pelting her face. 'Rajani's in a bit of state about leaving Nisha.'

'Let's get you to the station while we can,' I said. 'At this rate, the road to Rairakhol will be impassable in a matter of hours.'

Rajani and Nisha were in each other's arms in the front room.

'I'm going to miss you so much,' Nisha said.

Rajani wiped her eyes. 'I don't want to leave you.'

'No more of that,' Nisha said. 'You've got a whole new life ahead of you.'

Rajani held on to Nisha's arm. 'I'll write to you often. I promise.'

'Time to go,' I said. 'I'll get the cases loaded into the van.'

'Come on, Rajani,' Joanna said. 'Let's help Theo with the trunks. Maybe Nisha will come and see you in your new home.'

'Try and keep me away,' Nisha said. 'Don't you dare forget us when you're rich and famous.'

'You'll be guest of honour at the premiere of my first movie,' Zac said. 'I promise.'

Nisha beamed. 'Can't wait. I've always fancied getting all dressed up and walking down a red carpet.'

David Whittet

Outside, a group of townsfolk gathered in the teeming rain and showered Zac and Rajani with garlands. Joanna steered them towards the vehicle, the deluge washing the petals into the gutter as they clambered inside.

Everyone cheered and waved when I started the engine.

'Bon voyage! Godspeed! Good luck!'

'Make us proud,' Nisha said.

'I will,' Zac replied.

I glanced at the surface flooding on the street. Would I get them to Rairakhol in time for the train? With its multiple potholes, the road to the station was hazardous at the best of times. What would it be like today?

The wheels skidded in the mud. *Don't say we're stuck!* No way was the van going to move.

'Push,' Nisha shouted. 'Everyone!'

The crowd got behind us and shoved. The van hit a giant puddle and spun full circle, plastering the townsfolk in sludge.

The journey didn't get any easier. Flash flooding. Cracks in the road. I glanced at my watch. Less than an hour until the train left. Why hadn't we left earlier?

A concealed crater almost landed us in a ditch.

'Bloody hell,' I muttered. 'I didn't see that coming.'

'I want to go back,' Rajani said.

'It's going to be alright,' Zac said. 'We're nearly there.'

Were we? Was that the train whistling in the distance? Yes—there it was on the horizon. Trust it to be on time when we were late.

I was sweating when we pulled up at the station minutes before the train was due to leave. Zac helped me bundle the trunks out of the van and into the carriage.

Rajani clasped me in a mighty hug. 'Thank you for everything, Theo. You're one in a million.'

'No time for emotional farewells,' I said. 'Just get on the train before it's too late!'

What was Joanna doing dawdling behind?

'You're going to miss the train,' I said.

Joanna pointed to a bundle of newspapers on the platform. I glanced at the headline.

Meteorologists predict the worst monsoon floods in over a decade. Lives will be lost. Thousands will be left homeless.

The guard blew his whistle.

Rajani leant out from the carriage door. 'Quick. Joanna. Get on!'

'I'm not going with you,' Joanna said. 'I'm staying behind to help with the flood relief.'

The train started moving.

Rajani held out her arm towards Joanna, almost falling onto the platform. 'Jo!'

Zac hauled Rajani back into the carriage as the train gained momentum.

'Are you sure?' I asked Joanna. 'I can cope. We've got a great team at Madhapur.'

'Certain,' Joanna said. 'The lepers need me. Pastor Martin won't rest easy if anything happens to them.'

'Nor would Elisha,' I said.

We both waved furiously as the noise of the engine drowned Rajani's desperate cries, and the train sped away.

Two days of rain and the floodwaters were a metre deep in the leper colony. The residents' few belongings floated on the surface amongst the remains of broken chairs and mattresses.

'Why are the lepers always the hardest hit?' Joanna sighed, helping the last of the residents into the life raft. 'It's so unfair.'

'Because the colony is on low-lying land,' I said. 'We've Prasad to thank for that. Keep the lepers out of sight and out of mind.'

'You're soaking,' Joanna said to an elderly couple. 'Let me get you a dry blanket.'

'You must be Joanna,' the woman said. 'Rajani's sponsor from Australia.'

'That's right,' Joanna said. 'How did you know?'

'Rajani showed me your picture.' The woman held out her hand to Joanna. 'I'm Davinda, and this is my husband, Azad.'

'Davinda!' Joanna embraced the woman. 'I've heard so much about you from Rajani.'

'Rajani was like a second daughter to us, too,' Davinda said. 'Her parents saved us from the asylum.'

'Let's get you on the raft,' Joanna said. 'Then we can talk. I heard you were both in Zac and Rajani's film.'

'Wait,' I said. 'That wound needs dressing.' I stepped forward to take a closer look at the weeping sore on Davinda's arm. 'And we need to get her started on IV antibiotics.'

Azad was covered in boils, too. I rummaged through the emergency medical bag I'd put together for the evacuation. Did we have enough antibiotics left for both of them?

Wooden boards served as stretchers on the makeshift raft, and we laid Davinda and Azad side by side. Joanna cleaned their wounds and wrapped them with some bandaging.

'Hold on!' The raft lurched as Harija, one of the volunteers, steered us across the floodwaters.

Rashid, another volunteer, held up the IV line. Squatting beside Davinda, I searched for a vein to site the cannula. Surely to God she had an inch of skin somewhere that wasn't covered in pustules.

She hadn't. Both Davinda and Azad required venous cutdowns. Exposing the vein in a sterile environment was challenging enough, but on a swaying raft, it was a nightmare.

Joanna must have seen the panic in my eyes. 'Come on, Theo,' she said. 'I bet you've managed much worse situations than this.'

Maybe I had. It didn't stop the palpitations—or the wave of nausea that swept over me as the raft rocked from side to side.

Whenever I'd faced a situation like this in the past, Professor Rutherford's words had haunted me. *You will never make a doctor.* My mind flashed back to Saleh's lumbar puncture and Rajani's chest decompression. Today, instead of the professor telling me I couldn't do it, Elisha was there, watching over me and assuring me I could.

I held my breath and advanced the cannula along Davinda's vein, praying the needle wouldn't puncture the blood vessel.

'Brilliant! You've done it!' Joanna spoke the words, but it was Elisha's voice I heard. 'What did I tell you?'

Dry land at last. A group of young volunteers nailed a tarpaulin to the straw roof of the shack we'd built to house the displaced lepers.

'Great job,' I said. 'That should keep out the rain till the worst's over.'

We moored the raft and helped the lepers into the shelter. I found a quiet corner for Davinda and Azad.

'Don't worry about us,' Davinda said. 'Go back for our friends.'

'We will,' I said, 'just as soon as we've got you and Azad sorted.' I turned to Ishani, a nurse from the field hospital. 'Their IV lines are running smoothly. Make sure they get their next dose of antibiotics in an hour.'

Four more trips with the raft and we had all the lepers safely across the floodwaters and settled in the shelter.

Harija threw the stick he'd been using as a paddle onto the ground. 'Thank God that's over. I think I've broken my back.'

'We're not done yet,' I said. 'In fact, we've only just begun. There are loads more families stranded out on the plains.'

Over the next few days, the ever-resourceful people used every last piece of floating debris to transport the displaced to safety. Broken-down doors became canoes. Smashed tables turned into kayaks. Families waded through the floodwaters, carrying the possessions they had salvaged. Some youngsters tried cycling through the water but soon fell off their bicycles. We pitched tents for the weary and infirm to rest wherever we found solid ground. Mothers fed their babies. Fathers took care of the older kids, heating the rations we supplied on the campfire.

By the end of the week, we had evacuated everyone to our new base. Krishna blessed the ground, and we called the settlement Shanti, the Hindu word for peace.

The volunteers worked around the clock to construct new homes. It was back-breaking work, and the men were always hungry.

Nisha warned stocks were getting low, but she was used to making a little go a long way. At lunchtime each day, there was a bowl of mulligatawny soup for everybody, which she heated on a portable stove.

Joanna sat with Davinda and Azad and spoon-fed them their broth.

 David Whittet

'That's going to be your new house,' Joanna said, pointing to an almost completed hut.

I brought a young mother across to see them. 'Meet Ishwari,' I said, 'and her baby Rahini. They'll be your new neighbours.'

'What?' Davinda almost choked on her soup. 'You mean we're going to be living next to … um … non-lepers?'

'You are,' I said. 'You've been treated, so you can't spread the disease. We're all one big family here.'

My heart warmed as the young mother knelt beside them, and her baby reached out with his little hand to stroke Davinda's face. It had taken the devastating floods to see the lepers integrated with the community. If only I could tell Elisha and share the moment with her.

Joanna took a photograph with the baby on Davinda's lap.

'I'm sending the picture to Rajani,' Joanna said. 'She'll be thrilled.'

Nisha came over to collect the dishes.

'That was delicious,' Joanna said. 'Pastor Banerjee is coming to add his blessing to the site on Sunday. We should have a party to celebrate.'

Nisha stacked the bowls and shrugged. 'I'd love to but feeding everyone's a struggle as it is.'

'Fresh supplies are on their way,' I said. 'You'll see.'

The back road to Baripada had just cleared, and Harija had taken the jeep to collect provisions from the mission.

With a triumphant honk of the horn, Harija was back. 'Wait till you see what I've got,' he said.

Nisha's jaw dropped when we opened the back of the vehicle.

'There's enough here for a feast,' Nisha said. 'We're going to have a banquet on Sunday.'

Her eyes bulged so wide I thought she was going to faint.

There were no fairy lights or candles at Sunday's festivities. This was no Diwali, but it was no less magical. More than just surviving the floods, we had broken barriers and brought the community together with renewed purpose.

'Sure you won't have any more?' I asked a wide-eyed ten-year-old.

'I'm absolutely stuffed,' the girl said.

'Too full for an ice lolly?' Joanna said.

'Of course not.' The girl giggled and ran back to watch the puppet show some enterprising women elders had put on for the children.

The carnival atmosphere continued. After we'd finished helping Nisha with the food, Joanna and I sat back and watched the boys playing cricket.

'Have you heard from Rajani?' I asked Joanna.

'Nisha's had a letter from her,' Joanna said. 'Rajani's got a job as a costume assistant on the same film as Zac.'

Nisha came over to join us. 'Rajani's over the moon about what you've done for the lepers, and the rest of the community, too. If Zac wasn't so busy, he'd come and make a film about the cyclone relief.'

'Elisha would be proud of us as well,' I said. 'I wish she was here to see what we've done.'

Joanna took my arm. 'I miss her too. But her spirit was with us today. I'm sure of it.'

'I felt that as well,' I said. 'It was as though Elisha was standing right next to me while I was serving the food.'

'I believe I'll meet her again,' Joanna said. 'In Heaven. You will too.'

'Yes, I believe that.' A lump grew in my throat. 'Excuse me, Joanna. There's somewhere I need to be.'

I jumped into the truck. The engine spluttered as I drove along the still waterlogged roads. Through the mist, at the roadside, I spotted some plants that had survived the floods. My heart missed a beat—they were Elisha's favourite flowers. I pulled over and grabbed a bunch.

A flash storm broke. Rain pelted against the windscreen and the truck stalled. That wasn't going to stop me. Clenching the flowers in my hand, I clambered out of the vehicle. Knee-deep in mud and grunge, I trudged down the road, pushing myself harder than I'd ever done before. I stopped to catch my breath. There it was in the distance. Just a little further.

Soaking wet, I knelt in front of the wooden cross that Elisha had placed at the roadside in honour of her father. A simple memorial, but immensely poignant, and so typical of Elisha.

You were right about the floods. But we did it, my darling Elisha. Your spirit guided me, gave me the strength and the courage to bring everyone to

 David Whittet

safety. Now they have the chance of a better tomorrow—thanks to you. Tears welled in my eyes. *I promised you I'd carry on our work, and I will—till the day I die and we are together again.* The rain stopped as I laid the flowers at the foot of the cross. *These are for you, my angel.* Marigolds for the girl I loved and lost on the road to Madhapur.

Medicine is a constant source of inspiration for my writing. General practice, in particular, is about being interested in people's stories—they go hand in hand. The colourful cast of characters I have met throughout my career, colleagues and patients alike, breathe life into my writing.

The Road to Madhapur draws on my personal experience of family medicine in both New Zealand and India. While the novel is a work of fiction and not autobiographical, my first-hand knowledge of medicine in the raw and many real-life events helped shape the story.

I have relived these episodes while writing the book. Many have touched me deeply, and I hope my readers will find these life-changing events equally moving. I will never forget the smiles on the children's faces in those remote and impoverished Indian communities. Likewise, beyond the overwhelming sorrow and despair of the leper colonies, many were filled with joy, fulfilment and peace. They were among the happiest places I have ever seen and truly *houses of hope*, as Zac and Rajani call them in the story.

For the curious, the following are some of the real-world events that underpin Theo and Elisha's journey.

Like Theo, I sat through endless lectures at medical school from professors who had spent their entire working lives treating tuberculosis. I was as frustrated as Theo. Many years later, I saw my first case of tuberculosis—in a debilitated farmer on New Zealand's East Cape on the North Island.

My introduction to general practice was akin to Theo's, although not quite so therapeutic. Like Ralph Greenslade, my tutor was into psychological medicine. The first consultation I sat in on was also a young newly-married woman with a rash. My thinking was similar to Theo's: this was a textbook case of contact dermatitis. Not so, according to my tutor. He unwound a paperclip while telling her to forget about new detergents and washing powders. She had a nervous rash.

'It can't be,' she protested. 'I'm not worried about anything.'

'Adjusting to married life can be very stressful,' my tutor said. 'You've got a husband to cook for now.'

'No, I haven't,' she replied. 'My husband does all the cooking.'

'Now we're getting to the root of the problem,' my tutor shot back. 'You're subconsciously upset that your husband is usurping your rightful place in the kitchen. That's why you've got the rash.'

She entered that consultation a confident young woman with a rash. She left a nervous wreck with an even worse rash.

My time in the Mayurbhanj district of India was during a period of considerable unrest following the recent murder of Australian missionary Graham Staines by Hindi militants. Graham and his two sons, Philip, aged nine and Timothy, aged six, were burnt to death by a mob of over a hundred extremists while they slept in their car. The community remained in crisis, with the tension between the Hindu and Christian communities threatening to ignite at any moment. Graham Staines' widow, Gladys, stayed on in the Mayurbhanj and continued to provide a home for leprosy victims. I was privileged to meet Gladys and witness her extraordinary work caring for the poor and the destitute.

The Australian missionary in my story is entirely fictitious. Wesley Martin is not based on Graham Staines or any other missionary, alive or dead.

In Chapter Eighteen, Theo and Elisha mount an undercover operation to vaccinate the children. While this episode is also fictitious, we did raise funds for an immunisation programme but met with political opposition. And I did encounter a public health nurse in New Zealand who claimed childhood immunisation was the most shameful form of child abuse in modern times.

I made a keynote presentation on my work in India at the 2000 World Family Doctors conference in Christchurch, New Zealand.

During questions at the end of my presentation, an American man asked, 'If I gave you a million US dollars for your project, how would you spend it?'

Like Theo, the only answer I could come up with on the spur of the moment was to say, 'I'd use it as baksheesh to bribe the authorities to let us administer the vaccines.'

Reflecting on my time in India, I must acknowledge the World Organization of Family Doctors (WONCA) for supporting my work in the Mayurbhanj. Their encouragement and financial backing through the WONCA Foundation Award proved invaluable.

Many other non-governmental bodies provide aid to this community. In particular, I wish to recognise the work of World Vision in the Mayurbhanj. Their tireless efforts have lifted countless children out of poverty and provided them with education and the opportunity for a better future.

David Whittet

Closer to home, Theo's stint as a rural GP in a remote Māori community reflects my own experience. I, too, was the last in a succession of locum doctors, and there was standing room only in the waiting room when I arrived. Like Theo, with three or four sick people booked into each fifteen-minute appointment slot, I wondered what I'd got myself into and how I'd survive. While writing about the challenges Theo faced in rural practice, I relived the chaotic lifestyle. The call-outs to motor vehicle accidents in the middle of a busy clinic. Night after night without sleep. That sinking feeling after working for hours without food. All so vivid and ingrained in my memory.

There were rewards, too. Ariana Parata is wholly fictitious but reminds me of a real-life case. Theo struggled to get the care Ariana so desperately needed. I had the same battle while treating a student who had a pituitary tumour removed on her twenty-first birthday.

ACKNOWLEDGEMENTS

Writing *The Road to Madhapur* has proved both exhilarating and demanding. I must acknowledge those who have supported and encouraged me on this journey. Nicky Sinclair was my first beta reader, and her feedback gave me the confidence to progress the work.

An in-depth manuscript assessment by Caroline Barron helped me take the novel to the next level. Caroline invariably challenged me to 'linger' and 'go deeper' at critical points in the story. Going deeper strengthened the manuscript immeasurably but did increase the word count! I wrote a tongue-in-cheek blog post at the time titled 'Linger means Longer'.

As always, Caroline, your contribution has been immense. Your enthusiasm for my work and perceptive insights (including setting me right on some facts about the fashion industry) are the stuff of legend.

Sincere thanks to my editor and copy editor, Renell Judais at Proof Perfect NZ, for her meticulous attention to detail and expertise in perfecting the manuscript.

Thanks also to Stephanie McConchie, my proofreader at Focus Proofreading & Editing; Karen McKenzie, my publicist at Lighthouse PR; and Dave MacManus and the whole team at The Copy Press and Real NZ Books for their terrific support.

A special shout-out to Holly Dunn, whose stunning cover illustration brilliantly captures the essence of my story. You are an extraordinary talent, Holly, and I am proud to have your work on my cover.

Above all, heartfelt gratitude goes to my fantastic family, who have invigorated and sustained me throughout the project. My children, Mark and Rebecca, are the sounding board for all my new ideas, and their judgement is impeccable. As always, my wife, Siriporn, was the glue behind the scenes, holding everything together.

This book celebrates all those who strive to make the world a better and more equitable place. Like Joanna in the story, many people sponsor children in the developing world, providing them with the necessities of life and the promise of a new future. These children often become part of the sponsor's wider family.

During a twelve-year stint on the WONCA Working Party on Rural

 David Whittet

Practice, I met many passionate colleagues who pledged their lives to improve the lives of communities worldwide. Bold declarations on health for all rural peoples and the rights of indigenous people were followed by equally decisive action from this dynamic group.

Finally, I must pay respect to the work of Dr Derek Allen, to whom this book is dedicated. Derek has spent his entire career working in regions of extreme need. Whenever a natural disaster strikes, Derek is there to provide aid. His work amongst the most disadvantaged people on our planet is beyond inspiring.

ABOUT THE AUTHOR

David Whittet is a family doctor, a multi-award-winning independent film-maker and an author.

Storytelling has been in David's DNA for as long as he can remember. As a child, the serialisations of classic literature on television each Sunday teatime were the highlight of his week. A dramatisation of *Oliver Twist* had a profound effect on him. In its day, Dickens' novel brought reform to the poor law, which convinced David of the written word's potential to change the world.

He decided then that he wanted to be a writer. Subsequently, A J Cronin's novels inspired David to become a doctor, especially *The Citadel*, which pre-empted the National Health Service's foundation in the UK and beyond.

David's work as a GP brings authenticity and gritty realism to his writing. His twenty-plus years of practice in rural New Zealand inspired his debut novel. *Gang Girl* is the story of a notorious gang leader's daughter and her lifelong struggle to escape the gang and forge her own destiny.

IndieReader described *Gang Girl* as 'a memorable tale filled with drama, conflict and intrigue ... deftly painted characters, multilayered, and unique ... an extraordinary read.'

Enjoyed *The Road to Madhapur*? Learn more about the inspiration and the real-life stories behind the book at David's website:

www.davidwhittet.com

For the latest news on David's work, exclusive previews, events, short stories and advance reader copies, sign up for his newsletter at:

https://david-whittet.ck.page/subscribe